CINDY KOEPP

Animal Eye

a GameLit Adventure

First published by Bear Publications 2020

Copyright © 2020 by Cindy Koepp

All rights reserved. No part of this publication may be reproduced, stored or transmitted in any form or by any means, electronic, mechanical, photocopying, recording, scanning, or otherwise without written permission from the publisher. It is illegal to copy this book, post it to a website, or distribute it by any other means without permission.

This novel is entirely a work of fiction. The names, characters and incidents portrayed in it are the work of the author's imagination. Any resemblance to actual persons, living or dead, events or localities is entirely coincidental.

First edition

ISBN: 978-1-64633-406-3

Cover art by Mary Campagna Findley

Contents

Chapter 1	1
Chapter 2	8
Chapter 3	31
Chapter 4	57
Chapter 5	67
Chapter 6	95
Chapter 7	115
Chapter 8	137
Chapter 9	155
Chapter 10	171
Chapter 11	185
Chapter 12	201
Chapter 13	218
Chapter 14	234
Chapter 15	247
Chapter 16	270
Chapter 17	286
Chapter 18	310
Chapter 19	324
Chapter 20	343
Chapter 21	356
Chapter 22	383
Chapter 23	404
Chapter 24	420

Chapter 25	439
Chapter 26	466
Chapter 27	485
Chapter 28	505
Chapter 29	518
Chapter 30	529
Chapter 31	555
Chapter 32	569
Chapter 33	586
Chapter 34	606
Chapter 35	627
Chapter 36	649
Chapter 37	664
Chapter 38	678
About the Author / Publisher	688

Chapter 1

Khin May stepped out of her virtual landing pad and into the character generation module for *Animal Eye*. The decorator had chosen a dark wood with forest green cushions for the furniture and a maroon and green floral print wallpaper that would've been perfect in a 1980s home. Stainless steel cages off to one side held an assortment of dogs, birds, bears, and horses. Aside from a small terrier and a knee-high chocolate Lab, the animals were not the typical pet sorts. That gave the room more of a primitive zoo or exotic vet vibe than a pet shop.

She walked over to the cages. The terrier chased its tail while the Lab whapped the side of the cage with his. The next cage had a huge, furry *ovcharka*, a Russian bear dog. The dog cages were separated a short distance from the birds. A crow perched and preened while a gyrfalcon in the next cage stared at her. The harpy eagle was busy chowing down on some sort of rodent.

The next set of cages had bears. A black bear the same size as the *ovcharka* was curled up napping. The grizzly was sitting up. Like the popular animation floating around social media, the bear waved a huge paw as she looked in on him. She waved back. A polar bear was pacing from one corner of his cage to the other.

There were only two kinds of horses. One was a huge fuzzy-legged fellow that looked strong enough to pull a semi, and the other was a sleek reddish brown one with a white blaze down his nose.

"Welcome to *Animal Instinct: Animal Eye*, the newest AI-controlled VR from Horizon Systems." The rich voice came from the right. "My name is Alan Ivan Turning."

She turned toward the voice as the hard-soft clack of footsteps on the tile floor came nearer until a gray-haired old man joined her. He wore dark green trousers that stopped at the top of knee-high boots. His doublet matched the trousers, and a frilly white shirt peeked out at the collar and sleeve cuffs. His wide-brimmed, leather hat, also green, was pinned up on one side with fluffy white ostrich feathers flowing from the back.

He stood rod-straight, unnaturally so, and his movements had some suddenness in their starts and stops. In spite of his name, this guy wouldn't pass the Turing test. Smooth out the awkwardness in his motions, and he'd be a contender. Really, though, compared to some of the other AI avatars she'd met, this one was pretty impressive.

"Alan Ivan Turning?" Khin May smiled. "Not Porthos?"

"No, not Aramis nor Athos nor D'Artagnan, neither." He smirked. "Do you want a quick start–" He held up a file folder stuffed with papers sticking out at every odd angle. "–or would you rather take more of a role in designing a character?" He held up a magnifying glass and a clipboard. Khin May looked back at the different species. If the AI kept some sort of realism, each would have advantages. Her playtester notes gave her no instructions for character generation. "I'm up for a challenge. Give me a quick start. Random is fine."

"An excellent choice." Alan tossed the clipboard and magnifying glass over his shoulder, and both disappeared. "Solo play or team play?"

She stepped back to observe the whole wall of cages. *Specialists. A team would be better, but I don't want to coordinate with a boatload of people.* "Team play, but let's keep it to one other person."

He squinted into the corner of the room. "We do have some other players starting up now, so that's easily done, or do you have someone specific in mind?"

Khin May shook her head. Even at this late beta stage, they'd all be playtesters like her anyway. "Nah. Surprise me."

"Splendid. A moment please while I select your character and partner." He stared at the corner of the room for a moment then returned his attention to her. "Be advised that the initial parts of the game will have you and your human working independently, but your partner will come along once you've both gained a few levels. Likewise, your human may not be immediately available to you."

She nodded. "As long as he's not late."

"He'll be exactly on time." The old man pointed to a wooden door with ornate carvings like the result of a Spirograph picture. "Right this way, ma'am."

As Khin May approached, the door opened by itself with a quaint squeak of the hinges, and hazy images split by thin, gray stripes formed. A cacophony of voices occasionally yielded discernible words, mostly numbers and descriptors. A few times, someone mentioned "price" or "deal."

Khin May waved to Alan.

"I'm always here if you need me." Alan bowed and swept his ostrich-plumed hat from his head.

That was no doubt true, but Khin May hoped she wouldn't need the help screen in this game again. Something about talking to an AI just gave her the willies.

With any luck, when Horizon Systems had converted this kid game to an adult version, they hadn't taken out the user friendliness. She blew out a breath.

She stepped through a computer-generated door and morphed with each step. Her arms became broader and her body rotated forward as her legs became thinner. Her eyes slid around to the side of her head.

Meanwhile, the environment took form. Gray stripes became thin metal bars all around her. Beyond that, a crowd of giant people moved past the front of the cage in both directions. They were perfectly normal humans, as far as she could tell, but huge. Four times her height or thereabouts. Men and women alike wore the same kinds of clothes and came in two varieties. Pale-complexioned or tanned folks wore robes that were belted at the waist.

Darker-skinned people wore trousers and tunics, some much more decorated than others. For both sorts, browns, reds, and greens were the most common colors with accents in blue, yellow, and purple. Some hurried, but others strolled and stopped to look at anything that grabbed their attention. Most carried parcels, bags, or baskets, and only a few were empty-handed. About one in three had a medium- sized or larger dog with saddlebags or a cart attached to a harness. A couple had the cutest miniature horses pulling a cart.

CHAPTER 1

The doorway faded, leaving behind a cage interior. She stood on a wooden perch that was less of a dowel rod and more of a trimmed tree branch. The booth around her had a double handful of other cages, each containing a bird. She was the only black one in the bunch. The rest were eagles, hawks, bluejays, and falcons.

Nearby, a group of wood block, djembe, and flute players were giving a concert. The drummers established a syncopated beat while the flutes and woodblocks played an upbeat melody over them. The tune was catchy, but repetitive. She bobbed her head in time with the music while checking out the rest of the scenery.

The world around her was full color, and the images were unpixellated. Staring straight ahead, she could see in a full circle. Her solid black tail feathers were as clearly visible as her dark gray beak. She turned her head and the image shifted as if she were scrolling through a panoramic picture. She twisted her head almost totally backwards and could still see all the way around. Looking forward again, she ruffled her tail just to see the movement. Tipping her head down gave her a view of both the top and bottom of the cage.

Whoa. Killer peripheral vision, dude. Ain't nobody sneaking up on this bird.

When she looked up, a transparent menu bar formed like a heads-up display. On the far upper left, an icon like a cogwheel, which probably led to the settings screen, and a picture of a sassy crow with a glint of mischief in her eye. On the far upper right, a skills drop-down. She focused her attention on the crow picture, which summoned a character sheet.

Name: Ahva **Species:** Corvid – Crow
Class: Scout Level 1 **Gender:** F

Attributes

Attribute	Current	Skill	Current
Power	5	Sneak	20
Speed	38	Detect Enemy	20
Cleverness	63	Signal Human	20
Endurance	15	Stay Alert	15
Agility	60	Sound Alarm	15
Charm	33	Patrol	15
Vitality	5	Trek	15
Sight	63	Long Distance Mvmt	15
Smell	5	Sprint	15
Hearing	23	Nonverbal Communication	15
Health	25	Camo	15
Encumbrance 0 out of 5 oz		Fly	10
		Speech	10
		Bite	10

A female crow named Ahva? Stand back, villains, or I'll squawk you to death!

A caption window appeared midair above Ahva's eyeline.

Activate the menus to access some skills such as Sneak or Problem Solving. More basic skills such as walking or flying will not need to be activated. Just do them!

Ahva looked away from the window and it faded out. She returned her attention to the character sheet.

The skills were pitiful and weirdly distributed. Flying was one of her lowest. Shouldn't birds be aces at that? Signal Human shouldn't be that hard either. She could squawk, couldn't she? How did that differ from Sound

Alarm? Speech, now that might be fun after she invested some points into it. Combat skills, though, were lacking. Apparently, the game designers weren't Alfred Hitchcock fans.

She turned her attention to the attributes. What she lacked in Power and Vitality she made up for in Cleverness, Agility, and Sight.

At least crows have brains. She recalled a video of crows and ravens sliding pegs, unscrewing bolts, and using sticks to trip a lever. *Crow it is. First thing I should do is figure out how birds move.* Ahva willed the character screen away, but before she could move, a new window appeared.

Be a bird! Do things birds normally do like preen their feathers, collect shiny things, or mimic sounds. You'll gain XP as you behave like a bird.

That could be amusing! She'd had parakeets as a kid and thought back to how they moved around and how they acted.

Khin May thought about her right arm, and the crow's wing raised then lowered again. Her other appendages correlated properly, and moved with minimal lag time from the virtual reality system.

Ahva hopped to the side of the cage.

Chapter 2

Ahva perched on the stick that spanned the widest part of her cage. So far, she'd figured out climbing, perching, and drinking water without dribbling it all down her front. Ahva's food bowl was empty and the cage was too small to fly in, so that was as far as she'd gotten. The game hadn't gifted her with a quest yet, which probably meant she was still missing something. What else could she do?

A human, who looked taller than a city bus from her angle, strolled into the bird merchant's area.

"Good morning, my friend. What kind of bird do you need today?" The merchant spread his arms wide and strutted closer.

The shopper scanned all the cages. "I'm looking for a falcon."

Ahva looked up until the menu bar appeared over her head.

Skill.

A drop-down unfolded to show the non-automatic skills. Speech was an option.

That's got prospects! Let's try something easy, like "Hi."

Ahva opened her beak but only managed a hoarse hiss.

CHAPTER 2

She tried again and got a squawk after the hiss.

Come on! I can do this. How hard can it be?

After all, her best friend swore she never shut up.

She paced the length of the stick, then back the other way. Speech couldn't be that hard. Birds figured it out often enough, and she was definitely smarter than the average bird. As she turned to head back to the other end, she hissed then squeaked.

This game seriously needed hints, a tutorial, something! Complicating things, the djembe concert was still going on, and apparently the players knew only one tune.

When they started the same tune again, Ahva hissed. *Do y'all know "Take a Break?"*

Wait. What if that wasn't a concert? Did this game have background music? Ahva focused on the cogwheel next to the sassy crow pic. A Settings menu opened, and a quick scan through the options turned up a button marked "Music." Ahva tapped that with her beak.

A pop-up screen appeared. **You've turned off music. Cues in the music often let you know when you're about to be attacked or when you've received or completed a quest. Select the method you would prefer for those sorts of alerts.**

Color changes. The edge of your vision will turn red in combat and green for two seconds when you acquire a new level. Your notebook, which usually hides under your picture, will slide out and appear blue when you have quest-related information.

Banners. A banner with an announcement will appear at the top edge of your vision for five seconds.

No alerts. Not recommended, especially because of

the combat issue. You might take some serious damage before you realize you're in trouble.

Ahva picked the first option as least likely to get on her nerves.

The djembe concert stopped. Perfect. Now a bird could hear herself think. She willed away the Settings screen.

Now, back to speaking. *Animal Eye* had started as a kid game and this beta version was the final step in making an adult-level game out of it. Surely, they didn't throw kids in with zero help. Khin May paused the game and called up the help window. That returned her to the wall-papered room where she'd decided to go with a quickstart rather than slog through the character generation process.

Alan Ivan Turning, the green musketeer, strode into the shop from a door in the back. "Are you trying to use the Speech skill?"

"Yes." Khin May took a few steps toward Alan. "How does it work in this game? All I can do is squawk and hiss."

Alan nodded. "Naturally. You really shouldn't expect much at your level. At a skill of 10, you're lucky you can mimic and that not clearly. Free speech will become available at a skill of 105, which will require an augmentation. For now, to view the available vocabulary in full immersion mode, simply think 'Speak' and a window will come up." A transparent pop-up window appeared along the left of Khin May's view with a list of words. "This shows you what you've heard enough times to mimic as well as words or phrases you show particular fascination with."

Khin May frowned. "Every time I want to talk, I have to call up that window?"

"Certainly not." His eyes narrowed as he shook his head.

"That would be ridiculously tedious. If you happen to know a word on the list, then you may simply speak it. As your skill improves, you'll need fewer repetitions to gain a word or phrase on the mimicry list, but the first several attempts may not sound quite right. There's also a bit of a random component to acquiring words, so you might be surprised to find that you gain a word or phrase you've only heard once if it's something you're focused on. To gain skill, you can apply your points when you level up or continue to practice the skill whenever you can. Your skill will improve faster at lower levels. I assume I've answered your question?"

You know what they say about assuming. Khin May gave him a thumbs-up. "Got it."

"Marvelous. I'll return you to the game." Alan smiled and waved his hand.

The wall-papered room faded away.

Once the bird cage had reformed, Ahva squinted. *Speak.*

A sidebar flipped out of midair on the left listing a collection of words and quick phrases.

Organized by Frequency: Hello, Good Morning, Friend, Bird, How much, No, Yes

I can say "Hello" but not "Hi." Sure. Why not?

Ahva drew a deep breath. "Hello."

The voice rasped and strained but she formed the word well enough.

A small, blue notebook icon appeared in the top left corner of her vision.

What's that about? She focused on the book, and a transparent journal opened in front of her.

Oh, the Humanity! Find a human to acquire you.

Love it! She snickered, which sounded like a few short hisses.

Since the quest had held off until she'd figured out speech, she supposed that meant she needed to use the crow's speech and mimicry skills to get a human's attention.

Ahva hopped forward to her empty food bowl and practiced her newly understood skills on the humans that passed the merchant's booth. After mastering "Hello" and the others on her current list well enough, she listened to humans passing by.

"Look at the bird!" One kid hollered, dragging a parent leading a package-ladened dog to a stop.

"Loo' a' the 'ird!" Ahva repeated.

"Mom! Did you hear that?"

"Di' you 'ear 'at?" Ahva repeated. *That's some accent you've got there, bird. Don't suppose you've got better clarity than that.*

The parent rolled her eyes. "Yes, very clever. You already have two bluejays to help you tend the garden. You don't need another bird. Let's go."

Ahva hopped to the corner of the cage. "'ery cle'er."

Other humans, mostly kids, stopped as the sun climbed toward noon. Some even stayed for a while, but no one even mentioned trying to purchase her. At least she'd learned the names of the merchant and his family. Eavesdropping might not be polite, but sometimes it was the only way through these games.

The success rate in this quest stinks, or I haven't figured out the hidden trick to it yet.

A young man stopped. He was one of the fair-complexioned patrons in this market. His maroon-colored robes fit like an Omar the Tentmaker construction. The ID above his head said, "Patron" and his health bar was full with a simple smilie face emoji. She focused on the emoji and a tool tip popped up.

This is a Morale indicator. The happier it is, the better the person's morale. Characters with better morale are more confident. They're more likely to land attacks or stand and fight against a threat. If morale drops low enough, the character will flee or refuse to engage anyone.

"Hello." Ahva fluttered one wing.

"Aren't you smart." He stuck his finger through the bars. "Are you a fierce bird? Are you? Huh?"

The smilie emoji in his ID tag turned into a smilie with teeth showing.

Okay, so you're really, really, really confident. Got it.

"I wouldn't do that, if I were you." Callen, the merchant, glanced away from the customer he was helping across the booth. "Birds are territorial."

The man poked her beak. "You won't bite me. You're not that fierce. Are you?"

Ahva's head rocked back. *Try me, buster.*

"See? You're nothing." He poked again. "Come on. Try to bite me. Bet I'm faster than you."

Is that a challenge?

"Sir, I really wouldn't do that!" the merchant warned. "I'll be with you in moment, and we can talk about Ahva or any of the other birds."

The human smacked her beak, pushing her head to the side. "Slowpoke."

Ahva hissed. She fluffed up her feathers the way her budgies did when they were mad and glared. The edge of her vision turned red, and the emoji in the patron's ID tag became just a blah face. *Ooo. Did acting like a mad bird give him a Morale debuff? All right. Game on, foolish mortal. Try that again.*

"Y'wimp." The human tapped the side of the cage then jiggled the door.

When he poked his fingers through the bars again, she snapped her head forward and clamped down with her beak.

The human jerked his hand back. "Your bird bit me!" He backed away and inspected his hand.

She hadn't drawn blood, but two white lines marked where her beak had cut the top layer or two of his skin. His health bar had only dropped a few points, but his morale tag became a frown.

Serves you right. "Fierce."

Callen shrugged. "I asked you not to stick your fingers through the bars. If you want to see one of the birds closer, I'll be happy to take one out for you. Would you like to see Ahva?"

Ahva hissed like her friend's ticked off cockatiel. *You better say, "No." I'll bite you again!*

"That one? No, thank you." He slapped the side of the cage. "How about this blue one over here? He looks friendlier. I need one that will fetch small tools for me."

Then why were you so irritating about whether I was fierce enough? Try that stupidity on an eagle. Just try it! See if you come away with any fingers left.

The red at the edge of her vision went away.

Ahva watched Callen show off a silly bluejay who whistled a tune while retrieving different objects on command.

Show off!

After a bit of haggling, they came to an ultimate agreement. Callen swapped the bluejay for a pile of odd green chips. Coins maybe? What would they be made of if they were green? Corroded copper? As the pair went off together, Ahva wished them well and ruffled her feathers. She returned to practicing her speech skills and failing to attract a human.

In the distance, the horn like an Israeli shofar sounded one long note. The market cleared out like water down a small incline through multiple puddles.

A second horn sounded, and city guards strolled through, encouraging the rest to return to their homes more quickly. A pop-up appeared. **Hm… What would a bird do? Preen? Whistle? Explore?**

Ahva snorted. *Explore what? A half-meter cube doesn't give me much to investigate.* Ahva looked up and used the Skills drop-down. Her options included Sneak, Detect Enemy, Signal Human, and a pile of others. None of that offered a way out of this. She thought back to her budgies. They preened just about any time they weren't eating or chirping. She could do that.

Ahva preened her feathers when Callen started moving the birds back into one of the two tents where they would shelter from the night's cooler air. She was rewarded with **+10 XP** that glittered midair for a few seconds then vanished. A woman Ahva had learned earlier was Callen's wife Mirin came out of the other tent behind the booth as he came out from putting up the last hawk. "How did we do?"

Ahva went back to preening.

"Not bad. We sold two falcons, three bluejays, and an eagle." Callen numbered them off on his fingers.

"And that one?" Mirin pointed at Ahva.

Ahva looked up. "Dat one?" *And what exactly have I done*

to deserve that?

Callen shook his head. "Plenty of interest, but no takers."

"Mmhm." Mirin rolled her eyes. "I told you crows won't sell in this market. The nomads fear them."

Callen held up both hands palm out. "Some nomads fear them. Other Bakhari, especially some of the tribesmen, don't much care about the superstitions, and we get plenty of shoppers who aren't nomads. She'll sell."

"After we move to Nethanya or Ilion, maybe, which won't happen until next fall, and you know it."

"Not necessarily, Mirin." Callen leaned closer to her and spoke softer. "And we're not going to Ilion. I'm hearing too many strange things about that place. Weird half-rotting animals wandering the countryside and men that laugh hysterically while attacking people. No. When we move next fall, it's Nethanya. I'd even prefer Antwen over Ilion."

"Antwen taxes are too much." She huffed and took the cash box into the human tent as a boy ran up.

"Then we're going to Nethanya."

The quick movement drew Ahva's attention. The boy had sandy-colored hair and dark eyes. Like his parents, he wore loose robes, which he could be growing into for a long time.

"Hello!" Ahva tipped her head to one side.

The boy brought himself up short and leaned over to look in. "Hi, Ahva. Bite any fingers today?"

Ahva cawed. "Yes."

"Bite more tomorrow!"

Unless she figured out the quest, she planned to do that to any who decided to stick their fingers where they weren't wanted.

Mirin came out of the tent and frowned. "Darin, don't

encourage her."

"Oh, Mom, she doesn't know what I'm saying."

Ahva snorted. She understood every word. She wasn't some dumb chicken, after all. She was a crow, an intelligent breed by all accounts. Didn't this goofy kid watch vids on social media?

A man approached. He whipped off a loose robe and revealed dark, tight-fitting clothes. His gaunt face and long, thin nose gave him a rodent-like appearance. The ID above his head read "Ratnose." She'd been waiting for a human, but something about this man didn't sit right with her. His morale tag showed a smilie.

The red border formed around her vision, a confirmation of her suspicions.

That is not the human I'm looking for. If this fellow meant harm, acting hostile might give him some sort of debuff. She fluffed up and hissed to warn the man off, but he ignored her admonition and came on anyway. No debuff changed the morale tag in his ID.

Nice try, bird, but this guy's not impressed.

Callen stepped toward the man. "Good evening, friend. I'm afraid the horn has sounded for the day, but we'll be here tomorrow."

This human was not a friend. Even she recognized that. Ahva hissed more loudly and wove from side to side to prove how impressively dangerous she really was. This time, morale tag changed to a blah face. He shied away from her a single step. Not much of a debuff, but at her level, how could it be?

"What I'm here for I'll take right now." The man sneered. He pulled a knife out of a sheath on his belt and grabbed

Mirin, pulling her against his chest and pressing the knife to her throat. She tried to pull free but couldn't overcome the larger human's hold.

"Mom!" Darin screamed.

He rushed at the man. Callen reached for him and missed. Keeping a hold on Mirin, the unwelcome visitor swung his knife hand outward and struck a solid blow to the space between the collarbones with the knife's pommel. Darin stumbled backwards and whacked his head hard on one of the display tables. He collapsed, holding his head and crying. The health bar above his head had dropped by a quarter. Callen pulled him out of the man's reach.

Ahva jumped to the side of the cage and held on with her feet. She fluffed up her feathers and shrieked as loudly as any cockatoo in a snit. Maybe the debuffs would stack.

The blah face emoji didn't change.

Mirin stomped on the man's foot and jerked herself free but took only one step toward Callen before the man grabbed her by her long hair and yanked her back to him.

"Your cash box. Now." The man glowered and lowered his voice. "Else find yourself less one woman."

"All right. All right." Callen held both hands palm out. "Don't hurt her. I'll get it for you. It's in the tent."

"And be quick."

Callen ducked into the bird tent.

That's not where she took the money box.

"You, Ratnose. Let her go. Now!"

Ahva spun to the new voice. He was as dark as a nighttime shadow and dressed in brown trousers, a red three-quarter-sleeved shirt, and leather sandals. A largish bag on a long strap hung from right shoulder to left hip, and he held a bow and arrow at the ready. The ID over his head said "Osse Bente."

Huh. He has a surname, too. Is this a more important human?

Ratnose sneered. "Forget it, kid. You're fooling no one. You can't hit me without hitting her."

"Bakhari tribesmen start practicing archery the day we can stand up. It's nothing to me to shoot this over her shoulder and through your disgusting eyeball! Let her go!"

Disgusting eyeball? Now that could be a fun phrase.

Osse sidestepped, and Ratnose pivoted to track him, keeping Mirin pinned to his chest. Callen stepped out of the bird tent behind Ratnose and made as little noise as a hunting owl. An empty carrier cage hung from Callen's hand.

Osse led Ratnose most of a quarter circle around when Callen lunged forward and cracked Ratnose across the back of the skull again and again. The thief released Mirin and tried to shield his head with his arms. The carrier cage came apart, and he fell like a sack of birdseed.

And stay down!

The red border on Ahva's vision faded. She smoothed out her feathers. Mirin ran to Darin while Osse couched his bow and returned the arrow in the quiver on his back.

"My mother is an herbalist, and I learned the lore from her. I have supplies. Can I help your son?" Osse patted his bag.

Mirin had tears in her eyes. "Please."

He rushed over and crouched next to Darin and Mirin.

Ahva bobbed and twisted her head, weaving from one side or the other to get a peek at what Osse did, but he was too thoroughly in the way. Darin cried out all the louder.

"I'm sorry." Osse sat back on his heels. "It does sting a little, but it'll stop the bleeding and should stop infections. You'll want a physician to fully treat the injury."

Mirin snorted. "I thought you were an herbalist."

"Yes, but that means I can mix herbs to treat minor problems. I'm not advanced yet, and I'm no physician. If you can tell me where to find–"

Callen shook his head. "You'd never get back into the market. The horn has sounded. The physician will have to keep until morning."

"Are either of you hurt?" Osse looked up at Callen.

"I'm fine." Callen held one palm out.

Mirin stammered a few useless syllables then swallowed hard. "I'm all right."

"What's your name, lad?"

The tribesman bowed and touched his forehead with his fingers. "Osse Bente."

And I'm Ahva. Let's not forget me! Ahva squinted at them. "Hi, Ahva. Loo' at the 'ird!" *Seriously? I've known toddlers who speak clearer than that. Practice. Must practice.*

Mirin scowled. "If you're so fine with that bow, why didn't you take that one out?" She kicked Ratnose's leg.

Hey! Cut the kid some slack. He only saved your miserable butt. Ahva hissed.

"Your pardon, but that was a bluff. I'm accurate, but I don't know that I'd trust my aim enough to shoot past someone. Now my father, he could have turned the shot mid-air and landed it up Ratnose's left nostril without disturbing his mustache. But I'm not of that caliber yet."

"You did fine, Osse," Callen gripped his wife's shoulder.

Mirin shot a squint-eyed glance at the thief. "Yes,

I'm-I'm sorry. You saved our lives, and I chastise you for it."

Osse nodded once. "Think on it no more."

Ahva whistled. *I like him. Well spoken. Calm. Certain. Archer. Actually has a last name, unlike anyone else I've seen. Maybe he's the human I'm looking for?* She'd have to keep her eyes on that one.

Clicking and clattering drew nearer. Ahva hopped to the side of the cage nearest the noise.

Five sentries and three dogs approached. Instead of the robes of the locals or the tunic and trousers of the tribesmen, the sentries wore leather kilts that covered their thighs and a studded leather vest over a yellowish-brown shirt. Their boots were ankle-high with copper buckles. Their swords were drawn. The dogs were all Labrador types, two yellow and one black. The dogs wore leather armor that covered their back, neck, shoulders, and hips.

The lead sentry, who wore a cape, scowled. "You there! The horn has sounded and the market has closed!"

Osse stood. "Your pardon. I'm new here, and I got turned around on my way out."

"Any thief could say that. We'll have to take you in." The leader pointed with his sword. "Hand over your weapons peaceably, and there will be no harm done to you."

Callen stepped in front of Osse. "This one is my guest. He saved the life of my wife and son." He pointed to Ratnose. "Here's your thief."

The sentry surveyed the situation. "And the boy?"

Callen glanced back at Darin. "Struck his head. The bleeding has stopped. I'll bring him in to rest."

The leader sheathed his sword and turned to the others.

"Farl, fetch the physician. Neal, Patris, take the thief to the lock-up. We'll bring the physician to check him once the boy's tended." He returned his attention to Callen. "Let's get your boy inside. Then I'll need your statements to draw up the charges."

"Fine, fine."

Lifting Darin easily, the leader followed Mirin into the tent.

Callen waved for Osse to follow. "You can stay with us tonight."

Osse picked up his bow. "Thank you, but I have a room at an inn."

"The captain will need your statement as well. Come. Our hospitality is the least we can offer after this evening. We have plenty of food and space."

Osse bowed. "I am grateful."

Callen swept up Ahva's cage by the handle. "And you, little Ahva, were brave trying to scare that monster off like that."

Ahva watched the sentries cart off the thief and cawed. *"Disgussin' eye'all."* Or something like that.

Osse came over and looked in the cage. "Striking bird. All that posturing was a threat?"

Callen nodded. "Umhm. Fluffing up, weaving, beak clicks, and hissing are all an effort to show how large and threatening she is. Anyone who came at a bird in that kind of mood would do well indeed to come away with all fingers and skin intact. Unfortunately, the thief didn't much care."

And he obviously got a headache for his ignorance.

Callen leaned closer. "Fortunately for the thief, she didn't unhitch her cage door and come after him in person."

CHAPTER 2

Ahva studied at the cage door, held closed by a simple peg through a couple holes. She clicked her beak. Of all the stupid things! As soon as she knew he wasn't reasonably impressed by her display of ferocity, she could have unhooked the cage door and taken her complaint to him directly. She wouldn't forget next time.

"She can let herself out?" Osse snickered.

"I haven't seen her do it, yet, but other crows and bluejays I've had needed a padlock to keep them in." Callen tapped the peg. "This is too easy to circumvent, but I haven't had a bird escape a padlock yet."

Hey! There is no "lockpick" skill in my list, you dork.

Osse stood up straighter. "And you're not afraid she'll get away?"

Callen shook his head. "She's well trained and will return when told. Besides, her food is here, and she doesn't know how to forage in the wild."

You ain't got the brains God gave geese. How am I supposed to solve this quest if the first human we come across who's got skills gets an earful of how unskilled I am.

He carried her into the bird tent and set her in the last space, at the top of one of the shelves. After Callen doled out food to each bird, the humans left and strung a lace through the door flaps.

The bird tent was lined with shelves made of something like cinderblocks and wooden beams. Each shelf had bird cages. The largest cages containing the eagles were on the bottom, and each shelf going up had progressively smaller cages until the top shelf was all bluejays and crows.

Now, how am I supposed to attract a human if I'm away from where the humans are?

A green bar filling most of a black box appeared at the top edge of her vision then decreased to less than a quarter full while it changed colors from green to yellow to orange to red to maroon. A tool tip popped up next to it.

This is your fatigue meter. The more actions you do and the longer you go without eating or sleeping, the smaller this bar gets while the fatigue drains your endurance. In the case of birds, that can build up quickly. Birds have quite the metabolism, and that limits your maximum Endurance attribute. When the bar is empty, you're done for a while. To increase the bar, you should eat or sleep.

While she ate, she considered her available resources and the problem and watched the bar climb back up to full.

The cage bars were welded where they joined each other, the top, and the bottom. If she were an eagle, maybe she would've been strong enough to pop the welds, but a crow? Not hardly. Her Power attribute was a paltry 5 out of 100.

Lucky if I can pick up air molecules at that rate.

If she chilled until morning, she'd be right where she was out in the market waiting for a human. Osse wasn't dressed snazzy enough to be the sort to carry enough money to buy a bird, so if she wanted to go with him, she had some convincing to do, and that wouldn't happen here.

Gotta get that door open.

Her Cleverness and Agility attributes were good. Maybe they'd work together with the Sneak skill and do something worthwhile.

With her beak and feet, Ahva pulled herself around the cage to the door. The locking mechanism was a simple inverted cone-shaped peg crammed through the holes in the two metal plates that lined up when the door closed. Not exactly complicated. A smart, resourceful bird would have such an easy lock sorted out quickly. Social media was full of videos of parrots, ravens, and crows solving complex puzzles more robust than the "get the peg out" type.

Using her foot hadn't worked so well. Maybe her beak would be a better choice. Ahva tried first from the space between the bars on one side of the peg then the other. She could tap the peg, but her beak would need a hinge to be able to grab it. Next, she tried biting around the bar but her beak wouldn't close enough to get a purchase on the peg.

She huffed and hopped back to her perch. She had to get the peg out! Getting it from the top was no good.

Could nudge it from the bottom, maybe.

She hopped back to the front of the cage then slid down the vertical bars until her head was below the bottom of the peg.

Ahva reached through and smacked the bottom of the peg with the top of her beak. After sliding up a centimeter, the peg dropped back down to its original spot.

Okay. This can work!

Ahva pushed the peg up until the bottom was almost to the top of the rings on the cage and door. She twitched her head up.

For just a moment, the peg nearly flew free, but it lost momentum too fast. It tilted slightly and caught on the edge and wobbled side to side.

At least it didn't fall back in. Ahva nudged the door with her shoulder, and the hinge gave the smallest squeak as it slid open.

She hopped into the opening and squawked. "Done!"

The notebook turned blue, and Ahva opened it. **New skill: Problem-solving.**

She checked the other bird cages. They, too, had simple pegs securing the doors. *Should I spring them, too?*

Some of the larger birds eyed her with a combination of suspicion and disgust.

Nope. Don't need that headache. If they want out, I just showed them the way. Hope they were watching.

Ahva crept to the edge of her cage and peeked over. Naturally, her cage had been one of the highest, and the floor might as well be a few kilometers down to packed dirt. The confines of the cage hadn't given her a chance to figure out flying.

No time like the present!

Ahva climbed up to the top of the cage and held onto the bars with her toes. She spread her wings and flapped like mad. Her grip was harder to maintain but not because she was getting any vertical force.

What was she not doing?

Flight looks so easy when birds do it.

Ahva folded her wings and paced the diagonal of the cage top. Months ago, she'd watched a documentary on the miracle of flight. Whether bird, bat, plane, or helicopter, the concept was the same. Flight physics mattered. Her lift had to exceed gravity and thrust had to exceed drag. She needed more airfoil, the curve difference between the top and bottom surfaces of her wings.

She strutted to the cage edge again. Ahva flapped hard, tipping her wings at different angles to find the best one. When the beating of her wings created an upward pull, she let go of the cage and lifted off.

CHAPTER 2

I'm flying! I'm actually flying!

She looked down at the floor below for just a moment then back up again at the canvas wall of the tent filling her entire forward view.

Brakes! Whoa!

She closed her eyes and turned her head as she smacked straight into the canvas above the cage opposite her own. When she thudded onto the top of a bluejay's cage, the occupant fluffed up and hissed.

"Sorry. Sorry!"

Ahva twisted around as the jay climbed up the bars with murder in his eyes. Flapping like crazy, she took off again as the jay's beak closed on the bar where Ahva had been a moment before.

Grouch!

The far wall of cages raced closer.

Flight physics. Reduce lift on one side to turn.

She adjusted the angle of one wing slightly and started to roll but continued in a straight line.

Rudder!

Ahva swished her tail to one side and banked sharply, missing a falcon's cage by a couple centimeters. The wind ruffled her feathers and the cages swept past her at a phenomenal rate. A rush of warmth through her had her laughing out loud, a passable imitation of Callen's chortle.

WHOO!

She continued flying around until her fatigue bar had dropped to halfway. By then, she had figured out all the necessary maneuvers, including landing, with some measure of competence better than accidental humor.

Next step. Get next door and get that human's attention.

The door to the tent was closed and laced shut. Ahva hissed and landed on the packed dirt floor. She started to the door and stuck her beak under the canvas. If there was enough give in the material, maybe she could sneak out under the tarp.

The canvas wouldn't lift. She pushed harder and tapped something solid.

There has to be some way to get out of here. Time to use that new Problem Solving skill. She activated the skill from the menu and studied the problem. The laces zigzagging up the middle of the door.

Ahva stepped forward. A thought bubble appeared with the words "*If it isn't knotted...*" She pinched one of the cords with her beak and jerked her head from side to side. "*Please don't be knotted.*"

The cord slid, leaving a loop.

Yes!

She adjusted her grip and pulled again. The cord slid a few more centimeters before something hard smacked the other side of the canvas. When she tugged again, she gained no more room.

No.

The loop was only a few centimeters, not nearly enough for her to squeeze through, but if she could get the same space from the other lace, maybe she'd get enough. She looked up to get the Skill menu and selected Problem Solving.

The thought bubble appeared. "*Well, if moving one lace worked...*"

She grabbed the lace that formed the neat Xs with the first one and yanked. It slid more easily than the other and

CHAPTER 2

she tipped backwards, landing on her tail with a total lack of grace. Ahva scrambled back to her feet and stood proud, daring any other bird in the tent to mock her efforts. As she looked around at all the other cages, most of the birds, including the grouchy bluejay who'd gone after her toes earlier, were already beak under wing.

Early curfew, huh?

Soon, she wouldn't have enough light to do anything but sleep, and she wanted to be in the other tent by then. In the morning, Osse would be on his way, and with the skills he'd displayed earlier, he would be a perfect human to adventure with.

Now that Problem Solving had shown the way, Ahva resumed work on the second lace. Like the first one, she only managed to loosen it a few centimeters before the cord refused to slide any further. She rushed back to the door and stuck her head through the opening she'd made. Wiggling and pushing with her feet, she managed to squeeze her head and shoulders through, but after that, the edges of the tarp pressed hard against her and wouldn't budge.

If she were a raptor, she could tear the canvas or bite through the lacing. As a crow, she had to use other skills.

Think, think, think. She looked up and tagged the Problem Solving skill again.

"Beats me," the thought bubble said.

Helpful. Not.

She backed up and tried loosening the laces further. Nothing moved.

Come on, Problem Solving! She picked the skill again.

The thought bubbles appeared in the middle of her view again. *"What is keeping the laces from sliding free? Is there something I can do to remove the impediment?"*

Ahva stuck her head through the opening, looked down, and almost squawked. A bowknot tied the laces together. She grabbed one of the tails and tugged until the bow came loose. After that, the laces slid through the grommets easily, and in only a couple minutes, she had plenty of room to strut out into the merchant's booth in front of the tents.

That ought to boost my problem-solving skills some.

Ahva fluttered over to the other tent's door. Inside, someone's sleeping was like an intermittent chainsaw. Early to bed, early to rise, right? With the last of the failing light, she repeated the process and gained entry to the human's tent. The dull, reddish glow of a fire in the brazier gave her enough light to make out outlines and shapes in a warm grayscale, but it cast heavy shadows. The merchants and their boy slept on cots near the far walls. Osse was curled up on flat cushion on the ground closer to the door. His bow and arrows were inside the door, but his bag was near his head.

He won't be leaving without that!

She strutted over and perched on the bag. From the menu overhead she picked Sleep.

The image went dark.

Chapter 3

Jake smacked the Finished button and dearly hoped that was the end of the character generation process. Playing a game as a much larger version of his dog was going to be incredible! The view through his VR mask changed to black with a small cartoon terrier chasing its tail while a polar bear wearing a sandwich board waddled across. The sign read, "Please wait. We're processing your character and creating your world."

While that continued, Jake darted into the kitchen for a root beer from the fridge. By the time he got back, the terrier flopped spread-eagle on the screen as dotted lines spiraled over its head and tiny blue birds flew circles. The polar bear shrugged and carried the terrier off the screen by the scruff of its neck.

The view went black then faded in as a small, open-topped pen. As expected, he had a first-person point of view. He preferred that over the three-quarters overhead shot, but he'd wanted to know what Nagheed the Nethanyan Mountain Shepherd looked like. He'd have to watch for a mirror at dog height.

The background music started up, a very RenFaire kind of tune with a stringed instrument playing a lively song.

After a minute, the stringed instrument was joined by a recorder playing the same melody at a higher pitch. The tune brought him back to last spring when he'd gone to the local Renaissance Festival with some friends to watch jousting and fencing demos. He'd come home with a decorated tabard, an ornately designed knife, and a mild sunburn. When the tune restarted, he returned to checking out the environment.

In the top left corner of the view, the head shot of a shaggy dog gave him access to a character screen, and a cogwheel led to a settings window. Farthest right, a skill drop-down showed what he could do.

Jake adjusted his VR headset and thought about stepping back.

Nagheed took a step back from the nose-front view of the pen's chainlink fence and hit the rear. The sides were hardly wider than his shoulders.

A little close in here.

Jumbled voices competed with a trumpet fanfare. Nearer at hand, dogs whined and barked. Across the way, a merchant set up under a pavilion and displayed clay pitchers and bowls. His vision was a little weird. The whole view had shades of blue, yellow, gray, and a sort of yellow-ish brown, as if red and green had ceased to exist. Not the sort of colorblindness he had expected playing a dog, but interesting.

Everywhere he looked, words wafted up from various objects. The clay pots across the way exuded "paint" in dull, faded letters. Their merchant showed "human male," and after a few moments of looking, the word "anxious" tagged on. "Sausages" and "many humans" blew by on the breeze along with "leather goods," "sea salt," and "heated metal."

Some of the words were faint or disappeared quickly, but other lingered or stood out more. What a fascinating way to handle enhanced animal senses for humans!

After observing the scents for a while, Nagheed returned his attention to his current situation. Caged in a market. As big as he was, this wasn't much of a cage. He could hop out and bolt off any time he was feeling the urge, but he had to be here for a reason.

Am I acquiring my human or have I started the game with my human trying to sell me? What skills do I have to help me out? He focused on the dog icon in the corner.

Name: Nagheed **Species:** Canine – Mountain Shepherd
Class: Protector Level 1 **Gender:** M

Attributes

Attribute	Current	Skill	Current
Power	36	Detect Enemy	30
Speed	22	Sound Alarm	25
Cleverness	30	Stay Alert	25
Endurance	44	Nip	20
Agility	32	Bite	18
Charm	40	Claw	17
Vitality	44	Dodge	22
Sight	39	Posture	18
Smell	55	Intimidate	25
Hearing	55	Patrol	16
Health	124	Signal Human	20
Encumbrance 0 out of 50 lb		Trek	10
		Long distance movement	10

Sprint 10

He blew out a breath. *Not much.*

Charm, though. Maybe he could do something with that if the right situation came along.

Nagheed closed his character screen and harrumphed.

The computer pinged, and a notebook icon appeared in the top corner of the screen next to his dog headshot.

Jake looked at the icon and reached up with his VR-gloved hand to tap it.

It flipped open and expanded to fill the center of the screen.

How Much Is That Doggy? Find a human to acquire you. Jake rolled his eyes. *Really? Cheesy quest names for a quest he'd already figured he needed to do? He could already tell that would be one of the least-used features in this game.* He flipped it closed. It folded back down and shrunk as it slid back up to the dog image.

How hard can it be to get someone to adopt a cute, fuzzy puppy – the size of a small horse. Maybe I should have picked a different breed. Being adorable will be hard in this tiny box. Nagheed sighed. *All right. Gotta make this work. Time for that Charm attribute to do its thing.*

Standing, Nagheed had to tuck his tail between his back legs. Sitting, his hips hit the side, but he could curl his tail over his back. There wasn't enough space to lie down. Before long, a red alert box appeared at the bottom right corner of the screen. **-5 Agility. Try moving around some. You're getting awfully stiff!**

No kidding, computer. He arched his back as much as he could. He called up the Charm attribute and wagged his tail.

CHAPTER 3

Humans stopped by often, and left with small dogs. From listening to them talk, rats and other vermin were apparently a problem at the farms around here. The Charm attribute had him wag his tail, give the shopper sad eyes, or paw at the pen and whine. Invariably the shoppers made a comment about a curse and went on their way or purchased another dog. What was this nonsense about a curse? His character screen showed no debuffs active except for the stiff muscle ding on his Agility. Was that a curse?

Nagheed huffed. A couple more terriers and a yellow lab to go, and he'd be the last dog.

Jake tagged the menu in the top right corner and selected Charm again.

He tipped his head to the side and whined.

"Daddy! Puppies!" A girl ran up to Nagheed's cage and crouched. A basket dangled from her arm. A nametag that read "Zara" and a green health bar floated over her head. Her dress looked like an ankle-length shirt, and she wore hat that looked like a somewhat flattened chef's hat.

Jake winced and disabled Charm. Oh no. I do not need to be the pet of a little girl. I'd be old and gray by the time she's old enough to go adventuring.

Zara reached for him, but a man caught up, grabbed her around the chest, and picked her up. His nametag called him "Constable Simon Fishel."

Huh. A title. Must be an important guy.

The constable was dressed for trouble. He wore leather armor. A rapier and a dagger hung from his belt along with a blackpowder pistol and a belt pouch. The basic designs of his weaponry and the scuff marks suggested they were meant for use, not show.

"Not that one, honey." Simon set her down.

"Aw, but he's cute and fluffy!" She crossed her arms and frowned. "You said I could have a puppy for my birthday."

"Yes. One to be your companion. Help you do chores and the like as you both get older, but that's an adventurer's dog. Maybe you'll be an adventurer when you grow up, but for now, let's stick with something more practical. Besides, your mother would be in a right fit if we brought home a puppy half the size of a horse." He led her to the remaining terriers and the yellow lab. "Let's pick something smaller, hmm?"

Nagheed looked at anything but Zara. Was there an "anticharm" attribute?

The merchant identified as "Ibrahim" approached them. He was well-tanned and had clearly not missed too many meals. The tunic and pants he wore were simple in design like many at the Renaissance Festival last spring. "Happy birthday, young lady. How would you like a puppy that will fit perfectly in the basket you're carrying, even when full grown?"

Zara's eyes widened. "Really?"

He took a tiny terrier with long, silky hair out of the cage and set the pup right in her basket.

"But what does it do?" The father pointed at the terrier. "It doesn't look big enough to be useful."

"This one can fetch small objects for her and keep vermin out of the house." The merchant pointed to the yellow lab. "Now this one over here can do a good deal more. In addition to fetching, he can pull a cart or wear saddlebags to carry things. Not so good at the vermin problem, though, at least not in a house."

"No vermin issues in our house. We've got a cat for that. And I don't think she needs a cart dog. Fetching, though. That could be handy." Fishel crouched in front of Zara. "So, whichever you like. The yellow lab or this little terrier."

She held up her basket. "This one!"

"That one it is."

After they settled on the price, the girl skipped away with a dog Nagheed could swallow without chewing.

Glorified mouse. Probably for the best.

He needed to find a human old enough to go forth and do something more interesting than house chores, homework, and playing fetch.

"There you go! That's what I'm talking about!" a woman said.

Nagheed looked around as much as he was able and spotted a woman rushing over and a man trailing a few steps behind her. The man was decked out in chainmail and a sturdy metal helmet. A sword in its sheath hung from his belt. The woman wore gray-brown leather. Several pouches hung from her belt.

If those two weren't adventurers, he'd eat a shoe. Nagheed turned on the Charm and went for the sad eyes.

"You want a mountain shepherd?" the man raised an eyebrow and pointed. "A dog that size would be as stealthy as an elephant."

She propped her hands on her hips. "Oh, and you're so well camouflaged in all that clanking metal."

The man sneered. "Someone has to protect you when you trip alarms."

Trip alarms? Just what kind of adventurers are these?

"That was –" She stopped and lowered her voice. "That

was only that one time."

"Once was enough." He wrapped an arm around her shoulders and guided her away. "When we finish our next score, we can quit for a while. You can get whatever companion animal you want then. All right? Just not a mountain shepherd. They're huge. Too big to help us on a job. Now a ferret ..."

Nagheed blew out a breath. That didn't sound like the kind of adventure he wanted.

The merchant's wife stepped down from the back of the covered wagon and pointed at Nagheed. "'Don't worry,' you said. 'Plenty of adventurers would love to have a big dog,' you said. 'What about the eyes?' I asked. 'Don't–'"

The eyes? What was wrong with his eyes? He closed first one then the other. He could see just fine. Everything was still that same spectrum of gold, yellow, gray, and blue, but nothing was blurry or doubled up or anything weirder than that.

"That's enough. He'll sell, you'll see, and for a good price." Ibrahim jabbed his finger toward his wife and frowned.

She swatted his hand away. "You mark my words, Ibrahim. He's gone by sundown or the sea can have him. He eats more than both of us and the rest of the dogs together. We can't afford him." She climbed back into the wagon.

Nice, but if the computer gave me this quest, there has to be a way to solve it. So, Charm isn't working. What else do I have?

He summoned the character screen and scanned through the info.

Huh. Signal Human, maybe?

He picked that one and barked, a deep, resounding noise

CHAPTER 3

that came from the center of the planet. A few people paused, but none opened a pocketbook. He barked again. A loud clang rattled the pen. Nagheed cringed and shrank away as far as he could.

"That's enough of that. You'll scare people off." The merchant stood poised to swing the stick again.

"No need for that. The poor fellow's feeling a bit lonely."

Nagheed turned toward the voice as much as he could.

The man approaching was taller than the merchant, but not remarkably so. A wide-brimmed hat with a feather shaded his pale, bearded face. A rapier hung from his belt, and a ring with a large stone decorated his finger. The doublet and trousers were edged with detailed embroidery, clearly a man of some means. His leather knee-high boots creaked as he crouched. The nametag above his head labeled him "Baron Rafayel Dorcas."

A baron, wow, but does he go on adventures, or is he the administrative type?

"He'll scare off my customers." The merchant frowned.

Rafayel stood. "On the contrary, he may have attracted a sale. I'm in the market for a dog with some muscle. I heard his bark from the end of the row." He pointed the way he'd come. "I thought you only dealt in terriers and retrievers."

Ibrahim leaned closer. "Special consignment. Bought this one off an old friend. Dog knows his manners."

"Let's see them." Rafayel gestured to Nagheed.

"Sit!" Ibrahim ordered.

"Not in the pen. I can't imagine how the poor boy can breathe in such a tiny space, let alone display his good upbringing. Let's have a look at him where he's got some room."

Ibrahim stammered. "Um, Baron won't like that, sir. The guards told me strict that he doesn't hold with dogs running loose. If he gets away, it'd be my hide."

"It is true. I don't care for loose dogs, but–"

"What'd you say?" Ibrahim's eyes grew wide.

"I said, I don't care for loose dogs, but surely you have a leash or rope handy."

Ibrahim snatched the cap off his head and bowed. "I'm sorry, your Excellency. I didn't know you."

"No reason you should have." The baron smiled and indicated the wagon with a twitch of his head. "Be easy and fetch that leash."

"Yes, sir." Like a cowering dog afraid of getting smacked, Ibrahim hustled to the wagon and returned with a leather strip. A hole was cut in one end. "Now hold still, you."

Nagheed huffed. *Do I have a choice?*

He kept steady as the merchant made a loop by sliding one end of the strap through the hole at the other end. Then he slid the loop over Nagheed's head and pulled it tight.

"That'll do. Let's not choke the old boy." Rafayel reached over and loosened up the strap a bit.

Ibrahim handed him the leash and went to the other end of the cage. In a fit of mischief, Nagheed wagged his tail, whapping the merchant in the head a couple times.

"That's enough of that." The merchant blocked Nagheed's tail with his arm and yanked the peg loose. The door swung open with a creak worthy of any haunted house.

"All right, out you go," Ibrahim ordered.

Nagheed tried to turn in place but smacked into the side of the cage.

"Come on, out!" The man slapped Nagheed's rear.

Nagheed startled and whacked the front of the pen with his nose. At the top edge of the screen, his health bar appeared for a moment and lost a point.

Do that again, and I'll bite the end you sit on.

He shuffled backwards. Once clear, a tool tip on the Agility warning appeared.

To negate the penalty, choose the attribute from the menu. A blue arrow pointed to his skill drop-down.

Nagheed picked Agility from the menu. The game took over his movement. He shook like he'd just had a bath. His ears flipped back and forth, whapping the side and top of his head. He stretched all four legs then leaned forward to stretch his lower back then reversed directions with his tail in the air and front paws out as far forward as they'd go. The red warning in the corner showed the agility penalty dwindling.

"All right, that's enough," Ibrahim grumbled.

"Let him get the kinks out. If you were in a box barely bigger than you, you'd want a moment to limber up, wouldn't you?" He tipped his head down and looked up at the merchant.

The merchant studied his shoes. "Of course, your Excellency."

After the warning faded out, Nagheed sat, watching Rafayel.

Rafayel held his hand up, palm out. "Stay." He backed up to the end of the leash.

Nagheed stayed put.

"Good." He snapped his fingers and pointed to the ground at his feet. "Come."

Nagheed trotted over and wagged his tail.

The rest of the basic dog commands followed. Sit, stand, heel, speak, shake, roll over. Jake ran Nagheed through all the usual obedience stuff just like he'd trained his own pup, Prince.

"You're right. He's got a good command of the basics." Rafayel ruffled the fur on Nagheed's head. "Any special training yet?"

The merchant nodded. "Posture!"

Nagheed picked that skill from the list and bristled and growled.

"That'll be sure to frighten all but the most hardened criminals. Less likely to land their attacks if they're that spooked." Ibrahim winked. "I've only had him a day or two, so that's as far as we've gotten."

"How's his personality?"

"No issues with him, sir, except the barking."

The baron shrugged. "That can be trained out if it becomes an issue." He knelt and started running his hands along Nagheed's legs and back.

He twitched. *Hey! Hands off!*

"Any problems with hip or shoulder." The baron pressed his broad fingers against Nagheed's shoulder.

Nagheed side-stepped away.

"Not that I know of, sir, but are you sure you want this one? I've got a male retriever back here. Eight weeks old. The sire weighs some thirty kilograms. Very trainable, retrievers."

Rafayel frowned. "Too young. I need a well-behaved protector ready within a handful of weeks." He stood and frowned. "Why are you trying to steer me away from this old boy. Clearly you're not equipped to house him."

"Well, sir, it's, um–" After a glance over the baron's shoulder, Ibrahim studied his shoes. "It's the eyes, sir."

There we go with the eye thing again.

The baron lifted Nagheed's muzzle and studied his face. "Yes, he's odd-eyed. One brown, one blue."

And that's a problem?

Ibrahim glanced both ways, then leaned closer and whispered. "You know what they say?"

Rafayel waved his hand dismissively. "I don't hold with that old superstition."

"I dunno, sir. After taking him from my old friend, as a favor you understand, my wagon wheel broke. I got fined yesterday because I didn't hear the closing bell and sold a dog late. Then–"

Nagheed huffed. *And I suppose all that is somehow the dog's fault, right?*

"I can tell you with some certainty that I'm immune to the odd-eyed curse." He smiled widely. "The greatest blessing in my life has unmatched eyes. So, what do you say? Shall I restore your good fortune and take this 'curse' off your hands?"

A collection of clear, iridescent coins no sooner changed hands than the closing bell rang.

He waited for the system to declare the quest finished, but nothing happened.

"Thank you, your Excellency. May he serve you well." Ibrahim bowed.

"I'm sure we'll get along gloriously." He wrapped the leash around his hand twice. "Let's go introduce you to your new family, shall we? If my dear wife agrees...

But how could she refuse such a handsome fellow?"

So... Your wife is an adventurer? Sure, why not.

Nagheed trotted alongside his new human. He sniffed the air. Words, some brighter than others, floated on the sea breeze or fanned out from inside a tent or wagon: b**read, roasted meat, spices, vegetables, two squirrels, four species of birds, ocean salt.**

He looked around, following the words as they drifted by.

A pop-up appeared at the top of the screen. **Want to earn a little XP here and there? Act like a dog. What would the dog do on a walk?**

Jake thought about his half-chow, half-shepherd Prince curled up on the couch. What would Prince do, aside from peeing on every third shrub they passed.

Nagheed darted to the end of the leash to go check out a merchant booth that launched a constant stream of "??? Animal ???" into the air. **+10 XP** floated up from the booth then faded away.

"Heel!" The baron ordered. He wrapped the leash around his hand a few times. "You walk with me, not in front. Understood?"

Oh yeah?

Nagheed got about two strides ahead when another **+10 XP** floated up. The baron ordered him back and shortened the leash again.

He tried a few more times to get ahead. Each time he gained a few XP before he was ordered back and given less leash until he had no choice but to stay at the baron's side. Nagheed could have easily knocked the human over and pulled loose, but he supposed this was also part of the quest. As they strolled through the city, the baron periodically reached down and gave Nagheed's head or shoulder a gentle pat.

"Good boy."

Unable to go further away to investigate, Nagheed tried to observe everything with his eyes and nose. He got used to the red-deprived graphics and figured out how much information he could get from smelling. If he focused his attention, a person's emotional state appeared along with clues about identity. Hearing, too, was more interesting. Conversations behind closed doors were vividly clear.

They approached a gated and walled area near the center of town.

"Good boy." The baron ruffled the fur on Nagheed's head.

Something tapped his leg. Nagheed shied away and looked down at the long loop of leash hanging free.

Had the Baron been slowly playing it out? That made sense. The kudos had been for his obedience.

The gate opened as they approached.

Automatic door? That'd be weird for this environment.

As they slipped through, a man standing at the edge of the door bowed. He wore dark gray clothes less ornate than the baron but similar in style.

Not automatic, unless a stealthy servant counts.

The courtyard in front of them had a largish house of timber and stone. The gardens in front of the house sported flowers that would have had wonderful colors if Jake had picked a critter blessed with the right eyes. A cobblestone semicircle driveway looped in front of the house and then led off around the back. A half-dozen men and women tended the gardens. Others walked by with a purpose.

They entered through the iron-studded, wooden door

without knocking.

A new collection of scent words exploded on the air, concentrated in specific areas: **Lady, girl, boy, beef roast, carrots, potatoes, rosemary, woman, man, young boy.**

After a few seconds, the words shrank, and some vanished.

Nagheed followed the baron toward the back of the house. The food scents and the youths's, lady's, and woman's scents grew larger. They entered the kitchen where a lady sat at the table. Her embroidered dress spoke of nobility, strongly contrasting with the plain, unadorned older woman who stood at the fireplace stirring a pot.

The lady stood. "Rafayel Dorcas! Is that the thief the constable wanted to talk to you about?"

"Bettani, my dear, darling, light of my life, and air that I breathe, you know it is not."

Seriously? I'm going to hurl if this thing has a romantic subplot. He engaged Charm from the menu and tucked his tail and gave her the sad eyes.

Rafayel patted Nagheed's side. "This fine fellow is to keep you company while I travel abroad."

She smiled. "He is rather handsome."

Nagheed wagged his tail and looked up at the woman. One eye was dark. The other a pale blue.

"He's a good strong dog with a bark that would scare scales off a snake, including the two-legged kind that tries to break in." Rafayel stepped forward and embraced his wife.

Am I just a service dog and a guard beast?

Bettani leaned into his hug. "Thank you, but you've been teaching Micah and the other lads how to fight. We'll be fine. You should take him with you on your patrols and when you travel. I've never liked the thought of you going alone. Think how well he'll even out bad odds once you train him. You can get another one for me."

Rafayel stepped back and winced. "I specifically got him to keep you safe. I'll barely have time to train one dog, even if I'm able to find a second."

"Find him a friend when you get back. All the servants and Micah are much better trained, and you said yourself that our son's a natural leader. We're in better shape. The dog goes with you. I'll worry less."

Please. Getting stuck playing guard beast is not the adventure I signed up for.

"If you're sure," Rafayel said.

"I'm sure. Now, what's a good name for a mountain shepherd?"

Jake held his breath. *Is this where the game overrides my choice, and I get named Fluffy?*

"He's certainly a strong prince among dogs. Shall we call him Nagheed?" Rafayel suggested.

"Perfect."

Jake blew out a breath. *Okay, so, Rafayel travels, and I'm with him. That's better than being a housewife's pet.*

The computer pinged and gave him a brief trumpet fanfare as a notebook icon slid out from the dog avatar in the corner.

Yeah, right. Solved the quest, and it wasn't exactly a tough quest, so probably no level-up yet. He dismissed the notebook without looking and focused on the dog icon to get the character screen.

Name: Nagheed **Species:** Canine – Mountain Shepherd
Class: Protector Level 2   **Gender:** M

Attributes

Attribute	**Current**	**Skill**	**Current**
Power	36	Detect Enemy	30
Speed	22	Sound Alarm	25
Cleverness	30	Stay Alert	25
Endurance	44	Nip	20
Agility	32	Bite	18
Charm	40	Claw	17
Vitality	44	Dodge	22
Sight	39	Posture	18
Smell	55	Intimidate	25
Health	124	Signal Human	20
Encumbrance 0 out of 50 lb		Trek	10
		Long distance movement	10
		Sprint	10

Level 2? I did level up!

A banner across the top of the screen declared that he had five points to spend on attributes or skills. Health and Encumbrance were grayed out, but that still left him a terrific number of things to pick from. Oddly, the Signal Human score was higher than he remembered. Did he gain skills by using them? He'd have to watch that.

Now, where to distribute his five level points. Most games favored combat classes. Sure, the other stuff played into the scenario, but he'd always done the best with characters who could kick butt. He hadn't been in a combat in this game, though, so it was hard to tell what was important. The most likely attributes weren't too shabby, except maybe for speed, which was a pathetic 22. The combat skills, though, were laughable. Jake tossed two points into his Bite skill and the other three into Claw. After rechecking the modifications, he closed the screen.

* * *

As soon as there was enough light to discern shapes, red text in the lower corner warned Ahva that she was a bit stiff. She stretched her wings and feet and turned her head in that totally creepy backward-over-the-shoulder way that birds were so good at. Finally, the warning faded. The brazier had gone out some time ago, and the VR rig communicated a light chill in the air. The game overlaid a snowflake on her status bar. Ahva fluffed up her feathers to stay warmer. After about a minute doing a feathered tennis ball impression, the chill dwindled. The humans, of course, still slept. Birds were up with the sun. What better time to get some exploring in?

This tent was bigger than the bird tent. Callen and Mirin had bigger camp cots in one corner, and Darrin was on a smaller cot in the opposite corner. The brazier between them had burned low. Osse was crashed out on a pile of pillows nearer the door. One front corner of the tent was set up for a sort of mini-kitchen with a low counter and another lower brazier with a smooth slab of rock on it. The tent's ceiling was peaked in the center with a hole to let out the smoke from the fires.

Ahva strutted around the pillow pile Osse slept on, studying the human boy from all sides. He was a muscular guy but nothing like Mr. Universe. Sort of the high school athlete type without the awkward teenager-ness.

Should she wake him up? Get this party started? In a minute maybe. For now, she had to find out what kind of stuff he was carrying. Before she tried to recruit him for her human, she had to be sure he was worth recruiting. With all the trouble she'd gone through to get here, he'd better be. Ahva went first to the bow and quiver sitting next to his knife near the door. The bow was a simple recurve, without the string attached at the moment. The wood was nicely polished with no cracks or dings. The string, loose but ready to be stretched taut, had no fraying bits, even at the ends.

Next, she grabbed an arrow by the stiff black fletching and walked backward. Once she had the arrow clear of the quiver, she examined it from one end to the other. Odd, but there wasn't an actual arrowhead. Just a sharpened end. Easier to make the arrows that way, but wouldn't they do more damage with arrowheads? Well, they were early in the game. He'd be improving equipment along the way, no doubt.

The sheath for his knife was tough leather with a design stamped into it. Triangles and dots chased each other around the image of a bird on the one side. The other side was all dots and triangles in a lovely geometric pattern.

Ahva strutted over to the bag near Osse. A peg on a string secured it closed.

Easier than breathing!

After picking Problem Solving from the skill menu, a thought bubble appeared. *"Hmm, how did I solve the last peg-in-a-hole problem?"*

Right. Same thing but horizontal. She wrestled the peg loose then flipped the lid open on the bag. The contents were a bit sparse. A shirt, pants, a couple cloth-wrapped

CHAPTER 3

bundles, and some small jars like the one he'd used last night to take care of the merchant's kid.

You need to go shopping. You don't have anything interesting in here.

Osse rolled onto his back. He stretched both of his arms straight back over his head while he also stretched both feet. Ahva left his bag and stepped over to Osse's arm.

Time to practice her speech. "Hello."

He startled and twisted toward her. "Hi, Ahva."

Could she mimic noises better than she spoke? Ahva called up her skill list. There wasn't a "mimicry" skill, per se, but maybe Speech would get her in the right area.

Check out that mimicry thing. She climbed up onto his chest. "Hi, Ahva."

"I'm not Ahva. You're Ahva," he whispered.

Let's try, "Of course, I'm Ahva." "I not Ahva. You're Ahva." *Um, yeah. Missed. So, really locked into mimicry at this level. I'll have to practice more to build that skill.*

"Silly bird."

Nearby, Mirin inhaled loudly and sat up, yawning too much for such a fine morning.

"I'm sorry," Osse whispered. "I had a visitor when I awoke."

She jostled Callen's shoulder. "Callen, the crow's loose."

Callen groaned and rolled over. "Huh?"

"Crow's loose." Mirin scowled at him. "Did you sleep well, Osse?"

"Yes. I was very comfortable."

Mirin got up and rebuilt the fire in the brazier then filled the morning's teapot with water and hung it on the hook.

"How do I move her?" Osse asked.

Mirin shrugged. "Sit up. She'll adjust."

As Osse sat up, Ahva shifted around and used her toes to clutch his tunic through the light blanket covering him. Once he had situated himself, she fluttered up to his shoulder and perched. When he shied away from her, she leaned aside to watch him. Surely, he wasn't afraid of her. He was supposed to be her human, right?

The teapot whistled a boring monotone note. She tried to match the tone. Her pitch was a bit low, so she slid up the scale until she found the right tone.

Darin moaned and rolled over, covering his head with the extra blanket. Mirin finished preparing the tea and handed Osse a cup. Ahva leaned over to peek inside at the dark, greenish concoction. Some games used teas like potions. Maybe she should try that here, but what if it turned out toxic for a bird?

"Is she safe to drink this?" Osse tapped the cup.

Mirin waved her hand dismissively. "It's just a few herbs. Nothing hazardous."

Okay then! Safe for a taste test.

Ahva leaned further forward to get a taste of the tea, but the heat rising off of it gave her pause. Her sensitive beak might not find something that hot comfortable. She backed away and perched on Osse's shoulder again.

"They can eat nearly anything you do." Callen sat up and rubbed his eyes. "Ahva has definitely taken to you."

"Yes, I'm sorry. She was perching next to me when I woke up." Osse glanced at her.

"Does she bother you?" Callen stretched. "I can put her away."

"No, no, she's no bother, but I'm a little worried she

might bite me or scream in my ear."

"I don't think that's a worry for the moment. She's calm enough."

Just don't make me angry. You wouldn't like me when I'm angry.

Ahva started whistling a tune. Would that work toward the Speech skill? A glittery **+10 XP** fluttered in the air for a few moments, so that was nice.

"What do you plan today?" Callen asked.

"I need to finish my errands." Osse flipped the lid on his bag closed and latched it. "My family and the others in my village asked me to get some things while I'm here. Then I need to get some food for the journey home and start out, hopefully before nightfall."

"By yourself?" Mirin raised an eyebrow.

Callen nodded. "You're here to get your talisman, aren't you?"

Osse slumped and shrugged. "That's my main purpose for this trip."

Callen turned to his wife. "He has to take the journey to get his talisman on his own. That's the tribal way."

"I prove I'm ready to be a man that way." Osse hid an eyeroll from his hosts by turning away and taking a sip of tea, but Ahva caught the whole effect. Whatever this talisman business was about, he wasn't entirely onboard. Did he not like the tradition, or was he miffed that Callen had taken it on himself to explain it?

Callen smiled. "The way you handled yourself last night, I'd say you're ready."

"Thank you." Osse bowed his head.

Ahva thought about last night's excitement and remembered the interesting phrase Osse had used on Ratnose. "Disgussing eye'all!" *Hmm, getting closer. Still not there.*

Osse, with the tea halfway to his mouth, to quickly set it down as he laughed. "Did she say what I think she said?"

"She sure did." Callen smiled.

"Disgussing eye'all!" Ahva repeated.

"She's mimicking you. No doubt about it anymore. She likes you." Mirin cracked her first smile. "Why don't you take her with you when you go? She could be your talisman."

"I couldn't afford such a magnificent bird." Osse shook his head. "And she'd never work for a talisman. The ceremony requires sacrificing the talisman in a fire." Osse frowned.

And that would end this game real quick, wouldn't it? Ahva squawked.

Osse cringed. "Wow, she's definitely loud."

Callen chuckled. "That is a hazard of having a bird on your shoulder. Sometimes they cut loose with one of those shrieks."

"Then if not for a talisman, then how about for a sentry while you travel?" Mirin pointed at Ahva. "They're easy to care for. Callen could show you how before you leave. Birds make good sentries. They're almost impossible to sneak up on."

Not true. My brother used to spook my budgies. Just have to have enough background noise and catch 'em sleeping.

"I didn't bring much money." Osse patted his bag. "I have only enough for my errands."

What was this fussing about? All for show or was she supposed to do something before he agreed?

CHAPTER 3

Mirin shook her head. "I don't mean to sell her to you. I know Callen thinks we can sell her here, but there are too many who think crows are bad luck. She's costing us other sales because people won't enter our booth with her here. She obviously likes you, and we won't be moving on to Nethanya for months yet." She shrugged. "I'd say you earned her last night when you helped us with that-that thief."

Osse frowned. "I didn't do that for payment."

"Nevertheless, I mean for you to take her. You'll be helping us out again."

"She's friendly enough." Osse smiled.

Callen pointed at Ahva. "Birds are choosy about their people. She went right up to you, and even took some time to inspect your things."

"I insist. She needs a good companion to give her a home and a purpose," Mirin said.

Say "yes" already. We have quests to complete.

Ahva looked up at the skills drop-down, and picked Charm from the menu. She leaned over and rubbed her beak on Osse's cheek, then tucked her forehead against his shoulder.

"She wants you to pet the back of her head." Callen smiled. "She obviously trusts you."

Ahva waited while Osse carefully reached up and stroked the back of her head with his finger. Her fatigue meter gradually improved until he stopped.

While the humans continued to discuss her future, Ahva climbed down Osse's tunic and went over to where he'd set the tea. The drink had lost much of its heat to the air, and she took a few sips. Looking up, she summoned her character screen, but it showed no buffs or debuffs. If teas had powers in this game, this wasn't one of them.

Now I know, and knowing is half the battle. The other half is red and blue lasers.

Callen hopped up and left the tent briefly, returning with the carrier cage. "You'll need this until she gets used to being with you. Should only take a day or two."

I get to spend the game inside a cage? What's up with that?

Ahva sighed and hopped into the cage. This was just the beginning of the game. Surely, she'd be able to do something to gain her freedom. Callen closed and latched the door then handed the cage to Osse.

Won't you be surprised when you find out that I can open that door.

Osse bid everyone farewell and gathered his gear.

The edge of her view lit up green for a few seconds, and a blue notebook slid out from under the crow image.

Green edge, that was, what? Level up, wasn't it? Yay! And what's up with that blue book? She focused on the notebook icon next to her crow image.

The transparent notebook opened and filled much of her view.

Quest complete: Oh the Humanity! Find a human to acquire you. Level Up, Ahva!

At least that made the cage bearable. She opened her character screen to allocate her points to her Power attribute. That'd give her more strength and bolster her pathetically low Health points.

Chapter 4

A sudden whack on Jael's belly woke her from a nice, post-breakfast nap. She didn't have to wonder at the source of the attack. Oba's mini-roar echoed off the cave walls as he pushed off from her and tackled his sister who was sprawled on the floor nearby. Dina rolled to get away, and Oba rose up onto his back paws in preparation for a pounce. When he reached his full two hundred seventy kilograms of male grizzly, that pose would instill terror in the heart of any creature, but for now, he was too cute to be scary.

Cubs. Both the greatest joy of her heart and the greatest thorn in her paw. She hadn't gotten a proper sleep any time since they were born, but honestly, what would she do without them?

Jael yawned and stretched. Since she was awake anyway, she might as well take the cubs on a foraging expedition. Even though flowers dotted the landscape and the snow had all melted, she was still trying to get her weight up. Never too early to think about the winter.

She sat up as Oba tried another pitiful pounce on his sister. Dina shoved him away easily.

Jael lumbered toward the cave entrance and paused to

look over her shoulder. The rough-and-tumble, made-it-up-on-the-spot game had stopped and both cubs stared at her. A few more steps away, and the balls of fluff with endless energy ran, claws tapping on the rocky ground. They trotted along behind her.

Outside, she blinked in the mid-morning sun and sniffed the air. Words wafted upward from objects near and far or blew past on the wind: **two squirrels, feral wolf pack, berries.**

Berries would be a lovely snack. Jael twisted her head from side to side and figured out the direction then set off with the sun at her back. There were indeed a great many berry bushes this way. She'd stripped them of all ripe fruit not too long ago, but perhaps more were ready now.

Several steps closer to the berries, she stole a backward glance to confirm that her cubs were galumphing after her.

The word "berries" loomed larger and bolder. For a scant moment, "human male" paraded across her view.

Jael stopped. Humans were a mixed bag. Most were harmless if she didn't rile them up, but others came to these forests to cause trouble. Bear pelts could become clothing for some.

The cubs caught up to her and resumed their interrupted wrestling match. Jael took a couple steps away then circled them, trying to detect the humans again. The few times she spotted "human male," the words showed faintly. If there had been humans here, they were long gone.

She continued on with the cubs close behind. The bushes had no bright spots for new berries, but the smell came from a bucket full of fruit.

Jael rushed ahead to investigate her find before the cubs

got too close. Sometimes, humans were careless and left perfectly good food where bears could get at it. Sometimes they made a game out of it, challenging bears to remove or dodge around an obstacle. Sometimes it was a trap.

When she reached the bucket, she knocked it over with a swipe of her paw and gave it a good sniff.

"Berries, human male, decay?" formed a dome over the toppled bucket.

Nothing unusual there. The human had handled the bucket and the berries had been sitting here for a while. Some were a little past ripe. Jael ate a few big bites of berries then moved away to let the cubs eat their fill. Nice of the humans to leave her a snack.

* * *

Ahva clung to the smooth wood of her perch as the cage gently swung from side to side with Osse's gait.

The notebook image slid out from behind her picture and turned blue. She focused on it to open it.

Retail Therapy #1: Complete as many tasks as you can in one hour.

A countdown timer started in the top, right corner of the Ahva's vision, sort of like a heads-up display. Below that was a counter that read zero of seven. She dismissed the notebook.

Great, and exactly what could she do to further that along? "Ahva, the people of my village gave me errands to run. I need to find lace, beads, herbs, thread, a shirt for a man, a card-woven strap, and silverware." Osse held the cage up at eye level. "Sing out if you spot a merchant selling any of that, okay?"

Ahva bobbed her head. "Yes."

At least, that sounded easy enough. She repeated the list a couple times and watched the stalls when she could see something more interesting than the back of people's legs. She got her best looks down side streets off the main thoroughfare.

As they passed one, she caught a glimpse of a wooden sign decorated with a spool of thread and a needle.

"Dat one! Dat one!" She cawed.

Osse stopped and lifted her up to eye level. "Did you find something?"

She hopped to the side of the cage facing the side street.

"There. I got it. Good job!" He carried her down to that stall and ducked through the opening.

Spools of thread were arranged in rainbow order on pegs down one side of the tent. The other side had baskets of yarn balls. No sign of lace or card woven straps or finished garments.

Ahva huffed. Pity. Could have completed multiple tasks at once.

She had nothing to do but wait for Osse to finish the transaction. The countdown timer in the corner of her view bled seconds away. Ten spools of thread went in Osse's bag and a few green hexagons etched with coppery lines went out.

What kind of money is that?

"Come see me again!" the merchant called.

Osse waved and ducked out of the tent.

Ahva repeated the list. *Lace, beads, shirt, strap, silverware, and-and, uh, herbs! That's it. Herbs.*

A few stalls down, she spotted a sign with a fork, knife, and spoon. "Dat one! Dat one!"

Osse stopped. "Got it. Good job, Ahva."

The booth had shelves lined with tied bundles of silverware in various patterns. The vendor haggled with one man while a woman admired an ornately decorated bundle. As Osse selected a simple, unadorned set, the lady opened the basket on her arm and started to slip the silverware inside.

Oh no you don't! Thief. Speak.

The sidebar on the left flipped out and showed her list of available vocabulary. Some phrases had been added from listening to Callen sell birds. Ahva selected Signal Human from her skill list.

"What price! How much!" Ahva yelled. She changed voices. "Disgussing eye'all! Bite fingers!"

A small dog sleeping near a table hopped up and started barking.

"What's going on over there?" The vendor demanded.

The woman startled and returned the silverware to the shelf then scooted out in a huff.

The notebook turned blue, and Ahva opened it.

Stop, Thief! You prevent the theft of merchandise. The vendor will now deal favorably with your human. +200 XP

Yes!

Once the other customer was finished, the vendor approached Osse and shook his hand vigorously. "Thank you! If she'd made off with that set, it would have cost me plenty. One of the best ones I have in here. I'm indebted to you and your bird."

"Ahva's quite the bird! I've never seen one who could

mimic so clearly." Osse glanced down at her.

She snorted. *Just you wait until I get that skill up over 100.*
"You'd like that set there?" The vendor tapped the silverware Osse held. "It's a good set. Sterling silver, not as fancy as the others, but sturdy."

Osse reached into his bag and pulled out a couple copper-etched green hexagons with gray dots here and there. "Yes, sir. My village's chief wants it for his wife's birthday."

That's money? How peculiar! What are those made from?

"If it were up to me, I'd give it to you for free for stopping that thief, but my partner wouldn't like that at all." He took one of the offered chips, leaving the rest behind. "A third discount he'll accept. Use the rest to treat yourself."

Osse pocketed the money and silverware. "Thank you, sir."

"Thank you." The vendor patted his shoulder as another customer entered. "Have a good trip home."

"I will." As they left, Osse lifted the cage. "Good job, Ahva."

She chirped. "Good jawed, Ahva." *Jawed? Jawed? How about "job" with a B?* Ahva rolled her eyes. She checked the timer. *Forty minutes and five tasks to go. We better get a move on. Mush, human, mush!*

After a few minutes of wandering, Ahva spotted signs with beads, lace, and ribbons with a diamond patterns all within a few meters of each other.

Jackpot! Ahva flapped her wings. "Dat one! Dat one!"

"Wow. We are in luck!" Osse ducked into the bead stall and picked up a fist-sized bag that made a nifty rustling noise when it moved. He paid the merchant then darted across to the lace merchant where he purchased a roll of

CHAPTER 4

lace. Their next stop was diagonally across the street.

Rolls of colorful, heavy-duty ribbon, more like a car-towing strap, were stacked on shelves. Some had diagonal designs. Others had diamonds or dashes. A few were polka-dotted. The colors, wow. Some were such clashing choices, they vibrated in Ahva's vision. Thankfully, Osse chose a simple, single-color piece. He paid for it and dropped it in his bag.

Ahva checked the counter. *Two to go and twenty-one minutes. Unless these last two are hidden, we've got this.*

Ahva kept a close watch on the signs. The crowds were growing as they went deeper into the market. She spotted a sign with the shirt on it and sounded the alarm, but there were so many people there, Osse couldn't get into the stall to shop.

"Let's get the herbs first, then we'll be back," Osse suggested.

Good idea, human. There might even be another shop.

"Yes."

She watched the countdown timer as Osse wove his way through the streets until they found the one with a bunch of leaves sticking out of the jar. A table set up across the opening of the stall kept them from directly inspecting the jars and hanging bundles.

A heavy-set woman with narrow eyes approached the opposite side of the table. "Help you?"

"Yes, please." Osse produced a list. "I need one small jar of each please."

She nodded. Moving at a pace slightly faster than a dead tortoise, she moseyed around the little shop collecting jars one at a time and setting them on the table. A very obese cat was sprawled in the middle of the space.

Ahva kept an eye on the timer. Seconds flew away, becoming most of five minutes by the time Osse had his whole collection. The merchant took another two minutes to add up the total.

Osse paid her and moved the jars to his bag. "Hold on, Ahva."

He practically ran through the streets back to the clothing merchant. They arrived with only a few minutes left. The crowd had dwindled, but the shelves were nearly bare.

Osse stepped into the stall and sighed. Ahva scanned the remaining wares. Beadwork, embroidered flowers, and lace decorated everything.

"Can I help you, young man?" The tailor approached.

"Do you have any men's shirts left?"

He smirked. "Never had any to start with. I deal in women's clothes. There's a vendor five blocks east who deals in menswear."

Ahva hissed. With only three minutes left, they didn't have time.

"Do you have anything that might be suitable for a man. I'm not picky."

The tailor stared at Osse for a moment. "I might have something that would do." He kept talking as he went to a chest at the back of the stall. "Meant to be an under-tunic for a girl, but it's plain, no lace and the only embroidery is a geometric pattern around the hems." As he pulled garments out, he handed the hanger up to a hawk who distributed the rejects to pegs on the boards set up around the tent. "Nope, too small. Ooo, no, too small again. Nope, that one has flowers. Here's the one." He stood and held up a tan tunic with dark blue octagons around the hem. "You're a wiry lad. Should fit you fine." He returned to Osse and held it up to him. "A touch big, actually, but you're growing, yet. Suitable?"

"It'll work fine, thank you." Osse draped the shirt over his arm.

The timer was down to its last seconds, stopping on seventeen when Osse handed the tailor some money.

The notebook turned blue. Ahva opened it.

Quest complete: Retail Therapy #1: Complete as many tasks as you can in one hour.

Retail Therapy #2: Stay with Osse.

She closed the notebook. Stay with Osse? I'm in a dumb cage hanging from his hand. How hard is that?

Osse added the shirt to his bag. "Close call, Ahva. I have one more errand and we can start for home."

I go where you go, and remember this: wherever you go, there you are.

The crowds were much heavier now, and Osse threaded his way through. He stopped at a stall that sold necklaces. Each had a charm on it with the symbol painted on. The pegs the necklaces hung from were labeled. Ahva opened the notebook window and quickly recorded screen shots of the symbols. She'd been gaming long enough to know one or more of these symbols would be important later.

Osse picked up one of the Bakhari necklaces and hefted it. He started toward the merchant and sighed before returning the necklace to the hook.

What's up with that?

When Osse stopped at a food vendor's booth, Ahva's cage landed gently on the ground near his feet. She thought about letting herself loose so she could climb up his trousers and tunic to his shoulder, but she knew that would never last. She didn't think her new human would object, of course, but the crowds here were intense.

A hand swooped down and grabbed the handle of the carrier cage. As the stranger lifted it, the cage banged against Osse's leg.

Ahva engaged Signal Human and shrieked for all she was worth.

"Hey, you! Stop!" Osse yelled. "Ahva!"

The edge of her vision turned red.

Chapter 5

The cage bounced up and down, and Ahva jumped to the side where she could hold on as the thief darted between people. The fingers holding the cage's handle were too far out of reach. Ahva chose Posture then fluffed up and growled, weaving from side to side, but like before, this ruffian didn't recognize his peril. The morale emoji stayed on the blah face. Ahva lunged at the side of the cage to try to scare her kidnapper, but he gave no reaction. This knucklehead was as dense as a lead brick.

She recalled the previous night's escape and scrambled toward the cage latch. After sliding down the vertical cage bars, Ahva smacked the locking pin with her beak. The first time, it slipped up a little ways then dropped back. The second time, it flew free, and then she pushed the door open. The villain's hand reached down and slammed the door shut right into Ahva's beak. The screen flashed red, and she lost a few health points as the VR rig communicated a hit on her face and chest. She shrieked in protest and engaged her Power attribute and Bite skill. She sniped at the fingers pinning the door. Once she'd caught hold, she bit down as hard as she could. Flesh gave way to the sharp edges of her beak. The man screamed and retracted his hand. Ahva shoved the door open and flew out. The carrier cage smacked her tail as she jumped clear, and she spun out of control. Unable to right herself, she crashed into the cloth hanging from a vendor's display table. She clutched the material in her feet and beak and clung, trying to get her bearings again. A hand grabbed her across the back, and she sniped without hesitation. The villain screamed again.

"Ahva!" Osse called. "Ahva!"

She selected Posture and fluffed up, hissing her anger at her captor. His ID tag now sported a frown emoji.

"Ahva!" Osse's voice rose above the crowd noise.

"Ahva!" She kept an eye on the thief and sniped when he tried for her again. "I not Ahva. You're Ahva."

"I see the picture now," the man behind the booth said. "Mnyama! Threat!"

In Ahva's peripheral vision, a retriever sort of dog bristled up and growled, sounding bigger than the average elephant. The frown emoji turned into a fear face, like the one in Edvard Munch's *The Scream*. As the thief backed up a few steps, the dog barked and stalked forward. The fear emoji turned red a moment before the thief threw the carrier cage to the ground then ran off, bleeding from her well-aimed bites.

"Lad, your bird's here!" The vendor waved his arms. "Peace, Mnyama. Good girl."

The dog smoothed out her fur and sat panting. Ahva climbed up the cloth to the top of a table lined with little ceramic baubles. She shivered. How dare someone try to take her away from her human!

The edge of the screen was still red.

Ahva left the Posture skill armed. She fluffed up all her

feathers and fanned her tail to warn off any other idiots. Anyone who came too close to the vendor's table got a good, strong hiss. The crowd parted as someone slipped among the mass of shoppers. Finally, she recognized the red and brown clothes her human wore.

"Ahva!" He drew nearer and the furrowed brow and wide eyes melted to a smile.

She jumped off the table and flew straight to him, colliding with his chest in what had to be the worst landing she could ever manage. His hands awkwardly pulled her to his chest, and she squawked in protest, even as she realized the rough handling was her own fault. If she'd stayed put, he would have come to her, and she could have crawled up to his shoulder in a more dignified manner. The red edge of her vision faded.

Ahva found a purchase for her feet on the strap of his big shoulder pouch then climbed up to his shoulder where she perched as close to his head as she could. Safely back with her human, she quivered.

Take it easy! It's a game, goofball.

The blue notebook appeared in the corner. That was likely the "Quest Complete" announcement. No need for that.

Osse leaned over and picked up the carrier cage. One side had caved in altogether, the door was off one hinge, and the bottom had separated from the sides in one corner.

He frowned. "That's good for scrap metal, but I suppose you've gotten used to me by now." Osse approached the vendor where Ahva had taken refuge. "Thank you for getting her back for me."

"None of my doing, really." The vendor smiled and held his hands up, palm out. "Strangest thing. She let herself out, either that or the door failed. Anyway, she got out and flew here. Then when you called her, she answered. The thief fled quick as you please as soon as I had Mnyama give him her best growl."

"I thought Ahva lost for good." Osse preened Ahva's head, which restored a few fatigue points.

You can't get rid of me that easily.

"Might have been. No chance the sentries will find him in this crowd even if you did get a good look at him." The vendor pointed at the cage. "Y'know, if you take that cage to a metalsmith, he might give you a few chips for it."

"I need to finish my last errand and start for home." Osse handed the cage to the vendor. "You can collect whatever the smith will give you for it."

The vendor set the cage behind the booth. "I'll trade you a homemade bead for it."

"Do you have any that are bird-shaped?" Osse glanced at Ahva.

"Right this way."

While Osse inspected a glass bead, hordes of people continued past on their own business. Ahva watched them all in her peripheral vision while Osse shopped. Being able to see a full circle was handy. No need to keep her head on a swivel. She just had to watch moving shapes. The quest was officially done, but there were more problems to watch for than bird-nappers.

When Osse opened his shoulder pouch, the vendor smiled and pointed. "Y'know, that might be a good place for your bird. She might get a little nervous up there on your shoulder. In the bag, she wouldn't have to deal with all this madness." He took in the market places with a sweep of both hands. "The leather is a little stiff, so it won't collapse on her if you have some bulky stuff in the bottom. Probably a good deal safer in there, and quite a shock for anyone who made a try for your money bag."

They sure wouldn't know what bit them! "Bite fingers!"

Osse smiled and tucked a small, wrapped package down in the bottom corner of the bag. "That could be funny."

The vendor leaned closer. "And, after watching her deal with that thief, effective, too."

"I'll leave that up to her. Spooked as she is, I don't know if she'd appreciate me stuffing her into a bag. I might have to introduce her to the idea later when she's had a chance to settle a bit." Osse smiled and bowed, touching his forehead. "Thank you for the idea and for your help in recovering my bird."

"You're welcome. Safe trip."

Osse nodded once and walked away. "All right, Ahva, that's the last of our errands. Let's head for home."

Ahva chirped. *Let's blow this pop stand. Places to go. Quests to solve. Bad guys to squawk at.*

As Osse made his way through the market, the crowds thinned out. The noise declined from a perpetual roar to a reasonable conversation level. Osse's stride had changed from twisting and turning motions to a much more even gait.

Leaving the market through a high, wide gate reduced the crowd to a handful of people carrying small packages or baskets laden with food, clothing, and other articles. A bird could hear herself think.

Ahva took note of specific signs on shops or peculiar paint jobs on buildings. They might be back here later and having a general lay of the land would be helpful.

After about half an hour of hiking through the city, the gate stood wide open in front of them and the crowds grew dense again with people coming and going.

A street preacher stood off to one side declaring the end of the world while another a few meters away proclaimed peace and liberty for all if only they donated enough money to his cause. A third street preacher called for repentance of sins for forgiveness, and yet another declared that nothing in life mattered but personal happiness. Each had drawn their own crowd of fans and hecklers, but the one who had set up nearest to the gate railed at the abundant passersby from atop a large metal box. No crowd had stopped to hear her. As Osse came into range, Ahva focused her attention that way

"You heard me! Atrac and her priestess laugh at you!" The speaker cackled, but there was no mirth in the laughter. Nothing endearing. "They laugh at you all. You cannot survive the coming onslaught of her army! Even those she has rejected as imperfect will wash over you like raging water over a sandcastle, leaving behind nothing but blood and corpses. Those few, those precious few she deems worthy will be given the chance to become her new creations! They alone will fill this world. You cannot prevail. Atrac and her priestess will laugh at you all!" She cackled again, and the loop restarted.

"She's a cheery one," Osse muttered.

"No." Ahva tuned out the noise until Osse was out of range.

Other people coming toward them were an odd mixture. Most were the same sorts she'd seen in the market. Either dark-skinned like Osse and wearing trousers and tunics or lighter complexioned – but still pretty tanned – and wearing loose robes that gave them an almost Middle Eastern appearance. Some looked like they'd stepped out of ancient Rome with their togas. A few, very few, had taken their clothing cues from the AI. They'd fit nicely in any Technicolor Chivalry or *Three Musketeers* movie.

Most hurried on toward wherever they were heading, giving a wide berth to Atrac's cackling spokesman, but a few gave her and Osse a stern or suspicious look. Some spat over their shoulders. A couple rested a hand on the pommel of a knife or sword.

After picking Posture from the menu, Ahva glared at the gawkers and fluffed up her feathers. They might be trouble, but Osse ignored them all and continued weaving through the clusters of people. She stayed close to the side of his head and clutched the collar of his tunic as tightly as she could curl her toes.

When they were finally through the doors, a wide grassy field opened out ahead of them. There were no crowds here, and the only other humans Ahva noticed were the distant tents of a traveling caravan. Maybe they had a quest to do.

"Hello!" Ahva lifted one wing.

"Hi, Ahva." Osse looked off toward the caravan. "Don't worry. The heraldry on their tents is friendly. They won't bother us." He stroked the back of her head, giving her a boost on her fatigue meter. "No shrieking in my ear, okay?" Ahva leaned over and rubbed her beak on Osse's cheek.

No promises. A **+10 XP** floated up.

As he hiked onward, she kept her eye on the surroundings.

Nagheed finished his share of the family's evening meal. A fatigue counter next to his health points bar was now properly restored. The food had neither taste nor texture with his low-level VR, but a game world effect for food was a nice touch.

The selection of RenFaire music had continued to rotate, still mostly recorders and stringed instruments, but a few of the pieces had included a drum. Even the one with the bagpipes was starting to grow on him, but he still thought they could've left that one out and missed nothing at all. Some of the tunes were livelier than others, and he'd caught himself tapping out the beat on his knee while he played.

Acting like a dog, Nagheed had scarfed everything down in record time and parked himself at the fireplace. The **+10 XP** bonuses had floated up to the top of the screen and vanished.

After the family had finished, Rafayel stood. "That was glorious, as always, Marie."

"Thank you, sir. There is an apple torte for dessert."

"Wonderful, but let's have dinner settle a bit so I can properly enjoy the torte."

Her cheeks got a little darker. "Of course, sir."

Rafayel snapped his fingers. "Nagheed, come."

Nagheed stood and followed his human to a small but ornate room.

The system pinged and the notebook turned blue. Jake ignored the summons. He wasn't in the mood for another cheesy quest name and obvious instructions. When he needed to know, the regular game play would undoubtedly fill him in on what was next.

A countdown timer and a counter both appeared in the top corner of the screen.

Interesting. What's that for?

Rafayel crouched to Nagheed's height. "All right. You already showed me your basic commands. One more basic command, then we'll move on to other more complex things. There are other things I'll need you to do if we're traveling and run into trouble."

Ah. Time for training.

Rafayel led Nagheed to a rug in the fire in front of the fireplace. "Sit."

Once Nagheed obeyed, Rafayel snapped his fingers. "Good boy. This is your place."

Yeah, I taught Prince the same command.

Rafayel perched on the edge of an ornate wooden desk in the corner of the room. "Come, Nagheed."

He trotted over and stood next to his human to get a reward of kudos and a brief pat on the head.

"Place."

Bet you haven't had a dog learn this on one try. Nagheed went back to his rug and sat.

Rafayel's broad smile confirmed Nagheed's guess. "Good boy. Aren't you clever?"

They repeated the command a couple more times then went outside for a game of fetch the thing on command, followed by a bigger challenge: chasing someone and pinning the rascal until he was ordered out. A dummy made out of straw and old clothes served as the rascal being pulled along on a cart by one of the servants. He'd done similar drills playing football in high school.

Nagheed also practiced growling or barking on command, attacking on command, and even killing on command. Certainly not the sort of thing he'd taught Prince.

As an adventurer's dog, especially controlled by a human player, those made sense. In real life, though, did a real dog have enough brain to obey only his master's voice? Otherwise, how dangerous would it be to have a dog trained to kill?

The timer ticked down to zero as Nagheed pounced on a dummy made of straw and old clothes.

The sun set with some yellow and golden-brown streaks in the sky.

The computer pinged and the notebook turned blue. He ignored it. At worst, the notebook would tell him he ran out of time. At best, it might let him know how many commands he'd completed.

"That's enough for one day." Rafayel led the way inside and into a cozy sitting room.

The room's décor was a lot of ornately carved wood with a few squashy chairs, a couch, and a rug. Each place to sit had its own table. A long line of built-in bookshelves took up one wall. An assortment of books filled about half the shelf space. The rest was taken by knick-knacks.

Bettani sat in one of the chairs working on an embroidery project. The white material was getting flowers in various shades of gray. That might have looked more interesting if he could see more of the rainbow.

The lady of the house looked up from her work. "How did he do?"

"Quite well. A smart dog." Rafayel leaned over to pat Nagheed's shoulder. "I'd almost swear he had a human intelligence."

Funny that.

Bettani drew a pale yellow thread through the material. "When I was growing up, my mother had a companion dog that was smart enough to perform tasks given in full sentences. It was as if he completely understood what we were saying. Our Nagheed just might have that kind of aptitude."

"That would be perfect for what we need him for." Rafayel looked around. "Where are the kids?"

"Liora is pouting upstairs. She simply must have a puppy of her own, you understand. Micah has gone to the kitchen check on that torte Marie promised."

Rafayel snickered. "Typical on both counts." He pointed to the hearth. "Nagheed, place."

He trotted over to the rug near the fireplace and sat, earning more Be a Dog XP.

Bettani continued her sewing while Rafayel retrieved a dark blue book and sat in his squashy chair near her.

When Micah returned, a flurry of words erupted from him, or at least the bowl he carried. Nagheed sniffed the air to get the whole scent picture of the room. Words sprang from all the objects, some much brighter than others. From Micah, he got "Apples, honey, baked bread, Micah (content)." "Burning wood" wafted past from fireplace behind him. The bookshelves around the room exuded "old books." Rafayel was surrounded by "Rafayel (relaxed)" and Bettani showed "Bettani (happy)."

Nagheed's stomach growled. How could he be hungry after eating so much only twenty minutes ago? The fatigue meter was showing half empty. Well, it had been more than twenty minutes game time, and he had been running around like a crazy fool tackling a scarecrow.

He trotted toward Micah, but only got a few steps away.

"Nagheed, place." Rafayel's stern voice and glare encouraged a quick response.

After couple more sniffs, Nagheed trudged back to his rug and sat.

"Good boy," Rafayel said.

A few minutes later, Liora came in and flopped into a comfy chair. She huffed and threaded the needle with a dull brownish-yellow thread.

Rafayel flipped through the book to a bookmarked page. "Do you need to be excused for tonight, Liora?"

She huffed. "Why can't I get a puppy?"

Rafayel marked his place with his finger. "Two reasons. First, like the kitten you pleaded for a year ago, the puppy will cease to be cared for by you once it leaves the adorable stage and becomes more of a chore. Fortunately, the cat is doing quite well hunting rodents in the barn and the stablemen are looking after her. Dogs don't thrive in such situations. They crave more attention and need you to reinforce their good behavior. Second, what do you need a dog for?"

"To carry things?" she suggested.

"What do you need to carry that you can't do with your own arms? Marie handles the household shopping, and even she uses a simple hand-drawn wagon."

"Then, to –" She tapped her chin. "To catch rats."

"Your cat and the stablemen's cat handle that just fine. So, third, and most importantly, can you afford to purchase one?"

CHAPTER 5

"No." She huffed.

"There you have it. Now, answer my question. Do you need to be excused?"

She rolled her eyes. "No."

"Then make an end of pouting." He held up his book. "Chapter 9: The Judgment. Does everyone remember where we were?"

"Yes." Micah swallowed the bite of torte he was chewing on. "The judges were about to rule on whether Ilion could continue their experiments."

"This didn't really happen, did it?" Liora set her sewing aside.

Rafayel looked at the front cover. "Well, this is called 'A History of the Great Massacre'."

"Yeah, but it's talking about men that were half machines and people running faster than horses and animals that could talk. If it's real, where did all that stuff go? Why don't we have that now?" Liora shook her head. "Nope. I don't believe it."

Micah pointed at the book. "This book is supposed to tell us what became of all that."

"Let's see what happens next." Rafayel read out loud.

Nagheed curled up on the rug beside the fireplace and listened.

While Rafayel read out loud, Marie brought a tray with more dessert for the rest of the humans. Nagheed turned on Charm and gave Marie sad eyes, but she didn't even spare a look at him. He'd have to restore the fatigue meter through rest. After she left, Nagheed stretched out at the fire and listened. Coming in on the middle of a story could make this impossible to catch on to, but surely the computer would give him enough clues.

The story he read involved a conflict over whether human-monster crossbreeds had the same rights under law as humans. The conclusion in this one was a resounding no, casting the crossbreeds as an abomination, which resulted in orders to confiscate all properties owned by crossbreeds and handed down a death sentence on every one of them, man or beast. Any sign of the crossbreed culture was destroyed, including those that benefited the humans. Naturally, the genocide and confiscation efforts were imperfect, and a remnant of the crossbreeds, sitting on massive amounts of gold, silver, and platinum, hid somewhere.

Ominous, but was it there just for window dressing or did the story somehow play into the plot of the game?

Shortly after Rafayel finished the story, a prompt slid down from the top of the image.

Sleep? Yes or no

Nagheed chose **Yes**. The screen faded to black. A group of cartoon sheep danced across the screen like a chorus line.

Jake smirked and reminded himself that this had started out as a kid game.

When light faded back in mere seconds later, Nagheed blinked and lifted his head. *Wow, dogs sleep hard. The fatigue bar had only loaded to three-quarters. So, neither food nor rest alone fixed the fatigue issue? That made sense, actually.*

Rafayel and his family were gone, and the fire in the fireplace had gone to warm embers.

That's weird. When the family went to bed, shouldn't I have gone with them?

The dogs he'd had growing up and his own Prince could

be snoring, but the moment anyone moved, they woke up and followed.

Clearly this part was coded by a non-dog person.

Nagheed sniffed the air and watched the scents billowing in through the door: **Cooked bacon, bread, eggs, honey, porridge, berries, cheese, firewood, hot metal, one woman (Marie?).**

Most likely, he wouldn't be wanted in the kitchen yet, so he meandered through the rest of the ground floor, finding a library, a room large enough to host a good-sized gathering, and a pantry where a large assortment of household items was laid out. Just that little bit of exploring cost him fatigue points. He'd have to get food.

His stomach growled with some enthusiasm. Nagheed wandered into the kitchen. Marie stood at the fire again. Pots were bubbling, and the potbelly stove warmed sizzling frying pans. Covered dishes on the table gave off wonderful odors of sweet bread and berries. That'd take care of the fatigue problem.

He reared back, landing his front feet on the table, earning **+10 XP** glittering in the air as it floated upward.

"No, you don't!" Marie snapped a kitchen towel in his direction. "Get out! Out!"

Nagheed flinched.

Rafayel entered. "No need for the towel, Marie. Down and place are all you need. Give it a try."

"Nagheed, down! Place!"

And if I don't listen? He stayed where he was and sniffed the closed lid on the food.

-10 XP

What kind of game docks you XP? Fine.

The cook repeated the command.

He snorted and went to the rug near the door.

Marie nodded once. "Good boy."

"That's better." Rafayel walked further into the kitchen. "He's learning, but I expect him to answer to anyone in my family or my employ."

"Breakfast is nearly ready, sir." Marie piled sausages in a bowl.

Rafayel crossed to the door. "Perfect. I'll take Nagheed out for a few minutes."

Nagheed followed his human outside. He selected his Sprint skill and ran from one end of the estate to the other. Through the speakers, the wind rushed past him, and his running stride had him airborne for a long hang time each time he pushed off. The scenery zoomed past him at near blur speeds. He zipped through an orchard on one side of the estate and a cattle field on the other. That put a real ding in the fatigue monitor long before he was ready to stop. When it turned maroon, he returned to Rafayel and panted, which added a few points back to the fatigue bar.

A breakfast of bacon, eggs, sausage, dry toast, and more sweetbreads followed shortly after. Then it was back to training, more complex stuff now. The new tricks involved coordination with Rafayel and Ryder, a sleek pale gray horse. Funny name for a horse, but whatever. Then a couple meat and cheese sandwiches for lunch back in the kitchen.

As lunch finished up, Nagheed rested on the rug near the door and watched the family and servants eat. *They are so slow! Is this how Prince feels when I eat? No wonder he takes a nap under the table.*

When they finally finished, Rafayel stood, which brought

CHAPTER 5

all the servants to their feet. "Please, be seated and finish your meal. I'm going to take Nagheed and Ryder on patrol. We'll be back by nightfall." He stepped away from the table. "Excellent lunch, Marie. Thank you. Nagheed, come."

Good. I've been looking forward to seeing what the countryside looks like.

The computer chimed and turned his notebook icon blue. He dismissed the notification without looking at it. When he needed to know, he'd know.

Nagheed waited while Rafayel climbed onto his gray horse and stayed alongside as they left the manor grounds.

"All right, Nagheed, patrols involve riding part of a circuit around Yavne's perimeter. Being a country bounded by coastline down one long side, we tend to have trouble with pirates now and then, and we don't want them gaining any kind of foothold. In addition to potential pirate problems, there are the usual sorts of highwaymen and other miscreants. The boundaries are marked with a low stone wall, more boundary marker than anything meant to keep out an intrusion. We won't always go at the same time, nor cover the same ground, nor take the same route. The constable and his men take care of the parts we don't. Keeps the ruffians on their toes. We're looking for whatever doesn't belong. You'll get used to what's normal and what's alarming. For now, if you think it's out of place, alert me, and I'll confirm it."

Nagheed stayed alongside Ryder. *Okay, so I'm not the only one who talks to my dog like he'll understand complex speech.* They wove through the streets to a wall that was twice the height of the nearest buildings. As they approached, the guards at the gate snapped to attention, setting the staff of their halberds on the ground and leaning the blade forward.

Rafayel saluted the men. "Good work, gentlemen. Carry on."

The gate was iron-reinforced oak. A dense portcullis was retracted above their heads. Only the ends of the teeth on the lower edge showed.

The wall itself, not including the guardhouse, spanned a width greater than Ryder's length.

Wow! That's a wall and a half. That's not just for the odd pirate, highwayman, or other miscreant. Expecting trouble?

Once outside, the music changed. Rather than the recorder and strings, the new tune was much more of a picked guitar in a very minor key. A deeper, bass note kept the beat.

Rafayel spurred Ryder to a gallop. After selecting Sprint, Nagheed sped up to pace the horse. Just like his run across the estate, the terrain zoomed by at a phenomenal rate. Faint gray scent words whizzed past him, often too fast for him to clearly read. The best part? He was keeping pace with a horse and might even win the race to the border! Could this dog run! After a few minutes, the fatigue meter flashed dull red, but he pushed himself harder. No way would a horse win this endurance contest.

Moments before Nagheed seriously considered giving up, a low rock wall stretched out ahead of them. Rafayel reigned Ryder in. Nagheed ran all the way to the wall before he stopped. Then he sat and rested while the horse caught up.

Ha! Beat you!

"That was a lovely run. Thank you both." Rafayel dismounted and led the horse to a shallow stream nearby.

CHAPTER 5

Once the horse started slurping, Nagheed went further upstream and lapped up water, just the thing after that run. The fatigue warning faded and the bar climbed upward again. When he'd finished, he scouted around the area, not straying more than a dozen meters or so. No minus XP warnings came up, and Rafayel didn't scold him, so apparently, he was allowed a little freedom.

He sniffed around, watching words pop up from various places around the scenery or drift by on the wind: Horse, freshwater, damp rocks, squirrels, songbirds, owl, wolves, campfire.

Other words popped up and faded out as he continued to investigate, but nothing looked unusual.

After a nice rest, Rafayel climbed back into the saddle. "Let's go, Nagheed. Our patrol today is from here to the shore."

Nagheed trotted alongside the horse. He kept his nose to the ground and watched the vague scent words form and fade. A variety of animals and people had been through here, some recently.

They left the trees for a coastal plain. Grasses were tall enough to brush Nagheed's belly as they continued along the rock wall only slightly higher than the grasses. Faint gray words popped up or disappeared from objects as they walked. Squirrels, fox, grass, sea salt, Ryder, Rafayel, blood. *Blood?* Nagheed turned his head from side to side and watched the word move to the center of the screen. He turned his attention to the direction where the word was the biggest.

Nagheed chose Signal Human from the skill menu. He sat facing the strongest scent and whined.

Rafayel rode a few strides further before he stopped and turned back. "Find something?"

Nagheed looked up at his human then at a line of trees some fifty meters away. *It's gotta be somewhere between here and there.*

"Let's go see. Shall we?" Rafayel turned the horse toward the trees.

Nagheed rocked back onto his rear legs, ready to launch into another good run, but Rafayel kept their pace slower. All that prep for nothing.

Come on. Even a rock could escape at that pace.

Rafayel snapped his fingers as they reached the trees. Nagheed watched his human for the command and waited until Rafayel pointed forward.

Good. Nagheed trotted on ahead, turning his head from side to side and watching the size of the faint word "blood" to pick a way to go. As the scent grew stronger, a faint rustling from the trees ahead urged both caution and curiosity.

He slowed a bit as grass gave way to shrubs and scraggly trees.

Ahead, a man in a gray tunic and darker pants crouched over another, better dressed man lying face-down. The downed man's nametag read Ian, and his health bar was half gone. Three little Zs were next to his name. The crouching man, Aaron, looked back over his shoulder then took off running as his morale emoji became the red-faced version of the fear emoji for panic.

"Go, Nagheed!" Rafayel ordered.

Nagheed engaged Sprint and pushed off with his back feet. Within a few strides, he was running flat out, dodging trees and brush and closing the distance. Wind rushed past him through the speakers. When he was sure he was close enough, he launched himself at the fleeing human but hit the ground when the human's momentum carried him out of range.

Gotta be much closer when we're both running. Duh!

Gathering himself for another try, Nagheed took off again. He came close enough to be able to take a bite out of the human's rear end. Instead, Nagheed leapt. This time he drove the human to the ground and rolled a stride or two past before returning to his quarry and standing over him. He barked, an impressively deep sound that perfectly matched his immense size.

The human covered his head with his arms and flinched with every bark.

Yep. You better stay still. This dog's bite is worse than his bark.

Rafayel rode up behind Nagheed and dismounted. "Nagheed, out."

You sure about that? He's a slippery devil. Nagheed stayed put and continued barking.

−20 XP flashed across the screen.

"Nagheed! Out!"

Terrific. This has got to be the only game where you can lose XP. He stepped back, but stayed close enough to pounce if his prey proved too sneaky.

Rafayel grabbed the man by his arm and pulled him to his feet.

The man gasped, looked at Nagheed, then back at Rafayel. He bowed his head. "Baron Dorcas? I-I-I didn't know you had a dog. I-I'm sorry. I—"

"Aaron? Aaron Bethel? What's happening here? Why did I find you going through a man's pockets?" Rafayel let go of the man's arm.

"I was robbed. I sent my son for help soon as I saw the scoundrel and tried to lead him away from my boy. That thief said he had friends and a dog nearby, but once my son was clear, I fought back."

"And won, obviously."

Aaron blushed. "Thief stumbled into a low-hanging tree branch. His own attempt to get clever caught him. I was retrieving my purse when I saw your dog."

"I apologize for that. You weren't hurt, were you?"

Aaron twisted his arm around and rolled up his sleeve, revealing a quality case of road rash. "Nothing worth complaining about."

"Good. Let's go deal with that cur then get you to a physician."

Nagheed fell in next to his human as they headed back to where the chase had started. The "victim" still lay prone. The smell of blood was strong enough now to crowd out other scents. Further, a man on horseback approached the tree line from the direction of the city. A smaller human rode behind him on the same pale-colored horse.

While Rafayel and Aaron checked the thief's injury and restored Aaron's purse, Nagheed sniffed around the grass and pine leaves, trying to find a scent other than human blood. He caught glimpses of other letters behind the faint gray word, but never enough to identify anything.

Wonder if that has to do with my level? Will I get better at picking out faint scents as I advance?

The horseman, tagged Constable Simon Fishel, arrived

and dismounted after helping the boy down.

I know you. You're the guy who bought his kid the glorified mouse for her birthday.

"Your Excellency, I didn't expect to find you."

"Constable." Rafayel greeted the constable with a nod. "I was on patrol when Nagheed alerted me to trouble. After a brief case of mistaken identity, we took custody of the scoundrel." He pointed to the unconscious thief. "He may have confederates, or so he threatened."

Nagheed meandered back to Rafayel's side and sat.

The boy darted back several steps and stared.

The constable whistled. "That is some dog!"

"A magnificent animal." Rafayel patted Nagheed's side.

"Truly. If my daughter had gotten her way, he'd be mine because 'He's so fluffy.'"

I'm glad you turned her down.

Rafayel smiled. "He is that. I'll leave the victim and the thief in your capable hands and continue my patrol." He pointed first to Aaron then the thief. "Please make sure Aaron's injury is addressed. I will settle the account with the physician on my way into town."

"Very good, sir."

Rafayel swung up into the saddle.

The computer pinged then gave him the same brief trumpet fanfare as when he'd leveled last time.

Nagheed opened up his character screen and scanned through it. The skill list was longer than before. He looked through it one row at a time until he found the new entry.

Ooo. Tackle! That can be handy.

He allocated his level points to his attack skills then trotted alongside his human.

Sunlight blaring through Jael's closed eyes demanded she wake up, but her eyelids were weighted closed.

The computer chimed and displayed the notebook icon. Jael focused on it to flip it open.

Quest: Cubnapped! Find your missing cubs.

Find the cubs? Why would the cubs need finding? They were undoubtedly nearby sunning themselves or continuing one of their goofy games. Jael groaned and settled into her nap.

What if there really was a problem? She wouldn't have gotten the quest for nothing. She strained to hear some sound of the little fluffs, but weariness dragged at her. Before she could decipher any useful sound, sleep pulled her under again.

This time, she turned and rolled like meat on a spit. Dreams of two human men taking her cubs away nagged at her. She clawed her way toward awareness, but her efforts were as effective as climbing out of a sandpit.

After an eternity of futility, Jael rose from the depths of her fitful rest to full awareness. Her mind came up to speed before her body. Both eyelids weighed as much as a full-grown grizzly. They opened a sliver. The full light of day had become the dingy gray and heavy shadows of twilight. Her mouth was drier than brown pine needles, and her muscles were stiff. Her fatigue meter was leaning hard toward zero.

With all the effort she could muster, Jael rolled over and came to her feet for a moment. The forest clearing spun hard to her left, and she crashed to the ground again. The screen flashed red for a moment. Her second effort got her up on all fours. She was ready for the spin this time and widened her stance to keep her balance more stable. She didn't dare try standing erect.

The cubs were nowhere in sight, but the berry bucket was gone. She pleaded for some sign of them. The rustling of their games, the soft snoring they made in those rare times they actually slept. The cute mini roars Oba made from time to time. A distant owl hooted and a chorus of frogs chirped nearby but nothing from her cubs.

Scent maybe? Jael sniffed the air. Hazy words rose from objects. She blinked hard to clear her sight. "Berries, decay" were dim, barely visible in the air around her.

The clearest words were along a trail that showed her two favorite fluff balls and the humans, but the words were faint. The scent was getting old. How long ago had they gone?

Slowly, Jael turned in place, looking for stronger sign of her cubs. The smells of both humans and cubs were greatest along the path. If those humans did anything to her cubs, there would be fewer humans in this world when she was finished.

Her first few steps wobbled and swayed, but she kept her feet under her and cleared all the berries still attached to the bush, even if they weren't ripe yet. The fatigue meter crept upward. Once the bush was empty, she sniffed around to get her bearings then headed out, gaining speed and confidence as she traveled.

Most of her travels were downhill toward the broad plains. Humans were more plentiful there, but she'd face a whole herd of them to get Oba and Dina back with her where they belonged.

Twilight gave way to night as she left the dense woods for the scrub brush in the foothills. A waxing gibbous moon overhead gave her enough light to see.

The scents led her to a charred ring of stones. "Ashes" and "deer meat" drifted upward from the ring. There had once been a fire here, but the stones and ashes were cold. She sniffed around the area.

The campfire billowed "ashes," "pine wood," and "venison." Three wolves had been by, crossing from north to south. Intersecting that trail, Oba, Dina, and three humans – the males had been joined by a female – were equally strong, so they'd been here at the same time as the humans. Humans and cubs had left another scent path for her to follow. The words drew a line that led eastward.

Jael rose up on her back legs. She wobbled slightly but took a step backwards to reestablish her balance. In the moonlight, she saw no silhouettes, and the scent trail disappeared at the end of her range. Where were they?

She flopped back down, sending the terrain spinning for a few seconds. After sniffing around for the strongest sent, Jael continued. Although the moonlight didn't give her much, she'd use every scrap of remaining light to continue her search.

* * *

Ahva rode on Osse's shoulder and kept a good grip on the collar of his tunic. His somewhat bouncy gait had taken some getting used to, but she'd learned to keep her legs muscles loose.

The terrain hadn't been all that exciting. Aside from a

couple dust clouds to the east and southeast, there was waving grass and little else. The terrain was so flat, she could watch a dog run away for two whole weeks and never lose sight. At least here, unlike the more treed area near Fola, no nasty critters would be sneaking up on them. Without any real combat skills yet, random critter encounters didn't benefit her much.

There was that old, vintage movie about attacking birds. Surely, she had some kind of attack mode. She could "bite," sure, but she had to get awfully close for that. Next time they had some kind of fracas, she'd have to try something aggressive. In the meantime, she'd enjoy the scenery and wait for the AI to decide she needed a quest.

The notebook icon side out of her avatar in the top corner and turned blue. Ahva focused on it and the transparent book opened. Her earlier, completed quests were struck through, but a new one had been entered at the bottom.

What Do I Look Like? AAA? Help a fellow traveler.

Ahva dismissed it and stood up straighter. *Yay! As if on cue.*

She crouched and sprang off Osse's shoulder.

"Don't go too far!" He called.

No problem, human. Just need to find that "fellow traveler." I'm guessing those dust clouds.

She flapped her wings and gained altitude as she spiraled upward, away from her human.

To the east, a collection of covered wagons hid within the dust cloud. The cloud southeast was more of the same. Maybe one of them needed help.

She flew back to Osse. As she came closer, he held out his arm for a landing spot. She reared back to shed some speed and grabbed his wrist.

Ahva turned toward the east dust cloud and flapped her wings without letting go of Osse. "Dat one! That one!" *Whoa! Did I actually say that right?*

"That's just going to be a caravan, Ahva. Nothing we need there." Osse shook his head.

I still think we need to go check that out. She grabbed his wrist harder and kept flapping. "That one!"

He winced. "All right, all right. Wow, you have sharp toenails. Let's go look, but I'm telling you, a dust cloud that big will be a caravan. Nothing we need to see."

She stopped flapping and crawled up to Osse shoulder. *There, see? That wasn't so hard.*

Osse changed their path, turning almost perpendicular. He even sped up a bit. "They'll get past us, and I'm not backtracking no matter how curious you are. Got it?"

That's what you think.

His increased speed bounced her around more, but she held his collar tighter and crouched some to reduce the unnecessary jiggling.

The dust cloud grew. When they reached the edge of it, Osse slowed to a stop. A dozen covered wagons pulled by heavy-set horses plodded toward Fola. Each wagon had a red fan made of cards and a spray of stars painted on both the wagons and the blankets covering the horses.

He pointed. "See? Caravan. Nothing we need."

Ahva launched herself. *I'm going for a closer look, wimp.*

"Ahva! Come back!" Osse reached for her.

She flew straight at the caravan. A man driving the lead wagon whistled a shrill note. The edge of her vision turned red.

Chapter 6

Kids exploded from the back half of the wagons. While men strung bows and slipped quivers over their shoulders, each kid scooped up rocks and flung them at her.

Ahva squawked and tipped from one side to the other. Most of the rocks sailed past her. Others buzzed by her tail and wingtips.

"Ahva!" Osse called.

An arrow whizzed past. *Territorial much? All I did was fly in for a look.*

She wheeled around and headed back toward Osse. He met her halfway and offered his arm for perch. She landed, but momentum carried her forward, and she flopped into his chest. Osse opened the top of his bag. As she hopped in, he turned and sprinted away from the caravan. The contents of the dark bag rattled around her, but she crouched and tugged Osse's spare shirt around her for a cushion. At least she was safe from rocks and didn't have to hang on while Osse ran full tilt.

He'd been running forever before he slowed and open the bag. Ahva peeked out. Grasses. Lots of grasses. No covered wagons, no rock-throwing brats, no guys getting bows ready. Even the dust cloud was a distant blot on the horizon. She crawled out and returned to her spot on Osse's shoulder.

He breathed hard and fast, and his dark skin glittered with sweat. "What did I tell you? You don't go near the card fans and stars. They're superstitious and believe all you crows are bad news."

She growled like the dog at the merchant's tent. "Disgussing eye'all!"

"Right. I don't know if they're thieves, but they sure aren't friendly."

Then where are we supposed to find that fellow traveler who needs help? "Thanks!"

"No problem, Ahva." He sat down and fished the water flask from his bag. After he had a good swig, he poured some into the lid for her. Such a considerate human. Her fatigue meter recovered a few points.

Once she'd had her fill of water, he pulled out their bag of food. He broke off a few pieces of his cracker and tore a couple bits of jerky and set them on his knee where she could get to them.

Ahva poked at the food with her beak. *Mmm, hardtack crackers and jerky. Snack of champions.*

Someday, she'd learn how to do her own foraging. For now, bits of hardtack and slivers of jerky would do. Although they gave her a sensation of textures, they had real taste for her. She looked up and left, revealing the pop-up of her health and fatigue points. Full on the first and just over halfway on the other. They finished their meal.

Osse stood. "Let's go catch the other caravan, but wait for me to identify them before you go investigate, okay?

CHAPTER 6

Kids with rocks we can outrun. Adults with bows, not so easy."

"Yes." Ahva huffed.

Osse started for the southeast dust cloud. "I swear, sometimes I think you actually understand me."

Of course, I understand you, goofy. I may have a limited expressive vocabulary, but I understand you fine.

He hoofed it at a good clip. As they came close enough to see the heraldry in the fading light of the sunset, he slowed.

The caravan, seven wagons arranged in a ring, was decorated with a yellow bow shooting a sun.

"Not as bad as the last, but we can't approach them. They'll come to us if they want." Osse sat down. "Still. Safer for us here. We are less likely to be bothered by critters tonight so close to such a large group."

That would be nice.

Osse pulled his cloak out of the bag and spread it on the ground.

* * *

Jake returned to his computer after a bio break for both him and Prince. As he donned the headset, and unpaused the game, a pop-up window appeared with a cartoonish picture of Nagheed sitting in the corner.

The mini-image of Nagheed barked and ran off the screen to the right.

Presently, Nagheed lay near the fireplace, resting on a rug while Rafayel sat at an ornate wooden desk and wrote figures in a ledger. The selection of RenFaire music still played in the background and started on his favorite one, a happy tune with drum beat and two recorders playing the melody at different octaves in a round. He bobbed his head with the beat.

Footsteps approached the main door. Nagheed sat up and engaged Hear. His ears perked up.

The front door opened without a knock. Nagheed jumped to his feet and barked.

"Thank you, Nagheed," Rafayel said.

He barked once more.

-30 XP

Oh, really? And the number is higher each time. He sniffed. "Rafayel" surrounded the baron like a cloud. "Servant boy" squeezed in under the door. "Bettani," "Micah," and "Liora" drifted along on the air. "Burning firewood" flooded out of the fireplace.

One of the stable boys, the one who never spoke, slipped in with his cap in his hand. Halfway across the room, he stopped and bowed his head.

"Hello, Zev."

The boy waved for them to follow.

Rafayel looked down at his ledger and frowned then up at Zev, who waved more emphatically.

"Very well." He set the quill in the inkwell and stood. "Come, Nagheed."

Nagheed followed his human and the servant out the front door. Across the courtyard, the boy's father stood at the gate talking to someone on the other side through a tiny window inset into the right door. The voice coming from the other side spoke at a rate that could be measured in words per second.

Zev led the way, gesturing for Rafayel to come along.

CHAPTER 6

When Rafayel picked up the pace through the flower garden, Nagheed trotted to keep up.

"Take it easy. At this hour, I'll not let you in without the master's say so," The older servant waved them on. "Here he comes now. You can tell him what this is about." He stepped away from the gate and met Rafayel. "Sir, it's the constable going on about some kind of monster attack south of town. It doesn't make sense, sir."

Rafayel nodded once. "I'll take care of it, Eli. Thank you."

"Yes, sir." The servant corralled his son and led him away. "Come on, lad. We got our own business to attend to."

Rafayel lifted the bar on the gate and opened the door enough to step out. Nagheed followed and sat.

The constable stood there with his horse's reins in his hand. This horse wasn't the same pale one he'd ridden before. This one was darker with a black nose and socks. "You've never barred my entrance before."

"You've never come at such an early hour, Simon, but he should've let you pass. The ladies weren't ready for company, but I could have met you in the yard. I'll discuss better options with him." Rafayel brushed the concern away with his hand. "For now, you saw a monster?"

"Caught a glimpse of it as it fled. Might've been human once. Maybe." He scratched his head. "Doubtful now."

Rafayel crossed his arm over his chest and rubbed his chin. "From the beginning, please."

"Yes, sir. I was taking my patrol south of town when Karda got all kinds of skittish." He reached back and stroked his horse's nose.

Nagheed sniffed in the horse's direction but picked up no scent of fear now.

Rafayel pointed. "Karda?"

"The same." Simon glanced back.

"Hasn't she always been steady?"

"You've met mountains more jittery than this old gal." He ran his fingers through her mane. "Anyway, she got antsy, and I didn't see any reason for it, so I decided to check out the nearest farms, make sure everyone's all right and no one's seen anything worth investigating."

Rafayel nodded. "What did you find?"

"I went to the Benami place first." His face paled. "Sir, I've been to war more than once, as you know, but I never seen anything like this. Weren't anything alive in the whole place. Every cow, chicken, and person torn so thoroughly to shreds, I couldn't even say for sure which was Arn and which was his wife. Blood from one corner to the other. Weird symbols drawn on anything still intact enough to draw on. Just me and Karda, so I hightailed it out of there and headed for the Elazer place, expecting more of the same. I got there and found Misha brandishing a pitchfork at this two-legged monster."

Rafayel scowled. "Describe it for me."

Yeah. Animal, vegetable, or mineral?

"Not quite as tall as a man. Tattered clothes that were almost like they might have been fine some day long past. Stringy, matted hair. At first, I took it for an insane man or woman, but as I rode up, it turned toward me. One eye was normal enough. The other glowed."

Eyeshine? But then why only one eye?

"Glowed?" Rafayel shifted closer a half-step.

"Yes, sir, weird as that sounds. Not bright, but enough to see in the early light. And that wasn't all. The one hand, left I think, had skeletal fingers. Not like it hadn't eaten in a while, but actual pale, bony fingers. I drew my pistol and fired a shot at it. Caught it square in the shoulder. It reeled back, so I know I hit it, but it lit out faster than my horse can gallop. I tried giving chase, but less than a kilometer and it was gone. I went back to the Elazer place and helped him hitch the wagon, pile in wife and kids and whatever chickens were left, and I rode with them to town. They're holed up at the church now."

The computer pinged and showed him the blue notebook icon. Nagheed dismissed it.

Jake paused the game and sighed. If there wasn't a way to turn off those hokey quest notifications, he'd be sure to note it in his suggestions.

He opened the settings screen and scanned through all the options he had control over until he found Quest Notifications. He flipped that toggle to Off but left himself the option of being able to call up the notebook from the menu if he wanted it.

With that settled, he swiped the settings screen away and unpaused the game.

Simon blew out a breath. "I sent my men out in pairs and threes to check around the edges of town and warn the other farms. I sent a few others a couple kilometers down the road both ways. I'm headed back to the Elazer place to try to pick up the trail."

Rafayel nodded. "I'll ride out there with you."

Nagheed followed his human back inside and around to the stable behind the house. The groom already had the sleek, gray horse saddled.

"Thought you might be needing him." Eli cinched the

girth.

"Excellent, thank you." Rafayel entered the manor through the kitchen.

Nagheed trotted along with him and watched his human collect weapons and belt them on. Then he donned a leather doublet with steel rings fastened to it.

Bettani crept into the room. "What's happened?"

"The Benami farm and the Elazer farm were attacked by some manner of beast."

She gasped. "Are they all right?"

"The Elazers are. Short some livestock, I gather, but the family is sheltering with the priest. Benami and his family?" Rafayel scowled and shook his head.

She rushed to him. "You're not going alone, are you?"

Rafayel leaned over and ruffled the fur on Nagheed's head. "Certainly not."

Nagheed waved his tail and woofed.

"Nagheed is wonderful, I'm sure, but–"

"Constable Fishel will be with us, and I'm not so foolish as to neglect the better part of valor if the situation warrants." He finished buttoning the doublet as he kissed his wife's forehead. "Nevertheless, a few prayers wouldn't go amiss."

"You'll have them." She embraced him.

"I'll be back as soon as I can." He stepped away from her and slapped the side of his leg. "Come along, Nagheed."

Nagheed accompanied his human out the back door and waited while Rafayel swung himself into the saddle of his horse. They met the constable at the gate and left together. The constable led the way.

Once out of the city, they left the road and headed southeast. Nagheed sniffed the air and watched the horizon for smoke. "Damp earth" rose from the ground and hovered like a fog. "Fox" made a trail that wove off to the left.

Those were bolder. Dimmer, there were a handful of others: "**Horses, chickens, man, woman, two girls, Simon.**"

The constable had left a faint trail that went straight south and then another that came back from the southwest accompanied by the rest. Nagheed certainly didn't get a whiff of anything like a monster.

When they came to another road, the two men slowed.

Rafayel came even with the constable. "Let's check out the Benami place, then we'll head to the Elazer farm to try picking up that trail. Until we know what we're dealing with, I don't like the idea of anyone going off alone."

Simon looked away. "Probably some fellow who's not quite right in the head."

Who outran your horse? Not likely. He'd need more than a psychiatric issue to manage that.

Rafayel checked his flintlock pistol. "Perhaps, but if I have to be wrong, I'd rather be cautious than bold."

"As you say, sir." He turned and continued.

Nagheed kept the slow pace of the humans. For half a kilometer or more the scents didn't change. Then they crossed through a narrow band of trees and into what must've been an old farm. Dirt was turned up with trampled rows of yellow straw.

"Cow blood" and "chicken blood" drifted upward from overturned mannequins of farm animals. "Burnt grass" was remarkably strong closer to the house, which exuded "human blood" from every opening. Scattered all around the area were "Decay" tightly connected with "????."

What's up with that? Nagheed turned his head from side

to side then wandered a few steps away before reversing directions and crossing in front of the horses to go a few steps the other way. The faint scent words scrolling across shifted size and intensity as he moved, but the series of question marks never resolved into an actual word. What had they encountered that was so foreign he couldn't even hazard a guess?

He drifted back, crossing behind the horses this time to resume his place on Rafayel's left. The farmstead appeared on the horizon. Charred sticks, all that remained of the house, framed the rough outline of a box. Thin trails of smoke still rose, dissipating in the faint wind.

"It wasn't burning before." Simon squinted.

Rafayel pulled back on the reins of his horse.

Nagheed went a few steps further, but the scents didn't change. *Time for a different sense. How about hearing?* He lifted his ears and tipped his head from side to side.

Nothing. No birds chirped. No bugs chattered. What wind there was barely moved the grass. He wanted to bark just to be sure sound still worked in the area.

"Eerie, isn't it?" Rafayel stood in his saddle and looked around.

"Yeah," the constable whispered.

Nagheed looked up at the two humans and woofed.

"Stay close and be ready for anything." Rafayel sat again.

Always.

He kept pace with Rafayel as they crept closer. A chicken mannequin was flipped over in the yard. Nagheed stopped to investigate.

"Leave it." Rafayel snapped his fingers. "Stay near me."

Y'know, there might be clues or loot. He gave it one last sniff and watched the scent window. *Nope. Just dead chicken.*

Other mannequins of different sizes here and there accounted for the other chickens and cows. No loot to be had in any of them.

They plodded on, approaching what was left of the house and found other matted messes that scented human. A cursory search confirmed the game's total lack of generosity.

Heat radiated from the ruins like the embers of a huge campfire.

Hot embers, bare feet. Bad combination. He stopped and turned toward his human.

Rafayel dismounted, but the constable stayed on his horse.

"Wait here. Watch for unfriendly visitors."

Nagheed kept an eye on him and listened for other movement. Charred wood and ash crunched under the human's boots. He kicked over some of the larger boards and scorched pots. The game's stinginess continued.

Weird that there are no clues or loot to be had. Jake paused the game long enough to jot a note for his playtester report.

Noise behind Nagheed drew his attention. He spun away from the humans and scanned the landscape. Nothing there, but it couldn't just be his imagination.

There was something.

Engaging Hear, he perked up his ears and tipped his head. The rustling noise returned and something to the right moved. Nagheed growled. The hairs on the back of his neck stood on end.

"Your dog's got something." Simon pointed.

Rafayel returned. "What do we have, Nagheed?"

Trouble, no doubt.

A flock of birds flushed into the sky.

Nagheed trotted a few steps closer to the tree line. He sniffed the air, but burnt wood and blood overrode everything else.

"Nagheed, speak," Rafayel said.

He barked, a deep-throated sound that threatened destruction to anything dumb enough to approach. A deer sprinted out of the trees and darted across the farm.

Simon blew out a breath and muttered, "Dumb deer."

"Better that than the alternative." Rafayel swung up into Ryder's saddle.

"The Elazer place?" Simon twitched his head toward the west.

Rafayel pointed. "Lead on."

The humans kept to a pace that might get them there next year.

Nagheed snorted. *Come on! I could get road rage in the middle of this game!* He darted a few dozen meters ahead then stopped and turned back until the horses caught up then ran ahead a few dozen more meters before waiting again.

Simon chuckled. "I think we're annoying your dog."

"Patience is a virtue," Rafayel replied.

As they traveled at a pace slightly faster than a dead stop, Nagheed returned to his senses.

"Burnt wood" was faint at the moment, but directly ahead. "Deer" had been all over the place, some more recently than others. "Decay" and "????" were still tagging along together in a line along the general direction they were traveling. A gust of wind from the east brought him "horse manure."

CHAPTER 6

Whatever that unknown scent was, assuming it was the same thing as before, featured more prominently in the view now. Nagheed wasn't sure how he felt about that. Talk of monsters and the sight of corpses at the Benami farm sent a chill deep into Jake's gut, but he had to admit to some curiosity about exactly what the thing might be.

Nagheed focused on his hearing. The horses behind him crunched dry grass and rocks under their hooves. Various birds contributed to the wind rustling the tree branches, but nothing the size of a humanoid monster moved around out there.

Miraculously they reached the Elazer place before sundown. The ground was all turned up for planting in long rows. A modest log cabin on the far side of the plowed field hadn't been torched like the Benami place, but there was something odd about it. Nagheed couldn't quite see what it was, but the side left of the centrally placed door was splotchy with black, white, and gray patches.

Nagheed trotted forward, weaving from side to side to employ his nose to get some answers.

The "Decay, ????" combo was showing in bold letters from all over the farm, particularly closer to the house. A flock of "birds" had settled nearby in the field, probably looking for seeds or bugs. Rafayel and Constable Fishel each had their own cloud, but as Nagheed watched them for a moment, "(afraid)" joined the constable and "(nervous)" surrounded Rafayel.

As they picked their way across the plowed field, a lone figure came around the corner. The person? Creature? Had long, scraggly hair, matted almost to the point of resembling dreadlocks. Equally matted fur or maybe torn cloth, covered its body. With a burnt stick, it drew something on the side of the house. The nametag over its head showed the "????" that had been so prevalent since arriving at the first farm, and the scent cloud surrounding the monster showed both the nametag and "Decay."

Nagheed barked both to get the humans' attention and to spook the creature. No debuff icon added itself to the monster's nametag.

The RenFaire music abruptly changed to an aggressive drumbeat and ominous brass horns blaring warnings.

It turned and glared with a glowing eye before it laughed. The maniacal humorless sound pitched in a human vocal range still had a mechanical quality. Without first dropping the stick, the creature charged, still laughing. The nametag over the creature's head changed to "Maniac."

He ran, gaining speed with each stride. Rafayel hollered something Nagheed couldn't understand over the screechy laugh.

The moment Nagheed was in range, he pounced on the creature, knocking it over. He locked a mouthful of teeth on the thing's bony arm. After jerking its arm free, it threw him off. Nagheed flailed as he flew through the air and landed with a thud that turned the screen bright red. His health bar lost several points.

While he righted himself, two loud pops were followed by louder bangs. The scent of "gunpowder" billowed from both Rafayel and Simon. The maniac's health bar slid backward toward half. The maniac laughed.

Nagheed got his feet under him and headed back toward the fight. Every step with his front left leg brought a red haze to the screen. Rafayel guided Ryder and met the maniac's charge with a rapier. The cloud-to-ground slice left a terrific gash down the maniac's chest.

Without missing a beat, the maniac took a swipe at Rafayel's leg, doing enough damage to take a quarter of Rafayel's health. Simon rode around Ryder and came into range for a slash with his saber, but the maniac dodged and pulled Simon off his horse. He'd be dazed for a moment, and as fast as the maniac was, Simon might not get a chance to defend himself. Nagheed had to get there faster. He engaged Sprint mode to speed up in spite of the red haze.

As the maniac raised its hand to strike Simon, Rafayel drove his rapier into the maniac's face. A burst of sparks flew and the creature turned into a mannequin.

Nagheed snorted. *How weird!*

Both humans gasped and shied away from the expiring maniac. Ryder stayed steady, but the constable's horse whinnied skittered backward. Nagheed cringed, but Simon jumped up and caught the horse's reins.

"Whoa, girl. Easy there. Whatever it was, sure bet it's dead now." Simon patted the horse's neck.

The music changed back to the plucked guitar. Nagheed slowed to a walk. Every step with his injured leg still flashed the screen red.

Simon led Karda to Rafayel. "You're bleeding."

Rafayel leaned over and pried the torn cloth away from the injury. "Few centimeters down and my boot would've caught it. Doesn't look too bad."

"I'll help you down, and we'll see what we can do."

Rafayel shook his head. "If I climb down, I won't be getting back up. I'll be fine. Really. It smarts a bit but not too bad."

"All the same, visit a physician on the way in."

"I'll do that. Can you check Nagheed?"

Simon handed Rafayel his horse's reins. "Certainly, then we'll have a look at what that thing was carrying. Nagheed, come here, boy."

To stop the flashing red screen, Nagheed picked up his paw and limped forward.

"I was afraid of that." Rafayel leaned forward in his saddle. "He hit the ground awfully hard."

Simon grabbed his canteen then jogged over and knelt. "Now, is it your leg bothering you or the shoulder?" Simon ran his hands along Nagheed's left leg then inspected the pad of that foot. "Nothing there. Let's check your shoulder and ribs."

When Simon's hand pressed just behind Nagheed's leg the screen flashed red. Nagheed yelped.

"Right there, huh? Let's see if I can get through all this fur and find out what's happened." He gingerly parted the hair. "You're not bleeding. That's good." He pushed carefully making the screen go red again. "At best, you got yourself quite a bruise there. At worst, you broke something. You'll be visiting the physician, too." He ruffled the fur on Nagheed's head. "We'll go nice and slow until we get home."

Favoring the injured side, Nagheed followed Simon to the mannequin. As they came close, an inventory screen opened showing a white crystal, a handful of clear coins labeled "rounds," and a blue blob that resembled slagged plastic.

"What've we got?" Rafayel looked over Simon's shoulder.

Simon picked up pieces and showed them. "I say give the

money to the Elazers and whoever Benami's next of kin is. You can have the rest. I got no use for a chunk of quartz and I don't even know what that blue thing is."

Rafayel took the crystal and plastic. "I'll let you distribute the money however you like. In a few weeks, I'll be going to the Oligometa. Someone in Tel Caperna might know what this crystal and the blue thing are for."

"Fair enough. Let's finish checking out the Elazer place then head in." Simon grabbed Karda's reins and led her forward.

"Did you see how fast that creature moved?" Rafayel set a pace that kept him even with the other horse.

Simon whistled. "That was something else."

"I've never seen anything move that fast." Rafayel glanced from the Elazer place to the site of the battle.

"Your dog bit it, and it tore loose and threw him. And the gunshots. That's a total of three right through the chest and like it never happened, and then you landed that blow with your rapier. Nothing. Didn't even flinch!" The constable shook his head. "It isn't natural."

Rafayel frowned. "Only after I struck the glow in the eye did we have any real effect."

"I hope we don't find many more of those." Simon blew out a breath.

I've got a feeling this game will be totally loaded with more of those. Many, many more of those.

When they reached the house, Simon drew his sword and stepped inside. Nagheed sniffed around.

"Decay" was now accompanied by "maniac." There had been four humans around the area, too muddled to know where exactly. "Dead chicken" drifted up from five different overturned chicken mannequins.

The constable had downgraded from "scared" to just "nervous," and now Rafayel's word cloud included "injured."

Huh. The ???? is gone. Now he knew what to call the thing that had attacked him.

The outside of the house had been decorated with the same symbol over and over: a line with a loop below the line and another above the line a little further along. That symbol had been drawn with a charred stick and something like chalk. Other dark gray marks might have been intended to resemble the symbol, but whatever the drawing medium had been, it had skipped badly.

The cabin's door opened, and Simon stepped out. "Looks like it did when we left earlier." He swung up onto Karda's back. "Let's head back in. Get your leg treated."

This time, Nagheed didn't mind their slower pace.

* * *

Jael took a deeper breath.

The scents of Oba and Dina were faint but still recognizable. The two human males who had stolen her cubs still had a "human female" with them. Her heart sank. Three humans to deal with could really complicate getting her cubs back, but there was something more troubling. Something else was paralleling their path, and her sense of smell was not identifying it properly. A meandering line showed "Decay, ????" in bolder letters.

Whatever that other, unknown scent was, it took the same path as her cubs, and it better not do anything to harm them.

CHAPTER 6

She picked up her pace, sometimes losing the unknown scent for a moment, but always keeping track of her cubs.

The brush around her became more sparse. Small, scraggly bushes gave way to more grass until there was only grassland ahead of her. Jael stopped and stood on two feet. In the distance, clouds of dust marred the horizon. Near at hand, a tall, dark-skinned human traveled alone. Closer still, the trail of "????, decay" led directly to some kind of creature loped along, headed away from her at negligible speed.

What was it? Scrawny bear? A human? Some kind of mangy coyote on its back legs? She only knew one way to find out.

Dropping back down to all fours, Jael took off at a quick jog, gradually building into a full-speed run. She closed the distance with the unknown creature at a fantastic speed. As she drew close, the creature turned toward her and laughed, a high-pitched, eerie sound devoid of all humor.

It had the appearance of a human that hadn't groomed itself in ages. Male or female wasn't obvious at first. Greasy hair matted and clung to it in clumps. Dirt and blood were caked on what was left of its clothing. A glow, muted to red and orange, came from within its left arm.

Jael used her Tackle skill to drive the human beast to the ground. She picked up no scent of Oba or Dina on the thing, only the strong stench of decay and blood. It pushed her off, and she sailed backwards, landing with a thud on her back several meters away. Her vision flashed red.

What kind of human had that much strength? This wasn't time to find out. She had cubs to find. Jael rolled up to her feet and turned to retreat. Only a few steps further, something grabbed her back leg, dragging her backwards. Her front claws tore up the dirt.

Jael kicked backward. The smelly humanoid laughed as it staggered back. She came to her feet and turned toward it. The creature was almost on top of her. Jael swiped at it with her claw but didn't connect. The creature caught her by the arm in an impossible grip and swung her in a semicircle before letting her fly. She landed hard on her side, making her vision turn red again. Her opponent laughed and charged. As Jael came back to her feet, a black bird flew overhead and dropped a rock, narrowly missing the creature.

Nice try, crow.

The humanoid creature raced toward Jael again. Another direct attack would get her thrown off. Keeping an eye on it, Jael ran a quarter circle to her left. It ran at her, but Jael held her ground. When it was in range, she used Agility to duck under the attack and then used Claw and swiped with her paw, knocking its legs out from under it. It landed face down. Jael pounced, planting her entire bulk on the small of its back. She used her claws to strike at the glows in the arms. Sparks flew, igniting the cloth and turning her sight red for several seconds.

Chapter 7

Ahva dropped the rock, missing the glowing not-exactly-human monster. She hissed and looped around. There wasn't time for another attempt, and rocks were heavy. Time to get bigger help.

She flew back to Osse and landed on his outstretched arm. She held onto his wrist and kept flapping. "Bite fingers! Disgusting eyeball!"

Ossie winced. "All right, all right. Calm down. Something over there for us?"

"Yes!" Yep. Move it before that poor bear is toast.

As he turned back along the path she'd flown, Ahva crawled up to her perch on his shoulder and gripped his collar. He leaned forward and ran to the top of the hill. At the bottom, the bear was sitting on her attacker. She swiped at the glow on the monster's arm, and a mini-explosion caused a burst of sparks and fire, tossing the bear backwards. The monster's corpse became a mannequin.

Odd, but somehow strange. Bizarre, and yet usual. But y'know, for a former kid game, that makes sense. No graphic blood splatter to upset the squeamish, and it's still recognizable as a person, monster, or whatever.

The bear stayed still as they approached. Smoke wafted

from singed fur. When she did finally move, she tried to push up with her front feet, yelped, and fell flat again.

Ahva looked up to activate the menus then picked Chat. The transparent window appeared hovering just above the ground.

Who with? The pop-up window appeared with options for typing a name or choosing someone in sight. She picked Line of Sight, then stared at the bear.

Ahva: Hi, bear. I'm Ahva. Are you a player?

The text showed in the box like a heads-up display.

Jael: My name is Jael.

Ahva: Okay, Jael. My human is an herbalist. Maybe he can help.

Jael: My name is Jael.

The chat window closed.

I wasn't done yet. Ahva opened a new one.

Ahva: Hi, Jael. Are you a player? I'm looking for my partner.

Jael: My name is Jael.

The chat window closed.

Okay. You're either not my partner, an NPC, or incredibly rude!

Osse slowed has he got close to Jael. "Hi, bear. Can I see your paws?"

You know, if this becomes Androcles and the Lion scenario later, I'm going to be majorly unimpressed.

The bear whined but stayed still.

"I won't hurt you. I think you've burned your paws. I have a salve made of herbs. It'll heal that." Osse crouched out of the bear's reach and pointed. "Can I see your paw?"

Jael scooted closer and held one paw toward Osse.

CHAPTER 7

Osse pulled a canteen from his bag and poured some water on the smoking fur. Jael flinched.

"It's okay. Just cleaning out the junk." He set the canteen aside and pulled out a cork-stoppered jar. "This is the salve I mentioned. It'll heal the burns. Won't hurt at all."

Ahva leaned forward to watch. Under the bear's scorched fur, the skin was blistered. When Osse applied the salve, the blisters faded, but the fur didn't grow back.

Ahva snorted. *I guess that's not much different than other games where you drink red potions and poof! All better.*

Jael sat up and let Osse repeat the treatment on her other paw. Once he finished, she shied away from them then took off running.

"Thanks. You're welcome," Ahva said in two different voices.

Osse smiled and returned his jars to his bag. "A bear with a place to go."

The blue notebook icon appeared.

Quest complete, I'm sure.

Osse approached the mannequin. "She left her loot behind."

As he drew near, an inventory screen opened showing the loot available

"Yes!" *Like a bear needs green chips, a blue crystal, and melty orange stuff.*

Those green and copper chips really did look a bit like mini circuit boards, but what would that, and the plastic-looking blobs, be doing in a society that seemed to be stuck in the Medieval or Renaissance. Alternate timeline? Repelled an alien invasion? Way past an apocalyptic event? She'd have to watch for more clues.

"I think we'll keep all of it. Not sure what this orange thing is, but the crystal might be a sapphire." Osse scooped it all up and slipped it into his bag. "Come on. We should get home by tomorrow at our pace."

Okay, but we better not stay there.

* * *

After taking Prince outside to run around the yard a few times, Jake returned to his laptop, slid on his VR goggles, and unpaused the game.

Nagheed was sprawled on a rug in front of the fire in the den listing to Rafayel read while his wife and daughter sewed and his son carved a piece of wood with a knife.

This chapter described the retaliation of the crossbreeds. From within their mountain hideaway, they launched some sort of weapons that burned all the land within a long radius in a fire that swept along the ground to twice the height of a man. Tall buildings, hundreds of meters tall, toppled when the lower levels were compromised. Towns and cities were flattened. The only survivors were those holed up in the mountains. Millions of people died and all technology was lost.

After Rafayel finished reading the chapter, Nagheed went to sleep. Sheep in tutus twirled across the screen. Jake smiled and shook his head. When he woke up, the sunlight through the windows lit the empty den.

Still weird that the game doesn't send Nagheed to bed with his humans.

Nagheed wandered first to Rafayel's study then to the kitchen, where the cook was busy at work.

CHAPTER 7

He sniffed and filled the air with the words "**eggs, bacon, bread, plum jam, ham, potatoes, carrots.**"

Those last would be leftovers from last night, probably his breakfast.

"There's Nagheed! Sleepyhead!" Micah chuckled.

Hey! I'm a growing dog!

"Yours is over here," Marie, the cook, gave Nagheed's bowl a little kick.

I get the leftovers, right? He trotted over. *Yep.* He scarfed them down in no time, getting **+10 XP** for Dog Behavior.

"Wow. Does he even know what he's eating?" Liora snickered.

Of course, but I have better things to do in a day.

"Who knows?" Rafayel smiled. "Eat hearty, Nagheed. It's field rations for us until we reach the inn halfway to Vanya tonight."

"Vanya." Bettani glowered. "You have to go to Vanya."

"We talked about this last night. I need to know what that symbol means. That creature we killed yesterday took great pains to draw it, carve it, or burn it into anything it didn't destroy. I want to know what we're dealing with, and Yavne's library is still under construction."

"Tel Caperna has a library associated with the University there. You'll be there for the Oligometa–"

"A couple weeks from now. That was my original plan, but even if I go straight there and back, that will be almost a month. I can't afford to wait that long. I don't believe that thing was alone."

"Right, and you and Nagheed will be alone out there on the road to Vanya. What if you run into another one of those things?"

"I agree. It is not ideal. But I know no other way." He finished his food. "The way that thing moved and the way other travelers have described it and others like it, I'm not sure the city's walls let alone people's homes will be proof against them in any significant numbers. The time to go is now."

Bettani looked down at her lap. "Before they increase their numbers or get organized." She reached for him. "Just you be careful."

"I'll go and come back as quickly and safely as I can." Rafayel leaned over and kissed his wife. "Come along, Nagheed. Let's get our supplies packed and get moving before the sun gets much higher."

Nagheed followed his human to the den.

* * *

By Ahva's count, they'd been traveling forever. Maybe that was an exaggeration. A small one, anyway. A handful of days game time if she wanted to be picky, but she wondered if maybe Osse would hike off the edge of the world at this rate. At least the flat terrain had become rolling hills, and those were pretty. For an extra bonus, the game clock sped up considerably in this long-distance travel mode.

Currently, Ahva was checking out her flight skills. Her VR rig simulated the air rushing past her, and she experienced near weightlessness as she flapped her wings. As that drained her fatigue meter, she held her wings steady to glide and headed for an outcropping of dark rock. As she passed over, an updraft lifted her effortlessly higher in the sky. She turned a tight circle to stay in the thermal and rise

CHAPTER 7

ever upward.

When she reached the limit, she found Osse, as small as an ant in the distance. She'd been watching him scurry along for several seconds before it hit her. Her nerves were rock steady. Funny how looking off a second-floor balcony could give her the killer jitters, but in the game, she was literally as high as a skyscraper's top floor, and she felt fine. She felt better than fine. A song in her heart and pep in her step, well, wingbeats. Same thing, right? She could get used to this!

Ahva turned back toward Osse. She left the current and glided but dropped altitude like the downhill on a rollercoaster. Nearing the ground, she angled upward again, flapping constantly now to defy gravity. Her fatigue meter showed maroon. Time to land and get a bit of rest.

Ahva banked left and spotted her human. As she came in for a landing, Osse held out his arm, and she swooped down below the level then turned upward to shed momentum and dropped gracefully onto Osse's wrist.

"You're getting good at that," Osse said.

She cawed and ran up Osse's arm to his shoulder. *Of course! Gaining points in the skill.*

Her fatigue meter would be a while recovering. In the meantime, she'd stick with Osse and practice some of her less mobile skills.

Osse shielded his eyes with one hand to check the sun's position. "We're almost home, I think. It took me a week to get to Fola, and we've been hiking about that long. I thought I'd always recognize home, but after five days, this grassy hill is no different from another grassy hill. The treeline should be ahead. The river's on the far side of Kamali, and the village is nearer to us than that. Unless I drifted from the course."

Ahva whistled a quick tune to pick up a few XP. He'd figure it out. It's not like she had access to a map.

She continued riding on his shoulder and enjoying the cool breeze and the warm sun. They went up and down a few hills that started to become steeper.

At the top of one hill, Osse pointed at the dark green bumps on the horizon. "There. That's the tree line south of Kamali." He turned more toward the afternoon sun. "My village is over here."

He had to lean forward into the next hill and climb higher than they had before, and Ahva had to adjust her grip on his tunic, but they made it easily enough.

At the top of the hill, he froze, and his jaw dropped open.

Ahead, a few skeletal, partial frames of a dozen permanent houses resembled the remains of their campfires in the morning. A few still trailed wisps of grayish smoke. Was that Osse's village, or what was left of it anyway?

The system displayed the blue notebook in the corner and Ahva focused on it. A transparent notebook page showed the previous quests crossed out. The new one was written at the bottom of the list.

Home Fires Keep Burning. What happened here?

Ahva snickered. Cute. She was glad the game designers hadn't stripped the personality out of the game when they turned it into the adult version.

Osse started moving faster but with less certainty. He stumbled down the side of the hill then up the next one. Ahva tried to adjust her grip and hang on with beak and feet but couldn't keep her balance with the way he tripped

CHAPTER 7

and staggered. She launched from his shoulder. Much more fun to be in the air than trying to hang onto his collar. Her fatigue wouldn't tolerate a long flight, but maybe long enough for him to stop or adopt a steadier pace.

Circling around him in a wide arc, she kept him in sight. Osse made his way to what was left of a low wall made of mud and grass bricks. He picked his way among the debris to one particular collection of charred sticks in the corner of the low wall. Ahva's fatigue meter flashed. She'd better land before she crashed. Gliding in for a landing, she parked on his shoulder just as her fatigue meter hit zero. Tears streamed from the boy's eyes as he fell to his knees in the ruins.

Osse came uneasily back to his feet as Ahva gripped his shirt collar with her beak and one foot. Osse began rooting through the mess as if searching for something, but it must have been something large because he didn't overturn little bits of charred things. Finding nothing, he went from one wrecked dwelling to another, searching for something. He headed generally south and ended up at the edge of the village where several large stones had been set up. Each had writing in a language Ahva didn't recognize.

Gravestones? Memorials?

About halfway down the line Osse stopped and knelt so quickly Ahva almost lost her grip. He traced the writing with his finger and cried all the harder.

And this had been originally billed as a kid's game? What kid needed to see a completely destroyed village? Beyond removing the educational elements, was the AI tweaking the plot for adults?

Khin May paused the game and disconnected. She went to

the window and watched the rain fall. Her heart ached and tears burned in her eyes. Grandma spoke of her home in Myanmar. Burma. She always called it Burma. Government soldiers had come in and destroyed everything, burning every structure. Nothing left, just like Osse's home. She hadn't been there, of course. Grandma had been Khin May's age at the time, but Grandma's descriptions were so detailed.

She sniffled and brushed her eyes with her hand. "Way to make it personal, Horizon."

Khin May blew out a breath. Time to lighten up. Horizon Systems surely hadn't planned that scene in the game just for her. How many third-generation Burmese refugees played these silly games anyway. She dried her eyes and returned to the game.

Once more into the breach, my friends. Once more!

The computer restarted right where she'd left off.

She stared at the writing on the memorials but couldn't make anything of it.

Whatever was responsible for this might still be in the area, and he wasn't keeping a good watch. While he wrestled his grief, she activated her sentry-related skills. She became acutely aware of the local wildlife, but nothing was more treacherous than a squirrel.

The sun was halfway down to the horizon when he finally dried his eyes and stood.

"Come on, Ahva. We're going to find out who did this, and we're going to give the same to them." Osse glared at the memorial stones for a moment then turned toward Kamali.

Ominous words, but she passed it off as an artifact of his

grief. Hiking to and from Fola for a couple weeks total then finding Home Sweet Home reduced to cinders and smoke would rattle anyone's world. Likewise, Grandpa spoke that way any time Grandma brought up the destruction of their home.

He strode with purpose now and made a straight line for Kamali. Maybe they'd learn something there.

Ahva expected another day or couple of traveling, but the city was in view before the sun had set much further. A crowd had gathered around the gate to hawk wares and conduct matters of legal business just like in Fola.

"This will be like a market, Ahva, so watch yourself," Osse grumbled.

His voice sounded marginally steadier, but she still didn't care for the brooding overtone in his words.

Apparently, I'm going to have to be my own comedic relief in this game. Have jokes. Will travel.

She scooted closer to the side of his head and tightened her grip on his collar.

Some of the shoppers and many of the sellers gave Osse the stink-eye as he walked through the crowd. Ahva returned the favor. After the third person suddenly turned away after making eye contact with her, Ahva started counting how many rude humans she could stare down. She gave herself bonus points if they started spitting over their shoulders.

Osse approached a bald, wrinkled Bakhari man sitting under a shade tree by the gate. Instead of the typical tunic and pants worn by the majority of men in the area, he wore a brilliant red and tan toga, clasped at the shoulder with an ornate brooch. He wore a hat that resembled a mushroom cap with a short brim.

Osse stopped a few strides away from the man. "I don't wish to be a bother, sir, but if I might ask a question."

"Ask, young one," a man's voice answered in a tone that sounded older than the sky. He gestured to the ground in front of him.

Osse moved closer and sat facing the man. "The village to the west of here, what happened to it?"

"It has been eight sunrises since we saw the smoke rising." The old man drew one knee up to his chest and leaned forward. "Eight sunrises since we mustered a scouting force to go check on them. Eight sunrises since the scouts reported back."

Come on. Find another way to incorporate "Eight sunrises" into your speech. I double-dog dare you.

"The fires were still burning, and the villains were racing away from the sunrise, giggling like demented children. The scouts gave chase but lost their prey in the hills and plains. When they returned to the village, they found all destroyed and everyone dead. Your village?"

Osse brushed his eyes. "I was on my way to Fola."

"Your tears do them no good." His brow furrowed and his tone took on a scolding cadence. "You will never be a man if moved to emotion so easily."

Osse bolted to his feet, leaving Ahva's guts behind on the ground. She could've done without the VR simulating that for her. "I should take the murder of my people so lightly? My mother, my father, my grandmother, my sisters? Just like that?"

"A man is not ruled by emotion. That is for women." The old one made a slicing motion with his hand.

CHAPTER 7

Wow. Sexist much? Do you need sensitivity training or a whack upside the head?

"Then maybe it's best that I didn't pass my rite of manhood yet."

Ahva braced herself as Osse spun and strode into the city with a jarring pace.

"I am not done speaking. Come back!" the old man hollered.

She hissed at the useless man. "Nooooo."

"We'll need provisions for the trip." Osse brushed his eyes with his thumb. "I don't have many chips left, but we can sell some of the things we picked up in Fola. That should get us plenty."

Okay, so what kind of shop do you want? "Ahva look!"

"Young man! Young man, wait!" A middle-aged man called as they passed a shop.

"Hello!" Ahva waved with her wing.

The shopkeeper wore a decorated green tunic over dark brown pants and a necklace with a pendant that looked like a disk with a cross sitting on top of it. His ID over his head just said "Jeweler."

Osse sighed and turned back. "Yes, sir?"

"You're from the village, the one the maniacs burned, aren't you?"

Osse sniffled. "Yes, sir. I was in Fola this past week."

"I thought I recognized you. Tsidkenu be praised you were there, and may he give rest to those who were slain. I have your property in safekeeping." The shopkeeper gestured toward the store he'd come out of. "Please, if I can take a small amount of your time, I will return to you what is yours."

"My property?"

"Yours more than any other's." The shopkeeper ushered them inside then through a door to a workroom. "The attack was about a week ago. After the handful of guards chased the maniacs as far as they would, some of the less scrupulous decided to loot what remained. The memorial for the deceased hadn't even happened yet." He huffed and rolled his eyes. "Shameful. Anyway, the town elders wouldn't stop them, so some friends and I quickly collected everything we could and put them in baskets based on where we recovered them. We had hoped a survivor or a family member could be found. It usually is this time of year that one or more young people go to Fola, isn't it?"

"Yes. I was the only one of age this year, so I went alone."

The workroom had pieces of equipment behind magnifying lenses and piles of rocks. The rocks were in different stages of shiny and faceted, and some were set in brass bezels. Ahva craned her head around for a better look, but Osse moved through with a singular focus on the shopkeeper.

We'll check it out later.

They passed through a door into a store room. Labeled boxes filled the shelves on two sides of the room. A third set of shelves held some tools. The rest held some small baskets. Each was labeled with a number that corresponded with a hastily sketched map tacked on the front of one shelf. "We collected whatever belongings we could find and kept them organized by where they were found. We kept nothing for ourselves. It wasn't our place. We're searching for as many family members as we can. There have been some to claim their kin's belongings, and we're still seeking others." The shopkeeper led him to the map. "Which home was yours?"

Osse pointed. "Here, in the corner of the village."

"Yes, the farrier and herbalist's place. That would be baskets six through nine." He lifted each down and set them in the middle of the floor then gripped Osse's shoulder. "Take all the time you need." The shopkeeper stepped out and closed the door.

Osse crouched in the midst of the baskets. Pointing to each box in turn, he counted twice.

"What?" Ahva leaned forward.

"One short." Osse counted again.

He reached for the nearest, an old straw basket. Osse pulled the peg out of the latch and lifted the lid open. Inside, he found a roll of handmade lace, a few pouches marked with leaf drawings, an ornately carved silver ring with tiny stones, and a few green chips. "Grandmother's things. This ring was hers, and she never went anywhere without a couple pouches of healing herbs in case someone needed her. She made lace by hand to sell in the market." He slid the ring on the little finger of his left hand then added the lace and chips to his supplies.

Ahva whistled. *Wonder if that ring has special qualities.*

Osse opened the next nearest basket. Osse drew a heavy leather belt and sleeveless tunic from the inside. Beneath the tunic was a gray shirt. After tucking the shirt in his bag, Osse tapped one of the shelves. "This was Dad's. Perch over here while I try this on."

Ahva whistled and fluttered over to the nearest shelf.

After Osse had the leather tunic and belt situated, she returned to him and landed on one of the now empty baskets.

He sniffled.

Inside the third basket was a simple brown dress that showed no wear, a few more pouches decorated with leaves, and a cloth sack containing jerky, nuts, crackers, and dried fruit. "Mom's. She must have been returning from the market, and she was working on this dress when I left." As soon as Osse added the provisions to his own bag.

That left the smallest one.

"This would have to be either Maaska's or Mati's."

Inside was only a hand-sized porcelain case with pink flowers painted on it. Osse picked up the case, opened the lid, and pulled out hair ribbons.

He brushed his eyes with the palm of his hand. "Yeah. This was my present to her for her last birthday. She loved these ribbons. Never left the house without them attached to her hair, her dress, something." Osse added the porcelain box to his bag and stood up. "Where is Maaska's basket?" He went over to the map and turned his head to see the map at a different angle. "She always spent the day with Mom and Grandma while her husband and Dad were working in the forge out back. If she stayed home that day, she would have been–" He pointed a couple spaces away from his house. "–Here. Number Twelve." He stepped back and scanned the shelves.

Ahva spotted the twelve on the shelf and flew to that basket. "That one!"

Osse set it on the floor and flipped it open. He frowned. "A man's tunic, a tool belt, a few tools. No, that can't be Maaska's." He put it back on the shelf. "Where could hers be?"

Maybe Maaska hadn't been home. "Sorry. Bye!" Ahva said.

CHAPTER 7

"You want to leave? Not until I'm sure we're not missing Maaska's box."

Okay, so that was a logical conclusion, but not at all what she'd meant. "Noooo." *Speak.*

When the text screen popped open to show her the phrases she had available, she scanned through the list. Not much there.

"Nooo. Maaska, bye-bye."

"You think she'd left the village before the attack."

There you go. Smart human! "Yes."

"Maybe, but she's pregnant, so I doubt she would've gone far. I'll ask the jeweler." He adjusted the bag on his shoulder. "That takes care of getting provisions."

Ahva flew to another basket. *We're not done yet.*

Osse shook his head. "Those aren't for us, Ahva."

They could be for us. They might have important quest stuff. She strutted over to the nearest one, a wicker basket with the peg closing the lid.

"No, Ahva. That's not ours. Leave it, and let's go. I want to get going before nightfall."

Weapons, food, gold, armor. No telling what's in here that we'll need. What we don't need we can sell. She grabbed the peg with her beak.

-10 XP

-10? Minus? You can lose XP in this game? Of all the stupid–

"Ahva, leave it alone, and come here. Right now." Osse glared.

She hissed and flew back to Osse. *You're going to wish we checked those baskets. Who knows what nifty stuff we're missing?*

They left the storeroom. The shopkeeper stood at one of

the workbenches. He looked up as Osse approached.

"Thank you for taking care of my people's belongings." Osse bowed and touched his forehead.

"It was so little to do."

Osse glanced toward the storeroom. "My older sister's basket wasn't there. She would have been with my mother and grandmother during the day. Is there a chance it might have been stolen by the others before you and your friends took charge?"

Either that, or she wasn't home, or she wasn't carrying anything interesting.

The jeweler drew a breath through his teeth. "Possible, but unlikely. The looters started at the other end, closer to Kamali."

Osse nodded. "Near the chief's home."

"Mmhmm. They started where the money was most likely to be. Forgive me for saying so, but an herbalist and a farrier don't earn as well."

"No offense taken. We had enough, but we had nothing like the chief's family."

The jeweler glanced eastward. "I would hate to get your hopes up, but I would be remiss to keep the information from you."

Osse followed the other man's gaze. "What is it?"

Someone saw captives taken away.

"Rumors, really. Some children playing outside the town wall said that there was a fifth attacker. A different kind. Stronger and more in control. They said she gave the others their orders. The children insist that one had captives in a wheeled cart that had no horse or other animal but followed her everywhere she went. She herself floated a full meter above the ground."

"Then there were captives?" Osse asked.

"If the children were telling the truth, yes. One of the scouts also reported the four that ran west each had a captive." The jeweler perched on the workbench behind him. "As near as we can figure, accounting for what the looters took from the affluent corner of the town, we came up eight chests short. You're back. That means there are seven captives." He crossed his arms over his chest.

Ha! I was right. I should be a writer. We're going after them, of course.

"Four to the west. Three to the east." Osse pointed each direction.

"Mmhmm. If the children were telling the truth, at least about the captive part. One of those captives might be your missing sister." The shopkeeper winced. "I hope I haven't over-burdened your heart with that news."

Osse shook his head. "No, no. Thank you for telling me."

"If I might ask, what are your plans now?"

Osse brushed his eyes with his hand. "If there's a chance my sister has been taken captive, I'm going after them."

The shopkeeper frowned. "They've had a few days head start."

"Still, I have to try." Osse looked down then peeked up at the shopkeeper. "Even if the report of captives is false."

Whoo! Two for two!

The shopkeeper frowned. "To what end?"

Osse sniffled. "They destroyed my people."

The shopkeeper gripped Osse shoulder. "And that is truly a cause for grief, but be careful. Revenge always sounds good when plotted and spoken of, but when executed, it does not satisfy."

"Then at least they won't be able to destroy any other villages." Osse's hand clenched into a fist.

"True. My friends and I will pray for you, brother, and for the safety of the captives. We will ask Tsidkenu to guide you and draw you into his light. He alone knows whether your sister still lives." The shopkeeper led them back through to the front of the shop. "When your task is finished, if you have no greater plans, we would welcome you into our circle."

"Thank you, but I'm not thinking that far ahead, to be honest."

"No reason to. The offer stands no matter how far into the future it is." He stepped out onto the front porch with them. "Be careful out there. Atrac is on the rampage. Her prophets are declaring an end to all who won't submit willingly."

Osse nodded. "I heard one of them talking in the gate at Fola. 'Atrac is laughing at you' and some other business about destroying everyone. We'll keep an eye out."

"At least you have a good sentry to watch." The jeweler looked directly at Ahva. "You'll keep an eye out for trouble, won't you?"

Ahva bobbed her head. "Ahva, look!"

"She's good at finding strange things happening." Osse preened the back of her head.

"Travel safely. Perhaps we will see you again."

When Osse stepped off the porch, the notebook flashed blue a few times.

Wow! How many quests am I getting?

Quest complete: Home Fires Keep Burning. What happened here?

CHAPTER 7

I'm Not a Crook! You took only what belonged to you. +300 XP

Okay, so maybe it was best not to loot the other chests. Ahva chuckled. *And who came up with the quest names? Top marks, dude.*

The Hunt Is On! Track down and destroy those who burned your village.

To the Rescue! Find the fate of the captives, and if possible, rescue them.

Optional: The Path to Enlightenment. Learn about Tsidkenu.

After dismissing the notebook, Ahva got situated on Osse's shoulder and held on tightly as he headed out of town.

On the way, he stopped at the memorial stones and returned to the ones that he had studied so hard earlier. He reached into the bag and pulled out the wrapped package he'd tucked into the corner when she'd escaped the thief at the market. He unwrapped a small glass figurine, no bigger than his thumb. It was shaped something like a bird with a bright red beak, emerald green feathers, and a sky-blue tail. He stared hard at the shape then set it down on one of the stone piles.

"Is it enough, Father? Have I sacrificed enough to the fire to be a man now? Is that close enough to the rite of manhood? If so, was it really the loss that made me a man? If not, what more can I give? All I have left is what I carry now, and I'd give it all to get my family back. Your gods didn't help you against those attackers, did they? How could they? They're a piece of stone no different than the ones that make up your memorial now." Tears wet his face again.

"I'll get them, and I'll find Maaska. Count on me. I'll get them."

Okay. Enough tear-jerking. Khin May's heart ached with recollections of Grandma's stories about her old home. Ahva tapped into her Charm attribute. She whistled and tucked her head into Osse's shoulder as he reached up to preen her neck. That restored a few fatigue points.

"You may wish you'd picked a different human, Ahva; and I wouldn't blame you for leaving, but I hope you won't. I'm not ready to strike off alone, but I won't get any closer to their killers standing here staring at the memorials."

Nope, you're stuck with me, but cheer up, huh?

"What do you think, Ahva? Should we go west after the four killers who each took one captive or east after the one killer who took three captives in her magic cart?" Osse pointed to the west with one hand and the east with the other.

That's a good question. More risk and a greater chance of finding captives if we go west. Going east, though, we only have one opponent who apparently has weird equipment and could apply for a supervillain club. She floats above the ground and has a cart that follows her like a puppy. Let's not go after the weirder chick first. She flew to the hand pointing west.

Osse nodded. "Four captives were taken that way, so that does give us a better chance of finding Maaska. West it is."

She hung on tighter as he turned with a resolute determination and headed toward the setting sun.

Chapter 8

Jael's stomach growled as loud as a whole wolf pack cornering prey. She was back on the trail to find her youngsters, so there wasn't time for her to do any hunting or foraging. She really couldn't afford to delay her travels. If the trail ran cold again, no telling if she'd be lucky enough to find it. Still, she wouldn't do anyone any good if she collapsed or starved to death, and her fatigue meter was looking pitiful.

The smell of wood smoke in the air promised human habitation. They often had stores of food, and she might be able to get into it, at least enough to stop the rumbling. Jael tracked the wood smell to its source, a yurt near some farmland. Two humans, a man and a boy, were out in the garden, too far away to see her clearly in the damp grass. The smoke rose from the center of the yurt and a woman's singing came from inside. Next to the yurt, steps led into the ground.

Using the yurt for cover, Jael rushed to the steps and down to a door. When she pushed, the door budged in the top and bottom corners but didn't open.

No doubt, she could crash her way through. No simple wooden door would keep a halfway determined bear at bay.

A good charge and the door would be splinters, but that would surely draw attention and long years of experience had taught her that humans like the herbalist with the pet crow were rare indeed.

Something was blocking the door, and it had to be removable from the outside or the humans wouldn't be able to get to their own food. Humans might be confusing, but they did better than bar themselves from their own resources. Jael opened her skill list and selected Problem Solving.

Humans like knobs and sliders to secure doors like this. Could that be why the door won't open?

One side of the door had no extra hardware. The door slats ended at the frame, so the problem had to be the other side. Jael found the trouble: a couple wooden sticks that slid into the frame. Humans were silly if they thought that would keep a bear out. Wolf, sure, but never a bear.

Jael slapped the sticks, but they didn't budge. She huffed those had to be movable. How else would the humans get to their food? She tapped them downward with one of her claws, but got nowhere. Upward maybe? When she tried that, the stick spun out of position, turning a three-quarter circle around a point on one end. She repeated that move on the second stick.

The door opened, and she shouldered her way through. The dim light in the storeroom stole her sight, but after kicking in her sense of smell, she found smoked gazelle hanging from the ceiling and bags of root vegetables along the walls.

She couldn't stay for long, or she'd be trapped in here by an upset human, but what should she take? Her mouth watered for some of that gazelle, but root vegetables would

CHAPTER 8

give her more to travel on. No time to decide, Jael rose up on her back feet and chomped her teeth into one of the hanging gazelle pieces. Then she swiped one of the bags of root veggies and slipped the loops on the top of the bag around her paw and promptly left.

Running with a hind quarter of a gazelle in her teeth and a bag of potatoes on her paw gave her an uneven gait that would never do if the humans chased her, but the woman inside the yurt was still singing, oblivious to Jael. The two males at the far end of the cultivated land were far enough away she could reach the stand of brush nearby with time to spare even if they spotted her. Her heart raced until she was safely within the brush, out of the humans' sight where she could enjoy her feast. She hoped Oba and Dina were doing at least as well.

* * *

Nagheed trotted alongside Rafayel and Ryder. The sleek gray horse varied speed between a slow walk and a brisk trot, but Nagheed had no trouble keeping up. They'd been in a few minor scrapes on the trip south, one wolf pack and a few badgers. When the wolf pack took Nagheed for a pushover, some posturing and a shot past the alpha from Rafayel's pistol had convinced the pack to seek a less hazardous dinner. Two of the three badgers they'd encountered had run as soon as they were encountered, but the last had had foam around its jaws and a crazed expression on its face. Rafayel had shot it and then, without touching it, buried it deep. That chore had taken an hour out of their day, but Rafayel had declared the effort worth the loss of time.

Rabies was not something to take lightly. Nagheed had stayed safely out of the way.

As night fell, they came to Halfway Inn, a modest establishment. The innkeeper knew Rafayel on sight. A hearty meal, a good nap, and a generic breakfast later, and they were on the road again.

About midafternoon, the city walls and watchtowers of Vanya came into view. These walls were darker than Yavne but similar in architecture with high straight sides and crenellations along the top.

They approached the city as the sun neared the horizon. In this clearing next to the walls, a set of matching wagons, each decorated with three circles arranged in a triangle, were arrayed along the side of the road. They had set up like a flea market, selling various goods and offering services.

Rafayel dismounted and strode to the first wagon. A dark-complexioned merchant offered a selection of interesting rocks for sale. The nametag floating over his head said simply, "Mineral merchant."

"A talisman to protect you while you travel?" He held up a carved stone on a string. "One that will bring you better luck with the ladies?"

"I'm blissfully married, thank you." Rafayel produced a paper from his pouch and unfolded it. "A creature attacked two farms near Yavne. Upon whatever it didn't destroy outright, it drew this symbol in blood, chalk, mud, or ash. Have you seen it before?"

The merchant took the paper without looking. As soon as he glanced at it, he dropped it like it was hot. He spit three times over each shoulder, and the morale emoji on his nametag now showed the fear face. "Take it away! Take it away! Take it away! Take it away!"

That spooked by a picture? What could it be that has you that freaked out?

Rafayel return the paper to his pouch. "What does it mean?"

"Evil! Great evil. More than that I will not say." The merchant retreated into his wagon, spitting over his shoulder a few more times.

Rafayel looked down at Nagheed. "That was odd."

Nagheed woofed.

The next merchant, selling rugs, didn't stick around long enough to talk to. Before he vanished into the back of a wagon, Nagheed caught a glimpse of the fear emoji on his nametag, too. Other merchants they approached turned their backs, busied themselves with packing up for the evening, or simply ignored Rafayel.

"I think we may have made a terrific mistake, Nagheed." Rafayel frowned.

I think you're right. Too bad we can't revert to a previous save.

As they approached the city gate, a dark-skinned Bakhari nomad darted over to them. The man had graying hair, curled tightly and cut short. He had more wrinkles than a dried piece of fruit and a deeply furrowed brow. His nametag read "Grandfather," and the scents around him exuded worry that drowned out nearly everything else about him.

"Baron Dorcas," the elderly nomad said.

Rafayel turned toward him. "Have we met, sir?"

"Only by reputation." He smiled.

Rafayel nodded. "Ah. I see. How can I assist?"

"We can, perhaps, help each other." He took a deep breath. "My granddaughter wanted to go to the docks to see the sailing ships. I strictly forbid it as the docks are no place for a lady."

"Quite right, especially late in the day."

"I thought she went into the wagon to pout, but she's not there. I fear she may have disobeyed me." The old nomad glanced toward the ocean.

"Do you have something of hers?" Rafayel patted Nagheed's side. "Nagheed might be able to track her by scent, hopefully before she falls into the wrong crowd."

The old man hobbled over to the wagon and returned with a scarf.

"May I borrow this?" Rafayel pointed at the scarf.

The old man handed it over. "Yes, of course. Please find her."

Nagheed picked his Tracker skill from the menu and gave the scarf a good sniff.

"We'll be back as soon as we have news." He swung up into the saddle. "We'll start near the docks, Nagheed."

Nagheed stayed alongside his human. When they crossed through the city gate, the traveling music of a plucked stringed instrument returned to the RenFaire tunes he'd gotten used to in Yavne. The city was full of smells. Countless humans, animals, foods, and refuse were just the beginning. He was supposed to track one girl out of literally hundreds of people, a significant number of animals, and food. Scents rising from some objects, blowing on the wind, and forming domes over some things were constantly overwriting each other until they formed a vague static over everything.

CHAPTER 8

As they headed westward, an increasing number of human scents were decidedly male. That made the prospect of finding the girl somewhat less annoying.

When they passed the last building, a crowded street opened up. The setting sun backlit huge boats with multiple masts. Men crawled around the netting on the boats and wobbled around the decks as if they'd enjoyed too many stiff drinks.

Rafayel leaned down and held the scarf closer. "This will be a bigger challenge than finding our training toy, but do what you can."

After making sure Tracking was armed, Nagheed took a big whiff of the scarf and ranged back and forth in front of the horse. Transparent gray crowded the area, wafting upward from everything and drowning each other out almost as badly as the city streets they'd walked down to get here. How was he ever going to find anything in this mess? It was like trying to hear a whisper in a rock concert.

A woman screamed from somewhere up ahead and to the left.

Nagheed barked and led the way. The people on the docks backed away as he drew near. As he ran, a darker gray word took shape, forming a path for him to follow: **"Target."** **"Perfume"** was fainter, but strongly associated with **"Target."**

He followed the word path into an alleyway between two storehouses.

"Target" and **"perfume"** formed a dome in the corner around a cowering Bakhari woman. Her nametag read "Granddaughter." Three Nethanyan men identified as "Sailor" smelled of old fish. They beat up a guy dubbed

"Mentor Jood" wearing a black robe who smelled of herbs. His health bar was down a quarter and losing a handful of points with each hit.

Nagheed slowed and turned on Posture. He barked, baring his teeth. The woman and each of the men, including the one in the black robe, sported a blah face in their nametags. The music hadn't changed to the drums and brass of combat, so did that mean this wouldn't become a fight or would the change happen after someone threw the first punch?

"Let the monk and the woman go." Rafayel drew his rapier. "Do it now, or you'll have my dog and my sword to convince you."

Nagheed chose Posture from the menu again. He growled and stalked closer, hunching his shoulders and bristling his fur in a sign of extreme canine annoyance. The emoji on the woman's nametag changed to a frown, and the monk's changed to a smilie. For the others, blah face change slowly to a frown.

The pair beating up the monk stepped away and showed their hands empty. The one holding the monk sneered.

"Let him go. Now. I won't ask again," Rafayel ordered.

Nagheed darted a few steps closer and barked. The frowning emoji in the nametags looked more severe.

"Nagheed—"

He tensed, shifting his weight to launch into the attack.

The scruffy-bearded man shoved the monk into a couple crates at the end of the alley.

Footsteps ran in behind Rafayel. "Call off your dog. I'm the constable. I'll handle it from here."

"See, Constable? Just as I said." The new speaker's voice

trembled.

"I've got eyes, boy." The constable strutted halfway to the end of the alley. "Call off the dog, if you please."

"Nagheed, out." Rafayel dismounted and sheathed his rapier.

After smoothing out his fur, Nagheed retreated to Rafayel side.

"Now the boy told me about the sailors, the woman, and the monk. Who are you?"

"Baron Rafayel Dorcas of Yavne, and this fine fellow is Nagheed. We were sent to locate the missing girl and return her to the caravan."

"Caravan?" The constable stepped further into the alleyway then scoffed. "You three, get outta here and go mind your manners somewhere else."

Nagheed growled, stopping the trio in their tracks.

"Baron, I asked you to call off your dog!"

"Constable, those men attacked the monk, and that's just the part we saw."

"The Bakhari should've stayed with her own kind, and the monk should have kept his nose in his books and herb jars." He twitched his head. "Like I said, you three, get moving."

Rafayel turned the constable to face him. "You can't let them go!"

"If you try to stop them, I'll arrest you for disturbing the peace." He pulled a club off his belt.

Nagheed bared his teeth. Give it try.

Rafayel glared. "Your baron will hear of this. Be sure of that."

The constable snorted. "Won't matter. Who do you think

gave me my orders?"

The three scruffy sorts darted out and the constable followed them.

The monk sat on the ground rubbing his jaw and clutching his belly. The woman stayed in the corner.

The younger man, a backpack-wearing monk labeled "Learner," who'd arrived with the constable, ran past and went to Mentor Jood's side, retrieving a pale skullcap and a scarf from the ground along the way. "Mentor Jood, are you all right?"

Mentor Jood situated the skullcap and draped the scarf around his neck. "Fine. Sore, but fine. Just give me a minute to get my wind back."

Rafayel jogged toward the woman. "Are you injured?"

"No. The mentor and his learner arrived before those men did more than threaten." She stood and left the corner but kept her distance. Like the others in the caravan, she had a dark complexion and tightly curled black hair. "My grandfather sent you, didn't he?"

"He's quite worried about you." Rafayel crouched next to the monk. "Should we get you to a physician, Mentor?"

"No, no. I'm sure I'll feel that beating until we get back to the monastery, but once I'm there, the right set of herbs will mend all. I'd take care of it now if I'd thought to bring my supplies." He slowly came to his feet with the younger monk's help. "Young lady, dare I ask why you're alone on the docks at this hour?"

She glared but said nothing.

"Her grandfather says she wanted to see the sailing ships," Rafayel said.

"My cousin went alone." She clenched her jaw.

CHAPTER 8

"And since one was foolish, so must another be?" Mentor Jood sighed. "No matter. You've had quite a scare, I'm sure. We have His Excellency and a fine dog for protectors until you're safely home."

"We still need to finish our errand, Mentor." The younger monk leaned closer to the older one.

Mentor Jood nodded. "It will have to wait for tomorrow. The sun has set and no more fish will be sold today. Master Dan will understand when all is made clear."

The younger one leaned closer. "Master Dan will, but will Mentor Yudah?"

"He will have to tolerate corn and beans for supper, but he will live."

Can we go now? Nagheed sat and panted.

"Let's get the young lady home." Rafayel suggested.

As the men started toward where Nagheed and the horse waited, the woman came along more slowly, eyeing Nagheed.

Rafayel glanced back. "He won't hurt you. Nagheed has quite a bark and an impressive bite, but he won't use either if you're not a threat."

And if you are, then look out! Nagheed woofed and wagged his fluffy tail.

"I can find my own way back," she insisted.

"Maybe but I promised your grandfather in exchange for his help, and I refuse to be made a liar. Shall we?" Rafayel cupped his hands as if making a lower stirrup to help the lady onto Ryder's back.

She accepted his help up. "How do you know I won't ride off with your horse and leave you standing?"

"Try if you wish, but the horse, like the dog, will obey my

verbal commands over the verbal or physical commands of any other. You won't get too far."

The younger monk leaned closer to Mentor Jood and whispered, "She's not too grateful, is she?"

Mentor Jood shushed his younger companion.

Rafayel led Ryder by the reins and retraced their steps to the gate. The guard stood poised at the gate's mechanism.

"Come on. In or out. Time to close up for the evening. Fifteen minutes."

"We'll leave the young lady in your care." Mentor Jood patted Rafayel's arm. "Thank you for your help."

Rafayel nodded. "Thank you for stepping in when you did."

The two monks headed back into town and disappeared into the crowd.

As they walked away, Nagheed could still hear them.

"Maybe we can stop at an inn and get some fish there," the younger monk said.

"We will not be stopping in any inn, tavern, saloon, or other nocturnal establishment to purchase a fish for Mentor Yudah. He will live one more day without fish."

"Yes, but will we?"

Nagheed snorted and lost their voices in the crowd and distance.

A guard stepped in front of Rafayel as they approached. "Sir, if you leave now, we can't open the gate until morning. You'll be stuck out there with that caravan."

"Thank you, Guardsman. I appreciate your warning and fully understand your duties." Rafayel ruffled the fur on Nagheed's head. "After returning the young lady to her worried grandfather, Nagheed and I will withdraw and set up camp."

"As you wish, sir, but I wouldn't recommend it." The guard glanced out the gate and frowned.

"Duly noted." Rafayel nodded once.

The guard leaned closer. "Sir, you might try the south gate. Travelers usually camp there after nightfall to be ready to enter the city at first light. Safety in numbers, as they say."

"Excellent advice. Thank you!"

Rafayel led the way to the elderly nomad's wagon and helped the woman down. The old man, sitting on a stool near the campfire, rose and hobbled over. After a long embrace, he and the woman argued at a volume that would probably be lost on a human, but Nagheed still understood. There was nothing surprising there. Just the usual disciplining a rowdy teenager sort of thing. The woman darted to the wagon.

The old man gestured for them to join him at the fire. "Thank you for rescuing her."

"A pair of monks from the local monastery had a great deal to do with it, but I was glad to do my part." Rafayel sat on a stool near the fire.

The old man sat opposite, and Nagheed found a place at Rafayel's side.

"You had a symbol to identify?" The old man rested his elbows on his knees and steepled his fingers.

Rafayel produce the paper from the pouch. "If at all possible, yes. Anything you can tell me will help." He offered it to the old man.

He sat back. "Open your paper."

I guess he'll at least look at it without freaking out.

Rafayel unfolded the paper and held it up.

"That's enough." The old man spat over each shoulder three times. "I will say this only once. No more than that. It is bad luck to speak of it, but my granddaughter has been returned to me safely, so I think I have a little good luck to trade." He pointed at the paper. "The symbol belongs to Atrac, the Ilion goddess of change, twin of Motce, the god of constancy. Together with Elef, their grandfather, the god of balance, they seek the betterment of the world through causing changes that are sometimes successful, sometimes not.

"This is a constant struggle between the twins as the grandfather seeks to advance the world to a perfect state. When the change corrects a problem, they say Motce has won. When it improves some trait – sometimes with a negative effect on another, they say Atrac was victorious. Lately there is a rumor that Atrac has grown stronger. Others say Elef now favors his granddaughter over his grandson. Having the right knowledge is the honey of life, so I will answer three questions only. Then my debt will be discharged." He offered a stack of cards. "Each of these cards bears a question I'm willing to answer. Some will give you better information than others. You may choose three."

"Fair enough." Rafayel smiled and flipped through the cards once. "These are all good questions, Nagheed. Which ones do you like?"

Nagheed scooted closer and looked over Rafayel's arm as he flipped through the cards again and read them outloud.

Where are the changes happening?
How do I stop these changes?

CHAPTER 8

How do I restore the balance of power?
How do I help Motce gain dominance?
What is this crystal?
What is this blob of unknown material?
If this is happening in Ilion, how are the maniacs getting all the way across the continent?
If this is happening in Ilion, why are the maniacs here?
What should I do?
How much wood does woodchuck chuck if a woodchuck could chuck wood?

Nagheed huffed. *Woodchuck? Come on!* He rolled his eyes. *Since we are here to visit a library, we can probably skip the sort of fact-based questions. The library resources can likely answer basic stuff. Identify the weird artifact is probably also worthless.*

"Do you want to hear them again?" Rafayel asked.

Nagheed woofed.

"Okay. Raise your paw when you hear one you like." He read each card out loud then flipped it to the back.

Nagheed picked up his paw for the three least likely to show up in the library, ignoring the woodchuck question. Rafayel set each of his choices aside.

"He chose well." Rafayel picked up the first card. "You said Ilion is causing the changes as some plan to improve the world. Clearly, that's not working. How do I stop these changes? Those maniacs are creating considerable damage including killing farmers around Yavne." Rafayel leaned forward.

The old man shrugged. "And many others besides. It is not for you to eradicate another's faith, but if you wish to restore Motce's power or at least reduce Atrac's, you will have to travel to Ilion to Elef's main temple and undo the damage done by Atrac's followers."

"Why are the maniacs here?" He pointed at the ground. "We're so far from Ilion?"

"Elef has long hated Tsidkenu. Perhaps Atrac is trying to win her grandfather's favor by destroying Tsidkenu's followers, but that would not explain the troubles in Bakhar."

Equal opportunity maniacs.

"What should I do?" Rafayel asked.

"Gain information. You came to inquire at the library." He smiled. "That is no great secret. You didn't know we would be here, so the library is the most logical place to find information. You will also need an ally and supplies. If your god is calling you to restore Ilion's balance, you will have to travel to the temple of Elef."

The old man's granddaughter emerged from the wagon.

Nagheed snorted. *As if on cue.*

She joined them at the fire and sat facing away from them. She snorted. "Thank you for your help."

Your sincerity could use a little work.

"You're quite welcome." Rafayel tipped his hat.

The old man stood. "You will lose the light soon, and you still have to set up camp."

Rafayel slipped the paper back in the pouch. "Indeed. Come along, Nagheed. Thank you for your assistance, sir."

Instead of following the road back a distance from the city, Rafayel went around the city, staying near the wall.

* * *

Khin May returned from her snack break. A mini-cartoon

CHAPTER 8

version of Ahva flew circles on the screen. She hooked back into the system and mentally caught up to what was going on.

All right, computer, Ahva the Wonder Crow is back in the game.

They'd been hiking west on the trail of the creatures who had destroyed Osse's home. Not exactly a challenge since the things were leaving their symbol etched on rocks and trees every so often.

When she unpaused the game, the cartoon crow winked at her and flew off.

The darkness around her was broken only by a sliver of light from above. The small space was stuffy. Ahva stretched, reaching for the light. The things around her shifted, some colliding with her wings.

She squawked. "Bite fingers!"

The top of the small container lifted away, letting in sunlight. An extra shirt, herb jars, porcelain box, string, and assorted foodstuffs surrounded Ahva.

Osse peeked in. "Done with your nap?"

"Good morning." She climbed out of the bag and crawled all the way up his shoulder.

"Glad you slept well." Osse smiled, but the tightness in his face and the redness in his eyes suggested that his time alone hadn't done much to dispel his grief.

Hardly a surprise. Grandma and Grandpa still grieve for everything they lost.

Ahva turned on Charm and rubbed the side of her head against his cheek to get some Bird XP. *Dear programmer, people don't play games to be bummed out.*

The terrain had changed from rolling hills and grassland

to a rough trail through rocky hills and clumps of brush on both sides. The air was still but cooler than out on the plains. The few clouds in the sky were clumpy and white and scooted across at a good clip.

What would flying through that wind feel like? The clouds were far too high for her to reach and find out, but surely someday, she'd get a chance to fly in a good wind.

Jet-propelled crow!

To their left, screechy laughter moved through the brush. Osse stopped and clutched his bow.

Chapter 9

"Look, Ahva!" Ahva took off, spiraling upward while she flapped hard. *Any excuse to fly is a good one!*

"Who's there?" Osse nocked an arrow.

I'll find out.

Movement rustled in the brush moving forward along their path.

Ahva continue to climb as she scanned along the ground, widening the circle with each pass. Something dark moved through the brush.

It ran on two feet like a human, but somewhat hunched over like an ape. She adjusted her loop to center over the creature. The thing had a face that was human, but the eyes were opaque and the skin was torn and ragged like the clothes. A glow came from within the thing's chest.

As she completed another loop, the creature stared up at her with solid gray eyes then laughed, a raspy, high-pitched sound. Then it gradually gained speed. Ahva straightened out her loop to follow it directly, but even at her top speed, Ahva dropped further and further back until she lost sight altogether.

Ahva hissed and banked to come back around. She returned to her human.

Osse crouched next to a broken mannequin of large rabbit. She spiraled down and landed next to him. *Speak.*

The pop-up window showed the vocabulary she could choose from. There was nothing even remotely like "creepy zombie thing with glow-in-the-dark chest hardware that can outrun an SR-71." She closed the window.

He smiled at her. "I wish you could tell me what you saw."

Me, too. I'm working on it as quick as I can, though.

"Look. This is the same symbol we saw at the village." Osse pointed to a mark drawn with blood on a stone.

"Yes." *Horizontal line with the dot below on the left and a dot above on the right.*

Osse offered his hand. "Come on. I want to get as close as we can to Oni today so we can cover the rest of the distance tomorrow."

Ahva hopped onto his hand and scrambled up to his shoulder while he stood.

He set off at a brisk pace following the footpath that led upward into the hills. Ahva spent the time practicing her whistling and speaking skills to earn points in those areas.

Oddly, they didn't have nearly as many "random encounters" as Ahva expected. Most of the games she'd played wouldn't let a player get ten meters without having to fight a handful of whatever the creature of the sector was. As Osse hiked, Ahva spotted the occasional rabbit or bird but nothing major, and certainly nothing that bothered them. She didn't mind that really. Until she figured out crow attack modes, she couldn't be much good in a battle, anyway. Osse, although a skilled archer, didn't have a weapon for an up-close fight. That hunting knife was nifty and all, but how much good would that do? At some point, she assumed, the game would introduce them to their partner. With any luck, that person would be able to handle in-your-face battles leaving Osse to handle the long-range attacks.

When the sun was directly overhead, Osse fished some dried fruit out of his bag and offered Ahva a piece. "If you don't mind, I'd like to keep going until sundown. We'll stop and have a decent meal then."

"Yes." Ahva grabbed the fruit.

"Yes, indeed." Osse smiled.

After the meal of dried fruit with a peanut chaser, Ahva looked up to turn on the menus then selected her character sheet.

Name: Ahva **Species:** Corvid – Crow
Class: Scout Level 2 **Gender:** F

Attributes

Attribute	Current	Skill	Current
Power	10	Sneak	24
Speed	41	Detect Enemy	29
Cleverness	64	Signal Human	29
Endurance	18	Stay Alert	17
Agility	60	Sound Alarm	20
Charm	35	Patrol	24
Vitality	5	Trek	30
Sight	63	Long Distance Mvmt	30
Smell	5	Sprint	20
Hearing	23	Nonverbal Communication	21
Health	33	Camo	15
Encumbrance 0 out of 5 oz		Fly	34
		Speech	37
		Problem-Solving	14
		Bite	13

While the game was fairly stingy with the leveling, it was more generous with the practice-based skill increase. Her speech skill in particular was gaining some ground. Still not enough to speak freely but headed in the right way. Maybe she'd practice more speech later, but the red warning appeared low and on her right. Her muscles were getting a bit stiff from perching on Osse's shoulder while he traveled.

She crouched and leapt into the air, unfurling her wings as soon as she was on her way. Her VR rig simulated the wind rushing past her, and the objects on the ground shrank as she gained altitude. She had the exhilarating rush of seeing everything zoom past below and soon Osse wasn't in view. Banking as tight a turn as she could without stalling, she headed back his way and practiced weaving side to side, gaining altitude, diving both beak first and feet first, and seeing how far she could roll. She became her very own personalized rollercoaster!

After catching sight of Osse, she cawed to get his attention. He waved up at her.

Could she add a loop to her rollercoaster? Ahva started a climb but couldn't get enough pitch to complete the loop. Maybe later, when she had more skill. For now, her fatigue bar was drained by half. There was something else she wanted to try much closer to the ground.

The stiffness warning had long since faded out, so she returned to Osse, and spiraled down to land on his outstretched arm.

"Enjoy your flight?" He held her up level with his face.

"Yes!" She stretched out her wings and cawed a few times.

"Good. Spot any trouble ahead?" He asked.

"No."

Osse chuckled. "Good to know. Back to cawing?"

Maybe later. Right now, I'm going to work on another skill. "No. Fierce!"

He tipped his head to one side like a confused dog. "Fierce?"

She launched off his arm and landed on the side of the path some distance ahead near collection of rocks half the size of her head.

Ready, fire, aim! She picked up one with her beak and flapped like mad to overcome the weight and lift off. Once in the air, she needed more force on each downbeat of her wings to keep herself aloft. As soon as she was at an altitude that kept her out of reach of most normal bad guys, she picked a target and let go of the rock. Ahva did her best bomb drop whistle all the way to the ground.

Ahva hissed. *Nowhere near the target. If at first you don't succeed, give up on hang gliding.*

Her second and third attempts were no better. The fatigue meter turned maroon, and a different warning window appeared at the lower edge of her vision. One more attempt and then she'd rest. She grabbed another rock and flapped hard, but the rock slipped out of her beak. She landed to try again but when she tried to pick up a rock, her beak wouldn't close around it. The VR rig simulated a muscle ache in her chest and back muscles, protesting her foolish choice of activities.

Osse crouched next to her and offered his hand. "Having fun?"

She huffed and stepped onto his fingers. *I was until I ran outta steam.* "No."

He stood and resumed walking. "You know, Ahva, when I aim at a moving object, I have to aim a little in front of it. The faster it moves, the further ahead I have to aim." He mimed aiming his bow. "For you, your target isn't moving, but you are. You might have to aim behind your target and count on your forward momentum to land your rock on the target."

You mean, physics works here? Last couple games I played physics was semi-optional. I'll have to give that a try after I rest my wings a bit.

True to his word, Osse didn't stop until past sunset when the light turned too gray to make out colors. They stopped for the night under a rock overhang. In the last of the light, Osse collected enough wood to cook up a rabbit he'd brought down earlier. Some barbecue rabbit and fruit with hardtack for dessert made dinner.

"Tomorrow night we'll be in Oni. If they have an inn, we'll get some good food and something softer to sleep on," Osse said.

Ahva snored while she went to Osse's bag and tugged out the thin blanket he kept there.

Osse reached over and pulled the blanket out. "You go ahead. I'm not tired yet."

How can you not be tired? You hiked all day. Literally. All day!

Ahva crawled into Osse's bag and pulled out the shirt in there. With a bit of fussing, it made a passable nest.

"Comfy?" Osse smiled.

Ahva tucked her beak under her wing and imitated Callen's snore. *Good night. Sleep tight. Don't let the weird, creepy zombie things bite.*

CHAPTER 9

Osse chuckled. "Silly bird."

Ahva told the computer to sleep for the night. The view went dark and a cartoon of sheep hopping over a fence played until a dragon swooped in.

Okay, so that gave me the impression of danger in the area.

When Ahva awoke, dawn still hadn't come. Nearby, Osse wrapped in his blanket, bolted awake. The dim embers of the fire cast feeble orange glow around the camp.

Across from them, a coyote cowered. It stared at them for a moment, then ran off into the brush. Moments later, a startled yelp echoed off the rock wall behind them.

"Who's there?" Osse snatched up his bow and an arrow.

A high-pitched, screechy laugh preceded something crashing through the brush as it raced away from them.

Ahva turned on her Hear attribute and listened. She squinted into the darkness but found only shadows.

Nothing at all made a sound.

* * *

Nagheed snapped awake. In real-time, he'd been asleep maybe five seconds, but in the game world, the whole night had passed. The "sleep" screen showed a cartoon wolf sneaking up on sweater-knitting cartoon sheep, which suggested there was trouble, but he neither smelled nor heard anything immediately dangerous and the combat music wasn't playing. People milled around the impromptu campgrounds, so Nagheed sat up and kept an eye on Ryder, Rafayel, and all their things.

After leaving the caravan, Rafayel had led them around the city to the southern gate. They'd arrived shortly after darkness had settled and joined the rest of the people who had gotten to Vanya after the gate had closed. The crowd had gradually grown in fits and spurts after that.

Nagheed would have chosen somewhere less populated. Some of the other travelers had an appearance and a smell about them that Nagheed didn't care for. Rafayel, though, had chosen to bed down here, on the side of the southern road, with all the other humans. Before he'd gone to sleep, Nagheed had picked out a few who were likely thieves, as if he had any real knowledge of what a thief looked like. Ultimately, he supposed that the thieves were better than one of those laughing lunatics who had destroyed the farms outside Yavne.

While he waited on his human, Nagheed surveyed the impromptu campgrounds. So far, the other travelers were moving around but content to stay in their own spaces. That suited him fine.

Behind him, Rafayel drew a deep breath and sat up, keeping his cloak wrapped around him. "Good morning, Nagheed. Sleep well?"

Nagheed woofed.

"Good." He petted Nagheed's head. "I'm of a mind to eat something warm for breakfast. What do you say to that?"

All the same to me. Nagheed swept his big tail back and forth and panted, earning a **+10 XP**.

"Thought you might like that." He rose and tended to the horse.

By the time camp was packed and the fire was out, the guard had opened the main gate. The other humans flooded the road, jockeying for position to get into the city.

Rafayel swung up onto his horse. "Stay close, Nagheed.

CHAPTER 9

What do you say we let the crowd clear before we enter?"

"Oi!" The guard backed out of the way. "Gates won't be closing until nightfall. How about a little less pushing and shoving, eh?"

"You might have all day, friend, but some of us have business to tend to," a gray-bearded man on a covered wagon replied.

"That may be, but if you hurt someone, you will answer for it."

Once the majority of the mob was through the gate, Nagheed followed Rafayel onto the road and joined the end of the queue.

When they finally reached the gate, the guard blew out a breath.

"I hope it's not like that every morning." Rafayel looked down at the guard.

The guard rolled his eyes. "Sir, some days are worse."

"An inn would do a fine business, then." Rafayel pointed down the road to a flat, treeless area. "That would be a prime spot for it."

"Would, but his Excellency won't have any permanent structure outside the walls." The guard twitched his head northward. "North of town, there's an inn halfway to Yavne, but nothing south."

Rafayel shook his head. "That's too bad. Have a fine day."

"Yes, sir. You the same."

As soon as they passed the city wall, the music changed from the traveling plucked strings to the RenFaire tunes.

Nagheed followed his human to a stable, where they left the horse and got directions to the best place in town for a warm breakfast. An hour later, game time, they had a decent meal in their bellies.

Their next stop was a walled area at the center of town. They approached an iron-reinforced wooden gate.

Rafayel pointed to a rope hanging next to the door. "Nagheed, pull."

Easy enough. Turning his head sideways, Nagheed grabbed the rope with his teeth and gave it a good tug. A stout bell rang on the other side of the gate.

"Nagheed, pull."

He tugged the rope twice more.

"All right, all right, keep your boots on." A small square window opened at about human eye level. "What can I do for you?"

Rafayel produced a small card from the inside pocket of his doublet and handed it through the window. "If you could, please, let his Excellency know that Baron Rafayel Dorcas would much appreciate an audience."

The little window slammed closed and a mad scramble of scraping noise, huffing, and groaning came from the inside.

The gate guard opened the door and bowed them through. "Follow me, sir."

He was a stout, little man with rounded shoulders. His tabard matched the shades of gray on the flags flying on the corners of the house.

They threaded a path through a courtyard that had been meticulously tended with flowers and shrubbery around a swing.

The house itself was white stucco and timber strategically angled to make an interesting pattern.

The guard led them into the foyer and asked them to wait. Nagheed took a few steps away.

CHAPTER 9

"Nagheed, heel," Rafayel ordered.

Can't even explore a bit, huh? He returned to Rafayel's side before the computer started docking XP.

The foyer was much more form than function. A massive statue of a rather chubby man with a stern demeanor sat in the center. The statue bore a baronial crown and carried a book. Around the perimeter of the room, pictures of men with a strong family resemblance decorated the walls. Leafy garlands and small pale flowers were draped across the walls.

The gate guard hurried back through the foyer and out the door.

A moment later, the statue's model strutted in. "Rafayel!"

"Zofar! Good to see you." Rafayel shook his host's hand. Nagheed wagged his tail.

"Welcome, let's step out into the garden." Zofar leaned closer. "Aside from our own companion animals, I'm afraid my wife won't tolerate anything else with four feet in the house."

And why not? I'm housebroken. Nagheed followed them back outside.

"I assure you he's well-mannered." Rafayel patted Nagheed's side.

"Oh, no doubt on that, but our dog is more than a little territorial and wouldn't hardly make a snack for yours. Only she doesn't realize that and would go after him anyway." Zofar led them into the courtyard. "What brings you?"

"To Vanya? I need to visit your library." Rafayel glanced toward the docks. "To disturb your morning? An unfortunate matter with your constable."

"What's happened?"

"Last night as sunset approached, an elderly Bakhari gentleman asked me to seek out his headstrong granddaughter."

Nagheed listened as Rafayel related the incident in the alley and watched Zofar's reactions. The Vanyan baron let Rafayel relate the entire tale without hardly a blink.

Note to self: don't challenge this guy to any poker games.

Rafayel planted one hand on his hip. "I suppose we should be grateful the young lady and the monk weren't hurt more than a few bruises and a major scare, but your constable released the three men."

Zofar shrugged. "What else could he do? The monks never press charges no matter what happens to them. Everything that befalls them is 'the will of Tsidkenu' or so they say."

"What of the young lady? They attacked one woman, so what's to say they won't do it again?"

"You said the woman was threatened but not hurt." Zofar waved his hand dismissively. "In any case, no decent woman would be anywhere near the docks at dusk without an escort. I appreciate your concern, but I trust my constable to know his business. If he didn't think those men were a threat to a decent woman, then I'm sure he had his reasons. No real harm done, and next time, maybe these Bakhari will stay out of town. They can't say they've never been told."

No real harm done? Is he serious? Nagheed stared. *I should've bitten them on the kiester when I had a chance. Waste of time here.*

Rafayel nodded. "You know your man I'm sure, but I

would have held those men accountable for their actions. Nethanyan law makes no distinctions between Bakhari and Nethanyan ladies in this matter."

Zofar brushed Rafayel's comment away with a swipe of his hand. "Stay for breakfast?"

Rafayel ruffled the fur on Nagheed's head. "We've eaten, and I'm sure your good wife wouldn't want this big four-footer trespassing in the territory of your own dog."

"Definitely not." Zofar shook Rafayel's hand. "Well, good to see you, as always."

The local baron ushered him to the gate. They were well down the street before Rafayel spoke. "Instructive, if not productive. And sad. That attitude can't result in anything good. Let's take care of our errand and head back. Shall we?"

Nagheed woofed.

He walked alongside his human. They stayed to main streets, which were still fairly empty.

The scents of warm bread, fresh fish, and various roasted meats grew stronger as the crowds became denser. People waited outside a small gate into an area with a sea of tents. The words poured out of that gate and flew over the top of the wall like flocks of birds.

Nagheed paused, sniffing the air. The screen filled with "bread (fresh), roasted lamb, roasted beef, chicken, roasted pork, fresh fish, multiple humans."

Rafayel patted his leg. "Nagheed, come. Nothing we need at the market today."

After a few moments, Nagheed jogged to catch up.

"Although, I think my purse would be fairly safe with you along."

No doubt.

They took the next main street away from the market. It led up a shallow hill to a cul-de-sac and a building of stone and timber. Dark ivy grew along the stones giving an illusion of the building sinking into plant life. When Rafayel opened the door, Nagheed slipped inside.

Inside, the natural lighting from the windows was augmented by lanterns. The front room was empty except for a massive, hip-high wooden table. An athletic man sat on a stool behind the table and snacked on bread and jam – strawberry, according to the scent words drifting upward from his plate – while he jotted notes in a ledger.

The man set his breakfast and his ledger aside. "Good morning. How can I help you?"

Rafayel produced the paper from his doublet. "I've seen this symbol around Yavne quite a bit lately. Information I received recently suggested is a symbol for an Ilionite goddess. Would you have any resources to refute or confirm that? Perhaps provide more information?"

"Yes, but I think–" The man scowled and tugged the ledger closer. "–That–" He tapped the ledger. "Yes. Mentor Jood was here yesterday. He checked it out for Master Dan. That's the only book we have with information on Ilion's religions."

"Then, I shall pay Master Dan a visit. The monastery is only a few blocks away. Thank you." Rafayel folded up his paper and tucked it back into his doublet. "Nagheed, come."

"Oh, sir." The man reached after him. "The monks no longer live in town."

Rafayel paused at the door. "Oh?"

CHAPTER 9

"His Excellency and Master Dan had a disagreement." He leaned on the table. "His Excellency said that anyone living within the walls owed him taxes because they benefit from protection."

"The temple is exempt from taxes." Rafayel shook his head. "They repay the city through their charity."

The librarian nodded. "Exactly Master Dan's reply, but His Excellency said that applied to the temple itself, not monasteries or convents."

"So Master Dan has moved them out of town?" Rafayel pointed south.

"Yes sir. They're building a new monastery near the convent south of town." He squinted up at the corner of the room. "Some, what, five kilometers south of here?"

"Thank you again." Rafayel tipped his hat.

Nagheed slipped out the door ahead of Rafayel.

Rafayel closed the door behind him. "Let's go retrieve Ryder and head south."

I'm with you. Nagheed woofed.

After a jog back to the stable, they headed out of town to the south. Rafayel kept their pace more leisurely than Nagheed would have preferred, so he practiced his senses again. With a higher skill, maybe he would've done better finding the trail on the docks.

Near the town wall, the same wall of transparent gray scent words filled the screen, but as they traveled, the scents grew weaker and smaller on the screen until he could distinguish individual humans and horses. One scent, Mentor Jood, stood out among the others not by its size but because it was the only real name. Finally, only "Mentor Jood" and "Learner" were left and forming a trail along the road.

Another kilometer or so further, and "blood" closely associated with "Mentor Jood" formed a sort of dome off to the left. "Human man" was fairly dense in the area, too.

After Nagheed triggered Signal Human, he sat down and whined.

Rafayel reined in Ryder. "Something's not right? Lead on, Nagheed, and be wary."

No problem there.

The road curved away from the sea. Past the bend, a mass of rumpled cloth shaped roughly like a prone human was piled on the side of the road. Nagheed darted ahead and visually confirmed what his nose had already figured out. Mentor Jood had been injured.

Chapter 10

Nagheed nudged the monk with his nose.

Rafayel dismounted and knelt nearby. He pressed his fingertips against the monk's neck. "His pulse is strong."

Mentor Jood moaned and swatted at Rafayel's hand.

"Mentor?" Rafayel turned him onto his back. "Can you hear me?"

"Think so," Mentor Jood's voice had a sandpaper quality.

"This has not been your week, sir." He helped the monk sit up.

He winced. "Do you tell me? We headed home last night after leaving you at the gate. Attacked by bandits. They took everything including my learner then cracked me a good one on the head. I remember nothing else." He pressed his palm to his forehead. "Help me up? I must find my learner."

"With all respect, Mentor, you're in no shape to start such a search. I'll get you to the monastery then if Nagheed is game, we'll find him." He helped Mentor Jood to his feet and held him steady. "What do you say Nagheed?"

He woofed and wagged his tail.

Mentor Jood blinked hard. "That'll take too long. Most

of the day will be spent."

"I can't leave you here." Rafayel frowned.

"There's an elderly lady who lives near here." He pointed east. "Take me there, then."

Rafayel interlaced his fingers and boosted the monk onto Ryder's back while Nagheed sniffed around for the younger monk's scent. On the far side of the road, he found what he was hunting for. "Learner" along with a heavier concentration of "Human man" headed off toward the west.

"Nagheed, come," Rafayel called.

He scratched up the ground so he could find the spot again later and rejoined his human.

"It's a short way off the road, close to the crossroads with the road from Bakhar." Mentor Jood pointed.

Rafayel lead Ryder by the reins into the wooded area off the road. A few hundred meters in, they came to a clearing with a wooden structure that could only be called a run-down shack in an extreme effort at generosity. The wood planks making up the walls were worn to jagged edges near the ground and pockmarked with termite holes. The thatched roof appeared to have an unintended skylight. Near the shack, a chicken scratched around the yard and picked at bundles of straw, roofing material, probably.

The crooked door swung open, and an old lady wiping her hands on her ragged apron stepped out. Her poofy pants were heavily patterned with splotches and swirls and bound at the ankle. She wore an equally poofy, light-colored shirt, and a fringed scarf was wrapped around her head. The clothes were patched and faded. Her smooth movements had an old elegance to them that.

"Mentor Jood!" She hurried over.

CHAPTER 10

"I'm afraid he's taken quite a beating twice in as many days," Rafayel helped him down from Ryder. "His learner was abducted. May I leave Mentor Jood with you while I seek out the missing lad."

"Of course!" She led Mentor Jood by the arm. "You come right this way and rest your bones. I'll get you some water and a bit of bread then go collect the right sort of herbs."

"No, you don't have enough food for yourself."

"Now, Mentor, let a lady be as hospitable as she can."

"I'll be back directly." Rafayel swung up into Ryder's saddle.

They left the woman to fuss over the injured monk and returned to the road. Nagheed found the spot he'd marked. He led the way, chasing "Learner" as he went. The gray words thinned out as they left the road, giving him a varying handful of animals and human men.

At length, they approached a stony ridge that paralleled the sea. The trail led them to a narrow hole that led downward at a gentle slope through the rocks.

Rafayel dismounted and secured Ryder to a tree. He rooted around in his saddlebags and produced a metal and glass lantern and a handful of stubby candles to use in it, a carved wooden cylinder as big around as a man's thumb, and a small bag that smelled like jerky. All but the lantern and cylinder went into his belt pouch.

While the human continued his preparations, Nagheed took a few steps into the hole. The human men and the learner had indeed been this way. Up ahead, piles of sticks lined both walls. They were arranged in some kind of pattern, but there wasn't enough light that far in.

Rafayel's steps came up behind Nagheed. "Stay alert.

Let's not make noise we can avoid. I'd rather our situation involve a rescue but not a hostage."

Lantern in hand, Rafayel led the way into the pale rock cavern. Nagheed kept a half-step behind. The candle and the lantern cast a feeble glow that illuminated only a short distance ahead. As they approached the first stick pile, Nagheed darted ahead to investigate.

A couple dozen curved sticks were arranged nearly parallel to each other and aligned not quite perpendicularly with disc-shaped blocks. Larger sticks jutted out from the curved ones. He didn't realize what it was until he found the skull. Nagheed backpedaled into Rafayel's legs.

"Easy, boy," he whispered, patting Nagheed's side. "It's quite dead."

As far as you know. I've played enough games to really wonder. We're going to trip some mechanism and all of a sudden, skeletons. Everywhere.

In the lantern's glow, Rafayel picked a path around skeletons and rocks. Cobwebs filled every rough patch or pocket in the stone.

Let's hope the inhabitants of all these webs have moved on.

They rounded a U-shaped bend and found that the spiders' activity had been more strenuous. The stone walls were hardly visible through the fuzz of cobwebs lining the path. Weirdly, nothing encroached into the center. Nagheed had no complaints about that. He didn't want to think about the size of spider that could spin so much webbing.

The path widened out into a dome-shaped room as festooned with webs as the passage had been.

Lantern light glinted off the web but only in a specific

CHAPTER 10

spot. Nowhere else reflected light. Nagheed paused and took a step closer to the sparkle.

"Nagheed," Rafayel whispered. "We'll investigate more on the way out. For now, let's find our young friend."

He made a mental note of the location. There was something important there, maybe even something they needed.

The room narrowed again to a passage and spiderwebs thinned out to reveal the rock walls. Water dripped up ahead. The passage curved around in an S-shape and widened into a room. A natural pond in the center was ringed by stalagmites, stalactites, and columns. A flock of long, thin limestone sticks hung together.

A lizard-like critter the size of a cocker spaniel slinked out of the pond and hissed. Something around its neck sparkled. The music changed to a song that was mostly brass and drums. Jake tapped his toe to the beat.

The lizard ran forward, and Nagheed darted ahead to meet it. As he came into range, the lizard slapped at him. Nagheed used his Dodge skill and leapt over the attack but overshot the lizard and landed on the far side. It turned to face him, and Rafayel circled to come up behind the lizard. When it swiped a claw at Nagheed, he snapped and bit the lizard's leg. The health bar over its head shrank. Rafayel drove the point of his rapier through the lizard's neck. The lizard's health zeroed out, and it turned into a lizard mannequin.

The brass and drums ended and turned back into the traveling music.

After sheathing his sword, Rafayel crouched next to the mannequin. A pop-up screen showed what the creature was carrying. A key ring on a necklace with three keys was the total of what the lizard had. "Interesting." He stood and looked around the room, holding the lantern high.

Nagheed sniffed around. The "Human man" was joined by a couple others, and they all stayed close by "Learner." Those trailed off through the cavern's only exit. "Lizard" and "Lizard blood" crowded around him from the mannequin

"Let's explore later and get going now." Rafayel led the way to the other opening.

The single path out of the room branched like a Y only a handful of steps later. A glow glittered on the damp rock walls of the left passage, but the way to the right was narrow and dark.

Rafayel leaned closer. "Which way, boy?"

Nagheed took a few steps down the left passage and sniffed. "Human man" was pretty dense this way, but there was no sign of the "Learner."

He returned to Rafayel then went down the darker path. "Learner" definitely formed a trail this way, along with a dense concentration of "human men" and "lizard."

Of course. How else could it be? He looked up at his own human.

Rafayel nodded. "About what I expected, but I must admit I'm curious about the other way. Slow and easy, Nagheed."

He wandered on ahead, staying within the edge of the lantern's light. The stone glittered. The narrow passage wound around and generally downward for longer than Nagheed expected.

After several minutes of walking, the passage widened out into a cavern.

CHAPTER 10

"Stop." Rafayel whispered.

Nagheed retracted his last step and sat as Rafayel came even with him and held up the lantern.

This chamber lacked the pond of the last, but cave formations formed into more soda straws and a wavy curtain. Cages lined the walls each with chains that threaded through the ceiling. A massive lizard paced in each one. Although all were clearly the same sort, they ranged in size from similar to the one they'd killed to a huge one the size of a St. Bernard.

"Let us count our blessings that they are in cages." Rafayel crept further into the room. "And pray to Tsidkenu that they stay that way."

Nagheed followed his human forward, keeping a watchful eye, ear, and nose on the hissing lizards. They clawed at the cages and the biggest one rammed its head into the bars over and over.

Nagheed turned on Posture and growled back.

Rafayel shot a narrow-eyed his way. "Let's not rile them up any more than necessary?" He stopped in the center of the main room. "This appears to be a dead end. Are you sure this is the way?"

He woofed.

"Lead on."

With his Tracking skill still armed, he used his keen nose to find the way down the central aisle between the cages to a solid wall. When he crouched low and sniffed along the ground, "sea breeze" wafted in under the wall. Nagheed sat and whined.

"Are you sure?" Rafayel continued checking the part of the wall nearest him.

Nagheed crouched and got another good whiff of "sea breeze" coming from under the wall then whined again.

Rafayel joined him and held his hand near the floor. "Interesting. There's a draft here." He stood and searched the wall. When he peered around the stalagmite, he smiled and drew his sword. "Here's hoping this opens the door and not the cages."

Nagheed prepared to tackle the closest lizard. *If the cages open, it's me and you, and you're going down.*

Rafayel made a sudden downward motion with his hand, and the rock wall behind Nagheed shifted outward. The baron gave it a push with his boot. The rock wall swung open like a typical door but stopped halfway. Nagheed gave it another nudge. It opened slightly further then rebounded. Nagheed strained with his ears.

"Those last few chests and we are ready to go," a man said.

"What about the monk?" another asked.

"Him? Where we're going, he'll fetch a good price."

"But I belong to the temple!" the learner exclaimed.

"Not anymore, boy. You belong to me."

"Slowly," Rafayel whispered.

Nagheed led the way around the door into a dark corridor with walls hewn to form ninety-degree angles to the floor and ceiling. A flickering glow of fire from the room beyond lit the latter half of the hallway.

"No use you struggling so much now, boy. When the boss ties a knot, it won't come undone without a knife." Laughter retreated.

Rafayel tapped Nagheed shoulder. "Let's go."

They jogged the remaining distance and entered a room

the size of a tennis court. Torches and sconces lit the place to a reasonable facsimile of late dawn. A carved wooden chair with red velvet cushions occupied the far corner of the room. Other, smaller chairs ringed a rough table along the near wall. A collection of chests waited by a passageway leading out. Next to them, the learner was tied up on the ground. A red and purple bruise swelled one eye shut. The health bar above his nametag was down not quite a quarter. Four men in black denim each carried a chest. Their nametags all read "Bandit," and their health bars were full.

Rafayel deposited the lantern on the table.

"Baron!" The learner exclaimed.

Nagheed winced as the four bandits turned. They set the chests down, and drew long, thin daggers.

The music changed to brass and drums.

Nagheed followed the right wall around. The best way to prevent a hostage situation was to make sure no one else got to the learner. The four bandits split up. Two turned toward Rafayel while the other two turned toward the learner. Nagheed bolted ahead and interposed himself between the learner and the bandits. With Posture turned on, he growled and bristled, giving the bandits a frown for the morale emoji.

The pair of bandits slinked forward. Each tossed his dagger from hand to hand. Nagheed prepared to pounce but waited for the left bandit's knife to be in the air. Nagheed slammed into him, driving him to the ground and sinking long canine teeth into the bandit's arm. The bandit's health bar dropped a quarter. In his peripheral vision, he spotted the other bandit rushing in. Nagheed's vision flashed red as his health bar lost a few points.

Nagheed shook his head from side to side, doing more damage. His target's futile effort to push Nagheed off only did more harm.

In the edge of Nagheed's vision, the other bandit raised his dagger for another attack, but he stumbled aside. Nagheed swiped a claw at the one he had pinned, taking the last of his health and transforming him into a mannequin.

A distant horn sounded. Did that horn warn of round 2?
Reinforcements? We're not done with the first round yet!

Nagheed turned his attention to the other bandit, who waded into range. When the bandit drew his hand back, Nagheed swiped with his claw and scored a set of four deep cuts across the bandit's thigh. The descending dagger attack aborted as the bandit fell back. Nagheed tackled him and landed a killing blow to the throat.

The two new men swaggered in from the outgoing corridor, each with "Cutthroat" for a nametag.

"Boss wants to know what the holdup–" one of them began.

They froze, and their frowns deepened. The two cutthroats drew short swords. One charged toward Rafayel.

Nagheed darted back to the learner and growled at the cutthroat approaching them. The enemy acquired a frown for the morale emoji. Across the room, Rafayel slashed the throat of the last bandit then stood erect with his hand held straight out in front of him. The cutthroat charging him skidded to a stop in time to avoid impaling himself.

The cutthroat facing Nagheed threw a few fake attacks, but Nagheed knew better than to let himself be drawn into a vulnerable position. He'd played enough games to see that coming.

CHAPTER 10

Nagheed watched the cutthroat's hip. As the center of gravity went, so the body would go. When his enemy's hip shifted back, Nagheed launched himself. He knocked the cutthroat to the ground dislodging the short sword. It skittered across the stone floor and landed out of reach. The cutthroat swung a fist at Nagheed, but the thud on Nagheed's ribs hardly registered.

You are such a wimp!

A bite to the cutthroat's unprotected neck ended the threat.

Another horn sounded.

Round 3?

Nagheed retreated to his place by the learner.

Across the room, Rafayel thrust his rapier through the cutthroat he faced and created a new mannequin.

The new human strutted in sporting a nametag that read "Boss." "What is this?"

Nagheed expected a Boss Rant™, but the dialogue ended with that one-liner.

The boss drew a black powder pistol and took aim at Rafayel as Rafayel dropped his rapier and drew his own pistol.

Nagheed stayed frozen. He couldn't reach the boss in time, and Rafayel was going to fire second. Nagheed crouched in preparation.

"Hold, Nagheed!" Rafayel ordered.

The boss fired. The first pop of gunpowder was the flint igniting the powder in the flash pan before the bang of the main charge. At the sound of the first pop, Rafayel crouched and the shot missed him entirely. He returned fire. The pop-bang of Rafayel's pistol followed like an echo of the boss's gun. The boss dove for the ground, turning the potential killing shot into a blow to the shoulder.

"Go, Nagheed!" Rafayel ordered.

He didn't need telling twice. Nagheed charged. He pinned the boss down and attacked with claws and teeth until the boss turned into a mannequin and the combat music faded to their usual traveling tune.

Rafayel joined him. "Well done, Nagheed."

He wagged his tail and followed his human to the learner.

"You should have used that gun sooner." The learner smirked.

Rafayel shook his head and used a knife to cut the learner loose. "Takes too long to reload. With the boss, drawing and firing the pistol would've taken as long as running into rapier range, so the pistol was the better choice. Other than that impressive bruise, are you hurt?"

"Not really. They pushed me around some, but aside from punching me in the face when I tried to help Mentor Jood… Is he all right? Have you seen him?"

"He's a bit worse for wear, but we left him in the care of an elderly lady nearby."

He smiled. "Vehira, I assume. She's nice." He turned toward the opening the bandits had come through. "There were more of them. We should probably not stay."

"Nagheed will alert us." Rafayel approached the nearest bandit mannequin. "We'll divide the spoils when we're safe."

The inventory screen popped up showing a handful of clear, iridescent plastic disks – coins apparently, but they were labeled "rounds" – and a crystal. Rafayel pocketed everything and the window disappeared. All the bandits carried the same loot, even down to the number of rounds. The cutthroats carried a larger handful of rounds, a crystal, and a cylinder that looked like a AA battery.

Wonder if it still has a charge?

"What's that?" The learner pointed to a battery.

Rafayel shrugged. "We'll puzzle that out later."

The boss carried about the same number of rounds as the cutthroats, two crystals – one white, one black – and a paper-wrapped candle.

Dynamite? Seriously?

The learner's jaw dropped. "Don't light that candle unless you throw it fast. My father and uncles are miners. That stuff will blow a huge hole in solid rock."

Dynamite! Wow. The damage we could do with that.

Rafayel tucked the dynamite into his pack.

The rest of the chests that the bandits had been retrieving were padlocked. Rafayel fished out the keys they'd found on the lizard. He tried different ones until the littlest one popped the lock open. Rafayel winced as he withdrew a heavy book and a beaded leather pouch containing dried herbs.

A quick trumpet fanfare sounded over the traveling music and his notebook turned blue. He'd check that later.

The second chest opened with the same key. It held an ornate jeweled dagger and another beaded leather pouch.

The third chest also use the littlest key. Nagheed expected some other object and a leather pouch, but instead Rafayel gritted his teeth and pulled out a wooden case. When he opened it, gold plates and chalices shined in the firelight.

"Wow!" The learner ran his fingers along the details of the chalice. "Solid gold?"

Rafayel shook his head. "Not half heavy enough. Probably gold overlaid on a baser metal. Copper, probably, or maybe aluminum."

Footsteps approached in the outbound corridor. Nagheed turned that way and growled.

Rafayel handed the case to the learner then grabbed the nearest torch, handing it to the learner, too. "Let's go."

"What about the other chest?"

"No time. I'm not keen on another fight while we still have injuries from the first one. We go. Now." He gave the learner a little push toward the corridor they'd entered through. "Nagheed, lead us out!"

Nagheed charged into the lead but kept his speed to a rate appropriate for the humans. Each step flashed a red haze across the screen, reminding him that he'd taken an injury in that fight.

Behind them, exclamations and angry shouts echoed.

"There! I see them!" A woman shouted.

A man answered, but his words were lost in an onslaught of other upset voices.

Nagheed exited to the lizard room. Squinting lizards hissed. He didn't stop to exchange growls. Halfway to the pond room, metal clanked like someone was rolling up the chain.

Chapter 11

Nagheed glanced back the way they'd come then up at his human.

"Give me that torch." Rafayel turned toward the learner. "You take the lantern. Run. I'll catch up. Go, Nagheed. Lead him all the way out."

Nagheed kept going, but he looked back over his shoulder until he lost sight of Rafayel. *What are you doing?*

When he reached the pond room, Nagheed paused long enough to make sure the learner was with him. He kept going through the spiderweb-lined spaces and all the way to the mouth of the cave.

A loud rumble shook the ground. Nagheed crouched to keep his balance. The learner stumbled and fell. When a cloud of dust rushed out of the cave opening, Nagheed closed his eyes tightly and turned his face away.

The commotion settled, and Nagheed headed closer toward the opening. *Where are you, human?*

Vigorous coughing and footsteps drew nearer.

The learner joined him. "That's him. That has to be him."

A feeble torch light cut through the dust. Nagheed slinked back into the cave. The coughing came nearer until Nagheed made out a human form. Nagheed wagged his tail, earning a glittery **+10 XP**, and jogged to meet Rafayel and guide him out.

Once they were in the sunlight again, Rafayel sat on a large rock and jiggled his finger in his ear. "I think it'll be at least a month until I'm hearing properly again."

"What did you do?" The learner asked.

Rafayel looked up. "Again?"

The learner drew a deeper breath. "What did you do?"

"Used that explosive to keep the lizards and bandits away."

Not sure just tossing it down the tunnel would've worked like that. Game physics!

Rafayel retrieved a handkerchief and his canteen from Ryder's saddlebag. He tried to wipe the dust from his face with a damp kerchief but only managed to smear it around. "Let's get you back to Mentor Jood so I can find out what I need in that book and get you both back to the monastery."

"You're hurt, and so is Nagheed," the learner pointed to the injury on Rafayel's arm.

"Not too badly, and I'll stop at a physician on the way north." Rafayel took Ryder by the reins. "Nagheed, Mentor Jood, please."

Nagheed took the lead, favoring his injured side some to keep the red flashes to a minimum. The way back to the shack was shorter than the way from it. As they drew closer, the loud thuds of someone was applying an ax to wood punctuated the silence. They arrived minutes later to find Mentor Jood chopping firewood and stacking it alongside Vehira's shack.

The learner darted on ahead. "Mentor Jood! You're okay!"

CHAPTER 11

"Of course, I am." He froze with the ax midair then set it down. "You're a bit worse for your adventure. Come here and let me have a look."

The learner joined him and winced as the older monk gingerly prodded the swollen eye.

"Nothing a few herbs won't fix."

"The baron and his dog were hurt, too," the learner said.

"We'll tend your eye. Then, if there's not enough left, you can collect more herbs for me, and I'll tend the baron and his dog."

Vehira came out of the shack. She handed mentor Jood a board with a glop of gray grease on it.

"Now hold still." Mentor Jood smeared the concoction on the learner's bruised face.

At once, the swelling subsided and the bruise faded.

Mentor Jood sat back and smiled. "There. That's better, and unless his Excellency has done some greater mischief to himself, there should be plenty left for him and the hound."

Nagheed hung back with Rafayel. When they entered the clearing, Vehira chuckled behind her hand.

The stereotypical nobleman in these games would get in a snit right about now. Nagheed watched his human's reaction. He didn't seem to be that sort, but who knew?

"Oh glory!" Mentor Jood gave the learner a push on the shoulder. "Bucket of water near the door, if you please."

"I'm sorry, your Excellency," Vehira struggled to keep the giggle contained.

Rafayel smiled. "I'm sure I'm quite the sight."

"How did you come out so much the worse?" Mentor Jood asked.

The learner returned, leaning hard to one side as he

carried a bucket. "He blew up the cave while still in it."

"Only part of the cave and I made sure I was well away from the worst of it." Rafayel looked down at his dust-covered clothes.

"Not quite far enough," Mentor Jood muttered.

Rafayel leaned closer. "The bandits and lizards were deterred. That's all I really wanted."

With more than a canteen full of water, Rafayel did a better job of getting the dust off of his exposed skin and hair.

"Now, I feel more human." He looked at Nagheed then at the rest of the water in the bucket.

No, you don't. Nagheed backed away.

Vehira smiled. "I think he knows what you have in mind."

"Relax, Nagheed. A half-bucket full of water would turn you from a dusty dog to a muddy dog." Rafayel reached over and ruffled the fur on Nagheed's head, getting a miniature dust cloud.

Mentor Jood beckoned the learner closer. "Water Vehira's garden then fetch her some clean water."

She shook her head. "I can do that."

"You can, but my learner needs some chores today, or Master Dan will have him sewing tents until midnight."

"Still, less dust will help with treating the injuries." Rafayel pointed to an open area. "Nagheed, go out there and give yourself a good shake. Let's find out how much dirt you can shed."

Better than a cold shower, anyway. He trotted several meters away, crouched slightly, and shook like he had wet hair to dry. His injured side turned the screen red until he stopped shaking.

CHAPTER 11

A cloud of dust almost as bad as the cave formed in a three-meter radius around him. He sneezed several times and returned to his human.

Rafayel had taken off his leather doublet and rolled up his sleeve to reveal a shallow cut across his upper arm. Blood had smeared around it. Seconds after Mentor Jood applied the greenish concoction, the cut on Rafayel's arm faded.

"Thank you."

"Certainly." Mentor Jood made kissing noises. "Come here, boy."

If I respond to you, I bet I get a point loss. I'm only supposed to answer Rafayel and his fam.

"Nagheed, come." Rafayel patted the ground next to them.

Okay. That'll do. Nagheed joined his human.

"Down." He carefully combed through Nagheed's fur with his fingers. "We need to find armor for you or have some made. Chain would pull your fur, but some leather might do."

"There it is." Mentor Jood leaned closer. "A long thin slice across the surface. Not too deep."

Nagheed tensed, waiting for the screen to turn red.

As Mentor Jood applied the salve, Nagheed's health improved to full points.

"There you are." Mentor Jood wiped his fingers on Nagheed's fur.

Gee. Thanks. I don't suppose I get some kind of buff for greasy fur.

"Were you able to recover the book?" he asked.

Rafayel dug it out of his pack. "Yes, but I need to borrow it if I may, just for a few minutes."

"Certainly." Mentor Jood pointed at the book. "What do you seek?"

As Rafayel related the caravaner's tale, he scanned through the table of contents then flipped to a page in the center of the book. "I need to know where Elef's temple is, and if I can find out what some of these artifacts are, that might be something."

"You're assuming the old man told you true?" Vehira stood nearby. "In my experience, caravaners have their own agenda.

"He owed the baron a favor," Mentor Jood explained.

Rafayel ran his finger down the page then flipped to the next. "I'm hoping this book will confirm what he said."

"Trust Tsidkenu. Verify all else." Vehira smiled.

"Exactly."

Nagheed sat where he could read over Rafayel's arm.

Mentor Jood chuckled. "Your dog's interested, too."

And why not?

Rafayel scratched behind Nagheed's ear then held the book where they could both see it. "There you go."

Vehira stared wide-eyed. "You've taught him to read?"

"No, but he's a smart fellow. I wouldn't be too surprised."

Unfortunately, the game turned the writing to gibberish.

Figures.

Weird that he could follow conversations and complex directions spoken plainly, but not read. Both were skills Jake-the-gamer had that Nagheed-the-character would not. He added that to his feedback list.

For now, the best he could do was watch Rafayel scan through the words.

"The elderly fellow spoke truly. This says Atrac and Motce

CHAPTER 11

help their grandfather Elef in their own inimitable ways to varying degrees of success." He flipped the page and studied a map briefly. "Here. This would be the main temple to Elef, so if he's right about the rest, this is where I need to go."

The next few pages were pictures of objects, some of which they'd found either in the bandit's cave or on the maniacs.

Rafayel fished some of the artifacts out of his pack. "It says these crystals are used to 'select the enhancements.' Not sure what that means."

Mentor Jood shook his head. "Couldn't say."

Vehira held them up to the sunlight. "They might be used as some manner of complex code. Colors instead of letters."

Nagheed woofed.

Rafayel glanced over. "He agrees."

Vehira laughed and set the crystals down. "Smart boy."

"The cylinder here provides power for small objects temporarily." Rafayel picked up the blob of shiny stuff. "No idea what to make of this."

"Whatever it used to be, it's melted now." Mentor Jood frowned. "Possibly only good for the rubbish heap."

Vehira wagged her finger at the monk. "Not necessarily. I remake candles from melted wax all the time."

"I won't dispose of it until I know." He flipped a few more pages. "And look here. They've taken herbalism in a different direction by making fluids of different colors that have varying effects. Red for healing. Blue provides a temporary 'rubberized' coating, whatever that's about. Yellow recharges electrical devices. Not sure what that means, either. Gray chills the affected area. Pink offers temporary concealment."

"How very curious." Mentor Jood traced his fingers under the words again. "Well, you know to keep your eye out for red elixirs if you head to Ilion."

"Interesting." Rafayel handed Mentor Jood the book. "There you go. Thank you for the loan."

"My pleasure."

"Now as for the remainder of the materials the bandits contributed to our cause." Rafayel withdrew the iridescent rounds, the dagger, and the beaded pouches. Then he reached over and grabbed the wooden case from where the learner had left it. "If there are no objections, I'll take the Ilionite artifacts for my share. There's no telling what I'll run into when I get to Ilion."

Mentor Jood shook his head. "Part of your share. You and Nagheed took the lion's share of the risk. You deserve the lion's share of the reward." He opened the wooden case and gasped. "Oh glory! These are amazing! Master Dan has been trying to find replacements for ours."

"Replacements?"

Mentor Jood slouched. "Yes. When the baron expelled the monastery for 'failure to pay taxes,' he confiscated our ceremonial plates and chalices as payment due. We've been making do with lesser ones, but those cheapen our offerings to Tsidkenu."

"Take them with my blessing." Rafayel gave Mentor Jood the box. "Your learner did well helping Nagheed in the fight by distracting opponents. His share."

Nagheed woofed.

"That's settled then." Mentor Jood closed the case

CHAPTER 11

Another trumpet fanfare briefly blared over the music.

"Now, these pouches contain herbs, but I'm not sure what sort." Rafayel handed one to Mentor Jood.

He poured a small amount into his hand and sniffed it. "This one's healing." After returning the sample to the pouch, he checked the other. "Same. Mix the herbs with oil or water. Enough to make paste. Apply to the injury and wait. Without knowing exactly what it contains, I couldn't say if it's suitable for making tea. The monastery has plenty. You're not an herbalist, so keep it. Especially if you intend to go to Ilion. In fact, the dagger and rounds go to you as well."

Nagheed took a visual tour of the clearing. A stiff wind would turn the shack into kindling. The "garden" was a few scraggly plants in rocky ground. The only thing that wasn't falling apart was the chicken scratching around the yard.

He used his nose to flip a few of the iridescent rounds toward Vehira. By anyone's estimate, she could use them.

The old lady smiled. "That's kind of you, Nagheed, but I had no part in this adventure."

Rafayel piled half the rounds in front of her. "Nonsense. You tended to Mentor Jood, which freed us to rescue his learner. Even behind the scenes work deserves to be rewarded."

"My learner and I can take care of your shopping as per usual." Mentor Jood nodded toward his learner. "Just provide us with a list."

"Thank you." She blushed.

Rafayel piled his loot in his pack. "If we aren't needed, I would like to try to make our way back to the Halfway Inn. First, though, Mentor Jood, let's get you and your learner to the monastery without further misadventures."

Mentor Jood shook his head. "In broad daylight, we'll be fine. Our problem was traveling after dark."

"If you're sure. It's no trouble."

"I'm sure. Thank you."

"Very well." Rafayel stood and faced Vehira. "For you, my lady, I'm reluctant to leave you here alone. Not even one week ago, two of Yavne's outlying farms with sturdier structures than this were leveled and burned. There were no survivors in one case. There are enough rounds among us to secure you decent housing within the city for a considerable time."

Nagheed woofed. *Now you're thinking.*

She sighed and stared at her bare feet. "It's no good. Even if the guards let me into the city, no landlord, even in the slums, will rent or sell to me. Not even those who were once my most frequent customers. Makes no difference to them that I have been rescued by Tsidkenu and no longer practice my old profession."

"And meanwhile, your 'customers' enjoy the privilege of polite company." Rafayel shook his head. "Would you be willing to travel north with me to Yavne? I believe everyone rescued by Tsidkenu deserves a new start."

"Thank you, but I have lived my entire life in this city, and I want to spend the rest of my days nearby serving Tsidkenu. I have plans in the works to gain entry to the convent, and if I don't live long enough to realize them, then I move on to Tsidkenu's reward."

Rafayel frowned. "I don't like the idea of leaving you here alone, but I won't force you to do what you'd rather not."

"Thank you."

CHAPTER 11

Okay. Enough with the post-battle wrap-up. Let's go!

The learner returned. "I watered the garden, fetched clean water, and stacked the firewood."

"Excellent." Mentor Jood clapped his shoulder. "Gentlemen, I pray the rest of your week goes more favorably than last night." Rafayel gathered everything into his pack and swung up into Ryder's saddle. After bidding them farewell, he rode out.

Nagheed trotted alongside.

On the way back to Vanya, he opened his character sheet. The two fanfares were level-ups, which meant he had ten points to distribute. His skills and attributes had jumped from when he'd allocated his Level 3 points. All that practical experience was paying off. He'd planned to improve his smell and hearing to help with tracking, but somewhere along the way, he'd hit the max for his class, and now those were grayed out. With ten points to spend, he dumped a few into speed and a couple into each of power, agility, and endurance. That would improve his health and ability to dodge.

Name: Nagheed **Species:** Canine – Mountain Shepherd
Class: Protector Level 5 **Gender:** M

Attributes

Attribute	Current	Skill	Current
Power	40	Detect Enemy	35
Speed	26	Sound Alarm	32
Cleverness	33	Stay Alert	27
Endurance	53	Nip	20
Agility	34	Bite	32
Charm	42	Claw	28
Vitality	44	Dodge	27

Sight	39	Posture	25
Smell	70	Intimidate	34
Hearing	60	Patrol	20
Health	137	Signal Human	36
Encumbrance 0 out of 50 lb		Trek	15
		Long distance movement	15
		Sprint	19
		Tackle	20
		Tracking	22

He scanned through the list. By hovering over the various entries, the computer showed him the minimums and maximums. The range was remarkably tight on many of them, and soon, he'd max out. Awfully fast, wasn't it? At a measly level five, he was running out of room to grow? Jake made a note to bring that up in his report.

By the time he'd finished checking out his stats, the gate to Vanya was in view.

* * *

Ahva came in for a gentle landing on Osse's arm and scrambled up to his shoulder to catch her breath. Because of the rocky ground they'd been hiking over, she'd encountered more thermals, allowing her to scout for hazards for hours, game time. She could see for kilometers if she could get high enough. Flying was so much better than riding on his shoulder, but when there weren't thermals to ride, she had to give up fun of soaring until her fatigue bar caught up again. For today, she was probably done with any kind of distance soaring.

CHAPTER 11

The sun was setting on the second full day of hiking westward down what Osse generously called a "road." Unlike the stone-paved streets of Fola, this road through the hilly terrain west of Osse's wrecked village amounted to little more than a clear, foot-worn path among scraggly shrubs and clumps of spindly grass.

In the last couple days, Osse's mood had stabilized but not improved. He no longer started crying at random, but he wasn't nearly as chipper a chirper as he had been during the long trek from Fola to Kamali. He just hiked onward, stopping only with the setting sun to start up a camp and prepare a meal for them both. Their morning meal amounted to little more than the dried fruit and meat in his bag. Midday was often more of the same but eaten while they hiked. Last night, though, he'd managed to use his bow to bring down something he called a rock badger, which he'd roasted over their campfire. A little chewy, maybe, but it restored her fatigue meter.

Now the sun was leaning hard toward the horizon and Osse showed no sign of intending to stop soon.

"Goodnight." Ahva leaned closer to Osse's ear.

He gave her a smile she didn't exactly believe. "I don't know about you, Ahva, but I'm interested in dinner tonight. I haven't found any jackrabbits or rock badgers today. We should reach Oni soon. They'll have an inn where we can stop for food. I'm out of what we got in Kamali, but I still have money. That should be enough to get us through. Then if we don't start finding food to hunt down, I'll have to sell some things."

No food? We should have gotten more in Kamali. Ahva hissed and crouched lower on Osse's shoulder.

She tried not to be too mad at him. If she'd come home and found her village trashed and her whole family dead, she wasn't sure she'd be thinking all that clearly, either, and he did sound like he had a plan for making sure they had enough to eat. She'd stay nearer at hand, though. With the sun setting, she didn't want to be separated from him. Her vision in the dark was almost nonexistent.

With a quick turn of his head, he considered the sun then increased his pace. "A couple hours until sunset. I hope I have the distance right. I've only been there once, and that was a long time ago."

We'll get there. You'll see!

He needed to have the right mindset.

Grass rustled off to the left. She turned that way but saw nothing. For a moment, she wondered if her imagination was providing noise, but Osse spun toward the sound, too.

"On the other hand, if I can catch us a quick meal, that will do for now, and we'll have a late breakfast in the morning." He pulled his bow off his back and set the string then nocked an arrow but didn't prepare to fire yet. "Back, Ahva."

Ahva moved to the center of his collar, immediately behind his head. That way, she wouldn't get caught in his bowstring. She was safely out of his way and still close at hand. There was the added benefit of being able to watch his hindquarters for additional dangers. Teamwork!

Osse headed off the trail and into the brush.

Ahva listened intently and watched the ground. Although her fatigue bar would complain without breakfast in the morning, she liked the idea of stopping for the night, and she knew full well that they couldn't stop if they didn't have food.

CHAPTER 11

The edge of her vision turned red to warn her of a nearby threat.

The brush moved on the right, but when Ahva looked, she saw nothing. Osse turned, not suddenly like she'd expected but in slow motion. He stalked forward again in the direction of the noise.

A pair of voices spoke in unison but in a language Ahva couldn't understand. A creepy chill raced through her feathers, communicated through her full-immersion VR rig. They were on the wrong end of the predator-prey part of this game now. When she chose Posture from the menu, her feathers fluffed out, and she hissed.

"Who's there?" Osse drew the bow just enough to put a better bend in it.

The voices came again.

"I'm warning you. I'm no student with this bow."

There was a loud, high-pitched giggle then the sound of something running.

"Hold on, Ahva," Osse said.

He jogged forward, aiming the nocked arrow at the dirt.

The giggle came from a different direction then the sound of more running, away from them this time.

Osse slowed his pace. As he came around a tree, he stopped and gasped. Ahva climbed back up far enough to peek over his shoulder. A smashed mannequin of an animal – large enough to maybe be a human, but so mutilated she couldn't tell what it was – was scattered in largish pieces on the ground, obviously dead and just as obviously by unnatural means. What kind of inefficient predator destroyed the prey so totally without using the results of the kill? Worse, this kind of intense imagery was in a game originally intended for kids? Surely not. The AI had to be adapting to the audience.

Skirting well around the site, Osse jogged in the direction the last sound had come from, but they came upon nothing more than songbirds and bugs.

The red faded.

Ahva disengaged Posture, and her feathers settled.

"There's something unnatural about that creature." Osse couched his bow and slid the arrow into his quiver. "Another reason for us to reach Oni fast. I don't want to camp out in the open with something like that running loose."

He returned to the path and started off at a jog.

The sun was on the horizon before he stopped.

"It's further than I thought." He leaned forward, breathing hard and straining to catch his breath. "We can't have made a wrong turn. This road leads straight on into Oni. I expected to be there by now."

Ahva followed his gaze toward the horizon before he started off at a brisk march.

Night fell hard. Clouds overhead obscured the moonlight, which also did away with shadows. That might have been for the best. If she'd seen shadows, her imagination would start generating things to fill them.

Osse jogged again.

Not a good idea, silly human. She squawked in protest.

Maybe his eyes did better in the dark than hers did. She wasn't seeing much more than Osse, and even that was difficult. Would they walk right past Oni without realizing it?

The grass to Ahva's right moved. She turned but saw nothing.

Chapter 12

"That's the wind, Ahva," Osse said.

She was less certain. There was something out there, maybe even that laughing creature with the weird voice, the one who had killed so brutally. At least the red warning around her vision didn't show, but then would she see that in the dark when she couldn't make out anything else?

Up ahead, a steady glow moved from side to side, growing nearer with each of Osse's steps. Every creepy story and scary movie involving disembodied lights filled Ahva's imagination. Her guts threatened a full-scale revolt.

Those were just stories, and this was just a game, sure. She knew that, but her brain generated all the creepiness she could've asked for and more besides.

Another sound of motion in the grass turned Ahva's gaze that way, for all the good it would do. She could no more see that than she could identify the source of the moving light. "Wind," he'd said? She didn't believe it for a second. There was more than wind going on there. Could that be the destructive predator, or was it something else even more dangerous?

Osse moved a little faster, away from the wind-that-wasn't-wind and toward the light-that-couldn't-be-a-ghost. To keep her mind from conjuring up any further troubling explanations for the light up ahead, Ahva kept her eyes on Osse. She stole glances from time to time to find out if the unnamed glow had given up rambling. If anything, the distance was closing faster than she had expected.

Without warning, Osse pitched forward. Ahva launched herself into the air to avoid being pinned under him as he fell. Osse landed on the path with a thud and a groan as she headed for the ground herself. Before she expected to touch down, she hit and rolled over her beak and onto her back, but she didn't stay that way. Being belly-up was far too vulnerable, so she quickly rolled back onto her feet but stayed still and shook herself.

"Ahva! Ahva! Where'd you go?" Osse grunted and little rocks grated under his weight. "Ahva! Come here, Ahva!"

She'd like to, but she couldn't see where he was and had no chance of finding him in the pitch black.

Osse whistled.

That Ahva could do without moving anywhere. She whistled back to him, mimicking the tune he'd chosen. That wasn't too imaginative. They could do better.

Speak.

The pop-up window appeared, and she read through the list.

"Disgusting eyeball. Hello, Ahva. Bite fingers today? Goodnight, Ahva."

Steps came closer.

"Hello, Ahva. I not Ahva. You're Ahva. Silly bird." She continued through the list.

The vibration of footsteps stopped right in front of her.

"You camouflage well in the dark," Osse said almost on top of her.

Funny how black birds managed that.

"Up we go, Ahva," he said.

Another interesting phrase!

She felt something tap her chest and struck out before she realized what she was doing.

"Ow! Ahva! It's me, you squirrel," he said.

"Good bird. Bite fingers today?"

"Come on, Ahva. Step onto my hand," he said.

"Uhwe-oh!" she said.

That didn't sound right. She'd have to try again later after she'd practiced it a few more times.

She felt a tap on her chest and knew what it was this time. She stepped up and settled on Osse's fingers. Following his arm, she made her way back to his shoulder.

"Let's go a little slower now so I don't find any more chuck holes, huh?" he asked.

Brilliant idea. "Go slow, silly."

Osse picked up his pace again but kept to a more reasonable speed. She'd been anxious to reach their destination earlier, but the thought of losing him again scared her even more than the thought that something or someone was trailing them off to the side.

The light grew nearer and nearer, and finally Ahva saw that it was a lantern in the hand of human. Only then did the man's ID and health bar appear.

Ghost stories. Really, now!

"You! Stop where you are, and give your name and business," the man with the lantern called. Tension in his voice made him sound stern.

Osse stopped as ordered. "My name is Osse Bente. I'm headed westward to get to the inn at Oni."

"It's awful late for travelin', son." The sentry's voice lost the mildly ticked off quality.

"Yes, sir. Someone's been following us, and we found a mutilated animal on the side of the road. I thought shelter in the town would be better than camping in the open, but Oni is a little further down the road than I thought."

"Distances are deceiving on the road." The sentry leaned closer. "You said, 'We.' Who's with you?"

"Ahva, my bird," Osse said.

Ahva cawed to introduce herself. "Hello! I Ahva."

"Well, isn't that something. Come along, son. I'll take you to a house." He waved for him to follow.

"There's no inn?" Osse asked.

"Never been to Oni, have you?"

"Once, when I was younger. I remember wondering how a town could be so big." Osse took in the town with a sweeping gesture of one hand.

"When you're small, everything is grander than it really is. Oni is a village of the better part of a few dozen houses and a couple shops," the sentry explained. "No inn, so the folks hereabouts take turns hosting travelers in their homes."

Ahva kept her eyes on the surroundings as Osse followed the man along what was little more than a well-worn footpath. They stopped at a house made of mud bricks. The sentry knocked on an ill-fitted wooden door. When no answer came, he knocked louder.

"It's no good pretending you're not here." He huffed and rolled his eyes. "Heard you and your wife talking."

CHAPTER 12

"I don't want to be a bother." Osse leaned closer and whispered.

"Nonsense, son. We've all got our duties to take care of."

As he was about to knock again, the door opened and a man leaned on the frame.

"Traveler for you Kando."

"At this hour?" Kando groaned.

"It's your turn, and you get it easy. Just the boy and his bird."

Kando sighed. "Fine, fine. Come on in. Bring everything with you, or you may not find it in the morning."

Inside, Ahva could see clearly in the better light of a fire in the fireplace.

Kando stood a whole crow-height shorter than Osse and had lighter skin but the same dark, extra-curly hair. A woman ID'd as "Meesha," most likely his wife, sat near the fire with a bowl in her hand eating some kind of watery, chunky goo that Ahva was sure would stick to her beak. Her fatigue bar, however, suggested she either partake of what was offered or forego flying for a while. Being a permanent shoulder ornament was not on her agenda.

The inside of the house was plain. There were no chairs or tables nor even any cushions for Osse to perch on. She would be comfortable enough on his shoulder, of course. A dense pot with a blackened bottom hung on a hook in the fireplace. The dirt floor had been hard-packed by much use, and the mantle over the fireplace held a collection of baskets and pottery jars.

"You eaten?" Kando asked.

"No, sir. I was hoping to buy food here." Osse squatted and set his things down nearby. "I hoped there might be an inn."

Meesha snatched a bowl from the top of the mantle. "No inn, and we can't take your money, much as we need it. The town council would tax us the same amount if we did."

What a grouch!

"I'm sorry. I didn't mean to cause you any hardship," Osse said.

Meesha snorted. When Ahva snorted back, the woman glared.

"Let it go, Meesha. It's our turn, you know, and we're getting an easy one." Kando dished up some of the stuff in the bowl and handed it to Osse. "What does that one eat?"

"I'll feed her out of my own bowl." Osse sat on the hard dirt floor. "Is there somewhere in Oni where I could buy food in the morning before I continue on my journey?"

"The council runs a small exchange shop at the center of town." Kando gestured that way with the twitch of his head. "They usually have breads and salted or dried meats. You'll pay too much for it, though."

Osse nodded. "Then I'll get what I need to make it to my next stop." Osse stirred the bowl's contents. "It smells excellent, thank you."

He scooped some out and blew on it then held it up. Ahva leaned forward to sample the food and watched her fatigue counter creep upward. It'd do. After she'd scooped some of the goo into her beak, he swallowed the rest of what he had loaded onto his spoon.

"Where are you headed at this hour?" Kando asked.

Osse hastily swallowed a spoonful of porridge. "My village was destroyed by four creatures. There's a rumor they took captives. My sister might be one of them, so I'm

CHAPTER 12

searching for her."

"You think they went to Nethanya?" Kando picked up a piece of wood and a knife.

"I'm not sure, but they're definitely headed in that direction." Osse studied the porridge in the bowl and forgot to offer Ahva any for a while. "I've heard them several times on the way here, but every time I get too close, they run off. Fast, too."

Kando leaned closer. "You're bleeding."

Osse checked at his forearm and shrugged. "I tripped on the road when someone was pursuing us in the dark. I've done worse."

Ahva looked down at his arm. Hardly a scratch. He'd live.

"You brought blood into our house?" Meesha jumped up and retrieved a dingy cloth from a simple box in the corner of the room then dunked it in a bucket of water.

Couldn't find a dirtier rag, huh? Ahva did her best impression of a squint-eyed stare.

Osse shook his head. "It stopped bleeding before I came in."

Meesha mumbled and dropped the damp rag in Osse's lap. "Take care of it before you bring us any more bad luck."

He set his bowl aside and stepped out, grumbling, "Because somehow, having a scrape on my arm attracts bad luck? Stupid."

Probably not a bad idea to clean off the road dirt. Not sure using that particular rag to do it is exactly approved by the Surgeon General, though.

After finishing the task, he retraced their steps to the edge of the village.

The sentry glanced back. "Problem?"

"Scraped my arm when I fell. It's stopped bleeding, but Meesha is unimpressed." Osse cocked back like he was throwing a baseball and hurled the cloth.

"Can't blame her there. They've had a bad run of luck lately. Make sure you turn around seven times before you go back through the door."

"Right."

Ahva held on as Osse jogged back and slipped in.

"You threw the–" Meesha stared up at him without lifting her head.

Osse held up his hand to stop her. "I grew up in a Bakhari village. I know what to do."

You just chose not to do it. What they don't know...

The bowl of food Osse had left behind was gone.

Ahva hissed and made a noise like crunching nuts.

Meesha stared hard. "Is that a crow?"

"She's a corvid." Osse reached up and scratched Ahva's head.

You are not wrong. "I Ahva. Hello!"

Kando's eyes grew wider than saucers. "It talks!"

"Yes, she does. Totally harmless."

Until you stick your fingers in my face. "Bite fingers?"

Osse preened her head, which restored some of her missing fatigue bar. "No, don't bite fingers."

Meesha muttered something to Kando.

"Di' oo 'ear that?" Ahva leaned forward.

Kando shook his head. "It'll be fine. They're only here until morning." He retrieved a cloth worn enough to see through and pointed into the front corner of the house. "I don't have a guest room, so all I can offer is a patch of floor and a blanket.

CHAPTER 12

"That will do fine, thank you." Osse got situated where his host had pointed and fished his own cloak out of the bag to use for a blanket.

Ahva perched next to Osse and watched Kando and Meesha duck through a cloth hanging in a doorway into another room. Once the sounds of nearby movement stopped, she told the computer to sleep.

Everything went dark, and sheep played a poker game until a giggling maniac sent them running. The sheep and laughing loony disappeared.

Khin May smiled. *Bird, you need happier dreams.*

The darkness faded as the first light of dawn bled in through the cracks in the slats of the door.

Somewhere nearby, a woman screamed. Osse bolted awake, and Ahva squawked and fluttered to Osse's shoulder. Kando rushed out of the back room. He grabbed a hatchet by the door and mumbled something about "bandits" then ran out.

High-pitched laughter came from the same direction as the scream. Not a bandit. Definitely not a bandit.

"Back, Ahva!" Osse slung his bag over his shoulder.

She scooted around to the back of his neck and held on tightly as he stood and strung his bow. As he left the hut, Osse nocked an arrow, keeping a second in his hand. Ahva adjusted her grip. If he broke into a full run, she'd have to fly or hold on as solidly as she could manage.

A woman screamed again. Ahva grabbed the strap with her beak as Osse ran to join a growing crowd near one of the huts. Everyone in the group had the frownie face morale debuff on their ID tags, and a few had the fear face instead.

"He's still alive," someone said.

Maybe Osse, with his knowledge of herbs, would try to help the victim and leave hunting the giggly one to others. They'd be safer that way, but there wasn't much experience to be gained in playing with plant guts.

The laughter came from somewhere nearby. Osse ran toward it as the edge of the screen turned red. He came to the crest of a hill and took aim with his bow. The shot flew a moment later. When Osse lowered his bow, Ahva started up toward his shoulder. Then the maniac giggled again.

Osse quickly nocked the second arrow and took aim. "I hit him. Middle of the back. He should be dead!"

The arrow flew.

Other villagers, all men, ran toward him. They overtook Osse as he was readying a third shot. Ahva tightened her hold as Osse ran after the villagers. She didn't dare try to climb up to his shoulder while he ran flat out, but she had another option.

She launched off and flew a wide spiral, gaining altitude. Ahead of them and opening the gap at an alarming rate, that unkempt humanoid creature ran. Two of Osse's arrows stuck out of it, one in the middle of its back, and the other through its neck. Of the Bakhari giving chase, the one in the front twirled bolas and let fly. The weighted cords spun through the air, trapping both of the maniac's legs at the knees. The creature fell like a bag of rocks.

The Bakhari men caught up moments after, but Osse fell back through the group as he slowed down. In a flurry of swinging blades, the creature turned into a mannequin.

"That's one, Ahva." Osse slid his arrow back into his quiver and couched his bow. "I might not have brought him down, but at least I did have a hand in it."

CHAPTER 12

Ahva whistled and hissed at all the other Bakhari men. *Experience point hogs.*

Without waiting for the men of the village, Osse turned and trudged back to the crowd gathered around the house. A woman wailed and others gathered around her. As Osse came nearer, the group dispersed. The woman withdrew a bracelet and a tunic from a mannequin.

Meesha pointed at Osse. "You! You brought this on us. You came to into our village bleeding and carrying that-that black bird. This is how the gods repay us for showing hospitality to one like that. Get away from us, Osse Bente, before you kill us all!"

"As soon as the shop opens, and I get some traveling food, I'll be on my way without any hesitation." Osse's jaw clenched.

Ahva added her own hiss to match her human's displeasure. "Disgussing eyeball! Goodbye!"

Without any further words from either side, Osse turned and stormed away. He wove a random path through the dirt streets. Finally, he stopped in front of a door decorated with a picture of bread, a lamp, and a knife. He jiggled the door handle but couldn't open the door. After a moment of staring at the artwork they resumed the random tour up and down all the dirt paths among the houses. About the time Ahva thought they'd passed every possible building in the place at least twice, Osse returned to the weirdly painted door.

Ahva studied the artwork. It wasn't terribly exciting. The marketplace of Fola had better. Still, this was probably the place to get some kind of supplies.

After trying the door again, Osse sat against the building

and hugged his knees to his chest. "I don't know, Ahva. Somehow, I thought I would feel better after killing one of the four who killed my family, but I don't. The victim was alive when we started out and dead when we returned. What if I could have helped him? What if helping him would have saved his life? What if I had done nothing and because I did nothing, that lunatic had gotten away because I didn't hit him with my arrows? Where is Maaska? I have to find her." He sighed. "I wish you could tell me what to do."

Ahva climbed out onto Osse's arm. "Sorry. We find." She glanced at her paltry fatigue meter and made a noise like crunching nuts.

"Eat breakfast, huh? Is that your advice?" He managed a smile that was as legitimate as a fifth ace in a deck of cards.

"Yes." *Dinner was not that exciting, if you'll recall, and if my fatigue meter is that puny, yours will be worse.*

"You're still here?" The guard from last night approached. "I thought you'd left town after the morning's excitement."

Ahva knew the voice but didn't recognize the approaching man in the daylight. He had a bald head and coloring that would camouflage well with tree bark. His clothes were rough and repatched more than once with contrasting and clashing materials.

Osse stood. "I need food for the journey, and I'm told this shop is the only one here that can help with what I need. I plan to leave as soon as I'm done here."

"I don't normally open up on the day after I've had the sentry duty, but with Meesha riling up the town against you, you won't be safe here in another hour, let alone tomorrow morning." The man pulled a big key from a pouch and unlocked the painted door. "Come on. We'll equip you for your journey and send you on the way before she has the village blaming you for the bad harvest last fall."

"Thank you." Osse stepped away from the door.

"Good shot with the bow, I might say," the man said.

"I've had good teachers." Osse bowed and touched his forehead.

"I guess you have." The guard opened the door and ushered Osse in. "What will you be needing?"

"Just food. I'm not particular. Enough to travel to the next town." Osse pulled his coin pouch out of his bag.

Ahva preened while they discussed the prices and settled on the final cost. The food went into his bag.

"You travel safely now. No more of that hiking after dark business. Not safe for man or beast." The man wagged his finger at Osse.

Ahva nodded. "Yes. Goodnight."

The sentry chuckled. "Isn't he a character."

She, you gooberhead.

"Yes, she's funny. Great company on the road." Osse shrugged. "Traveling at night may not be safe but being in a village wasn't safe for the one who died this morning, either."

"All the same, watch yourself. The next town is most of two days away. You won't reach it by nightfall. A good fire will keep away most predators, the furry kind anyway."

"Thank you."

Ahva kept her eye on the man as Osse turned and left the store. They headed out of town, but as they approached the low wall, Meesha and a collection of people waited.

"Ahva, get in the bag." Osse flipped open the lid. "I'll tell you when it's safe."

She climbed down and situated herself in the cavity of the bag before he flipped the lid closed.

Osse shuffled forward again but slowly, deliberately, as if waiting for the predator to spring.

"I have the food I came for. I'm leaving now," he called out.

"What good is that going to do Heron's family?" Meesha demanded.

"About as much good as it does my own family. You think yours is the only village that was struck by these laughing maniacs?" Osse shouted. "At least Oni is still standing. I got back from Fola to find mine destroyed and nothing left but ashes and memorial stones for all but seven of the villagers. You speak of loss? You know nothing of loss! Now clear out of my way!"

"The gods are punishing you." Meesha yelled.

"All the more reason for me to hate and despise them. You say you want me gone, and yet you stand there in my path. Move away!" He started forward again.

Heavy things clattering around them. Once or twice Osse flinched hard or staggered, but he didn't run, and he didn't turn back. He kept walking at an even pace.

Once the voices faded and no more things hit the path near them, Ahva pulled herself out of the bag and climbed her way back up to Osse's shoulder. His health bar was down a bit. Not terrible, but no longer full. Osse muttered as they hiked, and she made out little for certain other than his extreme displeasure with the people of Oni.

They meandered down a path that was no better marked then yesterday's. Ahva's status bar was hovering just over half. She made a sound like crunching nuts.

"Oh, yeah, you were hungry, weren't you?" Osse stared straight ahead. "I'm not, but I suppose my bad mood shouldn't deprive you of breakfast."

He fished a piece of flat bread out of his pouch and tore a hunk off. Ahva leaned way forward to grab the bread in her beak. Pinning the bread to his shoulder with one foot, she tore off small pieces with her beak and swallowed them. The consistency wasn't as crunchy as she preferred, but it wasn't bad.

Osse smiled. "You are hungry."

Ahva chirped between bites.

"Guess it wouldn't kill me to eat something, too," he muttered.

He ate the rest of the flat bread. They finished their meal at about the same time, and the fatigue bar full again.

* * *

If Jael could trust her nose, she had gained ground on the trail of her missing cubs. The increasing strength of the scents hadn't been much, but she was closer. That meager encouragement drove her on.

She had trotted as fast as she could all day, even breaking into a run from time to time.

Her scents rising up from the trail her cubs had left showed a new human, female this time. If the pattern held, she'd pick up a couple more before one faded out. This steady increase meant either a town nearby or another of their common trails. Increasing chances of human encounters created a mixed assortment of blessings and curses.

Her cubs had gone this way. She had little choice but to follow their trail, even if that led her where bears ought not be.

Voices carried on the wind. Jael slowed. There were humans to watch for. She changed her course slightly to try to skirt around them. She would pick up the trail on the other side.

"Daddy, a bear!"

A collection of five humans watched her. As long as the three juveniles and two adults just watched, she didn't care.

"Wow! Can we go see it closer?" A different juvenile took a few steps closer.

"No, no." An adult restrained the juvenile. "We're close enough. That bear isn't your companion."

Good. You stay over there. I don't have time to deal with humans.

Jael was well beyond them before she cut back toward her original path. Her agitated nerves demanded more speed, but she kept her pace slower. Once she found Oba's and Dina's scent again, she'd do better.

* * *

Nagheed followed Rafayel out of Halfway Inn and stood nearby while the human prepared Ryder for travel.

After leaving the monks and the old woman yesterday, they'd passed through Vanya, noticing that the Bakhari caravan had already left. They'd made it all the way to the halfway point by nightfall. A nice dinner of roasted meat and root veggies and a good nap on a soft bed had restored

CHAPTER 12

their fatigue meters. Now with their bellies full of eggs, bacon, and bread, they were ready to finish the trip.

They started off at sunrise, and by the time the sun reached its zenith, they had encountered little more than a few birds and a couple rabbits.

Nagheed trotted alongside his human and the horse. He recognized the route, of course, but encountering it from the other direction gave him a feeling of déjà vu. A sparse tree canopy allowed sunlight to come through in shifting spots. The wind that ruffled the tree canopy also brought scents that reminded him of the Bakhari nomad camp a couple nights ago.

The wind carried indistinct voices to him. A man and a woman were calling out the same word or phrase repeatedly.

Chapter 13

Nagheed selected his Hear attribute, cocked his head to one side, and pricked up his ears.

"Levi!"

The couple called the name over and over. A lost kid maybe?

Nagheed sat and whined.

Rafayel turned Ryder back. "Lead the way."

After listening for a few more moments, Nagheed bounded on ahead. Ryder's hoofbeats stayed close behind.

"Levi! Levi, this is no time for games!"

"Levi!"

The voices grew louder until finally a man and a woman on the side of the road came into view. Their clothes were dull and unadorned but well-made. They wandered closer and further from the roadside calling the person's name.

Nagheed slowed as they approached.

Rafayel brought Ryder to a stop near Nagheed. "What's the matter?"

"My Lord, our son wandered off." The man came to the roadside but no closer.

The woman walked up behind her husband. "We've told him a hundred times to stay away from the road, but when we heard the caravan's music, he begged to come."

"We told him 'no,' of course." He pointed east. "Plenty of chores to do at home, and no time for any of that nomad nonsense."

"When I went out to find out why he was taking so long collecting eggs, he was nowhere to be found." The woman clutched a bundle of rags to her chest.

The man sighed. "I'm sure he went to see the caravan, and I have no doubt those nomads took him. They do that, you know."

Rafayel nodded. "I've heard that some do. How long ago did they pass through here?"

"Not long. An hour, maybe." The man shrugged.

"How old is your son?" Rafayel asked.

"He's eight," the man said.

Rafayel glanced down at Nagheed. "What do you think, Nagheed? Can we help them?"

Give that Track skill a workout. Nagheed woofed and wagged his tail.

"Excellent." He returned his attention to the parents. "Do you have something of his that Nagheed could get a scent from?"

The woman held out a bundle of rags to Rafayel. "His bear."

That's a bear? Here I thought your cleaning rags got tied in a knot.

"May I borrow that?" Rafayel pointed to the rags.

"Yes, of course, if it'll help." She handed it up to him.

"Nagheed is a stellar tracker. Where can I find you later?"

"Our farm is about a kilometer east of here." The man twitched his head eastward.

"I'll join you there as soon as I have news." Rafayel held the bundle of rags closer to Nagheed. "Find the lad."

We've done a few variations on this theme. At least I get tracking practice. Nagheed engaged Tracking and got a good whiff. He sniffed around, watching the scents rising from objects and floating on the air. One of them had to say "Target."

Clearly, the parents were there and each had "worried" attached to their scents. An entire sea of different "Nomads" had been through her recently. Then he saw it. A darker, bolder "Target" had goofed around on the side of the road for a while then left with the nomads. "Target" formed a path down the road.

As soon as he had a direction, Nagheed started off at a brisk trot with Rafayel and Ryder close behind.

The words "Target" and "Nomads" increased at the same rate. Accordion and tambourine music carried on the air long before the wagons were visible. When they came into view, Nagheed slowed.

They left the road and increased their speed to overtake the caravan. They'd passed half of the group when the word "Target" took over everything but led no further forward. Nagheed sat and whined.

"Good job, Nagheed. Heel." Rafayel urged Ryder on ahead and Nagheed fell in behind.

When they came even with the wagon in the lead, Rafayel matched the speed. The driver was a middle-aged man with tightly curled salt-and-pepper hair and a stern squint and his eyes. His name tag just said, "Nomad," but as Nagheed focused, "Annoyed" joined the scent cloud around him.

"Good afternoon, sir." Rafayel glanced his way.

CHAPTER 13

"We will be set up outside of Yavne tonight. You should come visit us then." The driver didn't even turn Rafayel's direction.

"Conveniently, I'm headed that way myself."

The driver shook his head. "We have no need for additional travelers."

Rafayel nodded. "Not my purpose for being here. I'm searching for a boy named Levi. Just a small boy. Eight years old according to his parents. They're quite worried about him."

"I'm sure I know nothing about him." The driver scowled.

Nagheed whined.

Rafayel gestured to Nagheed. "My dog disagrees, and I trust his nose."

The driver blew a sharp whistle and gradually slowed the entire caravan to a stop. "And so, what? You intend to invade our privacy and prove your dog right?"

You sound awfully modern for the Renaissance. Jake made a note on his feedback list.

He stood on the wagon's bench and drew a long, curved sword.

Nagheed picked Posture from his skills and darted forward far enough to stare the driver face to face. He growled and arched his shoulders as hair bristled down the center of his back. He waited for the combat music to start, but it stayed with their usual travel music of a plucked string instrument.

"You bring that cursed mutt to my caravan?" The driver shrank back as his nametag displayed a frownie face morale emoji.

Yeah, you'd better step back.

Rafayel rode a few steps ahead and turned back to face the driver. "I seek a lost child. That 'cursed mutt' is certain the boy is here. Turn the boy over, and the dog and I will leave."

"Just like that?" The driver glared. "You are one man and a dog. I have thirty men in my caravan."

Rafayel shrugged. "That's true. However, you left the Barony of Vanya a few kilometers back. You are now squarely in Yavne. I happen to be on excellent terms with the Baron of Yavne. Unless you prefer that he bar you from his territories, I would suggest you sheath the sword and we discuss this like proper gentlemen. What do you say?"

The driver continued trying to stare a hole through Rafayel's armor.

"Would you prefer to discuss it with Nagheed?" Rafayel gestured toward Nagheed.

Nagheed picked Posture again and flattened his ears. He growled.

The driver huffed. "You don't believe me? You try to tell me what to do? Is that it? Is that Nethanyan courtesy?"

"I am merely trying to find an eight-year-old boy who wandered away from his parents. He disappeared about the time your caravan pulled through the area. My dog is convinced he's here. What would you do if–"

He aimed his sword at Nagheed. "And I say he's not here. Are you saying I am less than a dog?"

Nagheed chose Posture again. He rounded his shoulders and bristled. *Let's go!*

Rafayel sighed. "Between Yavne and Vanya, there is nowhere for your caravan to go except this road. Toward the ocean, you'll find swamps, forests, and caves. Toward the

CHAPTER 13

mountains, nothing but forests, caves, and rocky foothills. I will be back, with the Yavne militia and the constable, and with or without your cooperation, this caravan will be searched. However, I have no doubt, that one of the consequences will include barring this caravan from ever crossing into Yavne ever again. Yavne is in a bottleneck between the ocean and the mountains. That's going to make your trade route from Vanya to Tel Caperna rather difficult. If I find the boy harmed, the consequence will be much more severe than simple banishment. Count on it."

"You threaten me?" His eyes narrowed.

"I warn you." Rafayel tipped his hat. "As a gentleman." He propped his right hand on his hip close to the butt of his gun. "I offer a compromise. Allow me to search one wagon. One wagon only. If I don't find the boy, I will go on. If I find the boy, you turn him over to me."

The driver smirked. "One wagon only?"

Rafayel nodded once. "That's what I said."

Nagheed stole a glance up at his human. *You trust this guy?*

The driver grinned. "Choose your wagon."

Rafayel leaned closer to Nagheed and held out the rag ball. "Nagheed, find Levi."

He selected Tracking. No pressure, though. Nagheed sniffed the rag ball and headed back along the row of wagons. Rafayel and the driver of the first wagon followed behind. Nagheed kept an eye on the scent words, until "target" overwhelmed everything else about halfway back. He went all the way to the end of the line then backtracked to where the scent was strongest. Nagheed sat and whined.

Rafayel dismounted and pointed at the wagon. "That one, right there."

The driver smirked and waved to the younger driver, also dubbed "Nomad." "Open the back."

No protest? No posturing? What are you hiding?

The young guy hopped down and jogged to the trailing end of the wagon then threw open the doors. Nagheed reared back on two legs and planted his front paws on the floor of the wagon, having to stretch considerably to get his nose above the floor. Jars were strapped to shelves along the walls, and parcels were piled on the floor, but there was no sign of the boy.

Rafayel and the lead driver argued, but Nagheed didn't listen.

I know I'm right. The boy is here. He hopped down and crouched low to go under the wagon and check his scent from the other side.

Nagheed stopped and turned back toward the wagon. *Hold up. I have to stretch to reach the floor where the door is but duck under the floor from the outside? Can you say "false bottom?"*

He ducked under the floor again and looked up. The word "Target" grayed out the entire area. Nagheed scratched at the floor and whined. When that didn't get his human's attention, he howled, sounding like an impressively large wolf.

Rafayel crouched and looked under. "You've never done that before."

Well, if you're not going to pay attention, what do I do?

"Nagheed, come."

He glanced back up at the floor, took two steps toward his human, glanced up at the floor again, then followed directions.

Rafayel indicated both drivers with a nod then twitched

his head toward the driver of the wagon behind them. "Keep an eye on them." He planted both hands flat on the doorframe of the wagon and pushed himself up.

"What do you think you're doing?" The lead driver demanded.

Rafayel leaned out of the opening. "Our agreement was that I could search one wagon. I'm searching. One wagon only."

The younger driver turned toward the leader. "But–"

The leader shushed him. "You buy whatever you damage."

Rafayel nodded. "Fair enough."

Nagheed kept a stern gaze on the three nomads facing him while thuds behind him suggested that Rafayel was reorganizing the parcels in the wagon.

Please find it. I have no doubt there's a hidden compartment.

"What have we here?" Rafayel asked.

Behind Nagheed, wood creaked.

"You do know that some of this is illegal in Nethanya." Rafayel leaned out.

The lead driver scowled. "Which is why it's packed away until we return to Bakhar and Ilion where it is perfectly legal."

"Be sure it stays there." He disappeared into the wagon again.

Wood creaked again.

The lead driver took a step forward, but when Nagheed growled, he backed up. "You had your search. Come down from there."

"I've searched the back half. I'll search up front," Rafayel said.

The kid has to be there.

More soft thuds of parcels being arranged preceded the wood creaking again.

"Not contraband, but definitely not supposed to be here." Rafayel's voice changed to a much calmer, much more comforting tone. "Easy there, lad. You're safe now. I'll get you to your mother and father again. Your mom sent your bear. That's a good boy."

Nagheed wagged his tail, earning a **+10 XP**. *I do like being right.*

The music changed to all brass and drums. The lead driver and the younger man who drove this wagon drew their swords while the fellow on the next wagon's bench whistled a loud, shrill note.

This dog's got bite. Nagheed settled into a slight crouch, ready to spring as soon as someone breathed wrong.

"Wait! Stop! What are you doing?" The old man whose granddaughter had gone missing on the docks ran into view along the side of the next wagon in the line. "Are you trying to make us a stink in the nostrils of Nethanya?"

On the one hand, Nagheed was itching to gain some more experience points and loot. On the other hand, thirty nomad guys and probably an equal number of women against him and Rafayel was probably a good way to get killed. He hadn't figured out about respawning in this game and didn't want to risk it now. Nagheed waited to find out if the old man could talk the others down. The combat music continued.

"What's this to you?" The younger man propped his fist on his hip.

The lead driver slapped the young one's head. "Respect your elders before he curses you to your mother's face."

CHAPTER 13

The old nomad slowed to a careful limp. They argued in harsh whispers Nagheed couldn't understand, but the combat music faded back to their traveling music. They were out of trouble. For the moment.

The old man approached. "Come on out of there, your Excellency, and do bring the boy."

Rafayel hopped out then lifted the boy down. "Thank you."

The lead driver squinted. "'Your Excellency?'"

"Of course." The old man wagged a finger in the lead driver's face. "You would do well to learn the faces of the nobility whose lands you travel through."

"You said you knew the baron." The lead driver propped his hand on his hip.

Rafayel nodded. "Does a man not know himself? How else would I have the authority to summon up the militia?"

The old man frowned. "Both of you return to your wagons now before you make us an even bigger stink in the nostrils of Nethanya than you have already. I will settle matters with His Excellency." He waited until both had left. "The arrogance of youth."

"We all have to be young once." Rafayel patted Levi's shoulder.

"And wisdom comes from experience, usually bad." The old man sighed.

Rafayel ruffled Levi's pale-colored hair. "This lad has gained some wisdom today. I would like to take him home."

The old man bit his upper lip. "And I would love to allow it, however, I fear the loss of potential income will result in, shall we say, less than favorable behavior toward the citizens of Yavne. This will result in punishment for my people – just punishment, I'm sure – and hardship for your people."

"Are you suggesting a ransom?" Rafayel took a half-step back.

"Not exactly." The old man smiled at the boy. "That would encourage more of what you received today and might actually endanger more people. This is not a thing either of us would like."

No, so you're going to ask us to do a favor to get the boy back when it was your people who unlawfully took him in the first place.

"I would suggest an exchange of properties. We returned to you what is yours." The old many gestured to Levi. "You return to us what is ours."

"And where do I come by your missing property?" Rafayel asked.

"Years ago, before the lands west of here became a swamp, I traveled here with my father."

And you think something's left after all this time?

"I hid a small box in the pocket of a tree. Above the pocket, I carved the symbol of our caravan. If you will retrieve that box and return it with the contents intact, I can convince the others that we benefited from returning your property, namely the child." He looked down at Levi.

See? I knew it.

"And what of the boy now?" Rafayel rested his hand on Levi's shoulder.

"If I have your word that the contents of the box will be restored to me by sunset tomorrow, you may return the boy to his parents now. I believe I can keep the others under control that long." He waved his hand toward the front of

CHAPTER 13

the caravan.

"Nagheed, are you up for a detour?" Rafayel pointed toward the west.

After trotting a few steps that way, Nagheed turned around and wagged his tail.

"Very good." Rafayel nodded and returned his attention to the old caravaner. "If your box is still there, I will return it to you with all haste."

"I am satisfied. We will meet outside the south gate before sunset tomorrow."

I'm up for looking, but what if the box is gone? You clearly haven't been a boy for many, many years. And why would you leave a box of valuable stuff in a tree anyway?

"I pray your box is still where you left it." Rafayel glanced toward the ocean.

The old man shrugged. "It is well hidden from the inhabitants of that swamp, and few others travel there."

Rafayel nodded. "Until tomorrow. Sooner if I can manage it."

"Safe travels, your Excellency."

Rafayel lifted Levi onto Ryder's back and climbed up into the saddle.

* * *

While Osse broke camp, Ahva supervised, and by "supervised" that meant practicing dropping rocks on things while making a bomb-drop noise. Finally, after what felt like eons of practice, she actually hit the things she was aiming for. She cawed a few times and repeated the performance.

The computer turned her notebook icon. She focused on it to open it up.

New skill! Bombing run.

Yes! "Good bird, Ahva."

Osse stirred wet embers from their campfire. "Did you get something?"

"Yes! Good bird." She landed and grabbed another rock. After a couple circuits around their campsite, she lined up for another run and dropped the rock. When it landed beyond the target, she hissed.

Osse chuckled. "Better luck next time." He slung his bag over his shoulder. "Let's get on the way. According to the sentry in Oni, we should reach the border town by nightfall. I'd like to get there sooner than that, so we don't have a repeat of the night we got to Oni." He held out his arm for a landing pad.

Ahva circled and landed on his head.

"You missed," Osse said.

Ahva settled in for a ride. "No." *I've got a better view from up here.*

He reached up and tapped her chest. "Come on. Off my head before your toenails get tangled in my hair."

Didn't think about that. When Ahva tried to step over to his hand, one foot came easily, but as he predicted, her other foot caught in his hair. She tugged and jiggled her foot until it came free and stepped over to his hand.

"See what I mean?" he asked.

Yeah, yeah. You were right. Don't rub it in. "Bite fingers today?"

Osse smirked. "No, please don't."

As he brought his hand down, Ahva stepped off onto his

CHAPTER 13

shoulder.

After one last glance around the campsite, Osse headed southwest down the road. Along the way, Ahva practiced talking and dropping rocks on targets. From time to time, she checked her character sheet and watched both skills and her flight skill improve.

She was on one of her bombing runs when a shrieky cackle somewhere nearby tensed every muscle she had. Ditching the rock, she bee-lined back to her human. Osse strung his bow and grabbed an arrow from his quiver. "Back, Ahva."

You got it. She crawled around to the back of his shirt collar and hung on.

"If you see anything, sing out."

"Yes!"

He moved ahead slowly, head on a swivel. Footfalls echoed from within the dense brush on the right side of the road. A scream, sounding far more natural than any noise their targets had made, came from the same direction. A sudden chill, communicated through the VR, shook Ahva from beak to tail feathers.

Osse stepped off the road and picked a path through the brush. "Who's there?"

Maniac laughter and thudding footfalls in the brush retreated toward the southwest at a high rate of speed.

The weird chill faded.

As Osse continued, light glinted off metal a little to their left.

"That one!" Ahva lean toward the metal.

Osse turned gradually. "I see it."

Still keeping an eye on the surroundings, he made his way toward the shiny object. Ahva leaned around the side of his head to watch.

A mannequin sat in the middle of a small clearing. A necklace reflected the dappled sunlight making it through the trees.

When Osse saw the mannequin, he sighed. "It's Saylou." He approached the mannequin and an inventory screen opened. The handful of slots were filled with a decorated falconer's glove, an embroidered shirt, and a necklace. He retrieved the loot and traced the intricate design on the glove cuff. "He was learning falconry, and his mother was a seamstress."

Ahva studied the detail. "Very pretty."

Osse nodded. "Now we know for sure that they took captives. We haven't seen Maaska or any sign of her. She might still be alive."

He tucked the loot into his bag and returned the arrow to his quiver. A few trips to and from the road to gather rocks – Ahva helped with smaller ones – resulted in a memorial for Saylou.

That accomplished very little.

They continue to the hike southwest. To her rotation of speech practice and bombing runs, Ahva added a patrol to watch for signs of Saylou's killer. Really, it was an excuse to spend more time on the wing. Her VR rig did an excellent job of communicating the thrill of rushing air. The artists gave her fascinating terrain to look at. She didn't have eagle eyesight, but the textures of the trees and the craggy foothills gained and lost clarity as she changed altitudes.

As usual, Osse continued their hike through lunch, sharing a meal of flatbread, nuts, and raisins with some canteen water to wash it down.

CHAPTER 13

After lunch she returned to her routine of bombing run practice, speech, and patrols. Ahva finished a round of bombing run practices and returned to Osse's shoulder.

They passed a large rock on the side of the road with that same weird symbol scratched in the rock.

Osse stopped for a moment. "They're still headed this way."

"Yes. There yet?"

"Not yet." He reached up and preened her head, which helped her fatigue recover a bit. "We've got to catch up to them before they kill anyone else."

"Uh we go!"

The sun was halfway to the horizon when Ahva spotted a collection of ten men camped on the sides of the road. She dropped her rock and smacked the target, a scraggly weed, with a satisfying thud before returning to Osse.

Osse came to the crest of a hill overlooking the campsite Ahva had spotted. The men, dressed identically in metal plate armor – except one who was a bit fancier with gold and purple accents – stood and formed a barrier across the road. Each one was armed with a massive shield and a short sword.

"What's this?" Osse slowed to a stop. "Did we cross into Antwen by mistake?"

Brother, I don't even have a good guess. "Disgusting eyeball?"

He snickered. "No, those are Antwen soldiers." He blew out a breath. "Let's hope they're not itching for a fight. We are kind of outnumbered. Let's find out what they want." He started forward again.

Chapter 14

After returning Levi to his parents at the farm, Nagheed followed Ryder and Rafayel back to the road and across to the other side closer to the ocean. The ground went steadily downhill until it leveled out and grew thicker with trees. The trees had stringy bark and wide trunks that tapered toward the canopy. The ground got muddier and squishier, and before long, Nagheed's feet were covered in black goo.

He looked up at Ryder. *I get the feeling this is not a good place for a horse. Dog or human, either, but definitely not a horse.*

"We need to find a safe place for Ryder. If we leave him tethered to a tree, I have no doubt the caravan will suddenly acquire a gray Nethanyan horse." Rafayel stopped and dismounted. "Seems to me I remember an old shack north of here."

They retreated out of the muck and turned north. About a half kilometer away, Nagheed spotted half-rotted building even worse than Vehira's shack.

Rafayel pointed. "There it is. That's the one."

Whatever you do, Ryder, don't sneeze.

After Rafayel secured some supplies and his weapons,

CHAPTER 14

they left Ryder at what was left of the shack and trudged into the swamp, taking a path that kept them out of the worst of the mud.

"Almost like trying to breathe underwater here." Rafayel slapped the back of his hand. "Blasted mosquitoes." He swiped at something in the air. "Be glad of your heavy fur."

A low, rumbling groan came from somewhere nearby. Rafayel froze then drew his sword with one hand and his pistol with the other. "Be alert. That sounded like an alligator."

Great. Who wouldn't want to fight gators?

The music changed over to the brass and drum tune as five small alligators climbed out of the water. Their nametags read "Caiman," each in a different font.

While the miniature alligators ran forward, Nagheed started a flanking move to the right.

Rafayel took aim with his pistol and pegged a caiman between the eyes. It became a mannequin. The remaining four split up. Two continued toward Rafayel, and the others turned toward Nagheed. After he circled a quarter of the way around, Nagheed held his ground and waited for the caimans to come into range.

As soon as they were close enough, Nagheed leapt over them. The second he landed, Nagheed bit the tail of the caiman on the left and swung it into a tree trunk. The other caiman snapped at his legs and got a mouthful of muddy fur. Swinging his head back around the other way, Nagheed smacked the caiman snapping at him with the one he had by the tail. The one snapping at him rolled away. A second impact with the tree turned the one he had by the tail into a mannequin.

Nearby, Rafayel fired his pistol again. A horn sounded, and five larger alligators crawled out of the swamp muck.

No way! Give the dog a chance!

The last caiman rolled back to its feet and charged Nagheed.

It worked once. Let's try it again.

Nagheed leapt over the caiman, but when he went for its tail, the caiman whipped around to face him.

Another, much larger alligator crawled out of the swamp. This one had a nametag that dubbed it "Augmented Gator."

And what does that mean?

The caiman charged again, jaws wide open. Nagheed jumped over it and went for the tail. When the caiman spun toward him, he clamped his jaws on the caiman's neck. He bit down as hard as he could until a crack reverberated through its body and a mannequin formed.

The gators hustled forward faster than Nagheed expected. Each one was at least three meters long, and their scales were heavier. He backed up. How could he take on something that big? He had no chance of tossing one at a tree, and the dense scales were probably more than he could bite through. Where was such a creature vulnerable? The belly?

Before they got close enough, Nagheed retreated to Rafayel who was reloading his pistol.

The augmented gator, twice the size of the others, caught up to last gator and dragged it into the murky water.

Is that thing friendly?

"Nagheed, don't attack the augmented gator until we know more." Rafayel took aim at the nearest gator and landed the shot between its eyes. He started reloading.

I hear you, but funny that you think it real dog would.

CHAPTER 14

A mannequin appeared at the edge of the water, and the augmented gator burst out of the muck and hit the ground running. It caught the next gator in seconds.

How can it be that fast?

A moment later, the augmented gator cracked that gator's neck.

Augmented Gator hustled after the third gator. The nearest was almost in range, but Rafayel was still reloading. Nagheed bristled and growled. He stalked forward, interposing himself between Rafayel and the gator.

I should be faster. On land, anyway.

He launched himself in the air and landed left of the gator's belly. The gator turned toward him, and Nagheed sprang again, narrowly missing a mouthful spiky teeth. He landed on the opposite side and waited for the gator to turn. Before he could jump again, the augmented gator arrived and cracked the gator's neck in one bite.

The combat music faded and the plucked instrumental returned. Nagheed trotted to Rafayel.

Rafayel held his hand in front of Nagheed's face. "Stay calm, Nagheed. I don't think it means to hurt us."

The augmented gator turned toward them. "She. I am not an it."

It talks? That's a little weird.

Rafayel's jaw dropped, but he recovered quickly. "I'm terribly sorry, madam. I was not aware."

"No. Most humans have not studied their herpetology."

Nagheed leaned toward the augmented gator and took a good sniff. "Swamp muck" still overwhelmed everything.

Rafayel tucked his pistol into his belt then removed his hat and bowed. "Forgive my poor manners. I am Baron

Rafayel Dorcas, and this fine fellow is Nagheed. We are most grateful for your assistance."

"My name is—" She groaned and grumbled in multiple pitches. "But you may call me Allie."

"A pleasure to make your acquaintance, Allie."

You don't find it slightly odd that we're having a cordial conversation with a large alligator?

"Is this your domain?" Rafayel took in the entire swamp with a sweep of his hand.

"I do live here, but I wouldn't say that I'm the lady of the land." Allie flattened herself on the ground, crossing her front feet under her chin. "What brings you here? We don't get many humans who venture into the swamp."

"I'm on an errand to retrieve a box from a hollow in a tree." Rafayel crouched.

Allie tipped her head to one side. "An odd thing, a baron doing a simple fetch chore."

Rafayel nodded. "Ransom for a kidnapped child. The parents are farmers."

"I understand. I believe I know the tree you are searching for. It has fallen, and it's half-rotten, but there is a box in it." Allie glanced to the west.

"That must be the one." Rafayel followed her gaze. "Could you direct us?"

Her tail swished to one side. "I will bring you straight to it and guarantee you safe passage there and back to your horse."

In exchange for what? Surely, you're not helping us out of the goodness of your scaly heart.

"Most generous." Rafayel nodded once.

Allie huffed. "Perhaps, but I do need your help."

CHAPTER 14

Here it comes.

"Of course. How may I assist you?" Rafayel asked.

"It's rather delicate, but I can't effect the repair myself." She scooted forward and spoke softly. "My augmentations gave me speech, speed, strength, and improved eyesight, but not opposable digits."

Rafayel glanced away. "Hence the need for a human."

"Yes, indeed. I'm afraid the battery that powers my right eye shook loose recently. It's still within its case, but it's rattling around. Enough to drive an old gator batty." She rolled her eyes. "I would be obliged if you could put the battery back in its place. No human I have encountered has been willing to assist."

"A battery?" he asked.

"An ancient piece of technology, from before the Great Massacre. For our purpose, no more complicated than sliding your sword into its sheath the correct direction."

"I see." Rafayel nodded. "How is the task done?"

Ancient tech? So, that Great Massacre you read about earlier was not relatively recent history. How much time has passed since the collapse?

Allie harrumphed. "Simply open the battery door, press the battery into place – it only fits one direction – then close the door."

Rafayel shrugged. "That sounds easy enough."

"It is. Except for one small detail."

The battery hatch is in your mouth?

Allie looked away. "The door for the battery is near the hinge of my upper jaw."

Ha! Got it in one!

"I can understand why that might make some people

nervous, but I am willing to help you." He crab-walked forward.

And soon all will call you Lefty.

Allie's eyes filled with tears. "Thank you. It is here, on the right. I promise I will not close my jaw." She opened her mouth wide.

As Rafayel approached the massive gator, Nagheed hung back. *Yup, you are certifiable.*

Rafayel crouched in front of the Augmented Gator and braced himself with one hand on her shoulder while he leaned over and moved a small lever. A panel, like the hatch on a handheld video game, dropped down and a metal cylinder fell into Rafayel's hand. The cylinder had a flaky coating of rust.

Rafayel turned it over in his hand. "I'm afraid this battery is showing corrosion. Is it supposed to be like that?"

"'O. 'ot 'u'ose 'o 'ook 'ike 'at."

"I believe I have an intact one in my bag." He swung his pack off his shoulder and fished out the battery they had found on the maniac. "Yes, this is about the right size. Let's find out if it fits."

Handy that they're all the same size.

"'Ank 'ou."

He snapped it in place. "Like it's meant to be there." He secured the battery hatch then stepped away.

Once he was clear, Allie's toothy grin snapped shut. She blinked several times. "So much better. Thank you very much."

"You're quite welcome." Rafayel stood and shouldered his pack.

"Come with me. I'll show you where the tree fell. Then

we'll return you to your horse and send you on your way." Allie turned and lumbered south. "I'm afraid your dog is still a little bit frightened of me."

Rafayel grinned. "He is rather young, and it's not every day that one meets a wonderfully courteous alligator."

"That is true."

His smile faded. "What's more, lately we have found other creatures that we believe to be human, but may not be, with glowing body parts, fantastic speed, amazing strength, and a most foul disposition."

"Oh dear." Allie rumbled. "That means Atrac has gained dominance, and her Priestess has done something unfortunate to Elef's Temple, likely the main one."

Rafayel adjusted his pack. "My plans are to collect some help and head across to Ilion to fix the problem, if I can. Would you like to come along?"

What? The player should get a say on big issues like this.

Allie groaned. "I'm afraid not. I have grown old. Today's excitement is more than I have done in over a month, and to my shame, I must admit my reasons were not entirely altruistic."

"I understand. I am grateful for your help nevertheless." He paused and followed behind Allie for a few steps through a narrow path of relatively dry ground before hustling to walk alongside again. "I've never been to Elef's Temple. Do you have any hints, any suggestions?"

She waded through some shallow water. "Without knowing what the priestess did, I'm afraid I would only be guessing. I would suggest, however, that you keep any more of those batteries, crystals, and other such artifacts. You never know when they'll be handy. Crystals determine the strength of the augmentations. Batteries power them."

"And the melted colored things?" Rafayel produced one from his pack and held it where she could see it.

She blinked a few times. "Building materials."

"Thank you. I'd wondered." He slid it into his pack again.

"Along those lines, we neglected to check those mannequins." Allie opened her mouth wide then snapped it shut. "They won't likely contain any batteries or crystals, but I understand your people use those shiny clear discs."

"Yes, rounds." Rafayel patted a pouch on his belt. "They are useful in our society."

Where would alligators keep a pile of coins? Ate them?

"We'll check on the way back. We have to go through there to get you to your horse in any case."

Hopefully, the area didn't reset after we left.

They came to a fallen tree. A small box covered with moss and mold peeked out of the decaying wood.

Allie nudged the tree with her snout. "There it is. Your box."

Rafayel strode forward and pulled the box out of the cavity in the tree. He brushed off enough muck and grime to confirm the caravan's symbol on the top. "Excellent. Thank you. I'm sure this is what we need."

"Good. Next the mannequins. Then your horse."

Rafayel gestured. "After you."

Nagheed followed them back out.

* * *

Jael finished off the jerky and bread she'd acquired from some sleeping campers. Her gut still rumbled, but the bag

CHAPTER 14

didn't even have an extra crumb for her. She'd keep her eyes open for a berry bush, but for now, she had to get moving. Leaving the bag behind, Jael sniffed around to find the strongest scent of her cubs. Once she found the best direction, she headed out at a jog. The sun hid behind clouds today. Without the evidence of the time, the day hadn't moved much at all. At least the sun didn't beat down on her dark fur. The rolling grassland was long on grass and short on shade trees.

Human voices carried on the wind, all male adult humans. They'd either be harmless, or they'd challenge each other to a foolish game of "annoy the grizzly." She hoped for the former, but her tumbling guts had her ready for the latter.

When the first rock sailed past her nose, she had her answer. The edges of her view lit red. The second hit her side hard enough to sting.

Jael wasted no time trying to challenge the humans. First of all, the odds were terrible. Second, she had more important things to do than become the subject of a bear hunt after defending herself against five idiots and being branded a "vicious bear."

She engaged Sprint, coming up to her full speed in seconds.

* * *

To get a good view of the road and the men blocking it and yet stay out of Osse's way, Ahva launched off his shoulder and circled above him. She stopped at the roadside, picked up a rock, and resumed circling. If the men ahead proved to be trouble, she wanted to be prepared.

In one of her close passes, Osse turned to track with her as she flew. "Don't start anything."

I don't plan to, but I don't want to be caught unaware either. She made another tight loop around him. "No." Weirdly, she only sounded slightly muffled talking around a stone in her beak.

When they came near the group, the one with the gold-and-purple-accented armor took a few steps forward and held his hand palm out. "That's far enough."

"I'm on my way to Nkamo. May I pass?" Osse asked.

The guard's smile belonged on a wolf sneaking into the sheepfold. "You passed the border. This is Antwen. We're collecting tolls."

"There's a Bakhari city nearby. How can this be Antwen?"

"Because it is." He sneered. "This road curves down into Antwen and then back up again into Bakhar. Pay the toll so you can pass by, and you'll come to your city in plenty of time."

"How much is the toll?" Osse asked.

"Twenty-five caps, that's Antwen currency."

Highway robbery. Literally.

Osse frowned and patted at his bag. "I have no Antwen money, and nothing like twenty-five even in Bakhari money."

"Then I guess you can't pass this way."

Extortion, that's what this is. Ahva lined up for a bombing run. *Pilot to bombardier. Open the bomb bay doors.*

"Ahva, come here. We're going a different way." Osse held up his arm for a landing pad.

I guess one boy with a bow and a rock-dropping crow are not much of a match for that many guys in plate armor. Ahva

CHAPTER 14

wheeled around and dropped her rock once she was clear of the soldiers. Then she returned to Osse and landed on his arm. "Disgusting eyeball!"

"If they're charging that much money just to pass through that chunk of road, I completely agree." Osse turned to the north and jogged through the brush and tall grasses lining the roadside. "We'll get enough trees and brush between us and them and loop around to catch up to the roadway a little further on."

There was only one problem with his theory.

Ahva imitated the laugh of the maniacs they'd been trailing.

Osse shuddered. "Of all the sounds you've learned, I wish you hadn't picked up that one."

Another laugh, from a real maniac, came from somewhere ahead and on the right.

Osse froze. "That wasn't you, was it?"

"No."

Footsteps belonging to a dark blur ran across their path behind them. Osse spun toward the sound but only waving shrubs and grasses marked the passage of whatever was.

While they were turned that way, it ran past behind them again.

Osse strung his bow. "Ahva, try to spot it from the air. If you do, circle it close so I know where it is. Stay out of reach."

Good plan, human. Ahva took off from his shoulder and spiraled up to a reasonable altitude.

The brush was dense in clumps and becoming denser toward the north. Movement drew her eye. A bipedal humanoid danced around a mannequin wearing a small crown. Ahva tightened her circle and flew a loop only twice her wingspan.

A bird could get dizzy doing it this way. If I reverse directions, will I unwind?

In part of her loop, she caught glimpses of her human making his way closer. When she couldn't see Osse, she turned her attention to the ground. The ragged creature dancing around the mannequin scooped up a stick.

The edge of the screen turned red.

Osse was almost there. Just a few dozen more meters, but dense brush would block his view of the enemy.

A hard strike on her tail threw Ahva off balance. She tumbled and smacked into the brush, losing not quite a third of her health when the screen flashed red. She floundered and caught herself, pulling herself up onto a branch.

"Stay there, Ahva." Osse called.

"Ow." She shook herself. *No problem there.*

An arrow sailed into the clearing, striking the maniac between the collarbones. The creature's health bar dropped by nearly half. Without missing a beat, it yanked the arrow free, threw it aside, and charged. A second arrow missed when the creature twisted. Its gait was unaffected. A third arrow drove into its arm.

Chapter 15

As the maniac passed out of Ahva's sight, she leapt into the air, careful to stay out of the path Osse's arrows traveled through.

A loud thud and rustling of branches came from Ahva's right. She wheeled around and found the maniac pinning Osse to the ground. The back of the creature's neck glowed. Its hand was drawn back to strike at Osse's face.

Ahva scanned the ground, but she found no rocks small enough for her to pick up and yet large enough to do some damage. The few twigs she found didn't have enough mass to be much more than annoying.

The maniac punched Osse's face, which cost him a handful of points.

Osse pushed against the creature with one hand while reaching for a knife with the other.

Ahva looped around again. *There's gotta be some way I can help him.*

Going to the Antwen soldiers collecting tolls for help would take too long, and they probably wouldn't help anyway, at least not without charging for the service. She wasn't an eagle, so she didn't have particularly strong talons. She did, though, have a beak with a good point.

Not razor-sharp, but certainly enough to get something's attention.

Osse blocked the maniac's second and third punches but only barely.

She selected the skill menu, but the only attack skills she owned were Bombing Run and Bite. *Not much help there.* She picked Problem Solving and the Power attribute. Neither were all that fantastic, but maybe together, they'd amount to something worthwhile. *What could she do?*

A thought bubble appeared. "Hmm... What might happen if I attack that glowing thing in its neck. My beak is pretty pointy."

Yep, that's what I thought, too! Ahva dove and landed on the back of the creature's head. She craned her head back and drove the point of her beak into the glowing spot on the maniac's neck. When nothing happened, she hissed.

Well, that was anticlimactic. If at first you don't succeed, don't go base jumping. Let's try again.

It flinched, and she repeated the attack, scoring a few points of damage about half the time. Maybe not her most effective attack, but it was surely getting some attention. Forgetting Osse for the moment, it swept both hands up and backward. She ducked under both swipes as Osse shoved it off of him.

As the creature reeled back, Ahva flew off to the nearest tree. Osse scrambled to his feet and grabbed his knife.

The maniac's entire body twitched, tossing it off balance for a moment. Once it recovered, it charged at Osse, and as it drew close, the maniac staggered. Its whole body shuddered. Osse slashed with his knife, doing enough damage to change the maniac's health bar yellow.

The maniac stumbled back a couple steps and pressed a

hand to the back of its neck as another shudder rattled its body.

It laughed then turned and ran.

"Bye!" Ahva called.

The notebook near her icon turned blue, and she focused on it. The book flipped open and grew larger.

New skill acquired: Peck.

Coool. I can do woodpecker impersonations now!

Osse stayed still, breathing hard and gripping his knife until the giggling had faded completely. He returned the knife to his belt and searched in the brush until he came up with his bow.

"You okay, Ahva?" Osse sat in the clearing near the mannequin and rested his forehead on his palm.

Although flew over and landed on his knee. "Yes. Maybe."

"Thanks for your help." He dug out his herb jars and canteen. "Whatever you did caused more damage than my arrows or my knife."

I think I hit it in the right place. Gotta aim for the glowing bit. "You okay?"

He smiled. "I think so. Maybe a couple bangs and bruises, but nothing much. Certainly not as bad as it could have been if you hadn't been here."

"Good bird."

Osse preened the back of her head, restoring a few fatigue points. "Very good bird." He fished out a couple jars of herbs and a jar with some greasy goo in it. After sprinkling some herbs on the palm of his hand, he scooped out an acorn-sized amount of the goo and mixed it all together before applying it to his bruises and scrapes.

"Hold still." He looked at the tiny amount left in his hand.

"I'm going to have to ruffle your feathers a bit to find out where you were hurt."

Easier than that. She twisted around and used her beak to left the feathers away from the minor hurts she had from colliding with the shrubbery.

"That helps." He applied the remaining goo, which restored her health, and offered his hand for perch. Osse shifted around to kneel beside the mannequin. "The chief's older son."

The inventory window opened. Inside, he found a simple crown made of gold and a pouch full of chips. Both went into his bag.

Osse searched the area and found the arrows he had shot. One was broken, but the others went back in his quiver.

"Can you scout around a bit? Spot that thing from the air?"

"Yeah." Ahva spiraled upward and flew several loops around, each bigger than the one before. She watched the ground, when she could see it, and tried to spot movement where the trees were dense. Plant life and plenty of it, but nothing that could be considered alive, or nearly so. The edges of her view were still red, so the threat was still too real. Where was that thing? It wasn't exactly colored for decent camouflage. After a few more rounds, the red edges faded. She returned to Osse.

"Anything?" He held out his arm for her to land on.

"No. Bye-bye." She imitated the maniac's laugh.

"That thing does move fast."

The screen edge turned green, and she focused on the notebook to open it.

Level Up, Ahva!

CHAPTER 15

About time! Man, this game is stingy with leveling. She opened her character screen to allocate her points.

Name: Ahva **Species:** Corvid – Crow
Class: Scout Level 3 **Gender:** F

Attributes

Attribute	Current	Skill	Current
Power	10	Sneak	24
Speed	41	Detect Enemy	33
Cleverness	64	Signal Human	29
Endurance	18	Stay Alert	17
Agility	60	Sound Alarm	20
Charm	35	Patrol	43
Vitality	5	Trek	30
Sight	63	Long Distance Mvmt	30
Smell	5	Sprint	20
Hearing	23	Nonverbal Communication	23
Health	33	Camo	19
Encumbrance 0 out of 5 oz		Fly	50
		Speech	51
		Problem-Solving	14
		Bite	17
		Bombing Run	20
		Peck	15

Her skills were coming along rather nicely. The game's leveling algorithms reeked, but practicing skills paid off. Some of her attributes, though, wow, did they need work. She threw all five points into vitality and closed the window.

Osse started walking again.

* * *

Jael yawned then yawned again. Her weighted eyelids closed for the second time before she snapped awake. The sun had passed midday by the slimmest margin, and she had to keep going. After traveling by moonlight for most of the night, her mind and body begged for sleep. Real sleep, not that one-eye-open nonsense she'd tried last night.

Yet she couldn't stop. If she did, the cubs would get further away. Without sleep, though, she was going to miss clues. She'd spend weeks traveling the wrong way, and by the time she backtracked, they'd be gone without a trace.

Jael scanned the surrounding terrain. A stand of brush beckoned for her to seek shelter from the sun there. She trudged toward the shrubs and scraggly trees, stumbling every few steps. Once safe undercover, she collapsed and fell asleep in moments.

* * *

Nagheed kept pace with Rafayel as they left the swamp for more solid ground. He glanced back over his shoulder at the augmented gator. Allie had turned away from them already and was slinking back into the muck and mire that was her home.

See you later, gator.

Mud weighed down the fur on Nagheed's legs, and the smell! It must have been impressive. The scents rising off of everything said only "swamp muck." A flatulent skunk eating rotten eggs probably compared favorably. Rafayel's boots, were likewise covered with swamp residue. At least

CHAPTER 15

Ryder was relatively clean.

Rafayel grimaced. "I do believe we are going to need a stop at the creek before we actually head in."

Nagheed woofed. *You're not exactly a bouquet of roses there, pal.*

"First, though, let's get this box back to the caravan. Then we can visit the stream. Maybe we'll be sleeping in our own beds tonight."

I like that plan.

When Rafayel urged Ryder into a swift canter, Nagheed stayed alongside.

Nagheed tried to get a whiff of the caravan as they drew nearer to the road, but all he could smell was swamp mud. Their accordion music declared their presence a quarter of an hour, game time, before they were actually visible.

"There they are." Rafayel pointed up ahead.

Nagheed stretched, but he didn't have half of his human's height, especially with Rafayel on the back of Ryder.

As they crested a low hill, he got his first glimpse of the top edges of the wagons. They were stopped on the road. Waiting for them, getting into more mischief, or taking care of some other business?

They drew near and a shrill whistle repeated itself down the line of wagons. From each, men bearing weapons ranging from repurposed farm implements through well-made swords formed a perimeter guard. The old man pushed his way through the line.

Only a half-dozen meters away, Rafayel reined in Ryder and dismounted. "I have something for you."

"You were able to find it? After all these years?" The old man took a few steps forward and held out his hand.

"With the help of a cordial alligator, it was actually easy to find." Rafayel fished the box out of his pack. "Is this what you wanted?"

Hard to tell with so much mess on it, isn't it?

"Did you open it?" The old man reached for the box.

Rafayel handed the box to the old man. "Not my property."

Gingerly, as if the slightest misstep would destroy it, he lifted the box out of Rafayel's hand. He withdrew an old key from a pocket hidden in his shirt. After sliding the old key into the lock and giving it a half-turn, he hugged the box to his chest and pried at the lid with weathered fingernails. The lid creaked as it opened, but it only came open about half way. The old man lifted the box closer to his face and squinted into the opening. "Yes, rounds, chips, and gems. You're as good as your word."

"Sometimes that's all a man has to go on. Does that settle all accounts?" Rafayel pointed to the box.

"I do believe so." He peeked into the box again and smiled. "I can convince the men that the contents of this box easily replace whatever we might have gotten from the boy."

He closed the lid of the box, but one corner stayed slightly propped up. "What will you do now?"

"Continue on our journey. I have more preparations before we can head across to Ilion. Still planning to camp outside of Yavne?"

The old man shrugged. "That decision rests with others. I go where the caravan goes."

Funny how your answers don't quite answer the questions.

Rafayel took a step back. "I won't keep you from your destination. I'm rather anxious to sleep in my own bed tonight, actually."

"And you still have a bit of a journey ahead of you, don't you?"

"Not too far." Rafayel slid his foot in the stirrup and pulled himself up into the saddle. "In spite of this detour, I still anticipate getting home by nightfall. Safe travels."

"Be wary. The further east you go, the more likely you are to find adversaries."

Rafayel glanced down at Nagheed. "I'll bear that in mind. Thank you."

He urged the horse into a quick walk. Nagheed trotted alongside.

* * *

Ahva circled over Osse, watching for signs of their crazy attacker. Nothing so far, but as fast as those things moved, that didn't mean much. Their wide arc through the brush and shrubbery brought them back to the road well out of sight of the Antwen soldiers. The cleared area on both sides of the road meant better sight lines. Since her fatigue meter had turned yellow five minutes ago, she could afford to take a rest. Ahva spiraled down for a landing on Osse's outstretched arm.

"Any sign of the city?" Osse asked.

"There soon!" Ahva crawled up the sleeve of his shirt to his shoulder.

Osse turned toward the setting sun. "Good. I really don't want to camp in the open tonight."

No kidding. Who knows where your attacker disappeared to?

"I'm afraid our detour around the tollbooth slowed us

down a little too much." Osse sighed and adjusted the strap of his bag. "Hang on tight. I'm going to jog for a while."

Not a bad idea in the daylight, but that means I'll be flying. So much for getting a bit of rest.

As Osse pushed off from the ground, Ahva took to her wings and flew long skinny loops from Osse out about a kilometer then back to him again. She glided as much as possible to keep the fatigue meter happy. His long strides covered ground at a fantastic rate. He might not medal in the Olympics, but Ahva found her return trips much shorter than the trips out.

When the sun neared the horizon, Ahva caught a glimpse of rooftops too densely packed to be a farmhouse or rural village. The buildings were very box-shaped with small windows and narrower than average doors. The rooftops were flat, and some had a short table and a few low chairs. Here and there, a dome poked out of the top of the roof. About half of the buildings had stone walls. The rest had been covered over in some kind of stucco.

Was that the city they were aiming for? She flew further away from Osse and found a high wall around an area. She banked into a turn and followed the wall around. The town was a decent size, but not nearly the huge monstrosity that was Fola. Only few people were out in the streets, hardly the bustling metropolis she would have expected. Where was everyone?

The sections of the city were easy to pick out. The affluent section was to the southwest, evidenced by well-kept, large structures. Nearly all of the buildings were stucco and painted in fun colors like red, green, and yellow. The opposite end of the socio-economic strata was not diagonally opposite like she expected, but southeast. Structures there were raw stone and had pockmarked walls that had never been shown a paintbrush. The rest of the town split the difference and included various shops. These had been painted some shade of brown or gray at some point, but many could use an exterior remodel.

After completing her tour, Ahva flew back down the path and found Osse sitting on the roadside taking a swig out of his canteen. She angled down for a landing on his knee.

Turning back toward the city, she got a tight grip on the seam of his pants and flapped her wings. "Loo' at da bird!"

"Found the city?" Osse took another drink.

"Yes."

He offered her a cap full of water. "Let me catch my breath, and then we'll head out and hopefully get there before dark."

Sooner would be better. I don't want to encounter that thing. At least, not until you've leveled up a few or I've improved my combat skills. Or both. Both would be good.

After his breathing slowed down to normal, Osse offered Ahva his hand. She hopped over and then ran up to his shoulder. He stood up and headed toward the city at a quick pace, but didn't start running again.

Ahva watched the terrain go by ticking off landmarks as they went. As soon as the top of the wall and the tops of the roofs came into view, the tension in Osse's shoulders faded. "We made it."

Not yet, silly human. Soon, but not yet.

Another half hour of quick hiking brought them to the gate. Although they hadn't closed up for the night, a guard stepped into their path and gripped the hilt of his sword.

"What's your business?"

Osse took a step back. "Just traveling. I would prefer to sleep at an inn. I'm almost out of food and we were attacked on the way by some kind of monster."

"I can understand that." He let go of his sword and nodded. "How'd you get past the tollbooth?"

Osse traced a half-circle in the air with his hand. "We went around. That's when we ran into the monster."

"Not surprised." The guard leaned closer. "With Antwen blocking the road, we haven't been able to do our proper patrols." He pointed through the gate with his thumb. "There are several inns in town."

"Thank you." Osse bowed and headed into the city.

The buildings in this part of the town were sturdy enough but most could use a fresh coat of paint. A wet rag on the small, dust-gray, rippled glass windows wouldn't hurt anything either.

Osse stopped at the first one, The Puzzled Potato. The sign showed a potato with a couple pieces missing on a brilliant red background, probably the only part of the building that didn't need new paint.

Good to know the priorities.

Osse stepped into the tavern. Five tables, each with a collection of four chairs, were arrayed across the near wall. Opposite, a long counter made of dark wood hosted a handful of stools. Two other doors led out of the room. One went down a long corridor to the right of the bar. The other was a swinging door behind the bar.

Huh. Not the interior I expected for the given exterior. I was expecting more rustic, perhaps.

The bartender leaned on the counter and spoke with

CHAPTER 15

the only other occupant, a somewhat homely woman who perched on one of the stools.

The bartender stood straighter. "Hello there. You wanting dinner or room?"

"Both if that's possible. How much are they?"

"Room is five chips. Per night. Dinner is barley and antelope, one chip."

Osse hustled over as he fished his coin purse out of the bag. He shook out six copper-etched green chips and plopped them on the counter.

Ahva squinted at them. *The circuit board cutouts for money still boggles the brain. Where did they get circuit boards, and why, oh why are they using them as money?*

The bartender took in the whole room with a sweep of his hand. "Find a spot. I'll bring your dinner out. When you're done, I'll show you to your room." He swept the chips into his hand and disappeared through the door behind him.

"Where's a good spot, Ahva." Osse looked around the room.

Ahva flew to the table in the corner of the room where they could keep an eye on the main door, the whole room, and both passages out.

"Nice choice." Osse sat with his back to the corner.

Shortly after, the bartender brought out a steaming bowl of grain with chunks of meat and carrots. A wooden spoon stuck out of the top of the bowl. He set the food down in front of Osse and then set a steaming mug next to the it. "You ain't man enough for a real drink, so it's tea for you."

"Tea is fine, thank you." Osse took a sip.

The bartender turned away.

"I am too man enough," Osse muttered.

Maybe, but if you think I'm dealing with a drunk NPC later ... Ahva hopped down to the table and tilted her head staring at the food.

"You might want to wait a bit. It's pretty hot. Don't worry, I'll leave enough for you."

Ahva leaned closer and snatched a piece of barley out of the bowl, swallowing it immediately. Her vision flashed red. She squawked and tried panting, but the red persisted. Her health bar lost a few points. Osse pulled out his canteen and poured her a cap full of water. She slurped the cool water down, and the red faded to normal.

"What did I tell you?"

"Ow. Pretty hot." *Okay, okay, you were right, but the fatigue meter is not happy just now.*

Osse dug in his bag again and pulled out a piece of crumbly bread. "Here. Nibble on that while your dinner cools off some."

Yum. Tasty. Ahva hissed.

He sighed. "I know. And I'll leave plenty for you, but that'll tide you over until your dinner's ready."

Ahva picked at the bread, making more mess than meal.

When Osse had finished half the bowl, he nodded. "Should be safe for bird beaks."

Ahva crept over to the bowl. She leaned closer, eyeing the barley.

Osse smiled. "I don't think it's going to jump at you."

It better not. She snatched a grain out of the bowl and held it in her beak figuring out if the temperature agreed with her before she swallowed it.

When no red tinged her vision, she returned to the bowl and ate her fill with gusto.

CHAPTER 15

When her crop was pleasantly stuffed and the fatigue meter looked better, she stepped back and let Osse finish the rest.

"Enough for you?"

Ahva nodded. "Good food."

"I'm glad you understand me. When I heard you speak the first time, I'd hoped you'd be one of the ones who could."

Just you wait until I get that Speech score over 100.

No sooner had he finished and the bartender had cleared their dishes, then the door opened to admit a man in heavily embroidered purple clothes and a weary expression.

The bartender held his hand up palm out. "Don't ask. Just don't ask."

The fancy-dressed man nodded in Osse's direction. "Just him?"

"Just him. Mayor, I told you I would let you know if any adventurous sorts stopped in."

"I'm sure he will do fine." The mayor's smile belonged on a fox in a hen house.

The bartender rolled his eyes. "He's a kid with a sentry bird."

The mayor strutted over and sat down without an invitation. "Son, how would you like to earn some serious money?"

"Doing what?" Osse sat up straighter.

"I'm sure you encountered the toll collectors on the road here."

Osse scooted his chair back from the table. "Yes, and we went the long way around."

"Most people won't do that. They turn around and go a different way. Or they give up and turn south into Antwen.

The toll is cheaper that way. As a result, most of the inns and many of the businesses are getting much less traffic." He held up one hand palm out. "I know what you're thinking. 'What about traffic from Nethanya.' We don't have many people coming this way from Nethanya. Most folks coming from Nethanya travel all the way up north to Tel Caperna and then cut across there to go to Fola. Nethanyans are not fond of Antwen, as you know."

Osse shrugged. "Actually, I don't know much about the politics between Nethanya and anyone."

"Take my word for it. Bad blood all around." He gritted his teeth. "The part of this that really grates is that Antwen is wrong. That road is solidly in Bakhar. If I can get a hold of the original map, showing the original boundaries, I could prove it."

"Sure." Osse nodded. "It's hard to argue with evidence."

So you think. Obviously yet you haven't spent much time on social media. Some people can argue with the wall.

"Exactly right. There's only one problem. The map is in the library vault where my predecessor also stored food up against a siege." The mayor grimaced.

"Then the library vault has been overrun by vermin of some sort?" Osse asked.

"Right. And for your troubles, should you retrieve the map for me, I would give you five hundred chips and you can keep any loot you recover while you're down there."

"What do you think, Ahva?" Osse offered Ahva his hand. She stepped onto his fingers. *What, so I get to do something other than ride on your shoulder, fly circles, and practice random skills? Of course, silly human.* "Yes."

Osse nodded. "We'll do it."

The computer turned her notebook blue, so she opened it.

Antwen Is Wrong #1: The Library Vault of Horrors. Retrieve the map.

Ha! Love it. She cawed. *#1, eh? How many parts to this progressive mission? They really should put a #1 of however-many-there-are.*

The mayor grinned like a kid at an all-you-can-eat candy shop. "That's great! I'll meet you in front of the library tomorrow morning right after sunup."

"Let's make that an hour after sunup. Ahva gets cranky without breakfast."

Hey! A bird's gotta eat. Gotta keep the fatigue meter happy.

The mayor pushed away from the table and stood. "Don't be late." He started to the door and left.

"Don't be late?" Osse rolled his eyes. "As if the monsters in the vault are going to be upset if we're late."

Maybe not upset, but let's not give them more opportunities to create smaller versions of themselves.

Osse finished his mug of tea and walked over to the bar.

"Take my advice. Don't even bother showing up at the library tomorrow. Six other adventurers have tried to clear that area. You can find their headstones in the graveyard."

Osse tilted his head to one side. "What killed them? Certainly not a few rats."

The bartender leaned closer. "The way I hear told, some kind of poison."

Osse opened his bag and dug through to the bottom. He frowned. "Is there a shop nearby that sells either pottery or herbalist supplies?"

"You'll find herbalist supplies a few shops down on the

left." The barkeeper pointed. "It's called Nightshades and Hemlocks. What you need that for?"

"Never start a journey unless you're properly prepared." Osse took a few steps toward the door then turned back over his shoulder. "I'll be back shortly."

Streets were relatively empty, more than expected at this hour of the evening.

"Let's hope they're still open." Osse strode to a shop that had a sign showing different plants.

When he opened the door, the shopkeeper stood there with key in hand. "We're closing. Are you browsing, or do you intend to buy something?"

"I need to buy some salve jars or vials."

"You an herbalist?" The merchant raised an eyebrow.

Ahva leaned forward. "Yes."

The merchant jumped back. "A crow? Why did you bring that in here?"

So I can curse you?

Osse scowled. "Ahva is my companion. Where I go, she goes. She won't hurt you. Do you have salve jars or vials?"

"What kind herbalist shop would I be without them?" The merchant snapped.

"Then let's complete the transaction, and I'll take my bird and go." Osse strutted to the counter and leaned his elbows on it.

"Salve jars are five for one chip. Vials are eight for one chip."

"Can I see one of each?" Osse took a quarter-sized piece of a circuit board out of his pouch.

The merchant heaved a sigh, but opened the box and took out a cork stoppered vial and a small jar with a lid that sat

CHAPTER 15

on top but didn't secure.

Osse frowned at the jar but picked up the vial. He handed the merchant the chip. "Eight vials please."

The merchant went back into the box and withdrew seven more vials then handed them all to Osse. He snatched the circuit board piece from Osse's hand. "What else do you need?"

"Noth – " His eyes widened. "Oh, I need a small bowl."

The merchant crossed to the room to another set of shelves and picked up a small ceramic bowl. "Will this do?"

Osse nodded. "It will serve. How much is it?"

"Two."

Osse paid the man and pocketed the bowl.

"What next?"

"The vials and bowl were all I needed." He secured his bag. "Thank you for staying open."

The merchant's smile was a little tight as Osse left.

"Friendly guy, wasn't he?" Osse glanced back at the shop.

Ahva hissed. "No good. Grouch!"

They returned to the inn, and the bartender showed them to a small room. Ahva had expected the inside to be as bad as the outside, but the room was really quite pleasant. It was a little sparse on decoration – the better to show off the art department's mastery of woodgrain, and the furniture was minimalist, but the homemade quilt on the bed was a nice touch.

For the rest of the evening, Osse mixed different herbal concoctions with the water in his canteen and filled the vials. The sun had set for a long time before Osse finished.

"Let's get some rest, Ahva. Tomorrow will be a long day."

As he stretched out on the bed, Ahva flew to the headboard

and perched there. She told the computer to go to sleep.

The screen went black, and a flock of sheep played volleyball against a sheepdog until the dog caught the ball in his teeth and popped it.

Ahva awoke the next morning when Osse groaned and stretched.

He sat up and yawned. "Are you ready for today?"

"Yes?" *Certain death. Small chance for victory. What could go wrong?*

He smiled. "I'll take that as a definite maybe."

After he collected his gear, Ahva fluttered to his shoulder.

Although the bartender was gone, the woman he had been talking to the night before served them a breakfast of eggs and two small muffins. "Are you really going to try to clear out the vault?"

Ahva squinted up at the woman. "Fierce!"

Osse smiled. "I'm going to try to retrieve the map. If I clear out the vault at the same time, bonus points for me."

She drew a breath through her teeth. "Be careful. There are many diseased animals down there and some of them use poison as an attack."

"Thank you for the warning. I think I'm fairly prepared." Osse patted his bag.

"Whichever god you worship, I suggest you offer a sacrifice before you go." She moseyed away before he could answer.

Osse split the muffin in half and scooped some eggs onto it, making an impromptu sandwich. He muttered, "Right, yeah, as if any of them are of any use." He split another biscuit in half and used it to scoop some of the eggs closer to Ahva then he set the biscuit-half nearby. "There you go.

CHAPTER 15

Breakfast for you."

"Thanks." Ahva hopped forward and scarfed down her breakfast while Osse took care of his.

As soon as they had finished, the woman returned to take their dishes.

Osse stood. "How do I get to the library from here?"

The woman set the dishes down and pointed. "The library is outside of the market. To get there, continue down the street until you get to Stitch in Time then turn left. That street will dead end at the library. You can't miss it."

Osse shouldered his bag. "Thank you. I'll be back tonight if I'm still in town."

"If you're still alive." She carried the dishes out.

You're almost as cheery as a mausoleum.

At this hour of the morning, the streets were completely empty. Apparently, no one in this town was an early riser except maybe the mayor.

Without a crowd to fight through, they made it to the library in record time.

The library was a tall, flat-roofed building with a domed overhang held up by marble columns at the door. A row of small windows ringed the building just lower than the roof line. Like the affluent part of the city, the library had stucco walls. These were painted a brilliant red.

The mayor, dressed in peacock blue and yellow, paced in front of the marble columns near the door. As they came closer, the mayor jogged to meet them. "You're early. I like that. No time like the present. Shall we?"

Osse gestured for him to lead the way.

The mayor led them through a small door. The inside of the library had been decked out in safari décor. The circulation desk in the middle of the room was an open-sided hut with a grass roof. Part of the wall directly opposite the door had been painted and textured to look like a tree trunk with branches spread across the ceiling and leaves hanging down into the room. Images of wild animals were painted along the walls above the level of the bookcases that lined every vertical surface and created a few new ones down the middle of the space. Detracting from the festive decorations, a layer of dust she could writer her name in covered everything.

They threaded their way through the shelving units to a door marked Employees Only in the back of the library. A key stuck out of the lock.

"Employees Only?" Holdover from the technology era, I'm guessing.

The mayor unlocked the door. "Through there and down the stairs. That takes you to the vault. The map is in room twenty-two which is the last one on the right side. I think. When you're finished, I'll be at town hall. That's around on the other side of the market."

"I'll take care of it." Osse nodded once.

The mayor clapped him on the shoulder. "I'll fire up the gas lights down there."

He left so quickly, Ahva expected of trail of flames in his wake.

Ahva clung tightly to Osse's collar when he opened the door and crept down the stairs.

Osse scowled and rubbed his nose. "Stinks down here."

I'll take your word for it. I don't pay for smellivision.

He paused and strung his bow then nocked an arrow. "That would've been stupid."

CHAPTER 15

Yep. Let's hope there are some rocks down here. Otherwise I may not be much help to you.

A whooshing sound preceded a warm light coming from the vault. Guttering shadows reflected off the walls for a few moments, then settled.

They reached the end of the stairs and found themselves in a passageway that ran left to right. About five meters to either side, perpendicular passages led away from them. Another was directly ahead of them.

"He said last room on the right, didn't he?" Osse asked.

"Yeah." Ahva leaned toward the right-hand passage.

Osse turned to the right and took the perpendicular passage. The doors, more numerous on the left side by two to one, had higher numbers.

"Think he might've gotten his left and right mixed up?" Osse stopped and scratched his head.

Ahva bobbed her head. *Unless the numbers get higher much faster. Or maybe if they skip around.*

They stalked forward, passing door number one on the right and doors nine and ten on the left. All three doors were closed. Something scrabbled on the hard stone floor behind the right doors. No sounds came from the left. Ahead, doors three and fourteen, if Ahva had her counts right, stood open. They no sooner passed doors two and eleven when a mass of gray erupted from door three and a pile of black boiled out of door fourteen.

Chapter 16

At first, she couldn't tell one creature from the other, but as Ahva stared, she made out individual forms of gray rats and black spiders. Both species were the size of a typical cat.

Osse backpedaled. As he took aim at the rat in the lead, the spiders overtook the rats in a flurry of clacking mandibles, hissing, biting, and clawing. Members of both species showed rapidly declining health bars. Osse held his fire until two large rats and a spider broke away from the main fracas and charged at them.

Before he could tell her, Ahva shifted around to the back of his neck where she'd be out of danger from his bow. Holding a couple arrows in his hand, he shot two in rapid succession then drew two more arrows from his quiver and loosed a third and a fourth. When he didn't reach for another arrow, she started scooting over to peek past his head, but she no sooner started moving than he made a hasty grab for the next couple arrows.

"Stay there until this is over, Ahva. They're coming two or three at a time." Osse shot the next two arrows and immediately drew two more. "Watch down the side corridor in case anything comes from that way."

CHAPTER 16

"Ahva watch!" She twisted her head around to get a better view that way.

Osse gasped and shot arrows as fast as he could draw them. In her peripheral vision, she checked his quiver. One arrow left. He drew it but didn't shoot.

Could she retrieve arrows? They were probably light enough, but could she carry something that unwieldy in her beak and still fly? Probably not without getting impaled. This corridor wasn't very wide.

Osse blew out a breath and returned the arrow to his quiver. "I think it's safe now."

She scooted around to his shoulder.

A couple dozen mannequins filled the corridor, looking like a kid had up-ended his toy box. Osse crept forward to the nearest mannequin. When they came close, the inventory screen popped open showing a few green and copper chips and a green crystal. All the rat mannequins contained a couple chips and either another crystal or melted piece of plastic. The spiders contained a blob of spider silk.

Okay, I get the spider silk, but where exactly were those rats carrying coins, crystals, and melty plastic? Marsupial rats?

If the game stayed true to form, all the mannequins of a given species would contain the same thing. He could handle that without her. Ahva launched off from his shoulder and flew to the nearest arrow. She pinched the middle in her beak and kicked off from the floor. The arrow wobbled back and forth like a teeter totter using her beak for the fulcrum. She tipped her head back and forth to keep it steadier. Trying to land it in Osse's quiver might end up stabbing Osse with it, so she set it down next to him and went for the next. Flying with an arrow drained her fatigue faster, but she kept at it, managing to keep the arrow steadier with each one she collected. By the time Osse had looted all the mannequins, his quiver was about half full again.

He helped her collect the rest of the arrows before they went to the end of the corridor where they found rooms four and fifteen.

"Guess he doesn't know is right from his left." Osse shrugged.

"No." Ahva said.

The end of the corridor was another passageway that paralleled the first. Osse turned and followed it to the middle passage. Door number twenty-two was there at the end. Osse held the bow in his right hand and reached for the doorknob with his left. Ever so slowly, he turned the handle and pushed on the door. It slid open without a sound.

Inside, gray spiderwebs covered everything. A shelving rack along one wall held a collection of scrolls, and one scroll sat on a table in the center of the room. Between them and the scroll? A knee-high tarantula on steroids. Her kitchen table wasn't as big as the leg-span on that thing. The edge of her vision turned red.

The spider reared back, snapping its mandibles. Ahva launched off of Osse's shoulder and took a quick spin around the room, trying to find something small enough that she could pick up and heavy enough to drop and do damage. Nothing. Books were too heavy, scrolls were too unwieldy, and other knickknacks were half her size or more. Osse fired his bow. The spider ducked as if it were taking a yoga position, and the arrow bounced off the exoskeleton on its back without penetrating.

Not good. Not good at all.

Osse dropped his bow and pulled out the knife he carried in his bag.

Ahva landed on the back of the spider. *A knife? Really? No good. You have to get way too close to use that.* The spider's leg took a swipe at her but missed when it couldn't get a good angle. She selected the Peck skill from the list and jabbed her beak at the back of the spider. The impact rattled her whole skeleton but did no damage.

As the spider started to tip toward one side, Ahva took off and circled the room again. That thing had to have a weakness. Surely the computer would not give them a quest they couldn't complete.

Think, bird, think. That thing's got an exoskeleton. Where would the weak spots be? Anyone have an enormous shoe?

As she completed another circuit of the room, the spider jumped at her and missed. She made eye contact and the answer occurred to her like a flash. She dove and landed on the spider's head. Before he could do anything about her arrival, she jabbed one of its eyeballs with her beak. Dark goo erupted from the eye.

Solid whack on her side sent her flying into the web. She flailed but couldn't get loose. The spider hissed and turned toward her.

"Ahva!" Osse jumped between her and the spider.

As the spider reared back for an attack, Osse thrust the knife at its face. It dodged and clamped its mandibles around his wrist. He took the knife with his other hand and completed the thrust, driving the knife through a compound eye and deep into its head. The spider crumbled up like a wad of paper and turned into a mannequin.

Osse shook his arm then inspected the injury. He staggered and fell to his knees. His status bar flashed a green-skull-and-crossbones. Fatigue and health bars gradually declined. Dropping the knife, he fumbled through his bag and took out one of the vials he had prepared the night before. He pulled the cork with his teeth and spat it out then up-ended the vial in his mouth. The skull-and-crossbones winked out. He set the vial aside and cut Ahva loose. By the time she was free, the spider injury had faded.

"You okay?" She checked his health bar above his head. Back to full points.

"Fine now." He glanced down at his arm then retrieved the stopper and returned it and the vial to his bag.

Ahva inspected her feathers. Threads of spider silk stuck to her in all kinds of directions. She picked at one, and it got stuck on her beak. She hissed.

"You're a bit of a mess." Osse cringed and offered his hand. "This won't be much fun, but you can't fly well with all that stuff attached you."

Without so much as a "by your leave," he pinned her to his lap with one hand and picked off all spider silk with the other. Ahva squawked in protest.

"I know. I know!" Osse kept picking at the silk threads. "No fun but has to be done."

An eternity later, he finally finished and let her loose. She gave him a halfhearted nip and fled up to his shoulder.

"Ow!" He frowned at her then at his hand and back at her. "Did you have any better ideas?"

"No. Dumb – " She squawked. *No, not "squawk."*

"Spider." "Dumb – " She squawked again. *Okay, so "spider" is not acceptable vocabulary. Fine.* "Dumb thing!"

He snatched up the map from the table, gathered his things, and headed down the center of passageway toward the exit. They had crossed the threshold into the stairwell when a loud bell rang. Scrabbling and hissing noises came from all three passageways in the vault.

"Uh we go!" Ahva sidled closer to Osse's head.

"Yeah, good idea." He darted up the stairs. They'd made it halfway when a horde of rats, spiders, and glowing worm-things reached the bottom step.

The three groups swarmed over each other, and individuals took damage. A glowing blob of muck struck the wall over Osse's shoulder. He opened the door enough to slip through and slammed it shut behind them. The key was missing.

Osse smacked the door with his palm. "The mayor took the key."

Ahva hissed. *Of course, he did. What could we possibly need with it?* "Not good. No."

Something hit the door from the inside.

He ran back through the library and out through the main doors and kept running until they found City Hall on the other end of the market. The stucco building was a flat one-story with a clocktower that soared above the tallest buildings in the area. A sign above the door read "City Hall." Without that, Ahva never would've guessed that's what the place was.

Effective but utilitarian.

Osse slowed and trudged up the steps to the door of the building.

As they approached, a uniformed man opened the door. "Can I help you?"

Osse held up the map. "I'm here to see the mayor. He is expecting me."

The uniformed man opened the door further and bowed them through. "All the way at the end of this hall. Then through that door."

Osse nodded. "Thank you."

Clearly, whatever funds had been dedicated for the decoration of the outside had been used to decorate the inside. The stone walls were festooned with tapestries, drawings, and paintings showing the mayor posing for "photo ops" with other people, in front of places of business, and even with plates of food.

He takes more selfies than a teenager!

The corridor ended in a door made of steel reinforced wood.

Interesting interior door. Expecting trouble?

Osse knocked.

"Yes, what do you want?" The mayor asked.

"It's Osse Bente. I brought your map."

Heavy footsteps raced toward the door from the other side. Several metal on metal slides and thunks came from the door.

"Wow, not a safe neighborhood?" Osse muttered.

The door opened and the mayor, breathing like he had finished a marathon a minute ago, stared at him. "You found the map already?"

"Yes, we did." Osse held up the map.

"Come in, come in." He snatched the map out of Osse's hand and spread it out on the desk. "Yes, yes, this is it.

Excellent work."

When the notebook in the corner turned blue, Ahva dismissed the notice. That'd just let her know she'd finished the map fetch.

"Did you get rid of all the vermin in the vault?" The mayor crossed his arms in front of his chest.

Osse shook his head. "That wasn't the deal. You said retrieve the map in exchange for five hundred chips. I did that. You said nothing about clearing out all the intruders."

The mayor rolled his eyes. "I would've thought that was understood."

You know what they say about assuming?

"That's not a job for one person. There are lots of rats, spiders, and glowing worm-like creatures. You need a well-armed, well-equipped party to tackle that. Ahva and I had enough trouble with a big spider." Osse held out his hand. "Our reward, please?"

"Very well." The mayor rolled his eyes. "Would you like another quest?"

Osse kept his hand extended. "We might be interested."

The mayor crossed to a safe in the corner of the room and stood where his back blocked the view of the number wheel on the front. "Retrieving the map was the first part. We need a copy of that map made so we can give Antwen proof of the original border without losing our only real proof. There is a scribe in the market who can make the copy."

"What does the quest pay?"

"Pay? What is with this generation? Won't do anything unless there's money in it." The mayor opened the safe and retrieved something from the inside then closed it again. "No money this time. How about a credit of five hundred chips in any shop in the market?"

Wow. The damage you could do with that! "That's nice."

Osse tipped his head toward Ahva. "What you think?"

"Yes."

The mayor walked back over to him and gave Osse a small bag. "You let your bird decide?"

I am the player, gooberhead.

"She's involved, too." Osse dropped the reward money in his bag. He rolled up the map. "We'll take your quest."

When the notebook turned blue this time, Ahva opened it to check out the goofy quest name.

Antwen Is Wrong #2: Human Copying Machine. Copy the Map.

She snickered. Not the best one so far, but not bad, really. She might have gone with "Paper Cloning" or "Seeing Double" or something like that.

"You'll have to be quick. The scribe leaves by noon if he doesn't have any business to keep him. He's rather fond a fishing." The mayor ushered them out. "I'm here until sundown and back at firstlight."

"Where in the market will I find him?" Osse glanced toward the market.

You're asking directions from a guy who doesn't know his left from his right? What could possibly go wrong?

"Three stalls left of the main entrance. You can't miss him. See you soon." The mayor closed the door.

Which translates to five stalls on the right, up a flight of stairs, around the corner, and down the third alley. Right?

As they walked down the hall to the main door, the thunks and metal-on-metal slides of all the door locks echoed off the stone walls.

CHAPTER 16

"Trusting fellow, isn't he?" Osse smirked.

Ahva squinted. "No."

The uniformed man at the door let them out.

Osse followed the marketplace wall halfway back to the library. Wide gates stood open to allow patrons to enter and leave at will. Osse entered and turned toward the left.

You actually trust those instructions?

They stopped at the third stall, which held a variety of decorated animal skulls.

Yep, nothing says scribe like decorated animal skulls. Ahva snorted. "Here?"

The merchant, a man who definitely had some years on dirt, wobbled over to them. "Help you, son?"

Osse nodded. "I was told to find the scribe here."

The old man laughed. "Been talking to the mayor, have you? Not sure that one could find the ground by dropping something two out of three times."

Osse snickered. "I'm starting to get that impression myself. Can you tell me where the scribe is?"

"Sure can. On the far side of the market, there are some permanent shops built into the market's outer wall. You'll find the scribe close to the northeast corner. His sign shows a feather and an ink bottle."

Osse nodded once. "Thank you."

"Say, you wouldn't want to sell that bird?"

"No." Ahva picked Posture and fluffed up, which had no effect.

"I'm afraid not." Osse reached up and pet Ahva's shoulder. "She's going to be stuck with me for quite some time."

"I'll give you an excellent price." The old man wobbled back to a metal box on a table in the back corner of his stall.

"No, sir. Thank you." Before the old man could ask again, Osse turned and strolled away. "At least I'm pretty sure you don't want to end up being one of his wares."

She leaned away from his head. "No."

"That's what I thought." Osse picked his way through the sparse crowd. "Remind me never to take directions from the mayor again."

"Deal!"

The market was much smaller than Fola or Kamali. They arrived at the opposite wall in about three minutes, game time. They turned to the left and headed for the northeast corner. Another couple minutes brought them to a small shop built into the wall. The sign hanging above the door showed an inkwell and quill.

Osse stepped into the shop.

Instead of the piles of books, scrolls, and ink, the shelves were lined with glass jars with colored liquids, feathers in a variety of shapes and sizes, and enough different kinds of paper to keep a scrapbooker amused for a millennium.

Osse stopped to look at the titles of a set of similarly bound books. "*Ilion and the Great Massacre*, *Prophecies from Ilion*, *The Ilionite Threat: Promise of World Domination*."

I sense a theme in these works.

A man, roughly Osse's age, came out of a back room. "Can I help you?"

Osse hurried over to him and offered the map. "I'm on a quest from the mayor. I have an original map here, but I need a copy made."

The scribe frowned. "That could be a problem. By Bakhari law, maps must be made on a specific type of paper. I don't keep it on hand. There's not much call for mapmaking."

CHAPTER 16

Osse leaned closer. "I can get the paper for you. Just tell me where it is."

"The stationery store has it." He pointed at the wall to his right. "If not, they can tell you where to get it or what they need to make it."

"Where do I find it?"

Oh boy. Here we go again.

"Right next door." The scribe smiled. "Convenient, no?"

For a change.

"I'll be right back." Osse turned back to the door.

The scribe reached after him. "Wait a minute. That map is old. You shouldn't be carrying it around in the open like that. If that gets damaged, what do we use to prove our border?"

"Do you have a map case?"

"No, but how about you leave that here with me." He grabbed a scrap of paper and scrawled a quick receipt. "There is some prep work I can do to get ready to copy it while you're retrieving the paper."

Osse traded the map for the receipt. "That sounds fair. Thank you." He stuffed the receipt into his bag and headed next door.

The stationery shop was another scrapbooker's paradise. Stacks of different kinds of paper had a variety of decorations. Some had matching envelopes. A massive printing press occupied the far corner of the room alongside a long row of drying racks.

A woman with an ear-to-ear smile bounced in from a back room while drying her hands on a stained towel. "Good morning. What kind of paper do you need?"

"Map paper," Osse said.

The smile stayed firmly in place, but the woman appeared to deflate a little. "I'm afraid I don't have any of that. Not much call for mapmaking."

Osse frowned. "So I hear. Can you make some for me?"

"Not without reeds, and those come from the river in Antwen." Her smile tightened. "You can guess how excited they are to trade those with us."

I'm sure they're as happy as a deer at a barbecue.

"Is there any reason I can't go collect them myself?" Osse asked.

The woman stared up at the corner of the room and tapped her chin. "I suppose not. You'll have to pay the toll to enter Antwen. They'll give you a token to prove that you have a right to be there. If I were you, I wouldn't be caught in that country without the token. You might not find your way back to Bakhar again for a long time."

"No. Good bird!" Ahva said.

Osse preened Ahva's head, giving her fatigue meter a boost. "I'll be very legal about everything. Don't worry about that."

"That would be great." She clapped her hands. "I need a minimum of ten reeds to make your map paper. If you happen to bring back more than that, I sure wouldn't complain. In fact, if you bring back fifty, I won't charge you for the paper."

"Is there any particular space along the river where I need to collect the reeds?" Osse asked.

"No, they grow pretty much anywhere along that stretch of the river due south of town. You might consider bringing some bug repellent, though. If you could catch those mosquitoes, they'd make good mounts."

Great. Where do we go for that?

"I have a recipe for that."

The woman's eyes grew to the size of a manhole cover. "You're an herbalist?"

"Yes. Learned from mother," Ahva said. *Hey, that wasn't half bad. Starting to get the hang of this!*

Osse nodded. "I focused mostly on healing and practical sorts of things."

"You might be my new best friend." She moved a few steps closer. "Can you make ink? Or dye?"

"No, I don't have any recipes for things like that. If you have a recipe yourself, I might be able to mix it for you."

She snorted. "If I had a recipe, I could make it. It can't be much harder than cooking dinner."

"There are a few tricks to it, but generally I guess you're right."

Silly human. Don't tell her that. How are you supposed to grow the mystique of herbalism?

"How late are you here?" Osse asked.

"Sundown. Same as most of the market, but if you're working with the scribe, you have until noon. Otherwise you wait until tomorrow. Doable. The river is not that far south of the border."

Osse backed toward the door. "I'd better get going. It sounds like I haven't much time." Once the door was closed behind them, he blew out a breath. "I can mix up some bug repellent, but we're short on time. What do you say we stop at an herbalist and buy some premade?"

A warning popped up in the lower left. **-5 Agility. Sitting still equals sore muscles. How about a nice stretch?**

"Yes." Ahva stretched her wings one at a time the way

her budgies used to.

"I'm glad you agree." He backtracked the route they had taken through the market earlier. "I think I saw another herbalist on our way from the skull merchant to the scribe."

About halfway to the skull merchant, they came across a booth with a sign showing several types of plants. Osse ducked into the stall and grabbed three vials marked "Don't Bug Me." After he paid the merchant out of the money they had gotten from the mayor, they left the city and turned south toward Antwen.

For roughly the length of a soccer field, all brush and trees had been cleared around the city. Beyond that, the trees were tall with broad-based trunks and a full, dome-shaped canopy, not like the dense, glorified brush on the north side of the road. The tree canopies didn't overlap, giving this area a look like an oversized mushroom farm. Insects buzzed and birds chirped.

They passed the corner of the city and the cleared area before entering the widely spaced forest. As they neared the first trunk, Ahva studied the structure. It wasn't one massive trunk like she'd expected, but rather a whole flock of narrower trunks that all grew together.

The sketchy sunlight making it through the canopy meant little more than moss grew on the ground. As they walked, small lizards skittered away from them.

They'd been walking for half an hour when they found a stone wall that was chest-high to Osse. It stretched across the landscape as far as Ahva could see. With his hands flat on the top of the wall, Osse hopped and pushed himself up before twisting to sit on the rock wall. He swung his legs over and slid off the other side.

CHAPTER 16

Five men on horseback, dressed in plate armor like the guys manning the toll both, rode through the trees and stopped in front of them.

Chapter 17

Ahva tensed as the soldiers approached. *We're definitely not in Kansas anymore, Toto.*

"Stop where you are. You have crossed into the sovereign territory of Antwen. The toll for entering our fair country is ten coins in any country's currency. Pay now, or turn back."

Osse reached into his bag. "I have the ten coins."

The lead rider waved for him to come closer. "Bring that here."

Osse dug out the coins and offered them to the rider. "I get a token. Is that right?"

"And don't be caught without it." The rider took the money and gave Osse a blue block that looked suspiciously like a big Lego half the size of his hand. "Don't go losing it either."

"Don't worry. I plan to do everything by the law." Osse slipped the Lego into his bag.

"You better."

The five riders turned and rode off, weaving through the trees

Another few steps further from the wall, and mosquitoes were everywhere, buzzing and whining past them in a bug fog. The whine got louder, passing from the right side to the left side before fading out again.

You crossed the magic line. We must be getting close to the river. Ahva snapped at a mosquito flying close to her head.

Osse slapped at a mosquito then pulled a vial out of his bag. "Good time for one of these."

He flipped off the cork and chugged the contents, scrunching up his face as he swallowed hard. "Ugh. Nasty stuff."

You drink it? I would've thought it was a topical application.

Mosquitoes still buzzed nearby, but they maintained their distance from Osse.

He shuddered and returned the empty vial to his bag. "I'm not sure how well this works on birds, so you should probably stay close to me."

"Yes. Good idea!" She sidled closer to his head.

Another twenty minutes of hiking and they arrived at the edge of a river. Reeds like cattails grew out of the bank to a height greater than Osse. He slipped his knife out of its sheath and started slicing through stalks. He kept count out loud as he piled them at the top of the riverbank. A pile of fifty made a rather impressive collection, but he collected an extra fifteen to be sure. He had only just piled the last reed when the mosquitoes crowded around them again making their whiny noises.

"Ugh. Nasty stuff." Ahva snapped at a whiny mosquito zipping past her.

Osse grabbed another vial out of his pouch and poured it down the hatch then shuddered. The mosquitoes backed off.

He stared at the pile of reeds. "I really don't want to do this in two trips, but how do I get this many back to town in one go? If I try to carry them all loose, they'll slide all over the place and we'll play sixty-five reed pick up a million times before we get back to town."

That's easy, silly human. You have a blanket. You have that card-woven strap. Make a reed-and-blanket burrito, bind that together with the strap, and carry the whole bundle at once.

Ahva crawled down to Osse's bag and nudged the flap up enough to slide inside. After rooting around for a moment, she tugged the corner of his blanket to the surface.

He flipped the bag open to watch what she was doing. "Aren't you clever."

That's what crows are good for.

Osse pulled out the blanket and spread it on the ground. As he piled the reeds into the middle of it and wrapped them up, Ahva continued to root around for the strap.

"What are you looking for?" Osse crab-walked back over to her.

She found the corner of the strap and tugged, but it wouldn't budge.

"I got it." Osse nudged her out of the way and retrieved the strap. Using that, he secured his blanket-and-reed burrito then picked up the whole bundle. "All right. Let's get moving."

The trip back to town took a little longer than the way out. As Osse walked, the blanket slipped little by little until the whole combination came loose, and reeds slid out in a cluster.

"Uh-oh!" Ahva called.

Osse sighed and crouched. He tucked the reeds back into the blanket and resituated the strap.

At the boundary wall, Ahva took off and flew a circle

CHAPTER 17

around Osse. He tossed the reed bundle over. When it hit the ground, one corner slid loose. After he hoisted himself up and over, Osse tucked the corner back into the cattail burrito.

Ahva spiraled up to patrol height. Sure, they were out of Antwen, but no telling what other hazards were here. The maniac that attacked them on the way here might be anywhere. When she got to altitude, Ahva flew long, skinny loops with Osse at one end.

The edge of her screen turned red.

In her peripheral vision, Ahva caught sight of something small and dark bee-lining for her. She wheeled around for a clearer view and found a hawk headed her way. Tightening her turn radius, headed back toward Osse at full speed. Her combat skills weren't half enough to take on a hawk in a snit, not yet anyway. She picked Signal Human from her skill set and cawed repeatedly hoping Osse would hear her before he could see her.

The hawk turned onto her path, but Ahva was pulling away from it.

Ha! Score one for the little bird.

She spotted Osse and cawed again. He squinted then dropped the reeds and strung his bow. A second later, she was staring down the shaft of an arrow and dove, aiming to land on the reed bundle to give him a clear shot at the hawk. As she got close, she reared back to shed velocity and landed then spun to watch the approaching hawk.

"Bad bird!" She hissed.

It must not have appreciated the view of the arrow's business end, because it veered off. He continued aiming at the hawk until it was out of sight then couched his bow and knelt.

"Are you okay, Ahva?" He offered his hand.

He hopped onto his fingers. "Yes. Thanks!"

"You did good leading it back toward me."

I knew where my help could be found. "Good bird!"

She ran up to his shoulder and held on while he picked up the reed bundle. Shortly after, they were back in town.

When they slipped into the stationery shop, Smiley the Paper Maker bounced on her toes and grinned like a pro golfer landing eighteen consecutive holes-in-one. Osse plopped the bundle of reeds on the counter and unfastened the strap.

"These are perfect! How many did you collect?"

"I think I got about sixty-five." Osse slid them off his blanket.

"Wonderful!" She planted a kiss on his cheek. "I'll get the paper made for you. It will take about an hour. That should still give you enough time to get back to the scribe and get that map done."

Really? An hour to make papyrus? Egyptians could've learned a trick or two from you. I guess that keeps the game moving.

"We'll be back in an hour." Osse left the store and wiped the smooch off his face. "What do you say we do a bit of shopping? If we're going to get a voucher for five hundred chips to use in the market, I'd like to use them wisely."

"Yes. New stuff!" Ahva bobbed her head.

"What do you think? Armor? A weapon? Food?" Osse wandered through the sparse foot traffic.

She leaned closer to him. "Yes. Good idea."

"To which?"

CHAPTER 17

"Yes." She straightened out an errant feather to get a sparkly **+10 XP**.

"Right. Thanks." He smiled and messed up the feathers on Ahva's head.

As the city clocktower sounded 11:00, Osse meandered up and down the rows in the market. The first place of interest they came to sold leather goods. He stepped inside and studied a set of leather armor decorating a dress dummy.

Ahva checked at the price tag and whistled. *Six hundred chips. Not saying it isn't worth it, but wow.*

Osse compared the thickness of the leather in the armor to his dad's tunic. "About the same."

The merchant came over. "That may be, but I guarantee my armor will outlast any blacksmith's tunic."

"I have no doubt, but my funds might be a bit limited. I might have to do with what I have and supplement." Osse turned toward him.

"If you're planning on some adventures, I sure wouldn't skimp on armor or weapon, but I can understand a budget, too." He led Osse over to another display of mismatched parts. "If you're going minimalist, I have a good set of vambraces, greaves, boots, and a helmet that I could let you have for two hundred. And, son, I don't haggle, so don't waste my time."

"No, that sounds reasonable." He picked up the helmet and inspected the stitching. "I'm working a quest right now, and when I get the payoff, I'll be back to talk to you."

The man returned to his seat in the corner of the tent.

After admiring a few other pieces, Osse returned to wandering the market. When they reached the end of the row, Osse stopped and turned back toward the leather work shop. "I should've asked if he could make armor for you."

Not sure I could fly with junk on. Tough enough staying in the air unencumbered, not to mention needing to pick up a rock or two from time to time. "No."

Osse looked up at her. "No armor for you?"

"Nooooo. Little bird."

"I guess flying with the extra weight would be a little tough."

"Yes!"

They stepped into a gunsmith's shop complete with taxidermied heads on the walls but promptly left after seeing the whopping price tag of five thousand for a small pistol.

Next, he stopped at a bowyer and priced out arrows and arrowheads. A fancy bow with pulleys hung high on the tent wall at the back. Ahva squinted and leaned closer, checking out the price tag. *Two thousand. Impressive.*

Down the last row, they found a weaponsmith in a permanent shop. Osse stepped inside and admired an ornate rapier and a huge zweihander before checking the prices on some short swords, daggers, clubs, and maces.

"What are you trained for?" The merchant stepped closer.

"The only formal training I've had is my bow." Osse tapped his bow.

The merchant shook his head. "I'll sell you whatever you like, of course, but my suggestion to you is to find a mentor first. Otherwise you might end up buying a weapon you'll never learn."

"I understand." Osse faced him directly. "Do you know any good trainers in the area?"

"A few." The merchant leaned back on his counter.

"Haven't seen you around here before. Are you moving here or passing through?"

"Passing through." He pointed toward the west. "I'm chasing down a set of four killers who might have kidnapped my sister."

The merchant frowned. "That does complicate things. Tell you what. Buy whatever weapon you want, and I'll give you a few pointers. Just quick lesson or two. You won't be a master, not by a longshot, but it'll get you on your way and give you something more effective for close-in fighting than that bow. My advice, however, is that you play to your strengths and take out your enemy from a distance until you get better instruction."

Osse nodded. "Thank you. What do you recommend for a complete novice?"

"A club or a mace should stand you in good stead." He directed Osse to a display of maces. "Most boys your age have swung a stick at a few things to be sure. Still takes a lot of practice to get good, but at least you have a start."

Osse joined him and checked the tag on a couple. "Good. I'll go with that, but I'm on a quest right now. As soon as I get the payoff, I'll be back."

He tipped his head to one side. "Don't wait too long. That offer's only good for a couple days."

"More than fair. I'll be back."

They returned to the paper merchant, whose grin was wearier than earlier. "You're just in time. I have your map paper."

She handed him a large sheet of paper, a palm-sized notepad, a small bottle of ink, and a quill.

Osse pointed at all the extra stuff. "What's all this?"

"The first fifty reeds paid for the map paper." She tapped first the paper then the other equipment. "The other fifteen paid for the rest of it."

Would have probably preferred the money.

Osse tucked the extra loot into his bag. When he flipped the lid closed, the clasps wouldn't come together. "Thank you."

"Thank you! You better hurry. The scribe will leave soon if he doesn't have something to do."

They darted next door and arrived as the scribe was approaching the door with the key in hand.

"I have your map paper." Osse handed him the paper.

A huge bell in the distance chimed noon.

The scribe slouched. "So you have. Copying the map will take two hours. Don't keep me waiting."

"I'll be back in under two hours." He slipped back out the door.

"You better be." The scribe's voice was muffled by the door.

Ahva checked their status. Osse's fatigue meter was solidly yellow and below half. They'd better get lunch. She imitated the sound of crunching nuts.

Osse chuckled. "Yes, I can do some food myself."

They returned to the inn where they were staying and bought a lunch that was composed of the leftovers of the previous night.

After they were both sufficiently stuffed, they retreated to their room and planned out what to do with the five-hundred-chip-credit while Osse sorted the contents of his bag to try to get a little extra room. With only a half-hour to go, Osse snatched up his bow and slid his bag across his shoulder then headed back to the market. They arrived at the scribe's shop with only fifteen minutes to spare. The scribe finished and traded the maps for one hundred green and copper chips.

Back at town hall, the uniformed man at the door waved them through without challenge. At the end of the hall, the mayor fumbled with his dozens of locks before he opened the door.

"You again? Finished so soon?" The mayor opened the door wider and stepped back.

Osse handed him both maps. "The original and the copy."

The mayor set both on his desk. "You aren't one to dawdle."

The notebook turned blue, but there was no green flash on the edge of the screen. She'd completed the mission but still didn't level up.

What? Come on! We solved two quests in a row.

"Would you like to help me with the third part?" The mayor handed Osse a paper marked "Market Credit: Five Hundred."

"And what would that be?" Osse pocketed the paper.

The mayor rolled his eyes. "Deliver the map and get rid of the tollbooth."

Because delivering the map guarantees that the toll booth goes?

"I can deliver the map, but what if Antwen still won't remove the tollbooth?"

"Bite fingers." Ahva snorted.

Osse chuckled. "No, let's not. They're much better armed and armored than we are."

The mayor sat at his desk and pulled out a stack of papers.

"Once they have the proof, how can they not?"

Because gooberheads are so good at following the rules, right?

"If you complete that task, the city will pay your room and board while you're here – up to five nights – then ensure you're properly provisioned before you leave. What do you say?" He picked up a quill and dipped it in ink.

Ahva bobbed her head. "Deal."

The mayor wrote without so much as a peek in their direction. "I need your word, Osse. You might do business with a bird, but I don't."

Well, excuuuuse me! Ahva hissed then muttered, "Hi, Ahva. Gooood bird."

"We'll do it." Osse nodded once.

When the notebook turned blue, she opened it.

Antwen Is Wrong #3: Just Go Away! Get rid of the tollbooth.

Not bad. How about, "You're in my space!"

The mayor handed him the copy of the map. "I suggest you start with the tollbooth. Show them the map. That should get rid of them."

With the map in hand, Osse left the mayor's office. As they hustled down the hall, Ahva turned around and watched the door, listening to get a count of exactly how many locks mayor had. Osse was out of the building before the mayor had finished.

Being paranoid doesn't mean they're not out to get you!

The path back to the city gate was familiar now, and the guards greeted them as they walked through.

"Another quest?" One guard called after them.

Osse looked back over his shoulder. "Going to get rid of

CHAPTER 17

the tollbooth."

"Good luck with that." The other guard rolled his eyes.

Instead of the detour through the scrub brush, Osse stayed to the road and reached the Antwen guards in only about ten minutes.

One of the guards blocked their path. "This stretch of road is controlled by Antwen. Pay the toll, or turn back."

Osse unrolled the map and held it up for the guard. "This map shows that the stretch of road is actually in Bakhar. You'll find the official cartographer's seal in the lower corner."

The guard snorted. "My kid could draw map and claim we're in the wrong place."

Another guard came over. He had shinier armor and a fancier sword but not the purple of the captain. "That may be, but if this is an official map, we're in the wrong place."

"Still, it could be a fake." The captain shook his head. "You'll have to get official orders from our garrison commander before we leave our post."

Osse rolled up the map. "Where can I find your garrison commander?"

"Just head straight south. You can't miss the garrison. It'll be on your left." The captain pointed toward the south. "But before you cross into Antwen, you'll need to pay the toll."

"I have already." Osse fished the Lego-shaped token out of his bag. "Just this afternoon."

"Don't lose that." The captain wagged his finger at Osse.

Osse tucked it back into his bag. "I'll keep it on me."

"On your way, then."

"Thank you." Turning to his right, Osse started off cross-country. "All right then, Ahva, keep an eye out for that maniac."

And that hawk. Good idea. Great time for a patrol. She launched off of Osse's shoulder and started an expanding spiral as she gained altitude.

As she flew her expanding loop, her path took her over the guards minding the road. She had half a mind and leave a "present" for one of them. No, maybe he was just doing his job.

Aside from the humans, the only movement she saw on the ground were small mammals, a few reptiles, and wind-blown grass. Nothing exciting, but after the "excitement" they'd encountered on their last cross-country trip, she could do with a fewer laughing loonies.

She passed over an area with a wide line of bare dirt, some trampled grass, and a wide scattering of stones. What was left of the wall, maybe?

The part of the stream that Osse approached was not hidden under trees, nor did it have a profusion of reeds. Five guards on horseback rode toward Osse.

She turned a direct course back to her human.

When she approached, Osse held out his arm for a landing pad. Ahva reared back to shed velocity and stretched out with her feet to come in for an easy landing.

"Find anything?" He held his arm up closer to his shoulder.

She hopped off onto his shoulder and turned around. "Yes."

"Bigger than the odd rodent?" he asked.

"Yes. Bigger."

"Dangerous?"

CHAPTER 17

She crawled down to his bag and squeezed under the flap. "No."

He opened his bag as she clamped her beak onto the corner of the Lego.

Osse took it from her. "Oh. The patrol?"

They rode up before she could answer.

"Stop where you are." The guard in the lead rested his hand on the hilt of his sword. "What's your business here?"

Osse held up the token. "I'm on an errand to find the garrison commander."

"Who sent you?"

"The captain at the tollbooth and the mayor of the town." Osse aimed his thumb over his shoulder.

The patrol leader nodded. "Veer a bit to the left. You'll find a bridge across the river which will take you much closer to the garrison than your current path."

Osse bowed. "Thank you. That will help."

The patrol turned around and galloped away. Ahva watch them until she lost sight of them in the trees.

Osse slid the token into his bag. "Why don't you stay with me now. As we get closer to the river, the mosquitoes might go crazy again."

Ahva climbed back up to Osse's shoulder. *Good idea, human.*

Unlike the near-swamp a kilometer or so downstream, the river here was narrower and moved faster, and that made the mosquitoes much less annoying.

The bridge was a sturdy rock affair, plenty high enough and long enough to accommodate moderate floodwaters. From the top of the bridge, a stone wall surrounded by a wooden palisade of spikes stood in the middle of an open field.

Osse pointed. "That's the spot."

Ahva took off from his shoulder and flew straight toward the structure. She covered the distance in a few minutes, game time. Inside the walls, there were a few low stone buildings. Clusters of men were scattered about an open area arranged in three columns of four men. Another fellow on a horse stood in front of them. Everyone clearly got their gear from the same armory as the toll booth guards. Another man in red and gold stood on a raised platform in front of all the groups. He was speaking, but the distance and her relative position behind him rendered his words meaningless. At the end of his speech, he punched the air, and all the men cheered.

The main gates opened and all the groups left, each going a different direction. The guy in red and gold watched them go, but stayed on his raised platform.

Bet you're the garrison commander. Ahva watched as she flew a few loops then returned to Osse.

"Are we too late?" Osse pointed to the group leaving.

Ahva fluffed up all her feathers and shook, a favorite trick of her budgies that gained another XP bonus. "No."

When they approached the main gate, a guard patrolling the stone wall jogged toward them. "That's far enough."

"I've come to see the garrison commander." Osse showed his token.

The man in red and gold joined the guard on the wall. "What do you want, lad?"

Osse held the map toward men on the wall. "The mayor of Nkamo in Bakhar sent me with this map. He says you are mistaken about the location of Antwen's border, so your

CHAPTER 17

tollbooth needs to move."

The commander rolled his eyes. "Lad, I've got bigger problems. There is some kind of two-legged monster harassing the farms in my jurisdiction. Eight dead. Three more wounded and probably dying. One missing. And that's just this morning. Until that monster is found and dealt with, I don't have time for your territorial dispute."

"I'm an herbalist. Maybe I can help your wounded."

"I have a qualified physician, thank you anyway. You want some of my time? Deal with the monster." The garrison commander left the wall.

"That was unproductive." Osse rolled up the map and slipped it into his bag. "Scout around and find that thing. I'm sure it's the one that attacked me earlier. It has to be. If you find it, either circle it until I catch up, or come back and lead me there."

Ahva took to her wings and spiraled away from Osse, keeping the spiral loose so she could cover more ground in less time. The trees had given way to grassland this far from the river. Although flat along this area, the terrain developed some rolling hills as it went on toward the south. The long, green grass might hide ground-level critters, but unless the maniac had taken to crawling on hands and knees, she shouldn't have much trouble finding it. After only a half-dozen passes, she caught up with the nearest Antwen patrols. Ahead of them, something dark skulked in the high grass. Ahva abandoned her loop and flew straight at the figure crouching in the grass. Stringy, matted hair. Shredded clothing. Intermittent twitching of its entire body. Yeah, that had to be the same thing that had attacked Osse yesterday. The health bar on its ID tag had only slightly recovered from yesterday, still yellow. The glow coming from the back of its neck was 'visible even in the bright sunlight, but whenever it shuddered, the light flickered.

She flew a tight circle above the monster. When her turns faced her in the direction of the garrison, she spotted her human sprinting toward her with his bow ready for business. She kept an eye on his progress and the patrol between them when she faced that way and checked on the sneaking monster the rest of the time. She didn't need the equations from her old algebra class to figure out that the patrol would arrive long before Osse did. She doubted that anyone in the patrol was bright enough to figure out that she could answer yes/no questions and fill them in on the danger. Either she had get the maniac to pop up from the crouch, or she had to slow down the patrol, preferably without turning them into enemies.

She turned her attention to the ground, searching for something small enough that she could pick up and drop on the monster. Nothing but grass, grass, and more grass.

Nothing else to do. She dove, staying out of arm's reach.

The edge of her vision turned red. It swiped at her and smacked the edge of her wing.

Ahva tumbled out of control and the ground flew up at her. She hit hard and rolled to a stop. The screen flashed red and nearly a third of her health bar disappeared as she rolled to a stop. *How'd that happened? I should've been far enough away.*

The maniac laughed.

Ahva scrambled to get upright then pushed off from the ground. Only one wing flapped. The other dragged. The screen went red again.

CHAPTER 17

Great. Maniac on the loose, and I can't fly.

The horseman leading the patrol pointed with his sword. "There it is!"

The Antwen soldiers charged at the monster.

That ought to keep them busy.

Unable to get airborne, Ahva ran as quick as she could away from the battle. Each step flashed the screen red, but she kept going. She did not need to get squashed under a horse's hoof or soldier's boot. Behind her the shouts of the soldiers and the clatter of their weapons and armor encouraged her to keep moving.

Over all the noise, the maniac's mirthless laughter increased as the sounds of the soldiers decreased.

"You have to strike the glow. Hitting anywhere else doesn't do anything." Osse's voice was closer than Ahva expected.

She turned to find him, but the tall grasses that hid her kept her from seeing anything useful. Ahva stopped and shivered. Other things lived in tall grass. Like, things that hissed. Not to mention a few dinosaurs that she'd seen in an old movie. Maybe it would be better to stay still. She was far enough out of range from the battle to avoid getting accidentally squished. Wasn't she?

"I don't see anything glowing." One of the soldiers yelled.

"Back of the neck." Osse yelled. "If it's the same one that attacked me, it's behind the neck."

The maniac's laughter was cut short by a gurgling sound. The clatter of weapons stopped.

"What was that thing?" One of the soldiers asked.

"I don't know." Osse breathed hard. "But a group of them destroyed my village and took several people captive. That one attacked me recently. All I can tell you for sure is that they move ridiculously fast, and they are strong. I saw one of these things pick up and throw a grizzly bear."

"Come on. That scrawny thing?"

"You saw how fast it moves," Osse said.

"Yeah, but–"

"I know what I saw." Osse said. Pottery jars clinked together.

"Here. Mix these herbs with some of your water. It should stop the bleeding and start the healing process. Your physician can do the rest."

"Thank you. What are you searching for?"

"My bird, Ahva. I sent her head to scout for me, and I lost sight of her when the battle started."

Ahva drew a deep breath. "Hello, Ahva."

"Black crow?" One of the soldiers asked.

"Yes, about so big." Osse said.

"Hello, Ahva." She called again.

"I hear her. Come here, Ahva." Osse's smile made it into his voice.

"No." The screen flashed red when she tried to move her wing. "Ow!"

"I saw that thing hit your bird," one of the Antwen soldiers said. "We didn't even know it was there until it jumped to hit her."

"Oh no. I thought it missed. Ahva! Are you hurt?" Osse asked.

Grass rustled as he moved.

"Yes. Bigger ow." Ahva walked toward the noise.

"It understands you?" the soldier asked.

"And answers." Osse projected his voice louder. "Ahva,

keep talking so I can find you."

Speak.

When the list of available vocabulary came up, Ahva read straight down the list.

The rustling noise in the grass came closer until Osse towered above.

"There you are." He squatted in front of her and offered his hand.

She stepped up onto his fingers then turned her injured wing toward him.

He winced. "You'll be okay. A few herbs, a little water. You'll be as good as new."

Now's good for me.

One of the soldiers, the one who had been riding horseback, approached and handed Osse a bag. "If you ever need a job as a physician, I'll put in a good word."

"Thank you, but I'm just an herbalist." Osse mixed some of the herbs with enough water to make a paste and spread it on Ahva's injured wing.

The red faded away in seconds as her health bar climbed back up to normal.

"Good bird," Ahva climbed up to Osse's shoulder as her human stood. "I okay now."

They followed the soldiers back to the garrison. The gates opened as they approached, and the commander met them. He looked Osse up and down. "You did your part. Come with me, and I'll honor our agreement."

"Good bird." Ahva waved one wing.

The commander squinted and leaned back. "It speaks."

She. Not it. "You're not Ahva. I Ahva."

"Sometimes." Osse preened Ahva's feathers, which

improved her fatigue points. "She can even manage fairly simple conversation."

"How long does it take to train one of those?" The commander gestured for them to follow and led the way toward the back corner of the garrison.

"Fully? I'm not sure. I've only had Ahva for a few weeks. I don't know how long she was with the merchant I bought her from."

I'd say about twenty minutes real time, one day game time.

"And she's a crow?" He stopped at a door to a white stone building made of the same stone as the outer walls. Red banners hung on either side of the doors.

"Yes, and she's good at solving puzzles." Osse preened the back of her head.

The commander opened the door and gestured them through. "They might be good messengers."

Osse glanced at her. "I think so."

"Something for me to think about." He gestured them through.

The commander's office had minimal decoration. A simple table and a wooden chair took the place of the desk. Pegs drilled into the wall served as storage for cloaks, weapons, and clothing. A cot in the corner of the room served for a bed.

"What did you need to see me about?" The commander perched on the edge of the table.

Osse produced the copy of the map. "The mayor of Nkamo in Bakhar sent me to discuss the tollbooth your men have set up on the road. I'm afraid this map shows that they are outside of Antwen and fully in Bakhar. The mayor does not want hostilities, but he requests that your men remove the toll collections station and retreat to the Antwen side of the border."

The commander spread the map out on his desk. He rubbed the paper between his fingers then held it up to the light of the window. "Everything appears to be in order. Where did this come from?"

"The map was found in the library vault. Then I had an official scribe copy it for me on special map paper." Osse pointed to the mark in the bottom corner.

"I can't fault that. I'll need to keep this copy." The commander studied the cartographer's symbol.

Osse tapped the map. "That copy is for you or for your king."

The commander retrieved a quill and ink set and a piece of paper. He jotted a note and folded the paper closed and sealed it with wax and an imprint of his ring. "Give that to the captain at the tollbooth."

"Thank you. I'm sure the mayor will be happy to hear about this." Osse tucked the paper into his bag.

The commander led them to the gate. "Don't suppose you would consider selling your bird."

"No." Ahva fluffed up her feathers and squinted.

"I wouldn't know what to do without her." Osse glanced up at her. "Crows are fairly common, so you should be able to find a good one to train as your messenger."

"Fair enough. Safe travels."

Osse left and turned back toward the north. They crossed the bridge and continued to the tollbooth.

As they approached, the captain of the guards strode to meet them. "You again. Back so soon?"

Osse handed him the sealed paper. "I bring you word

from your garrison commander."

He frowned and opened the paper. After staring at the paper for several seconds, he crumbled it and threw it down. "You had to interfere. We had a good thing going here, and you had to interfere."

"I'm just trying to complete a job." Osse stepped back and held both hands palm out.

Another soldier, the one with the shinier-than-most armor, snatched up the paper and flattened it out. He read it and passed it to the others.

Ahva fluffed up. "Disgusting eyeball!"

When the captain grabbed the hilt of his sword, Osse drew an arrow and nocked it. The edge of the screen turned red.

"Bite fingers!" Ahva selected Posture from her skill list and wove from side to side.

The soldiers didn't get even a frownie debuff for that. There were so many of them, they probably didn't much care about one crow in a snit.

"You're too close for that bow." The captain snarled.

"You might be surprised." Osse drew the bow but didn't aim.

Ahva hissed. "Fierce!"

The soldier with the shiny armor darted forward and interposed himself between the two of them. "We're ordered back to the garrison."

The captain pushed him. "And we'll go soon as I take care this troublemaker."

"You think the commander is going to stand for this?" The soldier stepped closer to the captain as Osse stepped back. "Are you really going to throw away your commission and all your years of service because you received orders you don't like?"

"Who's going to tell the commander?"

"I'm a priest. Or did you forget that? Do you want to be without your healer while I go do penance for lying? I'm already going to have to reconcile that the situation isn't as I was told. You said there was proof this was Antwen territory. Clearly it's not."

The captain glared at Osse over the priest's shoulder then growled and spun away. "Get out of here, kid. Before I decide that losing my healer for a month is not such a bad idea after all."

Osse couched his bow and return the arrow to the quiver then turned back toward town.

"Disgusting eyeball." Ahva kept her eye on the toll booth as they gathered equipment.

He didn't answer her until they were well out of earshot. "That was closer than I like."

"Yes, but okay now." *I think we disrupted his extortion racket.*

Chapter 18

When they entered the town, the first thing Ahva noticed was the increase in traffic on the main road.

She snorted. *That was fast.*

Osse took a direct path back to City Hall. The mayor met them at the door. "Congratulations! Business is booming in town again. People are arriving in town now, and the people who were here are no longer afraid to come outdoors. As promised, you have your money, you have your credits for the market, and you have lodging for as long as you're here and provisions for when you leave."

The notebook turned blue and the edge of the screen turned green for a few seconds.

Yes! Leveled up!

"Thank you. I'm glad the problem is solved," Osse said.

"Do enjoy your stay." The mayor returned to the City Hall.

Osse looked over at Ahva. "What do you say we go finish our shopping? Then a good night's sleep and an early start."

Sounds like a plan to me. "Yeah."

* * *

CHAPTER 18

Nagheed curled up on the rug in front of the hearth in Rafayel's study. Eating regular food and sleeping in familiar surroundings had been a welcome relief in between training and the regular patrols, but he'd had enough downtime. If the game programmers had half a storytelling ability, it was time to launch off into another quest.

A knock at the door promised that he might have something new to do soon.

Nagheed lifted his head from his paws and woofed.

"Thank you, Nagheed." Rafayel looked up at the door. "Come in."

A servant led the constable into the study. "Constable Fishel has a request for you, Excellency."

Rafayel stood and gestured to the chair across from him at the desk. "It's good to see you, Simon. How can I help you?"

"I have more than I can handle today." The constable flopped into the offered chair. "And with so many of my men out on patrol, I can't delegate one of these tasks."

Rafayel perched on the edge of his seat. "Tell me about it."

"Two major issues. First, there is a dispute to settle between the Bakhari nomads camped outside our gates and a local merchant accusing them of sabotaging his business. My preliminary investigation turned up inconclusive evidence. Naturally both sides insist they are innocent, so that one will require more digging and some book work." The constable shifted in his seat. "Second problem involves a strange report from one of the patrols. They found a small, curly-haired dog. It was injured, and someone had drawn that symbol we saw at the burned farmhouse on its back with mud. Its injuries are being taken care of, but someone needs to go out with that patrol and find whatever is responsible for causing the injury. Can you take one of the problems, and I'll take the other?"

"We just got back from a trip, but we probably could take one of the tasks. What do you say, Nagheed?" He pointed to the floor on his left. "Handle the trade dispute?" He pointed to his right. "Find out who attacked the poodle?" He pointed to the hearth. "Rest for today?"

Settling a trade dispute didn't sound like much fun, and besides, Nagheed had had enough of nomads for the moment. What had become their usual routine was comfortable enough, but it didn't help gameplay much. That left the poodle. He darted over to Rafayel's right side.

Rafayel smiled and sat back. "It sounds like you've already done a lot of the groundwork for the trade dispute, so I'll leave that in your hands. I'll go back out with the patrol and track down the thing that attacked the dog."

The constable stood. "Very good, sir. Honestly, I was hoping you would say that. My last encounter with one of those monsters was more than I wanted."

"I understand. That's not an encounter I want to repeat myself, but I will be heading out soon, and the more I can learn about them the better."

"I'll have the patrol wait for you at the southern gate."

"Excellent. Thank you."

Nagheed followed the two humans to the door. Once the constable had left, they returned to Rafayel's study. Nagheed sat by the fire while Rafayel traded his cloth doublet for the leather ring mail then belted on his rapier. He took a wooden box out of his desk and withdrew one of

CHAPTER 18

the matched flintlock pistols. After loading it, he tucked it into his belt. Nagheed followed him out to the stable to have the servants get Ryder ready to go, then accompanied Rafayel back inside. They found Bettani sitting in the family room working on embroidery.

Rafayel leaned over her shoulder. "That's coming along rather nicely."

"Thank you. It's almost finished, and just in time, too. It's promised at the end of the week."

He nodded. "You'll have it done in plenty of time."

She frowned up at him. "Problem on the patrol?"

"A wounded dog marked with the symbol that we saw at the burned farmhouses." Rafayel glanced in the direction of the ruined farms. "Constable's busy with a trade dispute with the nomads, so I'm taking the patrol out to go track the monster who injured the dog."

She patted his arm. "I'm glad you're not going alone this time."

He covered her hand with his. "Not with such an obvious threat. I expect to be back this afternoon, nightfall at the latest."

"I'll pray for your success and safety," she said.

"Always welcome." He kissed her cheek.

Nagheed followed him back out to the stable where Ryder stood saddled and waiting. Rafayel pulled himself up into Ryder's saddle and led the way to the southern gate where the other three men waited on horseback. At Rafayel's approach, the morale emojis changed from smiles to teeth-showing smiles. Their horses were not the same gray sort that Rafayel rode, but smaller versions in darker colors. Each of the three men wore a metal helmet and studded leather armor.

At least the monster has other targets.

"Show me where you found the dog." Rafayel gestured for them to lead the way with a wave of his hand.

They took off at a gallop heading to the southeast. Nagheed pushed off and kept his pace alongside Ryder.

One of the riders drifted back to come alongside Rafayel. "It was near the road to Bakhar."

Rafayel nodded. "That makes sense if they're coming from Ilion."

"Is it true what they say? That they're almost impossible to kill?"

"I wouldn't say that." Rafayel shook his head. "The constable and I were able to take one out rather handily once we knew what to do. Like most enemies, the more you understand their strengths and weaknesses, the better you do against them. That's all this is. Know your enemy."

As the ground became rockier, the group slowed. Nagheed picked his way around loose stones, sharp edges, and potholes. They stopped near a fat, low shrub and dismounted.

One of the men squatted and pointed to a small hollow under the bush. "That's where we found the dog, sir. It was whining and carrying on something awful."

Probably heard you coming and hoped you were friendly.

Rafayel lifted the low branches with the back of his arm. "Nagheed, try to pick up the scent of the dog, and trace it back toward its origin."

Nagheed opened the skill menu and engaged his Tracking skill then sniffed around the area. In addition to the human men traveling with Rafayel and their horses, faint signs of "Maniac" connected to "Decay" ranged all around the area.

CHAPTER 18

"Small dog" and a very closely attached "scared" formed indistinct trails and domes here and there. Nagheed roamed from side to side until he found the right angle where the path became clear. The small, scared dog had darted from tree to shrub to large rock and so on in a continuous path. The short trails connected the domes that represented each stop. Nagheed followed the path the dog had left toward the east then turned back to stare at the humans.

Y'all coming?

Nagheed waited until the riders were back on their horses before he trotted off, keeping the poodle's scent in front of him. Nagheed ranged from side to side, to stay with the strongest scent of the poodle. As they went, the scent grew weaker but new scents joined the target on the list. In addition to Rafayel's patrol and the small dog, scents in different fonts traced the path of three different maniacs, each of which had some heavy decay going on. There were also three other small dogs and another human male.

The stone path turned into more of a road lined with cobblestones. Dark-colored pawprints showed on the pale rock, headed the way they had come.

"Nagheed, stop," Rafayel ordered.

He trotted a few steps further then followed his human's directions.

"What are those? Bodies?" One of the patrolmen asked. His morale emoji degraded to a smilie.

"What's left of the other dogs and probably their trainer." Rafayel frowned.

"What could have done that?" Another patrolman's morale also decayed to a simple smilie.

The first one snorted. "I'm not sure I want to find out."

Nagheed craned his neck to try to figure out what they had spotted, but even at his size, he couldn't see over the next ridge in the way. He watched his human and waited for a command to move forward.

Shrieky laughter echoed around the stones, bouncing in from several directions without diminishing.

Nagheed triggered his hearing. He perked up his ears and tipped his head to one side. *No, that's not an echo. That's multiple voices.*

The smaller horses grew wide-eyed and pranced in place. The patrol riders held tightly to their reins and ordered their horses to be still. Ryder stood up taller. His head darted from side to side.

Rafayel patted his horse's neck. "Easy. Easy."

Nagheed used Posture to bark, his deep voice laden with a growl. That brought another round of laughter. One of the smaller horses bolted, tossing his rider.

"Sir?" The first patrolman rode closer to the downed man.

"There's more than one. Three, perhaps four. We're not enough for this." He rode back to the unhorsed man and offered a hand up onto Ryder's back. "Stay together. Let's head back to town. We'll need to come back with a much bigger force."

Once the patrolman was situated behind Rafayel on Ryder's back, the whole group started for the city at a gallop. Nagheed kept pace with his human. Terrain flew by as his terrifically long strides obliterated the distance. The sound system emulated the wind rushing past him as he all but flew alongside the horses. If his fatigue meter wouldn't get grouchy, he could travel like this all the time.

CHAPTER 18

As they rode, laughter returned. Maybe it was the sound of the horse's hooves distorting the laughter, but Nagheed would have sworn that the voices had split up even further. By the time they reached the city, horses and men were sweaty and Nagheed panted hard. His fatigue meter had declined through yellow to orange. At least they were safe, for now.

* * *

The next morning, Ahva was up with the sun. Apparently, that was common practice among all birds because outside, the whole chorus of songbirds was making ruckus. When Osse awoke, he dressed including his new armor to complement the old blacksmith tunic he had found in his father's equipment. Ahva perched on the bed's headboard and tipped her head from side to side studying her human's new equipment.

The helmet was padded leather, suspiciously like an old football helmet. The vambraces were leather cuffs that covered his forearm and cinched in place with buckles. The leather had been dyed black and decorated with intricate swirls. The greaves were dark brown and laced on. His new boots were simple undyed leather and came up to his knees. The gorget around his neck had a roaring lion's face. A new mace, bearing a strong resemblance to a baseball bat with metal studs, hung from a new belt. His quiver was full of new arrows.

Ahva snorted. *You, human, are decked out in the armor equivalent of grandma's early attic. I haven't seen a bigger mismatch since I moved into my college apartment and ac-*

quired every spare piece of furniture every relative I ever knew owned. But, hey, if it works...

Osse held out his hand. "Come on, Ahva. Let's get some breakfast and get on our way."

He slipped his bag over his shoulder and picked up his bow as Ahva flew over and landed on his hand.

Breakfast amounted to last night's leftover meat paired with eggs, pancakes, and a vaguely green-gray porridge. Ahva chowed down until her fatigue meter was maxed out then practiced building up her Speech skill until Osse had polished off the rest.

After weaving their way through surprisingly dense crowds on the way to the city gate, they were back on the road and headed into Nethanya.

A few hours into the hike, they came to a Y in the road. A signpost pointed down the southern fork to Vanya and the northern fork to Yavne.

Osse stopped and scratched his head under the edge of his helmet. "What do you think Ahva? Which is the most likely way those monsters would have taken Maaska."

She took off from his shoulder and flew down the northern road, high enough to get good sightlines and stay out of reach of most attacks.

"Come back, Ahva."

I'm busy. Back in a sec. Ahva had only been flying for a few minutes when she saw the first mannequin, a rabbit. No bigger than a Kleenex box. A little further down the road a collection of three wolf mannequins. Then a couple more dead animals and a couple more after that. The weird line-and-two-dots symbol was graffitied here and there.

Clearly a great way to go if you want to encounter more

maniacs. New armor or not, I don't think Osse is up for that on his own. I'm sure not much help. We both need more training or a dungeon crawl with easier monsters.

Ahva wheeled to the south until she found the second road and followed it back toward Osse.

A few deer, some odd rabbits, plenty of songbirds, but no mannequins, and no sign of maniacs.

This way, for sure.

When she caught back up to Osse, she landed in the middle of the southern road far enough from the fork to prevent all confusion about her recommendation.

Osse joined her and crouched. "You want to go south."

Ding! Ding! Ding! They can be taught!

"Trouble north?"

"Yes." She emulated the laughter of one of the maniacs.

He offered his hand and waited for her to climb on. Once she was settled, he darted to the north road.

Ahva flew off and landed on the southern road again. "No. Go here!"

He rejoined her and crouched offering his hand. "They may have Maaska, or have you forgotten that's why we're out here?"

Dude, for all we know, either she's dead, or she was taken east. We're only guessing that she was taken west.

He tapped her chest with the edge of his hand. "Come on, Ahva. We're going north."

She hopped backwards. "No. Bad idea!" *You really think that club makes you equipped take on these creatures? You've had, what, two lessons? You haven't even tried it in real combat yet.*

"Ahva! Stop messing around. For all we know she's

just a little ways ahead." He reached for her.

She hopped backwards and pecked at his hand. *I'm not getting any minus XP warnings, so I'm right. How do I convince you of that?* Ahva fluttered a few meters further down the south road.

He stood up and propped his hands on his hips. When he came after her, she flew down the road. Continuing that pattern, she led him another hundred meters. Off the road to the south, a loud thwack like an ax hitting wood made Ahva duck.

He glared at her and clenched his hands into tight fists. "Fine. You want to go that way? You go that way. I'm going the other way. I want to find Maaska before she's dead. Can't you understand that?" He waved his hand at her dismissively. "Of course, you don't. You're a dumb bird." He turned away from her and plodded toward the fork in the road.

"Hey! Dumb kid. Few pointers. Quick lesson."

Osse stopped and turned toward her. "What did you say?"

"Hey! Dumb–"

Another loud thwack preceded a startled cry from a woman. The voice had an old, grainy quality to it.

Osse flinched and turned toward the south.

"Did you 'ear that?" She crouched and launched into the air.

The trees along the roadway grew dense as she flew further from the road, but she was small enough to weave her way through even at full speed. Behind her, vegetation crunched and footsteps thudded as Osse followed her. She flew past a clearing on her right. An old shack and an even older human caught her eye. Ahva looped back around for another look.

The shack was built from half-rotted wood and looked like a soft breeze would turn it into kindling. Presently, it was not much better than a termite condo. Nearby, a few scraggly plants grew in somewhat ordered rows.

An old woman sat next to a woodpile and held her leg. She wore faded, threadbare walking shorts and a sleeveless tunic. A scarf was tied around her head. Next to her, an ax head separated from its handle dripped red. Her ID tag called her "Vehira" and her health bar was down a quarter while her fatigue was hazardously close to red.

Ahva landed nearby but out of reach. "Hey! Hey!" She selected Sound Alarm and whistled a high-pitched note as loudly as her lungs would do it.

"That's enough noise, you." Vehira winced.

Osse entered the clearing. "I'm here, Ahva." He pointed to the old woman. "Is she why you wanted me to come this way?"

Didn't even know she was here until she hollered, but if that will make you feel better... "Yes. Help. 'Erb'ist."

"Someday you'll learn how to talk to me clearly." He set aside his bow and took the bag off his shoulder. "Ma'am, my name is Osse Bente. Can I help you? I can stop the bleeding then run and get a physician?"

Vehira scowled. "The only one who would bother to come visit me is in the monastery it would take you good couple hours to get there and back."

"I don't mind the trip, but I can tend the injury as well as I can as long as you haven't broken anything."

"Lad, you don't know who or what I am."

"I know you're injured. I know I can help you, if you let

me."

"I would appreciate it." She looked away. "Aside from the mentors, not many will give me time of day."

Osse knelt next to the woman and inspected the injury. "Your ax head flew off?"

Ahva fluttered up to the top of Osse's head and perched on his helmet. A ragged-edged cut marred her shin.

"I think so. It happened so fast." Her face paled.

"I can heal this with some of my herbs. At least, I can stop the bleeding." He fished some jars from his bag.

"Is it worth the effort?" She sniffled.

"Yes. Ow!" Ahva leaned forward. *What kind of hokey question is that?*

"Of course, it is." Osse mixed a few herbs together with some of the oily goo in one of the jars until he had a paste then spread the paste on the injury.

Vehira grimaced and drew a sharp breath between her teeth. Within moments, the wound grew shallower, and the edges grew together.

"Good bird." Ahva fluttered to the ground.

"Thank you. That's much better already." She smiled.

Osse piled everything back in his bag. "I'm glad it worked."

"What brought a Bakhari tribesman to this part of the world?" The woman rubbed her shin.

"Some monsters destroyed my village. According to some reports, four of the attackers each took a hostage and fled toward Nethanya. One other took three captives and fled to the east. I think one of the captives might be my sister."

"Monsters? What sort?"

"They might have been human once. The ones I have

encountered have been insanely fast, strong, and hard to kill."

"That sounds suspiciously like the creatures–"

A shrill, mirthless laugh came from the other side of the shack. The edge of Ahva's view turned red.

Osse snatched up his bow and nocked an arrow. "Ahva, find it, but stay out of reach."

Chapter 19

She took off and turned a tight spiral, gaining altitude with each pass. Before she reached the roof level of the house, a disheveled creature stood on the peak. The building swayed and creaked. Ahva shrieked an alarm.

The creature had stringy, dark hair. An eerie glow radiated from its chest.

Osse stepped between the old woman and the house. "Stay behind me."

"Is that one of them?" The woman pointed.

"Yes, and watch yourself. They're fast, and they're mean." He took aim.

Ahva wheeled around out of Osse's sight line.

He shot a metal tipped arrow at the creature, striking the center of the glow before it bounced off. Sparks flew, and the creature tumbled off the roof and landed face down at Osse's feet.

Move! Move! Move! You're way too close! Ahva found a rock and grabbed it with her beak then started a Bombing Run.

Vehira grabbed Osse's arm and pulled him back toward her. "Let's not be too hasty. Baron Dorcas also mentioned that they're hard to actually kill."

CHAPTER 19

The two humans retreated to the edge of the trees. Osse drew another metal tipped arrow and nocked it and held a second one in his hand.

The maniac shuddered for several seconds then jumped to its feet and charged at Osse and the old woman.

Ahva looped around and dropped the rock on its head. It didn't even flinch.

That worked well. She hissed.

Osse fired the second arrow and immediately nocked a third, sending it in the path of the second. Both arrows hit the middle of the glow. The second bounced off like the first had, but the third pierced and drove all the way through the creature's chest. Sparks exploded, the light went out, and the maniac fell over backwards. Ahva watched, waiting for the maniac to turn into a mannequin, but then a new glow appeared a few centimeters below the first. The glow was faint but gradually gained intensity.

Osse led the old woman around the edge of the clearing while he prepared another arrow. "You've got to be kidding me."

That's what the billy goat said to its wife. Ahva landed on the maniac's chest and used Peck and the point of her beak to chip at the glow. *Figure I've got a few seconds.*

"Ahva get out of there!" Osse hollered.

Not yet. She kept pecking away as hard as she could until the glow started to approach the intensity of the original.

The maniac swiped at her. She twisted midair, but it still struck her tail. She tumbled and righted herself just short of the ground and zoomed back toward Osse. The maniac was back on its feet and hardly a step behind her. She veered off, looping around. It turned to follow her.

Better me than the humans?

"Climb out of range!" Osse ordered.

She followed his instructions, but their adversary jumped, and landed on the roof of the shack. The structure creaked and swayed then collapsed. Cracking and falling boards generated a deafening clatter and a huge plume of dust. Ahva arced away from it and then flew back toward Osse. She landed on a convenient tree branch and waited for the dust to settle.

"Is it gone?" The old woman took a few steps forward.

"I don't know, but I don't want to go check until we can see in there. Are you all right?" Osse kept his eyes on the dust cloud.

"Fine, except everything I owned, what little that was, was in that house." Vehira pointed at what was left of the shack.

Osse winced. "I'm sorry. Do you have any friends or relatives I can take you to?"

"I've been trying to meet the requirements to be accepted into the convent south of here, but I still have a lot to do."

"How can I help?"

"Let's be sure that thing is dead, and then we'll sit and talk about it. I would be grateful for your help if you're willing." She patted his shoulder.

When the dust cloud cleared up enough, Osse left her at the tree line and crept closer to what was left of the shack. Ahva kicked off from the branch and circled overhead. In the center of the structure, half buried by collapsed boards, a creepy mannequin had a piece of wood stuck all the way through it.

"Ahva, do you see it?" Osse asked.

CHAPTER 19

Ahva perched on the top of the wooden spike. "Yes, there."

"Is it alive?"

"No. Very dead."

He slid the arrow back into his quiver and picked a path through the boards. Many of them cracked under his weight. He offered Ahva his hand. "Step over so I can get that chunk of wood out."

Ahva hopped over onto his hand, ran up to his shoulder, and held onto the edge of the leather tunic. Osse grabbed the spike with both hands and yanked upward. The spike came free much more easily than expected and he staggered backwards a few meters, trying to gain his footing on the uneven ground. Ahva flew off his shoulder and circled while he fell back on his rear.

He laughed. "Grace has never been my strong suit." He picked himself up and approached the mannequin to open the inventory screen.

Wonky cylinder thing, blob of yellow plasticky stuff, two white crystals – both with major cracks, a couple clear disks with a chip in the middle. How weird is that? First circuit boards, now computer chips in clear plastic labeled "rounds." Not sure what to do with it all, but it's stuff.

Osse collected all the loot, he picked his way back to Vehira who was searching the yard. He offered her the loot.

She took one of the rounds. "You can have the rest, but please help me find Breakfast."

"I have food in my bag." He deposited the stuff and offered her a roll. "We can eat while you tell me what we need to do to get you to a safer place."

She patted his hand but didn't take the food. "I want to

find Breakfast first. She's my hen."

"Oh. I'll help you look." He tucked the bread back into his bag.

Ahva circled the clearing keeping her eye on the ground and watching for feathers, small mannequins, or blood splotches. When the clearing showed nothing, she extended her search into the edges of the wooded area. No signs of a chicken, but a fox stalked closer to a bush.

No, you're not suspicious at all. She banked sharply to the left and came back around at a lower altitude.

Sure enough, a red-feathered chicken cowered under the bush.

"Hey! Hey!" Ahva snatched a rock from the ground and initiated Bombing Run. She dropped it on the fox.

It flinched and snarled at her.

"Fierce!" Ahva hissed and snatched up another rock. She looped around at a higher altitude and dropped the rock, landing it between the fox's ears. It leapt toward her but missed by a kilometer or more.

"Disgusting eyeball!" She grabbed a third rock and set up for another pass. "Bite fingers!"

Osse crashed through the brush with Vehira following behind at a distance.

Ahva landed the next rock over the fox's left eyebrow. It flinched, but as Osse drew closer, the fox bolted.

She landed next to the bush. "Come here, bird."

The chicken did its best impression of a statue.

Come on, sister. Move it. Ahva crouched and slipped under the edge of the bush. She nudged the chicken. "Up we go."

The chicken pecked at her and backed away.

Oh yeah? Ahva darted forward and grabbed one of the

chicken's tail feathers.

The fat bird clucked and ran out from under the bush.

"Found her!" Osse called. "Good job, Ahva." He scooped up the chicken and ran back to Vehira.

The computer turned the notebook blue, so Ahva opened it.

You found Breakfast! Don't Be a Chicken. Level Up, Ahva!

Yes! More points!

She closed the notebook.

"Thank you. I know she's not much, but she's all I have." Vehira cradled the chicken in her arms and stroked its feathers.

Aww.

"I'm glad she's okay." Osse led the way back to the clearing. "How about this: I have food my bag. If you can make us lunch, I'll clear as much debris as I can from where your house used to be so we can find your things. You can tell me what I need to know to resolve the convent problem, and then I can get busy on it."

She stared at the dirt. "I do appreciate the help, but are you sure? This is hardly your problem."

"I can't leave you here. Taking out that maniac took three metal-tipped arrows, a gutsy crow, and a collapsing house. There might be more of them around here. And then we have winter coming."

Vehira snickered. "It's a few months away yet."

"Yeah, but even if I knew how to build a house, I don't think your building materials will withstand any kind of interesting whether. I'll sleep a lot better at night if I know you have somewhere to stay."

"All right. Thank you."

In the clearing, Osse handed Vehira his bag of food and started stacking decaying boards into piles: one for pieces that were mostly intact and one for pieces that were not much better than kindling. The second pile grew at a much faster rate than the first. Ahva found a place nearby and preened to gain some Be a Bird XP.

And now we start the exposition part of our day. Don't suppose there's a Reader's Digest version.

Before the Great Info Dump could begin, Ahva focused on the crow pic in the top corner of her view to summon her character screen. She noted which skills had improved by practice since her last visit. She tried to dump all five points into her incredibly pathetic Vitality attribute, but only three would allocate there before the field grayed out.

Really? My max is a whole, whopping 15? How pitiful is that?

She dumped the rest into her equally pathetic Power attribute, which grayed that stat out, too.

Wow. Must find technology to improve those stats further. A mini-Superman cape, maybe?

She closed the screen and waited for the exposition to begin.

"The biggest problem is that I need a token from Mistress Elisbet before I can join the convent." Vehira stacked some kindling on a blank piece of dirt then focused the sunlight using a glass lens hanging on a chain attached to her shirt. Within seconds, the wood smoldered then caught fire.

"And how do we get that?" Osse pitched some kindling at one of the piles.

"That's the problem. I haven't always been a follower of Tsidkenu, and in my younger days I did not have an exactly honorable profession. That all changed when I became a child of Tsidkenu, but Mistress Elisbet thinks I would be a poor influence on the younger learners."

Osse added to the first pile of wood. "I'm confused. I don't know a lot about Tsidkenu, but I thought he offered forgiveness for past mistakes."

"He does." She glanced upward. "Mistress Elisbet, on the other hand…"

"I see."

"When she knows it's me, she adds to the usual requirements." Vehira sighed. "When I meet those requirements, she adds another one."

Nice. Hypocrite. "Disgusting eyeball."

"Oh really?" Vehira laughed. "She's quite the character."

"That's what she calls people she doesn't like, usually thieves or other crooks."

"How funny."

Osse glanced over toward them. "What are the current requirements?"

"I need two thousand coins, in any country's currency, to donate to the convent to provide for my upkeep, she says. I also need to replace my clothes with something simple and in better repair to prove I have left my old life behind. I need five children of Tsidkenu to vouch for me to prove I have changed my ways. And I need a copy of Tsidkenu's law, even though I can't read it, to show that I'm serious about following him. If I have all those, Mistress Elisbet says she will give me the token."

Okay, doable. Not a cakewalk, but not nearly on the level of cleaning the Augean Stables.

Osse grabbed another board, which fell apart in his hands.

"Um, with two thousand coins, we could set you up in a modest room in town for a long time unless rent here is higher than home. No need to get the rest of that."

"If I were just looking for a place to live, I'd find a cave system near here and make a door across the opening. Problem solved, but honestly, I feel so much gratitude toward Tsidkenu for rescuing me from my old life that I'd like to spend the rest of it serving him directly. That's why I'm trying to get into the convent."

"Okay, then two thousand coins of some sort. The rest of that doesn't sound too hard. You're about my mother's size. In the equipment left behind when she died, there was a simple, brown dress. If it fits you, that should meet the requirement. Mother wasn't one for bold clothing choices." Osse sniffled and scratched his nose.

Vehira shook her head. "I couldn't take that."

"What am I going to do with it?" Osse smirked at her. "Believe me. She would approve." He recovered a lantern and brought it to Vehira. "I know a scribe in the last town we were in. If he doesn't have a copy of the law to sell me, he probably knows who does."

Vehira winced. "Books are expensive."

"I'm sure you can tell, but my bag is overstuffed." Osse nodded toward his bag while he added more wood to the growing piles. "I helped that last town out quite a bit, so I have a good reputation there. I can sell what I don't need or take on a few quests. Money, I can get. That leaves the five children of Tsidkenu to vouch for you. Is there no one in the area who would put in a good word?"

"The mentors and learners at the monastery. There are eight of them. Mentor Jood and his learner come out here to help me frequently. They've already agreed, and in a bag under my bed, I have sealed envelopes from them with their voucher." She pointed toward the back corner of the ruined shack.

"That's two. We need three more. Do you think any of the other mentors would be willing?"

"Perhaps. I don't know them personally, but if Mentor Jood has been telling them about me, they might know me by reputation – my new reputation, not the old one." She glanced northward. "There's also the baron in Yavne, but that's a two-day hike there and a two-day hike back."

"Not ideal, but if three of the others at the monastery won't help, we'll keep the baron in mind." He grunted and picked up another armload of wood.

"This all sounds good, but what about your missing sister?"

"Maaska would take my head off if she found out that I chased across the country after her and left a lady in distress. Let's get you somewhere safe, then I'll continue the search after Maaska." He dropped off the load of wood.

"But all of those things in your bag–" She poked his bag with a stick.

"Are taking up space. I'm a packrat. I keep everything. Now and then it's good to get rid of it all. That bag is really starting to weigh me down. I'll get you that token, Vehira."

She blushed and looked away. "Thank you. I don't deserve it."

Ahva hissed. "Silly bird."

Osse smiled. "Even Ahva disagrees with you."

"Then I suppose I'm outvoted."

When the notebook icon turned blue, she opened it.

Un-Convent-ional. Convince Mistress Elisbet to give Vehira a home.

Old Folks Home #1: Buy the Book. Get a copy of Tsidkenu's book.

Old Folks Home #2: Say 'Yes' to the Dress. Get Vehira a simple dress.

Old Folks Home #3: We're in the Money! Collect 2000 coins for Vehira.

Old Folks Home #4: Vehira's Fan Club. Find three more people to vouch for Vehira.

Ahva chuckled. *Un-Convent-ional. Cute.*

Vehira took the food off the fire. "Lunch is about ready."

Osse piled the last of the loose wood. "Just in time."

Isn't that convenient? The exposition finishes at about the same time as the chores.

"Will your bird eat with us?" Vehira glanced up at him.

"She eats whatever we eat." Osse joined them.

Vehira handed him a toasted sandwich of meat and cheese. Sandwich in hand, Osse darted over to the pile of scrap wood and came back with a short piece of wood. He set that in front of Ahva and loaded it with a piece of bread, a little cheese, and a piece of meat.

"The only thing that remains, is to find you a shelter where you can stay while I run these errands." Osse took a bite of his sandwich. "So good."

"Thank you. Perhaps a lean-to out of what's left of the wood?" Vehira suggested.

"There's not much of that, but maybe I can rig something that'll work. I'd prefer a harder structure." He turned west. "We're close to the ocean, aren't we? You mentioned caves."

"Lots of caves. One near here, actually. Due west, but it's

overrun by spiders and large lizards. The pirates should be gone now, or at least they can't get to this side of the tunnel. Baron Dorcas collapsed it with an explosive." She giggled. "He was a sight!"

Osse chuckled. "Wow, interesting guy."

She pointed at Osse with her sandwich. "And he may have information to help you with your search for your sister."

"I'll head north after we situate you." Osse took a swig of his canteen and offered it to Vehira. "What city are we close to? I might be able to take care of some of the errands there."

She took a couple swallows. "Vanya. We're near Vanya, but you stay away from there."

"Why is that?"

"Vanya has a baron who does not like Bakhari. That attitude has rubbed off on the people. You would not be safe there." She shook her head.

Osse scowled. "I have a lot to learn about Tsidkenu. His followers don't match what I've heard."

Vehira leaned closer. "There are some who follow him more closely than others. Is that not so in your religion?"

"I have none. It's too long a story to bore you with, but we have a plan now. I'll clear the cave, so you have somewhere safer to be. Then once we get you set up there, I'll go back to Bakhar and get the coins you need and the book you need. If the dress doesn't fit you, I'll get one of those there, too."

"I have some coins in that bag." She pointed to one of the recovered sacks.

Osse smiled. "I do, too. We'll take stock before I leave so I know what's left to do. When I get back from Bakhar, I'll go to the monastery and get the other three vouchers you need. Then I'll deliver everything to Mistress Elisbet to get your token."

"Perhaps you can find some poor farmhouse who could take in Breakfast. I do hate to part with her, but I'm sure Mistress Elisbet won't let me keep her, out of spite if not for a real reason." Vehira turned all misty-eyed as she stroked the hen's feathers.

Osse glanced at the hen. "We'll figure something out."

They finished eating. Ahva fluttered over to Osse's shoulder while he helped Vehira up. The humans rooted through whatever was left of Vehira's house and came up with a sack of food — mostly squished, a flask of oil for the clay lantern, and the bag containing a badly worn dress, a pair of pants, another shirt, two sealed letters, and a pouch of coins. Back at the campfire, Osse sorted through the contents of his bag, making piles of things he absolutely needed, things he would like to keep, and things he could do without.

"Now I wish I hadn't spent so much on armor pieces and arrows." Osse muttered.

Vehira frowned. "Nonsense. You need the armor to protect you, and those steel-tipped arrows were eventually effective against your target. I'm afraid the wooden ones wouldn't have been up to the task."

Osse piled everything back in his bag, most critical stuff on the bottom and the things he wanted to trade on top. "Okay. I think I'm ready to go. Do you want to come with me? You can wait outside the cave."

She shook her head. "No. I'll start moving things over like the wood for a fire and my bucket of water."

"I can do that once I have the cave cleared." Osse slipped

his bag over his shoulder.

Vehira scowled. "Let me do something useful."

"Fair enough." He stood up and started away.

"Wait!" Vehira lit her lantern and picked up the oil flask. "I didn't see any light sources in your equipment. It's going to be dark in there."

He smiled sheepishly. "Oh, yeah. That it will." He carried the lantern and put the oil flask in his bag, wedging it to stay upright.

She patted his shoulder. "You be careful."

He smiled. "I'll be back soon."

Finally. Dear programmers, I know exposition is important, but really now. Space it out some.

Osse headed due west until waves crashed against rocks in the distance. A rocky bluff rose in front of them and a cave yawned open to their right.

"This is it. Stay close." He charged the lantern and lit it.

Like I'm going to have much choice? Crows don't usually have night vision, I don't think. She adjusted her hold on his collar.

Ahva ducked as he slid his bow over his shoulder and drew the mace. Osse crept into the cave until the exterior light faded out. The lantern cast a glow only a meter or two in front of them. After that, the light dwindled off quickly.

Spiderwebs covered the walls and worked their way across the ceiling. The tiny mannequins of small birds, rats, and other little wildlife were caught up within the dense webbing.

Have I mentioned how much I hate spiders? Ahva found a songbird mannequin caught in the web and shuddered.

When they reached a point where the webs covered the

floor, too, Osse looked at the lantern his hand. "I have an idea." He strode back to the entrance of the cave where the webbing first started. "If this works, it should take care of the spider problem pretty quickly."

He touched the flame of the lantern to the nearest web. It lit like a candle wick and spread quickly. The flame raced down the wall then up and over the ceiling and down the other side, disappearing around a bend. Black smoke poured out of the opening. Plumes rose out of a few other places in the bluff. Osse hustled backwards into cleaner air. A flurry of bats erupted out of the entrance and a couple other holes further away.

Hisses and screeches were muffled by the distance.

They were still waiting for the smoke to clear when Vehira arrived with her first load of firewood. "What did you do?" She dropped the pile and pointed to the cave.

"Took care of the spider problem, I think. I'll have to wait for the smoke to clear before I can go in and check, so why don't I help you with another load or two."

"All right. I'll let you carry the water bucket. It gets rather heavy after a while."

When they started back for the clearing, Ahva flew a wide circle around them, practicing dodging around trees to improve her Agility. With her tight turn radius she could even fly a complete circle around the trunk of a tree keeping the edge of her wing just clear of the bark.

Whooo! Go bird go!

She tried looping around a branch but still couldn't get enough pitch to complete the loop.

Aww. Maybe later.

After they had made two trips with Vehira, Osse declared

CHAPTER 19

it was probably safe enough to go inside the cave to find out what the major conflagration had done. Ahva landed on his shoulder.

Inside, the air was heavy, like bad humidity or maybe chain-smoking tires.

Osse coughed. "Ugh. Didn't think about the smell."

What did you think it would smell like in here? Roses and perfume? "Ugh. Nasty stuff."

The webs that had lined the passage had turned into piles of ash along the walls and a dusting across the floor. The pathway made a huge U-turn into a small round room. A niche set into a wall on the left had a badly charred chest.

Standing to one side, Osse tapped the locking mechanism on the front of the chest with his mace. A small dart shot out of the mechanism and struck the far wall.

Ahva squawked. "No."

"It's all right, Ahva. I'll be careful."

You better. Pretty safe bet I'm not an herbalist.

He tapped the lock again. Something inside whirred, but nothing shot out of the lock. He reached across and slid the lever on the front of the locking mechanism. Ahva tensed, waiting for something to happen. Osse jerked his hand back and waited, but the lock may no further noise. Using the end of his mace, he flipped the lid halfway open but it slammed closed again. The wood splintered. His second attempt shattered the wood and a pile of rounds spilled out onto the floor. Osse scooped them all up and dropped them into his bag. As he got up to move on, something sparkly in the ash caught Ahva's eye. She fluttered off Osse's shoulder and landed next to the sparkle. After scratching away the ash with her feet, a gold ring shined up at her. She picked it up with her beak and flew back to Osse.

He offered his arm for a landing pad. "Find something?"

"Yes. Look at it. Nice stuff." She dropped the ring on his hand. *Check for elf writing on it, okay?*

He took it from her and inspected it in the lantern light. "Nice find."

"Good bird." She cawed.

The path made a wider U-turn into another more or less round room with a pond steaming in the depression along one edge. There was no ash in this cavern, but cave formations decorated the place, some of them broken and scattered along the floor. A short passage led east out of the room before splitting into a northern and southern route. A pile of rock blocked a pathway that led south, but the way north was still open. A mannequin's hand poked out of the rubble to the south. Ahva flew over and landed on a protruding stone.

"I'm not half strong enough to move most of that rock, and from what Vehira said, we might be wise to leave it."

She did mention something about pirates. Since we're supposed to be here to make the place safer, I suppose that opening up a passageway to a pirate stronghold would be imprudent. Y'think? She flew back to Osse as he turned north.

The passage wove around a few times before opening into a dead end. Stalactites and stalagmites grew from the floor and the ceiling. Other rippled cave formations lined the walls.

On the far side of the cavern. Gold glittered in the firelight.

"Maybe we won't have to travel back to Bakhar like I thought." Osse jogged over to the pile and crouched.

The "gold" was angular, and the color was not quite right.

No. We are traveling. All that glitters is not gold.

"Nice idea." He picked up a piece and tossed it back to the pile. "I think that covers it, Ahva. With all the spiders gone and the pirates blocked, I think Vehira will be safe enough here."

As they left, they passed the rock pile blocking the southern passage. Voices, muffled by the intervening stone, came from the other side. Osse paused to listen.

"You don't have this cleared yet?"

"These... heavy. Why don't you..."

"Shut your filthy mouth! Our new boss wants it done before he gets back."

"When's... getting back?"

"Next week. And if you don't have it done..."

"Then give me a hand or get me help!"

"You've got one week."

So no dillydallying, y'slacker.

Osse crept away from the pile of rocks and all the way through the next cavern and hurried back to the opening.

Vehira was there setting up camp. "All clear?"

"For now. There's even a fresh source of water in a pond where the cave system turns to limestone. That will give you clean water much closer than the stream." He hooked his thumb over his shoulder toward the cave entrance.

"That's good. That stream is a good hike." She looked off to the southeast. "But you said it's clear for now?"

"Those pirates you said the baron blocked in the other part of the cave? I heard them. They're digging their way through. It's slow going, but they expect to be through in a week."

She nodded. "If Tsidkenu is with us, we'll be well away

from here by then."

Osse sat next to her. "I hope so. My trip back to Bakhar should only take a day or two. I can leave now and get back to the town by nightfall. Take care of my errands in the morning, and return to you by nightfall again. Might take me another day if I have to do extra errands to get enough money. Next day, I'll deal with the convent and the monastery, and then you should be set."

"With plenty of time to spare." She smiled.

Osse turned back toward the cave. "Unless those pirates get help."

"If Tsidkenu is with us…"

Osse returned her lantern. "Thanks for your lantern. And I found a pile of coins. I'll leave them with you." He dug them out of his bag and then count of them and added them to the total. "About fourteen hundred fifty to go." He pulled the dress out of the bag and handed it to her.

She stood up and held it up to herself. "This will do fine. You're sure you want to part with it?"

"I'm sure. I have no use for it, I couldn't sell it for enough to buy a new one, and you need one to meet Mistress Elisbet's demands. You keep it. If mother knew the trouble you are in, she would give it to you herself."

Vehira teared up. "Thank you, lad. Be safe on the road. There are more hazards out there than those maniacs."

The notebook icon flashed blue.

Yeah. Completed the dress part of this adventure.

Osse gathered up the things they were taking and slid his mace into the sheath on his belt. "I'll be back as soon as I can."

Chapter 20

Khin May returned from her snack break and took the game off pause. Ahva awoke in the inn.

As predicted, they had arrived in Nkamo as the sun set. Naturally, all the businesses were closed in the marketplace so after a decent meal at The Puzzled Potato, where they'd stayed before, they'd turned in early.

Ahva paced the length of the headboard while Osse dressed. She had taken an inventory of Osse's bag when he'd sorted it at Vehira's place. Coming up with roughly fifteen hundred coins and enough to buy a book might be tricky. With some luck, Osse's good reputation in this town would ensure more favorable trading. Otherwise, she feared this errand running would take far too much time. At some point, they had to get to the main quest. Maybe. If not, the game designers needed their heads examined. They probably did anyway.

As soon as Osse was ready, they went downstairs for a quick but hearty breakfast of eggs, porridge, cheese, and bread.

"Let's find out what we need for the book first. Once we get that in the works, we can lighten this bag." He patted the satchel that hung over his shoulder. "How does that sound?"

"Good idea!" Ahva flew up to Osse's shoulder. *If you do it the other way, we might have to find that scribe's fishing hole.*

Osse strode out of the inn. "I thought you might agree to that."

Five minutes later, they entered the scribe's shop. The set of books about Ilion's plans for world domination were gone. Osse checked out the ones that took their place. They had green covers and gold-embossed writing.

"*Pre-Massacre Legends*, *Before the Fall of Man*, *The Age of Power: The Days of Mechanical Men*."

Weird. So, was this "fall" of mankind before or after Ilion's plans for world domination?

The scribe entered from the back room. "I didn't expect to see you back here so soon."

"I have an urgent errand, and you were the first person I thought of who might help me finish it." Osse walked over to the scribe's desk.

"What's the problem?" The scribe sat back.

"I need a copy of the law of Tsidkenu," Osse said.

The scribe frowned. "And what would you need that for?"

"I'm trying to secure shelter for homeless old lady. We have a place in mind, but the owner insists that she needs the law of Tsidkenu." Osse leaned his palms on the table. "Can you help with that?"

"If you bring me the book, I'll copy it for you." The scribe stared past Osse's shoulder. "I'm fairly certain our library has at least one copy that you could borrow long enough for me to make yours."

Library. The one that's overrun with rats, spiders, and glowing worms? That one?

CHAPTER 20

Osse winced. "That might be tricky. I'm sure you've heard about the vermin that were attracted by the food stored there against a siege."

The scribe nodded. "I know. Unfortunately, you won't find a temple to Tsidkenu here. You might find one in Vanya. In fact, I'm sure you would, but I'm told the locals aren't keen on visitors from Bakhar."

Osse nodded. "A local warned me to stay away. Do you know where I might recruit help to clear out of the library?"

The scribe squinted toward the corner of the room. "You might ask at City Hall. Other than that, I wouldn't know."

"How about special paper or ink? Do you need anything like that to copy the book?"

"No, this isn't an official government document, so any paper and ink I have on hand will do unless you want illumination or special calligraphy."

"No. Not special." Ahva leaned forward. *Simpler is better.*

"As the bird says." Osse reached up and preened Ahva's head. "I'll be back as soon as I have the book. You're here until lunch?"

"Right."

As Osse turned to leave, Ahva crouched slightly and adjusted her grip on his tunic.

They wove a path through the crowds and left the market. The City Hall hadn't changed.

Osse approached the door and knocked.

The uniformed doorman stepped outside to join them. "What do you need?"

"A book from the library. The scribe in the market suggested I check here for help in clearing out all the vermin." Osse glanced back toward the library.

"Don't know why he would've sent you here." The doorman scratched his head. "You might try Critter Ridder. Don't know that they've ever taken any job this big, but they can do it."

"Where would I find them?"

Oh boy. Not more directions.

"Far northwest corner of the town. Can't miss them. If the sign's not clear enough, the smell will get you there." The doorman pinched his nose.

"Thank you." Osse turned to leave as the doorman stepped back inside.

Let's speed this up. Ahva crouched and launched off of Osse's shoulder.

After taking a quick bearing from the morning sun, Ahva turned toward the northwest and flew over the roofs of all the buildings until she approached the corner of the city wall. A small building sat in the open space with no other establishments nearby. A sign on the front of the building showed silhouettes of a mouse and bugs exed out with drippy red paint.

That must be the place. Ahva circled around and went back to her human.

As she approached, Osse held out his arm for a landing pad. She dove below the level of his arm and then arced back upward to shed velocity and drop gracefully onto his wrist.

"Find it?" Osse held her up to his eye level.

"Yes. Look at the bird!"

"Show me the quickest way there."

If you could fly... But you can't, so, for you? The overland route. Ahva flew to the next corner and perched on a sign until Osse caught up.

CHAPTER 20

When he joined her, she flew to the next corner and waited again. Fly ahead. Wait for Osse. Fly ahead. Wait for Osse. This would be a lot faster if he could learn the flying skill. Several turns later, the pest control service was in view.

In faint, transparent gray letters, the word "bug spray" drifted around the building.

What is that supposed to be?

Osse's nose wrinkled and he fanned the air in front of his face. "Wow, they weren't kidding about the stench. Smells poisonous."

Oh. Is that what smell looks like in this game? My Smell attribute is in single digits, so that must be a real potent stench. "Ugh. Nasty stuff."

If that's how the game dealt with odors, she didn't plan on dumping points into the Smell attribute. Even without paying for smell and taste reception, the words floating around the environment were an annoying distraction.

Ahva fluffed out her feathers and shook. She returned to Osse's shoulder before he stepped into the building. Inside, a flurry of mask-wearing men carried knee-high truncated cones with knobs on them and a nozzle sticking out of the front. They darted around the room collecting equipment.

One of the men paused and lifted up his mask. "Help you with something?"

"I need a book from the library to complete a request. The–"

The man shook his head. "Wouldn't advise that. You know the place is overrun with rats, glowworms, and huge spiders."

"Yes. Big nasty spiders." Ahva clicked her beak a couple times to show her annoyance. *No kidding, Sherlock. Would we be here otherwise?*

"That's why I'm here." Osse nodded. "I need a way to get rid of all of the vermin. Hopefully, before noon, so I can bring the book to the scribe to have a copy made and then complete the request I was given. The doorman at the City Hall suggested you might be able to help me."

The man sighed. "Yeah, normally, that'd be right up our alley. Unfortunately, we are a bit busy at the moment. Someone played a prank on the mayor, and his house is overrun with grasshoppers and frogs. You might say he's unimpressed. Wants them all gone now. Yesterday would be better. You know how it goes. It's going to take us a couple days, at least, to clear out the mess."

"If I help you, would you finish faster?" Osse asked.

"No, not really. We have all the people we need. We have all the equipment we need. In fact, we have more equipment than we need. Any more men involved, and we'll start tripping over each other."

Osse frowned. "I have to complete this request in less than a week and it has multiple parts. I can't wait a few days to complete this part. What do you recommend?"

"You could clear the library yourself."

Ahva hissed. "No. Bad idea. Big spiders."

Osse held up one hand, palm out, and shook his head. "One spider was almost more than Ahva and I could handle. There's a lot more than that in there."

The man blew out a breath. "As I said, we have extra equipment. Potent stuff. I got these cones from Ilion a few months ago. Take a couple with you. They emit chemicals, shocks, and sounds guaranteed to scare off or eradicate vermin of all sorts. All you have to do is place them inside the library and push this button marked exterminate. Then get out fast. Wait thirty minutes then it will be safe for you to go into the library. Get your book, and then you're all set."

That's way too easy. What's the catch?

"What about the cones?"

The man shrugged. "As many vermin as I hear are holed up in the library? They'll be harmless at that point. Trust me. What could go wrong?"

Ha. Famous last words.

"I bring the cones back here when I'm done?" Osse asked.

The man shook his head. "No need. They can't be reused."

"How much do they cost?" Osse opened his bag and fished around for his money.

"You're doing me a favor, son. I don't want any part of that mess in the library. I told the last mayor that storing food down there was a dumb idea. Would he listen to me? No. Of course not. I only do this for a living. What do I know? Nothing. Apparently, nothing." He rolled his eyes. "I swore I would have no part in cleaning up that mess, and I meant it. If you do it, the job gets done, and I didn't have to do it. See? Perfect. I don't get nagged by our current mayor, and you get your book."

I smell a rat. I know birds can't smell much, but I smell a rat.

Osse nodded. "Deal."

No, don't ask the player for advice. Just go ahead and do it. Never mind that I might have an objection. Might think this is a bad idea. Might have a better idea. Maybe not this time, but on general principle.

"Stellar. You'll find a few extra cones around the side of

the building. Those are spares, so take as many as you need. Two or three should get the job done, but if you want more, take more. Seriously. Be my guest."

No, not suspicious at all.

Osse beamed a brilliant smile. "Thank you. I appreciate your help."

You know, goofy human, if you say "ice cream" slow enough it sounds like "gullible."

The man flipped his facemask down again and then rejoined the flurry of men gathering equipment. Osse slipped back outside the door.

"That was nice." Osse smiled.

Ahva squinted. "No. Looks good. Disgusting eyeball."

"Come on. He's giving us the equipment to do the job for free. It needs doing. He could've charged us quite a bit for the equipment." He headed around to the side of the building.

"Bad idea."

Osse chuckled. "You just don't like the smell."

What smell? Birds don't smell much. "Dumb bird. Bite fingers."

Osse frowned. "We can't wait a few days for them to clear out the library. Those pirates will be through the barrier in less than a week, and I don't want to think about what they would do to Vehira if we don't have her somewhere safe before then. There's no telling how long running the convent errands and getting the vouchers from the other three mentors will take, and you and I were not enough to take out more than one dumb spider. Let's try this. It shouldn't take more than a half hour, maybe forty-five minutes. If it works, then we get the book and get on our way. If it doesn't work, we only lost about an hour. Right?"

Ahva hissed. "Yes. Still bad idea."

"Otherwise, we have to travel a lot further to get a copy of the book, probably to Yavne. "He waved his hand in a vaguely northwest direction." That's at least two days there from Vanya and the same back from what Vehira said. That's cutting it too close."

Ahva slumped. "Yes." She mumbled, "Still bad idea."

Osse walked around to the side of the building. Several of the knobby truncated cones sat there. Each was about knee high, with a nozzle half the length of the body protruding from a cylindrical "head" at the top of the cone.

"He said two ought to do it. What do you say we try two? That will either do what we need, or create a bigger mess, but hopefully not too much of one." Osse picked up two of the cones, one with each arm, and headed back to the library. The only visible difference was the plant life now decorating a set of pots on the ends of the steps.

Ahva flew up to one of the high windows across the front of the building just below roof height. From her vantage point, she could see down several of the rows. The three types of critters had set up territories. Spiderwebs festooned one corner of the library, taking about one fourth of the space. An eerie green glow from the opposite corner suggested the worms had taken up residence there. That meant the rats either had free rein of the rest of it, or had set themselves up in some of the open spaces. She hopped further toward the corner of the window try to get a better view of the front door and the circulation desk, but the angle was too severe. Ahva fluttered to a couple of the other nearby windows but had the same problem. She darted back to the window closest to the front door and leaned against the glass.

"Anything in front of the door?" Osse asked.

Wish I could say for certain. "No."

"Good. You stay there and sing out if you see anything approaching the circulation desk. I'm going to turn these things on and then close them in there. Got it?" He reached for the doorknob.

"Yes. Ahva looks."

The door creaked open and Osse stepped inside. Her angle was too severe to watch him, but as he worked, a trio of rats came out of one of the unoccupied corners.

Ahva kicked in her Sound Alarm skill and squawked as loud and shrill as she could.

The door slammed.

"Okay, I'm out." Osse called.

"Good bird." Ahva watched the rats continue toward the front door.

Before Ahva lost sight of them, a burst of the electric blue light shot out and nailed one of the rats. It shuddered like it had been tasered then fell flat. The other two scattered.

Wow! This might actually work. She flew back to Osse.

"While we're waiting for those cones to do the job, let's go back to the market and figure out how much of the missing fourteen hundred fifty coins we can generate selling all the extra stuff weighing down my bag." Osse patted the bag hanging over his shoulder.

"Yes. Deal!" *Hopefully we'll get pretty close to the fifteen hundred. I have my doubts, but it would be real nice to proved wrong once in a while.*

The marketplace was busier today than the last time they

CHAPTER 20

were here. Removing Antwen's improper tollbooth had made this town a nice booming metropolis again. Yay for them. Not so great for her and Osse.

Osse turned to the right inside the main gate of the market and wandered up and down the aisles, stopping anywhere that dealt in merchandise similar to something he had for sale in his bag. Pretty much everything they had picked up in Fola along with the girlier stuff he'd inherited from his family, the crown from the chief's son's mannequin, and the ring they had found in the cave all found new homes somewhere in the market. No one showed interest in the slagged plastic or the weird cylinders. Likewise, the jeweler didn't much care for the crystals, which was odd. I mean, sure, they weren't diamonds and rubies, but they weren't all sandstone and quartz, either. Maybe they were quest items for later?

Ahva tried to keep mental track of how much money Osse was acquiring through the various sales, but she soon lost count and, in the end, could only roughly estimate that they were close, but no joy. Osse was going to have to find an errand or few or maybe even a quest. At one point, he stopped outside of the armorers and checked the various armor pieces he was wearing. After a bit of coaxing, he left that place behind and continued on their way.

An hour of reverse shopping later, Osse's bag was down to food, herbs, camping gear, and a few odds and ends, not to mention the possible quest items no one was interested in.

Osse sighed at his almost empty bag. "That's it. I don't think it's enough, but let's finish up at the library so we can get the book to the scribe, and then we'll go count and see if I need to find a few quick jobs to do."

I'm with you, kid. "Up we go."

Osse wove their way back through the crowds then around the marketplace to the library. Ahva flew up to the window. The spiderwebs still decorated the place, but the glow in the other corner had faded. Mini mannequins littered the floor. The two cones stood inert in the middle of the library.

Osse stood at the door. "All clear?"

I've got a bad feeling about this. That was way too easy. "Yes?"

Osse chuckled. "You don't sound certain."

Ahva flew back to his shoulder. "No. Bad bug guy." Not for the first time, she wished she had a better vocabulary. "Ex'er'nate Osse."

There's only one real way to find out.

He grimaced. "Oh, he was a nice enough guy, and those machines didn't look that bad. They're only as tall as my knee. Did you see anything moving around?"

"No." She fluffed up her feathers and squinted.

Osse studied her for a moment. "But you still expect trouble?"

"Yes. Easy. Too easy." Ahva bobbed her head once.

Osse drew his mace. "We'll be careful."

You'll be dead!

He opened the door and stepped inside the library.

Ahva's skin crawled, which the VR system accentuated. She resisted the urge to check for creepy crawlies in her feathers. *It's all in my mind. It's all in my mind. It's all in my mind.*

In the middle of the library, the two truncated cones slowly turned toward the main door.

CHAPTER 20

The edge of Ahva's vision turned red. "No good."

"I thought those were supposed to be dead. We were gone long enough." Osse crept his way around the circulation desk as the two cones turned to track their movement, aiming the nozzle that stuck out of their tops in his direction.

"Those are made of metal," Osse whispered. "I don't think my bow will do any good."

"No. Mace. Hit them." Ahva crouched lower on his shoulder.

His hand dropped to his mace. "Exactly. We'll have to find out how well this mace works. Find a place to hide. I don't want them thinking you're vermin."

Ahva flew up to one of the windowsills. *That should keep me out of range.*

When the two cones started rolling toward Osse, he darted toward them and closed the distance quickly. He raised his mace high above his head and brought it down in a cloud-to-ground strike that smacked the nearest of the two cones square on the top. A loud clang echoed through the library. The top of the cone now sported a terrific dent, but a noxious, brown fog burst out of the machine as it turned into a toppled mannequin.

Osse coughed and staggered backwards. He tripped over his own feet and landed in a sprawling mess on the floor, still hacking up a lung. His health bar flashed a green-skull-and-crossbones. The second cone turned to dodge around the mannequin that used to be its squashed companion and steadily made its way toward Osse.

Chapter 21

Get up! Get up! Get up! Ahva hopped from foot to foot.

Osse coughed into one hand while he rooted through his bag with the other.

I knew this was a bad idea. Ahva kicked off from the windowsill. She had nothing to drop on the thing, but the exterminator had mentioned a button. With any luck, it was a toggle. If she could press it again, maybe the dumb thing would shut down.

She dove as if in a bombing run and jarred every feather and bone in her body when she landed on the back of its head.

The cone had gotten around its destroyed counterpart and now aimed the nozzle straight at Osse, who was still hacking like a five-pack-a-day smoker. He up-ended one of the poison cures into his mouth. That took care of the skull and crossbones.

Ahva found a button and scowled at the gibberish written across the front of it. *Really, programmers? I can read store signs, but I can't read this button? Like they're in different languages or something?*

It was the only button there, so she hopped onto it. Naturally, it didn't move. She hopped a few more times, like the jig-dancing parrot video she'd seen a couple weeks ago. Still, no movement. Ahva stepped off the button and pecked at it. That was nearly as effective. Nearly.

Osse's coughing fit subsided as an arc of blue light shot of the nozzle. He rolled to one side, and the beam burned a hole through his tunic. Continuing his motion, Osse sprang back to his feet, with the mace at the ready. "Move, Ahva." His voice rasped.

She flapped hard and headed back toward the windowsill. The cone turned to track her.

If I can't turn the dumb thing off, maybe I can keep it pointing at me. She flew as erratic a pattern as she could, trying to make it hard for the thing to lead her. That should give Osse a chance to whack the tar out of it.

As soon as it had turned away from him, he darted forward. As he came into range, one of the knobs opened like a flower petal and emitted a high-pitched shriek.

Ahva squawked in protest.

A blue beam buzzed past her tail, singeing one of the longer feathers.

Make it quick, human.

Osse swung the mace like a baseball bat and hit the shrieky flower. That brought an end to the ruckus, but not the machine. Ahva turned into a sudden dive as another beam burned through the space she had been in a moment before.

Osse's next strike hit the nozzle, giving it a permanent downward bend.

Thanks, but could you kill the dumb thing already?

As another of the knobs started to iris open, Osse darted forward and slapped the button with the palm of his hand. The machine whirred and went inert.

As Ahva returned to Osse, he leaned forward with his hand on his knee and the head of the mace pressed against the ground. "Okay, so you were right, that guy wasn't being entirely honest with us. Surely, he knew that these things were still dangerous when the job was done."

His voice sounded like he had eaten gravel for breakfast.

Ahva landed on Osse's shoulder. "Disgusting eyeball."

"Yeah, no doubt." He slipped the mace into the sheath on his belt.

Ahva kept a lookout from Osse's shoulder while he toured the area and collected the loot in all the mannequins. Most of them had a few chips, some slagged plastic, a crystal, or a cylinder.

He headed for the circulation desk in the front of the library. "Let's find that book and be done with this."

Don't suppose they use the Dewey decimal system.

Osse scratched over his ear and turned a full circle. "This could take forever."

Ahva fluttered over to the circulation desk. If she were designing this game, there would be instructions on how to locate a book somewhere on the circulation desk. Because, you know, that made sense. Unfortunately, the programmers decided the writing on the papers would be unreadable. She engaged both Problem Solving and Cleverness.

A thought bubble appeared. *Hmm... I wonder if there's a pattern to the letters that correspond to sounds.*

Some of the writing translated, but it was still very much like a bad cryptogram. This would take some practice.

"Hey! Hey!" Ahva waved her wings.

Osse walked over. "Good idea. There has to be an index or something. Some kind of map."

CHAPTER 21

He sorted through the various papers while Ahva checked some of the circulation desk shelves for a map. She could recognize one of those, no matter what language it was in. After a few minutes of hunting, she found an aerial view of the library.

"Here we go." Osse picked up a paper and ran his finger down the list. "This list says that religion can be found under 200s, along with mythology."

Ahva snorted. *They are using the Dewey decimal system.*

Osse growled. "It doesn't happen to say where the two hundreds are."

"Hey! Hey! Look here!" Ahva tapped the aerial view with her beak. As she studied the map, some of the letters and numbers translated, including 200s.

Osse leaned over the circulation desk. "What did you find? Please tell me it's a map."

"Yes." She got the tip of her beak under the edge and pulled backward, but whatever adhesive held it there wouldn't let go.

He smiled. "You're kidding."

"No. Look!"

He darted around the corner of the circulation desk and squatted down to check out what she'd found. "It is a map. Good job, Ahva."

"Good bird." She tapped the map again. "200s." She jumped up and landed on his shoulder as he stood up.

Map in hand, he turned it to get oriented and headed straight for the right section. Naturally, she couldn't read the book titles, but he scanned through them, mumbling their names.

"*Morning Glory!: Prayers to Start the Day*, *Incensed: Making*

Your Own Incense, Smoking Section: The Proper Use of Incense, Altared States: Proper Arrangement of Sacrifices." He reached for one hand-sized, relatively skinny book. "Got it."

They returned to the circulation desk where he replaced the map, then he flipped open the book and found an extremely old school library card. He slid it out of the pocket and used a quill and inkwell to write his name on the card. After setting the card in a prominent place on the desk, he tucked the book into his bag. When they left, no weird alarms rang out.

The sun overhead was creeping into that straight up above position, which would indicate noon, so Osse hustled back through the marketplace to the scribe in the corner. As before, they arrived as the man was getting ready to lock up.

No fishing for you today.

Osse fished the book out of his bag. "I got it."

The scribe's jaw dropped. "How did you get past all the spiders and rats?"

Osse glanced toward the library. "It was a long, messy story. But it's done. How much will it cost to copy the book?"

"You do know, right, that books are rather costly." The scribe took the book.

"I know, but I need it." Osse frowned.

Buddy, you stink at haggling.

"A good, high-quality book will cost you at least two hundred chips." The scribe shrugged.

Osse shook his head. "I don't need fancy. I don't need leather binding, or fancy ink, or special paper, or pretty calligraphy. I'm sure you're a master of all of that, and I would be honored to have one of your best books at some other time when my need is less severe. I need the book to help a frail old lady meet the requirements to be admitted into a convent where she'll be safe and cared for for the rest of her days. What do you charge for the most basic, no-frills copy of this book?"

He thumbed through the pages. "Fifty. And that's quite a bargain for you. I'm only willing to do it because it's for a good cause."

Without pulling his money pouch out of the bag, Osse counted out the fifty circuit board chips and handed them over. "Thank you. When will it be ready?"

"How long are you in town?"

"Another day, maybe two."

The scribe blew out a breath. "Make it two. Come see me just before you leave. I'll have it for you then."

Osse nodded. "Thank you. I'll be here."

Without another word, the scribe went to his desk.

Ahva adjusted her grip as Osse turned and left.

They returned to the inn and grabbed a lunch that suspiciously resembled a burger and fries.

What, no shake?

Ahva stuffed her beak until her crop was full and her fatigue bar was maxed. She sat back and let Osse devour the rest. When they were both finished, they went back up to their room. Ahva perched on the headboard, and Osse sat cross-legged on the bed.

Your leg's gonna fall asleep that way.

Osse took his bulging coin purse out of the bag and dumped it on the bed. After splitting Nethanyan clear rounds with chips embedded and Bakhari mini-circuit boards, he made stacks of ten, but his starting pile dwindled long before they reached one hundred forty-five piles. The last couple stragglers went in a pile of their own.

Ahva bobbed her head as she counted each of the piles. *One, two, skip a few, ninety-nine, one hundred.*

She started her count again. For real this time.

"Two hundred sixty-two short." Osse sighed.

Yeah, and that doesn't count living expenses for the next few days. Don't forget that. Otherwise we'll be camping with the maniacs and living on crunchy air and pocket lint.

Osse blew out a breath and collected all the coins back into his pouch. "We'll have to find a few jobs to do. Surely someone around here needs an errand or few done."

"Up we go!" She fluttered over to his shoulder. *Lead on, valiant human.*

When he darted out to the main room, she had to hold on for dear life.

The bartender stood straighter as they entered the main room. "Headed back out again?"

"Yeah, I'm afraid so. Do you know where I might find some quick work or some errands that need running?"

"I hear tell the library is hiring temporary help."

I'd bet my entire comic book collection that the job is cleaning up the terrific mess.

"Thanks. I'll check it out." Osse spun on his toe and strode out of the inn.

They made it to the library in record time. Osse tugged open the door and walked in. A gray-haired lady sat with her head down at the circulation desk sobbing.

"Go away. We're not open. We probably never will be. Just go away." She shooed him away with her hand.

CHAPTER 21

"I'm here to help. I understand you need help, and I need a job. A temporary job. A day or two, tops."

She sniffled and dabbed at her eyes with a hankie. "Really? You can't mean that. This place is a mess! It'll take a year to get this place back in order. Spiderwebs everywhere. Dust you can write your name in. Books are out of order. The mayor wants this place open by tomorrow. A year from tomorrow, maybe."

Osse shook his head. "I'll help you. I need three hundred chips to finish a quest. For three hundred chips, I'll help you get this place back in order by morning. Then you can open up on time. How does that sound?"

"Like we would need to divert the river through here to accomplish that feat." The librarian muttered. "I would be grateful for your help. In fact, if you clear away all the cobwebs, dust the shelves, and reshelf the books, I'll give you four hundred chips."

Osse strode forward. "You've got a deal."

I love how you don't even try to figure out what the catch might be.

The woman shook his hand. "I'll start reorganizing the books. There are cleaning supplies in the far left corner of the basement." She pointed. "Collect those and then get rid of the cobwebs and handle the dusting. If you finish that before I do, then you can start from the other end of the books and work toward me. We'll meet in the middle."

Osse headed for the basement stairs.

"Bad idea. Very bad idea," Ahva muttered.

"What? The basement?" He strung his bow and checked his quiver. "Those cones should have taken care of all the vermin."

"Still bad idea."

He opened the door and descended into the basement. A chill communicated by the VR rattled Ahva.

"It's fine. Those cones should have taken care of everything."

"In basement too?" *This place needs parabolic mirrors at the corners.*

"We didn't check that, did we?" He paused halfway down.

"Noooo."

He blew out a breath and resumed his descent. "Well, if we need to, we'll go get another couple of those cylinders and just pound them to scrap after they've taken out the vermin."

Ahva snorted. *What could possibly go wrong with that plan?*

Osse paused at the bottom of the stairs.

Recalling the layout from their first visit, Ahva made a mental map. There were three parallel corridors connected at the ends by perpendicular ones, making a sort of Roman numeral III. Doors lined all the parallel corridors.

Squinting, Ahva listened for any sign of movement. Nothing moved in the corridor that led straight to where they'd found that huge tarantula.

"Do you hear anything?" he whispered.

"No." *Which isn't the same thing as "There's nothing to hear."*

He turned left and went down the parallel passage on the left side. Globs of glow-in-the-dark goo were splattered all over the walls. Spider, rat, and worm mannequins were scattered on the floor. The ones they came close to opened into an inventory screen, but none of them contained any loot.

CHAPTER 21

Has someone else been here? The librarian maybe? She doesn't seem the type, but who knows?

At each door they came to, Osse stood next to the door frame and opened it before peeking inside. Most of the rooms had a mannequin or two along with shelves of old books, office supplies, random papers, and decorations, but nothing like cleaning supplies.

They reached the door marked "Janitor" where the hallway they were in met the perpendicular corridor. A strange wheezing sound came from within the room.

Osse stood with his back to the wall then turned the doorknob and pushed the door open.

A glowing green glob hurled out of the door and splattered on the floor a few meters away.

"Ugh! Nasty stuff!" Ahva crawled to the back of Osse's collar and leaned around where she could see.

"Has to be one of those glow worms." Osse drew a couple arrows, holding both in one hand.

He nocked the first and darted down the hall they'd just checked. A glowing, green worm several meters long and as big around as Osse was coiled up in the janitor's closet on a pile of chips, rounds, crystals, melty plastic blobs, and spider silk. When he passed the glowing muck on the floor, he turned and shot the first arrow, a wooden one without a metal head. The arrow shattered on impact.

He nocked and shot the second arrow in a single, fluid move. It hit closer to the business end of the worm and pierced, but not by much. The health bar floating over the worm's head only lost a handful of points.

"I really don't want to use the mace on this one," Osse muttered.

The creature hissed and shot forward like a snake on a mission. Osse backpedaled as he drew a couple more arrows, one with a metal arrowhead and one without.

Ahva launched off his back and zoomed down the perpendicular corridor near the stairs then banked a sharp left into the parallel one then another hard left into the perpendicular hall with the janitor's closet.

Osse cried out. "Ahva, stay away from the front end of this thing! It's shooting some kind of burning chemical."

Yep. Figured that.

The worm was halfway to Osse as he continued to shoot arrow after arrow. His health bar was down a quarter and the right side of his blacksmith tunic was smoking. The worm's health bar was showing half now, so he was getting somewhere, but his arrow supply was dwindling.

In the janitor closet, she looked for something useful. If she could get that worm to focus on her, Osse could pound the holy fool out of it with his mace without having to dodge green goo. That had worked with the bug cones. So, why not here?

She grabbed a piece of the shattered arrow and flew down the hall. Osse had turned down the perpendicular hall with the stairs and the worm was still after him. She turned the left as Osse reached the end of the hall. Only a few arrows were left in his quiver and his health had taken a hit. The bar was down another quarter and the right edge of his shirt was smoking.

Ahva landed on the worm's tail and used the jagged piece of the arrow like an ice pick, poking the worm like a woodpecker after lunch.

In her peripheral vision, the worm twisted toward her

and started to double back. Osse slipped his bow over one shoulder and drew his mace, swinging it like baseball bat. He connected at the same time that the worm hurled a glowing glob. It splattered harmlessly on the nearest wall. The worm's health bar dropped a bit and changed red.

It whipped around to face Osse again, and he swung the mace but missed when slid sideways.

Ahva continued using her arrow fragment and on one jab managed to get it stuck between segments on the worm's armor. It wheezed and flipped its tail to the side. Ahva tried to kick off, but still slammed into the wall, which flashed the screen red. She hit the floor on her side and scrambled back to her feet.

Osse took advantage of the worm's distraction and whacked it with the mace again, turning it into a mannequin.

"Ahva?" Osse called.

"Ow. Bad worm." She crouched and leapt into the air. Each upstroke of her wings caused the screen to go red for a moment, but she landed on Osse's outstretched arm easily. "You okay?"

He inspected the pockmarked damage to his blacksmith tunic. "I think so. Someday, I'm going to need to replace this tunic." He slid the mace back into its sheath and pulled out his herb jars. "Let's get us both fixed up and then we'll have a look at the janitor's closet."

"Good idea."

She watched him mix the herbs into a paste with some water then held still while he applied them to her injured side. Once her health bar was back to normal, she launched to the air and went on a hunt for intact arrows. She'd made the whole loop of the basement and only found a couple, but she carried each one back to Osse while he pulled off his blacksmith tunic and damaged shirt. His right side was blistered and oozing, but when she came back with the second one, he was applying some herbal concoction, which took care of the damage in moments.

He traded his damaged shirt for the intact one in his bag then pulled his blacksmith tunic back on.

"Better?" she asked.

"Better." He approached the worm mannequin, but the inventory screen that opened contained only the arrows he's stuck into its hide. All but one had metal arrowheads. He retuned those to his quiver and frowned. "We'll need to visit the bowyer and pick up more arrows with metal arrowheads."

"Yes. Good idea. Metal good." She fluttered up to his shoulder.

For good measure, they checked all the rooms in the basement, finding no more vermin of any sort, and ended with the janitor closet. The worm had collected an impressive collection of Bakhari money, crystals, plastic blobs, spider silk, and other random flotsam. Osse sorted through it all and pocketed the money, crystals, and plastic. The silk and other junk could stay where the worm left it.

After gathering a small bucket of water, a rag, and a feather duster, they went back upstairs.

The librarian leaned around the end of a bookcase. "What kept you?"

Ahva hissed. "Bad worm."

Osse nodded. "A glowing worm as long as one of the hallways down there."

CHAPTER 21

"Is it gone now?"

"Yes. You might have warned me." Osse set the cleaning supplies on the circulation desk.

She crossed her arms over her chest. "How could I know it was there?"

Because someone else had cleared all the loot in the mannequins that littered the hallway.

Osse held the handle of the feather duster closer to Ahva. "You think you can manage to handle this thing?"

Not likely. Ahva tried to close her beak around the handle, but couldn't get enough leverage to hold onto it. "No. Too big." Ahva lifted off again and snatched one of the cleaning rags with her beak. To compensate for the extra drag, she flapped harder, and angled her wings for maximum lift. She flew to the nearest bookshelf and dropped the rag then circled back around and landed next to it. Grabbing it with her beak, she stepped backwards and swished her head from side to side. That left a cleaner trail than she expected.

Better than nothing.

The library and laughed. "What a clever bird."

"Yes, she is." Osse stroked Ahva's wing.

Khin May opened the settings screen and flicked the slider to speed up the game clock to maximum. The shadows moved across the library as Osse, Ahva, and the librarian raced around the room at a significant fraction of lightspeed. Gradually, cobwebs cleared, dust vanished, and books were re-sorted. When night fell in the game, the librarian fired up the gas lights, creating a warm glow around the room. Some time well after dark, the two NPC's trudged back to the circulation desk. Khin May slowed the clock back down to its usual speed and reentered the game.

Ahva joined the humans at the circulation desk.

"I didn't believe it possible. I really didn't." The librarian flopped onto the stool behind the desk. Tears welled up in her eyes.

Osse leaned on the desk. "We did it. You can now open on time."

"Yes, I can. But there's still a problem. I don't have the money I promised to pay you." She brushed her eyes with the back of her hand. "And I feel awful. I really didn't think we would get it done. That's why I promised you more than I could pay."

Ahva hissed. "Disgusting eyeball."

Osse glowered. "I made that agreement with you in good faith. I did my part. You can't do yours?"

"I don't have the money." She sniffled.

Turn off the waterworks, sister. I'm not buying it.

Osse sighed. "How much can you pay me?"

"Seventy-five. That's all I have."

This town is full of crooks.

"Can you pay me in goods? Something I can sell in town to get the rest?"

The librarian sighed. "If you find anything of value in the basement, anything that wasn't destroyed by the vermin, you can have it. Maybe that will get you enough."

There wasn't much down there, really. Maybe a book that we can sell to the scribe? Some paper to sell to the paper maker? Skull of a couple rats to sell to the decorated skull guy?

"I guess that will do." Osse scratched the side of his head. "I guess it'll have to, but I sure wish you'd been honest with me up front."

"I didn't think you'd help." She sniffled.

CHAPTER 21

Osse held out his hand. "I'll take that seventy-five now, please."

"You go search in the basement." She tapped the corner of the desk. "I'll leave it for you here at the circulation desk."

Ahva hissed. "No." She imitated the sound of the mini-circuit boards hitting the table. *Fool me once...*

Osse shook his head. "I'm sorry, but I'll take my payment now."

"I suppose I can't blame you for that." The librarian huffed.

She dug a ridiculously large ring of keys from her pocket, a set that would've never fit in there in the first place, and unlocked a drawer. She plopped a heavy bag on the counter then relocked the drawer. "I suppose you want to count this."

You bet your card catalog we want to count it.

He nodded. "That would be best, I think."

Osse made piles of ten hexagonal circuit boards on the surface of the desk running out short of the seventh pile.

That's sixty-eight.

"That's all there is. I am sorry. Take whatever you want from the basement."

"Let's go have a look."

The librarian yawned, which looked as real as her promise to pay them for their work. "I really need to go home and get to sleep."

"Then I'll be back in the morning." Osse piled the money back in the bag and then slid it into his shoulder bag. "We can go through the basement then."

"I suppose I can't blame you for that either."

Osse offered the librarian his arm. "I'll walk you home, and then I'll be back in the morning."

"That's decent of you. Thank you."

After depositing the librarian at a modest house on the edge of town, they returned to the inn and went straight to bed.

As usual, the computer zoomed through their sleep while it played a goofy cartoon of sheep jumping hurdles in a race and woke them up literally seconds after they'd stretched out or tucked beak under the wing. After a pile of Johnny cakes and gooey syrup for breakfast, they scooted on over to the library.

Osse paused outside the door. "What do you think? We need at least another few hundred chips to meet Vehira's needs, have our own traveling money, and buy some new arrows; but nothing about this library has gone the way we were told to expect."

No, sure hasn't. I'm half expecting that she'll either forget that she told you to come back and raid the basement or she'll pretend like she remembers it fine, and then accuse you of stealing.

"What do you think, Ahva? Library or market?"

She flew to the bottom of the stairs. "Dis way!"

Osse dropped his hand back to the side. "You're right. We'll come up with the rest somewhere. Just not here."

Smart human.

He jogged back down the stairs. They returned to the market and stopped in the first stall. Balls of yarn filled baskets lining the walls and filled shelves that reached as high as the top of the tent. The merchant, a sandy-haired man with a wiry build, rose to meet them. "What can I do for you?"

Ahva tuned out the gazillionth reiteration of their quest for money.

"Well, as a matter of fact, I do have something I need done." He pulled a wagon, more like an open-topped one-meter cube with wheels, over to Osse. "The shepherd I get my wool from has the next batch of wool ready. I've paid her for it, but two other errand runners came back saying they couldn't get there. Some nonsense about a-a-a bird in the way. I've never heard of anything so ridiculous. Anyway, I need that wool. If you bring back this wagon full of wool, I'll pay you two hundred fifty chips if you get it all in one trip."

Osse nodded. "Where is this shepherd?"

He turned and pointed. "Five kilometers north of town. There isn't much of a road, but if you go out the western gate of the city and take the trail north, it'll take you straight there."

Osse turned to her. "What do you say, Ahva? Should we take this errand?"

It sounded straightforward enough, and honestly, she'd die from the curiosity of how a bird could prevent two people from retrieving the wool. Sure, birds could be territorial, but that had to be some bird.

"Let's go!" She bobbed her head.

Osse took the handle of the wagon. "We'll be back."

"Good luck." The merchant returned to his chair.

They left the merchant's stall and headed for the western gate.

"Turned back by a bird?" Osse scratched over his ear. "Could be an eagle, I suppose."

"Big bird?" Ahva stretched her wings. "Could be—" She imitated the maniac's laugh.

Osse drew a breath between his teeth. "Oh, I hope not. Maybe you should stay closer to me this time. As quick as those things are on the ground, one in the air would be impossibly fast."

Not a bad idea, but if she stayed with him, that negated the benefit of having a bird to spot trouble before it found them. There had to be a nice middle ground. She could stay within the range of his bow, maybe.

At the western gate, the guard smirked and waved them through. Just as the merchant had described, the main road went further west, but a smaller trail led north. The wagon rumbled as they walked.

Ahva launched off Osse's shoulder and spiraled tightly as she gained altitude. Osse shrank down to toy size by the time she reached her maximum. She widened her circle and scanned for trouble on the ground. Although she spotted plenty of nests and smaller songbirds in the trees ahead, there was nothing avian that might pose a threat to them. So, what was the problem?

When Osse got close to the trees, Ahva reversed directions and spiraled down to land on his arm.

He held her up at eye level. "Anything?"

"Little birds." She fluttered up to his shoulder.

"I'm starting to wonder if there was some joke there, and I missed it." He shrugged and they continued on through the dappled sunlight that made its way through the maple trees.

After a half-hour of hiking, they left the trees for grasslands again. Ahva kicked off from Osse's shoulder and

CHAPTER 21

headed for her best altitude without going too far afield.

A loud raptor shriek came from behind them. In her peripheral vision, a pair of hawks took off from one of the taller trees.

I think I found the trouble! She dove for Osse, who was stringing his bow, and landed and his helmet. "Look!"

"I see them." He nocked an arrow.

As they came closer, Ahva got a better look. Their feathers were a matted mess to the point she wondered how they were getting enough airfoil to stay aloft. A glow came from their chests.

Ahva imitated the maniacs' laughter.

"Yeah. I see it." He loosed the arrow, and the hawk on the left dodged it.

He held his second shot as the hawks came closer.

Shoot! Shoot, shoot, shoot!

They were meters away when he shot the second arrow, hitting the glow dead center on the left hawk. The crystal shattered in a shower of sparks, and the hawk smashed into the ground on the far side of the wagon.

The second hawk was diving feet first.

Osse dropped into a crouch, and Ahva lost her footing on his slick helmet. She scrambled and fluttered to get some kind of stability, but there was nothing on the helmet to grab. She slid off and flapped like mad, managing to belly flop with minimal grace and wounded pride.

The hawk buzzed past them and arced upward again to try for another pass. Osse drew two more arrows, holding one and nocking the other. He stood, but Ahva ran under the wagon. When the hawk turned back, Ahva watched, willing Osse to take his shot, but like the first one, he waited far longer than she might have before finally releasing the arrow. The hawk wove to one side but not fast enough to clear the arrow entirely. The shot drove through its wing, which didn't even make the hawk flinch. It did develop a permanent left turn, though. As it turned, Osse shot the second arrow, creating a burst of sparks.

Movement behind Ahva caught her attention. The first hawk dragged its way toward her. The glow had transferred to its eyes.

"Bad bird! Bad bird!" Ahva yelled.

She bolted out from under the wagon and rushed past Osse.

"What's wrong?" He turned to follow her.

"Bad bird!" She imitated the hawk's screech.

"Third one?" He scanned the sky.

"No!"

The first hawk pulled its way out from under the wagon. The broken arrow was still lodged in its chest. It stood and screeched.

Osse scooped Ahva up with one hand and plunked her on his shoulder then drew two more arrows and backed away. From less than a meter away, he shot the glowing eye of the hawk, creating a new burst of sparks. It turned into a mannequin.

"Keep an eye on that one. Tell me if it comes back." Osse nocked the second arrow and stalked toward the second hawk.

I think we're safe from the first one. We haven't seen anything turn from a mannequin to a critter again. She nevertheless watched it. This wasn't the time to be proved wrong.

The other hawk shrieked, and Osse shot an arrow. The

loud crack of the crystal signaled his success.

He blew out a breath. "Any movement from the first one?"

"No. Dead." *D-E-D. Dead.*

"Okay. I think we found the problem that stopped the other two errand-runners."

"Yes. Big, bad birds."

He approached the second hawk first and the inventory screen popped open showing a few bits of wire, a crystal, one of those two-color batteries, and a melted mess of plastic. He transferred everything to his bag and found more of the same in the second hawk.

So, at some point, are we going to need to make a circuit board do something interesting?

Ahva launched into the air and resumed her usual patrol routines, but she found nothing more exciting than a few songbirds and rabbits. After another half-hour of hiking, they arrived at a hip-high stone wall. A flock of almost bald sheep wandered around inside. A stone cottage had a wisp of smoke rising from the chimney. The path ended at a gate with padlock and a bell. As Ahva landed on the wall, Osse rang the bell.

The door opened and a woman walked out, drying her hands on an apron. "Are you here for the wool?"

"Yes! Hello!" Ahva fluttered over to Osse's shoulder.

"The yarn merchant in town sent me." Osse pointed to the wagon.

"Good. Hold on." She disappeared back into the house for a moment then hustled over with a key to the lock. She swung the gate wide and gestured them through then locked it after them. "This way. The wool's in the barn. He's awfully late this time."

Osse walked alongside her, drawing the wagon along behind. "There was trouble along the way. Two others were turned back."

"Trouble?" She led them down a trail that went around the side of the house.

"Bad birds!" Ahva growled.

"I don't wonder. My dogs brought down the most bedraggled-looking hawk a week ago. Hideous thing." She shuddered. "Dead now, though."

"Your dogs?" Osse smiled.

"My sheep dogs. Two of them were hurt in the fight, but with they won in the end."

As they came around the house, the barn came into view. Obviously built by the same crew who'd made the house, it was stone with wooden supports and about the same size as the house but without a chimney.

She drew back the door of the barn revealing cloth-wrapped packages the size of a hay bale.

The shepherd pointed. "Those are them. They're already bought and paid for, so just load them up. I'll meet you back at the gate to let you out."

"Thank you."

While Osse loaded the wool into the wagon, Ahva flew up to the rafters and spent the time practicing her speech. As soon as everything was loaded, she flew back to him. He secured the barn door on the way out, and they followed the path around to the gate where the shepherd waited to let them out.

The trip back to town was less exciting than the way out, but they made worse time. The heavy wagon bogged down a few times, and it was late afternoon by the time they got back. The guard on the western gate stared at them slack-jawed as they pulled the heavily ladened wagon back in.

"Hello!" Ahva waved her wing.

"You did it! You got out there and back?" The guard pointed at the wagon.

"Yes. Good job!" Ahva nodded once.

"No trouble with a flock of mean birds?" The guard squinted.

"We took care of it." Osse shrugged.

"Took care of it? Just you and a crow?" The guard scratched under the edge of his helmet.

"That's it. Just the two of us."

"No. Just you." Ahva leaned closer.

"You saw them before I did and noticed the first one wasn't dead like I thought. That counts." Osse ruffled the feathers on her head.

When they arrived at the yarn merchant's stall, he stood up and met them partway. "You got it all!"

"She said it was all yours. Bought and paid for."

"So it is." He took the cart from Osse and pulled it to the back of the stall then dug around in a large chest before pulling out a bulging sack. "Two hundred fifty as promised."

Osse dropped the sack into his bag then opened the top and rooted around in the sack.

Getting suspicious, I see. There's hope for you yet!

"It's all there. You have my word." The merchant frowned.

"Sorry. I got cheated by someone else who had me help with a chore and kill a monster then gave me less than a fifth of what we agreed upon." Osse closed his bag.

The merchant shook his head. "They'll get what's coming to them. You'll see."

"I'm sure. Do you have any other chores I can help with?"

"The wool was the only thing I had." The merchant gestured toward the wagon. "I may have something you can help with tomorrow, but that's it for today."

Osse bowed and touched his forehead with his fingertips. "Thank you."

They left the yarn merchant and went next door just as the merchant was closing up for the night.

Osse frowned. "We'll have to finish the rest tomorrow."

"Yes. Time for dinner!"

After dinner at the Puzzled Potato, a good night's rest, and breakfast in the morning, they spent the morning, game time, chasing around the marketplace and the rest of the city running bizarre errands and nickel-and-diming their way to the grand total of two thousand coins, plus a bit for their own living expenses and more metal-tipped arrows. This time, Ahva was able to keep up with the count. The sun was high in the sky by the time the notebook turned blue.

That's the money part of the quest taken care of.

They wove their way through the crowds to the scribe.

When the scribe handed them two copies of the Law of Tsidkenu, the notebook in the corner of the view turned blue for completing the quest.

"Thank you." Osse flipped through the book. "I'm sure this will do fine."

The scribe shrugged. "Certainly doesn't bring joy to the artist in my soul, but if it will help the old lady you mentioned, I'm content."

Osse tucked the books into his bag. "It will be perfect for what we need. Thank you for taking care of it so quickly."

After a quick stop at the library to toss the original copy of the book through the book drop slot, they headed out immediately, enjoying whatever dried food was left in Osse's bag, and set off for Vanya.

* * *

Jael paused midstride and listen closely. As she expected, the grass crunched anyway. Someone was trailing her, probably someone with a bear pelt acquisition on his list of chores today.

Behind her, wood creaked. The edge of her vision turned red.

Jael selected Sprint and pushed off into a run, quickly coming up to her maximum speed. A line of trees and a natural depression in the landscape offered concealment, if not cover. Jael turned and bolted for that tree line as an arrow whizzed past her stubby tail.

Her heart pounded. If this hunter added her to his pelt collection, what would happen to Oba and Dina? Her muscles ached with the sudden exertion but she drove herself hard. The tree line was strides away. As she adjusted her course slightly, she stumbled over a large rock. An arrow grazed her hip, stinging more than it really hurt.

She dove into the tree line and tumbled down a steeper incline than she expected. Jael came to rest at the edge of the stream, but she couldn't spare a moment to catch her breath. Undoubtedly, that hunter would be pursuing.

Jael rolled to her feet and darted behind a stout shrub. She sniffed the air, but the wind was against her. The human's footsteps rustled the grass as he moved. When he crested the hill, Jael studied the Bakhari tribesman. His skin was nearly as dark as her fur. He had an arrow nocked, but his bow was aimed downward. If she waited until he came close enough, she could ambush him and take him out before he brought the arrow to threaten her.

Then what? If she killed him, the rest of his kind would chase her down for revenge. She would spend all her time dodging them, and her poor cubs would disappear for good.

His head jerked from side to side as he crunched river stones under his feet.

Jael waited, quelling her jittery nerves with her plans for eliminating the threat without killing the tribesman.

He crept ever closer. The moment he was in range, she darted out and slapped the bow. The nocked arrow launched into a bush and the bow clattered against the rocks and floated downstream.

The tribesman backpedaled, wielding another arrow as a dagger. Jael struck the ground with her paw and huffed. She chose Bluff Charge from her skills and ran half the distance and stopped, clacking her teeth.

The tribesman left at a run. Rather than pursuing further, Jael ran out of the ravine and hunted around for the trail of her cubs. The red faded from the edge of her vision.

Chapter 22

As they came close to the cave where they had left Vehira, Ahva launched off from Osse's shoulder and flew the rest of the distance. Vehira sat in the mouth of the cave with a man ID'd as "Mentor Jood" and a boy dubbed "Learner" each wearing a purple skullcap and scarf decorated with a cross sitting on top of a circle. Breakfast, Vehira's chicken, pecked in the dirt and short grass for her food.

Ahva landed on convenient tree branch. "Hello!"

The learner stared and pointed. "Did she just–"

Vehira smiled. "Speak? Yes, she did. That's the crow belonging to the boy I told you about."

"Have you not met talking birds before?" Mentor Jood turned toward his learner.

The learner shook his head. "I've heard stories, but no. Bird companions are rare in the far north. Plenty of dogs and bears, but not many birds."

"A treat for you then. If this is the lad's bird, then he must not be too far behind." Mentor Jood turned back toward the direction she'd flown in from.

"He's in time for dinner." Vehira went to stir a pot sitting on the fire. "Tell me, Ahva, were you successful?"

Ahva bobbed her head. "Yes." She mimicked the sound of clinking money.

Younger man laughed. "What a clever bird."

"Yes. Very clever bird." Ahva cawed. *I'm no chicken, mister.*

"I wonder if he was able to acquire the book?" The older man asked. "The bookseller here had several, but he wanted far too much. More than you or I have or can acquire in a lifetime."

"But what a fancy book that was." The younger man beamed.

"Hence the price tag."

If y'all would shut up for ten seconds, I'd answer you. "Yes. Book. Good price!"

"That's terrific!" The younger man punched the air.

"That means you just need the remaining three vouchers." Vehira frowned. "Until Mistress Elisbet decides to add another requirement. We've been down this road twice before. Remember?"

Osse joined them. "Then I'll have to be sure not to tell Mistress Elisbet who I'm doing this for."

"She will ask." The older man shook his head. "Tsidkenu does not approve of lying."

Osse frowned. "But he approves of denying an elderly lady a place to live? If Tsidkenu has forgiven her past, what makes Mistress Elisbet so much better that she can't?"

The older man held up both hands palm out. "I completely agree with you. Her actions are totally against Tsidkenu's design. According to his word, he himself would be incensed by Mistress Elisbet's actions. Believe me on that. Still, you can't break the law of Tsidkenu to circumvent someone who is breaking the law of Tsidkenu."

Osse shook his head. "Fine. I won't lie. I might be deliberately vague, but I will say nothing untrue. That's the best I can do." He bowed and offered his hand. "My name is Osse Bente."

The older man shook his hand. "I'm Mentor Jood. This is my learner."

"Good birds?" Ahva tipped her head to one side.

Vehira rejoined them. "They're the ones I told you who have already given me their vouchers. They also help me with errands since I'm not allowed in the town."

"Good birds." She nodded once.

"I'm glad some of Tsidkenu's followers are decent people. I was beginning to wonder." Osse took out a book and a large sack of clinking coins. "Here's the book. And the money."

"And the dress?" Mentor Jood asked.

Vehira nodded toward the cave. "With the rest of my belongings in there. I didn't want it to get it damaged before I present myself to Mistress Elisbet." Vehira hefted the bag. "You were able to get this much from the things you had in your bag?"

"Most of it came from that, but for the rest, I had to do some errand running and some housework." Osse shrugged. "It wasn't a problem."

"I'll never be able to repay you." Vehira's eyes teared.

"I don't need repaying."

Mentor Jood clapped Osse's shoulder. "You're a good lad."

Yep. I picked a good one.

"Do you have any ideas about who I can talk to for the

remaining three vouchers?" Osse looked toward the north. "I'd rather not travel to Yavne, but I will if needed."

"You'll never get in to see anyone in the convent. You're not woman enough, so you have to focus on the men in the monastery." Mentor Jood watched the wind through the tree canopy and rubbed his chin. "Who would be the most likely to give you a voucher?"

The learner smirked. "There's always Mentor Yudah. Just bring a fish with you. He'd sign anything."

Mentor Jood frowned and slapped the back of his learner's head. "That's not nice. True, but not nice."

Vehira laughed. "I do have a fishing pole and that stream near my old house happens to have some good trout in it."

"Then I'll go fishing in the morning before I go to the monastery." Osse held up two fingers. "Two more."

"I would say Mentors Ash and Naftil. Neither of them much likes Mistress Elisbet, so doing you a favor that would irritate Mistress Elisbet in the end might be all the incentive they need."

The learner shrugged. "You may have to do an errand or two for them."

"That's fine. Honest work is not beneath me."

Yep. Just make sure you know what the catch is this time.

"That'll do it. After you have all five vouchers, the two thousand coins, and the book, speak to Mistress Elisbet, answer her questions, and she should give you the token. Then we just need to bring Vehira to the convent, and all will be well." Mentor Jood stood up and dusted himself off. "We need to be getting back to the monastery. Master Dan gets rather nervous these days if were not back in time for dinner. I'll see you tomorrow, Osse, and I'll talk to Mentors

CHAPTER 22

Yudah, Naftil, and Ash and put in a good word for you and for Vehira. Maybe that will smooth the road a bit."

"Thank you. I appreciate your help."

"Son, I appreciate yours." Mentor Jood offered his learner a hand up. "I was fairly confident that I would be able to help Vehira meet all the requirements until Mistress Elisbet demanded two thousand coins for the deal. That's more money than any monk can get a hold of, which is why I think she did it."

"That's sad. That's truly sad." Osse shook his head.

Ahva flew over and landed on Osse's arm. "Disgusting eyeball."

The learner laughed. "Does she know she saying?"

Of course, I do, goofball. "Yes."

Osse smiled and ruffled the feathers on Ahva's head. "She understands what we're saying."

"That's terrific!" The learner smiled.

Mentor Jood bowed. "Until tomorrow."

The two monks left.

Vehira went over to the pot and returned with two steaming bowls of soup. "Speaking of dinner, you're in time."

Osse set the wooden bowl down next to his leg and dug out a cloth-wrapped loaf of bread. "This bread will go perfectly. Help yourself."

"Wonderful, thank you."

Ahva picked at a piece of bread that Osse broke off for her and waited for the soup to cool down enough that she could eat it without burning her crop.

Vehira picked up the book. "Can you read?"

Osse nodded. "Yes, pretty well. Why?"

"I'm afraid that in spite of all your efforts, Mistress

Elisbet will not admit me. I'm sure she'll lay some other requirement, like knowledge of Tsidkenu's law. I can't read. Could you read this to me, so that I'm at least familiar with some of the details."

Great. Was not expecting a sermon.

"After dinner, of course." Vehira added.

Osse smiled. "I'd be happy to."

Nope. Been to church four times in the last week for all the Christmas adventures. I don't need fake church.

Khin May called up the setting screen to speed up the clock. Everyone ate at warp speed, and then Osse picked up the book and read it out loud, sounding like one of the Chipmunks. That alone was worth it. As night fell in the game, he twisted around so the firelight provided him enough light to see. He flipped the page every three seconds, which still took him five minutes real-time. Khin May restored the clock and reentered the game as Osse reached the last page.

"–Will come again in glory and restore the perfection of the original world." Osse closed the book.

The notebook turned blue.

That was a quest? Or did I just acquire one? She opened the notebook.

Optional Quest complete: The Path to Enlightenment. Learn about Tsidkenu.

Become a follower of Tsidkenu?

Beats me, Bubba. She summoned up the help screen.

The cave entrance cross-faded with the pet store where she'd started. The green musketeer – Alan Ivan Turning, wasn't it? – strode out from behind some of the cages. "How can I help you?"

CHAPTER 22

"About religions in this game, are there any valid reasons to join one or not?" Khin May walked toward him.

A chair appeared behind Alan and he sat, crossing his left ankle over his right knee. "There are some advantages to each of the religions and some disadvantages to them as well. In this case, you and your human have had the opportunity to learn about Tsidkenu, so you have an opportunity to become a follower. If you agree, you'll gain the advantages of being a follower Tsidkenu, and you will gain some disadvantages. Followers of Tsidkenu gain advantages in the sorts of things that Tsidkenu values. The things that he hates, his followers are poor at."

"Okay, specifically, what would those things be?"

"Didn't you just–" Alan squinted. "No, you sped the clock."

"I know a bit of exposition is inherent in all games. Otherwise you have no idea what's going on, but listening to someone read a one hundred-page book? Really? Don't you think that's a bit much?"

Alan sighed. "I told the programmers it might be. I suggested that they take an opportunity to condense it down. Bullet points. It'll be more palatable to today's short attention span generation." He rolled his eyes. "All right. The short version. Tsidkenu values honesty, charity, and restoration. Consequently, his followers gain benefits to healing, especially the healing of others, and they are more likely to be successful at helping or securing help for others. They are harder to deceive, but they also find deceiving others difficult. Followers of a given religion will recognize each other on sight by the deity's symbol in their nametags, and they are more likely to do each other favors. Likewise, when encountering someone of a different religion, they are less likely to do each other favors. You would gain benefits to defenses, especially protecting someone else, but if you attack someone without cause, your attack is more likely to fail. I think that covers the best of it."

"What about the other religions?" Khin May asked.

"When you encounter them, you'll have an opportunity to learn about them and you can decide whether to join the religion or not. Honestly, the way you've been playing, if you choose to follow a religion, Tsidkenu would be the best match. Many of the others would run contrary to how you typically play. That's just my advice. Have I answered your question?"

She scowled. "Mostly."

"I can't tell you story information you have not yet encountered." Alan shook his head. "That would be cheating."

Without her say so, the pet store cross-faded and became the mouth of the cave again.

I guess I was done.

The notebook flipped open.

Do you wish to become a follower Tsidkenu?

Ahva fluffed up all her feathers and shook. *Advantages to dealing with other followers might help the current quest. Advantages to healing might be a good thing for an herbalist. God knows Osse could sure do with a little discernment about being deceived. The last couple days proved that in spades. Sneak attacks haven't been our thing anyway. Lying might be handy, but if we stink at it then will have to find other ways.* She pecked at the yes floating in midair.

The text in the notebook changed. **You have become a**

follower of Tsidkenu.

Advantages:

+50% to Herbalist skills when using healing concoctions

+20% to Charm when speaking to other followers of Tsidkenu.

+15% to Combat skills when defending noncombatants

New Skill: Detect Lies

Disadvantages:

-50% to Herbalist skills when making concoctions that cause harm

-20% to Charm when speaking to followers of other religions

-15% to Charm when attempting to deceive others

-15% to Combat skills when attacking without cause

When Vehira and Osse sprawled out next to the fire and covered up with their cloaks, Ahva told the computer to have them sleep. Cartoon sheep played volleyball with a sheepdog for a referee until one of the sheep spiked the ball and nailed the sheepdog on the head.

Khin May snickered. *Poor dog!*

A few seconds later she woke up again, but the sun was peeking over the horizon and the fire had burned itself out. Osse got up and started a fire then reheated last night's supper. Once they'd eaten, he borrowed Vehira's fishing pole and then hiked out to the stream where she said some good trout could be had.

You need some bait, dude.

"Need something on the hook," Osse muttered. He rooted through his bag and pulled out a piece of jerky. After stripping a small piece off, he speared it on the hook then tossed it into the water.

Come on fish! Ahva flew up to a nearby tree where she had a good view down into the water.

A few fish floated on by, but none of them were the eating kind. Finally, an arm-sized fish with polka-dots floated on down the stream. It swam on by Osse's hook, then turned back around and chomped down on the jerky. Osse started to reel in the line, but the fish pulled back the other way and broke loose.

If at first you don't succeed, base jumping is not the sport for you. Fishing, though, is probably safe enough.

Osse re-baited the hook and tossed it in.

Ahva watched for other fish and spotted a small one. *That might make better bait than a piece of jerky. My turn!*

She pushed off from the branch and circled a few times before she dove feet-first for the small, skinny fish. Her feet dragged in the water, and something slithery whipped past her toes as she closed them but she didn't have enough grip. When her tail and rear end got wet, Ahva flapped hard to gain altitude.

Nope. Missed. Come on now. Eagles do this all the time! They have way stronger feet than I do, though.

"Ahva, you're going to scare the fish away." Osse huffed.

She circled around and headed downstream where she spotted another bait-sized fish in the shallows. Diving beak first, she scooped up a veritable flood of water and clamped her beak down, but the top and bottom didn't meet up.

I got it!

She banked and returned to Osse. Ahva dropped the little fish next to his foot.

He smiled. "Good job, but I don't think Mentor Yudah will

CHAPTER 22

be impressed." He reeled his line in. "Might make better bait, though."

"Yes, it is." She shook splattering water all over.

While Ahva flew back to a branch, Osse baited his hook with the small fish.

A couple puny fish drifted on by, but they sure weren't the size for frying. When one showed interest in the bait, Ahva dove at it and pulled up at the last moment. The fish skittered away without taking the bait.

"Ahva, you're not helping."

Am too. You don't want that one. Hardly even bite-size. Mentor Fishy will laugh you out of the monastery.

She returned to her perch. After a few minutes, another big, fat trout lazily swam down the stream. Like the first one, it passed up the bait, then turned around and opened its mouth wide before going after it.

As soon as the rod bent, Osse started reeling the fish in. It pulled back, bending the rod nearly in half. He continued to pull back and reel at the same time, bending the rod into such a tight U-turn that Ahva was sure it would crack. With one last tug, the fish flew out of the water and bounced around on the end of the string as it flopped around.

"We did it, Ahva!" Osse held up the fish.

I saw that part. "Good bird!" Ahva flew to his shoulder and rode back to camp with him.

Vehira stood up as they came close. "That's a beauty! Mentor Yudah will be thrilled." She darted into the cave where the rest of her supplies were and brought back a worn sack that was barely bigger than the fish.

Osse unhooked the trout and slid it into the bag. He handed the rod to Vehira. "I'll be back as soon as I can."

"Take the money and the book with you. Along with the two vouchers from mentor Jood and his learner. That way, you'll be able to talk to Mistress Elisbet and get the token as soon as you have the other three vouchers."

Osse tucked everything but the fish into his pack. "Good idea. Once I have the token from Mistress Elisbet, I'll come back and get you."

Vehira patted Osse's arm. "Thank you, lad. The monastery and the convent are further down the road, right across from each other. The monastery is still being built, but the convent has been there for years. They're the only buildings around for quite a ways, so you won't miss them. You don't know how much this means to me. May Tsidkenu grant you victory."

With all those advantages we just picked up, I'm sure he will.

"I'll be back for you soon as I can." Osse waved and started off.

Yay! More flight time!

They continued down the road away from Vanya, headed generally south. As usual, Ahva spent the time either patrolling ahead of them, riding on Osse's shoulder and practicing language, or finding rocks to drop on targets. Aside from a few outside Fola, random monster encounters were decidedly missing in this game. Ahva wasn't sure she cared about that, given how her combat skills were fairly useless. At least Osse kept a pretty good pace. There wasn't a whole lot of lollygagging or stopping to admire the odd bug, bird, or flower.

After about an hour, game time, a large, multiple leveled castle came into view. The building sat on a plain near a cliff overlooking the ocean. In addition to the main building,

CHAPTER 22

there were a few smaller ones, an orchard, and a sizable garden. Across the road from it, a tent village had sprung up around a building site. The skeleton of a large, flat building was taking shape. Several workmen scurried about.

"That must be the place." Osse pointed at the structure.

They headed down the hill toward the plain and veered toward the monastery as they got close. Mentor Jood, trailing his learner, rushed out of a tent to meet them.

"Osse! I'm so glad you're here." He led them into the tent village. "We have a small problem. Master Dan is concerned that your interruptions will mean that all the chores will not finish on time today. I'm afraid the mentors will only talk to you if you agree to do something to free their time."

Osse nodded. "That's fine. Whatever gets this task taken care of."

"Come with us. I'll introduce you to the others." Mentor Jood led the way to the largest tent. "Probably best if we start with Mentor Yudah before that fish gets a little too old for his liking. We have a kitchen and dining area set up nearby."

Too old? We just caught the hokey thing.

Ahva adjusted her grip as Osse followed the two monks to a large gray tent. They ducked through the open flap and found a somewhat impromptu kitchen set up at one end with a few tables serving as workspace. The rest of the tent had simple tables and chairs. One notable exception in the east corner had a place setting of gold plates and jeweled chalices. The table itself was covered by an ornately embroidered white tablecloth decorated with swirls and flowers and various types of animals chasing each other around.

Osse pointed to the ornate set up. "Is that for Master Dan?"

Mentor Jood looked at Osse, the special set up, then back at Osse. "Oh, glory, no. That's the place for Tsidkenu, ceremonial of course."

Osse nodded.

Mentor Jood led them to the kitchen end of the tent where a monk was putting away the last of the dishes into crates that had been turned on their sides.

The monk grabbed a fishing pole. "I have no time for you now, Mentor Jood. I need to go catch us a trout for dinner." Mentor Jood took the fishing pole out of the monk's hand and set it aside. "No need, Mentor. This is Osse, whom I told you about last night. Osse, this is Mentor Yudah. Osse is helping the elderly lady I told you about, Mentor."

"Did you bring me a fish?" Mentor Yudah stared wide-eyed at the sack Osse carried.

Osse handed him the bag. "Yes. I brought this so you can spare the time to write the voucher for the elderly lady."

The monk pulled the fish out of the sack and caressed it as if it were a fluffy pet. "What a lovely trout. This will be a fine supper. Of course, I'll write your voucher for you. Come back in an hour. I'll have it ready for you then."

That was easy.

"Thank you, Mentor." Mentor Jood ushered Osse out of the tent. "Next we'll go talk to Mentor Ash. He's our quartermaster. I'll warn you. He's in a bit of a mood right now."

Osse's brow furrowed. "Why? What's wrong?"

"Master Dan hired a bunch of workmen. They all need tents. For the moment, they're sharing, but no one is happy about it, and they're all threatening to leave. So, Master Dan promised that every man would have a tent by the end of the week. That's a rather tall order. We all help out when we can be spared from our other duties, of course, but since tent making is not our main function, we're not nearly as efficient as he is. Still, every little bit helps, right?"

Osse shrugged. "The weather has been pleasant enough lately to sleep outside."

"I agree. The workmen however do not. We'll lose them at week's end if the tents aren't ready. A challenge, but a doable one." Mentor Jood leaned closer. "Mentor Ash is a little worried."

They ducked into another tent.

The monk sitting in the middle of it was surrounded by piles of canvas and hastily stitching two pieces together in his hands. "I haven't much time, gentlemen."

"I brought you help." Mentor Jood gave his learner gentle push toward one of the piles of canvas. "My learner and I will help you for the next couple hours. Then we'll have to go take care of our own chores, of course. And this is Osse."

Mentor Ash frowned. "Oh. You're the one who wants the voucher."

Osse nodded. "Yes. It's for a good cause. I can help, too, while you get it written."

"Fine." He heaved a sigh and sewed another stitch on the tent. "You finish a tent for me, and I'll write your voucher. You'll find needles and thread in the box in the corner. Each pile of canvas contains all the pieces you need to assemble a tent. They only fit one way. If you haven't made a tent before, you might want to lay out all the parts outside. By the time you finish the tent, I'll have the voucher written."

Mentor Jood handed Osse one pile of canvas and took a second pile for himself. They stopped at the box in the corner to pick up a spool of thread and a small box of needles before mentor Jood led Osse and his learner outside.

"Now, we just need to find the space big enough to lay out all these parts." Mentor Jood mumbled.

Ahva launched off of Osse's shoulder and spiraled upward searching for space of appreciable size. When she found it, north of the construction site, she circled the area until the humans caught up.

Without any prompting, the learner went to the far edge of the open area and started laying out pieces. Osse dropped his pile and started sorting through it. There were six total pieces one for each of the four sides, one for the top, and a flap for a door. The biggest square piece, was obviously the top, but the side pieces were trapezoids. It took a couple tries to figure out which way was up, except for the side the door was on. Obviously, the opening went to the bottom. That, of course, explained where the smallest rectangle was going to go.

The two monks had theirs laid out and were already sewing by the time Osse had his sorted out. He threaded the needle and started attaching one of the sides to the top. Osse jabbed the needle down through the material then angled it back up again. Before he could grab the pointy end and pull the thread through, Ahva turned on Problem Solving.

A thought bubble appeared. *Pulling the thread through doesn't look that hard.*

She fluttered down, grabbed the needle, and gave it a tug, stepping backwards to pull the string through the material until it was tight.

CHAPTER 22

Osse laughed. "You want to help, too?"

Ahva dropped the needle. "Yes." *Beats sitting here watching you do it.*

Osse got another needle from the box and strung it. "I'll get the stitch started, and you tug it through. Got it?"

"Yes."

While Osse started one stitch with one needle, Ahva pulled the other one through. Then she flew to the one Osse was starting and tugged it through while he started the first one. It became a race to tug the needle through and pull the string taut before he could get the other one started. Most of the time, sadly, he won. But every now and then, she got it tugged through and was sitting there waiting for him by the time he was ready for her.

Mentor Jood inspected the work. "Wow, you are fast. Have you made tents before?"

Osse shook his head as he started another needle. "Nah, Ahva helped."

"Keep it up! Mentor Ash will be highly amused." He returned to his own tent and continued sewing.

By the time Ahva pulled the last stitch tight, the two monks had theirs only half finished.

Osse and Ahva helped Mentor Jood finish his a lot faster, and then all three of them made quick work of the learner's. They gathered up the canvas, and Mentor Jood picked up the needle case and thread.

"Excellent teamwork. Too bad Mentor Ash doesn't have a well-trained crow to help him with his sewing. He'd be done with these tents in no time."

They returned to Mentor Ash's tent and ducked through the opening.

"Here you are, Mentor. Three completed tents."

Mentor Ash sealed a folded paper with a blob of wax. "That's impossible! How could you have done those so quickly?"

Ahva whistled. "Good bird."

Osse stroked Ahva's wing. "I had help. I started the needles, Ahva pulled them through. We had two needles going at a time."

"Don't suppose you'd let me borrow your bird for a while, say, 'til the end of the week?" Mentor Ash asked.

"No." Ahva shook her head. "Busy bird. Places to go."

"I'm afraid not, Mentor. I have some important work to do. That elderly lady's life depends on it, and I need Ahva."

Quite right. Me being the player and all.

Mentor Ash frowned. "I can't fault you for that." He handed Osse the letter. "Here's your voucher."

Osse tucked it into his bag. "Thank you. This will help tremendously."

Mentor Jood clapped his learner on the shoulder. "My learner still has an hour at your disposal. I'll be back to collect him at that time."

The learner grabbed a new pile of canvas and left the tent. Mentor Jood ushered Osse out of the tent. "It's been an hour. Let's get the voucher from Mentor Yudah. Then I'll take you to Mentor Naftil. Like you, he's an herbalist. I'm sure you'll be able to handle whatever he has for you."

They returned to the kitchen tent where Mentor Yudah was cleaning the trout Osse had caught that morning.

He pointed with his knife to the corner of one of the tables. "Your letter is there. Thanks again for the lovely fish."

Osse collected the letter and tucked it into his bag with

the others. "And thank you for the voucher."

"Any time! Anytime you have another fish, I'll be more than happy to take it."

He sure loves his seafood.

Mentor Jood led them out and all the way across the construction site to a tent marked with a mortar and pestle. Inside, shelves held a flock of small jars. Bundles of plant life hung from strings that criss-crossed the top of the tent. A monk was frantically rooting through boxes and reorganizing jars. "Where did I put that?"

Mentor Jood stepped forward. "Mentor Naftil. I brought Osse with me to visit."

The monk glanced up. "Yes, I remember him, and you said he needed a voucher to get that old lady past Mistress Elisbet." He muttered something about an old hag and returned to sorting jars.

"That's right. You mentioned you would be willing to provide the voucher when we spoke last night."

"Yes, and I will. Soon as I find what I'm looking for. Anything to teach that old hag lesson. Can't believe Tsidkenu allows her to be in charge of all those nuns. It's a wonder any of them have any compassion left at all."

Problem with Mistress Elisbet? Ahva snorted.

"How can I help, Mentor?" Osse walked closer.

Mentor Naftil stood up and ran his fingers through his messed-up hair. "What you know about herbs?"

"My grandmother and mother taught me herbalism." Osse tapped his bag.

"I need vervain."

"I have some. If there's a marsh, or maybe even a wet area, nearby, I might be able to find you more."

"I know where there's plenty. Only the place is overrun with mosquitoes, and I can't find my eucalyptus to mix a few vials of bug repellent." Mentor Naftil sighed. "Really, I only need one vial. That'll be enough for me to get in there, grab what I need, and get out there without getting eaten alive by mosquitoes."

Osse rooted around in his bag and produced a vial. "This is less than a week old. It gave me about thirty minutes of protection when I needed to go collect reeds for someone." Osse offered it to the monk. "Do you want to go collect the herbs that you need, or do you want to give me a list, and I'll go collect them?"

The monk took the vial. "I'd rather do it myself. You know how it is."

Osse smiled. "I understand. I prefer to collect my own, too."

"Thank you. I'll have your voucher ready in, say, half an hour?" Mentor Naftil shrugged.

"That's great. Thank you."

Mentor Jood led them out. "What do you say we help my learner finish that tent he's working on. With all of us working on it, it should be ready by about the time Mentor Naftil is finished."

"Yes. Good bird." Ahva launched off of his shoulder.

She flew on ahead of them and found the learner in the same place where they had been working. Ahva landed on the canvas, which from her perspective seemed big enough for an entire clan of giants. The learner smiled and started a second needle going. She tried to race him to pull the threads taut and get over to where he was working the other needle before he was ready for her. Unlike Osse, she was always waiting for him.

Slowpoke.

When Osse and Mentor Jood caught up, all four of them worked on the tent and had it done in no time.

While the learner took the completed tent back to Mentor Ash, Osse followed Mentor Jood back to Mentor Naftil's tent. Mentor Naftil was adding the finishing touches on his letter. Then he folded it and sealed it with a blob of wax.

He offered Osse the letter. "Here you go. I hope that's everything you need to remind that old hag that compassion is a virtue that Tsidkenu values."

Osse accepted the letter and tucked it into his bag. "Thank you. That was the last thing I needed."

The notebook turned blue to let her know the quest was done.

"Well done!" Mentor Jood shook Osse's hand. "From here, head across the road and knock on the convent door. Ask to speak to Mistress Elisbet, and present the requirements. I don't know how you're going to do this without her figuring out that we're helping Vehira."

"I'll deal with that when the time comes. I'm sure I can figure out something. I mean, Tsidkenu does not want Vehira sleeping out in the open with laughing maniacs wiping out people, animals, and entire villages, right?"

Mentor Jood nodded. "Quite right you are. Our prayers will go with you."

As Mentor Jood backed away, Ahva twisted toward the convent.

Chapter 23

The old castle was made out of gray rock. Gargoyles at each corner and at several points along each wall stared out at the landscape. Dark green ivy climbed up the walls.

That place would be a great spook house come October. Ahva adjusted her hold on Osse's tunic. "Up we go."

Osse skirted the construction zone and headed across to the convent. The path to the front door led them between a fenced in area with more than two dozen chickens and a garden growing a variety of different vegetables in rows. The door of the convent was made out of wood reinforced with metal. A heavy iron doorknocker akin to one of the gargoyles on the roof was attached to the center of the door. Osse pounded the knocker a few times. Seconds passed without any response, so he knocked again. The door opened a sliver.

"I can't let you in. This is a convent."

Osse nodded. "I know. I need to speak with Mistress Elisbet."

"I'll get her. Please wait here." The lady closed the door.

Osse sorted through the vouchers. Each was folded and sealed with wax. The monk who had written the

CHAPTER 23

voucher had addressed them to Mistress Elisbet with a return address that consisted of only the monk's name.

"I hope she doesn't open these. I forgot to tell the monks to forgo naming Vehira." He blew out a breath.

They know the score, and apparently, they've played a few rounds of this game already. Surely, they knew that. "It's safe. Good monks!"

Ahva flew over to the vegetable fence and perched there while Osse paced back and forth waiting for Mistress Elisbet. The door opened and a woman stepped out. After listening to Mentor Naftil call her an old hag a few million times, Ahva had expected the stereotypical Halloween witch. Instead, Mistress Elisbet was a middle-aged woman who could pass as a supermodel. She was tall and thin and the embroidered green dress she wore certainly wouldn't qualify as anything Ahva would call simple.

"What is it you want?" She leaned on the doorframe.

Osse drew a deep breath. "My village was destroyed by laughing maniacs."

Mistress Elisbet folded her arms in front of her. "Unfortunate. Are you here seeking assistance?"

"Yes." Ahva squinted at the "old hag."

Osse glanced at her. "Not for myself. I'm a young man. I can find my own way. Unfortunately, a sweet, elderly lady I know also lost her home because of the same maniacs. One of them, anyway. I'm seeking a space for her. She really can't travel with me because I may be on the road for a long time. A woman I met outside of Vanya told me that a sweet, elderly lady might be given asylum here by meeting certain conditions. She said I needed to get a token from you." He flipped open his bag and withdrew objects as he spoke. "I collected everything I was told we'd would need. I have the two thousand coins for this elderly lady's upkeep. I have a book of the law of Tsidkenu. I have five vouchers from other children of Tsidkenu vouching for how kind this lady is and how sincere she is in her faith. I understand the lady also needs a simple dress. She has a simple, brown, undecorated, ankle-length tunic that my own mother made. May I have the token?"

Mistress Elisbet frowned. "Where is this sweet, elderly lady?"

"As I said, she's not keen on travel. I didn't want to bring her with me all the way here without knowing that she could stay. If you'll give me the token that proves she will have a place to stay, I will go get her and bring her back. Before nightfall. She is currently camped out in a cave. The Baron of Yavne blocked pirates out of it, and then Ahva and I took care of the other vermin. She has nowhere else to live, and I'm afraid those pirates will return. Surely the cause is just. Tsidkenu would approve, would he not?"

So how will this work. Deceiving people now comes at a disadvantage, but he gets a bonus for working with other Tsidkenu followers, but then she would have the Detect Lies skill, but really, nothing he said was actually a lie. It simply wasn't the whole story, which is kind of like lying but not exactly lying. But then he's doing this whole charade to take care of a defenseless lady, and by all accounts this chick in green is working contrary to what her god values. So... wow. What a tangled web we weave.

Mistress Elisbet took each of the vouchers one at a time and glanced at the monk's names written on the outside. Without opening them, she tucked them into an ornately

CHAPTER 23

beaded pouch at her hip. Then she took the money and the book and handed Osse a palm-sized stone inlaid with gold. "By nightfall. Or she may not stay here at all."

Osse slipped the rock in his pouch. "I promise you; we will be here in time."

Without another word, Mistress Elisbet returned to the convent and closed the door with a bang.

"Good bird." Ahva flew back to Osse's shoulder.

Osse jogged between the chicken coop and the garden. "Let's not let too much time go by. We don't want her to change her mind."

When they reached the road, Osse started running. Ahva took off and circled around him spiraling their way down the road. By the time they made it to the camp at the cave, Osse was out of breath. For both of them, the fatigue meter was too far the wrong way. He flopped down in the shadow of the cave and took a long swig from his canteen then offered her a bit of water in the lid of his canteen.

Lantern light from deeper inside the cave came around the first U-turn. Vehira carried a bucket of water toward them.

"Osse! You're back so soon? Was there a problem?"

Osse shook his head and pulled the rock out of his bag. He held it up where she could see it.

She set the bucket down and hurried toward them. "You got it! She actually gave it to you?"

Osse set his canteen aside. "I don't think she was happy about it, but she gave it to me."

She reached for the stone then stopped. "She doesn't know it's for me, does she?"

"No? Maybe. Probably not." Ahva leaned forward.

"Won't she be surprised?" Osse handed her the stone. "But I did get it without lying. Unfortunately, this is only good until nightfall. What do we need to do to get you ready to go?"

"Douse the campfire. Whatever food I have remaining, you can take with you for your travels. It's only fair. I'll change into the dress you gave me. My old clothes aren't worth saving. I can't take them with me, and you couldn't sell them for dust. They can stay here and rot. Then we take Breakfast and go. I have nothing else that matters."

"You change. As soon as I catch my breath, I'll take care of the campfire."

Tears welled up in Vehira's eyes and she collected the dress from her belongings and headed deeper into the cave.

"Aww. Good bird." Ahva flew to the nearest tree where she could supervise the breaking of camp. Osse collected the water bucket Vehira had been carrying and refilled his canteen before he used the rest to douse the fire. Vehira's bag of food contained a stale loaf of bread, a piece of cheese that was getting a little green around the edges, and a few raw carrots. When Vehira returned, she was dressed in the brown, ankle-length tunic Osse had given her. With Breakfast the chicken cradled in her arms, they started off toward the south. Osse kept to the pace Vehira set, which was considerably slower than their usual rate of travel, so Ahva spent her time zooming up and down the road, dropping rocks and pine cones on targets while watching for more of the laughing loonies.

As they descended the last hill toward the plain where the convent and the monastery were, Ahva landed on Osse's arm.

CHAPTER 23

"What do you think Ahva? How should I approach convincing Mistress Elisbet to honor the agreement? Remind her what Tsidkenu's law says about caring for the unfortunate? Maybe I could tell her what I, as a new believer, think of her double standards?"

Vehira smiled. "Tell her some jokes to put her in a better mood. I don't think I've ever seen her anything but horribly grim."

Ahva snorted. Telling the "Old Hag" off was no good. Aggravating people was no way to convince them to change their minds. Jokes might be funny, but effective? No. Start quoting the law? Maybe?

"Law." Ahva nodded once. "Few quick lessons for dumb bird."

"Okay. Sounds like a good idea." Osse preened the back of her head, which restored a few points on the fatigue meter.

A bell sounded from the monastery's construction area. A group of monks quickly assembled and met them at the side of the road.

Mentor Jood ran forward. "We are somewhat concerned that Mistress Elisbet will not honor the token. We're coming along for moral support."

An older, taller monk with purple edging his robes in addition to the skullcap and scarf stepped forward. "And, if necessary, I am prepared to remind her of the law she swears that she upholds."

There ya go. That'll help. With a passel of monks with us, surely someone can rebut any lame argument she comes up with.

"Thank you all very much." Vehira brushed her eyes with her hand.

Ahva flew ahead to the fence around the garden and perched on one of the poles. Osse led the whole procession to the main door and slammed the knocker a few times.

Half an eternity later, the door opened and Mistress Elisbet stepped out. She stared, eyes roving from the top of Vehira's head to the bottom of her dress and frowned. "I knew it. I suspected this was some kind of a trick." She jabbed her finger at Osse. "You told me it was an elderly lady from your village."

Osse shook his head. "I told you my village was destroyed. It was. In fact, I might be the only survivor who is not also a captive of the attackers. One of those attackers destroyed Vehira's house. I gave you everything you asked for in exchange for the token. Does that mean nothing to you?"

Mistress Elisbet drew a deep breath.

Osse stepped forward and spoke over Mistress Elisbet. "The Law of Tsidkenu says, 'Do not turn away the destitute from your gate. Nor refuse mercy to the repentant. No, instead invite them into your home. Provide them with the food, shelter, and mercy they require. Do this, and I will show mercy to you. Refuse, and I will withhold my mercy.' Do you hear in that any exceptions? I don't. She has met your requirements, which were much more stern than Tsidkenu required of you. Do you follow him? Or do you follow your own will?" He squinted.

Mistress Elisbet glowered. "She will corrupt my learners."

"On the contrary." Vehira looked away for a moment then back at Mistress Elisbet. "With my experiences, I can tell them with all authority and certainty what kind of a trap living apart from Tsidkenu places one in." She offered Mistress Elisbet the token. "I would never suggest my old way of life to anyone as a preferred path. It brought me nothing but shame and useless, temporary happiness that left me rejected and helpless. Without Tsidkenu, I am nothing."

"Yeah." Ahva flew to Osse's shoulder.

Mistress Elisbet took the token out of Vehira's hand. "I am not convinced. However, may Tsidkenu strike you dead if you even try to corrupt one of my learners."

"Then I will live a long life indeed." Vehira's eyes teared up as she handed Breakfast to Osse. "Find her a good home."

"I will." Osse pet the chicken.

When the notebook turned blue, Ahva opened it.

Fly the Coop. Find a home for Breakfast.

Ha! "Fly the Coop." Love it!

Mistress Elisbet open the door and gestured Vehira through. The door closed with a heavy bang, but the cheer from the assembled monks was louder.

The blue notebook told her she'd been successful in the quest. She'd no sooner dismissed that announcement than the edges of her view turned green for a few seconds.

Yes! Level up for the bird!

As the humans threaded their way between the chicken enclosure and the garden, Mentor Jood cast a glance back to the convent then took Breakfast from Osse. He opened the door to the enclosure and set the bird down with all the other hens then quickly closed and secured it.

"Can't think of a better place, can you?" Mentor Jood winked.

"Works for me." Osse smiled.

Ahva imitated the clucking chickens, gaining a few XP.

The notebook turned blue, and then the edge of the view turned green.

Level up again? That wasn't much of a quest. I must've been right on the edge after the last one.

"You've done a wonderful thing, Osse." Master Dan clapped him on the shoulder. "The sun is setting. Why don't you and your bird stay with us for the evening. You can leave at first light and have a full day's travel wherever you're going."

"Yes. Good idea." Ahva whistled a tune.

"Thank you." Osse bowed and touched his forehead. "Vehira mentioned that the baron in the Yavne might have more information about the creatures that destroyed my village and kidnapped my sister. I think I'll try there next."

And maybe, just maybe, somewhere along the way we might run into our partner. You never know. Could happen.

Mentor Jood nodded. "Yes. His name is Rafayel Dorcas. He was here not that long ago seeking information about those strange laughing lunatics. I'm not sure what all he found, but that would be an excellent place to start."

"But you stay out of Vanya." Master Dan wagged his finger at Osse. "They don't much like your people. Not sure why, really."

"I'll go around the city."

The troop headed across the street and bee-lined toward the kitchen tent where Mentor Yudah was serving dinner to the various workmen. They joined the end of the line.

While they were waiting, Ahva called up her character sheet to allocate her new points.

CHAPTER 23

Name: Ahva **Species:** Corvid – Crow
Class: Scout Level 6 **Gender:** F

Attributes

Attribute	Current	Skill	Current
Power	15	Sneak	26
Speed	50	Detect Enemy	43
Cleverness	70	Signal Human	41
Endurance	22	Stay Alert	26
Agility	69	Sound Alarm	32
Charm	40	Patrol	65
Vitality	15	Trek	53
Sight	64	Long Distance Mvmt	43
Smell	5	Sprint	21
Hearing	25	Nonverbal Communication	40
Health	52	Camo	20
Encumbrance 0 out of 5 oz		Fly	88
		Speech	86
		Problem-Solving	36
		Bite	30
		Bombing Run	40
		Peck	26
		Detect Lies	11

After checking out all the numbers, she maxed out her endurance to 30 and plunked the last two points into Peck.

* * *

Nagheed ran alongside Rafayel and Ryder at the head of a much larger group of men. Including the constable and the baron, he'd counted ten men and horses, which according to the way the humans were talking, amounted to most if not all of the constable's men. Really, though, heading out now was a little pointless. A few days had passed since they'd found the poodle. Surely whatever had attacked that group was well past gone now. Whatever clues there might have been would be gone, too, blown away by the wind or trampled on by the wildlife. Nevertheless, this is what the humans wanted, so Nagheed tagged along. The excursion gave him more chances to run and check out his dog-eye view of the world.

When they came upon the area where the injured poodle had been found, the group slowed to a crawl. Nagheed turned on Smell and sniffed around the area. Scent words for the dog trainer and the dogs were there but very faint. One of the maniacs, too, was old news. The other two, differentiated by fonts, were brighter, but they'd been all over the place. A wolf pack of at least ten different wolves, each with its own font, had been through here. Coyotes, too, had frequented this area. Five human males had been by very recently. Those scents were bold.

Busy area.

The wrecked wagon that had been there two days before was gone now, but the symbol of the Ilionite religion still adorned the rocks and trees.

Up ahead, animals growled and humans shouted. Rafayel held one hand up high and then pointed in the direction of the noise. He set a slow, reasonable pace. Shrill, mirthless laughter echoed off the rocks in the path and the cliffs that lined one side. Rafayel stood higher in his saddle as a second maniac's laughter joined the first.

"Whoever they are, they're about to be overrun." Rafayel

CHAPTER 23

urged Ryder into a canter.

Nagheed kept the pace, but Jake leaned forward. The music changed, becoming an aggressive tune with a lot of trumpet and snare drums. Each of the patrolmen and the constable gained a smile-with-teeth emoji for their morale.

They rounded a bend in the road and came upon five men battling as many coyotes, but these were small, maybe the size of a small Labrador. Nagheed had an easy seventy kilograms on them. Two of the men were about dead. They were hanging onto life by a handful of health points. Two of the others were also injured. The last was still in good shape. The coyotes were all short a few points but none were in mortal peril yet.

Really low-level humans? Stronger-than-you'd-expect coyotes?

The patrol arrived.

"Engage the coyotes," Rafayel ordered.

While Rafayel and the rest of the patrol dispersed, Nagheed charged at the nearest coyote. The coyote broke off its attack against one of the men and crouched, snarling and growling. Rather than take advantage of the coyote's distraction, the man stormed toward Rafayel.

Without breaking stride, Nagheed tackled his target, bowling it over and landing on top. The coyote snapped at him, but he swiped a claw across its face. He bit the coyote's neck, rendering it into a mannequin. At the same time, a pair of patrolmen took out another coyote, and another two severely injured a third.

The man, apparently the leader of the beleaguered humans, stopped out of reach of Rafayel. "You take your men and your mutt and clear out. You're not wanted here."

Rafayel's stern glare belonged on a parent getting ready scold a bratty kid. "First, you do not issue me orders on my own land. Second, two of your men are badly injured, and the coyotes by comparison were rather healthy before we intervened. Third, much, much worse is coming. You may ultimately be glad of our arrival."

A horn sounded.

Here comes the second wave.

Nagheed left the last of the coyotes to the humans and watched for the next challenge. The five men who had been losing the fight gathered together and left. With their injuries, retreating was prudent, but leaving their allies with a mess wasn't exactly nice.

The patrolmen dispatched the last coyote the moment seven wolves came out of the trees. They strode onto the battlefield in an inverted V. Overall, the wolves were much closer to Nagheed's size. The leader, who stood at the center of the V, had a dark streak down the middle of its back and pale fur.

A reverse skunk. Great style choice.

When the leader started to howl, a few of the patrolmen swapped the smile-with-teeth emoji for a blah face or a frownie face.

Both Rafayel and Simon fired their pistols. Both hit, knocking the leader's points down by three-quarter.

The wolves maintained their formation and charged at the patrolman nearest to Nagheed. The patrolman's horse spooked and threw them off. He hit the ground like a sack of potatoes, which dropped his health points to less than half, as his horse ran off. Nagheed interposed himself between the nearest wolf and the fallen man. When the nearest wolf leapt, Nagheed triggered Tackle and launched himself. He collided with the wolf midair. The two landed with a thud that made the screen flash red. Nagheed rolled away from the wolf and came to his feet as a pistol shot echoed off the stone cliffs.

Nagheed chose Posture. He bristled and growled at the wolf as it approached, which had no effect on his opponent. When the wolf charged the last few meters, Nagheed crouched and timed his attack. At the last moment, the wolf dodged. Nagheed held his attack and spun. He pounced on the wolf, knocking it flat less than a meter from the injured patrolman. Nagheed clamped his teeth on the back of the wolf's neck and shook his head side to side. The wolf tried to roll and throw him, but Nagheed dug in with his back feet and planted his front feet on the wolf's shoulders. He kept shaking his head until the wolf became a mannequin.

Another patrolman rode up and dismounted. He pulled a clear jar of green goo out of his pack. "Good work, pup. You kept him safe." He smeared the goo on the injuries.

Nagheed woofed. *All part of the job.* He stayed near at hand while the herbalist did his work.

The status screen showed all the patrolmen, Rafayel, and Simon in fairly good shape. At least they were over half their points. Only four wolves remained, and as he watched, one of those zeroed out. Another horn sounded, and a howl with a grainy, metallic quality answered. Nagheed turned the direction of the sound, back the way they'd come. The maniacs had circled the group.

"They're behind us!" Rafayel shouted.

Nagheed glanced back at the herbalist. The fallen patrolman was back on his feet, sword in hand, and the other swung up into his saddle.

Now that you two are up and active again, we'd better knock down the rest of those wolves.

He surveyed the battle. With men outnumbering wolves by nearly three to one, anywhere he tried to get involved would increase the odds of a friendly fire incident.

"Nagheed! Heel!" Rafayel ordered.

He found his human, mostly because of Ryder's stature and sprinted across the battlefield, dodging horses along the way. He stopped next to Ryder's left side, away from Rafayel's sword arm.

A large, black wolf with a glowing disc in its chest and a second glow behind its head charged over the ridge and slowed down. "More humans. And I was hoping for a challenge. What about it, dog? You got any fight in you?"

"Hold, Nagheed." Rafayel reloaded his pistol.

"'Hold, Nagheed.' Do you always do what you're told, dog?" The wolf stalked closer.

I do when I don't want to lose experience or get shot.

The two maniacs came over the ridge. One had glowing eyes and the other had glowing discs in its upper arms.

Nagheed glanced back at the wolves. The patrolmen would have the last wolf taken care of momentarily. Creatures approaching them had been dubbed Maniac, Maniac, and Maniac Wolf.

"Aim for the glow." Simon waved the patrol closer. "Nothing else will do any real good."

The patrolmen, many of them at or below half their health, formed a line.

The maniac wolf paced. "Come on, dog. Are you at all

CHAPTER 23

useful?"

You're about to find out.

Rafayel and Simon exchanged a look then fired their pistols at the nearest maniac. As soon as the powder flashed in the pan, the maniac dodged one shot with a blurred sidestep, but the other hit one of its glowing eyes, causing a shower of sparks. The glow in that eye flickered and went out.

The maniac wolf and the other maniac charged.

"Go, Nagheed!" Rafayel ordered.

Nagheed leaned back then pushed off with his back feet. When the maniac wolf leapt, Nagheed initiated Tackle and jumped at the same time. He didn't get the height his opponent managed and collided with the wolf's belly, flipping the beast midair. The maniac wolf came down on its back. Nagheed landed on his feet and jogged a few steps forward then turned to take advantage of his opponent's bad position, but it was already back on its feet.

"You think that was clever, dog?" It snarled.

Not half as clever as I'd hoped.

The maniac wolf charged again.

Try that jump again.

His opponent didn't oblige. They collided on the ground this time, a rolling ball of bites and scratches that made the screen flicker red. His glanced at his health bar, which had dropped below half.

That momentary distraction got him pinned under the maniac wolf.

Chapter 24

Nagheed tried to roll but he couldn't manage the leverage. He snarled and snapped at the maniac wolf.

"Goodbye, dog." The maniac wolf bared a mouth full of sharp teeth.

Horses ran closer. One of the patrolmen and Rafayel drove the points of their rapiers at the back of the maniac wolf's head. Sparks flew. Maniac Wolf fell to one side. Nagheed rolled to escape.

"Nagheed, out!" Rafayel aimed his pistol.

Backpedaling, Nagheed cleared the range of even a bad shot. Between the pop of the powder in the flash pan and the bang of the main charge, the maniac wolf scrambled to get to its feet. The shot still hit it, but it missed the crystal. The patrolman with Rafayel thrust the point of his rapier at the glow, eliciting a terrific shriek from the crystal as the blade scraped across it. Three other patrolmen gathered around. With five humans ganging up on the maniac wolf, Nagheed stayed out of range. He surveyed the battle. The maniac wolf was the only remaining opponent. Simon and three of his patrolmen were in sorry shape, two them below a quarter of their health. As he watched, one of them jumped

CHAPTER 24

to half. That had to be the herbalist patrolman doing his thing.

Nagheed watched the maniac wolf's health bar dwindle in fits and jolts. Then sparks flew and it zeroed out altogether. The combat music cross-faded with their typical traveling tune.

While the herbalist took care of the worst injuries, Rafayel checked out all the mannequins. Nagheed limped along with him. Each step flashed the screen red for a moment. The coyotes' and wolves' mannequins contained only a pelt.

Rafayel delivered the herbs to the healer and distributed the rounds among his men.

The two maniacs and the maniac wolf carried a couple crystals each, a couple cracked crystals marked "broken," slagged plastic, and a few batteries. In addition, one had wires.

Rafayel kept those for himself.

Simon joined them. "You ever hear a wolf talk like that? I know some birds can manage it, but a wolf?"

"Only in legends." Rafayel glanced at the maniac wolf's mannequin.

The herbalist jogged over. "I've done what I can for all the men. Will your dog let me treat him?"

Rafayel nodded. "Yes. Thank you."

Nagheed sat still and watched his health bar jump up in brief spurts as the herbalist parted his fur and applied oily goo.

When the herbalist had finished, the Constable pulled the unhorsed man onto the back of his horse and they set out for town. At about the place where the wagon had been, they found six more mannequins. Five were clearly the men who'd been fighting the coyotes, and the other was a horse, likely the one that had run off after tossing its rider. The horse had the saddlebags. The other five had a sizable collection of rounds, a handful of varied jewelry, armor, and weapons.

"Hm. Do you think those men we came upon acquired all this loot honestly?" Simon hefted a handful of jewelry.

Rafayel shook his head. "Not for a moment. Do you?"

"Not nearly this much of it."

Bandits in training?

Rafayel turned the loot over to Simon. "Ask around and find out if anyone's missing things. If they are, and they can properly describe it, return the property to them. What's left, give to the church. As for the weapons, add the ones that are worth anything into the armory. The rest can be disposed of however you see fit."

The constable nodded. "I'll take care of it."

They headed back to town.

* * *

With Vehira settled in the convent and enough provisions to get him safely to Yavne, Osse and Ahva left when the sun was barely over the horizon. Ahva flew circles around Osse, trying a new game. After seeing those creepy hawks earlier, she assumed that wouldn't be the last hostile bird they ran into. Smaller than an average hawk, she should have greater agility. To improve those numbers, she darted in and out of the trees that lined the road.

For the first quarter-hour or so, she treated the trees like a slalom course, weaving around the boles of the trees.

CHAPTER 24

Then she tried to see how close she could get before she dodged, keeping the movement as small as possible. More than once the bark brushed past her wingtips, but she kept up the practice until she could scoot around the obstacle without touching.

Now she was ready for the next part. As Ahva approached the next tree, she zoomed over a branch while dodging around the trunk. The next one, she went under and kept alternating over, under, left, and right. This was like creating her own rollercoaster while playing dodgeball!

When her fatigue meter turned maroon, she hissed and flew back to the road. She'd have to play again later. She turned and flew back toward Osse, gliding as much as possible to conserve what fatigue points she had left. As she approached her human, he held out his arm for a landing pad. She dove under the height of his arm then arced up to drop onto his wrist.

After running up to his shoulder, she checked her stats and whistled a cheery tune. She had maxed out her Agility attribute, and her Flight skill was getting close to its max score.

She'd come a long way from that first day in the tent. Other skills also showed considerable improvement, but some noticeable ones lagged significantly behind. She was going to have to find a way to practice sneaking and camouflage.

As they approached Vanya, Osse held out his arm. "Ahva, stay closer until we get around the other side of the city." He left the road and followed a footpath along the side of the city wall. "At least we have no crowds this way."

Nicer scenery, too.

Like Nkamo, all trees and shrubs had been cleared for at least the length of a soccer field. To the east, foothills led into the snow-topped mountains that reached high enough to tickle the clouds. Trees here were pines, making the whole place look like a gigantic Christmas tree farm. The only thing missing was a layer of snow on the ground.

In about half the time it took them to go from the monastery to the city, they made it around the outside wall to the northern gate where they rejoined the road. The crowds here were a little thicker, as people entered the city. Once the crowds thinned out, Ahva took to her wings and resumed her previous game of darting in and out of trees.

About midafternoon, game time, Ahva was out on one of her scouting runs when she spotted a few men approaching a lone traveler. When the three men each drew weapons, Ahva turned a tight loop and flew back to her human.

"Disgusting eyeball. Bite fingers!"

"Problem?" Osse asked.

"Yes. Bad men. Other needs help." She pushed off from his arm and flew down the road again.

About fifty meters down the road, she peeked back over her shoulder to find Osse jogging to catch up.

Voices came from up ahead.

"Listen! I don't have anything."

"You really want us to believe you're out here for a lovely stroll. Hand it over."

Ahva turned back and flew a tighter circle around Osse. He stopped and held out his arm for her land on.

"Here's an idea. You stay on the move and stay hidden. From time to time say something loudly in one of your mimic voices. I'll come at them from the side. Maybe we

CHAPTER 24

can scare them off."

"Good idea." Ahva flew into the trees.

When she came even with the traveler and the three men, the three had the other man surrounded.

"Hey! Did you 'ear that?" she called.

One of the men turned toward her and scanned the tree line. When he turned away, she flew further down the road.

She lowered her pitch. "You okay?"

The same man who had scanned the trees her earlier turned her way again. "Who's there?"

She flew further back into the trees then climbed up above the canopy, flew across the road to the other side, and then dropped down into the trees there.

This time she went for woman's voice. "Ugh! Nasty stuff."

Between her and the road, Osse crept through the underbrush with his bow in hand. The trio of men had weapons drawn. Two of them had the business end of a sword pointing at the victim's chest while the other had a knife raised. The edge of Ahva's vision turned red. The ID tags identified the trio as Thieves. The other was labeled Traveler.

She flew to a different location and chose a deeper man's voice. "Who's there?"

As one thief drew back for an attack, Osse popped up out of cover, fired his bow, and drew a new arrow all in one fluid move. The arrow caught the attacker in the throat and turned him into a mannequin that fell like a piece of dead wood.

Ahva flew to a different location. "Good job."

The traveler lashed out at the second thief, launching a

flurry of kicks and punches that drove the attacker backwards. A small pouch fell from the traveler's belt. The third thief stepped in with a knife and led with an overhand strike. The traveler twisted, turning the fatal blow into a deep cut down his arm. When the traveler staggered, Osse popped up again and shot an arrow. The knife-wielder lost a third of his health.

The traveler pulled a small knife off his belt and threw it, hitting the one Osse had just shot. A third arrow from Osse turned that thief into a mannequin. The remaining thief snatched up the pouch and fled into the trees toward the ocean.

"Ahva, follow him," Osse ordered.

She pushed off from the tree and zipped between branches. Her quarry was quick, but his moves were uneven. Snatching up a pinecone, she dove for him and dropped it, pegging him in the middle of the back. He scooped up a rock and hurled it at her. She watched it in her peripheral vision and folded her wings in tight when it got close. Without the airfoil, she dropped fast, and the rock flew over her.

She circled back to keep him in view. Checking his health points on is ID tag, she hissed. Her pinecone attack had accomplished exactly nothing. When he slowed to a limp, Ahva fluttered from one tree branch to the other to keep an eye on him.

As if he had drunk something sturdier than coffee for breakfast, the man wove a convoluted path, sometimes doubling back, sometimes stepping high as if over an obstacle.

Ahva flew closer, perching in a tree directly over his head. Light filtering through the canopy glinted off something in the leaf litter. As she turned her head from side to side, the length of wire shined at her.

Tripwire?

She followed along, making note of the weird turns the man made. After a few minutes, he arrived at a cabin and ducked inside.

You stay there.

Ahva circled up to a good altitude that kept her out of arrow range. From that height, a worn path was noticeable.

She flew her straightest course back to where she'd left Osse and the traveler.

As she approached, Osse and the traveler were dividing the loot from Thieves 1 and 3. The gash on the traveler's arm was no longer bleeding. His shirt was still bloody on that side, but the wound no longer leaked.

Ahva landed next to Osse.

He smiled at her. "Did you find out where he went?"

Ahva preened to pick up some bird XP. "Yeah. Home. Look at the bird!"

"Good job, Ahva."

"Does she mean that?" The traveler stared at Ahva. "She really understands what you asked, and she gave you a real answer?"

Osse preened Ahva's head. "She's a good scout."

That is my job.

"Can you get her to take us there?" The traveler pointed at Ahva.

"Yes. Up we go!" Ahva spoke each word slowly. "Look. At. The. Bird."

"Are you sure you're up for that? All I've done was stop the bleeding. Healing a wound that deep will take a physician." Osse pointed at the bandage.

The traveler frowned at his arm. "I have to get that pouch back. I was entrusted with an errand. I would appreciate your help, but I will understand if you cannot."

"We'll help," Osse said.

The notebook turned blue, so Ahva opened it.

Give That Back! Retrieve the traveler's pouch.

Ah, see? Missed opportunity. They should have named this quest, "Mine! Mine! Mine!" She closed the window.

"Let's go." The traveler stood up and dusted himself off.

"Ahva, lead the way." Osse pointed toward the trees.

"The bird knows. Very clever!" Ahva flew to a tree at the edge of the road and waited.

To guide them, she flew about five meters at a time and waited for them to catch up. For their part, the traveler set a brisk pace, faster than Ahva would have thought given his recent injury. They arrived at the spot where the thief had started moving like a drunkard.

"Stop! Wait for me." She watched for an acknowledgment from Osse before she flew up through the canopy. From her height, the vague path was clear again. She picked out a couple of waypoints before she dove back through the canopy and rejoined the humans. She landed in front of them.

"No good for humans. Bad thing here."

The traveler turned at Osse. "Is that just chatter does that mean something?"

"It means something."

"Look." Ahva fluttered over to the first tripwire and stared at it.

"Something that would hurt us, maybe?" The traveler

CHAPTER 24

squinted at her.

"Yes. Good. Look." Ahva stared hard at the hazard.

"The pathway is trapped." Osse squatted and pointed to a tripwire.

Smart human. "Right. Few quick lessons."

"Do you trust her to lead us through here?" The traveler squinted at Ahva.

"She has stopped me from taking dangerous paths before. If she reaches a point where she refuses to go further, that's probably the end of her ability to direct us." Osse stood.

"Lead on then. Watch for tripwires." The traveler waved her on.

Ahva flew ahead one tree at a time keeping an eye out for the willow that marked the first waypoint. For their part, the humans moved forward much more slowly than before. They poked at the ground with sticks and brushed leaf litter aside when it piled up strangely. A few times, Ahva spotted a glint of sunlight where there shouldn't have been any. Without fail, that turned up a piece of wire or some sort of spring-loaded projectile. Whenever she passed a waypoint, she paused the humans and flew above the canopy to get the next one. It was slow going, but they finally reached the cabin where the thief had hidden himself. The humans crouched behind some of the brush and studied the cabin.

"I say we rush the place." The traveler drew a knife.

"You're sure there's only the one of them then?" Osse asked.

"Do we have any reason to think otherwise?"

"No, but we don't have reason to think that's true, either." Osse looked up at Ahva perched in the tree. "Ahva, can you get a peek in one of the windows and then tell us how many people you see?"

"Yes. I go look." She launched off from the tree and flew to the cabin, perching on the windowsill. Inside, the thief scrambled around, piling equipment into a bag. The traveler's pouch sat on the table.

She checked as many other windows as she could find but never spotted anyone other than the one man.

Let's hope this is not an elaborate game of hide and seek.

She flew a straight path back to Osse and landed on his arm.

"Just the one?" Osse held up one finger.

"Yes." She held up one foot and curled three of her four toes.

"Did you see my pouch?" the traveler asked.

"Yes. Dinner time." She imitated crunching nuts.

"Dinner time?" The traveler scowled.

Osse nodded. "It's on a table."

"Yes!" Ahva bobbed her head.

The traveler nodded. "All right, then I say we go straight through the front door."

Osse turned to Ahva. "Is there a back door?"

You didn't tell me to find a door. She thought back through the path around the house and recalled the second, narrow door in the back corner. "Yes."

Osse tapped the traveler's shoulder then pointed toward the house. "You go in the front door. But give me a minute to get around to the back. I'll enter through the back and make sure that thief doesn't escape with your stuff. He probably knows the layout of the traps, so he would get through the gauntlet much faster than we would and then you would lose him. And your pouch."

CHAPTER 24

The traveler nodded. "Not a bad idea."

Ahva led Osse through the edge of the tree line around the side of the house that had the fewest windows. Before they reached the back corner, a loud bang and a crack came from the front of the house. Muffled shouting came from the inside.

"Nice of him to wait for us." Osse sprinted the rest of the distance. He grabbed his mace and flung the back door open.

The door led into a kitchen. Opposite them, another door came out into the main room where the thief was packing his gear. The thief had a black powder pistol in his hand aimed at the traveler.

"I only want my pouch back. I don't care about whatever else you have. Then you can then go your way, and I'll go mine." The traveler took a step forward.

"Oh sure. You say that now. Next thing I know, there will be militia or a constable on my tail. No, this ends now. Here. Permanently. Too bad you didn't bring your friends from the road."

The edge of Ahva's vision turned red. The traveler's health bar showed about three-quarters, and the thief was just south of half.

Osse cocked his arm back as if getting ready to swing a tennis racket. "But he did."

The thief spun, leading with pistol. Osse swung the mace downward and struck the thief's forearm. The pistol went flying and landed on the floor. The thief lost a handful of health points and clutched his hand against his belly. The traveler darted forward and grabbed his pouch.

Ahva ignored the notebook turning blue. That might be

the end of the quest, but it wasn't the end of the fight.

Then he collected the gun and aimed it at the thief and Osse.

"Hey! Disgusting eyeball! Bad human!" Ahva chose Posture and fluffed up.

The traveler showed a slight frown on his morale icon. "Get out of the way," the traveler yelled.

Osse kept hold of the mace and held up one hand. "There's no reason to kill him. You have what you came for. Let's leave."

"So he can steal from someone else? No. Either get out of the way or risk getting shot."

The thief pushed Osse out of the way and ran out the back door. Ahva followed him. The traveler was not far behind, and as soon as he had cleared the door, he took a quick aim and fired. A pop preceded a loud bang, but he missed his target. The thief disappeared into the trees.

The traveler growled in disgust and stormed back into the house. Ahva turned and flew back, but the traveler closed the door before she could get there.

"Disgusting eyeball!" She banked sharply and flew around the house to the front door and darted inside. She landed on the table where the thief's gear was splayed out.

Osse slid the mace back into its sheath. The red at the edge of Ahva's sight cleared.

The notebook turned blue.

We finished another quest or got one? She opened it.

Spare Me! You didn't kill when you didn't have to. +200 XP

The traveler sighed. "I would've had him if you hadn't been in the way."

CHAPTER 24

"He would've had you if I hadn't been there." Osse pointed at the man's bandaged arm.

The traveler leaned against the table and studied his shoes for moment. "Yes, I suppose you're right. We could wait here for him to get back."

"No point to it, really. You have your property back. You can finish your errand. Ahva and I are on the way to Yavne to get some more information for our mission. We both have what we need, and I'm not in the mood for trouble. Honestly, it finds me without any trying on my part."

The traveler shrugged. "Take whatever you want of the loot. I'll take the rest and will get on the way."

Take the loot? We didn't kill anything. This isn't loot. It's someone's stuff. She inspected the mismatched, heavily worn, and rusted equipment. *Besides, who wants it?*

Osse shook his head. "Nothing here I want."

The traveler ducked back into the kitchen and rooted around for a few minutes, coming back with a loaf of bread and taking a bite out of an apple. "I got what I want."

The trip back out was quiet. Removal was the reverse of insertion, and they arrived at the main road in a few minutes.

The traveler drew a deep breath. "Thank you for your assistance. And thank your bird for me."

"I'm glad we were able to get you in time." Osse bowed and touched his forehead. "Safe travels."

"You the same." The traveler continued on his way south, and Osse turned north.

Ahva circled a few times then returned to Osse and landed on his outstretched arm.

Osse blew out a breath. "You wonder if we came in on the

right side of that argument?"

"Maybe?" *Three "thieves" attacking one "traveler" makes it pretty obvious which side we needed to come in on, especially since the three were after the property of the one, but something doesn't quite sit right about the one.* "Three all bad. One less bad."

"Yeah, I suppose they were all a bit shady." Osse blew out a breath. "Let's get a move on, I want to reach that inn at the halfway point before sunset."

When he picked up the pace to jog for a bit, Ahva took off and resumed creating her own personal rollercoaster-dodgeball game, weaving in and out of the trees, trying to get as close as she could get without hitting one.

* * *

Nagheed curled up next to the hearth in the kitchen and waited while his humans finished eating. He'd had a long day of training and patrolling. Now he was anticipating a lovely evening of watching the computer play for a few minutes while he sped up the clock so that it would become morning again. He'd already made a note that this game sure had a lot of down time. Maybe it couldn't all be action and adventure, but he would like a bigger helping of it. And when was his partner supposed to arrive on the scene? Hopefully he had a partner who wasn't interested in playing for ten minutes at a time every fourth day. He wanted to get a move on.

Micah snickered. "Poor dog. He looks so sad."

Rafayel smiled. "He had a long day. We patrolled twice the distance, since we're now sending people out in force.

CHAPTER 24

Everybody has to cover more ground."

Bettani nodded. "That's not a bad idea, actually. You're all much safer that way. Those strange attackers from Ilion are becoming more prevalent. I would not want anyone out there alone and encountering one of those."

"I quite agree." Rafayel blew out a breath. "I'm not complaining, but it makes for a long day."

A heavy knock sounded on the front door. After a short pause, maybe a few seconds, it repeated. Nagheed lifted his head and barked.

Rafayel swallowed a bite of food. "Thank you, Nagheed."

One of the servants excused himself from the table and darted out of the kitchen. He returned moments later.

"Sir, one of the constable's men is here. He's asking for you. Something about the constable's kid and a dog. Child's been kidnapped."

"Oh glory!" Bettani's eyes grew wide.

Rafayel wiped his mouth with a napkin and dropped it on the table before he stood. He slapped the side of his leg. "Come, Nagheed."

Nagheed stood up and trotted over to Rafayel. He followed his human into Rafayel's study where one of the patrolmen was waiting.

"Make your report." Rafayel crossed his arms over his chest.

The patrolman bowed. "The constable's girl, sir. She's gone missing along with that little dog of hers."

"You told my man that she was kidnapped?"

"I don't know about that for sure, but that's one guess. The constable asked if you could come. He thinks the girl's in trouble. He wants to take the patrol out and sweep the area while we still have some light "

Rafayel retrieved his leather doublet and his sword. Then he took his pistol from its box and loaded it. "Let me saddle my horse. Did he say where he wants to meet?"

"The south gate, sir."

"I'll be there directly."

We will be there directly. If you're going, I'm going.

The patrolman bowed then let himself out. Nagheed followed Rafayel out through the kitchen doors. The two men who minded the horses in the stable were getting the gray horse ready. Once they finished, Rafayel swung up into the saddle.

"Go open the gate, lad," the older stable hand ordered.

The youngster, the one who never spoke, ran around to the front of the house while Nagheed stayed close to Rafayel. He led the horse around through the courtyard, and out the gate, waiting open when they reached it.

Rafayel stopped and smiled at the boy. "You did well, Zev. Close the gate after us and return to your father, all right?"

The boy nodded as he tugged on the gate.

Nagheed increased his pace as Rafayel brought the horse up to a nice canter. They reached the main part of the city within moments and turned south to the main gate. The constable was already there along with eight other armed men on horseback. All the patrolmen and the constable gained a smilie or smile-with-teeth emoji as Rafayel approached.

Rafayel rode closer to Simon. "What's happened, Constable?"

"Oh, sir, my girl's gone off." Simon drew a deep breath and blew it out. "I got home yesterday to find Galice fit to

CHAPTER 24

be tied. That dog of the girl's got into the linens and made a mess of everything, including Galice's favorite tablecloth, the one her mother made for our wedding."

"Oh, no." Rafayel winced.

"Yeah, well, that set it off. She and I, we had it out over what to do with the dog this afternoon. Galice wanted it gone, and I said to give someone a chance to train it properly. Galice wouldn't hear any of that and said to sell the dog. That was the only way she'd have it." Simon took off his hat and ran his fingers through his hair. "Only you know my wife, sir. Can't use one word when there are fifty at hand, and won't whisper when she can holler. The girl heard it all, I'm sure. When I went to get her for supper, she was gone and so's the dog. I brought one of her dresses in case your shepherd can get the scent."

"All right. We'll ride out." Rafayel looked down at Nagheed. "Nagheed might pick up her trail. He's a good tracker, but if that doesn't work, we'll split up into a few bands and start searching."

The sentries opened the gates and Rafayel led the way out with Nagheed and the constable beside him and the rest of the men behind.

They had ridden several dozen meters when the constable gave Rafayel the dress. He held it low where Nagheed could reach. "Track her, Nagheed."

He knew the routine. Nagheed selected Tracking from his skill list. He got a good whiff of the scent then started sniffing around. The scenery exploded in scent words rising off some objects or blowing around on the wind. In addition to a wild assortment of human scents and wheel grease along the road, he got a whiff of a maniac closely associated with the word "Decay," a female pup, and the target.

The pup and the target followed a trail into the nearest trees. The maniac also made a trail that intercepted them before they all traveled together.

Nagheed whined and followed the trail toward the trees.

"He's got it," Rafayel said.

Once Rafayel was alongside, Nagheed picked up the pace and led his human and the other men on the way. The trail was strong, and he had no problem following it through the loose stands of scraggly trees and over the rocky terrain. Faint scrabbling ahead drew his attention.

He stopped and engaged Hear, which perked up his ears.

A little girl screamed as a dog yelped then a maniacal laugh drowned out both. Nagheed turned toward the sound. Using his Signal Human skill, his hackles raised and he growled.

"Come on. That came from this direction," Rafayel ordered.

The music changed to the combat tune.

Chapter 25

Nagheed stayed alongside as Rafayel spurred his gray horse into a gallop. There was movement ahead where the scream and the laughter had come from but also coming on an intercepting path from the right. Nagheed peeked toward the other direction and caught sight of another human. This one was dark-skinned, armed with a bow, and accompanied by a black bird that flew long, narrow loops. The nametag over the archer's head said, "Osse." And the bird was "Ahva." Names! They had actual names! Was he about to meet another player or were they important NPCs like the constable?

The girl screamed again, and Nagheed turned his attention back toward the sound. The little girl was bound on the ground and the small tuft of tan and gray fur had to be the dog. A maniac with glowing eyes stood, raising a knife high over its head.

The archer was closer to the child. He stopped some two hundred meters or so away and aimed his arrow at the creature. "You! Leave the girl alone!"

His voice carried well to Nagheed's ear, but would anyone, or anything, else make it out as clearly?

The eerie laughter came from the maniac again. It turned

and spoke as it ran at a horse's galloping speed for the archer. "You? I'll kill you!"

The crow picked up a rock and dropped it on the advancing maniac, which didn't slow it down at all.

"Constable, get your daughter," Rafayel ordered.

Simon took half the patrol and went left.

Nagheed stayed with Rafayel and the rest of the group and headed to help the archer.

The archer let one arrow fly after another. The first two hit the head of the advancing maniac. Sparks flew from one eye and a new glow started in the maniac's shoulder. The bird landed on the maniac's head and pecked at its other eye a few times before the maniac swung its arm upward. The bird ducked and narrowly missed the swipe.

Two of the archer's arrows went drove into the maniac's shoulder. The next arrow bounced off the maniac, generating a burst of sparks, and yet the creature kept advancing.

Dropping the bow, the archer snatched a mace from his belt.

Nagheed and Rafayel were nearly to them now.

As the maniac came close to the archer, he swung the mace, but the maniac ducked. Starting from a steep dive, the bird dropped a rock on the maniac, doing no significant damage.

The maniac knocked the archer down and pinned him. A moment later, the crow landed on the maniac's head and pecked at its face.

"Go, Nagheed!" Rafayel yelled.

Nagheed sprinted the remaining distance as the maniac pummeled the archer, totally ignoring the bird pecking at its head. The archer protected his head with his arms.

CHAPTER 25

When Nagheed was a few strides away, the bird flew off. He engaged his Tackle skill and leapt at the maniac. The momentum carried them both off the archer. Nagheed rolled further and righted himself quickly. The maniac laughed and turned back toward the human on the ground. Nagheed rushed forward and bit the maniac's leg. He dragged the maniac backward and crouched lower as Rafayel approached. Rafayel drove his rapier at the maniac's shoulder throwing a shower of sparks from the crystal before the maniac turned into mannequin.

The drums and brass faded back to the non-city music of plucked strings. Nagheed waited for Rafayel. He dismounted from his horse to check on the archer, who pressed his hand to his head but didn't try to move much more than that.

"Blood" floated on the air, and Nagheed tracked it back to the fallen archer, Osse according to the nametag. The bow lay nearby, and arrows had fallen from their quiver at his shoulder. Ahva flew back and landed on Osse's chest. All her feathers ruffled and she leaned low, growling and hissing.

The bird hissed and growled as Rafayel came close to the archer.

Rafayel stepped back. "I don't mean to hurt the lad. I just want to help him."

A new transparent window opened along the bottom of the screen. It showed his name and a blinking cursor. A label in the top corner of the window said **Player Chat (Ahva)**.

This is new.

Nagheed: Hey, bird, you wouldn't happen to be a player, would you?

Ahva: Howdy, Pilgrim. You'd better believe it. I'm Ahva. The kid with the bow is Osse.

Around them, the NPCs froze like statues.

Nagheed: I was starting to wonder if I was the only player in this goofy game.

Ahva: I knew there would be others. I told the AI I wanted one partner.

Nagheed: That's what I said. But you sure took a long time to show up.

Ahva: Hey. I've been busy. Your name is very ... foreign.

Nagheed: I like it.

Ahva: It's lovely. The computer dubbed me Ahva.

Nagheed: What? Didn't you generate your character?

Ahva: Nah, I went with a random quick start.

Nagheed: That explains why you're a little bird.

Ahva: What do you mean?

Nagheed: Most games of this sort will assign random quick starts to a class no one else has been picking. Horizon got a few negative reviews about small birds in the kid version of the game, so I'm guessing nobody picks them.

Ahva: Yeah. Leveling was slower than my granny with a walker at first. Y'know, "Get a move on. It's going to snow soon." I haven't done too shabby lately, though. Have you been chasing these crazy maniac things, too?

Nagheed: All over the countryside. I don't know if you're supposed to be my partner, but how about we try to con our humans into pairing up so we can chase these maniacs across the countryside together?

Ahva: Sounds like a plan to me. I'll have two humans to fly circles around while we hike halfway across the universe. And I didn't even bring my towel. Find anything interesting?

Nagheed: Loads.

Ahva: Let's not get into the exposition now. I'm sure the computer has it worked out where our humans outline everything that we've each learned. I'm not interested going through the same burst of exposition twice.

Nagheed: Right. Good to meet you, finally. Partner.

Ahva: Charmed, I'm sure.

The chat window stayed open but shrank down to a single line. The NPCs resumed whatever movement they were doing when the chat started.

The bird stopped hissing and smoothed out its feathers.

Rafayel crouched next to the archer. "What kind of mischief you've done yourself."

While he checked for injuries, Nagheed sniffed around the area to find clues about another maniac. The one they killed might've been the third one they'd heard when they'd found the dog show wagon, but maybe more had moved in. The bird stayed with her human.

He wasn't sure what to think about a crow for a partner. Certainly not half a powerful as an eagle nor as swift as a falcon, but crows were supposed to be smart. If she was actually putting some points and practice into her speech skills, this could be a handy way for him to communicate with the humans via a translating crow. He could chat with Ahva, and Ahva would talk to humans. A literal bird's eye view of the terrain might also make for an interesting complement to his tracking skills.

If nothing else, the bird's human was a decent archer. With some luck, the player had learned the strengths that a bird had and would use those and stay out of his way for the rest.

Nagheed returned to his human and sat next to him.

Rafayel had pulled Osse into a sitting position and was lying him flat again as Nagheed approached. Ahva hopped onto her human's chest and preened a few errant feathers.

"He's had quite a knock on the head." Rafayel stood. Shielding his eyes with his hand, he scanned the rest of his men. "Not as bad as it might've been, so the herbalist should be able to take care of it pretty quickly." Rafayel tapped the nearest of his men on the shoulder. "If he's not busy, ask him to come join me here."

The patrolman darted uphill.

Nagheed trotted a few steps that way and stopped. Up ahead, the constable picked up a young girl and came down the hill toward Rafayel. One of the other men led two horses.

At least the girl was okay.

The man darting uphill met up with the one leading the horses and took control of them before the other jogged down to Rafayel. As he drew near, Rafayel pointed to the bird's human. "He's got a nasty knock on the head. Can you do anything with that?"

The herbalist dug in the satchel that hung from his shoulder. "I'll do what I can. You may want to have a physician treat him later. Just to be sure."

"We'll stop on the way in. For now, do what you can so we can get him back into town."

Rafayel headed uphill and met the constable partway. Nagheed trotted along beside.

"She's all right. Little scared, I'm sure, but she'll be okay." The constable rubbed the girl's back while she sobbed on his shoulder. He jiggled a small dog collar looped over a couple fingers and mouthed, "The dog died."

Nagheed harrumphed. Being a small dog around here was not safe.

After the herbalist finished his job, Osse sat up.

"Hello." The bird tipped her head to one side and stepped onto her human's hand.

He blinked hard. "Ow. What happened?"

Rafayel crouched nearby. "You protected the constable's daughter by drawing off her attacker then fired several well-aimed arrows as the creature ran at you. It tackled you before Nagheed and I could reach you. My herbalist did what he could, but I suggest we stop at a physician on the way into town."

He pressed his hand against his forehead. "I think so. That's not the first one that I've run into that didn't go down after I hit the glowing part. Like it had some sort of backup."

"I counted a total of three glows. You destroyed two by the time it reached you." Rafayel shifted to kneel on one knee. "You've encountered these before?"

"Yes, they destroyed my village. I think they may have abducted my sister. One group headed west and another east. I picked the group to the west because they took four captives this way and only three the other, but now I think I picked the wrong group." He sighed heavily. "I went the wrong way."

Rafayel gripped his shoulder. "Let's head into town and get your head checked out. Then I would appreciate it if you would accompany me back to my manor. We can compare notes about these monsters and perhaps help each other out."

Osse nodded. "Thank you. My name is Osse Bente. This feather ball is my crow, Ahva."

Ahva waved a wing. "Hello! You're not Ahva. I Ahva!"

Rafayel stood and offered Osse a hand up. "I am Baron Rafayel Dorcas. Pleasure to make your acquaintance. This fine fellow is Nagheed."

Osse accepted Rafayel's hand up then stared slack-jawed at Nagheed. "That is a big dog."

Thank you, Captain Obvious.

Rafayel ruffled the fur on Nagheed's head. "That he is, and I wouldn't have him any other way."

Nagheed stood off to the side while the men mounted up on their horses. Rafayel offered Osse his hand and helped him up onto Ryder's back. They headed back into town less one dog, but with the girl in one piece.

* * *

Ahva perched on the back of a chair behind Osse's shoulder. The constable and his men had dispersed upon reaching the city gate leaving her human, her partner, and her partner's human to continue on to the physician alone. Yavne continued the Technicolor Chivalry vibe going on with the rest of Nethanya. The buildings were brick or stone with heavy wooden timbers. The men walking around were either wearing a belted tunic and pants or doublet and knee-length trousers and boots. Women wore floor-length dresses or a doublet and split skirt. No one was hat-free. If she hadn't known better, she'd've sworn they'd stepped into a Three Musketeers or Robin Hood movie set.

CHAPTER 25

The visit with the physician hardly took five minutes, real time, before their quartet headed up to a walled enclosure containing the baron's manor, a timber and stone building surrounded by pretty little flower gardens. The humans settled into squashy chairs in Rafayel's study while Nagheed curled up in front of the fireplace. Ahva hopped down to Osse's knee.

Then, as she had expected, the long run of exposition had started in which each human caught the other one up on the adventure so far. Unfortunately, the option to speed up the clock was grayed out now that she had a partner. When Osse's turn came to tell the tale for Rafayel and Nagheed, Khin May had fired off a quick "BRB" to her partner and gone off on a bio break. A PB and J, glass of milk, and trip to the privy later, she settled back in and hoped they were at least getting close to the end of the exposition.

"–Followed the sound of the girl screaming and the rest you know." Osse concluded.

Yes! Perfect timing.

"You never ran into more than one at a time?" Rafayel asked.

Darn. Maybe not so perfect timing.

"No. Well, a couple hawks, but nothing larger and a good thing we didn't. I'm barely managing against one. Ahva tries to help, and she has actually managed some good damage against couple of them, but I'm afraid we would be overwhelmed by two or more."

Rafayel nodded. "I'm sure. I've usually had at least part of my patrol with me when we ran into these things. Certainly when there was more than one. Fortunately, I have not found any sign that suggests your sister was out this way.

Likewise, I have not found any other injured Bakhari who didn't belong to the caravan. Nor have I heard of any being held captive by these creatures. We can only conclude that if your sister yet lives, she was taken east."

Osse looked down. "I only hope I can get to her fast enough."

Ahva stood up straighter. "Up we go!" The faster they got moving the better.

When the humans ignored her, she hissed.

"I have a proposal." Rafayel stroked his short beard for a few moments. "Clearly, these things are getting stronger. You say you have encountered more than one that jumped back up after you had knocked it down. The last couple I encountered were harder to kill than the first. Truly, I don't think it's wise to continue chasing them alone. I suggest we join forces."

Oh fine. Ignore the bird. I'm just the player, after all.

Osse winced. "That's prudent, but I'm not sure how helpful I would be."

Ahva mimicked the sound of his arrows hitting objects.

Rafayel smiled at her. "As your bird is suggesting, you're an excellent archer. My best archer can't shoot as cleanly as you can under that much pressure, and you're an herbalist with some skill. Other fighting skills can be trained. I noticed that you have a mace, but you're a bit awkward with it."

"I've only recently acquired it, and I'm afraid I'm not that good." He cast a look at the mace sitting with the rest of his equipment near the wall.

"There's an excellent trainer in town. A few lessons would not go amiss."

Osse nodded. "I'll find some work in town to earn the money. It was totally worth it, but my most recent work outside Vanya drained my resources to nearly nothing."

Rafayel sat back and steepled his fingers in front of his chest. "You may find that you qualify for a discounted rate. A man in my employ does have certain privileges. In any case, we leave for the Oligometa by week's end. That'll give us some training time and some time to collect our resources."

"Oligometa?"

"A quarterly meeting of Nethanyan nobility. We discuss things of mutual importance such as threats to the nation. I do believe these maniacs infiltrating the country from Ilion definitely qualify as a national threat. With any luck, I'll be able to secure some help from the crown and we can go together with a significant force. Worst case scenario, it's on the way toward Ilion, so we lose no time either way. From there, I suggest we move on to Ilion with or without the assistance of the crown and set things right to stop these attacks. What do you say?" He offered his hand.

Yeah. Isn't that the whole point?

"That sounds like an excellent plan." Osse shook Rafayel's hand.

The blue notebook signaled the quest, so she checked it out.

Oligometa. Get to Tel Caperna so Rafayel can petition the crown for help.

Oh, boo hiss. That one's not even funny.

Nagheed: Ahva? I think we need to plan out how this is going to work?

Ahva: How what's gonna work?

Nagheed: How we play. When are you available?

Ahva: All week. My whole office goes on vacation this week.

Nagheed: So, what? You're online twenty-four seven?

Ahva: If I want to be. How about we just play. The game will unfold as we go. Elaborate plans never survive first contact with reality in any case. Virtual or otherwise.

Great, so her partner was one of those hyper-analytical sorts who planned out everything including the number breaths to take per minute. That was going to make for fun gameplay.

Nagheed: What do you want to do if one of us needs to take a break in the other one doesn't want to?

Ahva: Either I take a break anyway or maybe you give me control of both characters. That's gotta be somewhere in the settings. But don't stay gone long, you know? If I need a break and you don't want to stop, I'll give you control of both characters. As long as we don't get ourselves dead or do anything critical to the quest, should be good to G. O. We'll work it out. 'Kay?

Nagheed: If that works, okay.

"Excellent." Rafayel stood. "Smells like dinner's about ready. What do you say we go see about filling our bellies then we'll consider what we need and what we have? Tomorrow I'll introduce you to the trainer. While you gain some skill with your mace, I'll start collecting our supplies."

Ahva fluttered up to Osse's shoulder as her human followed the baron from the room.

* * *

CHAPTER 25

The last few days had passed as if Nagheed had not acquired his partner. Ahva and Osse spent their day with the trainer both for mace and herbalist. Rafayel had also given Osse some horse-riding lessons. He could now hit a target with his mace on purpose more often and could mix herbs that did more than stop bleeding and heal minimal damage. Not much more, but that was a good start. Nagheed and Rafayel started assembling the equipment they would need to take this trip first to the Oligometa and then across the continent to Ilion. Fortunately, he and Ahva had discovered that if they went to the setting screen simultaneously to change the clock speed, that was still an option. As a result, the last few days in game time had passed in less than an hour real-time. With the computer running the clock at high speed, he secured himself a quick lunch and took Prince out for a potty break.

Morning had come early on the game clock, which didn't bother Nagheed at all. The humans had decided that they would leave for the first leg of their journey as soon as the sun was up. With breakfast eaten, horses saddled, and gear stowed, they were finally ready to go.

Nagheed stood at the back door from the kitchen and stared at it, wagging his tail.

Bettani chuckled. "Guess who's anxious to go."

"He is the adventurous sort." Rafayel smiled.

Of course, I am. I didn't play a game so that I could sit around the house and do chores.

Rafayel hugged his wife. "You'll be okay here. I'll be back as soon as I can, but I'm not sure how long it will take."

Bettani leaned into the embrace. "Don't worry about us. You spent a lot of time training Micah and the men. They'll be able to handle whatever comes up." She disengaged from the hug and crouched in front of Nagheed. "Keep an eye on him now. I'm counting on you to bring him back."

Nagheed woofed. *Not a problem.*

Osse carried Ahva in on his hand.

All right, all right, the gang's all here. Nagheed yawned while the humans continued wishing each other well and all that other silliness.

Finally, Rafayel opened the door and led the expedition out back where the servants had two horses saddled and waiting. The humans mounted up and guided the horses around to the front gate where the boy stood ready to open it for them.

Ahva: Happy trails!

"Bye-bye!" Ahva waved with one wing.

Ahva: Wait! Wait! I think they forgot to say goodbye to the potted plant in the foyer.

Nagheed: Don't remind them. We'll have to go back.

Ahva: But then the plant will get its feelings hurt.

Nagheed: It'll live.

Ahva: I suppose.

Nagheed trotted alongside his human toward the north gate of Yavne. The sun was popping over the horizon as they crossed through the gate and into the wilds. Or at least the suburbs of the city. The land had been cleared for a considerable distance away from the wall. Little farmhouses littered the landscape for a couple kilometers further before they left the suburbs. A mix of evergreen and deciduous trees lined the sides of the road.

A loud fluttering noise drew Nagheed's attention. Ahva launched off her human's hand and flew a long thin loop

CHAPTER 25

away from them and turned around and came back. He expected her to land, but she turned right back around and headed out again.

Nagheed: What are you doing?

Ahva: Stretching my wings. Scouting for danger. Practicing my birdliness. You have noticed that most of this game involves hiking from one part of the universe the other.

Nagheed: I've noticed, but the scenery is lovely. You're lucky your human lets you get that far afield. I start wandering too far off from Rafayel, and he calls me back.

Ahva: And if you don't obey then you lose points, right?

Nagheed: Yeah. Only game I've ever played were you lose experience.

Ahva: Irksome, but that's handy. I've run into a few occasions where the only reason I knew I was taking the right action was that I defied my human and didn't lose points.

Nagheed: Huh. I haven't encountered that yet. So, what do things look like from above?

Ahva: Oh man. Wish you could see it. Maybe we'll find a trampoline, and you can jump real high. Find a doggie hang glider. Something.

The road passed through dense trees. Many creeps hunting for a good spot for an ambush would pick here. Sure, Ahva was out scouting backwards and forwards crossing over the same distance, but the enemy might be hiding were she couldn't see them.

Nagheed trotted a few steps out ahead of the group and put his nose to the ground, ranging back and forth across the path trying to pick up some sign of trouble. He kept his eye on the scents blowing by on the wind or emanating from objects on the screen. Squirrels, birds, and rabbits made up the bulk of what he picked up. Not terribly dangerous. Once, he caught a trace of a wolf, but it was gone as soon as he saw it.

They'd been traveling for a while when Ahva flew back to her human and came in for a 'graceful landing on his hand. She took to whistling a tune.

Nagheed: You have to do that? You'll attract every baddie in the area.

Ahva: What baddie? I've been scouting since we left town and the most violent thing I found was a bluejay chasing a squirrel for a nut. Trust me. There's nothing there.

Nagheed: Don't say that! It's always after someone says that that the manure hits the rotating air circulation device.

Ahva: Bring it on! I could use the XP.

Still, they continued on down the road a few kilometers and didn't find anything worth noticing. As she had suggested, Nagheed found nothing more exciting than the occasional squirrel. He was starting to get an idea for why dogs liked to chase things.

Ahva took off again, but this time, instead of scouting a couple kilometers ahead, she grabbed a small rock off the side of the path and dropped it, complete with a bomb drop whistle, and hit a larger stone. She made several more attempts with variable success.

Rafayel turned toward Osse. "She's really quite good at that."

Osse smiled. "She's been practicing."

CHAPTER 25

"You know, if we can find small enough blades, or something weighted that she can pick up, she could do more damage. At least more than a simple rock."

Ahva: Or maybe even a bomb. Now that would be the thing. Then my bomb drop whistle actually have a boom at the end.

Nagheed: Because bombs are thing here?

Ahva: Well, with batteries, circuit boards, computer chips in plastic, and zombie cyborgs, I figure we're either alternate timeline or post-apocalypse.

Nagheed: Post-apocalypse. Very post-apocalypse. Rafayel reads a book to his family about Ilion and the rest of the continent going to war because Ilion went a little overboard on creating "crossbreed" humans and monsters. Long enough ago that it's considered legend more than real history.

Ahva: I knew something was up when I saw the books about Ilionite prophecies and world domination. So, y'see? A bomb. I could drop bombs.

Nagheed: The burning wick would scorch your tail.

Ahva: Okay, fine. How about a grenade.

Nagheed: Yeah, but don't slip with the trigger.

"Are there craftsmen that make blades or weights that small?" Osse asked.

"There might be. Many adventurers take a bird with them, even small ones like Ahva. We might have to search a bit to find one, though." Rafayel shrugged. "I suppose we could commission them made."

"That would take a while, unfortunately."

Rafayel watched Ahva's next bombing run. "Not necessarily. We're not talking about anything exactly huge.

Might be as simple as an arrowhead with a short shaft or a loop she could grab with her beak. Weighted and sharpened properly, she could drop it and strike an opponent. It wouldn't do as much damage as if you shot the arrow from your bow, but it might get someone's attention."

"Maybe we could try it tonight after we get camp set up." Osse patted his bag. "I might have a few arrowheads in my bag."

"Worth a try."

Ahva: Will you be my target?

Nagheed: Um, no. I don't think so. You'll have to make do with a piece of fruit.

Ahva: Eat your food don't shoot it.

Nagheed: What?

Ahva: You've never played-? Oh, how tragic. That is something that you simply must remedy. I'll send you a link.

Nagheed: To what?

Ahva: A totally fabulous vintage game. The one-liners are worth it. But the gameplay itself was kind of fun. Vintage, but fun.

He'd rather stick with the modern stuff. The pixelated images of the older games made him wonder if his glasses were out of date. When the sun was overhead, the trees surrounding them thinned out. They became scraggly brush in open fields with scattered farmhouses. Ahead, the wall of the city loomed.

"That's Salomon." Rafayel indicated the city ahead with a nod.

"Are we passing through or stopping?" Osse squinted into the distance.

CHAPTER 25

"Hopefully, we'll pick up another traveling companion who will go with us as far as the Oligometa. He may have left already. If he has, we'll pay our respects to his wife and continue on."

They entered the town shortly after and headed toward the middle of town. The stone and timber architecture of Vanya and Yavne were continued in Salomon. The people were dressed similarly, too, if perhaps a little more toward the doublets and trousers instead of tunics. Unlike Vanya, which had smelled strongly of fish, and Yavne, which had smelled of ocean, the scents rising up in Salomon read "sewer" to the exclusion of all else. The word formed a haze over everything. The lack of sensory input was a definite advantage to playing the simpler VR modes.

Osse waved a hand in front of his face. "Wow. That's some stench."

Ahva: It must be. Even I'm getting a few gray words floating around the screen, and birds don't have a sense of smell worth speaking of. Except vultures. Vultures are weird.

Nagheed: What do you know? There is an advantage to being a bird.

Ahva: Stinks to be you. My Smell attribute is a puny 5. I spect a dog's sniffer is much more interesting. Can you even see the background art?

Nagheed: Yeah. There's a haze from the word "sewer" overtaking everything, but it's transparent. At least my set up doesn't have full sensory perception.

Ahva: Who would want a stinky game anyway?

Little by little, the overwhelming "sewer" faded from the view. Nothing replaced it, but the word grew smaller and fainter. At least he wasn't trying to see the background through the haze of the word.

At the center of town, they found a sprawling manor made of the same timber and bricks that constructed most of the rest of the city. Wrought iron artwork shaped like a variety of sea creatures decorated the walls. Unlike the baronial manors in Vanya and Yavne, there was no tall stone wall. Instead, wrought iron spikes fashioned to resemble kelp had been driven into the ground surrounding the manor. The cobblestone pathway led to a gate composed of two massive iron sea shells. Each was taller than Rafayel on Ryder's back. Nagheed nudged one with his shoulder. It stayed still in the dirt, but would it survive a push from something really meant to break it down?

As they approached, a gate guard came out of a guard house built from driftwood festooned with old fishing nets, an oar, and some impressively large starfish. Jake smirked. The hokey decorations on this place reminded him of Fish Food, a local seafood joint near campus.

"Good afternoon. I am Baron Rafayel Dorcas. Is your lord in?"

The guard shook his head. "He's already left for the Oligometa."

"Very well. I should like to pay my respects to the lady of the house before I continue on myself." He withdrew a small card from an inside pocket of his doublet and handed it to the guard.

"Wait here." After reading the card, he hustled to the main door of the manor.

The guard ducked inside. When the door opened again, a lady with a rounded physique and a heavily decorated gown stood in the doorway as the guard jogged back to the gate and opened it for them.

"She'll meet with you." The guard ushered them through.

"Thank you." Rafayel dismounted and led his horse inside.

Nagheed followed and Osse stepped down from his horse and trailed behind. After the humans secured the horses to a post near the door, they followed the woman inside to a sitting room. Scent words drifted in the air, giving evidence of garlic, chicken, apples, cinnamon, three human females, two human males. The food and all but one of the people scents came from somewhere off to his right while one human female's scent came from the left.

Nagheed's stomach rumbled. Sure enough, the fatigue meter could use some food.

Another, older woman with graying hair and a simple dress joined them and sat in the corner of the room. The baroness gestured to a padded couch before perching on the forward edge of an ornate chair.

Without being told, Nagheed went to the simple gray rug in front of the hearth and sat.

"I'm so glad you came, Rafayel. I don't know who else I could have turned to." The baroness smiled, showing her blinding white teeth.

Nagheed: I hear a side quest coming.

Ahva: Enh, I don't mind the odd side quest. Adds variety.

Rafayel leaned forward. "What's the matter?"

"My cousin usually comes to visit while you're all in the capital being very official. This time, with all the strange attacks going on in the countryside, he's afraid to travel alone. I was wondering if you would be willing to go escort him back here."

"We would be pleased to have a bit of a diversion." Rafayel stood.

Nagheed got up and wagged his tail.

"Where can we find your cousin?" he asked.

"Follow the road east out of town." She pointed away from the ocean. "As you head into the mountains, the path will split off to the north, but continue following it to the east. It dead-ends at my cousin's home. It's not far at all. I don't imagine it would take you half an hour to get there and bring him back. I'd be so grateful if you'd return him here. I'd love to visit with him again."

"We'll be back as soon as we can." Rafayel stood.

Nagheed darted forward and walked alongside his human, who led the procession out to the horses.

"We'll leave the horses here. They could use the rest and the mountain paths around here are steep in spots." Rafayel patted Ryder's side.

As soon as they were outside again, the "sewer" odor took over everything in the words drifting on the air to represent his olfactory's perception.

Nagheed: So glad the smell doesn't really translate through the computer.

Ahva: Advantage to the bird.

Nagheed: You mean your rig translates smells?

Ahva: For a fee. I usually won't pay it. The programmers overstink these games. The place ends up smelling like an explosion at a factory that makes air stinkifiers. I'd rather have in-game anosmia. Are you VR?

Nagheed: Yeah, but lower tech. I don't get much for

sensory perception.

Ahva: Wow. Very Old School. I like it! Wouldn't want to play that way, though. Flying with my current rig is a trip.

They left through the eastern gate. The road led up into the foothills. The further they were from the city, the smaller and fainter the word "sewer" became until it nearly vanished. Now he was treated with the usual birds, trees, ocean air, and a few others faded in and out or drifted by on the breeze as they walked.

They'd gone only a few hundred more meters when the path turned north and a second path, hardly more than a well-worn footpath continued to the east.

Rafayel kept on to the east. The path wound back and forth through numerous switchbacks. New scents wafted by: **Bear, mountain lion, pine trees, small birds, and an eagle.**

Nagheed: Oh good. Bears and mountain lions in the area.

Ahva: Bears aren't all bad news. We ran into a nice one on the way from Fola.

Nagheed: We should be so lucky.

Ahva: Too bad we didn't have a pic-a-nic basket to give her.

Nagheed: What?

Ahva: You really need to catch up on your vintage arts.

Nagheed: Who's got time for that?

The trail turned steeper, and Nagheed dug in with his back feet to launch himself forward. When the path leveled out some, a gray stone house appeared fifty meters to the left. That had to be the place. They veered to the left and approached the door.

Rafayel knocked then stepped back a pace. "I'm surprised that he doesn't have better protection so far from town."

Osse looked around. "That's what I was thinking too, what with–"

The door opened and a portly man peeked out. "State your business."

"The baroness of Salomon has sent us. She desires a visit with her cousin and sent us as his escort."

The man's brow furrowed. "Cousin? There's–" His eyes widened as realization set in. "Oh. Right." He opened the door wider. "Do come in. I'll fetch him directly."

Nagheed followed the humans and the bird in.

Ahva: No, that wasn't suspicious at all.

Jake snickered. There was more going on here than a friendly visit from a cousin.

Nagheed: Do you get the feeling we haven't been given the entire story?

Ahva: Now whatever gave you that idea? :D

Some mild rattling and banging came from the next room. The portly man returned carrying two small suitcases. They simple box-shapes made of plaid cloth that had some sort of internal structure and a long zipper that went around thee sides. They had a simple U-shaped handle.

Wow! So, did they retain the ability to make zippers or has that suitcase survive this long after the technology decline?

A few moments later, a short, wiry man dressed in a lace-endowed doublet and trousers pranced into the foyer. The word "Cologne" surrounded him like a fog.

Rafayel stepped forward and offered his hand. "Good morning. I'm Baron Rafayel Dorcas, and this is my friend

CHAPTER 25

Osse Bente. Your cousin sent us to invite you to visit.

The young man ignored Rafayel's hand. "My name is Johan. I knew she would come through. Carry my bags, and let's be off, shall we?"

Ahva: Nice guy. The sort you'd want to feed to a bear.

Nagheed: There are bears in the area, so don't give me any ideas.

Ahva: Is this where the guy comes back with twenty extra suitcases for you to carry?

Nagheed: Do I have hands?

Ahva: You're big enough to pull a cart.

Nagheed: I specifically avoided that character class.

Ahva: That doesn't mean you don't get to try.

After casting the bird a sidelong look, Nagheed backed away from the suitcases. Rafayel took both and handed one to Osse.

They left immediately, which didn't upset Nagheed at all. The faster they got off this hokey side quest and back to the main one, the happier he'd be. One step after the house disappeared, a growl came from the right.

Johan jumped. "What was that?"

"Nothing we need to worry about as long as you don't lose your head." Rafayel glared back at him.

Ahva leapt off of her human's shoulder and wove a path through the trees. Nagheed turned on Smell to get more than the passive readings and sniffed around. More than the usual scents bloomed all across the screen along with a couple new ones: "Maniac bear" and its closely associated "mild decay." Other scents that registered from various directions included squirrels, songbirds, mountain lion, and bear.

Nagheed sat and whined.

"What's wrong with your dog?" Johan pointed.

Rafayel set the suitcase down and drew his sword. "Osse, your mace." He turned to Johan. "Stay behind us."

"What is it?" Osse set the suitcase down grabbed his mace from the carrier on his belt.

Nagheed: Where are you? I've got a whiff of maniac nearby.

Ahva: A bit north of you – Oh no. Zombie cyborg bear.

Nagheed: Black bear? Grizzly?

Ahva: Uh... Not as big as the one we saw earlier. Definitely black fur. So, I'm going to go with black bear. The only animal zombie cyborgs I've run into were not good. Definitely bad.

Nagheed: Yeah. There are good ones, though. I ran into a friendly alligator, but I think that one was just a cyborg.

Ahva: An alligator? Wow! What will they think of next?

The music shifted from stringed instruments to snare and brass.

A black blur flew back into the area and landed on Osse's outstretched arm. She imitated the maniac's laugh with startling accuracy.

Nagheed: Okay, that's creepy.

Ahva: You like that one?

Nagheed circled away from Rafayel. A bear with two glowing eyes lumbered out of the trees. It smacked the ground with its paw and huffed. Johan shrieked and hid behind a tree.

"Fierce!" Ahva fluffed up and hissed.

Nagheed picked Posture out of his skills then growled and bristled. The maniac bear didn't acquire a debuff.

CHAPTER 25

Ahva: Wow. You're pretty scary all fuzzed up. Sic him, Shaggy!

When the Maniac Bear charged Osse, Nagheed initiated Tackle and leapt at the bear, sinking long canines into the scruff of the bear's neck. As the humans closed in for an attack, Nagheed gave his head a good shake. Although that didn't move the bear, the bite damage increased. He retreated so they could attack the glows without hitting him.

Chapter 26

Rafayel thrust his rapier at the bear's face. A crack accompanied a shower of sparks.

A rock flew in from the right and clipped Rafayel's shoulder, doing minimal damage.

"Johan, stay out of this, or do something constructive." Rafayel rolled his shoulder.

The bear reared back with one massive paw.

Nagheed bit the bear's back leg and dragged it backwards. The bear aborted its attack. Osse stepped in and swung his mace like a bat. A loud crack preceded a burst of sparks. The bear shuddered. Nagheed drew back with a paw as the bear turned toward him. Ahva swooped in and dropped a pine cone on the bear's nose. It flinched, and the attack faltered. Rafayel thrusted his rapier and struck the bear's face, producing a much more impressive burst of sparks. The bear turned into a mannequin.

The combat music cross-faded back to the stringed instruments.

"That took you long enough." Johan stepped out from behind the tree.

Ahva landed on the bear mannequin and hissed. "Fierce! You try!"

At the same time, both Rafayel and Osse glared at the useless "cousin." Nagheed growled.

"What?" Johan came out from behind the tree. "You're supposed to be my protection."

"Are you hurt?" Osse pointed at Johan.

He looked himself over and readjusted a piece of lace. "No."

"Then we did our job." Osse turned away.

Johan continued to grumble.

"Is anyone hurt?" Rafayel looked at each of them.

"I don't think either animal took a hit. Are you okay?"

"Fine, fine. None of its attacks were leveled in my direction." Rafayel squatted in front of the mannequin. "Excuse me, Ahva."

Ahva fluttered up and landed on Rafayel's head.

Osse chuckled. "Ahva, come here."

"No."

Osse strode over and tapped the bird's chest. "I said, 'Come here.'"

"I said, 'Nooooo.' See good here."

Rafayel snickered. "She's got a bit of an attitude. She's fine where she is for the moment." The mannequin's inventory screen opened, and he withdrew another battery, slagged plastic, and a crystal. Then he reached into the inventory again and picked up a printed circuit board with some scorch marks at one end.

Ahva: Oh look. Bakhari money. Unminted yet.

Nagheed: Bakhari money?

Ahva: Yeah. Looks like little hexagonal circuit boards without chips. Some bigger than others. Lighter than carrying a pocket full of gold coins, I suppose.

Nagheed: How odd.

Ahva: Maybe, but Nethanyan money is plastic-encased chip, right?

Nagheed: Yes.

Ahva: Also odd. In a weird way. I wonder where all the real money went. Y'know, gold, silver, platinum.

Nagheed: Oh, Rafayel's book explained that. The surviving remnants of the crossbreeds are holed up somewhere with a huge hoard of gold, silver, and platinum.

Ahva: Would be funny if their boss is a dragon.

Johan strutted up behind Rafayel. "Anything interesting?"

"Not particularly." He slid his backpack off his shoulders and stashed everything in there.

"You're not even going to share with us?" Johan huffed.

Rafayel stood. "Osse and I are on the same mission. My resources are his resources. You, sir, were not a part of that combat."

"I threw a rock." Johan propped his hands on his hips.

"And hit me."

"You got in the way!" Johan jabbed his finger at Rafayel.

Rafayel picked up a suitcase. "Let's get going. I want to drop you off at your cousin's house and get back on the road. I have places to go."

Osse picked up the other suitcase and followed as Ahva flew back to his shoulder. Nagheed fell in alongside his human.

The rest of the trip to town saw nothing more exciting than a couple squirrels and a few songbirds, but Nagheed didn't relax until they were safe inside the city walls.

When they reached the iron seaweed fence, the main door

of the manor opened and the baroness rushed out. She stopped halfway to the gate and waited while one of her servants let them into the yard. Johan rushed forward and embraced his cousin. Rafayel took both suitcases and set them next to the front door. He untied Ryder.

A brief trumpet fanfare announced that he gained level.

Ahva: *sigh* Still no level-up.

Nagheed: I did. You must have just missed it.

Ahva: I suppose. Missed it by that much!

Nagheed opened his character screen and allocated the points.

"Thank you both for your help." The servant closed the gate.

How rude. No offer of hospitality? No farewell from the lady herself? Nothing from the guy they protected on the road?

Ahva: Can you feature that? He didn't even say goodbye.

Nagheed: Seriously.

Ahva: Some people's kids.

Rafayel and Osse walked their horses out of the gate before mounting. Ahva hissed at the house.

Osse twisted in the saddle toward Rafayel. "That's not what I expected."

"No. That was rude even for her. We still have the bulk of the day. Shall we see how close we can get to Geva."

"I'm with you."

* * *

Ahva looped around and landed on Osse's arm. The trip

to Geva took a few hours of travel in the game, but they arrived shortly before sunset. She been highly amused by a random encounter with a couple coyotes. They'd had one good glimpse at Nagheed and bolted. The dog did have a good intimidation factor, no doubt about that.

Osse followed the baron through the city gate. Without stopping to ask for directions, Rafayel led them down a couple streets to a large house overlooking the coast. Although a high fence surrounded the property, the gate was wide open.

"Shouldn't this gate be secured?" Osse pointed at the gate and looked at Rafayel.

"Most of the time, I should think so. Three months ago, when I passed through here on my way to the Oligometa, the baron had been stricken ill. He'd made little recovery by the time I passed back through a week later. I do hope everything's okay."

Ahva turned to Osse. His healer skills might come in handy shortly.

Nagheed: I predict a fetch quest to acquire medicine for the sick baron.

Ahva: Yeah, that, or an escort quest to get a higher leveled healer.

The humans rode the horses closer to the main doors and dismounted. As they approached the main door, muffled shouting came from within. The two humans exchanged a glance before Rafayel pounded on the door.

"Go away! We're not receiving visitors!" A man's voice hollered.

"That's not the baron. The voice is all wrong." Rafayel drew his sword and threw the door open.

CHAPTER 26

Osse hung back while Nagheed followed his human in.

"Nagheed, go!" Rafayel ordered.

Ahva flew into the house ahead of Osse and veered toward movement on the right in time to watch her partner tackle a heavyset man and pin him face down. Nagheed was all bristling fur, bared teeth, and growls. He punctuated his growls with the occasional bark, a deep, menacing sound that challenged his target to give an excuse for an even harsher reaction. The brute he had pinned sported a fear emoji in his nametag.

Circling the room, Ahva got an impression of the rest of the story. A middle-aged woman in an ornate split skirt and doublet picked herself up from the ground and dusted herself off. She wiped blood from the corner of her lip. A younger girl in simpler attire cowered behind her and rubbed her left arm. A young man, also dressed plainly, lay sprawled on the floor, apparently unconscious. Books and papers were scattered on the floor around the desk. A maroon curtain hung askew on one of the windows.

Ahva looped the room one more time before returning to Osse.

Rafayel approached the man Nagheed still had pinned and stopped a meter away. "Nagheed, out."

After one last bark, Nagheed retreated to Rafayel's side.

"Don't move." Rafayel kept his rapier pointed at the man and glanced at the well-dressed lady. "Are you all right, Mary?"

She blew out a breath. "Much better now, thank you."

Without taking his eyes off the man, Rafayel waved Osse forward. "Mary, this is my friend, Osse. He's an herbalist."

"If he could take care of James." She pointed to the

unconscious fellow on the floor.

Ahva flew ahead and landed next to the kid.

"Do you have someone to send for the constable?" Rafayel asked.

"I am the constable, you idiot." The man rose up onto one elbow and scooted back from Nagheed.

Osse knelt across from Ahva and swung his bag off his shoulder.

"Indeed? Then how about an explanation for what I saw?" Rafayel switched his rapier to the other hand and rested his palm on the butt of his flintlock.

"And who are you to be issuing orders?" The constable asked.

Osse checked for obvious injuries and then felt along James's skeleton before carefully turning him over. A dark red stain on the light tan material around a hole in his belly blared at them. Osse carefully lifted James's shirt, revealing a puncture wound, too big around to be a knife. In the edge of Ahva's peripheral vision, she found a fireplace poker stained with blood on the business end.

"Baron Rafayel Michael Nicolaos Dorcas of Yavne, so I suggest a much more civil tongue in your head."

"He came in here ordering me to give him Samwel's signet ring." Mary jabbed her finger at the man.

"And when you rightly refused, he resorted to a more physical response?" Rafayel suggested.

"Yes, and when my servants tried to get in the way, he pushed them both." She glanced at the kid sprawled on the floor. "James tripped into the fireplace tools. Anna hit the edge of the window."

Osse dug herbs out of his pack and prepared a paste with

some of the water in his canteen.

"There are things I need to have done that old Sam can't do while he's laid up, and the boy's not here to take care of it. The barony doesn't run itself."

Rafayel shook his head. "Not relevant. If Samwel is not able to take care of things, the baroness is quite capable of handling the administrative duties of the city whether her son is here or not. She is the proper authority in this barony, not you."

Osse used scraps of James's destroyed shirt to make a bandage and applied to the herbs to the injury on his belly.

James drew a sharp breath between his teeth and squeezed his eyes closed.

"I'm sorry." Osse winced. "It does sting a bit, but you'll be okay. Try not to move around too much. The wound doesn't look particularly deep, but you're going to need some rest and a several more applications of those herbs or the aid of a physician before you're ready to get up again."

"Mary, what's to be done with this man?" Rafayel kept his eyes on the constable.

"I want him charged and jailed until the judge can hear the case." She crossed her arms over her chest.

Rafayel nodded. "Do you have someone in mind who can take over as constable at least until the trial?"

She studied the corner of the room for a moment. "His deputy is a good man."

The constable snorted. "He's a brat kid."

"With more common sense and decency than you'll ever have not to mention a proper respect for the law." Her clipped words lacked the hysteria Ahva expected.

"Osse, can I leave you here to attend the wounded while I

take care of this errand?" Rafayel asked.

Osse nodded. "Certainly."

The notebook in the corner turned blue.

You Are Healed! Help your human heal the injured and investigate the area.

Khin May smiled, getting a mental image of the old TV faith healers high-fiving someone's forehead.

Rafayel kept the business end of his sword aimed at the constable. "Get to your feet. Slowly. And in case you're wondering, no, you are not faster than Nagheed. He can give my horse a good challenge."

Ahva: No kidding! You can outrace a horse?

Nagheed: Close. Real close. I think my stamina might be a shade better.

Ahva glared at the brute. "Disgusting eyeball. Bad man need a few lessons."

Nagheed: Disgusting eyeball?

Ahva: When I first met Osse, he helped catch a thief and said something about putting an arrow through his "disgusting eyeball." I didn't have a whole lot of vocabulary when I started. I used what I had to create a communication mode with Osse. Besides, it's funny.

Nagheed: You have a weird sense of humor.

Ahva: You say that like it's a bad thing.

Her partner, his human, and the knucklehead "constable" all left. Ahva fluttered up to the desk. She strutted to the edge nearest the cowering servant. The girl was a teenager with all the usual cute kid awkwardness of that age. She backed further into the corner of the room, still cradling her arm.

"Good bird." Ahva waved with one wing. "Hello!"

CHAPTER 26

Osse left James and approached. "Ahva won't hurt you. She's just curious." He stopped an arm's reach away from the baroness. "Are you injured?"

What a dumb question. The trace of blood was still on the corner of her mouth.

"Not too badly, I don't think. I cut my lip on my teeth. I'll be fine. Take care of Anna. She hit the wall pretty hard." She led him over to the girl.

While Osse did his herbalist thing with the girl, Ahva rooted around on the desk, peeking under papers.

"Ahva, don't be a pest," Osse said.

Who was being a pest? There might be quest related information here, and her quest did involve investigating. She wouldn't find it if she didn't try. This game was not exactly forthcoming with the clues. On the far side of the desk, something shiny in a brighter green than naturally found in this kind of environment showed under the edge of a few stacked papers. Ahva darted over to the green thing and slid her beak under the edge of the papers. When she lifted them, she turned her head sideways to keep an eye on the green thing. Slagged plastic? Ahva dropped the papers and got a tenuous grip on the plastic. She hopped backwards, tugging it with her until her last hop landed one foot in the air and the other on the edge of the desk. Ahva flapped her wings like mad trying to get air but only managed to slow her fall. She landed on an area rug with a thud, and the melted green plastic bounced off her side and clattered on the wooden floor nearby.

"Sorry." Ahva hissed.

"Ahva! I told you not to be a pest." Osse scolded.

"What did she get into?" The baroness asked.

Ahva rolled and righted herself. "That one! What's that? Good bird."

The baroness came around the desk but stopped well out of reach. "Oh. That thing. I don't care if she plays with that."

"There you go. You're going to be fine. I think you sprained the wrist. It'll smart for a few days, but it will heal. We'll use your scarf for a sling so you remember not to put any strain on that hand. Okay?" Osse said.

Ahva fluffed up her feathers and shook before she pulled the green blob out from under the desk. When Osse crouched nearby, Ahva flipped the plastic up to him.

He caught it, offered her a hand, and stood up. "Your Excellency, have you ever encountered the glowing maniacs around here?"

"I've heard rumors of them." Mary pointed at the plastic. "My son brought that back from school when he graduated. He said he found it alongside the road. Is that thing somehow related to the glowing creatures?"

Osse nodded. "Whenever we kill one of them, they leave behind something like this, a metal cylinder, and one or more crystals. The colors vary, but those artifacts are fairly consistent."

"And you found these creatures near here?"

"I've traveled here from a city in South Bakhar. Ahva and I have run into a half-dozen of them ourselves, and Baron Dorcas has encountered about that many on his patrols. They're all over the place. He did mention, however, that he and Nagheed found a friendly alligator. Apparently, they're not all bad, but most of them have been. I would be very cautious." Osse set the green blob on the desk. "You mentioned that your husband is unwell. Is it something I can help with?"

"I don't think so. We brought in the best healers and physicians in all of Nethanya." Her eyes became watery. "They tell me there's nothing to be done. He'll either recover on his own or remain an invalid for the rest of his days."

Ahva looked down. "Awww. Poor bird."

"May I ask what happened?" Osse leaned on the desk.

"I can't say for sure." She shrugged. "We were out riding. Then without warning he became dizzy, couldn't speak clearly, and went all numb on the right side."

Osse frowned. "I've heard of things like that. My grandmother said it was a condition of the nerves. She knew of nothing to do except to make the patient as comfortable as possible. I'm very sorry."

"Nethanya's physicians agree with your grandmother."

A knock on the door preceded the return of Rafayel and Nagheed.

Ahva: Find anything interesting?

Nagheed: The deputy just returned from chasing down one of the laughing maniacs.

Ahva: The game is getting better about dropping clues. I found a green plastic blob hidden on the desk.

Nagheed: I'm not surprised to know that they're in the area. They've been all over this game.

Ahva: Did the deputy have anything interesting say about the one he ran into?

Nagheed: It sounded like a werecritter.

Ahva: A lycanthrope zombie cyborg? Come on! This is starting push the edge of "you gotta be kidding me."

Nagheed: Might not be an actual lycanthrope as much as a furry like the bear. He described it as walking on two feet like a human, but decidedly doglike in appearance. It had hands with opposable digits, wielded a sword, and wore clothing. Or at least what was left of clothing.

Ahva: Weird, but still strange.

Nagheed: Yeah. What about yours?

Ahva: Not half that exciting. The baroness's son found the plastic on the side of the road.

Nagheed: Then the important part is that there are laughing maniacs in the area. What about the sick baron? Are we going on a quest to get a healer or some meds?

Ahva: Doubtful. Based on the baroness's description, he's had a stroke.

Nagheed: That doesn't preclude a solution. This is a game. Not real life.

Ahva: True, but so far, no quest assignment.

Rafayel removed his hat as he came closer. "The constable is taken care of, and the deputy was appalled to hear about what happened. I think we can count on his sense of duty to keep the constable under wraps until the judge is ready for the trial. I stopped to talk to the physician. He'll be out as soon as he can to take care of James. I assured him that Osse's skills would keep James steady in the meantime. Is there anything that we can do for you or for Samwel before we leave?"

Mary glanced at James. "If you could help me get James to his bed, I would be most grateful."

"Of course."

Ahva fluttered up to Osse's shoulder as the two men lifted the injured servant and followed the baroness to a small room off the kitchen. They set the kid on the bed.

The notebook turned blue.

Completed the quest. Yay!

"Rafayel, it's late afternoon. Are you sure you want to travel this late? Stay here until morning and get an early start." She pointed upstairs. "We have plenty of room, especially with my son away."

He shook his head. "I wouldn't want to impose. There is an inn in town. We'll stay there so we don't disturb your household in the morning. You do have sick and injured."

She frowned. "You're no imposition."

"With your husband ill and your son away–" Rafayel held up his hand, palm out. "No, the inn is more appropriate, but I appreciate your offer. I'll stop by again on our way back through. That may be some time, however. We may have an extended journey."

She nodded. "I suppose you're right. Travel safely."

"Tsidkenu watch over you."

Mary ushered them to the door.

Ahva stretched her wing. "Bye!"

* * *

Ahva gobbled down the last of the eggs, waffle, and fruit that Osse had set aside for her. As usual, she and Nagheed were finished first and had to wait for the humans to catch up. Realistic, sure, but it gave her a chance to earn some bird XP by preening her feathers and whistling a tune.

As soon as the humans finished eating, Rafayel paid the innkeeper for their room and board. Ahva fluttered up to Osse's shoulder, and they went to the stable to retrieve their horses. Once the horses were saddled and their equipment was packed, they were on the way out the main gate and headed north again.

After they were clear of the city walls and the traffic of people waiting to get in or out, Ahva launched off from Osse's shoulder and flew a long, narrow loop down the road and back again. She watched the terrain for signs of aggressive animal life, two-legged or four-legged.

Tall pines crowded close to the road, casting enough shadows to create a twilight. The dirt road was dry now, but wagons had cut some impressive the last time it had rained.

She made a total of three passes without finding a threat. They should be safe enough for a while.

Ahva completed her third circuit and landed on Osse's arm.

"Find anything interesting?" Osse held her up at eye level.

Ahva hissed. "No one here."

Rafayel chuckled. "It almost sounds like she wants to find trouble."

"She might." Osse preened her head. "Too bad we couldn't get those little blades like we wanted for her. This be a great time to practice them."

Rafayel shrugged. "It was rather late in the day to ask someone take on a new project. We'll be in Tel Caperna for at least a few days. We'll talk to a smith there. I'm sure we can arrange something."

Ahva snorted. *It can't be that complicated.*

Osse frowned. "And you think the stop in Tel Caperna is going to be important for our trip?"

Rafayel glanced over. "I know you're worried about your

sister, but once my duties are discharged and I know for sure whether the crown will consider sending us any help in our trip to Ilion, we'll be on our way."

"If I hadn't taken off after the wrong group, I might have found her by now." He slumped in the saddle.

"Perhaps. But these creatures are getting stronger, and you yourself have said you don't think you could take on two of them." Rafayel offered a sympathetic look. "I have a feeling we're going to find more than two in one place by the time we're finished."

Osse glanced at Rafayel. "She's the only family I have left."

"I understand." Rafayel nodded. "But you do no one any good, least of all your sister, charging into enemy territory without thorough preparation."

"You really think they'll send help?" Osse frowned.

Rafayel shrugged. "These laughing maniacs have been found from Vanya to Geva. Probably even further north. I will be more surprised if any of the barons think they can shelter in their own cities and withstand the threat."

Nagheed trotted out ahead of them and then sat down facing east and whined.

Ahva: Whatcha got?
Nagheed: Smoke.
Ahva: ... on the water.
Nagheed: On the wind actually.
Ahva: It's the name of a song.
Nagheed: Not one I'm familiar with.

The humans stopped their horses and Rafayel stood up in his saddle. He shielded his eyes with his hand and scanned the horizon. "I see smoke rising. Too much to just be someone's campfire."

"Ahva, check it out and come back, but stay too high to get hit by any thrown or shot weapons. Got it?" Osse pointed toward the gray column.

Ahva pushed off from his shoulder and spiraled up before she headed off toward the column of smoke in the east. Her flight took her over increasingly dense brush and scraggly trees. Those thinned back out as she approached a rocky footpath. The terrain zipped past her staying relatively level and clear. Ahead, a collection of huts was distributed around a larger stone and wood building. One of the huts was on fire. A group of non-glowing humans on horseback chased villagers around. Beyond the village, indistinct forms moved around in a dense stand of trees. Ahva looped around and headed back the way she'd come. She flapped hard to gain speed, which dropped her fatigue meter into the red. About two thirds of the way back to the road, she found the rest of her group and glided to shed both velocity and height to make a decent landing on Osse's outstretched arm. Her fatigue meter was a dull red. When she tried to speak, all she could manage was hyperventilation.

"She came back in a hurry." Osse preened the back of her neck, which scooted the fatigue meter upward to a drab orange.

Ahva forced herself to regulate her breathing so that she could actually tell them what she found.

"Too bad she can't give us a regular report." Rafayel scratched under the edge of his hat.

That's not for lack of trying.

"Yeah, but she does pretty well." Osse shrugged.

They weren't capable of flying. It balanced.

CHAPTER 26

"Did you find any of those glowing killers?" Osse held her at his eye level.

She drew a deep breath. "No. Maybe in trees."

"Is someone in trouble?" Rafayel leaned closer.

"Yes. Town people. Bad humans."

"That explains the speed of her return." Rafayel drew his sword. "Let's go."

He urged their horses into a gallop and Nagheed ran alongside, keeping pace with them easily.

Nagheed: What did you find?

Ahva: A bunch of knuckleheads on horseback attacking a village. There's something moving in the trees beyond them. I didn't see anything glow-in-the-dark, though.

Nagheed: A bunch? Define a bunch.

Ahva: I didn't stop to count. More than a couple, less than a platoon?

The view from Osse's shoulder didn't match her aerial view, but she recognized enough to have a good feel for their location. As they got closer, the crackling of the fire and galloping of the horses and the screams of the villagers became louder.

"Do you think you can shoot from horseback?" Rafayel asked.

Osse winced. "I haven't practiced that. I probably could, but I don't know what my accuracy would be."

Rafayel shook his head. "This isn't a good time to find out. You and Ahva stop within bow range try to pick off attackers. Nagheed and I will ride in and make the fight a little more personal. When you run out of arrows or decent shots, join us."

"Got it."

The village was in full view now. Weirdly, the situation hadn't changed. There should have been fewer villagers running around. Surely, the attackers were gaining some ground. It wasn't like the villagers were offering much of a challenge. Mostly, the "attack" resembled a hyperactive, energetic game of tag. Apparently, no one in the village had thought that perhaps one or more of their farming implements would make a decent weapon. Nobody was standing their ground.

Some fifty meters from the village, Osse stopped and dismounted. "Are you going to stay with me, Ahva, or see what kind of mischief you can get into?"

She had a choice? "Bite fingers!" She kicked off from Osse's shoulder and followed after Nagheed and Rafayel.

Chapter 27

Ahva's vision developed a red edge as soon as Nagheed cleared the low wall around the village. As she flew in, she scanned through the crowd looking for bad guys. Five guys on horseback were labeled "Bandit."

Ahva: You know, they should have given the bad guys interesting names like Rex Karz, and Bob Frapples. That would be so much more fun than Bandit.

Nagheed: At least that would be easier to recognize at a quick glance.

As Ahva flew past, Nagheed bit one of the bandits on the ankle and dragged him off his horse.

Let's see how many bombing runs I can get in. She swooped down and picked up a pine cone then flapped hard to come back up to speed. *Nice and spiky. Not good for eyeballs.*

Ahva picked the bandit ahead of her and tried angling the attack to hit him in the face. The pinecone bounced off the front of his helmet, but that still made him flinch.

Threw off his attack, anyway. She grabbed another one and set up for another pass.

Nagheed: Whoa! I wish your human wouldn't try shooting past me!

Ahva: At least he's a good shot.

Nagheed: Accidents happen!

Ahva: Yep. And friendly fire isn't. That's one of Murphy's corollaries.

Nagheed: Who's Murphy?

Ahva: Seriously? Have you not heard of Murphy's Law? Anything that can go wrong will and in the worst possible way.

Nagheed: Oh. That Murphy.

Ahva: There's another one? Do you know Cole's Law?

Nagheed: Uh... no.

Ahva: Thinly sliced cabbage.

Nagheed: *groan*

Ahva: You're welcome.

She flew over a bandit-shaped mannequin.

One bandit kicked the bucket!

Ahva built up momentum and tossed the pinecone. It smacked a bandit on the forehead as he was setting up for baseball bat practice with a villager's head. He glared at her and swiped it away. She snatched up another pinecone. When she lined up for her next bombing run on the same bandit, he held his mace like a bat and watched her.

No, you don't. You're not playing badminton with this birdie! She veered off and instead delivered the pinecone to a different bandit's cheek, wrecking his aim.

The spear thrust at Nagheed's back went awry and hit dirt.

Nagheed: Thanks for that.

Ahva: Anytime, Shaggy.

She grabbed a pinecone. As she came up to speed again, she passed a second bandit mannequin. Taking a quick glance at the others, two weren't very healthy, and the one in the best shape was chasing down a villager. Ahva flew across his path and dropped the pinecone right in front of him. She looked back over her shoulder in time to watch it hit his nose. He snorted and swatted at it, aborting his attack. Multiple scratches across his face trickled blood.

Not exactly fatal damage, but it'll do for now.

She turned forward again at a wall coming up at her fast. Ahva banked hard, scraping the wall with her wing tip.

Watch where you're going, bird.

When she picked up another pinecone, a horn blast made her jump. The remaining bandits were joined by four dogs, which resembled beefed up greyhounds, at the edge of the tree line.

Ahva: Not exactly my idea of dangerous. They breathe fire? Teleport?

Nagheed: They wouldn't be Round 2 if they weren't more dangerous. You might want to stick to bombing runs rather than strafing. Stay above their range.

Ahva: Right.

Two of the dogs charged toward Osse. She started in that direction and quickly realized she'd never catch up. Osse shot an arrow at the one in the lead, but it dodged. The arrow hit the second dog, a critical hit that turned it into a mannequin.

Ahva: Oh, no, that's not overpowered at all.
Nagheed: What?
Ahva: Dumb dog dodged Osse's arrow.
Nagheed: Wow. They're fast.

Osse dropped his bow and grabbed his mace and knife in time to get bowled over by the dog. He came up to his knees as the dog growled with its hackles raised. Osse stood, mace in hand and watched the dog slink closer. When it charged, he swung the mace like a major league baseball player and slammed the knobbed head of the mace into the dog's shoulder. It yelped and hit the ground. When I got up, it heavily favored one side.

He's got this.

She looped around and dropped her pinecone on a dog's nose while Nagheed went for the jugular, literally, and took out another bandit. He faced one of the dogs and bristled up, which actually gave the dog a slight frown for morale. As she grabbed another pinecone, Rafayel killed the last bandit while the fourth dog caught the business end of Ryder's hoof.

I don't care what planet you're from. That's gotta hurt.

With all the bandits gone, the villagers gathered at the side of the only stone structure and turned into an audience.

No, no. Don't try to help. Just stand there. We got this.

She picked up another pinecone and pegged the dog going after Ryder's legs right between the eyes. It pawed at its face, which gave Rafayel an opening to create a new dog-shaped mannequin.

She picked up a pinecone just as a horn blared.

Ahva: Uh-oh. Round 3.

Nagheed: You'll have to help with whatever it is while I deal with the last two dogs.

Ahva: Let's see what it is first. Might make more sense to help you. And you've got the only dog left. Rafayel just took out the other.

Nagheed was too tangled up with the last dog for her to risk pegging the enemy with another cone. She banked into a turn and watched. Nagheed's superior strength and mass pinned his target. A well-placed bite to the neck, and that dog bit the dust.

An arrow whizzed out of the trees and caught Rafayel in the shoulder. He guided Ryder behind one of the thatched roof houses, and Osse sprinted to the corner of the nearest one.

Nagheed crouched behind the mannequins that used to be a dog and a bandit. Ahva continued her circle, altering course slightly to take advantage of the peaked roof of one of the buildings. She lost sight of the tree line, but better that than getting skewered. When she emerged from the other end of the building, a bipedal dog carrying a fancy, pulley-empowered bow stood at the edge of the tree line. One of Osse's arrows stuck through its arm.

The augmented dog, as the computer called it, jerked the arrow out of its arm and shot it back at Osse, sheltered behind the nearest building.

Ahva: Get ready. I'm going to drop a pinecone on its face.

Nagheed: Stay high.

Ahva: Yep.

The augmented dog was nocking an arrow when Ahva dropped the pinecone. She smacked the mutt on the nose, causing it to release the arrow into the dirt. The augmented dog laughed, jumped straight up, and swung its bow. The upper arm of the bow struck Ahva's side. Her view flared red. She tumbled out of control and hit the side of a house, causing another red burst. Her health points dropped to one quarter.

Ahva: Ow! How tall is that thing?

Nagheed: It jumped. You're out. Find cover.

Ahva got her feet under her and hustled to a pile of straw behind a nearby fence post.

Nagheed: You call that cover?

Ahva: When you're my size, you can hide most of Rhode Island back here.

"Hold, Nagheed!" Rafayel ordered.

The pop-bang of his pistol resulted in half the augmented dog's health points vanishing.

Nagheed: I can't close the distance and attack before it shoots.

Ahva: Leave that to me.

Nagheed: You don't have much health left.

Ahva: Yeah, so I have to be more careful.

She grabbed the straw on the ground with her beak and then lifted off. The screen flashed red with every downbeat of her wings.

Osse had given up archery and was moving closer, one house or barn at a time. The augmented dog shot an arrow at him then at Nagheed's fluffy tail. The glow in one of its arms flickered, but the other was still strong.

"Go, Nagheed!" Rafayel yelled.

As Ahva flew over the augmented dog, much higher than last time, and dropped the straw in its eyes, Nagheed bolted out of his hiding place and clamped his jaws around the augmented dog's good arm. Ahva came in for a heavy but not entirely graceless landing on one of the mannequins. Nagheed dragged the augmented dog down. It raised the bow, ready to brain Nagheed when Osse ran up and gave it a permanent concussion before bashing the flickering crystal. The augmented dog turned into another mannequin.

The edge of her vision turned green for a few seconds

then returned to normal and the notebook turned blue. She focused on it to open it.

Good job! Save Me! Rescue the village from the raiders. +500 XP Level Up, Ahva!

She closed the notebook.

The couple dozen villagers dispersed. Most returned to whatever chores villagers had to do, and the rest – distinguishable by their snazzier clothing – strutted toward Osse. Osse ran straight for where Rafayel had hidden, bypassing the villagers who were intent on visiting with him.

Ahva: Well! I'm his companion. Does he come check on me? No. Humans first, is that it?

Nagheed: Arrow to the chest is slightly more dangerous than getting smacked by the arm of the bow.

Ahva: Easy for you to say. I only have a quarter of my health left.

Nagheed: Yeah, and Rafayel could bleed out. He'll keep taking damage from blood loss.

Ahva: I suppose that would complicate things.

Nagheed: Hop on, and I'll give you a ride.

Ahva fluttered over to Nagheed's head and landed between his ears. **Ahva: Onward, gallant steed.**

Nagheed kept a slow enough pace that Ahva didn't get dislodged.

When they joined Osse and Rafayel, Osse was mixing a handful of herbs.

"This will stop the bleeding and give some healing, but to do a proper job, we need to get you to a physician. How far are we from Tel Caperna?" Osse added some oily goo to his hand and mixed everything together.

The upper class of the village arrived as Osse was speaking.

The most dapper of them, clothed in tunic, vest, and pants that had no patches and showed minimal wear, stepped forward. "A couple hour's ride. We can keep him here while you retrieve the physician."

Rafayel shook his head. "That'd take too long, and there's no need to inconvenience you. If we avoid any further battles, I'm sure I can ride in."

"Suit yourself." He frowned, resembling Aunt Say Paw when she held a losing lottery ticket. "I'm the mayor of this little town. Although we appreciate your assistance, we have no means to pay you for your service."

"No need." Rafayel winced as Osse applied the herbs to his injury. Rafayel's health bar recovered only a quarter of what it was lacking. "Whatever the enemy left behind for loot is sufficient."

"Fair enough. We'll leave you to it. If you change your mind about staying with us while he rides into town–"

"I won't, but thank you for the offer."

The mayor and his entourage left.

"Wait here. I'll go collect the loot." Osse stood and adjusted the bag on his shoulder.

Of all the rudeness! Treat the human, ignore the bird? And the dog?

Ahva fluffed up her feathers and hissed. "Hey! Hello! Look at the bird! Poor dog."

Osse's jaw dropped when he looked at her. "When did you get hit?"

"When that augmented dog first showed up, she flew over its head, and it jumped up and smacked her to the ground

CHAPTER 27

with its bow." Rafayel mimed the actions one-handed.

"I missed that altogether." Osse prepared another set of herbs and pressed it against Ahva's back. Her health bar returned to full.

"Thanks." Ahva shook herself and hopped onto Osse's shoulder.

He turned to Nagheed. "He also took a few hits." After inspecting the injuries, Osse frowned. "He'll need a stronger healer, but I'll do what I can here."

Osse prepared another set of herbs and applied it to Nagheed's injuries. That restored only about a third of his missing health bar.

"Now, I'll go check for loot." Osse stood.

Rafayel reached after him. "Be careful. Some of the villagers may not appreciate it."

Osse nodded. "Back in a little bit."

As they made the rounds to each of the mannequins, villagers gave Osse the side-eye while he collected the loot, Ahva returned the glare with her own squint-eye. She chose her Posture skill and fluffed up her feathers, weaving from side to side.

"Take it easy, Ahva." Osse spoke through his teeth while he smiled. "We don't want any trouble."

"Fine." She smoothed out her feathers but still kept a watch on them.

The bandits each had a handful of rounds, the weapons and armor they'd been using, and random camping equipment. The dogs had a pelt but nothing else. The real haul came with the augmented dog. That mannequin contained a bag of rounds, two crystals, two batteries, two blobs of melty plastic, a book, a compound bow, and a quiver of metal-tipped arrows.

After he had collected all the loot, they retrieved his horse and rejoined Rafayel to show off their haul.

"That's impressive. We'll sell the excess weaponry, equipment, and pelts in town. I suggest you keep the bow and the arrows and sell your bow with the excess. That's an upgrade for you. If any of the armor fits, keep it. Mine can be repaired in town. The book is written in what looks like ancient Ilionite. We'll have to find a translator. The crystals, batteries, and plastic we'll keep with us until we figure out what to do with them. The money, I suggest we split in half. Give the mayor half earmarked to compensate villagers who suffered loss in the raid. The rest, we'll keep to get supplies and training. What do you say?"

Osse nodded. "Sounds fair. I'll take care of it then we'll get on the way."

With Osse's help, Rafayel stood and started packing the loot in their saddlebags.

Osse split the money in half then split one of the halves in half again. When the number didn't divide evenly, he added the extra in the town's pile. He gave a quarter part to Rafayel and kept a quarter part for himself then toured the village hunting for the mayor. Not surprisingly, he was hanging out near the door of the stone building.

Osse approached and handed him the rounds. "This is for the people who lost something in the raid. My friend and I will be leaving now."

"Thank you for your help." He accepted the money with a smile that belonged on a hungry great white.

"I'm glad we were in the area."

As Osse turned away, the notebook turned blue. Ahva

checked the note.

Nice work! Hey, Brother, Can You Spare A Dime? You shared at over half the money collected from the raiders with the village. + 200 XP

They returned to Rafayel and Nagheed in time to watch Rafayel manage to climb up into Ryder's saddle while keeping one arm tucked tightly against his belly. "From here, we can head northwest instead of following the path back to the road. We can pick up the main road closer to Tel Caperna and save some travel time."

"We're more likely to encounter trouble if we get off the established roads." Osse climbed into his horse's saddle.

"The sooner we reach town, the sooner we can get to a physician and replenish supplies. Your herbs helped, but my shoulder is not in good shape. Nagheed is also not quite up to his fighting trim, and you got banged up some in the fight, too."

Ahva: They both make good points.

Nagheed: Yeah, but there haven't been many random encounters. I've run into a few here and there, but nothing I'd call a real challenge. You?

Ahva: Nah. Just a coyote or two and a ticked off hawk.

Nagheed: Let's see if we can get them to take the shortcut. If you scout ahead, you should be able to find anything aggressive.

Ahva: Works for me.

Ahva flew to the nearest northwest tree. "This way!"

Nagheed trotted over and sat near the tree trunk.

Rafayel smiled. "I think we have their vote."

"How about we send Ahva to scout the way while we start out northwest?" Osse pointed that way. "If it's not clear, she can find us."

"Fair enough."

Ahva launched and came up to speed. Her VR rig simulated wind rushing past her. She swerved from side to side both for the simple amusement of it and to give her different angles to see from in case there were any knuckleheads hiding in the shrubberies.

When she found the road, the walls of a huge city were just visible over the trees.

Nagheed: Anything?

Ahva: Nope, at least not that I can see as far as the road. Your sniffer getting anything interesting?

Nagheed: Just the usual wildlife. No augmented or maniac anythings.

Ahva: 'Kay. Headed back now.

She wheeled around and reversed her course. A large bird shriek drew her attention to the right.

Hawk?

She looked back over her wing as an eagle took off from a branch and came straight at for her.

That's not the right call for an eagle. They pulled a Hollywood-ism and used a red tail's screech.

Still, not a favorable development for her. She was nowhere near Osse's bow range.

Ahva: Not good. Definitely bad.

Nagheed: What? Find something?

Ahva: Eagle on my tail.

Nagheed: Can you outrun it?

Ahva: Probably? At my size, I've definitely got maneuverability.

Nagheed: Stay ahead of it. I'll try to alert the humans.

Ahva: Yep. Going for the dense tree branches. Let's see if I can get it to face-plant into a tree.

She dropped below canopy level started one of her rollercoaster-dodgeball games of weaving around tree branches. The eagle stayed on her, but wasn't duplicating her path. Figures. It knew it didn't have the agility. She'd have to make it try a tight turn radius to get her plan to work.

Ahva pulled a U-turn around a tree trunk and zoomed back toward the eagle in a seriously lopsided game of chicken, only she had no intention of staying the course. She folded her wings as she got close and dropped a couple meters to pass under the eagle before she unfurled her wings and resumed flying. The larger bird shrieked in protest and started the turn, narrowly missing a tree trunk.

Nuts. Missed. Let's try that again.

She waited until the eagle was back on her tail and slowed down a bit to let the bigger bird catch up. As she neared a large tree, she started the U-turn and found a branch right in her way.

Yikes!

She dropped under the branch and completed the turn. A loud crash was followed by a few others, and the eagle didn't make it around the tree.

Ahva: Yes! One large bully bird down.

Nagheed: Excellent. How'd you do it?

Ahva: Pulled a U-turn around a tree trunk with a very conveniently hidden branch that was right in the way. I had the agility. The eagle did not. On my way back now.

She slowed her flight to a more normal cruising speed and took advantage of gliding whenever she could. Her fatigue bar was a solid orange by the time she landed on Osse's arm.

"All clear?" He held her up at eye level.

"Yes. No problem now." She fluttered up to his shoulder.

"Now?" Rafayel asked. "Nagheed seemed to think there was trouble."

"Big bad bird. Gone now." She mimicked the sound of crunching nuts.

Osse opened his bag and rooted around. "Maniac bird like the hawks?"

"No. Big bad bird. Nice tree."

Rafayel stared at her. "Nice tree?"

Osse smiled. "She used the tree to take out the large bird somehow. Maybe we'll find a clue on the way." He pulled out a piece of flatbread from his bag. "Here you go. A snack before you go out to scout again."

"Good idea!" She pinned the food to his shoulder with one foot while she ripped off small pieces.

* * *

When Rafayel followed the physician out of the back room of the medical clinic. He moved more easily now, and the color had returned to his face. Nagheed sat up and wagged his tail. He was rewarded with a glittery **+10 XP** for acting like a dog.

Rafayel shook the physician's hand. "Thanks for your help."

"My pleasure." He leaned on the doorframe. "That village was lucky you and your friend were nearby, and so was I. You spared me a trip. Travel safely."

"With Tsidkenu's blessing." Rafayel settled his hat on

CHAPTER 27

his head.

Nagheed followed him out of the little clinic.

"Where do you think Osse found for us to stay?" Rafayel looked up and down the street.

The Bakhari had finished with the physician first and gone in search of accommodations.

Nagheed: Where are you?

A familiar whistle came from above them.

Rafayel startled. "There you are. Come to show us the way?"

Ahva fluttered down to Rafayel's offered hand. "Yes. Look at the bird. Up we go!"

She flew to the next sign and waited. Once they'd caught up, she flew to the next one and waited again.

The buildings here were identical in design to the other cities Nagheed had been in: stone and brick with supporting timbers. In fact, a few looked similar. Repeating the artwork in similar places would be a good way to save a little money, and there were whole subdivisions in the real world that had the same five houses repeated over and over.

Ahva landed on a sign for Drop and Roll Inn, and went no further when they caught up.

Rafayel glanced up at Ahva. "This is the place?"

"Yes."

"Posh. I didn't think this establishment would allow animals." He opened the door and led the way in.

The main room could have been any great room of any inn in any fantasy novel. In fact, the architect responsible for Halfway Inn had designed this place, too. Dark wood tables and chairs were scattered about the middle of the floor and booths ringed the edge of the room. A bar directly opposite the door had a collection of stools in front of it and casks behind it. Scents wafting around the screen showed candle wax, alcoholic beverages, cooked meat, and cooked vegetables. The man behind the bar was a tall, heavyset fellow who would have fit in as a running back on any NFL team. The sleeves of his green tunic were rolled up past his elbows. He leaned on the bar talking to a lady wearing abbreviated attire, but still not showing enough to violate Horizon Systems' All Audiences rating.

The lady waved at them. "You must be Baron Rafayel Dorcas. Either that, or there are a whole bunch of travelers in town with a large dog and a blackbird."

Rafayel bowed. "I am he."

The barkeep inclined his head toward an opening in the right wall. "Your friend's in room eight. All the way at the end of the hall. Can't miss it."

Rafayel nodded. "Thank you."

Ahva took off and headed down the hall without them. Nagheed stayed alongside his human. The hallway was dark except for a few sconces backed with curved mirrors. As promised, room eight was the last one. The door, sitting open enough to allow a certain bird to squeeze through the opening, faced down the hallway.

When they entered, Osse was using a cloth to carry a steaming bowl from the fireplace and set it on the table across from another one. A third bowl, not steaming nearly as vigorously as the other two, sat on the floor.

A fire burned in the grate casting flickering shadows in the room. The room had three small but well-appointed beds taking up three corners of the room. Osse had laid claim to the one nearest the window by spreading out the contents

CHAPTER 27

of his bag across the top of the bed. He'd set Rafayel's pack on the one diagonally opposite. Their saddlebags were in a pile on the third.

"You're looking better." Osse gestured to the bowl he had set down.

"I'm feeling much better, too." Rafayel replied as he sat at the table and picked up a spoon.

Ahva: It's a BOGO arrangement.

Nagheed: BOGO?

Ahva: Buy one. Get one. You don't go shopping, either?

Nagheed: That takes money. I have tuition to pay for.

Osse retrieved some of the crusty bread they had in their saddlebags and set it in the middle of the table. "I hope soup is agreeable for Nagheed. It's all they have for the evening."

"It will do fine." Rafayel snapped his fingers and pointed at the bowl.

That was Nagheed's cue to chow down. He didn't waste much time.

"Excellent. I'm afraid for the next few days you're going to be mostly on your own, and I'll have to leave Nagheed with you. Visitors are unwelcomed in the Oligometa, and the space isn't large enough for Nagheed."

"That's fine. What errands can we take care of while you're busy?" Osse asked.

Rafayel blew across a spoonful of soup. "I've been thinking about that. I thought perhaps you could take care of selling our excess equipment and purchasing our supplies."

"That sounds doable." Osse numbered off items on his fingers. "We need food for the road, herbs, I could do with some more arrows – running out before the end of that battle was not a good feeling, your armor needs repaired, the book needs to be translated, and what else?"

"A little training might not go amiss." Rafayel pointed at him with the spoon. "You're skilled at what you do with your herbs, but more potent concoctions might serve us better as we continue to the east. I've had another thought, too. If Ilion's pantheon is causing all this trouble, it stands to reason that our own priests might have valuable information. A visit to a couple temples might yield beneficial results."

Osse's brow furrowed. "Will they allow a Bakhari tribesman to even set foot inside?"

"You're a follower of Tsidkenu, are you not? I don't see how they can refuse."

Nagheed finished his bowl and licked every available surface on the inside hoping for a little bit more. The fatigue bar was still a little short. His stomach rumbled.

Osse chuckled. "Uh-oh. Soup wasn't enough."

"He's a growing boy." Rafayel tossed him one of the larger rolls.

Nagheed caught it in the air and lay down on his belly so he could hold the role with his front paws while he chewed pieces off.

He finished before the humans and went to the rug in front of the fireplace.

Ahva: No, no, no! Dogs are supposed to keep begging for food until the food is gone and then for at least another thirty minutes after that. What kind of dog are you anyway?

Nagheed: When you can't taste anything, the food's not that exciting.

CHAPTER 27

Ahva: It's kind of all texture, no flavor for you, too, is it?

Nagheed: Not even texture. Just sound. I'm not surprised, though. I'm not playing full immersion.

Ahva: That's a shame. You really ought to invest in a sim chair. They're expensive, but they're worth it.

Nagheed: Maybe when I graduate.

When the humans finished eating, Rafayel stood and gathered up their dirty dishes. "We still have a few hours. I'm curious to learn if my idea of visiting priests will gather results. What do you say we try a couple?"

Osse stood and packed a few things into his shoulder bag and flung it over his shoulder. "Sounds good."

Ahva: Beats hanging around here.

Nagheed: I go where they go.

Ahva: Besides, I get to fly more.

They climbed uphill until they came to a place that shined in the light. Sparkles glittered all over the surface in strange patterns. Nagheed squinted into the brilliance. Stairs led up to seven tall pillars in front of the place, but the metal towers didn't appear to be holding anything on top of them. Ahva whistled.

Osse pointed. "Is that the palace?"

Rafayel chuckled and started up the steps. "That's the temple. The palace is further up the hill."

The big doors opened and a man wearing almost as much gold as the building pushed out a man wearing patched clothes. "I said, 'No.'"

"But Reverend, just for two days then–" The man in the repaired clothes landed on his knees.

The man in the shiny clothes slammed the door. The one

on his knees slumped.

Chapter 28

Nagheed kept pace as Rafayel jogged up the stairs. Osse followed close behind.

The man in worn-out clothes picked himself up and dusted himself off with his left hand. His right was missing above the wrist. "Stupid superstitious–. And a man of Tsidkenu, too, so they say." He spun as Rafayel approached and backed away.

Rafayel made a sharp downward motion with his hand. "Nagheed, sit."

He obediently parked his fuzzy tail on a step.

"I'm afraid I saw the end of that exchange." Rafayel went on alone. "Are you well?"

The man huffed. "Not hurt, if that's what you mean, but no better off than when I came. I was welcome enough here when I was recovering from those laughing fools that destroyed my place and sawed off my hand. A miracle the Reverend said I was, least 'til I was all healed. No one wanted to hire a man with only his left hand. Afraid there's somethin' more wrong with me than my hand on account o' I gotta do everything with my left now. I finally found honest work, but it doesn't start for a couple more days when the smith's boy leaves t' get himself married down south in Vanya."

"So, you came here for a roof and a meal?" Osse asked.

His face turned bright red and he shook. "I came here for a job so I could pay for my own roof and meal. Thought maybe he could spare me a couple rounds to sweep out the floors or polish the silver or empty chamber pots even. Honest work. That's what I wanted. The good reverend–" He spat on the ground. "–couldn't even give me an audience on account this." He held up his right arm. "From miracle to dirt just like that."

Jake fumed. His older cousin had faced the same kind of outrage after the sudden end to his military service.

Prince came over and laid his head on Jake's lap.

"I'm okay, Prince." He petted his dog's head.

Ahva: Who's "Prince?"

Jake winced. He'd forgotten his rig could do voice recognition.

Nagheed: My dog. He thought I was upset and came over to check on me.

Ahva: Aww, that's sweet. Give him a Scooby snack for me.

Nagheed: Do I want to know what a Scooby snack is?

Ahva: Dude. Vintage cartoons. Watch them.

Nagheed: Maybe someday.

Rafayel took a step closer to the man. "I'm here for the Oligometa, and I do have a job that needs to be done if you're interested. I can't pay you in rounds. I'll need every bit I have to buy supplies for the next phase of my trip, but the room I'm staying in has an extra bed and I'll pay your meals until I leave."

"You're kind, but I don't want charity." The man studied

the ground at his feet.

"Who said anything about charity? I wouldn't insult a strong, able man that way. I have a job for you. I'd have to do it myself otherwise, and I'd as soon have someone else do it. Those meetings are exasperating, and I don't relish having to do work afterward. Are you interested?"

The man glanced up then went back to staring at the ground. "I'm interested, all right. What's the job, sir?"

"Care for my horses." He held up two fingers. "There are two of them in stable behind The Drop and Roll Inn under the name Rafayel Dorcas. Take care of both properly, and you'll have your room and board in exchange until your other job with the smith starts or I leave town."

"All right, sir. I'll take that and thank you kindly." He started to reach forward with his right arm but then scowled at where his hand should be and tucked it against his belly.

Rafayel stepped forward and caught the man's left hand in both of his. "I'm glad to hear it. That'll spare me a great deal of work, but no man works for me if I don't know his name. You are?"

"They call me Eezak, sir."

"Eezak, I am Rafayel Dorcas, and this is my friend Osse Bente. My dog is Nagheed. He won't hurt you unless he thinks you're a threat. The bird is Ahva." Rafayel let go of the man's hand and stepped back. "We're staying at The Drop and Roll. Finish with the horses and meet me there this evening for your wages."

"I'll do a good job for you, sir. I will." He jogged off down the steps.

The man strode away with his head held high and a spring in his step. Nagheed wagged his tail.

+10 XP

Rafayel stayed still while Osse took a couple steps further up toward the cathedral.

Osse stopped and turned back. "Don't you want to talk to the priest?"

"You read the scriptures. Did that priest act like he belongs here?" Rafayel waited for Osse.

"No, not nearly." Osse glanced at the gilt temple.

Rafayel shook his head. "I don't know that I'd trust what he says."

"This is a big city. Do you think we can find another temple?" Osse joined Rafayel.

"I'd bet on it." Rafayel led the way down the steps. "Yavne is not half this big, and I've got two."

Nagheed followed them down the steps. When they reached the bottom, Osse turned toward Rafayel and pointed first left then right. Rafayel shrugged and pointed left, away from the inn. As they continued down the road, the neighborhood declined from gaudy and ostentatious down into a more middle-class kind of area. The houses were still in good repair, but they were considerably smaller. Shiny brass accents and complex murals gave way to plain paint colors with contrasting trim. The people hustling through the streets in this area wore less velvet and brocade and more tunics, pants, and dresses made of finely woven materials.

Rafayel stopped at a storefront where the proprietor was sweeping off the sidewalk. "Say, could you tell me where to find the local church?"

The shopkeeper leaned on his broom and pointed back the way they'd come. "Turn yourself around walk about eight, maybe ten blocks. Can't miss it. Huge building. Tsidkenu's symbol on the door. Lots of brass. Lots of brass."

Rafayel pointed back that way. "We saw that. Lovely place, I'm sure, but I'm from a small town. I'm afraid I get quite lost in those large cathedrals. Would you know of a smaller church?"

The shopkeeper winced. "I do know of three others, but two of them are in a rough neighborhood. Constable does quite a bit of business in that area." He smirked at Nagheed. "Though I daresay your dog might give any ruffians a chance to think about it."

"No doubt he would." Rafayel leaned over and scratched between Nagheed's ears. "How about that third place you mentioned?"

"Quite a ways from here. Do you know where the Royal Council Hall is?"

Rafayel nodded. "I do indeed. I'm here for the Oligometa."

"Ah. Then you're familiar with the place. From the back of the Council building, walk five blocks south, turn right, go another–" He bobbed his head. "–Three blocks? Six? Can't say for sure. Not exactly a big place, but it's nice. You'll know it by the sign on the door. Pastor's a bit of an old-fashioned sort, though. You know the kind. All fire and brimstone, and they say he's a scholar of some kind."

"I'm sure we'll find it. Thank you for your help."

Nagheed stayed alongside his human as Rafayel led them away.

After they were a couple blocks away from the shopkeeper, Osse glanced over his shoulder. "Fire and brimstone?"

"Down toward the opposite end of the spectrum from

what we saw earlier." Rafayel mimed drawing a long line. "Very stern. Very serious. The sort who believes that Tsidkenu was not kidding, even with the more difficult teachings in the book."

"Good." Osse nodded once. "He's more likely to know the kind of information we need."

"I hope so, particularly if that 'scholar' part is related to what we need to know."

As they wove their way through the streets, Nagheed kept an eye on the scents his sniffer was picking up. Mostly, it was the sort of things he expected. "Fresh baked bread" came from one window. "Beef roast" from another. Small birds, squirrels, and chipmunks of various sorts and both genders had been all over the place. An angry man had been by a while ago. That scent was barely detectable and mostly hidden by more recent scents of men and women.

They rounded a corner and headed down an avenue to a low building with four spires, one on each corner. A wrought iron fence surrounded the place. A pair of small guard houses flanked a gate large enough to drive a carriage through.

"There's the Council Hall." Rafayel pointed at the structure.

"That's where you'll be for the next three days?" Osse asked.

Rafayel nodded. "Yes. All the barons will meet there, and the king will preside to discuss various concerns affecting the kingdom."

"Useful discussions, I hope," Osse said.

"Sometimes." Rafayel shrugged. "Sometimes it's a waste of aggravation. As you'd expect. Attendance, however, is mandatory, so even if it were a complete waste of time I would still be required to attend."

"And the baron who was too ill to travel?"

"He'll have sent a regent. His son, if the lad has reached his majority."

Ahva: And thank you for the civics lesson.

Nagheed: Hope you're taking good notes. There will be a test later.

Ahva: I wouldn't be surprised. This was a kid's game.

Nagheed: Enh, not really a problem. We learned something about the game world anyway.

Ahva: There is that, I suppose, but I still mean to put it in my playtester notes.

Nagheed: Yeah, wouldn't hurt. They did ask for feedback.

As they strolled down the avenue, the door of the Council Hall burst open and a man charged out. Handcuffs were tightened around one wrist with the other end dangling free. Instead of going to the gate, he bolted for the fence. Jumping, he caught the top horizontal bar and hoisted himself over. Men in uniform ran out of the Council Hall.

"Stop!" One of them hollered.

Another drew a black powder pistol and fired but missed.

"Nagheed, go." Rafayel pointed at the Council Hall.

Nagheed blasted off and came up to his full speed in a handful of seconds. His long strides ate through the distance. The escapee saw him coming, and turned down one of the side streets, but that wouldn't keep him away for long. Uniformed men came out of the gate as he passed and fell in behind him but quickly lost ground. Nagheed made a wide arcing turn and spotted the fleeing man weaving in and out among the pedestrian traffic. People cleared the way as Nagheed continued the chase. The music changed from the RenFaire city music to all drums and brass. The villain he chased was labeled "Escapee."

Nagheed: That's weird. I've chased people down without entering combat.

Ahva: You be careful. That probably means this knucklehead is up to something. And I doubt it's favorable.

Nagheed: Where are you? I could sure use some extra eyes.

Ahva: Flying over the buildings. I'll cut the corner and catch up to you.

The escapee grabbed a knife from the belt of a man he passed and turned to face Nagheed. He grabbed a woman and held her in front of him. Nagheed slowed and picked Posture. He growled, bristling as he stalked closer. The Escapee's nametag sprouted a mild frown emoji.

Nagheed: Now we know I went into combat mode. I can't attack him without getting the woman hurt.

Ahva: No worries. We got an Osse.

Nagheed: I'd rather not hurt civilians.

Ahva: Admirable. But still not a problem. I've got an idea.

Nagheed: Oh?

Ahva: Yep. Bark.

Nagheed: What? What's that going to do?

Ahva: I need to hear you again so I can try to mimic. If I come in behind the guy and bark like a crazy fool while you're barking in front of him, he may think there are two mountain shepherds. Don't know about you, but I would be a little bit nervous facing down two mountain

CHAPTER 28

shepherds, five Council Hall guard type people, and two other humans. One of whom can all but split hairs with an arrow.

Nagheed: He won't know that last part.

Ahva: Bakhari tribesmen are notorious. At least, that's what the game said earlier.

No harm in trying it her way. Nagheed barked and growled as he stalked closer.

Ahva: Perfect. Now let me call up my list of acceptable verbiage. Yep. There it is. Nagheed Bark and Nagheed Growl.

She landed on a street sign behind the escapee and part of the crowd. A scratchy, somewhat higher pitched version of Nagheed's bark came out of her beak. That ratcheted the escapee's morale emoji to a deeper frown.

The escapee looked around for the other dog, but kept his eye line low, where a dog was supposed to be.

Behind him, running people approached. The scents blowing past on the wind showed Osse and Rafayel. Nagheed glanced back. Rafayel had his pistol out, and Osse was armed with his bow. An arrow was already nocked but not aimed.

Uniformed men came closer but left Nagheed a considerable space.

One of the guards pointed a sword at the escapee. "Best you give it up before the gentleman who owns those dogs releases them."

Nagheed growled and barked to punctuate the man's words. Further down the street, Ahva echoed him. That stacked another debuff on the escapee.

"I'd listen to them, if I were you. My friend here is deadly accurate with this bow," Rafayel called.

Nagheed stalked closer, closing half the distance while he growled. Ahva flew to the next closer sign and barked. The escapee kept his eyes too far down to notice Ahva was anything other than a bird. The debuff stacked again. What was the max on that?

"Throw the knife away and surrender." The guard drew a rapier.

Ahva landed on the sign nearest the escapee and growled. Nagheed matched her.

The escapee tossed his weapon down, let the woman go, and showed both hands empty. The combat music faded back to RenFaire.

The guards came forward and took custody of the escapee. Four of them escorted him back to the Council Hall. The fifth waited for Rafayel and Osse to catch up. When Nagheed turned off Posture, he smoothed out his fur and sat until Rafayel was closer. Then he stood up and wagged his tail, earning some dog XP. Rafayel crouched in front of him and ruffled his shaggy fur. "Good work, Nagheed."

The guard bowed. "You're the Baron of Yavne, are you not?"

Rafayel stood. "I am, and this is my friend Osse."

"Thank you for your help. That's some dog you have. Where's the other one?" The guard looked around.

Osse held up his arm as a perch for Ahva moments before she landed. "This is the other dog."

The guard's jaw dropped. "That bird?"

Ahva barked a few times.

"That's amazing. How long did it take you to train him to do that?"

"You know, I've never deliberately trained her to do any noise. She just picks it up, and she's smart enough to know when to use them."

"I've seen birds that do that. Still amazes me. Thank you both and both your animals." The guard bowed and returned to the Council Hall.

Ahva: What, no loot?

Nagheed: Never do good deeds for money?

Ahva: What a gyp!

Nagheed: We got experience out of the deal. And, you learned how to bark.

Ahva: Oh yay. My life is complete.

They returned to the Council Hall building then walked around the perimeter fence to the back. One street headed south. They followed the shopkeeper's directions and ended up at a building that had none of the ostentation of the Cathedral, but the door was decorated with Tsidkenu's cross-on-a-circle symbol. Rafayel tried the door, but it was locked. He knocked.

"You won't find him there." Someone called from across the street.

Nagheed spun toward a woman leaning out a window.

Rafayel turned and shielded the sun from his eyes with his hand. "Would you know where to find him?"

The woman tapped her chin. "What is today? Oh yeah! He's at The Snorts and Giggles. He and one of the local physicians run a clinic to help out the poor folk who need medical care."

"Admirable. How would I get to The Snorts and Giggles?" Rafayel asked.

"Keep heading southwest until you reach the corner of

the city." She waved roughly in that direction. "It's right there."

"Thank you." Rafayel bowed. He turned to Osse. "Shall we?"

Osse shrugged. "Sure, but I get the feeling this is a goose chase."

"If we don't find him at the next stop, we'll give up the search." Rafayel pointed at the descending sun. "It's getting around to dinner time."

Ahva: We should get frequent walker bonuses.

Nagheed: Yeah. This game could do with a teleporter.

Once again, they wove a zigzag path taking one block south and one block west than one block south again all the way down into the furthest corner of the city. They knew the place by the line snaking out the door. As they approached the door, muscular guy with the demeanor of a bar bouncer blocked their way. "End of the line's over there." He pointed.

Rafayel shook his head. "I'm not here for the clinic. I need to have a word with the priest."

"Priest is busy now. End of the line or find him at his church."

Osse stepped forward. "I'm an herbalist. Is there something I can do to help?"

"One minute." The bouncer stepped through the door but stayed close. "Sir, there's a Bakhari kid out here who says he's an herbalist. Says he wants to help if he can."

"Thank Tsidkenu. Send him in. We're gonna need all the help we can get to get through this queue before you fine folk open for business in an hour."

The bouncer stepped back out. "Go on in, kid." He turned

his stare on Rafayel.

Rafayel nodded. "And I need to stay out here. Understood. I'm not here to cause you any trouble."

"Make sure you don't."

Nagheed studied the waiting crowd. Most of the people wore worn clothes and many were trailing one or more children. All of them yawned, fidgeted, and shifted from foot to foot. Hardly surprising. Waiting in line was not the most fun pastime.

A woman huffed. "How much longer is this going to take?"

"Sorry, ma'am. You're always welcome to go to one of the regular physicians," The bouncer pointed down the street.

"If she could afford it." Rafayel crouched to Nagheed's level. "Shall we make ourselves useful?"

Nagheed woofed.

Chapter 29

Nagheed sat in front of his human and waited for the first command. Rafayel started with some basics. The usual. Sit. Rollover. Play dead. Speak. Then they advanced to more complex things like fetching specific objects and the other sorts of tricks Jake had taught Prince. At first, no one noticed, but then first the children, then their parents started cheering whenever Nagheed finished a trick. The line moved no faster, but instead of lamenting about the wait, the kids at least were reluctant to go inside. Finally, the last person in the queue got their turn.

The bouncer nodded. "Nice work. How long did it take you to train him to do all that?"

"Not long at all, actually. He's a remarkably smart dog, well beyond the basic obedience and fetch type of tasks. I've only met a handful that were such effective companions."

There will be more coming after the official release.

The bouncer waved them inside. This tavern was laid out exactly like the one they were staying in, lending support to his idea that they spared the art department by reusing some basic designs and redressing them. The biggest difference was the quality of the building materials. This

CHAPTER 29

place could have used a little upkeep. Cobwebs hung from the corners and the floor clearly hadn't been swept in a while. Tables and chairs had been repaired a time or five. Three stations were set up in different corners of the room. Osse and Ahva were in one of the spaces checking out a cut on a boy's foot. A young man wearing an apron was talking to a woman who flexed her hand carefully and smiled. At the third station, a man wearing a simple monk's robe along with the purple skullcap and scarf was combining an assortment of herbs. He applied it to a man's arm.

The woman, still flexing her hand, left. The man in the apron waved Rafayel over.

Rafayel held up one hand. "I'm not a patient."

Young man pointed. "The blood on your shoulder?"

"Already tended."

The bouncer followed Rafayel in. "That's the last for the day, Doc."

The young man sighed. "We had quite a crowd today." He hustled over to Osse and led him through treating whatever was wrong with the kid. "Good job. You learn quick."

"Thank you for teaching me." Osse smiled.

The boy and his father left about the same time the priest finished with his patient.

The priest blew out a breath as the last patient left. "What a day!" He turned to the bartender. "Thank you for the use of your building again."

"No problem." The bartender beamed a wide smile. "Spares me a bit of taxes on the place and helps the locals to boot. Can't hurt business."

"We'll clean up and be on our way."

Nagheed found a spot to park his tail in front of the fireplace, even though there was no fire in it, while the humans rushed around picking up trash and putting supplies back in the bags.

When they finished, the physician clapped the priest on the shoulder. "Same time next week?"

"I'll be here. Thank you for donating your time."

"My pleasure."

The priest shouldered his bag. "Do you mind if we travel while we talk?"

"That's fine with me." Rafayel gestured toward the door.

They started on the same zigzag path back toward the center of town.

Ahva: Joy. More exposition.

Nagheed: Got your notepad going?

"What can I help you with?" The priest asked.

As expected, Rafayel launched into a description of the weird attackers, including information that he had found in their travels and deferring to Osse on some points that he had personal experience in.

Ahva: I got this part.

Nagheed: Stop interrupting. You have noticed that whenever we go into chat mode, the game pauses. Right?

Ahva: Oh, nuts. Okay. I'll shut up.

"We were wondering if you had any information that would help us either in the quest to find the temple of Elef or how to deal with the strange mutant creatures or how to set things right again."

The priest took most of a block to think about it. "I've never heard of this happening before, but it does make sense. Atrac seeks to improve humanity at any cost, so if any of her followers damaged or repurposed the artifacts in Elef's temple, it would stand to reason you would get more chaos."

"Should we be seeking to destroy that temple?" Osse asked.

"I wouldn't do it that way. You would have to destroy every one of the temples on the entire continent. That would take more of an army than all of Nethanya owns. Your best bet is to restore the artifacts to their original function and eliminate the Priestess who caused all the trouble."

"And we wouldn't be violating any of Tsidkenu's laws in the process?" Rafayel dodged a pedestrian coming the other way.

"That is a bit of a touchy area." The priest adjusted his equipment bag on his shoulder. "On the one hand, we are not meant to promote another religion. On the other hand—"

Ahva: There are five more fingers.
Nagheed: Shhh.
Ahva: Right, right. Shutting up.

"If we don't do something, those artifacts will continue to produce mutilated creatures bent on destroying anything that lives." The priest shrugged. "Really, though, there's a common misconception about Ilion's religion. Although it's changed over time to become a worship of the three deities, it didn't start out as a typically faith-based religion, not like ours. The Ilionite religion originated as a way to make machines work to enhance living creatures. More technological than religious. That changed after the collapse of Ilion's economy and government."

Rafayel frowned. "Then we're not supporting a foreign religion, but rather correcting a technology problem. That's good to know. Our only viable choices are to destroy the temples of Ilion, which will take in enormous force and start a war; or reestablish the balance of power and let Tsidkenu sort it out when he comes again."

The priest shrugged. "That's about the size of it."

Ahva: How about trashing the equipment so it can't produce any more wackos?

Nagheed: You're assuming there's only one set of equipment. You know where the rest of them are?

Ahva: Pff, I don't even know where this one is.

"What if we disable the artifacts altogether but leave the temple itself intact." Osse asked.

"There's more than the one set. You're back to chasing down every temple of Elef and figuring out which ones have been overrun by Atrac."

Nagheed: See?

Osse squinted. "In that case, how do we know that the only set of artifacts that are damaged are the ones in the main temple?"

The priest shrugged. "Unfortunately, you don't. But, if you correct the main temple, that should restore enough power to Elef that his own followers will take care of the rest."

Rafayel blew out a breath. "All at once, this feels like the entirely wrong thing to do and yet the only possible option."

"Just remember the Ilionite religion has become a religion recently, but in its original incarnation, it was just the technology, which has either been sabotaged or broken down."

Ahva: Well, whaddya know? Useful exposition.
Nagheed: Definitely backs up with Rafayel read from

CHAPTER 29

his book.

Ahva: Takes it out of the legend arena and plunks it in history.

Nagheed: Yeah.

The priest nodded. "In any case, the threat needs to be ended before these creatures get too strong to defeat. You say you have noticed an increase in their power."

"That's the truth." Osse scowled. "I can't kill one on my own anymore."

"Do you think Tsidkenu will honor our actions?" Rafayel asked.

"I believe he will. You're acting to protect the innocent. You're stopping Atrac, not empowering Elef. We will, nevertheless, pray that Tsidkenu guide you and bless your efforts. Trust him to lead you, and if there is another way that we haven't thought of, he will reveal it to you when the time is right."

Their zigzag course dropped them off in front of the temple.

Ahva: It's about time.

Nagheed: Just wait, we might go inside for more.

Ahva: Bite your tongue, Shaggy.

"Will you come inside?" The priest pulled his keys out of pocket.

"No, but thank you for your help. You had a rather long day and I'm sure you're interested in your supper." Rafayel cast a glance at the setting sun. "It'll be dusk soon, and I'm afraid I don't know the city as well in the dark as I do in the daylight. I appreciate your wisdom on the matter."

The priest nodded. "It's a difficult path you've chosen. I'll pray for your victory." He opened the door and went inside.

They reversed their path toward the Council Hall then went to The Drop and Roll. Rafayel led the way around to the stable where they checked out their horses's stalls where their own horses were. Both stalls were cleaned to near shine, and the horses had both food and water.

Rafayel smiled. "Good. I was afraid we'd have an awkward situation."

Osse shrugged. "He seemed sincere enough."

Nagheed followed them to the inn.

* * *

Ahva awoke with the sun, as usual. Why the computer decided that she had get up before anybody else was a mystery she had yet to solve. But nevertheless, she was up, and everybody else was asleep. Rather than simply wait for everybody to wake up, Ahva decided to take a proactive approach. She did her best impersonation of the songbirds outside at full volume.

"Ahva! Is that really necessary?" Osse muttered.

She leaned closer to his ear. "Yes."

There was a book to translate, junk to sell, supplies to buy, and, most importantly, food to eat to complete the refill on her fatigue counter. None of that was going to get done with all the sleepy heads investigating their eyelids for holes.

Nagheed, parked on the rug in front of the fireplace, lifted his head.

Nagheed: The computer gets you up first?

Ahva: Yep. Every time. When we're camping, I inves-

CHAPTER 29

tigate the area. There's not much here in this room to investigate. Trust me. Been there. Done that.

Shortly after, all three humans yawned, stretched, and rousted their lazy butts. To Ahva's great relief, "getting ready" for the day amounted to nothing more complicated than washing their faces at a wash stand and gathering up their gear. The game's All Audiences rating spared her a view of the rest of the masculine anatomy.

As a group, they traipsed on down to the great room where they were served pancakes and bacon. Osse moved one of his pancakes off to the side, and Ahva picked at it.

Eezak finished his breakfast and pushed his plate away. "After I take care of the horses, is there anything you'd have me do?"

Osse swallowed a mouthful of pancake. "Do you know the marketplace well?"

"Sure." Eezak shrugged. "Merchants come and go, but I can at least steer you away from the ones who won't deal fair."

"How about I help you with the horses this morning, and then you can help me with the errand running."

"Sounds good." Eezak nodded once.

Rafayel looked from one to the other. "I'm afraid I won't be back until supper. The Oligometa is an all-day affair. I will, however, take a miss on the 'reception' that usually follows these meetings."

"Just an extension of the meetings?" Osse stuffed another piece of pancake into his mouth.

"No, exactly the opposite. Plenty of strong drinks and other activities that I don't care for. I'm happily married."

Osse picked up some bacon. "Then we'll meet you back

here around sunset. Is today the day you will find out if we have any support?"

"That depends on the king's agenda. Usually he has certain points that he wishes to discuss before he opens the session to concerns raised by other nobility. The time will come, but it might not be today."

When they finished eating, Rafayel took his leave of them.

She perched on Osse's shoulder as they headed out to the stable behind the inn. Watching the humans muck out the stables was as exciting as staring at the woodwork, so she hunted around for clues, while Nagheed nosed around the empty stalls. She ran out of places to investigate both inside and outside the stable by the time the humans had finished. They returned to Room Eight and took an inventory.

"Okay, so what is it you have to sell?" Eezak perched on one of the beds.

"I have pelts, these weapons, this jeweled knife, and all this armor." Osse laid out the wares on one of the beds. "I also need to have this book translated, get Rafayel's armor repaired, and buy arrows, herbs, and food for the journey. I'd like to talk to a weaponsmith about making small weapons that Ahva can pick up and drop on enemies, and Rafayel has mentioned getting some barding for Nagheed."

"That might take us more than today."

"That's all right. Rafayel says he'll be at the Oligometa for three days. We've got the time."

"I say we start with the book. If we find a translator who's willing to take it on, you'll probably need more than a day to get it done. Likewise, the armor repair, the dog's barding, and your bird's weapons. That is, if you have the money to pay for those without selling the other first."

"I've got some. Let's find out what it costs. If I don't have enough, we can always take care of the other errands first and then come back to it."

Ahva: And then we need to pick out our outfits for the ball. I was thinking something in a nice yellow chiffon. Nice contrast, don't you think?

Nagheed: You'd look like a bumblebee.

Ahva: More than meets the eye.

They packed all the equipment up into Osse's bag and one of the saddlebags. The handles of the axes, swords, and maces stuck out of the top of the saddlebag.

To Ahva's unending relief, the marketplace was only a few blocks away. She expected the crowds to be huge. After all, it was the middle of the day, but there was hardly anyone around. Everyone she saw was clearly upper-class or maybe middle-class. Maybe. And those were probably servants of some upper-class, hoity-toity trust fund brat. Assuming of course that this game had trust funds. Was there another marketplace somewhere where the poor folk did their business?

"Are we here on an off day?" Osse slowly turned.

Eezak shook his head. "No, well, sort of. I'd be willing to bet the Oligometa sale is on."

"Oligometa sale?" Osse's brow furrowed.

"When the Oligometa is on, the prices usually go up. Three, four times. More even. Most townsfolk don't do business in the marketplace for those three days. You get enough to get you through, and you don't show up. All the barons, their servants, and the wives who came with them do their shopping here. You want my advice, don't buy more than you absolutely need to get to your next stop. Unless maybe..."

Osse peeked at Eezak from the corner of his eye. "Maybe?"

"Don't want to say till I know for sure." Eezak shook his head. "I'd hate to commit people to things I got no business committing them to. But hold off on buying at least your foodstuffs until the day you leave. Might have a better solution. Let me give it a think and talk about it to the other folks."

"Fair enough."

"But I'll show you where we need to go to get good prices on the rest of your stuff. Usually the buy prices don't change with the sell prices. You know how it is."

Ahva: What do you think the big mystery is?

Nagheed: Um, totally guessing, but maybe a farmer's market?

Ahva: That could be. We probably need the Super-Secret, Mystic Handshake of Doom or something.

Chapter 30

Ahva gave up trying to remember the meandering path Eezak led them through. He stopped in front of a permanent shop that had a fake book hanging from a steel rod above the door.

Inside the shop, Horizon Systems had chosen to use the same artwork as the scribe in Bakhar. The only difference was the color scheme. Light wood there, dark wood here. But otherwise, even the scribe was the same. Twins, apparently. Not the first game to reuse artwork in different places, and certainly wouldn't be the last.

The scribe stood up. "Eezak! We missed you last night."

Eezak embraced the scribe. "Got me some temporary work to hold me over 'til my job starts beginning of next week. Had to meet with my employer and make sure my room and board was covered. You know how it is. I'll be there tonight, though."

"Glad to hear it." He sighed. "I know about what happened at the cathedral. What a mess."

"It's all right." Eezak brushed the thought aside. "Skunk showed his stripe. That's all. I landed right enough with one of the barons. Taking care of his horses and helping out with the shopping."

"That's excellent. So, stopping to chat?" The scribe perched on the edge of a desk.

Eezak aimed his thumb at Osse.

Osse dug the book out of his bag. "He said you might be able to help me with the translation. We found this in the loot of one of those laughing maniacs that have been harassing the countryside. It's not written in a language that any of us can read." He set the book on the scribe's desk.

"Aha. Seen this before." The scribe flipped through the book. "Ancient language. They say it originated before the Great Massacre. This one, though, is intact. The other ones are a wreck. Pages missing, what's left of the pages are torn, burnt, stained, or smeared. This is in such good shape I can restore the others."

"This book is fairly common?"

The scribe shook his head. "I wouldn't say common. Since I opened the place, though, people have brought in partial copies of this book. They end up selling it to me, but there's not much I can do with them. With this one to help me out, though, I can make sense of the others and then sell them to collectors. They're not doing me any good sitting in a chest in the back room. When do you need this back?"

"We're only here for the Oligometa. Once that's finished, we'll move on."

"Hm." The scribe drew a breath through his teeth. "Tight, but I think I can do it if I set a couple journeymen on it. Come back when you're ready to leave, and I'll have it translated for you. If you don't mind, I'd like to make a copy for myself at the same time. I have an apprentice who needs to practice his penmanship. That way I will have an

CHAPTER 30

intact version that I can use to restore the others. All right by you?"

Osse nodded. "I'm sure it's fine. How much do I owe you?"

The scribe stared at some point past Osse. "Call it fifty rounds?"

"Would you consider forty?"

"Let's say forty-five, and it's done." He offered his hand.

Osse shook the man's hand and counted out the money. "I'll be back when we're on our way out."

Eezak waved. "See you tonight."

They left the store.

"Armorer next?" Osse asked.

"Yep. The guy I'm taking you to will buy your excess, fix your broken, and maybe even make the dog's."

They wove another convoluted path through the almost nonexistent crowd and ended up at another permanent shop. This time, Ahva was not surprised to find that the interior of the shop exactly matched the one in Bakhar except for the color scheme.

The armorer came out of the back room. "What do you need?"

Osse dug the extra armor and his father's blacksmith tunic out of the saddlebag and plunked them on the counter then pulled out Rafayel's armor and set it down nearby. He tapped the first pile. "These are for sale." He tapped Rafayel's armor. "I need this one repaired."

The armorer sorted the first pile then inspected the leather doublet Osse had picked up from the loot. "Looks like what you're wearing came out of this pile."

"I thought this would serve better than that blacksmith

tunic."

"That's a little big on you. Can I see it?"

Osse un-laced his leather doublet and handed it over. "It fits better than the blacksmith's tunic. Mostly."

Ahva: I smell a hard sell coming. Wanna bet the quality sucks and he's gonna try and sell Osse a new one?

Nagheed: No bet.

The armorer inspected the doublet inside and out and even give it a hard tug on a couple seams. "Well-made, actually. I don't recognize the work, but armor that doesn't fit you won't do you much good. Gaps too much under the arms and at the belly and at your neck. What do you say you let me cut this down to your size? It will serve you a lot better."

Ahva: You should have taken have bet. You would have been one No Prize richer.

Nagheed: No Prize?

Ahva: You don't know what the infamous No Prize is? Friend, you need to read more comic books.

Nagheed: If I could afford the subscription.

"How much would it cost for the repair work and resizing that one considering the sale of the rest." Osse tapped the excess armor pile.

The armorer inspected the rest of the doublets. "All the same except for this smith's tunic. I'd be willing to call it a wash."

Osse nodded. "I'll go with that." They shook hands on it. "When do you need it by?"

"I'm here for the Oligometa. We're leaving in three days." He held up three fingers.

"Won't take me that long. You can pick it up any time

after tomorrow."

"And Nagheed. Would it be possible to make barding for him?" Osse gestured at the mountain shepherd sitting next to him.

The armorer came around the counter and paused. "How friendly is he?"

Osse patted Nagheed's side. "He only attacks if something threatens him or if the baron orders him."

The armorer crouched next to Nagheed and pet his head. "I've seen mountain shepherds, but this one's a beauty."

Ahva: I think he would prefer "ruggedly handsome."

Nagheed: LOL

"If we keep it to something simple to protect his back, chest, and belly, and maybe the neck, I can get my journeyman on it and have it done by the time you leave." He stood. "It'll be functional, but not pretty to look at."

Osse shook his head. "It's not for show. We're going to be taking on strong enemies soon, and he needs better protection. In some of our other encounters, he's taken some blows to the back and shoulders."

The armorer tapped his chin. "Okay. I can do basic leather for four hundred."

"I can give you one hundred sixty now and the rest when we come to pick it up." Osse fished his money pouch out of his bag.

"That'll do. I'll see you then."

Ahva: He really thinks those other weapons will sell for at least 240?

Nagheed: That dagger we found in the pirate's den will likely do the trick.

Ahva: Oh, yeah. Forgot about that.

When they left the store, Eezak turned to Osse. "That takes care of the stuff that takes time. How about we sell these extra weapons and pick up your new arrows. We can take care of your bird's weapons at the same time."

Ahva was expecting another convoluted path, but they only went a couple doors down. And, she guessed correctly, the inside matched the shop in Bakhar. Big surprise there. The weaponsmith had a twin in Bakhar, too.

"Buying or selling?" The weaponsmith leaned on the counter.

"Both." Osse laid out the excess weapons on the counter.

Weaponsmith inspected Osse's recurve. "Nice bow. Obvious Bakhari styling. You make it?"

Osse nodded. "With my grandfather's help."

Next, he checked the weapons they'd collected off the village raiders. "Not as impressive, but workable." He picked up the jeweled dagger. "Nice. Easy on the eyes, but not too functional." He set the dagger aside and gestured to the rest. "These, I'll give you seventy-five for. That dagger, though, I don't usually deal with eye grabbers like that. To the Point in the southeast corner of the market is where you'll find that sort."

Eezak snorted. "Now come on, Dev. You know full well that thief won't give the boy any kind of price. You-know-who would pay you plenty for it, and you'll turn a quick, easy profit. Give the boy half for it, and it'll still pay your rent for two months."

The weaponsmith frowned. "I hate dealing with that guy. I always leave feeling like I need to count my fingers to be sure they're still there."

"I know." Eezak held up his hand palm out. "I know, and

CHAPTER 30

I'm not his greatest fan, either, but you know I'm right."

The weaponsmith blew out a breath. "All right. I'll give you four hundred for the dagger."

"Thank you." Osse pushed it toward him.

"Now what can I get for you?"

"I need some arrows with metal arrowheads, and then I have this little gal to arm." Osse offered Ahva his hand.

She hopped over. "Hello! I Ahva. Bite fingers?"

"No biting." Osse held her at eye level.

The weaponsmith chuckled. "What do you have in mind?"

"She has been picking up small rocks and pinecones and dropping them on our opponents' heads, but that's not doing much more than creating a distraction. I was wondering if you had anything more dangerous she could drop on them that's light enough for her to fly with."

"Hmm. That's the problem. You get the force of the attack from the weight and the speed of the weapon. Ravens–"

Ahva: That's "crows," goofy goober.

Nagheed: There's a difference.

Ahva: Yeah? I think? Y'know, I've never seen either one in the feather.

"–Aren't strong like eagles or fast like falcons. Awful smart, though, from what I hear. Maybe an arrowhead on a short stick? Be right back." The weaponsmith disappeared into the back room and rummaged around then returned with an arrowhead on a two-centimeter shaft. "See what she can do with this."

Ahva grabbed the shaft with her beak and lifted off. After she zipped around the room a couple times, she picked a knot on the wooden floor for a target and let go and whistled as the arrowhead fell. It stuck in the floor next to the knot. She returned to the counter.

The weaponsmith looked from Ahva to the arrowhead stuck in the floor and back again. "Wow. That's not bad."

Osse retrieved the arrowhead. "I think that'll work. She won't get anywhere near the damage I can do with my bow, but she'll do more than she's doing with a little rock."

"I've got scrap bits of shafts I can use in back. They were going for kindling in the fire, so I'll just charge you for the arrowheads. I charge two rounds per arrow if you want a metal head on it, and the arrowheads alone are a round each. Good and sharp, so I suggest you find yourself a sturdy leather pouch to keep them in so you don't cut yourself reaching into your pack."

Eezak leaned closer. "Armorer will have a simple leather pouch that'll do the trick. Good price, too."

Osse nodded. "Thank you. I'll take two dozen arrows for me and a dozen arrowheads for Ahva. Do you also sell balls and powder for pistols?"

"No, but the gunsmith down the street will have all you need. Come back in an hour and I'll have your order ready."

Money changed hands and they left.

The rest of the purchases and sales were straightforward. They sold the pelts in one shop and used that money to buy the balls, patches, and powder for Rafayel's pistol in another. In spite of Eezak's dire prediction that it would take them all three days to run all the errands, they were actually done before the sun set, except for waiting on the other orders. The only thing left to buy was the food, which Eezak had suggested they wait on.

CHAPTER 30

Next came another exciting adventure in cleaning out stables. Then Eezak took his leave and headed off on his own. Ahva and Nagheed followed Osse to the great room of the inn and found a place to sit until Rafayel joined them shortly after.

"How'd it go?" Osse asked.

Rafayel sighed. "We didn't get to personal concerns today." He scanned the room. "Where is Eezak?"

"He had something he wanted to do this evening. Somehow, it relates to acquiring our food." Osse shrugged. "He said not to buy the food at the market. The Oligometa sale is on."

Rafayel scowled. "That's not supposed to be legal anymore, but I'm not surprised. I usually buy enough to get me back to the nearest city on my way home. That, alone, costs me more than the entire rest of the trip."

"I'm curious about what Eezak has in mind."

"So am I. Did the rest of the errands go well?"

"Wonderfully. I sold everything else. The book is being translated. It will be ready by the time we leave. We're supposed to stop on our way out of town. Your armor is being repaired, and mine is being sized down to me. Those will be ready day after tomorrow. Nagheed's is being made. I'm afraid that, because of the time constraint, Nagheed's is going to be fairly simple."

"That's fine. Anything complicated would require him to relearn some skills."

"The weaponsmith made a dozen arrowheads with short shafts for Ahva, and I found a gunsmith who restocked your supplies for your pistol."

Rafayel smiled. "Well done. What are you going to do

with yourself for two more days?"

"The priest we talked to yesterday said that he runs one of those clinics in each corner of the town on a rotating basis. I'll try to lend a hand. Maybe he'll teach me another herbal preparation. Yesterday, I learned more advanced versions of combinations that will purify toxins and heal injuries."

"That's excellent." He nodded.

"He said that if I meet him at his church an hour after dawn, he'd take me with him."

"An honorable way to spend your day."

They went to their room with supper in hand. Osse set Eezak's dinner next to the fire to keep it warm.

Ahva: You really need to do the dog thing and try to eat his dinner.

Nagheed: And lose experience? Thank you, no.

Ahva: You get experience for acting like a dog, and a dog would definitely try to eat it.

Nagheed: Maybe next time. Speaking of dinner, though, Prince and I would sure like some.

Ahva: What kind of dog is Prince? I'm guessing a big Labrador.

Nagheed: Half-shepherd, half-chow mix. Kind of like Nagheed, but smaller.

Ahva: With the purple tongue and a curly tail?

Nagheed: Yep.

Ahva: That's so cool!

Nagheed: So, meet back here in a couple hours?

Ahva: Couple hours? Planning a seven-course meal?

Nagheed: No, but I have to feed me, feed him, then I'm sure he would like an opportunity to run around the backyard for a while.

Ahva: Okay. Two hours. Probably do me some good to eat something other than pop tarts, chips, and soda pop.
Nagheed: That's the spirit.
Ahva: I think I'll order pizza.
Nagheed: Whatever floats your boat. Back in a bit.
Khin May paused the game and disconnected.

* * *

On the third day of the Oligometa, Ahva awoke before the rest of the group and stretched away a stiffness warning before she started her chirp festival. That got the humans up and ready in minutes, game clock. After a breakfast of ham and eggs, Rafayel stood to leave and Ahva fluttered up to his shoulder.

"Going with me today?" Rafayel looked at her from the corner of his eye.

She bobbed her head. "Yes. No doctor today for the bird."

He turned to Osse. "Do you mind if she comes with me?"

Osse shrugged. "If you don't mind her company."

"Fine with me, but Ahva, you can't be calling people disgusting eyeballs or threatening to bite fingers."

Nagheed: You want to go sit in meetings all day?

Ahva: Variety. Day one was shopping. Day two was fetching the medical stuff. Day three might as well be finding out what the final verdict is on this meeting thing. Are you going to go put on the dog show?

Nagheed: Sure. I gain some fair experience, improve my agility, and stuff like that.

Ahva: Okay. See ya later, gator!

Nagheed: I'll be around.

Ahva: You'd look funny with corners.

While they wove their way through the town to the Council Hall, Ahva kept a grip on Rafayel's collar. He moved differently than Osse, stiffer and jerkier than Osse's gentle swaying motion. Getting used to his gait took a little more doing.

They turned the corner onto the same street where she'd done her impersonation of Nagheed. The crowds were not as dense as the time before, so Rafayel was able to travel without dodging people.

At the gate into the fenced area around the Council Hall, the guard bowed him through, and Rafayel entered the building. The foyer was larger than some whole houses and decorated with tapestries, marble statues, and shiny metal accents. Signage directed people to the left and right for various courts and government offices.

A man in brilliant red tunic and tights strode toward Rafayel and bowed. "Good morning, Your Excellency."

"Good morning. How has the day found you?"

"Well, sir." The man conducted Rafayel through a set of large, brass doors into a small room. Six identical chairs, two on each of three walls, faced into the center of the room. The fourth wall had a more ornate chair on a dais with a crown painted on the wall above it.

Three of the lesser chairs were already occupied by other men. Rafayel greeted each of them on the way to his spot next to a kid who bore a striking resemblance to the baroness in Geva, the one whose husband had suffered a stroke. As the two of them talked, the kid's shaky hands steadied, and his furrowed brow faded some.

Ahva looked around. Other people had brought their

critters, too. A yellow Labrador was curled up next to the seat of one of the barons, a hawk perched on a stand next to another one, and a cat occupied someone's lap.

As soon as the last two of the lesser seats were filled, the man from the foyer entered and stood in the center. "Your Excellencies, please rise for your king."

Everyone stood while the herald bowed and backed out of the room. A door on the fourth wall opened behind a tapestry and a tall, muscular man entered and took his place on the throne. Like all of the barons, he'd stepped out of a Three Musketeers movie, only the silver embroidery and beadwork on his blue doublet and pants was more ornate by a couple orders of magnitude. He took in the room with a sweeping gesture of his hands, and everyone sat.

Well, aren't you the bag of chips that comes with all that?

Nagheed: Hey, unless you're really into the meetings today, whaddya say to speeding up the clock a bit.

Ahva: And make everyone sound like the Chipmunks? Score! You do know who the Chipmunks are, right?

Nagheed: Of course I know what chipmunks are. Small, squirrel-like critter.

Ahva: Well, you're not wrong, but those aren't the ones I mean.

Nagheed: More vintage cartoons?

Ahva: Naturally!

Nagheed: How about moving the slider to half?

Ahva: You got it!

She focused on the cogwheel next to the crow image in the corner of her vision to open the setting screen then scrolled to the game clock control and slid bar to halfway. It zipped back to regular speed.

Slowpoke partner.

When she tried again, it stuck. She closed the settings.

The king was speaking, a pretty passable imitation of Alvin the Chipmunk. He started with some opening remarks, recapping what the previous sessions had covered. Then he opened the floor to whoever wanted to bring a concern.

Various people stood in the center of the room and gave speeches, each one sounding like an audition for a kid's cartoon voice. Pirates, trade imbalances with Bakhar and Antwen, and a border dispute between two of the barons, which only lasted until the king sent for a cartographer who proved that they were both wrong. Sure, the border once followed the river, but the river had since moved. Not as far as one of them claimed, but it had moved. The king ruled in favor of keeping the original border. Moving shadows in the room indicated the passage of time.

Somewhere toward late afternoon based on the shadows, Rafayel took the spot in the middle of the room. When he launched off into a recap of the events so far. The goofy cartoon voice made hearing the repeat of their adventures totally worth it. His heavily abbreviated retelling was only a couple minutes long.

Around the room, some of the barons were whispering to the others. Were they providing translations or ignoring the seriousness of the problem?

"What are you proposing we do?" one of the barons asked.

"They're coming from east of here, Yurial." Rafayel made a sweeping gesture with one hand. "As I said, I have it on good authority that they're coming out of

CHAPTER 30

Ilion from the main temple to Elef. I suggest we go there and set things back to their proper order to stop the attacks on Bakhar and Nethanya."

Yurial laughed. "You propose to march an army across Bakhar, and you think the Bakhari will accept that and not meet us with their own forces?"

Rafayel scowled. "Did I say anything about summoning an army? No. That would be foolish. Not only would we leave our own lands undefended for far too long but we would anger Bakhar, if not also Antwen and Ilion, who would likely misunderstand our purpose. I suggest a small force, not more than a dozen men and mounts, to go to Ilion and restore the balance of power there."

"And you believe Tsidkenu will bless this venture to restore the power of a rival?" another baron asked.

"I believe he would have us stop the kidnapping and murdering of his children. I have it on a priest's authority that this will only happen if we either eradicate all the temples in Ilion or restore the balance."

"And who do you volunteer for this certain-death mission of yours?" Yurial leaned back in his chair.

Rafayel stood straight. "I am volunteering to lead the expedition and pay the expenses of any man who travels with me. I have already found a Bakhari tribesman who is seeking his missing sister. He's agreed to help. Whatever other able men would like to volunteer would be appreciated."

"You're going in any case?" Yurial picked at his fingernails. "Got your affairs in order then?"

"Nice guy," Ahva muttered.

"Always." Rafayel shrugged. "But I don't think it'll come

to that."

Yurial jabbed his finger at Rafayel. "Why should we have any part of restoring an Ilionite religion?"

Rafayel shook his head. "The priest I spoke to recently tells me that the Ilionite gods and goddess aren't deities as much as misunderstood remnants of the Ilionite society that was there before the Great Massacre. So, it's not restoring a religion but correcting a malfunction in their equipment."

"And you understand how to fix the equipment when you get there?" the king asked.

Rafayel turned to face him. "No, Your Majesty, but if I don't find the information I need to make the repairs myself, my intention is to clear out the people who have created the malfunction so that the ones who do know how to fix it can do so."

Ahva looked around at the group. Of the five other barons, only the kid of the one who'd had a stroke wasn't frowning or scowling. The king would be a terrific poker player.

If it's up to a vote, they're not going to go for it. If the king decides unilaterally, might have a chance.

One of the other barons, a tall, wiry fellow with blond hair. "You would start a war with Ilion with your interference and aggravate Bakhar by leading a band across their lands."

"Not with a small band of men, not even a significant fraction of the army." Rafayel gave the whole group a hard gaze. "Osse and I will go alone if we must, but I warn you now. We've consulted experienced priests about this and we've observed an increase in the strength of the enemy. You cannot hide behind your walls indefinitely. They'll weary of striking at outlying farms and travelers. Stone and

CHAPTER 30

timber will not keep them out."

Yurial jumped to his feet and drew a quick breath, but the king cut off his response. "When do you plan to leave?"

"That depends on your decision. If others will be joining us, clearly, we'll have to wait a few days before we set out to give them time to assemble and prepare. Otherwise, there's no reason we shouldn't leave at first light tomorrow." Rafayel took a step toward the king. "Your Majesty, can I at least request that the assembly pray for our safety and success, regardless of the final decision?"

"That we can all do. Let it be so by decree." The king waved Rafayel back to his seat.

Rafayel resumed his seat.

"Remain here while I consult my priest." The king stood, bringing everyone to their feet again. He left through the door behind his throne.

"Bye-bye." Ahva fluffed up her feathers and shook, earning a few bird XP and sending a cloud of feather dust into the air.

Samwel, Jr., the son of the disabled baron, leaned closer. "I could go with you."

Rafayel patted his arm. "And I'd be glad to have you, but your mother needs you at home. We arrived to pay our respects in time to interrupt your constable making unreasonable demands. He'd injured two servants and had started pushing your mother around."

"Bad bird." Ahva hissed. "Bite fingers!"

His eyes widened. "I thought he might be a problem. I've never liked him. Is Mother all right?"

"She's fine. The tribesman traveling with me is an herbalist and took care of everyone as well as he could. The constable is awaiting trial in prison, his deputy is in charge of peacekeeping, and the physician was on the way to treat all the injured when we left."

He sighed. "I'd better get home soon."

The herald entered and announced the return of the king.

* * *

Nagheed stood to one side and watched Osse, the priest, and the local physician cleaning up the mess that had resulted from treating patients all day. They'd borrowed an empty storefront for the clinic today, and Nagheed had entertained the waiting masses again, playing fetch and tag with a bunch of kids. His "dog cam" view while moving around was amusing. Everything was taller than it should be. He wished his VR rig would communicate how it felt to have the wind rushing through his fur while he ran, but it'd be a while before he could afford a full-immersion set-up.

After the humans finished tidying, Nagheed walked back to the inn with Osse. Rafayel and Ahva were actually waiting for them this time. He waved them over.

"What was the final verdict?" Osse settled into one of the chairs.

Rafayel shook his head. "I'm afraid they won't help us. All the same excuses I expected and a few new ones. If we're going to do this, we're on our own."

"How can they not see the danger?" Osse sighed and rested his chin on his palm.

"I don't know. It's blatantly obvious to me." Rafayel rubbed his forehead.

"Are you having second thoughts about going to Ilion?"

Rafayel shook his head. "No, no second thoughts here. I'm every bit as certain now as I was when we left Yavne. This needs to be done. I'm tired of finding mutilated farmers who were trying to do nothing more treacherous than grow vegetables in dirt. You?"

"I need to find my sister. She was taken east into Ilion, so that's where I'm going." Osse pointed at Ahva. "Are you still with us?"

"Yes. Of course! Good bird." She fluttered to Osse's shoulder.

"And Nagheed is coming along, too, right? Or do we need to take him home so he can help your family?" Osse asked.

Rafayel smiled. "What do you say, Nagheed? Go with us?"

Nagheed woofed and wagged his tail.

Osse chuckled. "We'll take that for a 'yes.'"

The notebook in the corner turned blue, and Ahva focused on it to flip it open.

Get Outta Here! Oust Atrac's Priestess from Elef's temple.

Call a Repairman. Restore the artifacts in Elef's temple to working condition.

Optional: Better, Stronger, Faster. Receive an augmentation.

Ahva: Wow. That triggered a pile of quests.

Nagheed: What do you mean?

Ahva: Didn't you just get a pile of quest alerts?

Nagheed: Oh, turned those off a long time ago. They're hokey and annoying.

Ahva: Hokey? They are the bombdiggity! Well, open your notebook and check it out. Apparently, we get to fix

the broken stuff, evict the priestess, and turn ourselves into zombie cyborgs.

Nagheed: Theoretically, if we fix the stuff, it should work right.

Ahva: And not make zombie cyborgs. That'd be nice. I can become the six-million-dollar bird. We can rebuild me so I can become stronger and faster. Wouldn't that be fun?

Nagheed: Might be interesting.

Osse turned to Eezak. "And what about you? Are you coming along?"

"My new job starts in the morning." He twitched his head to indicate somewhere east. "I appreciate the opportunity to work for you over the last few days, but I'll be okay now."

"Good." Rafayel clapped him on the shoulder. "Then in the morning, we'll have breakfast and then head out."

"After a stop at the market. We need to pick up the translation of that book and our armor and some food," Osse said.

Eezak smiled. "Food I don't think you need to worry about."

"How's that?" Osse asked.

"Bit of a surprise." He waggled his eyebrows.

Rafayel ordered dinner for them to enjoy in their room. After they ate, it was time for a nap, which on the real-world clock only lasted a few seconds of watching sheep skydiving. When the sun came up, Nagheed awoke to Ahva's extremely loud singing again. The humans were soon on their feet and their gear was packed. Nagheed followed the whole troupe down to the great room where they scarfed down a morning meal of fruit, toast, and bacon.

CHAPTER 30

Eezak finished first and stood up. He bowed to Rafayel. "Thank you, your Excellency. I'll be sure to remember your generosity to Tsidkenu."

"You're a hard worker, Eezak." Rafayel stood and shook Eezak's hand.

"Thank you."

He and Osse shared a wave and then he was gone.

"Bye-bye, bird." Ahva waved one wing.

Once the humans finished, they left. In the street, a mob of people wearing unadorned clothes crowded around them.

A dozen people, mostly women, lined the street in front of The Drop and Roll. Each had a basket hooked over her arm.

A woman approached and lifted the lid on her basket. "Loaf of bread, sir? Made it fresh this morning with wheat and barley. Good bread, sir. For your trip home?"

"What are you asking for it?" Rafayel fished out his coin purse.

"Just two rounds, sir. Much less than the market. Eezak said at church last night that you were a good man, sir, not like the others who kick us poor folk around."

"I see." Rafayel smiled. "Yes, I will gladly take the bread for my journey and give you a fair price."

Nagheed sat and wagged his tail.

Ahva: And you're not going to do the dog thing and try to snitch the food, are you?

Nagheed: Nope.

Ahva: Party pooper.

After that, each person approached and offered them something for the road. Dried fruit, jerky, dried vegetables, fresh vegetables and fruits, salted meats, nuts, hard tack, and even some other non-food items like candles, herbs, and oil in flasks.

In the end, they had acquired a small pile of paper-, leaf-, or cloth-wrapped packages at their feet.

Rafayel crouched and started loading the haul into their packs and saddlebags. "I believe that sets us up rather handily for the next stage of our trip. And so Tsidkenu has provided both ways. We have most of the provisions for the first stage of the journey for a good deal less than we would have had to pay at the market, and all those fine folks now have a few rounds more than they had."

Osse continued packing. "I hope they weren't selling us their day's meal. The money they gained wouldn't buy the replacement for it until the Oligometa sale ends."

"I must admit that it occurred to me only after I made the first couple purchases, but really, a few of them did suggest to us that they were only selling what they could spare." Rafayel held the door for them. "We will have to trust that they are more prudent than to sell their day's bread for less than they need to buy their supplies."

Once they had everything stowed, Osse led the way back to the marketplace. By some incredible miracle, he found his way along the winding the path Eezak had charted for them and landed at the scribe's shop.

The scribe stood up and picked up the book. "Good morning! I've only just finished the last few pages. Kind of confusing, even with the proper translation. But here it is."

Osse took the book and flipped it open, holding it where Rafayel could read over his arm. Nagheed harrumphed and sat down. The least they could do was hold it where he could see it.

CHAPTER 30

Nagheed: Okay, you've got the bird's-eye view. What is it?

Ahva: Weird. Definitely weird.

Nagheed: Not helping.

Ahva: I can actually read it. Usually, the computer renders writing into gibberish.

Nagheed: Must've advanced your cleverness enough, I'm guessing.

Ahva: I suppose. Anyway, the cover said Elevated Life Engineering Foundation. "ELEF" if you make an acronym of it. There are two tabs. The first is marked MOTCE and the second is ATRAC.

Nagheed: The names of the Ilionite gods? Okay.

Ahva: Probably also acronyms. Remember what the priest said about technology? Maybe ELEF was a company.

Nagheed: And the other two names are acronyms for divisions in the company? Rivals?

Ahva: Probably divisions. Anyway, on the inside, there's a picture of some body part. Then there's a description. A paragraph or two, not a lot. Really, it looks like an old magazine ad. Reads like an ad, too. Following that, there's a list. Like the one on this page says two green, quartz, amethyst, four. Finally, at the bottom of the page, there's a number. Most of them have five or six digits and they all end with this symbol that kinda looks like a mini sun. It's a catalog, I think.

Nagheed: Catalog?

Ahva: Yeah. Back in the old days, before you were born apparently, big stores would send out paper catalogs. The catalogs showed what the store had to offer.

In this case, the body part shows what augmentation you're buying. Then you have a description of what the augmentation's going to do for you. Then it shows the parts you need. The color is probably those melty plastic bits. Next you have the crystals. Then probably the number of batteries.

Nagheed: And the last number is the cost?

Ahva: Makes sense, doesn't it?

Nagheed: Yeah, it does.

Ahva: That would also explain why there are multiple copies. The catalog would been sent out to whoever.

Nagheed: Could be handy where we're going. Especially if we need to do that optional quest.

Ahva: Yeah, but if that number is typical coins, we're gonna need a lot more money.

Nagheed: That's probably why it's an optional quest. Maybe we have to find where the crossbreed humans hoarded their gold?

Ahva: Could be. Given the number of digits on some of these catalog pages, it'd take a dragon hoard.

Osse tucked the book into his bag. They thanked the man and started the long hike to the armorer.

When they walked into the armorer, he came forward out of the back room and smiled. "Be right back." He returned with two leather doublets and handed Rafayel his. "There you go. Good as new."

Rafayel inspected the work, paying close attention to where the arrow had pierced him. "Very nice. I think that will hold well."

Then the armorer presented the other set to Osse. Now, the padded leather had metal rings over key areas. "Try

CHAPTER 30

that on. Let's make sure I got your size right."

He set his equipment down as Ahva fluttered up to the top of his head. He shrugged into the doublet. At first it felt a little loose, but once he had laced up the front, it fit properly. "It fits well. But you did more than simply resize it."

"I was able to sell what you sold me for quite a bit more than even I expected. I split the difference with you and used it for your armor. The rumor has it you're headed in the territory that might not be all that safe. I try not to miss many opportunities to do another follower of Tsidkenu some good. We're square, and you have better protection."

Rafayel inspected the work. "You do know your craft. Ring mail will give him better passive defense without slowing him down. Thank you."

"This is great. Thank you so much." Osse moved his arms through their range of movement.

"You're welcome. Now for the last." The armorer ducked into the back room and returned with a collection of overlapping leather strips bound together. He came around the counter and approached Nagheed. "Dogs move different from men, so this will flex more when he's moving around. It won't bind at the joints or give him a pinch." He draped the armor over Nagheed and tightened the lacings.

The armor covered his back, chest, belly, and even had short extensions like epaulets to cover his shoulder and hip joints. Another short extension covered the back of his neck. Like Osse's armor, small metal rings had been attached in key areas.

Ahva: You're a lot smaller with all your fur contained.
Nagheed: Yeah. You should see Prince after he's been

bathed.

They stepped outside, and Nagheed ran full tilt to the end of the row and back, dodging around people. As the armorer had promised, the leather didn't restrict his movements, but the terrain wasn't moving past him quite as fast. Perhaps that was an artifact of being in the city. There was more to update than being in a field, so maybe the processor was bogging down slightly. Or, maybe that was an encumbrance effect of the weight. In any case, no red flashes popped up.

When he made it back to Rafayel, he spun in a circle and barked, picking up a little dog XP.

Back inside, Osse paid the rest of the bill.

Rafayel shook the man's hand. "Thank you for the repairs and the excellent craftsmanship."

"Glad to be of service. Safe travels." He retreated back into his work room.

With all the errand running finished, they returned to the inn to collect their horses and headed across town to the east gate.

Chapter 31

Nagheed trotted alongside the two horses. They'd gone uphill steadily since leaving Tel Caperna that morning.

Near the top of the ridge, the land leveled out. A shallow pocket in the rock on one side had a blackened patch in the middle of a ring of stones. Rafayel held up his hand and stopped his horse. "This will do for a good campsite."

Nagheed went the last few steps to the top of the ridge and looked down a hill as steep as the one they'd climbed.

Osse grimaced and slowly stretched his arms and legs. "This has been used for a campsite previously."

"It's a reasonable, defensible location. Good view of the trail in both directions." Rafayel unhitched the horses' saddles and set both of them aside. "Can you take care of the horses while I scout around for firewood?"

"Certainly."

"Stay alert." Rafayel retrieved a small ax from his horse's bag and snapped his fingers. "Come, Nagheed."

He jogged over and received a scratch behind the ears for his obedience. Rafayel led the way off the trail and into the sparsely wooded area south of their campsite. Nagheed stayed close by as they ranged back and forth in a widening half circle around the camp.

Ahva whistled and chattered, making enough noise to summon every maniac and monster in the country, but if she could be that loud, then she was clearly not in trouble. She'd stop goofing around if they had a problem.

Nagheed found a dead tree limb with some smaller branches sticking out of it. The leaves were scattered around the ground. There were many spots where little branches had been broken off, suggesting other travelers had used this tree for firewood. Rafayel used his ax to hack off a couple of the larger branches then dragged them back to camp. They made a second trip to the dead limb.

High pitched laughter bounced off the rocks, and a brisk wind blew through the scraggly bushes and sparse trees.

Nagheed turned on Smell and sniffed the air as transparent gray words bloomed all over the screen. In addition to an assortment of squirrels, deer, songbirds, and wolves, "Maniac" with "Decay" all but glued to it wafted in on the wind coming from the north.

He sat and whined. The piercing laughter came from somewhere nearby.

Rafayel attacked the tree limb with his ax and soon had a couple big branches to bring back to camp. "Let's go and be quick."

He set a fast pace straight back for their camp, but Nagheed kept up easily.

When they arrived, Osse stood with his bow ready. The horses were nearby munching on grass. A bunch of little sticks were arranged in the ring of rocks all ready to turn into a fire.

"It is I." Rafayel stopped at the edge of the camp.

CHAPTER 31

Osse couched his bow and slid the arrow into the quiver. "Did you hear it?"

Ahva flew circles above their heads.

"Yes." Rafayel came into camp and dropped off the new limbs with the old. "We'll have to set a watch tonight."

While Rafayel hacked at the tree limb, Nagheed sniffed around the camp, adding scents from a variety of people and pack animals to his view. The maniac's scent was more distant, carried on the light wind rather than the rocks, shrubs, and trees.

The burning wood smell overtook his view. That meant dinner would be soon. He returned to Rafayel's side and stretched out on the huge, solid rock that made up that part of their camp.

Their dinner of roasted veggies, salted meat, and bread was no sooner ready than eaten. Then Rafayel took the first watch and Nagheed selected Stay Alert from his skill menu.

* * *

Ahva rode on Osse's shoulder and preened to gain some bird XP. The trip down the mountain had taken twice as long as going up. From time to time, a high-pitched laughter came at them from behind, but her patrols had found nothing. She checked her fatigue meter. Almost full. Time for another circuit or two, maybe three. She kicked off from Osse's shoulder and flew a quick patrol to make sure nothing was within bow range.

They entered the foothills at the base of the mountain. The huge pine trees had been replaced by a mix of smaller pines and deciduous trees. Further from the mountain, trees gave way to shrubs and finally to long grasses.

After several loops, she returned to Osse. The maniac laughing nearby on and off had something other than them on its mind. When her fatigue bar dropped below half, she returned to her perch.

After about an hour of travel, game clock, they entered an area much like the road from Fola to Osse's village. Rolling hills were covered with grass as tall as Ahva and few shrubs or trees. In the distance, an antelope herd grazed.

Osse pointed ahead and left. "Nomads."

Ahva crawled across the back of his shirt collar to the other shoulder where she could see. A long caravan of wagons, horses, and humans were visible from the top of the hill.

Do you think they'd be willing to let us travel along with them?" Rafayel brought his horse to a stop and squinted into the distance. "We'd likely be safer in the group."

"We wouldn't be able to join them tonight." Osse shook his head. "First, we need to get close enough to see the heraldry clearly. There are some nomadic tribes we would do well to associate with and others who would kill me and sell you into slavery for coming within arrow range. Others still who would welcome us fine, but we wouldn't want to be associated with some of the things they do."

Ahva recalled the card fan heraldry on the group that had thrown rocks at her. "Fierce! Bad men." She hissed.

"Let's close the distance as much as is prudent. They're headed in the right general direction." Rafayel turned his horse toward the caravan. "I've only encountered nomads in their impromptu markets and on the road in Yavne. If they do prove to be one of the benevolent groups, how would

CHAPTER 31

we make contact?"

"Anything we do would raise suspicion. Nomads are cautious people when they're in the open like this. If we want to discuss the possibility of traveling with them toward Fola, then we need to shadow them for a while. When they decide we're harmless, they'll make contact with us."

Rafayel started off in the direction of the nomads. "Then we can ask?"

Osse shook his head. "No, we have to wait for them to invite us."

"They really are a cautious bunch." Rafayel snorted. "We might arrive in Fola before they get up their nerve."

Osse chuckled. "That's a real possibility, but if they do invite us, we'll enjoy their hospitality and their protection."

"Then it's worth trying." Rafayel cast a glance at Osse. "If they ever do work up the nerve, though, I suggest we hide my identity."

Osse's brow furrowed. "Why's that?"

"Noblemen traveling abroad have been held for ransom."

"Bite fingers!" Ahva fluffed up and hissed. "That's not nice."

Osse preened her head, restoring some fatigue points. "Then, what should I call you?"

"Since I usually only use my first and last names, few people know my other names. We'll call me Michael Nicolaos."

"Michael Nicolaos." Osse nodded. "I'll remember that."

Nagheed: Y'know, that's who we didn't see coming north.

Ahva: Who? Nomads?

Nagheed: Yeah. There was a nomad group we ran into outside Vanya then again near Yavne. They had a little mini-market set up outside town. When they disappeared, I assumed they'd continued on north, but we didn't find them on the way to Tel Caperna.

Ahva: There's a road to Bakhar from Yavne. Maybe they headed that way instead.

Nagheed: Must have.

The shadows across the prairie were long. They'd be stopping soon for the night.

* * *

Jael watched the scents wafting on the wind or blooming from different objects. "Oba" and "Dina" made a path along with a few humans. She'd been getting closer all day. They had to be only a short distance ahead. Her guts fluttered. They were close, real close. She might even catch up to them if she hustled.

She accelerated into a full speed run, keeping one eye on the terrain and one on scents around her. "Oba, Dina, two human males, human female," and a few other animals all moved along together along the same path. Ahead, "Burning wood, Cooking meat, Cooking vegetables" joined the others in a large dome.

Ahead, human voices were talking. Jael slowed and listened. There were two male voices and one female.

Using the high grass and scattered shrubs for cover, Jael crept closer until she spotted them in a depression in the rolling hills. Two men and one woman sat around a campfire enjoying roasted meat and vegetables speared on

CHAPTER 31

sticks.

Beyond them, a strange, four-wheeled cart had cages on the back. Each cage had one or two juvenile creatures: a white bear, a horse, and a few dogs. Behind the white bear, Oba stood up on his back feet and whined.

Jael's breath caught. Her precious babies. They were here. She had to get them out of that cage. That couldn't be too hard.

One of the men took some of the meat and vegetable skewers and distributed them to all but the horse in the cart.

Jael picked Posture and Charge from her skills. She rushed into the camp, baring her teeth and flattening her ears to her head. Her vision edged red and the status bar appeared identifying her targets as an Ilionite Researcher and the other two as Ilionite Technicians. The two at the fire dropped their food and scrambled toward the cart. The one at the cart picked up a metal tube with a wooden end. He held it to his shoulder. When Jael darted forward, the man with the tube aimed it at her. The woman got another one from the front of the cart. Two clicks were followed by two puffs and something sharp pierced her neck and shoulder. Jael stopped her charge and swatted at the stinging pain. A third click and pop preceded a new sting on the back of her neck. She pushed onward to get to her cubs.

Oba and Dina were both standing tall and watching her.

Her vision swam in and out of focus. Her paws felt mired in thick mud. She staggered forward, and her vision blurred. Jael fell flat. She struggled to get up but only made it to her feet long enough to fall again. Oba and Dina whined. Jael managed one last feeble attempt before the world went dark.

* * *

Ahva came in for a landing on Osse's arm and raced up to his shoulder. After two days of shadowing the nomads, the hills had flattened out considerably. The nomads were clearly in sight all the time now, but they hadn't yet come out to chat.

A rumbly sound accompanied by piercing shrieks drew Ahva's attention. A group of three men on horses came over the distant hill in the north and charged at the nomads. At the sound of a bugle, the nomads scrambled to form a perimeter defense, but the men rode through the back edge of the caravan then turned west and continued at a full gallop.

Osse shielded his eyes with the edge of his hand on his forehead. "They've grabbed a couple people."

Rafayel stood up in his saddle. "I see skirts and scarves. Let's go. It'll take the nomads time to unhitch a few horses to go after them, and a group like that probably doesn't have the girls' best interests in mind."

Both humans urged the horses to a gallop, and Ahva flew on ahead to keep an eye on the riders. Osse and Rafayel changed their angle to go directly at the fleeing brutes, making a constantly changing triangle with the kidnappers at one point, the nomads at another point, and Ahva's party at the third point.

Ahva lost sight of the kidnappers off and on as they got into the hillier terrain, but each time they appeared, they were closer. Beasts who relied on their feet to move them were so slow. Except maybe Nagheed, who was doing a fair

CHAPTER 31

job of keeping up.

When Ahva got close enough, she got a better view of their targets. They weren't chasing men at all. Each one had faint glows that bled through their clothing. When they carted the girls into a cave, Ahva looped back. As she flew past Osse and Rafayel, she did her imitation of the maniac's laugh. She banked around and headed back for the cave.

After landing next to the entrance, she crept inside. The cavern was bigger inside than she expected, but it was only one large, low-ceilinged room. She wouldn't be able to drop anything on anyone's heads in here. She hissed. When was she going to get a chance to try out her new weapons?

The rock wasn't natural. The walls were too smooth and too perpendicular. Scattered scraps of paint suggested a mural of some kind. Someone had used this place for a home or some kind of official structure some time ago. The three maniacs had bound the girls in the back of the cave. The horses were closer to the entrance. They breathed hard. When one of the maniacs came back toward the horses, Ahva stepped into a dark shadow and crouched.

Behind her, other horses arrived. She retreated and returned to Osse.

He dismounted. "Did they spot us?"

"Unless they're particularly dense, they had to. We made no effort for stealth." Rafayel drew his sword. "We'll approach more carefully and try to assess the situation. If we go charging in there, the captives might get hurt."

They left their horses and continued on foot to the entrance of the cave.

The dog sniffed around and whined.

A high-pitched giggle came from the cave followed by a

young girl's scream.

Although these three maniacs weren't as completely disheveled as the ones they'd encountered before, they still had matted hair and tattered clothes. The edges of her vision turned red.

Osse whispered. "Let me try to hit them from here. We might be able to draw them out into the open."

The three maniacs approached.

Osse rose up into a crouch and nocked an arrow. He fired at the glow in the throat of one maniac and hit straight on. The crystal cracked and threw sparks. The maniac flailed backward a couple steps then righted itself as a new glow started in its eye.

Rafayel drew and fired his pistol. His aim was true and put out the glow in the eye. A third glow, muted by the maniac's shirt, started in its chest.

Flying straight at the second maniac, Ahva landed on its head. She pecked as hard as she could at the glowing stone embedded in the back of its neck.

The first maniac drew a short sword and hobbled toward them. The second twisted and awkwardly tried to swat at Ahva but managed to land nothing. The third continued on.

"Back up a little, Nagheed." Rafayel tapped Nagheed's back.

Nagheed retreated several steps.

Ahva continued her woodpecker impersonation and actually managed to damage the crystal.

Osse's next arrow turned the first maniac into a mannequin.

Rafayel dropped back a few steps and reloaded his pistol.

The second maniac twisted hard and Ahva lost her hold.

CHAPTER 31

She fluttered and managed to slow her unintended flight before she smacked into the stone wall. The third maniac darted on ahead.

Ahva gave up on fighting maniacs. She didn't have enough room to use what tools she had. After scrambling back to her feet, Ahva flew to the girls in the back. Maybe she could untie them.

She landed near the girls. The two younger ones shrank away from her.

The older one scowled at Ahva but stayed still. "You can't curse me, crow. I'm not afraid of you."

"Good bird. Hello! I Ahva." She strutted to the girl's ankle and studied the knot for a moment before she picked one of the loops and gave it a tug. Nothing budged. *Wrong one.*

Ahva picked a different part of the knot and tugged that one. This time the string moved. She kept tugging until the end came loose. She grabbed one of the loops on the second layer of the knot and pulled until she was left with an unknotted string.

After strutting up the girl's legs to her lap, Ahva studied the knot in the rope binding her hands. It was the same type as the first and untied the same way.

When Ahva hopped toward one of the other girls, the kid cowered away from her and kept scooting away when Ahva tried to get near enough to get at the knots.

"If you're not scared of it, it can't curse you," the older girl said.

She couldn't curse them anyway, at least not that she knew of.

If the others wouldn't let her help, she'd go do something

else useful. Ahva flew back toward the cave's opening. Only one maniac remained. Ahva hissed. She wasn't needed here, either. She found a perch and watched.

Nagheed charged at the third maniac and locked his jaws around the maniac's leg.

Osse shot an arrow at its glowing shoulder, and Rafayel followed up with a thrust from his rapier, and that took care of the last maniac.

The red edge faded.

While Osse treated everyone's injuries, Rafayel checked the mannequins, finding the usual assortment of chips, crystals, batteries, and plastic blobs. One had an additional artifact: a small butane lighter.

Ahva stayed perched on her human as he led the way into the cave and approached the three girls. Now that the conflict was over, Ahva took more time to observe them. Each wore long skirts of brightly colored material and a shirt of a different color. They had long black hair that hung loose and wore sandals on their feet.

He bowed and touched his forehead. "I am Osse Bente." He pointed to Rafayel. "This is Michael Nicolaos."

Rafayel bowed slightly.

"Hello!" Ahva waved her wing.

Osse pointed. "You met Ahva earlier." He looked down at the dog. "That is Nagheed. Are you hurt?"

The three girls shook their heads.

"A little shy?" Rafayel nodded toward the girls.

Osse shook his head. "They are not permitted to speak to an unrelated man until they marry. Some of the stricter nomadic tribes won't even allow unspoken communication.

"I understand." Rafayel started toward the horses. "Let's

CHAPTER 31

collect these horses and get the girls back to their families."

Osse conducted everyone outside the cave.

Rafayel followed them leading the three maniacs' horses by their reins. "It won't surprise you to learn that these horses have not been well-tended, and I think this one is injured, but the other two should be able to bear the girls well enough." Rafayel lifted two of the smaller of the girls up to the worn-out saddle of one horse.

"What do we do with the third?" Osse gave the older girl a boost into the second horse's saddle.

Rafayel sighed and checked the horse. "I don't know. If it's injured too badly, we'll have to destroy it. We haven't time to sit and nurse a wounded horse."

The older girl pointed to the horse then to herself.

"Or, we can give it to the nomads and let them figure out how to handle it." Rafayel gave her the reins.

"It might be theirs to begin with." Osse followed Rafayel to get their own horses.

Ahva adjusted her grip as Osse pulled himself up into the saddle.

They rode back toward the nomad caravan leading the girls on their borrowed horses. Nagheed kept pace on Rafayel's side while Ahva kept watch on Osse's side. The steeper hills leveled out a little allowing Ahva to see further ahead. A group of humans on horseback galloped toward them.

"Wait." Osse stopped his horse. "That's probably the search party from the caravan."

Rafayel chuckled and pulled his horse to a stop. "Better late than never, I suppose. Would we still be unwelcomed to approach?"

Osse nodded. "I'm afraid so."

"Even after we rescued three of theirs?" He glanced back at the girls.

"Give them a chance to relate the events to their people, and they might change their minds." He twisted around in the saddle to face the girls. "If those are your people, ride on without us. We'll wait here."

The older girl nodded, and all three trotted on ahead. Ahva kept her eyes on them until the two groups met. All of them got off their horses and several of them shared embraces.

The notebook turned blue. Ahva focused on the notebook to open it.

Kudos! What's a Nice Girl Like You Doing in a Place Like This? You rescued the three captive nomads. +200XP

Rafayel smiled. "Good deed done for the day. Let's go set up our camp within sight of the caravan and take care of our own poor horses. I don't think either of them has run that hard in weeks."

Ahva fluffed up her feathers and shook, earning a few XP for bird behavior.

Chapter 32

Ahva perched on top of Osse's bag while the humans took care of the horses. Another uneventful day of riding toward Fola hadn't really accomplished anything interesting. At least the game clock moved faster during these travel segments.

Nagheed barked. Ahva answered with another bark but didn't pitch her voice down on his level. She sounded like one of those little yapper dogs that way. She chirped and did a few more small dog barks.

Osse and Rafayel stopped the care and feeding of the horses and came back to where they'd left their own gear near the fire. Ahva flew up to Osse's shoulder where she could see better.

A group of four nomads were riding toward them at a brisk pace.

Rafayel took a few steps. "Have we finally overcome their caution?"

"I don't think so." Osse smiled. "It's too soon."

"Too soon?" Rafayel smiled and shook his head. "We've been shadowing them for a most of four days."

"Right. It's too soon."

Rafayel chuckled. "Cautious is not the word for them.

Paranoid might be better."

"They want nothing to interfere with their way of life, so they only deal with the outside to trade." Osse sat on his bedroll.

"What do you think the purpose of this envoy is?"

Osse drew a breath between his teeth. "Trade?"

"Not that we have much." Rafayel ran his fingers through Nagheed's fur. "Could they mean us harm?"

"I don't know, but I don't think so."

"I'll let you handle the conversation. You understand the nuances better than I."

The nomads stopped about twenty meters from the camp and dismounted. They unbelted swords and set them and bows next to the horses. The four men all wore long, open-fronted robes in shades of gray over not exactly white pants and shirts. They had wide cloth belts in bright colors. None of them had a hat. Their skin was darker than Rafayel's but not nearly dark as Osse's. One of them was ancient but the other three were between Rafayel's and Osse's ages. All of them had long hair and short beards. Their hair was bound in back with colorful beads. The old man's hair was streaked with gray, and his beard was nearly white. The whole group stopped out of reach.

Ahva stepped around to the back of Osse's neck. He would no doubt be greeting the visitors after his usual way, and Ahva didn't need to get tossed around.

"They're being polite, anyway." Osse stood and bowed, touching his forehead with his fingertips.

When he straightened up again, Ahva returned to his shoulder where she could see.

He gestured to the ground across from him and Rafayel.

"Please sit with us."

The men bowed and touched their foreheads before they knelt and sat back on their heels.

"I am Osse Bente, and my friend is Michael Nicolaos."

"I am Gowon." The oldest one pointed to himself then to each of his friends in turn and spoke Bakhari. "My companions are Hodid, Javar, Kwame."

Osse sat on his heels like the nomads. "What has brought you to us?"

Gowon rested his hands on his knees. "You returned three slaves and three horses to us. We wondered why you went to such a risk on such worthless creatures as slaves."

Ahva: I'm not likin' this guy much.

Nagheed: Why's that?

Ahva: Arrogant twerp? Devalues people? Dunno.

Nagheed: Fortunately, I don't think we'll be dealing with him much.

Ahva: Better not.

Osse gave the man a lopsided smile. "Sir, I have seen the results of those creature's actions, and I would not leave a snake in their possession if I could avoid it. Your own people must value slaves highly, as well. A rescue party met us on the way back and there was a great deal of affection for those slaves."

"A parent will miss its child even among animals." Gowon pulled out a drawstring pouch that clinked when he handled it. "We wish to give you a gift for your efforts." He tossed the pouch toward Osse.

"We acted in the interest of the children, not in the interest of our purse." Osse picked up the pouch and tossed it back.

"Money is useful for many things." Gowon threw the pouch closer to Osse. "Do you not wish to know how much we are willing to pay for your service?"

Ahva couldn't decipher anything out of the man's flat tone or his stillness. No emotion showed in his face.

Nagheed: Don't play poker with this guy.

Ahva: That's it! That's why I don't like him. He makes Vulcans sound emotional.

Osse threw the pouch beyond Gowon. "It would not matter if this pouch contained the wealth of two nations. Money is helpful, but we are not mercenaries who do good works for payment."

Kwame retrieved the pouch.

"I will double the amount." Gowon twisted to the man and retrieved his purse.

Ahva hissed. "Bite fin–"

Osse covered her head with his hand. "Triple it, and then keep it. We assisted your lost ones for our own reasons and not for your money."

When he removed his hand, she hissed and made a half-hearted snipe for his finger. *Just for that, I ought to holler, "Disgusting eyeball!" at them.*

Gowon tucked his purse back into his belt and stood, bringing the other three to their feet. They bowed and touched their foreheads then returned to their horses, retrieved their weapons, mounted up, and rode off toward the caravan.

That was it? No goodbye? No offer to travel with the caravan? Maybe Osse should have taken the money after all.

Ahva waved. "Bye-bye!" *And don't come back.*

CHAPTER 32

Once they were well out of range, Osse sat more comfortably on his bedroll.

Rafayel stroked his short beard. "A test?"

Osse grimaced. "I think so. I only remember that my grandfather beat it into me once, literally, that I should never do a kind act for payment." He studied his feet. "I'm sorry I couldn't find a way to talk to you before I spoke for us both."

"You did fine, Osse. I would have told him the same." Rafayel shifted around toward Osse.

Rafayel groaned and stretched out on his bedroll. "Wake me when you tire, and I'll take the rest of the watch."

Nagheed curled up beside Rafayel.

Ahva rubbed her beak on Osse's cheek and picked up some bird XP.

* * *

Jael awoke with a headache that threatened to explode her skull. She opened her eyes a sliver in the blinding light. She listened hard, hoping for the whine of one of her cubs, but the wind rustled the grass, bugs clicked and warbled, and birds chirped. She sniffed the air.

The "burnt wood" and "cooked meat" odors still permeated the area, but the humans, the cart, and her cubs had left a trail of faint words heading further east.

The scents were fading. She had to get moving before she lost them altogether. Jael rolled and came up to her feet, which doubled the intensity of the splitting headache. She roared her frustration and heartbreak and stayed upright through determination.

Squinting in the bright sunlight, Jael sniffed at the food the humans had left behind. She found the skewers propped up against rocks around the ashes of their campfire. Jael scarfed down all she could find then staggered north. She'd find her cubs again.

* * *

Ahva perched on Osse's shoulder after another exhilarating flight around the grasslands. They weren't running into crazies, yet, and every day was the same thing. Wake up, break camp, ride for a long time while keeping the caravan in sight. Stop for a lunch of dried fruit and bread. Get back on a horse and keep riding with the caravan in sight. Stop a couple hours, game time, before sunset so Osse could go hunting for their dinner while Rafayel set up their camp. Osse stayed up to watch for the first half of the night. Rafayel watched the second half of the night. Get up a little while after the sun woke up and do it all over again. Plenty of flight time for her, which was a terrific bonus, even though the game clock was running a bit faster in this long-distance travel mode.

One nice thing about traveling parallel to the nomads was that every night, they played interesting music.

Far ahead, the nomad caravan slowed. Kids bolted to the edge of the group and shoved sticks into the ground. The sticks had flags that fluttered in the wind. Each flag showed red horse rearing back on a white background.

Rafayel held up his hand and pulled his horse to a stop. "They're stopping for the day."

Osse dismounted and readied his bow. "I'll hunt down

dinner."

"Wait. Someone's coming." Rafayel climbed down from his horse. "A single rider."

"Hellooo!" Ahva waved first one wing then the other. *They'd better be friendlier.*

Osse went around to join Rafayel. "That's a good sign."

"You mean they may actually trust us now?"

"We'll see." Osse smiled and set his bow down.

The rider stopped a short distance away from the group but stayed on his horse. He was about Osse's age and armed with a sword strapped to his back.

Khin May snickered. If that wasn't a short sword, he'd have to unbelt it to draw it. Bad design. His clothes were the same dark gray robe over white pants and tunic as the other caravan visitors, but with a bright green belt that covered from his ribs to his hip bones.

"I bring greetings from the elders. I am Khal."

Ahva scooted around to the back of Osse's collar.

He bowed and touched his forehead and then introduced himself and Rafayel – still using his middle names. Osse stepped forward. "What brings you?"

"We travel on the trade routes to Fola." He pointed east. "If you go the same way, our elders advise that you seek safety in the company of your father's people and leave this foreigner and his cursed pets to handle his own affairs."

"You would have me abandon my friend? There are insane killers roaming the countryside." Osse took in the whole prairie with a sweep of his hand. "What manner of friend would I be to leave Michael to their designs? It's hard enough minding the camp with the two of us and our animals for sentries."

Khal leaned forward. "What good is it to risk your own life for one such as him?"

Osse's back straightened. "He has taken care of me when I was injured, treated me with respect the entire time I've known him, and endangered himself to rescue three of your children. Are these the acts of a man I should now betray for an off-chance of improving my own safety? Go back to your elders and tell them to offer me no more insults." His last words were clipped.

He spun away from the rider and returned to Nagheed and Rafayel.

Ahva chose Posture from her skills. She fluffed up and shrieked. "Disgus —"

Osse covered her head with his hand and muttered, "Ahva, don't rile them up."

Because you were tact and diplomacy personified, right?

The rider wheeled his horse around and galloped away.

Osse blew out a breath and glanced back over his shoulder. "I hope I read that right."

Rafayel snickered. "Your own people? You're no more of that tribe than I am."

"No, I'm not."

"And 'cursed pets?' I know many Nethanyans are superstitious about odd-eyed animals, but nomads, too?"

"Yes, some are. And Ahva is solid black, which makes her evil by default. It looks like the best we can hope for from this caravan is that I get an invite. You might get an invite. The animals? No. They're bad luck."

Rafayel nodded. "I say it's all or nothing. I'm not keen to leave such wonderful companions to fend for themselves."

"I agree." Osse picked up his bow. "I'll go try to catch us

CHAPTER 32

some dinner or we'll be having jerky and hard tack."

"If it gets too late, then we'll eat from our provisions." Rafayel clapped him on the shoulder. "You've done so well hunting in the last week, we aren't using our dried provisions at half the rate I anticipated."

Osse smiled and looked down. "I'll see what I can find in the area."

Rafayel started unloading the horses while Osse nocked an arrow. Ahva flew a circle over his head to keep watch for hazards and help with locating dinner.

Osse padded across the prairie, keeping the light wind in their faces, which her VR rig made an effort to translate for her. Something moved in the grass ahead of them. Osse twisted but didn't shoot.

"I have no interest in skinning a rat, Ahva," he muttered.

Tastes like chicken?

"Osse, more riders!" Rafayel's voice was distinctive but faint.

Ahva glanced back over her shoulder at Rafayel standing on the near edge of the camp with his hands cupped around his mouth.

As he turned back toward camp, Osse couched his bow and waved one arm way over his head. "I guess we're having hard tack and jerky for dinner, Ahva."

Six of one, eight minus two of the other to me.

Osse sighed. "Y'know, I almost liked it better when the nomads ignored us."

When they reached the camp, Osse set his bow aside then sat on his bedroll.

Two riders were galloping toward them. As they came closer, Ahva recognized one as that disagreeable twit Khal and the other as the equally irritating old leader Gowon.

"What do you think about this group?" Rafayel nodded toward the approaching nomads.

Osse kept his eyes on the riders. "I think either we're about to get an apology, or I'm going to be chastised for refusing their offer. Most likely the latter."

Twenty meters from the camp, both horses stopped. The riders dismounted and set swords and bows aside before coming closer. Nagheed sat next to Rafayel and panted, which probably got him some dog XP.

Gowon and Khal approached. Osse bowed and touched his forehead then gestured for them to be seated. The two nomads sat on their heels.

"I wanted to be sure my grandson delivered the message faithfully. We are extending our hospitality to you." Gowon gestured toward the caravan.

Osse nodded. "To me, but not my friend, and clearly not to Ahva and Nagheed, or did I misunderstand?"

"You would be much safer in the caravan."

Ahva squinted at them. "Fierce!"

-20 XP floated up.

"Knock it off, Ahva." Osse muttered as he covered her head with his hand. "I completely agree. Traveling with numbers is far safer than traveling alone, and that's why I will not abandon my friend. You, yourself, have encountered the laughing killers loose on these plains. You would have me be disloyal to my friend and leave him to an almost certain death. What good am I as a man if even my friends can't trust me? No, until the invitation extends to my friend and our companions, I cannot accept."

"As you wish. We will not bring bad luck into our camp."

CHAPTER 32

Gowon rose and led Khal back to their horses.

They collected their gear, mounted up, and rode off.

Ahva picked Posture and fluffed up and hissed.

Once they were out of earshot, Rafayel nodded. "We're still safer if we camp close to them. We'll be their shadow."

"The leader had a horn on his belt." Osse patted his belt. "He'll use it to signal the caravan if there's trouble. That'll give us a warning."

"Good." Rafayel reached for his saddlebag and fished out some food. "Three potatoes, bit of jerky, and some hard tack. Sound good?"

"All right."

Ahva crouched and leapt into the air. She had enough light for one more patrol.

* * *

The sheep batted a balloon around until it popped. Nagheed awoke and lifted his head. His human measured out some powder and poured it into the barrel of his pistol, then he put a piece of cloth in his mouth for a moment before placing it over the barrel. He selected a ball from a pouch and used the ramrod to push the ball and cloth into the gun. Finally, he added a small measure of powder to the flash pan and closed the lid on it. He tucked the pistol into his belt and looped his leather gloves over the flash pan.

Nagheed had watched the care and feeding of the flintlock almost daily, and so far, it hadn't gotten old. In fact, if the AI were doing it correctly, Jake could probably load a real one himself now. The sun was already up and Ahva and Osse were missing, probably trying their luck at catching breakfast.

He stopped to listen to the music. Once they'd crossed into Bakhar, the RenFaire selections had gone away in favor of a very Middle Eastern sounding tune in a minor key with a flute, string instruments, and drums. As much as he'd liked the RenFaire tunes, the selection for traveling in Bakhar was fun.

When it started over, he stood and inspected their surroundings.

About fifty meters away, the caravan was inert. Even the sentries impersonated statues.

Osse returned with a smallish gazelle-like creature over his shoulder.

"Good shot!" Rafayel helped Osse dress the game.

"I thought I was going to have to argue with a lion." Osse drew his knife.

"Lion?"

"A male lion was stalking gazelles. When the gazelles bolted, I let him take the first pick, and I picked a different straggler."

Rafayel smirked. "Prudent."

By the time they'd started eating their barbecued gazelle, the caravan had come to life. Kids ran around the collecting perimeter flags, and a single horn blast started them on the way.

"Bye-bye!" Ahva lifted one wing.

Osse chuckled. "We'll catch up."

Ahva: Are we there yet?
Nagheed: No.
Ahva: Are we there yet?
Nagheed: No.

CHAPTER 32

Ahva: Are we there yet?

Nagheed: No.

Ahva: Are we there yet?

Nagheed: Are you imitating an annoying younger sibling or is this from a vintage movie?

Ahva: Not that vintage, but definitely a movie.

Nagheed: How did it end?

Ahva: With a knife. Fortunately, birds don't have fingers.

Nagheed: What?

Ahva: Another movie for you to see. Seriously. I'll have to send you a list.

Nagheed caught pieces of gazelle that Rafayel tossed his way while Ahva tore strips of meat off the piece Osse gave her, and the humans ate theirs off the bones.

"Are we in any danger from that lion you saw?" Rafayel asked around a mouthful of meat.

Osse shook his head. "He brought down a good-sized gazelle, and he appeared to be healthy. If we leave him alone, he should leave us alone."

"How far we from Fola?" Rafayel asked.

"Not sure. A day? Maybe two? I haven't seen the map in Kamali's City Hall in a while, but I don't think the distance from Kamali to Fola was much different than the distance between Fola and the Nethanyan border. Although shadowing the caravan is a little slower than going forward alone, we're still moving faster than I did on foot."

When they were down to hide, bones, and entrails, they doused the fire and packed up camp. In the distance, a horn sounded a long note. Ahva kicked off from Osse's shoulder and flew on ahead.

Ahva: Back in a bit.

Nagheed: Careful out there. You did mention finding maniac birds earlier, and there's not much for trees to get one to face-plant into.

Ahva: You had to remind me of that.

Nagheed: You're welcome.

Nagheed trotted ahead of the humans on their horses and sniffed. The wind blowing in from the west carried scent words in pale gray for Osse, Rafayel, horses, and Ahva. Much fainter, multiple copies of "gazelle" in different fonts and a "male lion" had roamed the area.

No sign of maniacs, so Nagheed waited then trotted alongside Rafayel.

Osse shielded his eyes with his hand. "I think that's Ahva."

"And she's coming fast." Rafayel stood in the saddle and peeked through the gaps between his fingers. "Let's meet her on the way."

Nagheed crouched. When the humans urged the horses into a gallop, he pushed off and came up to full speed in a few strides.

As they closed the distance, they slowed, and Osse offered his arm. Ahva changed from full-time flapping to gliding. She dove below the level of Osse's arm then arced upward and, shedding speed, dropped gracefully onto his wrist.

Nagheed panted, which restored a few fatigue points while walked alongside his human.

"Problem?" Osse held Ahva up at eye level.

Ahva impersonated the maniac's laugh.

Rafayel pointed. "Smoke ahead."

"The caravan?" Osse asked.

CHAPTER 32

"Yes. Big trouble." Ahva bobbed her head and imitated the maniac's laugh. "Lots of them."

"Will they accept help from us?" Rafayel asked.

Osse scowled at the smoke curling up from the horizon. "In the moment, they might, or we might find ourselves fighting two battles at once."

Rafayel frowned. "Let's get close enough to observe, at least. We'll interfere if we're needed or asked. Otherwise, there were several able men in that caravan."

They headed out at a faster pace than usual but nothing like emergency response speeds. The smoke rising ahead dwindled to wisps and changed color from inky black to the palest gray.

A few kilometers later, they crested a ridge and found the caravan. The wagons were nothing but smoldering skeletons. People were scurrying around like ants in a disturbed hill. Some tended the injured. Others put out the fires. A few were herding wailing kids into a larger group. A mounted man with a spear galloped toward them.

"We're about to get blamed for this." Osse sighed.

Rafayel twisted toward him. "We weren't even–"

The rider came within spear throwing range. "Came to see the results of your evil?"

"Evil?" Osse rode a few steps closer and stopped. "We've done nothing to your caravan except rescue 3 girls and 3 horses. That's what you call evil?"

"We didn't ask you for any help. We offered you hospitality, and you repay us like this?" He pointed at the wrecked caravan with his spear.

Ahva fluffed up and hissed.

"No, you didn't offer us hospitality." He pointed to

himself and Rafayel. "You offered me hospitality." He pointed to his own chest. "Now you see why I couldn't abandon my friend."

"Less than a day from Fola, and you brought those things on us! Your evil bird led them straight our way." He lifted his arm as if to throw his spear.

Rafayel drew his pistol. "Don't. I'm a remarkable shot at this range."

Ahva scooted around to the back of Osse's collar.

Ahva: Outta sight. Outta his mind.

Osse nodded. "Those creatures didn't come from our direction, which means Ahva had nothing to do with leading them to you."

"Didn't hurt you. Go 'way or bite fingers!" Ahva peeked out from behind Osse and fluffed up. "Fierce!"

"Your cursed mutt and that black bird brought bad luck to us because you stayed so close to our shadow," the rider continued. "While one of the creatures rounded up people into cages on a horseless cart, the other four ran around the caravan killing people, mortally wounding others, and setting fire to the wagons."

Osse nodded. "That's same pattern used against my village."

"So you knew about them and still lived in our shadow? We lost half our people and most of our provisions. You brought your bad luck to us!"

"I'm saddened by what happened here." Osse patted his bag. "I'm an herbalist. I can help you treat your wounded."

"No. Bring us no more of your help. Be gone or I'll kill you now." He raised his spear.

As Rafayel aimed his pistol, Nagheed stepped forward and

CHAPTER 32

chose Posture from his skill list. He bristled up and growled. That gave the nomad a very serious frown emoji for morale.

"Hold, Nagheed," Rafayel said.

"Hold" was not "out" so Nagheed stood his ground and growled.

"That was an offer of help, not a threat." Osse's clipped words carried a hard edge. "If you don't want our help, we'll move on. It's no harder than that." He turned his horse and led the way east. Rafayel followed. Nagheed stayed behind with hackles raised, ready for a fight until the nomad rode back to the caravan. When he was back with his own kind, Nagheed jogged and caught up to his human.

Osse blew out a breath. "I understand their superstitions about bad luck, but honestly, I thought we stayed far enough away."

"And how could Ahva lead the attackers to them? They came from opposite directions." Rafayel rolled his eyes. "In any case, they refused our help. They'll have to do for themselves."

Osse shrugged. "Wish they'd let us do something."

"As do I, but they've made their choice." Rafayel sighed. "Even if we had a pile of provisions to leave them, they'd likely ignore it or destroy it for fear that our 'bad luck' will curse them further."

"At least we know we're less than a day from Fola."

Rafayel nodded. "That's something. Stay alert for more maniacs, and let's find out how early we can get there."

As Ahva left on another scouting flight, Nagheed darted several steps ahead and sniffed around.

Chapter 33

Fola was exactly how Ahva remembered it. Exactly. Like, she wouldn't be surprised if all the NPC extras were in the same locations as when she left. It was a little creepy, actually. Didn't they have lives? Weren't there other players?

Ahva: Know something weird that I've noticed?

Nagheed: That you can't go more than ten consecutive seconds without a chat?

Ahva: No, silly. Sometimes I go an entire minute and a half. Before you ran into me did you encounter any other players?

Nagheed: Now that you mention it, no. Running into you was the first time the chat window appeared on its own. You?

Ahva: I ran into a bear. When I tried to chat the bear, she told me her name was Jael. Never anything else, mind you, but her name was Jael. I don't know if that means she's a player or not. Are we, like, the only two players in the game?

Nagheed: Doubtful. There'd be a whole pile of playtesters, wouldn't there?

**Ahva: This late in the beta testing, sure. Then where is

CHAPTER 33

everybody?

Nagheed: Beats me. Maybe the AI is running several parallel worlds. Or, this planet is huge and everybody is on a different continent.

Ahva: Wow. That would be a nightmare to keep up with.

Nagheed: It'd probably be easier than trying to keep up with several thousand people in one place. You'd have to track their interactions and remember who hates whom and all that junk. Much simpler this way, I think.

Ahva: Maybe.

As they passed through the gate, they found the street preachers out in force. A crowd had gathered around all but the creepy one nearest the gate.

"You heard me! Atrac and her priestess laugh at you!" The preacher laughed, a barely passable imitation of one of the maniacs.

Ahva provided the correction for her.

The preacher glared at Ahva. "They laugh at you all. You cannot survive the coming onslaught of her army! Even those she has rejected as imperfect will wash over you like raging water over a sandcastle, leaving behind nothing but blood and corpses. Those few, those precious few she deems worthy will be given the chance to become her new creations! They alone will fill this world. You cannot prevail. Atrac and her priestess will laugh at you all!" She cackled again, and the loop restarted.

Ahva hissed. "Not new for her."

"What do you mean?" Rafayel turned toward her.

"Same words. Different day." Ahva fluffed up and shook, earning a few bird XP.

"The same four street preachers." Osse pointed to

each one. "As near as I can tell, they're using the same speeches."

"Yes. No different." Ahva bobbed her head.

Not far past the street preachers, they found a stable where they secured lodging for their horses and arranged for a farrier to work on the horseshoes. With their saddlebags and other equipment in hand, they headed out into the city.

The notebook turned blue. Ahva opened it.

A Place to Lay My Head. Find an inn.

Ahva: *snicker* There's a quest to find an inn. What? Is there a convention in town or something?

Nagheed: Maybe they have an aversion to animals.

"You've been here, haven't you?" Rafayel asked.

"Right. I made my pilgrimage here, ran a bunch of errands, acquired Ahva, and then headed for home." Osse preened Ahva's head, restoring a few fatigue points. "That seems so long ago now."

"I know what you mean. Let's find an inn. We can leave the bulk of our things there and take care of our errands."

Osse pointed down the street. "The place I stayed before wasn't fancy, but it was nice. We can try there, if you'd like."

"Sounds perfect to me."

Ahva whistled a tune while they traveled. **+10 XP** glittered in the air. She didn't remember the inn from the first visit, but then again Osse had stayed with her the night before they'd left. He led them to The Bubble and Squeak.

As soon as they entered, the innkeeper turned red in the face. "Out! Out! You're not bringing those things in here!"

"Things?" Rafayel asked.

CHAPTER 33

"That black bird and your odd-eyed dog. Get them out. Now."

They stepped back out to the street.

Osse closed the door with some gusto. "I'm sorry. I didn't have Ahva with me the last time I was here. I stayed that last night with the bird merchant."

"There are other inns. We'll find one." Rafayel waved his hand dismissively.

Ahva took off from Osse shoulder and flew down the street. When she found another inn, The Four's Alehouse, she made note of it and returned to Osse. "Look at the bird!"

Osse smiled. "Lead on, Ahva."

Ahva led the humans to the place she'd found then fluttered back down to Osse's arm.

When they slipped through the door, the innkeeper approached them. "I'm afraid you can't bring those in here."

"I promise you they won't cause trouble." Rafayel assured him.

He petted Nagheed's head. "I'm sure they won't, but my wife will sneeze her head off."

Osse stepped forward. "Can you tell us a place where we can bring them?"

"My cousin doesn't mind animals that mind their owners. He might ask you to hide the bird, though. He's not superstitious, but some of his patrons are. His place is The Beer Hug. You'll find it across from the north entrance to the market."

"Thank you." Rafayel looked north.

They found the marketplace couple blocks away then followed the perimeter around until they saw a sign for The Beer Hug and stepped inside to find the standard tavern art.

Ahva: Haven't we been here before?

Nagheed: In every town we stopped in.

Ahva: They need to pay their art department.

Nagheed: Enh, these inns aren't that important. Maybe they've got the good art in the endgame.

Ahva: One can only hope.

Beaming a huge smile, the innkeeper darted across the room, deliberately placing himself between Osse and the rest of the patrons. "And how can I help you gentlemen?"

"Room and board for the duration of our stay in Fola. At least one night, possibly two or three." Rafayel patted Nagheed's side. "I assure you, our animals are well-behaved."

"I don't mind animals if they mind you. But you'll need to keep the crow out of sight. Many of my countrymen are not fond of dark birds. Bad omen, so they say."

"She can ride in my bag when we're passing through the main room. Will that work?" Osse flipped the lid of his bag open.

Ahva: You notice he didn't ask me.

Nagheed: The tribulations of being your size.

"Yes." Ahva crawled down Osse's doublet, using the rings for beak and footholds and settled inside.

Ahva: Seek and go hide. Seek and go hide.

The innkeeper snorted. "That's funny. As long as she's out of sight in the company of my other patrons, that's fine."

"And Nagheed?" Rafayel asked.

"Isn't he handsome. I don't get many Nethanyans or nomad merchants here, so an odd-eyed dog should not be a problem. You can have room seven. Fourth door on the left." The innkeeper jingled something several times. "Room and board will be twenty chips a night for the whole lot of you."

Rafayel counted out chips that clacked. "Once I figure out the rest of our plans, I'll settle the remainder, but that should suffice for tonight."

"That'll do fine."

The notebook turned blue. Mission accomplished!

Ahva listened for the door to open and close before she stuck her head out the side of the bag under the flap for a moment.

Ahva: And we've teleported back to Tel Caperna.

Nagheed: There are certain similarities.

Ahva: All the way down to the wood grain. The bed quilts, though. Those are different.

Nagheed: Wasn't paying that much attention to them.

Ahva: Log cabin quilts in Tel Caperna. Double wedding rings here.

Nagheed: I'll have to take your word for it.

They dropped off their saddlebags then headed back out. When the crowd noise got louder, Ahva assumed they were back in the great room, but she didn't peek. Osse twisted and turned as he threaded his way through the crowd.

Ahva: Lots of people all of a sudden?

Nagheed: Bunches. They must've come out of the woodwork.

Ahva: Literally.

Their movement stopped.

"Excuse me. Can you tell me if there is a temple to Tsidkenu in town?" Rafayel asked.

"I think so." The innkeeper sounded close. "Not a

follower, myself, but I hear tell there's one on the east side of town somewhere near the gate. I'm sure you can't miss it."

"Thank you. We'll be back later this evening."

When Osse started moving again, Ahva listened for a door to open and close. After the faintest squeak, the noise level suddenly dropped.

Osse flipped open the lid on his bag. "Come on out."

She crawled back up to his shoulder and fluffed up her feathers and shook like her budgies did, picking up some bird XP and filling the air with a dense cloud of feather dust.

They continued to follow marketplace perimeter around until they found the east entrance then turned ninety degrees and headed for the outer wall. A block away from the market, they found a tall, narrow building that had Tsidkenu's symbol etched into the door.

The door opened as they approached, and a man in delicately embroidered robes gestured for them to come in. "Welcome! Welcome, august travelers through our bountiful land of milk and honey."

And maniacs. Don't forget maniacs.

He continued. "May the ever copious and profuse grace of our glorious lord and savior Tsidkenu rest eternally upon your redeemed souls throughout this life and the next and may his magnanimous and inexhaustible graciousness flow in a never-ending stream from your own richly blessed life to all around you bringing his cornucopian and vast peace unto the whole unredeemed world."

Ahva: Wow. Laying it on a bit thick?
Nagheed: What gave you that idea?
Ahva: He forgot the next part. "And help us continue

our ministry by donating ninety-eight percent of all your income. You will be blessed in the next life." Or something like that.

Nagheed: Ninety-eight percent? You slacker. You're supposed to send everything.

Ahva: This is one of the enlightened televangelists.

Rafayel smiled. "My friend and I are on our way to Ilion to neutralize the threat that has been plaguing Bakhar and Nethanya. I was wondering if you might spare a few minutes to discuss the quest with us. We could certainly use a bit of wisdom in our endeavor."

"You're naturally making a clear reference to our brilliantly glowing Ilionite kinsmen?" The priest leaned closer.

Ahva: Don't know if I'd want to claim any kind of kinship to those wackos.

Nagheed: Speaking figuratively?

Ahva: I figure so.

Rafayel nodded. "The same, though I've never heard them called that."

"I do indeed have a word of grace and wisdom from our great and generous lord explicitly for no other weary soul but your very own." The priest beamed a smile full of whiter than white teeth. "However, before I can even remotely consider disseminating the beneficent verbiage proclaimed to me for the singular benefit of yourself, I require the specialized need for well-armed and -armored men such as yourselves to execute a critically important errand for me first."

Ahva: What do you think? Fetch or escort?

Nagheed: Fetch. Definitely fetch.

Ahva: That would be handy. You're pretty good at fetch.

"Very well. What's the quest?" Rafayel rested his hand on his rapier hilt.

"Proximate to this metropolis, north to be precise, rubble exists of a miniscule hamlet." The priest pointed. "In that flotsam, you will locate a tome. I have a dire need for that tome. If you retrieve that book in my stead, I will convey the efficacious information I have for you."

Ahva shook her head. *Wow. Someone take this guy's thesaurus away.*

"How far north of town?" Rafayel glanced that way.

The priest shrugged. "Not far. Were the ruins of the hamlet closer, we would exist in contiguous spaces. Half-hour at most."

"We'll be back directly."

When the notebook icon turned blue, Ahva opened it.

What's the Word? Fetch the book from the ruins north of town.

Ahva: You're right. Fetch quest.

Nagheed: I win! So far, they're all fetch quests.

Ahva: Nope. I had an escort earlier. Fairly detailed one, actually. And we did escort that baroness' cousin.

Nagheed: Enh, escort quests are just fetches with living objects.

Ahva: *snerk* You are not wrong.

The priest showed them out. "May our resplendent and exalted lord Tsidkenu bless your brief but victorious travels and protect you, keeping you safe and protected at all times and in all modes in his impregnable embrace."

The door closed behind them.

"Are we going to get our horses?" Osse aimed his thumb toward the city gate they came through.

CHAPTER 33

"No, I don't think so. By the time we hike all the way to the south gate, collect our horses, and then come all way back over here, we could have been there and back again. I could use the stroll. Could you?"

Osse nodded. "I hiked from Fola to Yavne by way of Kamali and Vanya. I'm sure I can handle thirty minutes north of Fola."

They headed east to the gate. Like the southern gate, several people were set up as a sort of minimarket and a few street preachers were trying to outshout each other, including one from Ilion who worked from the same script as the southern gate preacher. They turned north and started hiking.

Osse glanced back toward Fola. "About that priest."

"He was something, wasn't he?" Rafayel chuckled.

"You see many of that type?" Osse asked.

"Thankfully, no. I think he might base his piety on his word count."

Osse frowned. "Then, do we really want the information he has for us?"

"I don't know." Rafayel shrugged. "On the one hand, I think it might be as frivolous as everything else that comes out of his mouth. On the other hand–"

Ahva: There are five more fingers.

" – Sometimes wisdom comes from the mouth of a fool," he finished.

"I suppose."

"Besides, there might be something worthwhile at the ruins themselves." Rafayel indicated the ruins with the twitch of his head.

Osse snorted. "I had nothing else to do this afternoon."

They hiked in silence for a while. The terrain around them was the grassland that extended between Fola and Kamali.

Ahva: You wonder where the quarry is that all the rock came from?

Nagheed: What rock?

Ahva: To build the city. I mean, the whole city is made out of rocks. Big, hulking rocks. They had to come from somewhere. I'm just wondering where the quarry is.

Nagheed: In the artists' source file?

Ahva: Don't be a nooge. I mean within the game, you knucklehead.

Nagheed: Do you think they planned it that carefully?

Ahva: A girl can hope. I'll be disappointed if they didn't.

She kicked off from Osse's shoulder and flew a spiral over them until she had gained some altitude then she headed more directly north. A quarry should be visible from the distance, right? A big hole in the ground was not exactly easy to hide. She'd been flying for a few minutes when she spotted a rock outcropping. She veered to the left and went closer. Stone discs were arranged like collapsed dominoes. A stone wall was still impressive in some parts but collapsed in others. In the center, there was a large stone platform and a raised dais.

Ahva: I found it!

Nagheed: The quarry?

Ahva: No, silly. The ruins. No sign of the quarry.

She looped around and headed back.

As she drew closer, Osse held up his arm.

Ahva spiraled down and gracefully landed on his arm. "Come on!"

"Did you find it?" Osse held her up at eye level. "You know where the ruins are?"

She bobbed her head. "Yes. Yes. This way! Close now."

"Are we headed the right way?"

"Almost." She leaned to her right, his left.

They adjusted their course slightly.

"Good bird." Ahva turned around to face forward.

They traveled along in silence for another bit.

The ruins appeared ahead of them, looking hazy and indistinct at first, but gaining clarity as they come closer.

Ahva: Poof! There it is.

Even though there was a hole in the wall significantly closer than the gate, they still made for what was intended to be the actual entrance to the ruins. When they passed through where the gate should've been, a path led further north with a couple side streets into a rundown neighborhood. The houses, though small, were in states of disrepair ranging from "this could be workable with a renovation" to "bulldoze and start over" all the way down to "was there something here?" Rafayel veered off on one of the smaller side streets into the right-hand neighborhood. After checking out a couple spots that were really nothing more than the crumbling foundation, if that, they picked a way through the debris to one of the places that might have dealt with a nice renovation.

The front door of the place was gone. Rafayel knocked on the doorframe and leaned inside. "Is anyone here?"

Ahva: Nobody here but spiders and cobwebs.

They stepped inside and gave themselves the quick nickel tour. The skeletal framework of a couch and armchair filled the front room. While Nagheed was sniffing around, he stopped and suddenly backed up.

Nagheed: Huh. Interesting.

Ahva: Oh? Whatcha got?

Nagheed: There's an actual gold coin back here.

Ahva: Real money? You gotta be kidding me.

Nagheed: No joke.

Ahva: Ooookay. Kind of like finding money in the couch cushions. Think this city used to be a crossbreed neighborhood?

Nagheed: Possibly, but we're not even close to Ilion yet. Weird.

Ahva: But strange. Odd, and yet still unusual. Mind blown. Brains everywhere.

Nagheed: That'll make the zombies happy.

Ahva: They don't seem to be that kind of zombie.

Nagheed sat and whined until Rafayel came over.

"What did you find?" he asked.

After glancing up at him, Nagheed pawed the gold coin.

Rafayel leaned over and picked it up.

"What is it?" Osse asked.

"If I'm not mistaken, it's gold. An ancient coin, to be precise. This is all supposed to be in some stronghold somewhere in Ilion."

Osse smirked. "They missed a piece."

Rafayel tucked it into his bag. "All the better for us."

They entered the kitchen, which was laid out like any average house. There were counters that ringed the walls, leaving spaces for a stove, a sink, and a refrigerator.

Osse approached the refrigerator. When he tugged on the door, it fell off one hinge and hung at a wonky angle. "What do you think this is?"

CHAPTER 33

Rafayel scratched his head. "Storage for valuables? Hiding place?"

Valuables. Like snackage.

They went from there into a large bedroom. As soon as they crossed the threshold, the edges of her vision turned red.

Ahva: Oh boy. Here we go.

Nagheed: There had to be something.

The closet door to the right squeaked open. Two creatures dubbed Resident staggered out. Unlike the laughing maniacs they had run into all over the continent, these two had little that described them as human. They resembled the undead skeletons of most role-playing games combined with a construction site disaster. The skeletal structures were made from metal tubing and wire. There was no rib cage. The spine was articulated, but not nearly as much as a normal human. The heads did resemble real skulls made out of rusted steel. The eyes glowed, but that glow flickered often, like an old fluorescent light with a bad ballast. The pair wobbled a couple steps forward. Further away, two other closet doors creaked open.

Nagheed darted forward and pounced on the nearest Resident. Knocking it into the floor turned into a mannequin.

Ahva: Did we stumble into a newbie zone?

Nagheed: These are here to lull us into a false sense of complacency. Just wait. The fun stuff comes later.

Ahva: Maybe. Or maybe I was supposed to tackle this ruin and this errand when I first started here.

Nagheed: If so, walkthrough for us. I wouldn't count on that, though.

Osse pulled his mace off his belt and clocked the second

Resident. It, also, didn't survive one blow.

Rafayel ran down the hall with his sword in hand. Ahva followed him. Two other Residents stumbled to the doors of their respective rooms. These two were half the height of the other two.

Ahva: We have mommy, daddy, and two kids.

Nagheed: I'm not as surprised as I should be. Everything we've seen here so far suggested a family home.

Ahva: Four zombie cyborgs who want the middle-class American dream. It'd make a great sitcom. You know what a sitcom is, right?

Nagheed: Yes...

Ahva: There's hope for you yet!

Nagheed and Osse ran out of the bigger room and joined them.

Ahva: You guys be careful. This narrow corridor is going to create some friendly fire type incidents.

Nagheed: You think you can get one of them to follow you back into the room it came out of?

Ahva: I can try that.

Rafayel took the last two steps into range of the nearest mini-resident and bell punched it in the face. The mini resident collapsed backwards and kicked the bucket.

Nagheed pranced from foot to foot behind Rafayel, who blocked the narrow hallway. Osse, likewise, queued up behind Nagheed. Ahva zoomed over everybody's head and ducked through the door into the room the last resident was coming out of.

"Come 'ere, little monster." Ahva imitated the maniac's laughter.

It awkwardly pivoted and took a step toward Ahva.

CHAPTER 33

When Rafayel stepped into the room, he used his momentum to deliver a bell punch to the back of its head. As soon as it collapsed into random parts then formed a mannequin, the red edge faded. She circled the room a few times before zipping out the door and landing on Osse's shoulder.

Rafayel checked the mannequin from the last resident while Osse stepped into the other room and checked the other mini-resident.

Ahva: Melted plastic thingy, crystal, battery.

Nagheed: We must need a trainload of these things at some point.

Ahva: That or the designers figured people would leave them behind or chuck them after finding out these things don't sell. Good thing they don't weigh much.

They backtracked to the larger bedroom and checked out the other two residents. In addition to the usual assortment, one had been carrying a palm sized device that had both a miniature keyboard and a screen.

Ahva: Oh look. Smart phone. Think we have cell reception?

Nagheed: Doubtful. I haven't seen any cell towers, have you?

Ahva: Have you ever been to Phoenix?

Nagheed: No. Why?

Ahva: They disguise their cell towers as palm trees.

Nagheed: Cute, but I don't think they did that here.

Ahva: Yeah, and without a second one, who ya gonna call? Ghostbusters?

Nagheed: What? Never mind. I want to know where it was hiding the thing? They don't exactly have pockets.

Ahva: Don't ask questions you don't want the answer

to.

The other mannequin contained the usual and a slip of paper with writing on it.

Nagheed: What's it say?

Ahva: $F_n = F_{n-1} + F_{n-2}$, $n > 1$ **Ooo, that's familiar. Where have I seen that? I know that. If I can remember why I know that, we'd be in good shape.**

Nagheed: No cheating.

Ahva: I am not going to go check a search engine. Wish I could do a search engine on my brain, though. I really have seen that before or something kinda like it.

Nagheed: It'll come to you when you start thinking about something else.

Ahva: Yeah, like at four the next morning.

All the loot went into Osse's or Rafayel's pack before they left the trashed house. A cursory search through the rest of the ruins on the right side of the main entrance turned up more of the same. The area left of the entrance also turned up a few residents who were none too happy about the home invasion but couldn't put up much of a fight. Among the loot, they turned up another an old pamphlet called "The Use of Mathematical Patterns as Passcodes." The inside of the pamphlet was warped and faded, but the equation from the other resident was mostly there along with the separate heading for "Binary" something and "Skip Patterns."

Their next stop was a huge, flat area on the west side of town that had nothing left but foundations. They continued around to another housing area that took up the whole north side of the ruins. These houses were larger but in no better repair. In fact, second stories had crumbled down into first stories rendering the whole place impassable. The few that had survived enough to enter had obviously fallen prey to previous visitors. What was left of furniture had been flipped around or torn apart. They encountered no residents.

The east side of town was a dead-on match for the west. Foundations and nothing else. That left the center of town, a flat area with the dais in the center. Pillars around the dais had collapsed like dominoes.

As they ascended into the outer platform, Khin May tensed, which made Ahva's feathers all stand on end.

Ahva: This place gives me the willies.

Nagheed: Don't worry. If something comes at us, the combat music will start.

Ahva: Combat music? Ugh. Turned off all music a looong time ago. Bleck.

Nagheed: Seriously? I'd've thought you'd be all over it. Ever since we entered the ruins, it's been a techno version of a classical piece. It's cool stuff!

Ahva: I'll take your word for it.

Rafayel picked his way through the debris to the edge of the dais, which was shoulder height on him. "What do you make of this?"

Ahva: A brooch, pin, pterodactyl.

Nagheed: What?

Ahva: I picked the wrong week to stop sniffing glue.

Nagheed: What are you talking about?

Ahva: A vintage movie your life is tragically incomplete for not seeing.

Osse joined him. "Why would there be numbers in order on the wall?"

The numbers zero through nine were arranged like a

standard keypad. Next to the keypad, there was a small, cracked screen.

Ahva: Because we're going to have to enter a code that has something to do with that formula the resident was carrying.

Nagheed: Remember what that formula is yet?

Ahva: No, it's going to drive me crazy. Short trip.

Nagheed: So I gather.

Ahva: You have no idea.

Rafayel fished the paper out of his pocket. "Something to do with this, maybe?"

"Possibly." Osse looked at the paper then at the keypad. "I can't imagine what else it would be good for."

They continued around until they found a short run of steps on the north side of the dais.

Ahva: Betcha walking up the steps to the dais triggers something.

Nagheed: No bet.

Instead of taking the steps up, Osse and Rafayel continued the circuit around the dais then returned to the steps after finding nothing that exciting. The two humans filed up the narrow steps with Nagheed following.

Ahva: Hold on to your butts.

She waited for the top of the dais to open and spewed forth legions of unpleasant things, but they made it to the top of the dais without anything really happening.

Ahva: Seriously?

Nagheed: I should've taken that bet.

On the top of the dais, there were evenly spaced holes in the rock forming conjoined rectangles, if you assumed there was a wall around the edge of the dais.

CHAPTER 33

Ahva: Zoo? Jail?

Nagheed: I vote jail before zoo, but maybe? I mean those are spaced about right to have been bars.

Rafayel took another step forward. The floor clicked under his weight as if he'd triggered something, and a warbling, pathetic-sounding alarm rang out from somewhere below them.

Chapter 34

Ahva tensed when the middle of the dais floor slid open unevenly about half a meter on the right side and a bit less than that on the left. The mechanism grounded to a halt with a grating metal sound. Loud whirs and clanks came from the opening. The edge of Ahva's vision turned red.

Ahva: Not good. Not good at all. Definitely bad.

Nagheed: Something's coming. Remember that code yet? I'm betting that'll turn them off if you tap it into the keypad.

Ahva: Let me think. Let me think. Let me think. Come on brain. Why do I know that equation?

Nagheed: I don't know. But math is not my thing. I've only been taking history and English classes at college, so far.

Ahva: That would rule out history and English, which leaves math and science.

Nagheed: What if you start trying numbers?

Ahva: Right. We don't even know how many digits are in the code. You know how many combinations of numbers you get with ten possible options for each position?

Nagheed: I'm guessing a lot.

Ahva: You guess right. Millions. Literally. Millions.

Nagheed: Maybe the computer will give you feedback if you start guessing right.

Ahva: Worth a try, anyway. Maybe after I get a couple good guesses, I'll place the rest of the pattern.

With a harsh metal-scraping-metal sound, a sphere labeled Sentinel squeezed out of the opening on the right. The sentinel was about a half-meter in diameter and made of blue-painted metal with a terrific scratch on two sides from squeezing through the tight opening. On the side of the sphere facing them, presumably the front, there was a small cylinder like a camera lens. The air beneath the sentinel shimmered like a heat mirage. It hovered midair about a meter off the ground. From the camera lens, a beam of electric blue light that moved slowly enough to see shot out and burned into the ground about a meter short of Rafayel.

The other sentinels managed to smack into the opening that wasn't wide enough to get through.

Osse shot an arrow at the Sentinel. He hit his mark, but the arrow glanced off.

First Nagheed, then Rafayel ran toward the sentinel. Ahva flew to the edge of the dais where the keypad was and leaned over. The numbers were within reach if she stretched. Ahva activated Problem Solving.

A thought bubble appeared. *"Hmm, that pamphlet said something about mathematical codes, didn't it? This civilization had science. What kind of number patterns occur in science?"*

The pamphlet had also mentioned skip patterns and binary. In science, fractals and the golden ratio were also available along with the anti-patterns of irrational numbers like pi.

She tapped the zero button. The keypad pinged and a zero appeared on the screen.

"What is she doing?" Rafayel asked.

"Who knows? I'm not sure she can help us with these things, so as long as she stays out of the way..." Osse said.

Ahva: Thanks a lot. I'm over here doing useful work, thank you very much.

Nagheed: An unsung hero.

Ahva: I'll have to supply my own music later.

She glanced back at him and hissed.

A sentinel took a potshot at Rafayel, burning a hole through his cloak while another sentinel scraped its way through the opening. The panel in the center of the sphere started to open, but got caught on some internal mechanism that clicked but allowed no further movement. Others jockeyed for position. Ahva returned her attention to the keypad.

Nagheed: Hurry up with that keypad. These things take more than one hit.

Ahva: I'm on it.

Still leaning over the side, Ahva studied at the keypad and tried to sort out which number she should try next. Problem Solving had suggested a science-based equation, those tended to start small and grow big in a hurry. She tapped the nine and got the mechanical equivalent of a Bronx cheer before the screen wiped clear. She tapped the zero again. Nine didn't work, might as well try the other end. She stretched and tapped the one. The computer pinged and set a one next to the zero. She recalled the formula. To

CHAPTER 34

define the next one, she added the previous two. The mental lightbulb came on. She tapped one again and confirmed her guess.

Ahva: I got it! It's the Fibonacci sequence.

Nagheed: The what?

That needed to be his mantra. She might have to find out how many times she could get him to say, "What?" Bonus points for extra question marks.

Ahva: The code for the keypad? It's the Fibonacci sequence. Anyway, you start with zero, then one, and then to find the next number you add the previous two and keep going as far as you like. Look it up later.

Nagheed: As long as you know what to do.

She tapped the two, then the three, then the five, eight, thirteen …

The red edge of the screen went away.

She flew back to Osse and checked everyone. Nagheed looked fine, but both Rafayel and Osse sported a few scorch marks. Rafayel checked the sentinels' mannequins one at a time and found the ubiquitous collection of crystals, batteries, and melted plastic blobs.

Rafayel stood. "Let's get off this dais before we trigger something else."

"I'm with you." Osse nodded and led the way.

They retraced their steps, taking a huge step over that chunk of the floor that had caused this mess and then headed down the stairs.

"That's the whole place." Osse took in the ruins with a sweep of his hands. "I didn't see a book, did you?"

"We missed it. Somewhere we missed it." Rafayel pointed to the front corner. "Let's start again and search methodically from the front corner to the back."

Osse set his bag down and sat. He pointed to another patch of ground across from him. "After I patch up that arm."

Ahva: No, they found it. It's the smart phone. It might be an ereader instead.

Nagheed: Maybe. How do we prove it? Neither one of us can exactly explain complex concepts like smart phones and ereaders.

Ahva: I think I can get it across if we use props.

Ahva crawled down Osse's tunic to the bag and slid in under the lid.

Osse flipped the lid up. "What are you doing?"

She clamped her beak around the edge of the smart phone and tugged backwards. "Here is book."

"I don't know what that is, Ahva, but I don't think it's a book."

She tapped the phone again. "Book!" She dug around in the bag for a moment and found a battery and picked it up and dropped it on the keypad for the smart phone. "Here is book."

"She's insistent." Rafayel smirked.

Ahva: That's because I'm right, you knucklehead.

She grabbed the edge of the smart phone and twisted her head to the left, trying to flip it over. It had too much mass to cooperate. "Turn over." She tried a couple more times, hoping her human would get the idea.

"Here, Ahva, I've got it." Osse flipped the smart phone over.

She found the ridged surface that would mark the battery door. Standing on the smart phone, she pushed against the ridges with her beak. "Open says Ahva!" Her beak skipped off the ridges a couple times, but third time it caught and popped the door open about a half of a centimeter.

"That was unexpected." Rafayel leaned closer.

Osse picked up the cell phone and slid the battery door off. Then he picked up the battery and popped it into place before sliding the door back on. The smart phone screen lit up.

Ahva: Score one for the bird.

Nagheed: Huh. The battery is even the right size.

Ahva: In the future, all devices are required to use AA.

"What do you know. She was right." Rafayel sat back.

Of course, I was right. Me are smart. I has brain.

Rafayel tipped his head to one side. "What's the book?"

Osse squinted at the screen. "Eloquent Discussion: On the Effective Utilization of Effusive Dialogue."

Rafayel picked it up and studied it then tucked it into his pocket.

Nagheed: I don't think that priest needs it.

Ahva: He may have written it.

Osse used his herbs to heal Rafayel's injuries and his own before they started the hike back to town.

As with a lot of trips, the way back felt shorter than the way out. Ahva stayed perched on Osse's shoulder and whistled the tunes on her approved list of learned sounds. By the time they reached the eastern gate of Fola, Ahva had been through the entire list of tunes twice. The crowd at the gate was not as dense as it had been earlier so they slipped through easily and made their way back to the church.

Ahva: Twenty.

Nagheed: Twenty whats?

Ahva: The number of words in his greeting. I'm gonna guess twenty. What about you?

Nagheed: Thirty.

Ahva: Bold. I like that.

When they entered the church, the priest in the extremely loud robes approached with his arms spread wide. "Most auspicious greetings to my benevolent fellow travelers in this gloriously pulchritudinous creation that Tsidkenu, our ever-munificent lord, has fabricated for our mutually beneficial use. What have you done to further his glory today?"

Ahva kept count of the words as he spoke.

Ahva: Twenty-five if you count only the first sentence. Thirty-four if you count the second. Not a bad guess.

Rafayel pulled the smart phone out of his pocket and offered it. "Here's your book. It's a little strange, but it's the only portable thing we found in the ruins that had writing on it." He pulled out the pamphlet with the codeword instructions. "Oh, and this."

The priest crept forward, and his hand shook as he reached for the smart phone, but he waved off the pamphlet. "I've heard of these, but I've never seen one. They're rumored to come from Ilion."

"The ruins were full of Ilionite artifacts. I wonder if perhaps Ilion once had a colony here in Bakhar." Rafayel suggested.

Ahva: Me? I'm wondering why a book intended for a follower of Tsidkenu is on an Ilionite device in the middle of a Bakhari ruin.

Nagheed: Remember that Ilion's "religion" isn't a religion. Not really. Maybe pre-apocalypse the religions

CHAPTER 34

weren't mostly confined to certain countries.

Ahva: Possibly. Maybe even probably.

The smart phone disappeared into a pocket of his voluminous, brilliantly colored robes. "Only Tsidkenu, our tremendous and omniscient lord, can properly answer such an astute interrogative. One of my numerous devoted disciples is from Ilion, our closest neighbor. Perhaps he can guide me through the utilization of this peculiar compendium. You have satisfactorily completed the indispensable errand I sent you on. The word I have for you is–" He leaned closer. "–Unity. Tsidkenu, in his unending wisdom, compels us to perpetually seek unity. We must not insist that others metamorphose to indulge our whims, especially those we don't comprehend. This inauspicious quest you have undertaken to change the unique people of Ilion is not in compliance with what Tsidkenu, our omnipresent lord, requests. You must utterly abandon it immediately. Thank you for the book. And may Tsidkenu guide and protect you as you wend your way through this world so that you may do only that which he seeks and which pleases him." With a flourish, the priest turned and went deeper into the church.

The notebook icon turned blue and the screen edge flashed green.

Ahva: Level up for me! If it hadn't granted me a level up, I would've grouched. I really would have.

Nagheed: Well-deserved. I got one, too.

Rafayel indicated the door with a twitch of his head.

When they stepped outside, Osse blew out a breath. "That was interesting."

"Wasn't it, though? I'm not sure I trust his advice."

Rafayel snorted.

"I'm sure I don't. Should we seek out another church? Maybe one that's not quite as obvious?"

"We can if you want, but it'll be dusk soon." He turned toward the setting sun. "What do you say to dinner?"

Osse nodded. "I like that idea."

"Good. In the morning, we'll restock our food and ask around in the market about another temple of Tsidkenu. If we find one, we'll check it out. Otherwise, let's head out."

Ahva: Nah. Don't ask us. We're just the players.

Nagheed: Think about this way. If there's something else useful to do here, the computer will set it up. If there isn't, no one will know anything about any other church.

Ahva: Yeah, I suppose you're right.

While they walked, Ahva called up her character screen and allocated her level points.

* * *

Jael was getting closer. Except for brief naps and pausing long enough to eat what she managed to find along the way, Jael had been chasing the kidnappers nonstop since so nearly rescuing her cubs. The scents were stronger now, no longer tagged as "old."

The scents parading across the screen grew dense with a variety of animals and humans. A wide path cut a line through the grassland.

Jael's heart thudded hard in her chest as the scents of Oba and Dina were crowded out by a flock of random travelers and their animals. After adding Cleverness to her Tracking skill, she darted to the side of the path and sniffed, ranging

CHAPTER 34

far to the right and left in and ever-expanding arc. They had to be here. They had to! As she moved, the words shifted relative to each other, and some were revealed or hidden behind others.

Finally, she got far enough away from the road that the travelers' scents faded out. She spotted Dina's name first then Oba's and tightened the arc. Once she had narrowed the direction down, she increased her pace.

The sun neared the horizon as she came to a large, flat human structure. The cart her cubs had been in sat empty near the only visible door. Jael thoroughly checked the cart before she went to the door. The scent stopped there. Jael pushed on the door and slapped it with her paw.

* * *

After a decent breakfast and a stop in the local market to replenish their food supplies, Nagheed and his party were back on the road. They left Fola out the east gate without bothering to stop to talk to the loquacious priest and beat feet toward Ilion. As they crossed through the city gate, the music changed from the Bakhari city song with a djembe, flute, and woodblocks and returned to the Bakhari traveling music with the Middle Eastern feel to it.

Strangely, they had run into very little wildlife. Not even the odd bird or few. Had something scared off the local wildlife or destroyed it? The only other signs of life so far had been a caravan they'd passed about an hour ago. Nagheed couldn't be happier than when Osse had declared the heraldry unfavorable. After their last travels near a "favorable" caravan, Nagheed wasn't waiting with eager anticipation for another opportunity. He liked the idea of traveling on their own. Especially when the option was to line up with a caravan whose people might try to kill them at any moment.

They came to a crossroads where a trail coming up from the southwest crossed their path obliquely. Nagheed kept Smell armed and his nose to the ground, trying to find other signs of life. He watched the gray words floating around the screen for something that didn't belong. Then the word bear popped up. Bear? Out here? Weren't they more of a woodsy type?

Nagheed: Weird.

Ahva: What? Did you find something fun?

Nagheed: Bear. A bear has been by recently.

Ahva: And that's weird because why?

Nagheed: Aren't they forest critters?

Ahva: I thought they were anywhere-you-can-find-food critters. Especially food in pic-a-nic baskets.

Nagheed: Picnic baskets?

Ahva: Vintage cartoon you need to watch.

Nagheed: What is it with you and vintage stuff?

Ahva: Throwback to my childhood. Someday you'll understand.

Nagheed: Maybe.

Osse stood up in his saddle and shielded his eyes with his hand. He pointed. "Smoke? Do you see smoke that way?"

Rafayel leaned forward and squinted. "I think so."

Ahva kicked off from Osse's shoulder.

"Let's follow her. If there is something that way, we'll be closer to it." Rafayel aimed Ryder that direction.

They turned and followed the oblique road until it veered

CHAPTER 34

more to the west.

Ahva: Found your bear.

Nagheed: So, it is actually a bear.

Ahva: You know, it kinda looks like the same one Osse and I ran into on our way from Fola to Kamali.

Nagheed: How can you tell? Recall that the art department hasn't been real bold with their variations.

Ahva: Her paws got burnt. Osse healed her, but the fur didn't grow back. I mean, we ran into that bear a long time ago, but this sure does look like the same bear. Hang on. I'm going to try and chat with her.

Nagheed squinted into the distance and saw the black speck that was probably Ahva banking into a turn.

Ahva: Hey, bear. You, grizzly with the fur. Are you a player?

Jael: My name is Jael.

Ahva: Howdy. How in the world are you? I'm Ahva. My human and I helped you with the laughing maniac on the road to Fola.

Jael: My name is Jael.

Ahva: Right. Got that. We're headed the same direction, generally speaking. You want to team up?

Jael: My name is Jael.

Nagheed: I would take that for no. I think you're done there. Best turn around and come back.

Ahva: Goodbye, Jael. Catch up with you later, maybe. Nagheed, I haven't yet found the source of the smoke. I'll turn back toward the north and see what I find.

Nagheed: Fair enough. We're headed that general direction.

As Nagheed trotted alongside the horses, the scent of

the bear became stronger, not a surprise given Ahva's Jael encounter. Fortunately, it was headed away from them. He didn't relish tangling with a bear.

He noted Ahva's return before the humans made mention of it and watched her flight as she zoomed in, then shed speed suddenly by kicking back almost vertically before landing on Osse's arm.

"Trouble ahead?" Osse held her up at his eye level.

"Yes. Smoke. Lots of smoke." She bobbed her head.

Osse frowned. "Is that something still on fire?"

"Maybe. Didn't look close." Ahva fluffed up her feathers and shook.

He glanced at Rafayel. "Let me try a different question. Should we investigate?"

"Good idea!" She bobbed her head.

"Good." Rafayel smiled.

"Did you find any sentinels or residents?" Osse asked.

"Nooooo, and no –" She imitated a maniac's laughter.

"Is anyone in immediate danger that you can tell?" Rafayel asked.

"Maybe. Didn't look close."

Rafayel pointed toward the north. "Let's see what she found."

They continued on at a reasonable pace and arrived within a half hour, game clock. The building itself was bigger than some of the villages they had encountered. It sort of resembled one of the big box stores with an entranceway jutting out front of it. The smoke came from the center and out of the crashed in front door.

They left their horses in a stand of scraggly oak trees and then continued on foot.

CHAPTER 34

When they entered the building, the music changed, leaving behind the Middle Eastern flute, strings, and drums for became a techno version of a classical piece Jake recognized but couldn't place. He air-drummed to the beat.

The foyer turned out to be deeper than Nagheed expected. The air inside was heavy with a scent labeled "**Burnt Artifacts**" mixed with enough steam for a pro-quality sauna. They crept into a defunct reception area. A wooden desk had been smashed to splinters. Hallways led further north on both the right and the left flanking a room behind the desk. Six smaller rooms, three on each side, were on the outer walls. While Osse tried the different doors, Rafayel rooted through what was left of the desk. Nagheed nudged debris around with his nose. Between them, they came up with a set of keys, a few ballpoint pens, some mechanical pencils, and a couple notepads. Except for the keys, everything else had been chewed up or decayed.

Osse returned. "All the doors are locked."

"I found keys." Rafayel tossed them to him.

They tried each of the six small rooms. They'd all been decorated by the same guy and contained a desk, the skeletal remains of chairs, and torn and faded abstract artwork of streaks and blobs. In the desk, they found an assortment of decrepit office supplies, a few chips, and the ever-present crystals, plastic blobs, and batteries. Next, Rafayel opened the larger room behind the reception desk. Shelves lined the walls and contained piles of what was left of old office supplies.

"This room isn't big enough." Rafayel took in the storeroom with a sweep of his hand.

"What do you mean?" Osse slid a pile of batteries into his

bag.

Rafayel paced off the width of the room. "When we checked all the side rooms, this room went back almost to the door leading into the larger area. This isn't deep enough."

"There's another door." Osse led the way around to a broken door that led into the big-box part of the building. Opposite that, there was a second door into the storeroom block marked "Break Room." They stepped inside.

In one corner of the room, there was a vending machine with a cracked face and what was left of candy bar and potato chip wrappers all over the floor.

Ahva: Want a snack? There might be some left.

Nagheed: Not a chance. I think they're all past their expiration.

Ahva: You know, most of these ready-made snacks have enough preservatives to outlast the end of the world.

Nagheed: Help yourself.

Ahva: Nah. I gotta keep my girlish figure.

In addition to the vending machines, there were cabinets, a sink, and a coffee pot with a cracked glass carafe. Rafayel checked the upper cabinets while Osse checked the lower ones. Rafayel turned up cans of food with faded labels, and Osse found the can opener in a drawer. He pulled out a black stick that had a button on it. He pushed the button and a laser dot lit up the wall.

Ahva: Want to chase the dot?

Nagheed: I think I'll pass.

Ahva: What kind of dog are you? I can keep my sister's dog occupied for hours with a laser pointer.

"Curious. It's not doing any damage." Rafayel ran his

fingertips along the wall where Osse had shined the laser.

"Maybe it's used to draw attention to something?" Osse suggested.

"Let's hold onto it for now. Maybe we'll figure it was used for."

Ahva: For keeping my sister's dog busy. For hours.

Nagheed: Your sister's dog isn't here.

Ahva: But you are.

They left the break room and entered the big-box area of the building. Like a typical big-box store, this was one big open space. Unlike the stores, however, this had more in common with a mad scientist's lab that had been redecorated as a horror movie set. There were stations of beakers, flasks, burners, and test tubes. Interspersed with those, were stations that resembled a surgical theater with robot arms that ended in dastardly appendages. A few of the stations in a straight line to a stairwell in the left front corner were streaked black with scorch marks, but no longer on fire. Overhead, some vents in the ceiling had opened, at least partially. One in particular slid a few centimeters back, hit an obstruction, then closed and tried again.

Ahva: This place gives me the willies, too.

Nagheed: Same answer. We run into something unpleasant, the computer will let us know by changing the music or turning the screen red.

Ahva: Do you really mean to tell me that this room does not give you the willies?

Nagheed: Nope.

Ahva: You half Vulcan?

Nagheed: No, I just have a plan for dealing with weird stuff.

Ahva: You do know that no plan survives first contact with reality.

Nagheed: We'll figure it out.

After checking out a few of the science stations, Rafayel led the way to the stairwell and down to a basement level. The space down here was as big as above, but instead of a mutant science lab, this level was a high-tech zoo. Glass enclosures lined up in rows contained an assortment of wildlife ranging from deer to squirrels to songbirds to birds of prey to people. The desk at the end of the stairs had a map of this floor with buttons next to each representation of the enclosures. A gray metal cabinet mounted to the wall had a numbered disk on the front.

Ahva: That means there's a combination around here somewhere.

Nagheed: Check around the desk. Some people are crazy enough to leave their passwords in plain sight.

Nagheed left the searching of the desk to Ahva and instead took a tour of the various enclosures. Aside from a few scrawny coyotes and a few nonplussed birds of prey, none of the animals in these enclosures were particularly dangerous.

"Hey! Look at the bird!" Ahva said.

"She's found a code. R13, L9, R42," Osse said.

Nagheed wove his way back to the desk. He arrived about the time Rafayel finished turning the combination lock. The door clicked and opened. Inside, there were two 9 mm pistols, a box of bullets, and a couple magazines.

Rafayel picked up one of the pistols. "How interesting. I've heard about these. There's even a diagram in one of the books in my library."

CHAPTER 34

"That reminds me of your pistol but more, I don't know, rectangular," Osse said.

When he searched the gun safe, Rafayel found a small book. He took it out and flipped through it. "Instructions for using it." He tucked both pistols and the book into his pack.

Osse tapped the desk next to the map. "Do you think these buttons open those cells?"

"I'd bet on it. Before we start pushing buttons, though, let's go talk to the people. I wouldn't want to release them if they're lawfully here."

Nagheed knew the way and led them directly to the cluster of five enclosures that contained humans. They all had the gray and white attire of the Bakhari nomads they'd shadowed on the way to Fola.

The nearest one pounded on the glass wall. "Let us out."

"How did you get here?" Osse stepped closer to the enclosure.

"Why does that matter? Just get us outta here." He slammed the side of his fist into the glass.

"Answer our questions first." Rafayel shook his head. "How did you get here?"

"Our caravan was attacked by people from Ilion. We were taken captive and locked in these glass cells. We tried breaking the walls, but they won't break. There used to be more of us, but people from Ilion showed up and took a group of us away."

Rafayel gestured for Osse to follow him to one side. "These might be the people that the followers of Atrac turning into our adversaries."

"You're probably right." Osse glanced back at them. "I

think we should let them out of here."

Rafayel winced. "That may alert the people of Ilion about our arrival. We'd lose the element of surprise. Nagheed, Ahva, what do you think?"

Ahva: What do you say?

Nagheed: They both make good points. If this really is the source of the people and animals that are being turned into laughing maniacs, releasing them will reduce our remaining foes.

Ahva: I say that's worthy. I sure don't want some boss battle where I have to fight ten of these things at once.

Nagheed: With you there. If Ilion is alerted to our impending arrival, though...

Ahva: They'd have to be dopes to not think we're coming. We've been making steady progress in that general direction the whole time since leaving Tel Caperna. Surely, they've had some kind of recon.

Nagheed: You'd think so.

Ahva: Let's let everyone out. The fewer the number of laughing loonies, the better.

Nagheed: All right.

"Out! Let them out!" Ahva fluttered her wings.

Nagheed scratched at the glass.

"And the animals? What about them?" Osse pointed to the rest of the room.

Ahva: Same answer, I say. I sure don't have any wish to fight a maniac eagle. A real one was fun enough.

Nagheed: Sounds good to me.

"Out! Out!" Ahva turned around to look at the trapped animals.

Nagheed went to the nearest one and scratched at the

CHAPTER 34

glass enclosure there, too.

Rafayel pointed. "The controls are probably back at that desk."

After following them back to the desk, Nagheed hopped up and planted his front feet on the top and looked at the bank of buttons. There was writing there, but it was total gibberish.

Nagheed: Can you read that?

Ahva: Grid coordinates. Probably correlates to the locations of the cells.

Osse hit the buttons one at a time and the glass partitions sank into the floor.

Animals of all sorts rushed past them and up the stairwell to the nightmare science lab. When the nomads were released, they all left together.

An incredibly loud alarm blared, and the lights turned red. Nagheed whined and shook his head. A television screen slid up from the top of the desk showing a disheveled woman in robes that had once been fine but now were shredded in some parts and intact in others. "Your intrusion has been noted. You should have left the others and saved yourself. We will take special care of you when you are captured, and soon you will join my army and leave blood and corpses in your wake. The glory of Ilion will rise again!"

Behind her, other people in similar mixed array gathered captive humans and animals into pens on wheels and left with each going a different direction. The woman giving the orders pressed a button marked automated defenses. With a joyless smile on her face, she stepped through a double door and watched it close. The red light stopped flashing on the screen, but the alarm was still going strong in the lab.

"Time to go!" Rafayel gestured Osse through the door first.

The door slid closed as they ran up the stairs. The door into the science lab made a horrific grinding noise but didn't move.

Ahva: You were right. We alerted the bad guys.

Nagheed: Yeah, but I think it'll be okay. They cleared out.

Ahva: Except for that one creepy gal.

Nagheed: And whatever the automated defenses are. Really, though, I think we'll be fine.

Ahva: Probably. I mean, we're going to have a grizzly bear helping us.

Nagheed: Yeah, if she'll ever say more than, "My name is Jael."

Ahva: We haven't triggered the right response yet.

Nagheed: Probably, but let's not hang out here.

Ahva: Right. Places to go. Maniacs to kill. The world to save. We've got a busy day planned.

The humans retrieved their horses, and they got on the way.

Chapter 35

As they continued traveling east, Ahva had expected to find more bear signs. The grizzly had been hauling some serious butt through here. Although it was evident that something with some mass had gone crashing through the knee-high grasses, if she hadn't actually spotted Jael doing the running, she wouldn't have known it was a bear.

Ahead, a low rock wall extended north and south, disappearing over the horizon. The one gap accommodated a road coming down from the north then veering east through the wall. A guard house, or what was left of one, had been knocked over flat and stomped on a few times by something large and unhappy. Jael was her guess. That bear had an attitude.

If this was the border of Ilion, she had a bone to pick with the game designers. Logistically speaking, it would've made a lot more sense for there to be an established road between Fola and the next largest city in Ilion, not a puny footpath. That's where this guard post should have been.

Ahva flew over the smashed guardhouse, taking careful note of the bear claw marks on the wood, before she looped around and headed back for the humans. They were a good distance out so she went from flapping her wings to gliding. When she was a few dozen meters away, Osse held out his arm for a landing pad. Ahva descended, and before she came in for a landing, she reared back vertical and flapped her wings to shed speed and drop nicely on his arm.

"Find anything interesting?" Osse held her up to his eye level.

"Yes." She imitated a low-pitched growl. "Bear. Gone now."

"An angry bear that's gone now?" Osse glanced toward the border.

"Anything dangerous now?" Rafayel asked.

"No. Bear gone." She nodded.

"Okay, then how do you know it was a bear?" Rafayel shrugged. "I guess we'll find out when we get there."

Nagheed: What did you find?

Ahva: Ilion border and a guard station that been squashed flat by a certain bear we both know and love.

Nagheed: I haven't been able to figure out yet if that's another player or an NPC.

Ahva: Me, either. But I haven't been able to chat any other NPCs. Have you?

Nagheed: No, I suppose not. So, she's a PC with major attitude problems? Having technical problems? Found an autoplay feature and is just watching?

Ahva: One or more of the above? In either case, if she's also heading to our objective, we need to hurry up or she's gonna hog all the puzzles and all the experience, not to mention the loot.

Nagheed: We have one major advantage.

Ahva: My wild sense of humor?

CHAPTER 35

Nagheed: No. Opposable thumbs. We have humans with us. They're going to be better able to manipulate puzzle parts and open doors and stuff like that.

Ahva: Yeah, but she's got brute force backed up by one hundred thirty kilograms or more of really ticked off bear.

Nagheed: I get the feeling that won't be quite enough.

Ahva: We can hope.

About an hour later on the game clock, they reached the Ilion border and the trashed guardhouse. The humans dismounted and started checking the wreckage while Nagheed sniffed around. He sat down and whined, facing south.

Ahva: Zombie cyborg?

Nagheed: Kinda smells like one.

Ahva: The nose knows.

Ahva's view turned red around the edges. Two maniacs, an Augmented Human, and Augmented Khal all darted out of the trees and stopped at the edge.

Ahva: Khal. That was the nutcase from the caravan, wasn't it? The caravan leader's grandson or something.

Nagheed: Yeah.

Ahva: Great. I hate leaving strings untied.

Nagheed: From a storytelling perspective, you knew he had to be back.

Ahva: Yeah. I mean, he had a name, and he was a real twit.

Osse dumped Ahva's arrowhead pouch on the ground.

Ahva grabbed one of the arrowheads and spiraled upward as the two maniacs ran forward. The two augmented humans stayed in the nearest stand of trees.

While taking shelter behind the wrecked guard station,

Osse shot arrows in rapid succession and Rafayel fired his flintlock pistol before fishing out a 9 mm from his pack. Nagheed joined them.

After picking Bombing Run from the skills list, Ahva dropped the arrowhead on a maniac. Another arrow from Osse turned the maniac into a mannequin. Rafayel fired a couple bullets at the other maniac as Ahva returned to her arrowheads. By the time she lifted off again, second maniac was a goner.

Nagheed: If you can't hit the glow, you're just going to annoy them.

Ahva: That's been useful before.

A brilliant streak of red from Khal's bow shot toward Ahva. She tucked in her wings and dropped most of a meter. A blue streak from the augmented human's arm zipped over her.

Ahva: Uh, Houston, we have a problem.

Nagheed: Can you muck up the lens on the laser, or blaster, or whatever it is? That'll mess up its aim so I don't get fried on my way to attack it.

Ahva: Find me some mud.

Nagheed: This prairie has been as dry as a popcorn fart, but one of the horses left a road apple.

Ahva: Eww, gross!

Another blue streak flew past her.

Ahva: All right, all right. Road apple it is.

She swooped down to the path and found the mess left by the horse. She grabbed some of the horse manure with her feet. Osse and Rafayel exchanged shots with both augmented humans. As long as they ignored her, she didn't mind.

CHAPTER 35

Nagheed: The augmented human fires five shots and has to wait.

Ahva: Handy. What's the count?

Nagheed: Three.

Ahva: If I get there after five, I should be golden.

She lifted off and flew straight on toward the stand of trees where the augmented human was crouched. A blue beam flew from the augmented human's arm and burned a hole in the wood of the collapsed guard station.

Ahva: That's four.

When it turned toward her, Ahva's heart beat harder. The lens from the augmented human's left arm glowed blue. Ahva dove. The tug on her tail feathers told her she wasn't quite quick enough.

Ahva: Hey! I need those!

Nagheed: That's five! It has to wait.

Ahva landed next to the augmented human and smeared the manure all over the lens.

The augmented human swatted her away. The screen flashed red and she rolled beak over tail into the trunk of a scrawny tree. She glanced at her health bar and winced. A hair over half her points were gone. She flipped herself right way up. The bottom of a boot headed her way. Ahva squawked and scrambled to get clear as a huge mass of black and tan fur soared over her and tackled the augmented human. Ahva left the brute to Nagheed and lifted off. Each downbeat of her wings turned the screen red.

Ahva: Thanks, Shaggy.

Nagheed: All part of the service.

She returned to Osse and landed in the grass next to him. Several metal arrows were stuck in the wood. Rafayel popped up and fired his 9 mm. Ahva didn't see what he hit, but he nodded. The red edge of her vision faded.

"Got it." He looked down at her. "Take care of Ahva. I'll help Nagheed."

Ahva scraped as much manure off her foot on the grass as she could.

Ahva: Eww! I've got horse poo on my foot!
Nagheed: Could be worse.
Ahva: So you say.
Nagheed: You could have it all over.
Ahva: Gross!

Rafayel ran out from behind the barricade, rapier in hand.

When she'd cleaned her foot as well as she could, Ahva stayed still while Osse applied the herbs. Her health points shot back up to full. She stepped onto his hand. Osse stood, and Ahva surveyed the background.

They went to check the mannequins. The maniacs had left behind — surprise, surprise — a crystal, a blob of plastic, and a battery. Khal had left behind his compound bow, which had some extra fancy widgetry at the ends of both arms. There was also a collection of metal arrows, a pile of coins — both Nethanyan and actual gold, a few different crystals, four blobs of differently colored plastics, three batteries, and a still photograph that showed Osse and Rafayel standing at the desk in the basement of that laboratory.

Ahva: Hey, we're famous. I'm ready for my close-up.
Nagheed: They were hunting for us.
Ahva: That's weird. Because you found them first.
Nagheed: Um, they stink at their jobs?
Ahva: Or you're really good at yours.

CHAPTER 35

In the augmented human's mannequin, they recovered yet more crystals, another pile of plastic blobs, a few more batteries, a set of three lenses, one of which was marked as dirty, and some weird car-part-looking thing marked "Micro-reactor."

Ahva: Uh-oh. We're going start glowing in the dark.
Nagheed: Hopefully it's better shielded than that.

Once they had collected all the loot, they headed back out to the east following along the road that came down from the north.

* * *

Crossing into Ilion gave Nagheed a new piece of music to enjoy. Like the lab outside of Fola and the ruined city north of Fola, this one was a techno version of a classical tune. This time he recognized it as Moonlight Sonata.

Nagheed sat next to Ryder and waited for Ahva's return. They'd made better time following along the road. In fact, in less than ten minutes on the real clock, they'd arrived at the edges of a walled town. This wall, however, was not made of simple rock. It had rusted steel supports and curls of razor wire along the top. The road led directly to an unsecured gate. Unlike the guardhouse at the border, however, this one had not been smashed down by an unhappy bear. Scorch marks marred the surface and the metal was slagged near the hinges. When Ahva returned, she landed on Osse's arm.

Nagheed: What's in there?
Ahva: Parts the town look like they were bombed. I didn't see any normal people but there were bands of

augmented humans patrolling the area.

Nagheed: Did you see the bear?

Ahva: Yeah. There's a big-box store kinda place in the north central part of town. The bear is there pounding on the door. And you were right about brute force being useless.

Nagheed: It'd have to be. Otherwise characters would specialize in big strong brutes and beat everything they came across to dust. Takes all the fun out of the game.

After Osse and Rafayel heard Ahva's report, in her usual inimitable conglomeration of words and sound effects. Nagheed led the way. They picked their path through the collapsed gate and into the northwest quadrant of the town. She did her usual flutter ahead and wait routine to lead them to the courtyard around the place she had dubbed the "big box store."

The glass walls were decorated with etched imagery showing Mr. Universe types in impressive poses and supermodel gals clothed barely enough to maintain the all audiences rating. Someone with the imagination of a ten-year-old artist had come through and drawn spectacles, mustaches, dripping fangs, an out-sized ears on most of the images.

The courtyard in front of the building had overgrown flowerbeds that back in their day must have been impressive. Now, they were colossal weed patches. At the main door, a grizzly bear with dark brown fur stood on two feet and took out her incredible frustrations on the door.

Ahva: Ready for a bear fight?

Nagheed: Me?

Ahva: You do have that Caucasian Mountain Shepherd vibe going on. Did you know that they're used in Russia

hunt down bears?

Nagheed: How do you know that?

Ahva: I am a fountain of much useless information. That just happened to be one of the points.

Nagheed: I don't think we're meant to fight this bear.

Ahva: You sure about that?

Nagheed: I'm not getting combat music. Are you seeing red?

Ahva: Good point. I don't think anyone will notice if you put a hat on, though.

Nagheed: What?

Ahva: Bad joke. Never mind. And, I suppose that you are on your own. I suspect the Russian dogs usually have a friend or two when they go after a big bear.

Nagheed: Likely. Unlike that black bear maniac we ran into, this one's a good bit bigger than me.

Nagheed trotted forward about half the distance to the door and stopped.

Nagheed: Hello, Jael. Having some trouble with the door?

Jael: My name is Jael.

Ahva: So we heard.

The humans dismounted and crept closer to the bear.

"Any guesses how to get the bear away from the door?" Osse asked.

When they came within twenty meters of the door, Jael dropped to four feet and turned toward them. She ran a few steps forward and stopped then struck the ground with her paw.

Ahva: Nice bear. Good bear. We really like bears.

Jael: My name is Jael.

Ahva: Are you sure it's not Groot?

Nagheed: Have you noticed? No combat warnings.

Ahva: Yeah, I noticed. There's some other way to get her away from the door long enough for us to get in.

Nagheed: I got it!

Ahva: Hopefully there's a cure.

Nagheed: No, I know how to get the bear away from the door. Food.

Ahva: Nice! I'll tell the humans.

She made a crunching nuts sound. "For bear."

"Do you think she's hungry?" Osse dug around in his bag.

Rafayel shrugged. "I don't think I've ever met a bear who wasn't, but will that keep her at bay long enough?"

Osse pulled a small jar out of his bag. "If this stuff works on bears, I might be able to get her to take a nap. I don't know how long she'll sleep, though."

Jael clacked her teeth and struck the ground with her paw again.

"She's not terribly interested in attacking us, so I'd hate to kill her for being an inconvenience." Rafayel kept his hand on his flintlock.

Osse pulled a medium-sized loaf of bread out of his bag. He slit the side open and stuffed some herbs inside before he gave it a slight underhand toss toward Jael. "Okay. Let's back up and see if she goes for it."

Rafayel snapped his fingers and patted his leg. "Nagheed, come."

He trotted back to his human.

They retreated back to the horses. Keeping a wary eye on them, Jael crept forward and gave the loaf a good sniff before she chowed down. Less than a minute later, Jael staggered over to a weed patch and flopped on her side. She was snoring a second later.

Ahva: Come on. Tranquilizers don't take effect that fast.

Nagheed: Would you rather hang out here for the next half hour waiting to see if it took effect?

Ahva: No. No, now is good. Now is perfect even, but it is funny what the AI decides is worthy to go full realism on and what gets a miss. Let's get this road on the show.

They tiptoed past the bear to the door. The horizontal line joining a smaller circle to a bigger circle had been carved into the door, and it was still visible through the slash of black paint.

Rafayel pointed to the symbol and whispered. "Elef's symbol."

Osse nodded.

Next to the door was a keypad and a screen. The screen was lit up and showed "1, 5, 6, 3, 7,____,____, 9,____, 7." A blinking cursor sat in the first blank.

Nagheed: Okay, bird brain. You're on.

Ahva: That's "brainy bird." A bird nerd, if you will. She leaned closer. **That's a skip pattern. All I have to do is figure out the rule.**

Nagheed: It's all yours.

After about half a minute, Ahva jumped over to the screen and clung to the edge with her toenails. She leaned over and tapped 8, 5, and 10 on the keypad. The door slid open.

Rafayel chuckled. "How did she know that?"

Osse shrugged and led the way in.

The music changed again, now becoming a techno version of a Mozart song that Jake couldn't remember the name of.

The entrance didn't lead to any kind of a reception area or antechamber. The corridor they entered led left and right and ran straight into a wall dead ahead. To the right, the floor had a heavy layer of dust that made Nagheed's nose itch. He sneezed a couple times.

Ahva: Good golly. I mean bless you.

To the left, the corridor went about five meters and turned right. At one time, the place had been a pristine silver white, but someone had redecorated by tossing entire cans of paint along all the walls in whatever random color happened to be on sale that week.

Ahva: I just love what they've done with the place. It's got that whole modern art chic going on.

Nagheed: I bet it would sell for gazillions of dollars.

Ahva: I'm hoping one of our quests is not to clean up the place. I already got to clean a library.

Nagheed: Shhh. Don't give anyone ideas.

This corridor was wide enough to pass two across, but Nagheed led by a few paces. As he approached the L-bend in the corridor, the combat music interrupted techno Mozart.

Nagheed peeked around the corner. Three blue sentinels floated in the corridor. Like the ones at the ruined city, these were half-meter spheres with what looked like a camera lens sticking out on one side. The air under them shimmered.

Osse joined him. With Khal's bow in hand, Osse looked up at a parabolic mirror in the corner then darted forward and shot two arrows at the front sentinel. Each arrow glowed red as it left the bow. One shot hit the sentinel dead on and sapped half its health. The other arrow missed the first sentinel as the sphere dropped half a meter but struck the

CHAPTER 35

sentinel behind it. It, too, lost half its health.

Ahva: I'd wait, if I were you. You'll be in the way of Rafayel's shot. Once he's blown a hole in one, you can zip in there and do your thing.

Nagheed: I think you're right.

Rafayel leaned around the corner and blasted the front sentinel with his black powder pistol. It lost about a quarter of its health, and the bar turned red.

The sentinel fired back at Rafayel, but hit the wall instead. The middle sentinel darted left and shot Osse's leg. He fell back against the wall. The sentinel in back darted to the right and shot the wall near Rafayel.

Ahva zipped out and landed on the arrow sticking out of the lead sentinel, tilting it sideways. Whatever mechanism it used to hover instead accelerated it into the wall. Ahva jumped clear in time before the sparks flew, and the sentinel's health bar dropped to nothing.

Ahva: Woo hoo! What a ride.

Nagheed darted forward and swatted the second sentinel into the floor. Sparks flew, and its health bar turned red.

Osse fired two glowing arrows. The first one hit the second sentinel and took it out. The second arrow speared the back sentinel through the aperture on the front. The sentinel glowed and exploded showering them with pieces the size of Legos.

Techno Mozart returned after a brief trumpet fanfare signaled a level-up.

Nagheed opened up his character screen and allocated his points.

Ahva: How much fun was that?

Nagheed: I don't know. At least you got a ride out of it.

"Nagheed, watch." Rafayel ordered.

While Nagheed used Stay Alert and stood between Rafayel and the next intersection, Rafayel helped Osse treat the leg injury. After they finished, they checked the mannequins. To Nagheed's surprise, the sentinels did not have the usual assortment of crystals and nonsense. Instead, each one had a few bits of wire and a circuit board. They also had Osse's arrows. A couple metal ones were still usable, but other metal ones had developed a significant bend, and the wooden ones were cracked.

Ahva: Look! An arrow with its own built-in U-turn.

Nagheed: Not sure it works that way.

Ahva: Probably not, but it'd be funny if it did.

They stuffed the equipment into their packs then continued down the hall to the intersection, which went left to a door and doglegged around to the right into another wide corridor.

The door on the left had a keypad and a screen next to it. The screen showed more mathematical foolishness.

Nagheed: Ahva, another one for you.

Ahva: Oh, goody. I love algebra.

The screen showed, "$2X=1Y, 4Y = 2Z, Z=$____X"

Ahva: Come on. This isn't even hard.

Nagheed: Remember, this was originally meant for kids.

Ahva: Yeah, but the computer could adapt.

Nagheed: Careful, or it'll start giving us calculus.

Ahva: Bring it on! I passed Diff EQ. What's a little calculus?

She fluttered over to the screen and hung on to the top with her toenails and leaned over and tapped the four.

CHAPTER 35

The door slid open.

Nagheed: Show off.

Ahva: Hey, you handle the muscle stuff. I'll handle the nerd stuff.

They entered the cubicle village with shoulder-high walls forming cubicles barely two strides on a side. The wacko paint job had not happened in here. In fact, evidenced by an impressive layer of dust, the room hadn't been disturbed.

Ahva: You know, it might be fun to play laser tag in here.

Nagheed: If another set of the sentinels show up, you might get your wish.

Ahva: Yeah, but it's no fun if you can't shoot back.

Nagheed: I don't think they make laser pistols for birds.

Ahva: And that's an oversight. I could be a bird with a laser! Pew! Pew! Pew!

Nagheed: Some other time, maybe.

Ahva: Or get the equipment fixed and get augmented.

Nagheed: Not sure that's possible, but would be interesting.

Ahva: A different meaning to laser eye surgery.

As he started checking all the desks in the cubicle village, Ahva flew to the far corner. Nagheed went from desk to desk grabbing the drawer pull with his teeth and walking backwards to open the drawer. Most of the desks had the typical office-supply kind of things. About one in five had wire bits and one in ten had a circuit board.

When they got to the last row, Nagheed found that Ahva had spent the time drawing in the dust on the desk surfaces. Most were games of tic-tac-toe, but he also found a smiley face on a sun beaming down on a tree next to a river and a flock of butterflies. The last one had a cartoonish guy peeking over brick wall. Above the guy, she'd written the words "Kilroy was here."

Nagheed: Who's Kilroy?

Ahva: You don't know who Kilroy is?

Nagheed: Never heard of him.

Ahva: Maybe it was before your time. Come to think of it, it was definitely before mine. Kilroy was an inspector during World War II, I think. Might have been World War I. Anyways, the story goes that whenever he finished inspecting something, he wrote "Kilroy was here" in yellow chalk so he wouldn't have to inspect it again. The actual cartoon guy peeking over the wall was a British World War II cartoon about shortages. In the original cartoon, he says "Wat, no tea?" or whatever else was running short at the time.

Nagheed: You must be hard to beat at trivia games.

Ahva: Only if I get the right questions.

Inside Kilroy's desk, they found a thick book.

Nagheed: Can you read that?

Ahva: Yep. Yay for being clever! Y'know, this game should have a reading skill. I figure it's basing reading ability on cleverness, but you can be awfully clever and still be illiterate.

Nagheed: Add it to your feedback.

Ahva: Done!

"Elevated Life Engineering Foundation International Systems. Instructional Manual for the DNA Alteration for Genetic Nucleotide Access and Basic Biologic Enhancement Technology." Rafayel read.

CHAPTER 35

Ahva: LOL! That's great!

Nagheed: What's the joke?

Ahva: Starting with DNA, turn the rest of it into an acronym.

Nagheed: I can't read it. It's scribble to me.

Ahva: Oh. DNA Alteration for Genetic Nucleotide Access and Basic Biologic Enhancement Technology. Make the acronym.

Nagheed quickly sorted it out and rolled his eyes.

Rafayel flipped through the book. "It's instructions on how to operate some kind of equipment."

Osse looked over Rafayel's shoulder. "Better hang onto it until we figure out what."

Rafayel tucked the book into his backpack.

They threaded their way out of the cubicle village and back into the hallway. After following the dogleg around, they went to the nearest door south. Here, the keypad had been taken out of the wall, and the door was already open.

As they approached the door, Techno Mozart cross-faded with the drums and brass of the combat music. Five sentinels streamed into the corridor. Four were the same sort they'd seen before, but the fifth was larger and painted a golden brown. They were all labeled "Damaged Sentinel."

Ahva: Red's a boss sentinel, y'think?

Nagheed: The gold one? Probably. If not a boss, then definitely a stronger version.

Ahva: Oh, right. You don't see red. That makes it tougher for you.

Nagheed: It works out. The blue one is blue, and the red one is sort of a gold-brown kind of color, but let me know if there are any other weird ones.

Ahva: You got it!

Before the floating sentinels could get themselves properly set up, Osse fired two arrows in rapid succession. One bounced off the sentinel in the front and ricocheted off the wall before it clattered on the floor, but the other pierced the sentinel's metal hide near the lens and stuck out. Rafayel shot the big one with his black powder pistol, but bullet flattened into a disk short of the droid before it fell.

Nagheed: Big one's got a shield?

Ahva: That or B.O. so bad even bullets don't want to get too close.

Ahva zoomed to the sentinel Osse had shot and perched on the arrow. It rolled midair and accelerated into the one next to it. They collided with a loud clang, and the health bars above both of them dropped. Ahva fell off the arrow and fluttered to the ground.

After Osse shot the one that already had an arrow stuck in it and turned it into a mannequin, Nagheed charged toward the big one. A beam from its lens hit the middle of his back, burning the armor.

"All right, dog?" Ahva asked.

Nagheed: Yes. No damage to me.

Ahva: This time.

The other sentinels fired beams at Osse and Rafayel, but Nagheed didn't see them land.

Launching off his back legs, Nagheed leapt at the big sentinel and batted it. The screen flashed red as the sentinel careened sideways and slammed into one of the smaller ones. The little one spewed a shower of sparks and became a mannequin. As Nagheed landed, the screen flashed red again.

CHAPTER 35

Note to self. No smacking the shielded ones.

"Nagheed, out!" Rafayel flattened a bullet from his 9mm on the shielded one.

A sphere a few centimeters from the shielded sentinel flickered. Rafayel shot it again, and this time the bullet hit, putting a major dent in the side.

Nagheed kept his injured paw tucked up as he hobbled to the humans. Osse stuck another arrow in a smaller sentinel, and then Ahva landed on it and flipped the sentinel onto its side. It flew sideways and smashed into the wall hard enough to take it out of the fight. That left one more smaller one and the big bruiser.

The small one pivoted, tracking Ahva's flight. She flew toward the larger one and zipped around it as the smaller one fired a beam from the lens. It missed Ahva by a couple spare millimeters and hit the larger sentinel, leaving it only a handful of health points.

"Clear out, Ahva!" Osse lined up a shot on the large one.

She zipped down the hall away from them, with the smaller sentinel still tracking her.

Osse loosed two arrows in rapid succession. The sentinel hit the first with a beam from the lens, but the second hit the lens and shattered it, taking the rest of the health points.

Rafayel shot the smaller sentinel a moment later and turned it to mannequin.

The music cross-faded back to techno Mozart.

"That's got it. How bad is your arm?" Osse slipped his bow over his shoulder and stepped over Nagheed to get to Rafayel.

Rafayel looked down at two dark burn marks on his armor. "Hurts like the devil, but I don't think the damage is too bad. Check Nagheed's paw while I get my armor off."

Osse crouched in front of Nagheed. "Okay. Let's see your paw."

He looked at the blisters oozing on his paw then picked it up as if giving Osse a high-five.

"Ow. That's a pretty bad burn." He winced and rooted around in his bag. "Best if you leave the big ones for people with distance attacks, at least until we get the shield knocked down." He took out a dark gray crockery jar and popped the lid off. "This is just burn salve. It'll heal the damage."

When he smeared some of the goop on Nagheed's paw, the health bar recovered to full points.

Ahva flew in for a landing on Osse's shoulder. "Good job."

Nagheed: What's down the hall?

Ahva: A door marked "Repair Droids Only." No keypad or screen, so may not be a way in. Nothing else looked interesting.

After Osse treated Rafayel's arm, they checked the mannequins and found more wires, circuit boards, crystals, batteries, and plastic blobs. Osse was able to recover a few arrows, but about half of the metal ones were curved and all the wooden ones were cracked.

While they were stowing the new loot, Nagheed walked to the door the sentinels had come from and peeked inside. This room had been spared the wild painting done to the corridors.

Two roughly human-looking droids labeled "Repair Droids" were standing near a workbench with a variety of tools and electronic parts neatly arranged on the surface. Both droids had been decorated with necklaces made of

CHAPTER 35

nuts and bolts and a hat fashioned from a curved piece of metal.

There was a single, closed door in the far corner, and to Nagheed's right, a cabinet that had a collection of buttons on it.

Nagheed crept into the room, watching the droids for movement, but they didn't even turn his direction. The humans came in behind him and Ahva flew circles around the room.

Osse pointed to the button-empowered cabinet that took most of one wall. "Doesn't that match the artifact pictured in the book we found?"

"I think so." Rafayel dug out the book as they walked over. "Yes. It's the same machine. If we can repair this thing, then that should end the maniac generation."

"Worth a try." Osse shrugged.

Nagheed joined him to check out their discovery. The machine was more like a long metal countertop and cabinets. A screen was embedded about halfway along it with a regular keyboard built in and a slew of other buttons. A red one was flashing. To the left of the screen, an empty cubical container had a lid that would slide back into the top of the machine.

Osse ran his fingers under the text on the screen. "Run self-diagnostic. Refer to page 427 in the User Manual."

Rafayel flipped open the book to the indicated page and found a list of step-by-step instructions. "Press the flashing red malfunction indicator light."

Ahva fluttered off Osse's shoulder and landed on a button that was flashing red, which turned it off.

"Enter **run self-diagnostic** at the prompt." He typed in

the text using the keyboard below the screen. "The self-diagnostic will take 2 to 5 minutes."

While that was processing, Osse and Rafayel checked the rest of the room.

Osse pressed his ear against the door in the southeast corner. "There's something on the other side of this door."

Chapter 36

After turning on Hear, Nagheed trotted over and tipped his head to one side, raising his ears. Whirring noises and faint buzzing sounds came from the other side.

"Let's not seek trouble if we don't have to." Rafayel waved Osse away.

Nagheed sniffed around the corners of the room. In the northeast corner, scents of "machine oil" and "Ilionite tech" wafted in from under a narrow strip of the wall.

Nagheed: There's a hidden door over here.

Ahva: I wondered if we were going to find anything hidden like that. The mazes in this game have been woefully short on hidden passages.

The self-diagnostic program ended with a chime. The light that had flashed before was flashing again. Ahva jumped on it to turn it off. Nagheed followed Rafayel and Osse back over as the sliding lid opened to the left of the screen.

Rafayel picked up the book. "When the self-diagnostic is finished, the screen will list the components necessary for self-repair. Place these components in the hopper to the left of the screen." Rafayel consulted the screen. "Fifteen pieces of wire, nine circuit boards, one mini-reactor, and five batteries."

Osse and Rafayel opened their packs and dug out as many wires and circuit boards as they had collected. As they added them to the hopper, the screen updated. Then they set five batteries in the hopper and dug out the mini reactor they had collected from the Augmented Human and set that in there. In the end, they were still short three pieces of wire and a circuit board.

"Where should we look now?" Osse glanced around the room.

Nagheed darted over to the corner where he'd found scents coming under the wall. After picking Signal Human from his skill list, he scratched the wall then turned back at Rafayel.

Nagheed: Check out that console. There has to be a button to release the door.

Ahva strutted from one end of the machine to the other and only found a button that had once been marked, but the words had been worn off by constant use.

"Did you find something?" Rafayel crouched next to Nagheed. "There's a draft here."

Ahva jumped on the unmarked button and the wall in front of Nagheed slid open.

Ahva: There you go.

She fluttered over to Osse's shoulder.

This corridor was long and narrow stretched on to a dead end.

Several scents of "Ilionite tech," each with its own font, drifted out from under the wall.

Ahva: That was anticlimactic.

CHAPTER 36

Nagheed: Wait. Another secret door.

Rafayel pushed on the wall in front of them, then on the wall beside them. Both slid open. The opening to their right led into another long corridor. The one ahead went into a store room. Nagheed led the way. That was the place they were most likely to find one more circuit board and three more pieces of wire.

Inside, industrial, metal shelves lined the walls and filled the center of the room. The first row of shelves to the left was neat and orderly. Everything had its place and every place was marked. Boxes were neatly labeled. In the rest of the room, several crates of a shipment had been thrown around at random. Equipment of all sorts was strewn from one end of the room to the other and piled knee-deep.

Osse whistled. "It'll take us a month to sort through this."

"We don't have time for that." Rafayel led the way out. "In fact, I don't know that I would recommend trying to move through any of this. Who knows what's hiding under all that garbage? Remember what happened at the ruins?"

Osse nodded. "Yeah, and we could see the floor there."

They instead took the long corridor that led south. There were no doors on the left side of the corridor, but on the right side, doors occurred about every five meters or so.

Rafayel tried each door they came to, but found every one of them blocked. Unlike the hidden doors they had encountered at the north end of this hall, pushing on the door had no effect.

At the end of the hall, they found a door with the keypad. The keypad had been torn off the wall and tossed aside. An assortment of wires hung out of the opening.

Osse pulled the knife off his belt and cut some of the

longer wires loose. "That takes care of the wire. Now we need one more circuit board."

The door was open a crack. Rafayel slipped his fingertips into the opening and pulled as hard as he could. He got it open about a meter and couldn't move it further. Nagheed walked through the door into another storeroom that was in better repair. Labeled crates filled the rows of shelves that lined the wall and filled the center. On the shelf about nose height, he found a circuit board. He carefully bit down on the outside edge of the board and carried it back to Rafayel.

Rafayel took the board from him and ruffled the fur on Nagheed's head. "Well done."

Osse counted his arrows. "I'm running out of arrows. Do you think there are any in here?"

"We can check, but be quick."

While they checked the labels on the various crates, Nagheed searched up and down the aisles of shelving for a bundle of arrows sitting out in the open. When he had no success, he went back to the door and watched for shenanigans in the hallway. When the humans joined him, there were no new arrows in Osse's quiver.

They followed the bend in the corridor to the west and then north again, continuing to try doors on either side of the hallway but having no luck.

Nagheed led the way as they backtracked around the corridor to the room where the repair droids were hanging out. Osse added the wire bits and the last circuit board to the hopper on the machine. The panel slid closed and the screen changed.

"Estimated time to repair fifteen minutes. Queued augmentations: full speech, hand with opposable thumb," Osse read.

The two repair droids stood up from the workbench and left the room.

Nagheed: Where are they going?

Ahva: Fix the junk we just equipped them to fix?

Nagheed: Isn't that the thing you're standing on?

Ahva: Apparently not. Maybe they're fixing the machinery that's been making the zombie cyborgs.

Nagheed: Uh... okay. Sure.

He darted to the door to watch where they went, but the hallway was empty.

Nagheed: I think they can teleport.

Ahva: Then why didn't they do it from where they were sitting?

Nagheed: That's a good question I can't answer. Game glitch?

Ahva: Droids with a place to be? Put it in our playtester notes!

"We still have the northern parts of the complex to investigate. Let's check there, then we'll see how the repair is going." Rafayel waved for them to follow.

They left the room and returned to the north-south corridor with the dogleg. This time they went north to the end of the hall where there was a door to the left and another to the right. The door on the left had a large screen next to it but no keypad. On the screen, there were ten equal sized blocks with different numbers on them. Toward the bottom of the screen, a row of lines made a perfect spot for those blocks.

Nagheed: What do you think?

Ahva: I think that "daughter" and "laughter" should

sound the same.

Nagheed: About the screen.

Ahva: Blocks. With numbers that are spaced weirdly. They probably need to be arranged in a proper order in the lower part.

Nagheed: You're the nerd, bird. Can you figure out the order?

Ahva: Like breathing. It's easy. It's a doubling pattern starting on one.

Nagheed: Get to it.

Ahva: How? There's nothing for me to hang onto, and that screen is too big for me to stretch from one end to the other.

Osse squinted at the screen. "What do we do here?"

Rafayel shook his head. "I'm not quite sure."

"Look at the bird!" Ahva fluttered her wings.

Osse chuckled. "It's kinda sad when my bird is better at solving these puzzles than I am."

"Hold her closer to the screen." Rafayel smiled. "She might have it already."

When Osse offered his hand, Ahva hopped over. He held her close to the screen, and she tried to tap and drag the block marked 1 2 4. It wouldn't move.

Rafayel tapped the edge of that block, and it scooted itself down into the lower portion of the screen. "How about you show me which ones are next."

Ahva tapped 8 16, then 32 64, then 128 2, then 56 51, then 2 102, then 4 204, then 8 409, then 6 819, then 2.

The door slid open.

To the right of the door, there was a long, chest high countertop. Behind that, there were several cabinets arranged on the wall. They may have been locked at some point, in fact they probably were, but the doors had been torn off. Inside were racks for weapons ranging from bows and quivers of arrows like the one Osse had acquired from Khal to shotguns and pistols. To the left, filling most of the room, there were square glass enclosures similar to the ones they had found in the lab outside Fola. Many of the cells were broken, and a few of the intact ones were empty. In the far corner of the room, though, the cells contained a very pregnant Bakhari woman, two nomads, and a Nethanyan.

Nagheed: I think we found the missing sister.

Ahva: Awww, a big family reunion coming soon with much weeping and many smiles.

Osse, however, had not paid any attention to the rest of the room. Instead, he had darted around the counter to replenish his supply of arrows.

Ahva: *Snicker* Good to know where his priorities are.

She flew off to the glass cell imprisoning Maaska and landed on top. "Hey! Hey! Osse! Look at the bird!"

Inside, Maaska backed as far away from Ahva she could and banged on the cell wall. "Go away! Go away!"

Ahva: That's gratitude for you.

She looked down. "No!"

"Just a minute, Ahva." Osse finished stuffing arrows in his quiver before he turned around. "Maaska!" He ran over and pressed his hands against the glass. "Are you okay?"

"I think so. Get me out of here!"

"Okay. Hold on." He ran back over to the counter. Nagheed followed Rafayel around to the back of the counter and then stood up with his front feet on the edge of the counter. Like the lab, there were labeled buttons for each of the cells. Nagheed wagged his tail. When Osse arrived, Rafayel pointed to the cluster of buttons in the corner.

"These will control the cells over there, but if we press those, we'll probably set off an alarm like we did at the lab." Rafayel frowned.

"I know, but I don't think it's a secret that we're here."

Rafayel nodded. "True enough. What do we do with them, though? We still have to find Atrac's priestess and oust her so Elef's people can get in here and clean up this mess. I don't believe taking a group of unarmed men and a pregnant woman into a battle is a good idea."

Osse pointed to the weapon rack behind Rafayel. "We can arm the men with that."

"And your sister?"

Osse blew out a breath. "I don't want to leave her here. If something happens to us, I want her to have a chance to actually escape, but you're right. If we bring her into the last confrontation with the priestess, she's liable to be hurt or killed. Do you think she'd be safe out with the horses?"

"Either there, or we can hide her in a room we've already cleared."

Osse pressed the buttons for the remaining cells. The glass walls retracted into the floor. The two nomads bolted straight for the door. Osse reached after them and missed. Maaska waddled along at a better rate then Nagheed expected, and the Nethanyan man hung back and offered his arm. Osse rushed to his sister and pulled her into an embrace. As he led her back over to the counter, she described her capture and waking up in the cell. When the trio arrived at the counter, the Nethanyan man bowed.

"Your Excellency, thank you."

CHAPTER 36

"You're welcome. How are you? Are you hurt?" Rafayel looked the man over.

With Smell engaged, Nagheed leaned closer and sniffed. No hint of blood or decay appeared.

"They didn't hurt us, sir. They wanted us for some kind of experiment."

"I'm glad you're all right."

Maaska blew out a breath. "Osse tells me you have one more battle. I don't want to stay in this creepy place any longer than I have to. I'll wait out with your horses."

"I completely understand." Rafayel turned to the man. "Can I prevail upon you to accompany the lady and protect her until we're finished here."

"You can count on me, but I would feel better with a weapon."

"Easily solved. Do you prefer a bow or a gun?"

"Bow for me, thanks. Never used a gun."

Rafayel retrieved one of the bows and a quiver of arrows from the cabinet behind him and handed it across. "Here you are. Thank you."

Osse led his sister. "Let's escort them out and then we'll come back and deal with that last door."

Nagheed led the way reversing their path to the main door.

Rafayel drew a breath between his teeth. "I've just had a disturbing thought. I do hope those nomads haven't taken our horses."

"If they did, they called five generations of bad luck on themselves." Maaska shook her head. "On the matter of bad luck, does that thing belong to you?" She indicated Ahva with a twitch of her head.

"That's Ahva, and she's been anything but bad luck. If not for her, I wouldn't have found you." Osse preened her head for a few seconds.

"Hello, silly bird." Ahva waved a wing.

Maaska huffed. "I guess I'm not too surprised. You've never participated in our traditions willingly."

As they came around the dogleg in the corridor, the two nomads were backing down the hall toward them. Nagheed stopped. Best to wait. As the two men continued to back up, a shadow formed in the corner, then grew larger until Jael lumbered into view of the parabolic mirror. Maaska gasped and stepped back.

Osse stepped in front of his sister. "Don't worry. She hasn't been any harm to us. I think she's hunting for something."

The two nomads retreated behind Osse and Rafayel, and the whole group backed up until they were out of the dogleg. Jael turned in the cubicle village. Nagheed quickly resumed the path to the main door and out into the courtyard where they had left the horses.

Osse walked over to the nomads. "If you can stay here until we finish, then we can all leave together. We'll be safer in a larger group."

The nomads backed away.

The older of the two nomads snapped back a response. "Keep your cursed raven and the mutt to yourselves."

As the nomads hightailed it for the exit, Nagheed ran ahead and stood between them and the horses. Sure, Maaska insisted that they would leave other people's property alone, but that other group he and Rafayel had encountered outside Vanya had kidnapped a kid. Whether they had designs on the horses or not, they gave Nagheed a wide berth on the way to the main gate.

"You'll be okay here. We'll be back as soon as we can." Osse gave his sister a quick hug.

Rafayel snapped his fingers and tapped his leg. "Come, Nagheed."

As they retraced their steps back to the remaining door, the computer gave him a quick trumpet fanfare twice.

Finished two quests and leveled up! Now that's the way to do it.

Ahva: Hot diggity. More points to spend.

Nagheed: Did you just get caught by the profanity filter?

Ahva: No. I actually said, "Hot diggity."

Nagheed: Who says that anymore?

Ahva: Me. Anyway, for all I know you're a kid, so why would I try to cuss in front of you?

Nagheed: I'm not a kid.

Ahva: See? A kid would say that. You sure aren't old enough to know quality entertainment.

Nagheed rolled his eyes and called up his screen to allocate his points.

They arrived at the final door, the one leading east from the cellblock. The keypad on this door had only the numbers one through four. On the screen was a picture of cable spaghetti. All the cables were attached at the top and bottom of the image. The connections at the top were labeled A through D. The ones at the bottom were labeled one through four. In between the two was a total rat nest of twisted cabling. Below the picture, was **A=** and a blinking cursor.

Ahva: This one's for you, Shaggy. These things make

me cross-eyed.

Nagheed: This one might be more my speed. No numbers except as labels.

He reared up on his back legs and planted his feet on the wall.

Osse chuckled. "I think your dog's going to give it a try."

"It's only fair." Rafayel shrugged. "Ahva had the last few."

Nagheed started at A and followed the wire around through the cable spaghetti until he got to the other end. With one of his long, thin toenails, he tapped the 3. He tracked B around to 1. C was 4, and D was 2.

The door slid open.

Rafayel ruffled the fur on Nagheed's head. "Good work."

Nagheed wagged his tail and hopped down. They passed through the door into another weird science lab. There were typical lab workstations ringing the perimeter of the ten-meter square room. The tables on the left and right sides of the room had racks of small vials containing fluids. In the middle of the room, there were two operating tables with dastardly robotic appendages. In the northeast corner of the room, there was a glass-enclosed chamber with a door into the room and another through the wall into the next room. Another bare patch of wall on the east side interrupted the spacing of the lab stations. That was probably another hidden door.

Proving his expectation, that panel of the wall slid away, and techno Mozart changed to the horns and percussion of the combat music. Three maniacs stepped through.

Ahva: Here we go! Progressive battle ending with the boss.

CHAPTER 36

All three maniacs had one glowing eye. A second glow on each came from somewhere in the torso, arm, or leg.

Osse grabbed the edge of one of the metal lab tables and flipped it on its side. He ducked behind it.

Ahva: Not a bad idea, actually.

Nagheed joined Osse behind the fallen table. Rafayel flipped table on the opposite side of the door and hid behind it. Ahva joined him.

Nagheed: How do you want to play this?

Ahva: Um, kill the bad guys? Don't get killed ourselves?

Nagheed: You're not one to strategize, are you?

Ahva: Who needs strategy? As the situation develops, observe, adapt, move on. For now, we have three maniacs. They don't have distance attacks, so get out there and do your growly, bitey, scratchy dog thing. I'll drop arrowheads on them. We may have to change tactics when the next round shows up, but for now, that sounds pretty good to me.

Nagheed huffed. Not quite the planning he preferred, but it did accomplish something.

He peeked over the top edge of the table and checked out all three maniacs. Dodging equipment was slowing them down, but not by much.

"Hold, Nagheed. Osse, go for the middle one's chest. I'll get the eye," Rafayel ordered.

Both humans popped up long enough to fire a flintlock and two glowing arrows at middle maniac. After a terrific burst of sparks, it fell flat but didn't turn into a mannequin.

"It's going to pop back up." Osse nodded toward it.

"We'll deal with it when it does. Nagheed, go!" Rafayel raised his hand then dropped it and pointed forward.

Nagheed bounded over the overturned table and charged at the nearest maniac halfway across the room. It crouched lower and drew one hand back in preparation for an attack.

Ahva: Look out, Shaggy!

The moment before Nagheed was in range to pounce, Ahva flew past him and dropped an arrowhead on the maniac's head. It swiped at the bird, missing by a light-year or more, but that left an opening for Nagheed. He tackled the maniac, biting down hard on the glow in its arm. The maniac threw him back toward the overturned table, but sparks flew, and the glow in its arm went out. A bright arrow from Osse pierced the maniac's eye. It also fell flat but didn't turn into a mannequin.

Rolling back up to his feet, Nagheed checked the room. The third maniac was missing, but the other two still showed about a quarter of their health.

Both downed maniacs jumped back up to their feet sporting glows in new locations.

Nagheed ran toward middle maniac, going after the glow in its left leg. When he used Bite to clamp his jaw on its leg, the crack of the crystal reverberated through the maniac's body a moment before it turned into a mannequin.

A horn blast heralded the arrival of the second wave. Movement in the edge of Nagheed's vision drew his attention to the door. Jael skidded to a stop between the two overturned tables.

Ahva: What do you know? We get reinforcements, too.
Nagheed: Let's hope she's on our side.
Ahva: She has been so far.

Ten meters away, Nagheed watched the indistinct figures silhouetted in the far door. He counted five shadows, and

CHAPTER 36

at least one of them was enormous.

Nagheed: Get ready.

Ahva: Why? Do they have a cave troll?

Nagheed: No, but could be about as bad.

Chapter 37

As Jael skidded into the room, a glowing arrow turned a maniac into a mannequin. She rose up onto two feet and assessed the situation.

The room was large and square with a high ceiling. Silver metal tables around the edge had wooden racks of small, thin containers. Each container in the rack a set of vials, one each in pink, yellow, gray, and blue with a red one off at one end by itself. There were three maniac mannequins sprawled on the floor near the odd tables and their strange brass instruments. On the far side, a doorway stood open, but there was no sign of an actual door. Indistinct shadows milled around. In one corner, a glass cage had a door into the next room.

The leather-clad herbalist who had healed her injuries and given her a snack was crouched behind a table to the left of her. The herbalist's friend was set up similarly on the right. The crow was circling the room with something clutched in her beak, and the massive reverse-brindle dog was standing in the middle the room next to one of the mannequins. The scent of her cubs was strong in here, but there were no physical signs of them. Were they in the next room?

CHAPTER 37

Ahva: Wait there, Jael. We're about to get a whole bunch of new bad guys, and it's safer for you if you wait until Rafayel and Osse take their shots. Then you can charge in. Do that bear thing with your bear feet. Get it? Bear feet?

Nagheed: You're still assuming she understands you.

Ahva: You understand what everybody is saying without being able to say anything back. Why shouldn't she?

Across the room, a creature that resembled a dog on two feet led a similar companion, two humans, and a huge white bear through the door. The two augmented dogs wore dark brown and gray leather armor covering their torso and held bows in their hands and quivers of arrows at their hips. The two augmented humans wearing different colored tunics and pants carried weapons that looked like the metal tube the Ilionite researcher and technicians had used against her when she'd tried to rescue her cubs. The augmented polar bear wore a leather helmet and a metal breastplate, but it carried no weapons. At nearly double her mass, did it really need one?

The two humans on either side of her – labeled "Rafayel" and "Osse" in their nametags – popped up from their hiding places. The herbalist shot arrow after arrow at the newcomers while his companion made a terrific amount of noise with some sort of handheld device. One of the augmented humans and one of the augmented dogs had barely cleared the doorway when they turned into mannequins. The remaining augmented human flipped a table on its side and hid behind it. The other augmented dog crouched behind one of the platforms in the middle of the room. The polar bear, remaining on two feet, waddled further into the room at a remarkable speed Jael wouldn't have thought possible on hind legs.

After selecting Tackle, she dropped to four feet and ran flat out, tackling the polar bear before it got to the middle of the room. They wrestled, trading claws and bites that made the screen flash red. The polar bear threw her off, and she crashed into one of the platforms. As it charged at her, glowing arrows pierced the polar bear creating a burst of sparks from the glow in one arm. Jael spared a glance at her health bar and the polar bear's. Her own health was down by half, but she'd given as good as she'd gotten against the polar bear.

Ahva: You gotta hit the glowing bits, Jael. Otherwise, you'll never get the upper hand.

Glowing bits, huh? The only glowing part on the polar bear was its eye. Jael rolled back up to her feet. Holding her ground, she used Posture, clacking her teeth and striking the floor with her paw. With arrows flying around the room, she couldn't risk standing tall, so how was she supposed to hit the glowing spot in the polar bear's eye?

The huge black, stripy dog in armor ran up behind the polar bear and bit its leg. The dog pulled backwards, and the polar bear belly-flopped on the floor. The polar bear kicked, but missed the dog entirely. Jael rushed in and delivered a terrific slap to the polar bear's head. The polar bear swiped a claw at her, scoring only a glancing hit when the dog jerked the polar bear backward. She delivered another hard slap, and a crack preceded burst of sparks. The polar bear turned into a mannequin.

A horn blast announced the arrival of more enemies. Jael followed the big dog toward the back of the room where the rest of this round's opponents were hiding.

* * *

When the dynamic duo of Nagheed and Jael got the better of the polar bear, Ahva aborted her bombing run and instead disrupted the plans of the augmented human by dropping the arrowhead on him.

A horn blast signaled round three.

Ahva: What do you think? Seven of something or the creepy chick?

Nagheed: If this is the endgame battle, I'm guessing there's a fourth round. So, I'm gonna say seven of something.

She wheeled around and returned to the arrowhead pouch next to Osse where she found nothing but the pouch. She stuck her head in the pouch and then flipped it over.

Ahva: Oh, PBTH! I'm out of arrowheads.

Nagheed: Are there any you can recover and use again?

Ahva: Not without getting way too close to something that really doesn't like me.

Nagheed: What about the test tubes on the side tables?

Ahva: Those aren't just props?

Nagheed: If the game will let you pick up individual ones, I don't see why they can't become your new distraction device.

Ahva: That's fabulous!

She flew to the nearest side table and checked out the test tube rack. Each table had one rack and each rack had five test tubes in five different colors. Four – pink, yellow, gray, and blue – were grouped together. The fifth one, red, was by itself at the other end of the rack.

Ahva: What do you think? Each color mean something different?

Nagheed: Ooo. Hadn't thought about what affect they would have. Earlier in the game, we found a book that labeled elixir colors with effects. Unfortunately, I don't remember which was which.

Ahva: Nuts. Okay. I'll watch where I throw them until we know what they do.

Seven sentinels – painted red this time – cruised through the door and joined the augmented dog and the augmented human. As the sentinels filed into the room, Rafayel and Osse popped up from behind their tables and rained bullets and glowing arrows on the sentinels. Unlike last time, their efforts didn't immediately kill any of their opponents. In fact, none of them even showed damage.

Nagheed: They're shielded.

Ahva: Yeah. They're the red ones. That complicates things.

Nagheed: I don't see any blue ones?

Ahva: Nope, so back off until the shields are gone.

The sentinels returned fire, and Osse and Rafayel ducked back down behind their tables. The bolts from the sentinels acted more like sci-fi blaster bolts than actual lasers. Handy, since that meant they were slow enough to be visible before they hit the target.

Ahva picked up a pink test tube and flew to the far corner of the room where the augmented human was hiding behind his table. She dropped the vial on its head and sped out of range. A pink cloud erupted from behind the table and filled that whole quarter of the room.

CHAPTER 37

Ahva: That was interesting.

Nagheed: Doesn't do any damage, though.

Ahva: No, but creatures that aim for their attacks can't do that if they can't see. That effectively takes them out temporarily.

Nagheed: Unless they have some kind of radar.

Ahva: Let's hope not.

She flew to the nearest table and picked up a blue vial. As Ahva lifted off, an electric blue beam burned in the space where she'd been standing, hardly missing her by a millimeter.

Circling the room and dodging blue beams, Ahva delivered her test tube to one of the sentinels. When the test tube shattered, a dark blue goo encased the sentinel. It dropped, but when it hit the ground, it bounced like a rubber ball.

Ahva: ROFL! Boingy! Boingy! Boingy!

As she returned to the nearest table, she checked everyone's health bar. Jael and Nagheed were not doing well. Both were down to less than a third of their health. Osse and Rafayel, however, showed a few dings, but nothing potentially fatal.

In most of these games, red potions were for health. Could it be the same here? Was that one sitting off by itself because it wasn't an attack? There was only one way to find out. Ahva picked up the red vial and flapped like mad to take off.

Sorry, bear, but you get to be the test subject.

Ahva passed over Jael as she and Nagheed were finishing off the augmented dog. Watching Jael's health bar, Ahva dropped the vial. When it shattered, Jael regained half the points she'd lost.

Nagheed: How'd you do that?

Ahva: Red is for healing. Want one?
Nagheed: Might not be a bad idea.

The pink cloud cleared, and Jael charged at the augmented human behind the table.

As Ahva circled, she dodged under a blue beam from a sentinel and skidded to a stop on one of the tables. She grabbed the red test tube, flew back over Nagheed, and dropped it on his head. Nagheed's health points recovered to three quarters.

Jael went airborne from behind the overturned table. After flying over the platforms in the middle of the room, she bounced off the furthest one, landed on the ground with a thud, and slid several meters.

Ahva winced. *Let's see if I can help you out back there.* She went to the nearest table and paused long enough to pick up a yellow vial. She zipped across the room and dropped the yellow tube on the augmented human. Electrical sparks ignited from the tube and spread around the augmented human's body. The crystals glowed much brighter then exploded. The augmented human collapsed but didn't turn into a mannequin. As Ahva flew back to the nearest table, Jael hopped over the edge of the table and whacked the augmented human hard enough to permanently take him out.

Ahva landed on the table and grabbed a gray test tube. *I wonder what this one does.*

* * *

Nagheed nodded to the beat of the combat music as he checked his fatigue meter. Under half. Even with a grizzly bear helping him out, the fight had been intense. He looked around the room for a status check in time to witness Jael's victory over the augmented human. That left four sentinels, one of which was still encased in goo and bouncing around like a rubber ball. A different sentinel was only a few points short of becoming a mannequin. If its health was down, that meant the shield was off. Nagheed ran toward it and batted it into the wall. It hit the wall then fell to the floor, no longer a threat.

A horn blast announced the next wave.

Ahva: Please tell me were not about to have nine of something.

Nagheed: Surely not.

Ahva: I hope not. And don't call me Shirley.

He didn't even bother asking what that meant this time. Probably another vintage movie reference. Nagheed rolled his eyes and ran to the nearest operating table to hide behind until they saw what the next opponent was going to be.

Ahva: That was anticlimactic.

Nagheed: What did you do?

Ahva: Dropped a test tube of gray stuff on the sentinel.

Nagheed: And?

Ahva: It got a little frosty. That's all. No damage. No weird effect. Just a little frost.

Nagheed: Maybe works better against non-machines.

Ahva: We can only hope. Oh. It's the creepy chick.

Nagheed peeked around the side of the operating table. The woman who had been giving all the orders on the screen at the lab floated into the room. The nametag over her head dubbed her Priestess of Atrac. The spot between her collarbones, both feet, both arms, and both eyes glowed brilliantly even in the lit room. Like the augmented human that they had met at the collapsed border guard station, the priestess's left hand and forearm had been replaced by a metal tube with lenses at the end.

Ahva: I get the feeling she's not happy to see us.
Nagheed: What gave you that idea?

As the priestess floated to the middle of the room, Rafayel and Osse pelted her with arrows and bullets. All of them fizzled out mere centimeters away from her.

Ahva: And she's shielded.
Nagheed: You'd be disappointed if she was a pushover.
Ahva: True story.
Nagheed: We'd better take out the rest of the sentinels. I think we're going to have our hands full with this one.

He waited until Jael and Ahva chose targets then he went to the remaining one. The sentinel saw him coming, and the aperture on the front glowed. Nagheed slipped on the slick floor and landed spread eagle, which saved him from a bolt in the face.

Ahva: Graceless but effective.
Nagheed: Whatever works.

He scrambled to his feet and jumped at the sentinel, headbutting it into one of the operating tables. It bounced off the edge of the table and careened past Jael before hitting the priestess's shield and blowing up. The priestess whirled toward Jael. She picked the bear up one-handed and threw Jael more than ten meters into the glass enclosed chamber in the northwest corner of the room. The door of the chamber slid closed and a conveyor belt carried the bear into the next room.

CHAPTER 37

Ahva: That's not good. I think we're about to see that bear from the other side.

Nagheed: Then we'd better be quick.

Ahva: You mean end this battle before Jael returns?

Nagheed: Might work.

Ahva: Shot in the dark, but let's try it.

Nagheed took a quick look around the room. Only the priestess remained. Rafayel aimed his 9 mm and pulled the trigger but only got a click.

The priestess aimed her left arm at the table Rafayel hid behind. A light beam shot from her arm and disintegrated the table.

Ahva: Because that's how lasers work?

Nagheed: Typical sci-fi trope.

Ahva: Hokey sci-fi trope. They should've made it all glittery while it disappeared. That would've been the way to do a disintegrator beam.

As Rafayel darted to the nearest operating table to hide behind, the priestess zapped Osse's hiding place, too. Ahva flew over the priestess's head and dropped a vial. A billowing cloud of smoke filled the center of the room. Rafayel bolted to the table the augmented human had used for cover and popped back up with its rifle.

The smoke clouds swirled and dissipated revealing the priestess in the center spinning like a top. She slowed and beckoned them closer.

Rafayel and Osse both shot at the priestess. The air around her shimmered.

"Go, Nagheed!" Rafayel ordered.

He left his hiding place and charged at her. She was focused on the operating table Osse hid behind. A beam from her arm obliterated the table. As she took aim at Osse, Nagheed picked Tackle and drove her to the ground. She laughed, a shrill, piercing sound that threatened to blow out speakers. The next thing he knew, he was airborne. After a hang time that felt like years, he struck one of the walls, which flashed the screen brilliant red.

Ahva: Wow. You okay, Shaggy?
Nagheed: This time.

He got back to his feet and ran to help Osse who had left his bow behind in favor of his mace. Rafayel likewise discarded his gun and charged in with his rapier. When the priestess raised her left arm to zap another hiding place, Osse swung his mace and connected with the metal tube. It threw a burst of parts and sparks on impact, and the glow in that arm winked out.

Instead of going for another tackle, Nagheed bit the priestess's leg just below the knee where the glow was. The crack of the crystal reverberated through her body. She kicked him off and he flew backwards again into the wall, causing another red flash.

Nagheed checked his health bar. Well under half.

After stopping at a rack of test tubes, Ahva took off with one.

The priestess's shrill laugh made Jake wince.

While flying past, Ahva tossed the test tube at the priestess.

Ahva: Put a sock in it, sister. Ahh, she was supposed to bounce.

Nagheed looked up. The priestess was encased in goo.

Nagheed: That stuff takes forever to dissolve. We're supposed be getting rid of her in a hurry.

CHAPTER 37

Ahva: Betcha it doesn't last that long.
Nagheed: Why shouldn't it?
Ahva: Smokescreen didn't.

Nagheed got to his feet and moseyed over to the priestess. Every other step flashed the screen red.

Osse dug into his pack and pulled out a jar of herbs. "Come here, Nagheed. Let's take care of some of your injuries while she's in that muck."

A crackling noise came from the priestess.

"Never mind that for now." Rafayel drew back his rapier. The goo smoked and evaporated.

Osse pushed his equipment out of the way and jumped back to his feet, mace in hand. Nagheed crouched, ready to go after the glow in the priestess's right arm. The moment the goo was gone, Nagheed rushed in and bit down on the glow in the priestess's forearm. After a loud crack, she dropped to the ground and kicked Nagheed away. The screen flashed red again.

When Nagheed tried come back to his feet, the screen turned red, and he couldn't get his left leg under him.

* * *

Ahva cringed when Nagheed flew into the wall yet again. *He flies pretty well for a dog. Landing stinks, but he flies well.*

When Nagheed tried to stand up, his left front leg didn't move. He yelped and fell flat.

Ahva: Stay put, Shaggy. I got a red vial with your name on it.

She picked up a red test tube from the kit behind her and dive-bombed her partner. The vial broke on impact, and his health recovered to just over half.

Ahva: I got one more of those. Want it?

Nagheed: Save it. Someone might get hurt pretty badly again.

Ahva: If you say so. But you be careful. Landings are only good if you can walk away from them.

She flew to the nearest table and picked up a gray test tube. It hadn't done much against a sentinel, but Nagheed had suggested maybe it would be better against something that was alive. She was game to try. At near ceiling height, Ahva circled the room and timed her drop. The vial struck the priestess square in the chest as she drew back to whack Rafayel with her left arm. Ice crystals spread all across her chest and down both arms, slowing her movements. Rafayel easily ducked her attack.

Ahva: That was more useful.

Nagheed: Stun it.

Ahva: You mean the yellow vial?

Nagheed: Yeah, I think? Two of them are kinda yellowish to me. Whichever one isn't healing.

Ahva: Okey dokey. One yellow stun juice coming up.

As she landed on the table that still had a yellow vial, a loud crack and a fizzling sound preceded another piercing laugh. Ahva picked up the yellow vial and flew a circuit of the room to gain momentum before starting her bombing run. It broke on impact, but instead of doing damage, it restored a third of her health. One of the crystals that had gone out in her leg started glowing again.

Ahva: Whoops.

Nagheed: Okay. I was wrong. Don't do that again.

The ice crystals disappeared.

CHAPTER 37

The priestess stomped once, causing a ripple through the floor that knocked everybody off their feet and threw them backwards a few meters. Ahva landed on another table and grabbed the third of four blue vials. She landed the vial on the priestess's shoulder, creating a shell of blue goo that lasted just long enough for everybody to get back to their feet and get back in range for battle. Rafayel's rapier thrust to the eye and Nagheed's dog bite to the knee cracked two crystals at once, and Osse's mace deflected a punch bent on giving Nagheed a concussion.

Only one crystal remained.

The priestess's shrill laughter rattled the walls. She stomped again, sending a ripple through the floor that knocked everyone backwards. Ahva grabbed the last of the blue vials and dropped it on the priestess's head to buy everyone time to get back in position. Without waiting for the outcome, she flew to the nearest table that had a gray vial and snatched it up. As soon as the blue goo dissipated, Ahva dropped the vial on the priestess. Ice crystals spread and slowed the priestess's movement, giving the humans enough of an opening to eliminate last crystal.

Ahva: Now if she pops back up again…

The priestess collapsed into a mannequin. The notebook in the corner turned blue as the screen edge flashed green.

Ahva circled the room one last time while Osse and Rafayel sat checked mannequins for loot. She came in for a landing on Osse's shoulder.

Chapter 38

Nagheed followed Rafayel while he checked out the different mannequins. Most had a larger quantity of the usual assortment of loot in addition to whatever weaponry and armor that opponent had used. That was a little disappointing, really. A missed opportunity by the designers to award some really cool stuff for completing the whole point of this exercise, maybe some unique items that would carry into the next iteration of the game. Jake made a note to include that suggestion in his feedback.

After they checked everything, Osse and Rafayel sat in the middle of the room, and Nagheed flopped next to Rafayel. Osse mixed various herbal concoctions to heal everybody's wounds.

The door their adversaries had come through slid open. Nagheed jumped to his feet and growled. He took a couple steps closer to the door and sniffed. "Jael" wafted through the door.

The bear waddled in from the other room, but something about her was decidedly different. Her bear paws had been changed. Although not exactly human, they were not quite bear either. Each digit had been elongated and the fifth one had been rotated to an opposable position. All the injuries she had taken during the battle were healed. Unlike the augmented critters and maniacs they had encountered, no part of Jael was glowing.

She plodded up to them and sat. "Hello. My name is Jael. Thank you for your help. I may not have been the most hospitable creature, but you must understand that someone stole my cubs from me. They were here. I can smell their scents clearly, but they're gone now. I can't wait here any longer. I must find my cubs." She rose and headed for the door.

Rafayel reached after her. "If you can wait a little while, we'll go with you. We can help you."

Ahva: Go with her? With a pregnant woman in tow? I mean, the guy we rescued, sure, but Maaska looks about ready to pop any microsecond now.

Nagheed: We could always send Maaska back to Kamali or Yavne with the man.

Ahva: Risky, but yeah, I suppose. I wouldn't agree to that if I were Osse seeing all the trouble we had getting here.

Nagheed: We fixed the stuff.

Ahva: So, *poof* all the baddies dropped dead?

Nagheed: No, probably not. You're right. There will probably be some mopping up to do for a while.

"Thank you, but no. The longer I wait here, the colder the scent grows. It lingers longer here inside, but out in the elements, it will fade faster. I must go now." Jael turned toward the door. "Thank you again."

Ahva waved with her wing. "Bye-bye, Jael. Find cubs!"

Without a look back, she raced out.

Osse finished healing everyone as well as he could with his supplies. "Is there anything else we need to do here?"

"Not that I can think of." Rafayel groaned as he stood.

"We've done what we came to do. I was hoping that we would encounter someone who belongs here so we're not just leaving it standing wide open, but that might take some time. Let's collect your sister and the gentleman we left to watch over her. We'll shelter here tonight and leave in the morning." Osse nodded.

Ahva: If the designers did this right, we'll be here when the handoff to Elef's folks occurs. Then the credits will roll.

Nagheed: Credits?

Ahva: Yeah, credits. The list of who did what. Usually comes after the last snazzy cutscene.

Nagheed: What games have you played lately that rolled credits?

Ahva: Recent games? Uh... ooo... Now that you mention it, I've been playing the VR adaptations of vintage games. No endgame cutscene?

Nagheed: Not likely.

Ahva: No credits, either? What a missed opportunity! They could have soooo many funny jokes in there.

Nagheed: I'm sure you can access the credits somewhere and find out.

Ahva: How do you know you've ended the game without rolling credits?

Nagheed: You complete all the quests and run out of special things to do. Then you can explore the world if you want.

Ahva: Uh-huh. Weird way to do it, but I guess if that's how it works for them...

Nagheed led the way back out through the corridors. When they left the building, the door slid shut behind them with a loud click.

"Hey! Open up!" Ahva cawed.

Osse returned to the door. "We can't get back in."

Rafayel spun toward him. "What?"

Nagheed walked toward the door. A metal plate now covered the keypad and screen that had given them access earlier.

"Well, that complicates things." Rafayel frowns. "We'll just have to make camp out here."

"Would we be better off camping outside the city?" Osse pointed to the horses. "If Maaska rides my horse, we have enough daylight to make it back to Bakhar before we set up camp."

Ahva: We can't leave yet.

Nagheed: Because?

Ahva: Optional quest. We haven't even been given the option to get an augmentation.

Nagheed: Maybe we missed it when we left.

Ahva: The door wouldn't now be inaccessible. It'd stay open so we can still get the quest done, wouldn't it?

Nagheed: Good question.

"That's a thought." Rafayel rubbed his chin. "Ahva, when you patrolled the city earlier, did you find many other potential hazards?"

Ahva bobbed her head and imitated the maniac's laughter. "Everywhere. Little groups."

"Can you do another patrol now?" Osse asked.

"Fly, Ahva!" She launched off his shoulder and cawed a few times as she spiraled upward.

While she circled, Osse and Rafayel checked the horses. Nagheed walked his own patrol around the courtyard, looking for recent sights and smells indicating potential threats. He picked up scents of grass, dirt, and fading scents of maniacs, but no hint of songbirds, squirrels, or even rats. The urban wildlife population was apparently non-existent here.

Crowd noise came from outside the courtyard. Nagheed ran to the entrance and engaged Hear. Multiple people were talking. He focused on individual voices, and they sounded far too clear to be maniacs.

Ahva returned and buzzed over his head before landing on Osse's arm. "People. Lots."

"Maniacs?" Osse asked.

"No. People. Green and white. Big group fighting – " She imitated the maniac's laughter. "Small group here."

A dozen men and women wearing robes rounded the nearest corner and approached the temple. The one in the lead carried a staff with Elef's symbol across the top of it. They strode into the temple courtyard as if they owned the place. The door opened as they came near.

Nagheed barked.

Rafayel smiled. "The owners of the establishment, I think. Nagheed, heel."

He retreated to Rafayel's side.

The one with the staff turned aside. He was a taller man with gray hair and some extra embroidery around the hems of his garment. He held his hands wide. "You have restored the balance of power. I knew it would take someone from the outside to do it. I did not expect followers of Tsidkenu." He frowned and gave them an impressive stink-eye before he smiled again. "Nevertheless, the enemy of my enemy is my friend. At least for now. As a show of gratitude, I offer you augmentations. You need not fear becoming the creatures you just destroyed. Your repairs were quite effective. The equipment now works flawlessly as you saw with the bear. You are only limited by the crystals, plastic blanks, and batteries that you were able to collect on your way here. I will grant you each a maximum of two augmentations. Do you have a catalog?"

Osse rooted around in his bag and pulled it out. "We have a translation of one."

"Perfect. Please make your selections."

An input window zoomed out of the catalog. Across the top, their names were listed. Maaska and the Nethanyan gent they'd rescued weren't there. That made sense. They hadn't been in the game until just a while ago. In the lower half of the screen, there was a long list of different types of augmentations that could be picked. At the bottom, there was an option that said, "No augmentation, thank you."

Before Nagheed could respond, increased strength and increased speed filled in under Rafayel's name. A moment later, Osse chose increased agility and cleverness.

Ahva: Have you heard about part two? Does this really matter? I mean, the game is over, right?

Nagheed: I've heard rumbles. I think they're coming out with an expansion set of side quests or mini quests or something like that. Then, the storyline of Jael was wide open. There might be a sequel regarding that.

Ahva: You thinking to take any of these augmenta-

tions?

Nagheed: Sure. Fills the optional quest.

Ahva: That's true, too.

Ahva chose increased cleverness and increased strength. Not a bad choice for bird. If she got her cleverness up high enough, she'd be able to speak freely, and such a small bird could certainly do with more strength. That would give her more health among other things.

Nagheed scanned through the list and chose vocal chords - basic speech and mimicry for himself. A talking dog could be interesting to play. For his other option, he chose hands with opposable digits.

As soon as he made his last choice, the input screen zoomed out.

The priest took the catalog from Osse. "Excellent choices all, and I'll take the remaining augmentation equipment off your hands. We need it. You do not. Follow me."

He led them through the temple again. His entourage was now armed with cleaning supplies and working hard at tidying up the terrific mess Atrac's people had left behind.

They passed through the lab where the final battle had occurred and into the back room their opponents had come out of. Six cylinders in the corner stood open.

"If you'll each take your place in one of the chambers, please." The priest pointed to the cylinders. "I'll program the equipment with your choices."

Ahva flew into the one furthest left, and the door closed with a click. She fluffed up and shook out a cloud of feather dust. Her beak moved as if she'd said something, but the chamber muted whatever she said.

Osse took the one next to her. Rafayel directed Nagheed

to one. He trotted over and stepped inside. He'd expected a cramped space given his size, but standing in the middle, even his tail didn't hit the side. Rafayel took the last spot.

Gray mist filled the cylinders and lightning flashed. When the mist faded, Nagheed looked down at his paws. His forepaws had lengthened digits like Jael's and the dew claw had been moved down to form an opposable thumb.

Nagheed flexed his hands. *Nice!* When he tried to speak, he merely growled.

Nagheed: Dumb question. How do I talk?

Ahva: You'll only be able to mimic for a while. To see what words you've acquired, think "Speak" and the pop-up window will show you what you've learned. The more you practice what's on the list, the more you learn from hearing people talk.

The door clicked and swung open.

Nagheed walked forward. His movement now lacked some of the grace he'd grown accustomed to.

Nagheed: Walking is going to have a learning curve, too.

Ahva: I imagine so. Dogs are usually digitigrade, so you'll have to get used to walking on your fingertips. You'll get the hang of it. We have a looong walk back to Kamali and Yavne.

Ahva flew out of the chamber and zoomed around the room. "Wow! Here I am to save the day!" After a few loops, she landed on Osse's hand.

"I have one last gift for you." The priest approached them. "I will transport you back to your hometowns along with your companions, horses, and the people you rescued. It will take me a few minutes to prepare. I'll leave you to make your farewells."

"Do you plan to stay in Kamali?" Rafayel asked.

Osse nodded. "I think so. I had an invitation from a jeweler to set up there. There are physicians, but they charge too much for most people and some of their folk remedies aren't agreeable to people who don't follow one of the Bakhari religions. I want to set up a little herbalist shop and run clinics like the priest in Tel Caperna. Some people will be leery of Ahva, but they'll have to learn she's no harm to them."

"Yeah! I'm a good bird." Ahva leaned closer to Osse. "Most of the time."

Rafayel clapped his hand on Osse's shoulder. "A noble pursuit. I'll miss your company, and if you find you can't make a go of it there because of religious pressure or superstition, I can always find a good use for an honorable and trustworthy herbalist in Yavne."

Osse smiled. "Thank you. I'll miss your kindness and good advice."

The priest returned leading their horses by the reins. "All right. This way, please."

Ahva: Wow, that was quick-like-bunny. Prepped the equipment and retrieved horses in 2 minutes flat.

Nagheed: He's got things to do today.

Ahva: I guess so! Well, fun playing with you, Shaggy.

Nagheed: Likewise, bird nerd.

The priest led them through another door into a small room with a raised platform. As soon as they stepped onto it, the view faded to black.

* * *

CHAPTER 38

After a few seconds of blackout, Jake found himself sitting character generation room with Alan Ivan Turning.

"I have just a few questions to ask you." Alan took out a paper scroll and flung out about ten meters of it.

Jake rolled his eyes.

Alan laughed. "Just kidding. He tossed the scroll way and pulled out a small notepad. "This won't take long. Your feedback will be used to improve not only future versions of this game, but also the coming sequel and the expansion pack."

This wasn't exactly the most fun part of Jake's job, but it was part of the job. He settled in for the list of questions.

About the Author

Originally from Michigan, Cindy Koepp combined a love of pedagogy and ecology into a 14-year career as an elementary science specialist. After teaching four-footers – that's height, not leg count – she pursued a Master's in Adult Learning with a specialization in Performance Improvement. Her published works include science fiction, fantasy, and GameLit novels; a passel of short stories; and a few educator resources. When she isn't reading or writing, Cindy is currently working as a tech writer, hat collector, quilter, crafter, and strange joke teller.

About the Publisher

Bear Publications seeks out and publishes highly original stories in science fiction, fantasy, and horror from Christian authors or with a Christian worldview.
Find out more at: www.bearpublications.com

CPSIA information can be obtained
at www.ICGtesting.com
Printed in the USA
BVHW081934030720
582841BV00001B/1